MURDER HOUSE

JAMES PATTERSON is one of the best-known and biggest-selling writers of all time. His books have sold in excess of 300 million copies worldwide and he has been the most borrowed author in UK libraries for the past nine years in a row. He is the author of some of the most popular series of the past two decades – the Alex Cross, Women's Murder Club, Detective Michael Bennett and Private novels – and he has written many other number one bestsellers including romance novels and stand-alone thrillers.

James is passionate about encouraging children to read. Inspired by his own son who was a reluctant reader, he also writes a range of books for young readers including the Middle School, I Funny, Treasure Hunters, House of Robots, Confessions and Maximum Ride series. James is the proud sponsor of the World Book Day Award and has donated millions in grants to independent bookshops. He lives in Florida with his wife and son.

Also by James Patterson

A list of more titles by James Patterson is printed
at the back of this book

JAMES PATTERSON
& DAVID ELLIS

MURDER HOUSE

arrow books

1 3 5 7 9 10 8 6 4 2

Arrow Books
20 Vauxhall Bridge Road
London SW1V 2SA

Arrow Books is part of the Penguin Random House group of companies
whose addresses can be found at global.penguinrandomhouse.com.

Penguin
Random House
UK

First published by Century in 2015
First published in paperback by Arrow Books in 2016

www.penguin.co.uk

A CIP catalogue record for this book is
available from the British Library.

ISBN 9780099594888
ISBN 9780099594895 (export edition)

Typeset in 10.5/13pt Berkeley Old Style
by SX Composing DTP, Rayleigh, Essex, SS6 7XF
Printed and bound in Great Britain by Clays Ltd, St Ives Plc

MIX
Paper from
responsible sources
FSC
www.fsc.org   FSC® C018179

Penguin Random House is committed to a
sustainable future for our business, our readers
and our planet. This book is made from Forest
Stewardship Council® certified paper.

To Matt, Libby, and Zach Stennes

Prologue

BRIDGEHAMPTON, 1995

WHEN HIS EYES pop open, it is still dark outside, the air cool and crisp through his window. Normally, he wouldn't be up for another hour yet, but he could hardly sleep last night waiting for today. He's not sure, in fact, that he slept at all.

He sees the long, narrow trombone case in the corner of his bedroom and his heartbeat ratchets up. All those rehearsals, all those hours of practice until his hands and shoulders ached, until his head throbbed, all of that preparation comes down to today. It's finally here!

He quickly brushes his teeth and puts on his Halloween costume. He picks up the trombone case and his school backpack and heads downstairs quietly, not wanting to wake his mother.

He rips open the cellophane and drops two Pop-Tarts into the toaster and pours himself a glass of milk. He drinks the milk but doesn't touch the pastries. His stomach is churning too wildly. He will eat later, after his performance.

It is still dark, a nip in the fresh air, as he leaves his house, backpack over his shoulder, trombone case in his left hand. At the end of his street, he looks to his right, where a half mile away he can see the fog of the Atlantic, dark and endless. His eyes invariably move to the house by the ocean, perched up on the hill, the haunted mansion that, even from a distance, scowls at him.

No one ever leaves alive
The house at 7 Ocean Drive

A shiver runs through him. He shakes it off and turns left, moving north on Ocean Drive. He alternates the trombone case between his left hand and his right, because it's heavy, and he doesn't want it to affect his performance today.

He perks up as he approaches the school from the south end. The morning air begins to warm, a refreshing break in the chill. The sun peeks through the treetops. Leaves of assorted colors dance in the wind. He stifles the instinct to skip along like an eager little boy.

But he's no little boy. It's not like he's eight or ten anymore.

He's the first one here, just as he planned, alone with an acre of grass, nothing but an expanse of open field, leading up to the baseball diamond and playground to the south of the brick building. No trees, no shrubbery, no brick walls, nothing for the length of half a football field at least.

He turns toward the woods on the east side and finds

4

his perch. He opens the trombone case and removes the rifle, already fully loaded.

He holds the rifle in his hands and takes a deep breath to calm his nerves. His heartbeat is at full throttle, catching in his throat, bringing a tremble to his limbs.

He looks at his *Star Wars* watch, which he is wearing over his Halloween costume. The first bell, the warning bell, will come soon. Some of the students will arrive early, congregating near the back door, dispersing into their little cliques or tossing a football or Frisbee around. The playground equipment, for the younger kids.

But it's not the younger kids he wants.

He looks back at his watch, where Darth Vader tells him the time is drawing near. He wanted to dress up today as Darth, fitting for the occasion but too clunky with the oversize helmet—visibility through the rifle's scope was nearly impossible when he tried it out.

He loses himself in his thoughts, in his fantasies, in the dancing leaves, and suddenly time has crept up on him. They are arriving. Small kids holding their parents' hands, bouncing with animation. Older ones walking together. Superman and Batman and Aquaman, vampires and clowns, kittens and bunnies, Cinderella and Snow White and Tinker Bell, Pocahontas and Woody from *Toy Story*, Ronald Reagan and Simba from *The Lion King* and Mr. Spock—

—and the oldest ones at the school, the juniors and seniors, a few of them with some obligatory face paint or semblance of costume but generally too cool to dress up like their younger classmates—

"Showtime," he says. He heard that word in a cable

movie he wasn't supposed to watch and thought it sounded cool. His body temperature jacks up beneath his costume.

"Showtime," he says again as he raises his rifle, but this time he finds his voice, strong and confident, and then everything changes, like the flip of a switch inside him. A sense of calm sweeps through him, itself exhilarating: Look at him! Look at him patiently walking out from the tree cover, rifle raised, aiming and firing and clicking in the next round, aiming and firing and clicking, *aim-fire-click* while he walks toward the unsuspecting masses. The pop of the rifle, with each pull of the trigger, is the most invigorating sensation he's ever felt.

Jimmy Trager howls in a combination of pain and surprise as his back arches and he staggers to the ground. Roger Ackerman, that asshole, clutches his arm and tries to run but stumbles into the leaves.

Visible in the clearing now, he drops to one knee to steady himself as screams and cries fill the air, as fifty, sixty kids scatter in all directions like cockroaches, bumping into one another, tripping over one another, dropping their school bags and covering their heads, unsure initially which way to run, heads whipping in all directions, only knowing they should run, run, run—

"By the trees!" one parent yells.

"The parking lot!" cries another.

He fires and clicks in the next round, *aim-fire-click*, while panic propels the population of students like a strong gust of wind. Their squeals are like music. Their terror is his oxygen. He wishes this moment would never end.

Six hit, seven, eight in the clearing near him. Another half dozen farther away.

And then he raises his rifle with a dramatic flair and takes a moment, just a moment, to savor the delicious scene, the power he holds, the havoc he has created. It's like nothing he's ever felt. It's beyond words, this rush, this thrill coursing through him. And then his vision blurs, and it's a moment before he realizes it's not the wind causing it but his own tears.

There are probably a dozen pellets left in his BB rifle, but he's out of time. Faculty will pour out of the building any second. The STPD will be called. And he accomplished what he wanted, anyway. Just some superficial pellet wounds.

But wow, was that fun!

And I'm only twelve years old, he thinks. *You ain't seen nothin' yet.*

Book I

BRIDGEHAMPTON, 2011

Chapter 1

NOAH WALKER STANDS carefully on the roof of his house, takes a moment to ensure his balance, and removes the Yankees cap from his head to wipe the sweat off his brow under the scorching early-June sun. He never minded roofing work, but it's different when it's your own roof, the place you're renting, and the only reason you're doing it is the landlord will take six months to get to it, and you're sick of water spots on the ceiling.

He runs his hands through his thick, wavy hair. *The Matthew McConaughey look,* Paige calls it, noting that he has the physique to match. He's heard that comparison for years and never thought much of it. He never thought much of what anyone thought or said about him. If he did, he sure as hell wouldn't still be living in the Hamptons.

He hears the crunch of car tires down the road, the hum of a powerful, well-maintained engine. The unpaved roads just off Sag Harbor Turnpike are uneven at best, sometimes bumpy and other times outright treacherous. Not like the roads by the ocean, by the forty-thousand-square-foot mansions where the elite like to "summer." Not that he should bitch too much about the blue bloods; he makes twice as much from May to August, doing their bidding, as he does the rest of the year combined. He fixes what they need fixed. He digs what they need dug. He stomachs their condescension.

"Paige," he says to himself, even before her black-on-black Aston Martin convertible pulls into his driveway and parks next to his nineteen-year-old reconstructed Harley. She's not being discreet. She should probably be more careful. But back here in the woods where he lives, people don't mingle with the wealth, so there's no real danger of this getting back to Paige's husband, John Sulzman. It's not like his neighbors are going to run into Paige's husband at some high-society event. The closest people like him have ever come to a tuxedo is watching penguins on the Discovery Channel. Same zip code, different world.

Paige floats out of her convertible with the same grace with which she always carries herself. Noah feels the primal yearning that always accompanies the first sight of her. Paige Sulzman is one of those people for whom beauty is effortless, a privilege, not a chore. In her white hat and polka-dot dress, one hand holding the hat in place in the wind, she looks every bit the Manhattan socialite she is, but she hails from upstate originally and has maintained a sense of proportion and humility.

Paige. There's something refreshing about her. She is

a natural beauty, with her shiny blond hair and killer figure, her softly upturned nose and stunning hazel eyes. But it's not just her looks. She has a sharp wit, the ability to laugh at herself, the manners of a well-raised girl. She's one of the most sincere and decent people he's ever known.

She's pretty good in bed, too.

Noah climbs down the back and meets her inside the house. She rushes to him and plants her lips against his, her hands on his bare chest.

"I thought you were in Manhattan," he says.

She gives him a mock pout with those juicy lips. "That's not much of a greeting, mister. How about, 'Paige, I'm *so* very thrilled to see you!'"

"I *am* thrilled." And he is. He first saw Paige three years ago when he was cleaning the gutters on the Sulzman estate. Her image lingered with him long after. It was only six weeks ago that the stars aligned.

The prospect of Paige has always been both exhilarating and terrifying. Exhilarating, because he's never met someone who could light that flame inside him quite like she can. And terrifying, because she's married to John Sulzman.

But all that can wait. The electricity between them is palpable. His big rough hands trace the outline of her dress, cup her impressive breasts, run through her silky hair, as she lets out gentle moans and works the zipper on his blue jeans.

"I'm going to leave him," she says to him between halting breaths. "I'm going to do it."

"You can't," says Noah. "He'll . . . kill you."

She lets out a small gasp as Noah's hand reaches inside her panties. "I'm tired of being afraid of him. I don't care what he—what he—oh—oh, Noah—"

He lifts her off her feet and they bump against the front door, pushing it closed with a thud, a sound that seems to coincide with a similar sound, another door closing outside.

Noah carries Paige into the family room. He lays her down on the rug and rips her dress open, buttons flying, and brings his mouth to her breasts, then slides down to her panties. A moment later, her underwear has been removed and her legs are wrapped around his neck, her moans growing more urgent until she is calling out his name.

He moves upward and works his jeans down, freeing himself. He braces himself over Paige and gently slides inside her, her back arching in response. They find a rhythm, first slow and then urgent, and the sensation courses through Noah, the intensity building, a dam about to burst—

Then he hears another door closing. Then another.

He stops, suddenly, and raises his head.

"Someone's here," he says.

Chapter 2

NOAH PULLS ON his underwear and scrambles to his haunches, staying low. "Are you sure your husband—"

"I don't see how."

She doesn't see how? John Sulzman has endless resources, more money than some small countries. He easily could have tailed someone like Paige, who is far too innocent to notice something like that.

Noah takes one deep breath; his heartbeat slows and his veins turn icy. He finds his jeans on the floor and fishes the knife out of his back pocket.

"Go upstairs and hide," he tells Paige.

"I'm not going anywhere."

He doesn't bother to argue the point. Paige wouldn't listen, anyway.

And besides, they're not here for Paige. They're here for him.

Noah hears movement outside, not voices and nothing deliberate, which makes it worse—they aren't announcing themselves. He stays low and slips out of the living room, but not before catching a glimpse through the window of bodies in motion, some rushing around the side of the house, others toward the front door.

A small army is descending on his house. And he has nothing but a roofing knife.

In the hallway now, he faces the front door. There is little point in hiding. If he hid, they'd find him, and they'd be braced for action when they did, their guns poised, fanned out in some defensive formation. No, his only option is to get them when they come in, when they think they're sneaking in on a lovers' tryst, when they think Noah won't be ready for them. Surprise them, hurt them, and escape.

He hears the back door slam open at the same time that the front doorknob turns slowly. They're coming from both directions at once. He has almost no chance.

But he has nothing to lose, he figures, as he tightens his grip on the knife.

He moves one leg back, like a sprinter locking into his blocks before a race, ready to spring toward the front door with his knife, as the doorknob completes its rotation, as his pulse drums in his throat, as the front door pops open.

He lunges forward, ready to sweep the knife upward—

—a woman, a redhead dressed in blue jeans and a flak jacket, a gun held at her side, a badge dangling from a lanyard around her neck—

—*A badge?*—

—he tries to halt his momentum, falling to his knees,

sliding forward. The woman spins and kicks up her leg, and Noah sees the treads of her shoe just before impact. His head snaps back from the kick. His body arches and his head smacks the floor, stars and jagged lines dancing on the ceiling.

"Drop the knife or I drop you!" she says evenly. "STPD."

Noah blinks hard, his heartbeat still hammering. *STPD.*

The police?

"Toss the knife, Noah!" says the redheaded cop as several other officers flood in behind her.

"Jesus, okay." Noah drops the knife to the floor. Blood drips into the back of his mouth. A searing pain shoots through his nose and eyes.

"Don't move!" the other officers yell at Paige. "Hands in the air!"

"Don't hurt her!" Noah says. "She didn't do any—"

"Noah, you resist me again and I'll put you in the hospital." The redhead puts her foot on his chest. Despite his predicament, and the pain drumming through his head, and the fear gripping his heart, he registers this cop for the first time, her striking ice-blue eyes, her shiny red hair pulled back, her confidence.

"What—what is this?" he manages. His initial reaction of relief—nobody's going to kill him—is short-lived, especially with the crew of cops flooding in from the back now. Ten officers, he guesses, all wearing bulletproof vests and heavily armed.

Why?

"You don't have the right to do this!" Paige shouts

17

from the other room. It comes out as half protest, half lecture, the kind of thing a person with money would say, someone who doesn't shrink in the face of the cops like others might.

About the only thing Noah can see, through his blurred vision, is the female cop staring down at him. He's in his underwear, flat on his back with her foot on his chest and a pretty good shiner developing from the kick to his face. But hearing Paige's cry sets off something within him.

"This is my *home*," he hisses, his hands forming into fists. "You have a problem with me, knock on my door and tell me."

"We have a problem with you, Noah," she says. "Feel better?"

Noah's eyes catch Detective Isaac Marks, whom Noah has known for years, going back to school days. Marks doesn't give much of a reaction, save for a small shrug of one shoulder.

The redhead orders Noah to roll over. She cuffs him and yanks him to his feet. The sudden movement, coupled with the concussive effects from the kick to his face, leaves Noah's legs unsteady.

"This is ridiculous," he says. "Does Dr. Redmond say I took his Rolex again? Tell him to look in the couch cushions." It wouldn't be the first time one of the gazillionaires misplaced something and accused the help of pilfering it. A movie producer once had Noah arrested for stealing his golf clubs, only to realize later he'd left them in the trunk of his car. "And do you think you brought enough cops?"

"Is that why you rushed me with a knife?" asks the redhead. "Because you thought I wanted to question you about a watch?"

"He knows this isn't about a Rolex." Noah recognizes the voice before he sees Langdon James swagger into the house. He's been the chief of the Southampton Town Police Department for over fifteen years. His jowls now hang over his collar, his belly over his belt, and his hair has gone completely gray, but he still has the baritone voice and thick sideburns.

What the hell is the chief doing here?

"Detective Murphy," the chief says to the redhead, "take him to the station. I'll handle the search of his house."

"Will someone tell me what's going on?" Noah demands, unable to conceal the fear choking his voice.

"Be happy to," says the chief. "Noah Walker, you're under arrest for the murders of Melanie Phillips and Zachary Stern."

Chapter 3

THE FUNERAL FOR Melanie Phillips is heavily attended, filling the pews of the Presbyterian church and overflowing onto Main Street. She was all of twenty years old when she was murdered, every day of which she lived in Bridgehampton. Poor girl, never got to see the world, though for some people, the place you grew up is your world. Maybe that was Melanie. Maybe all she ever wanted was to be a waitress at Tasty's Diner, serving steamers and lobster to tourists and townies and the occasional rich couple looking to drink in the "local environment."

But with her looks, at least from what I've seen in photos, she probably had bigger plans. A young woman like that, with luminous brown hair and sculpted features, could have been in magazines. That, no doubt, is why she caught the attention of Zach Stern, the head of a talent agency that included A-list celebrities, a man who owned his own jet and who liked to hang out in the Hamptons now and then.

And that, no doubt, is also why she caught the attention of Noah Walker, who apparently had quite an affinity for young Melanie himself and must not have taken too kindly to her affair with Zach.

It was only four nights ago that Zachary Stern and Melanie Phillips were found dead, victims of a brutal murder in a rental house near the beach that Zach had leased for the week. The carnage was brutal enough that Melanie's service was closed-casket.

So the crowd is due in part to Melanie's local popularity, and in part to the media interest, given Zach Stern's notoriety in Hollywood.

It is also due, I am told, to the fact that the murders occurred at 7 Ocean Drive, which among the locals has become known as the Murder House.

Now we've moved to the burial, which is just next door to the church. It allows the throng that couldn't get inside the church to mill around the south end of the cemetery, where Melanie Phillips will be laid to rest. There must be three hundred people here, if you count the media, which for the most part are keeping a respectful distance even while they snap their photographs.

The overhead sun at midday is strong enough for squinting and sunglasses, both of which make it harder for me to do what I came here to do, which is to check out the people attending the funeral to see if anyone pings my radar. Some of these creeps like to come and watch the sorrow they caused, so it's standard operating procedure to scan the crowd at crime scenes and funerals.

"Remind me why we're here, Detective Murphy," says my partner, Isaac Marks.

"I'm paying my respects."

"You didn't know Melanie," he says.

True enough. I don't know anyone around here. Once upon a time, my family came here every summer, a good three-week stretch straddling June and July, to stay with Uncle Langdon and Aunt Chloe. My memories of those summers—beaches and boat rides and fishing off the docks—end at age eight.

For some reason I never knew, my family stopped coming after that. Until nine months ago when I joined the force, I hadn't set foot in the Hamptons for eighteen years.

"I'm working on my suntan," I say.

"Not to mention," says Isaac, ignoring my remark, "that we already have our bad guy in custody."

Also true. We arrested Noah Walker yesterday. He'll get a bond hearing tomorrow, but there's no way the judge is going to bond him out on a double murder.

"And might I further add," says Isaac, "that this isn't even your case."

Right again. I volunteered to lead the team arresting Noah, but I wasn't given the case. In fact, the chief—my aforementioned uncle Langdon—is handling the matter personally. The town, especially the hoity-toity millionaires along the beach, just about busted a collective gut when the celebrity agent Zach Stern was brutally murdered in their scenic little hamlet. It's the kind of case that could cost the chief his job, if he isn't careful. I'm told the town supervisor has been calling him on the hour for updates.

So why am I here, at a funeral for someone I don't know, on a case that isn't mine? Because I'm bored. Because since I left the NYPD, I haven't seen any action. And because I've handled more homicides in eight years on the force than all of these cops in Bridgehampton put together. Translation: I wanted the case, and I was a little displeased when I didn't get it.

"Who's that?" I ask, gesturing across the way to an odd-looking man in a green cap, with long stringy hair and ratty clothes. Deep-set, creepy eyes that seem to wander. He shifts his weight from foot to foot, unable to stay still.

Isaac pushes down his sunglasses to get a better look. "Oh, that's Aiden Willis," he says. "He works for the church. Probably dug Melanie's grave."

"Looks like he slept in it first."

Isaac likes that. "Seriously, Murphy. You're looking for suspects? With all you know about this case, which is diddly-squat, you don't like Noah Walker for the murders?"

"I'm not saying that," I answer.

"You're not denying it, either."

I consider that. He's right, of course. What the hell do I know about Noah Walker or the evidence against him? He may not have jumped out at me as someone who'd just committed a brutal double murder, but when do public faces ever match private misdeeds? I once busted a second-grade schoolteacher who was selling heroin to the high school kids. And a teenage volunteer who was boning the corpses in the basement of the hospital. You never know people. And I'd known Noah Walker for all of thirty minutes.

"Go home," says Isaac. "Go work out—"

Already did this morning.

"—or see the ocean—"

I've seen it already. It's a really big body of water.

"—or have a drink."

Yeah, a glass of wine might be in my future. But first, I'm going to take a quick detour. A detour that could probably get me in a lot of trouble.

Chapter 4

LANGDON JAMES CLOSES his eyes for just a moment and raises his face to the sun shining down on the backyard cocktail party. In these moments, with a slight buzz from the gin and the elite of Southampton surrounding him, he likes to pretend he is one of them, one of the socialites, the mega-wealthy, the trust fund babies and personal injury lawyers, the songwriters and tennis pros, the TV producers and stock speculators. He is not, of course. He wasn't born with a silver spoon, and he was always more street-savvy than book-smart. But he has found another route to power, through a badge, and most of the time, that is enough.

There are at least a hundred people in the sprawling backyard, most of them blue bloods, all of them here to support the reelection of Town Supervisor Dawn McKittredge and her slate, but really here to be seen, to eat elaborate hors d'oeuvres served by waiters in white coats and talk about their latest acquisition or conquest. They don't live here year-round, and the only relevance the governing authorities of the town hold for them is the rare zoning issue that may arise—water rights, land use, and the like—or in Chief James's case, the occasional drug bust or DUI or dalliance with prostitutes from Sag Harbor.

"Nice day, Chief."

Langdon turns to see John Sulzman. He's had a place on the ocean in Bridgehampton, a tiny hamlet incorporated within Southampton, for over a decade now. Sulzman made his money in hedge funds and now spends half his time in DC and Albany, lobbying legislatures and cutting deals. His net worth, according to a *New York Post* article Langdon read last year, is upwards of half a billion. Sulzman's on his third marriage—to the lovely Paige—and what appears to be his third or fourth Scotch, judging from the slurring of his words. He's wearing a button-down shirt with the collar open and white slacks. He is overweight, with a round weathered face and a full head of hair if you count the toupee, one of the better ones Langdon has seen, but still—don't these guys realize everybody knows?

"John," says the chief.

"I understand Noah Walker is in custody," says Sulzman, as if he's commenting on the weather. "I understand you were there, personally."

"I was." The chief takes a sip of his gin. No lime, no tonic, no stirrer. To all appearances, he could be drinking ice water, which is the point.

"I saw the police report," says Sulzman. "What was in it, and what was not."

His wife, he means. The chief didn't mention Paige

26

in the police report, thus concealing her presence from the media. John Sulzman probably thinks he did it to curry favor, but he didn't. There was no need to include her. She had nothing to do with the arrest, other than being a bystander.

But if Sulzman sees it as a favor—well, there are worse things.

"It's not a well-kept secret that you have your eyes on the sheriff's job, Chief."

Langdon doesn't answer. But Sulzman is right. The Suffolk County sheriff is retiring, and it would be a nice cap-off to Langdon's law enforcement career.

Sulzman raises his glass in acknowledgment. "Ambition is what makes the world go round. It's what drives men to excel at their jobs."

"I always try to do my best," says the chief.

"And I try to reward those who do." Sulzman takes a long drink and breathes out with satisfaction. "If Noah Walker is convicted, I'll consider you to have excelled at your job. And I'll be eager to support your next endeavor. Are you familiar with my fund-raising efforts, Chief?"

It so happens that the chief is. But he doesn't acknowledge it.

"I can raise millions for you. Or I could raise millions for your opponent."

"And who would my opponent be?" The chief looks at Sulzman.

Sulzman shrugs and cocks his head. "Whoever I want it to be." He taps the chief's arm. "And do you know who else is familiar with my fund-raising efforts? Our town supervisor. Your boss."

Chief James takes another sip of his gin. "Would that be a threat?"

"A threat? No, Chief. A promise. If Noah Walker goes free, there will be people in this community—maybe I'll be one of them—who will call for your head."

John Sulzman is not known for his subtlety. When you're worth five hundred million dollars, you probably don't have to be. So if Noah is convicted, the chief is a lock to be the next sheriff. If Noah walks, the chief can kiss his current job, and any future in law enforcement, good-bye.

"Noah Walker is going to be convicted," says the chief, "because he's guilty."

"Of course he is." Sulzman nods. "Of course."

This conversation should be over. It never should have started, but it should definitely end now. A guy like Sulzman is smart enough to know that.

And yet Sulzman hasn't left. He has something else to say.

"There's a . . . new officer on the case?" he asks. "A woman?"

The chief whips his head over to Sulzman.

"Your niece," says Sulzman, clearly pleased with himself for the knowledge he's obtained, and happy to throw it in the chief's face. "Jenna Murphy."

"Jenna's not on the case," says the chief. "She handled the arrest, that's all."

"I only mention it because I understand she had some issues with the NYPD," says Sulzman.

"The only 'issue' she had is she's an honest cop," Langdon snaps. "Truth is, the day she arrived, she was

28

the best cop on our force. She's as smart as they come, and she's tough and honest, and she wouldn't put up with corruption she found in Manhattan. She wouldn't go along with dirty cops, and she wouldn't look the other way."

Sulzman nods and purses his lips.

"It's not her case, John," says the chief.

Sulzman appraises the chief, looking him up and down, then square in the eye. "I just care about the result," he says. "Make it happen. Make sure Noah Walker goes into a very deep hole. Or there will be . . . consequences."

"Noah Walker is going into a hole because—"

"Because he's guilty," says Sulzman. "Yes, I know. I know, Lang. Just . . . don't forget this conversation. You want me as a friend, not an enemy."

With that, John Sulzman makes his exit, joining some acquaintances under the shade of the tent. Chief Langdon James watches him leave, then decides he's had enough of this party.

Chapter 5

AS THE FUNERAL for Melanie Phillips ends, I say good-bye to my partner, Detective Isaac Marks, without telling him where I'm going. He doesn't need to know, and I don't know if he'd keep the information to himself. I'm not yet sure where his loyalties lie, and I'm not going to make the same mistake I made with the NYPD.

I decide to walk, heading south from the cemetery toward the Atlantic. I always underestimate the distance to the ocean, but it's a nice day for a walk, even if a little steamy. And I enjoy the houses just south of Main Street along this road, the white-trimmed Cape Cods with cedar shingles whose colors have grown richer with age from all the precipitation that comes with proximity to the ocean. Some are bigger, some are newer, but these houses generally look the same, which I find comforting and a little creepy at the same time.

As I get closer to the ocean, the plots of land get wider, the houses get bigger, and the privacy shrubs flanking them get taller. I stop when I reach shrubbery that's a good ten feet high. I know I've found the place because the majestic wrought-iron gates at the end of the driveway, which are slightly parted, are adorned with black-and-yellow tape that says CRIME SCENE DO NOT CROSS.

I slide between the gates without breaking the seal. I start up the driveway, but it curves off to some kind of carriage house up a hill. So I take the stone path that will eventually lead me to the front door.

In the center of the wide expanse of grass, just before it slopes dramatically upward, there is a small stone fountain, with a monument jutting up that bears a crest and an inscription. I lean over the fountain to take a closer look. The small tablet of stone features a bird in the center, with a hooked beak and a long tail feather, encircled by little symbols, each of which appears to be the letter *X*, but which upon closer inspection is a series of crisscrossing daggers.

And then, *ka-boom*.

It hits me, the rush, the pressure in my chest, the stranglehold to my throat, I can't breathe, I can't see, I'm weightless. *Help me, somebody please help me—*

I stagger backward, almost losing my balance, and suck in a deep, delicious breath of air.

"Wow," I say into the warm breeze. *Easy, girl. Take it easy.* I wipe greasy sweat from my forehead and inhale and exhale a few more times to slow my pulse.

Beneath the monument's crest, carved into the stone in a thick Gothic font, are these words:

Cecilia, O Cecilia
Life was Death Disguised

31

Okay, that's pretty creepy. I take a photo of the monument with my smartphone. Now front and center before the house, I take my first good look.

The mansion peering down at me from atop the hill is a Gothic structure of faded multicolored limestone. It has a Victorian look to it, with multiple rooflines, all of them steeply pitched, fancy turrets, chimneys grouped at each end. There are elaborate medieval-style accents on the facade. Every peak is topped with an ornament that ends in a sharp point, like spears aimed at the gods. The windows are long and narrow, clover-shaped, with stained glass. The house is like one gigantic, imperious frown.

I've heard some things about this house, read some things, even passed by it many times, but seeing it up close like this sends a chill through me.

It is part cathedral and part castle. It is a scowling, menacing, imposing structure, both regal and haunting, almost romantic in its gloom.

All it's missing is a drawbridge and a moat filled with crocodiles.

This is 7 Ocean Drive. This is what they call the Murder House.

This isn't your case, I remind myself. *This isn't your problem.*

This could cost you your badge, girl.

I start up the hill toward the front door.

Chapter 6

I'M TRANSPORTED BACK hundreds of years, to a time when you rode by horseback or carriage, when you lived by candlelight and torches, when you treated infections with leeches.

When I close the front door of the house at 7 Ocean Drive, the sound echoes up to the impossibly high, rounded ceiling, decorated with an ornate fresco of winged angels and naked women and bearded men in flowing robes, all of them appearing to reach toward something, or maybe toward one another.

The second anteroom is as chilling and dated as the first, with patterned tile floors and more of the arched, Old Testament ceilings, antique furniture, gold-framed portraits on the walls of men dressed in ruffled shirts and long coats, wigs of wavy white hair and sharply angled hats—formal-wear, circa 1700.

The guy who built this place, the patriarch of the family, a guy named Winston Dahlquist, apparently didn't have a sense of humor.

My heels echo on the hardwood floor as I enter the airy foyer rising up three stories to the roof. Every step I take elicits a reaction from this house, fleeting coughs and groans.

"Hello," I say, like a child might, the sound returning to me faintly.

The stairs up to the second floor are winding and predictably creaky. The house continues to call out from parts unseen, aches and hiccups and wheezes, a centuries-old creature drawing long, labored breaths.

When I reach the landing, it seizes me again, stealing the air from my lungs, pressing against my chest, blinding me, *No, please! Please, please, stop*—

—high-pitched childlike squeals, uncontrollable laughter—

Please don't, please don't do this to me.

I grasp the banister so I don't fall back down the stairs. I open my eyes and raise my face, panting for air, until my heartbeat finally decelerates.

"Get a grip, Murphy." I pass through ornate double doors to the second-floor hallway, where the smell greets me immediately, the coppery odor of spilled blood, the overpowering, putrid scent of decay. I walk along a thick red carpet, the walls papered with red and gold, as I approach the bedroom where Zach Stern and Melanie Phillips took their last breaths.

I step onto the dark hardwood floor and look around the room. Gold wallpaper is everywhere. Against one wall is a king-sized canopy bed with thick purple curtains and sturdy bedposts. The bed is dressed in a purple comforter and ruffle with velvet pillows, some of which are still on the bed, some of which lie on the floor. The dark wood dresser holds two pewter statuettes that were probably bookends for the thick volumes of short stories that also now lie on the floor. The statuettes, as well as an antique brass alarm clock, are knocked to the side on the dresser.

Opposite the bed, made of wood that matches the dresser, is a giant armoire. And in the far corner of the room, south of the armoire and west of the dresser, is the bathroom.

I remove copies of the crime-scene photos I xeroxed from the file. Zachary Stern was found lying facedown on the floor, his head turned to the right toward the door, his feet pointed toward the bed. Beneath him was a pool of blood and other bodily excrement from the horrific stab wound to his midsection. Several of his fingers were crushed as well. Melanie Phillips was found by the armoire opposite the bed, the back of her right hand touching the armoire's leg; she was lying on her stomach like Zach, her head to the left, her eyes open and her mouth frozen in a tiny o. She was stabbed more than a dozen times, in the breasts and torso and then in the face, neck, back, arms, and legs.

Now back to the scene. The comforter on the bed has been pulled back on the left side, showing a large blood pool where Zach was first stabbed while lying in bed. There is blood spatter on the wall behind the bed, and a thick sea of blood embedded in the floor where he died. There is blood spatter on the armoire and all over the nearby floor where Melanie lay as she died.

Two more facts: Judging from the fresh semen found

inside Melanie and on Zach's genitalia, it seems clear that the two of them had had sexual intercourse not long before they were killed. And as of now, barring DNA testing that is still pending, there is no physical evidence putting Noah Walker in this house—no fingerprints, no carpet fibers, no shoe or boot prints.

And now the theory the STPD and the district attorney are running with: Noah was obsessed with Melanie. He somehow learned of her affair with Zach and followed her here. We don't know how he got in. The front door should have been locked, and no damage was done to it. In any event, he lay in wait until they had completed their sexual intercourse, when they were relaxed, when their guard was down, to spring into the room.

Noah surprised Zach in bed, plunging his knife into Zach's chest and dragging the blade downward, causing a vertical cut of roughly five inches, tearing open the esophagus and stomach. At this point, Melanie, who was in the bathroom cleaning up, came out. Noah subdued her by the dresser, knocking over the books and alarm clock and stabbing her multiple times in the breasts and torso before throwing her to the floor by the armoire, where he continued to stab her from behind, slicing her cheek and ear and neck and then her back, arms, and legs. He then returned to Zach and threw him out of the bed and onto the floor, stomping on and crushing some of Zach's fingers in a blind rage.

I move to the corner beyond where Zach's body was found and squat down, trying to get the angle right and using the photos to make sure I'm accurate. Where Zach would have been lying on the floor, with his head to the right, his sight line travels beyond the edge of the bed to the armoire. I repeat the same exercise from Melanie's vantage point and get the same line of vision, from the opposite end.

I remove my compact from my purse and squat down by the leg of the armoire that Melanie's right hand touched. I curl the compact under the armoire and around the leg so I can see the back of it. As I thought, the wood is abraded—scraped and cut.

Ten minutes later, I'm walking on Ocean Drive toward Main Street, on my cell phone with Uncle Lang. "Melanie Phillips was handcuffed to the armoire's leg," I say. "He made her watch the whole thing. This wasn't an act of blind rage, Chief. This was a calculated, well-executed act of sadism."

Chapter 7

I GET BACK to my car and drive to see the chief, who is away from the office this afternoon (don't ever tell him he has the day off, because he'll spend a half hour explaining that the chief of police never has a day off). My uncle lives on North Sea Road in a three-bedroom cottage set back from the road and flanked with well-manicured shrubbery that always reminds me of a defensive military formation.

The front door is unlocked and open. It smells like it always smells in here, musty guy scent: dirty socks and body odor combined with the latest fast-food takeout he ate. A bachelor pad, ever since Aunt Chloe left him two years ago.

On my way to the back porch, I detour to the kitchen, open his fridge, and peer inside. Cartons of Chinese takeout, half a Subway sandwich in its wrapping, a twelve-pack of Budweiser with three cans remaining, a long stick of summer sausage, a pizza box shoved in the back. Oh, yes, and then a tall plastic container of sliced fruit that's packed to the rim, and a batch of veggie lasagna, still in the shrink-wrapped casserole dish, with only one square cut out of the corner.

I find Uncle Lang out back, sitting in a chair overlooking his lawn, a water sprinkler doing its thing, the air steamy as a sauna. Lang is wearing a button-down shirt and slacks and decent loafers. I'd forgotten he had that fund-raiser earlier today.

"Heya, missy," he says to me. His eyes are small and red. The glass of gin in his hand isn't his first of the day. He probably drank gin at the fund-raiser and pretended it was ice water.

I kiss his forehead and sit in the chair on the other side of the small glass table, the one holding the bottle of Beefeater.

"You haven't touched the fruit I cut up for you," I say. "And the veggie lasagna? What's the deal there? You preserving it for posterity?"

He sips his gin. "I don't like spinach. I told you that."

"Yeah?" I turn to him. "And what's your excuse for the fruit?"

He waves me off. "I don't know, it's . . . mushy."

"It's pineapple and melon and cantaloupe. You like them."

"Well, it's mushy."

"That's because you let it sit there for a week. I cut it up a week ago and you didn't touch it. Not one piece." I whack the back of my hand against his shoulder.

"Ow. Don't hit me."

"I'll hit you if I want to hit you. You're like a child.

You're like a little kid. That spinach lasagna is delicious."

"Then you eat it."

"Hopeless," I say. "You're hopeless. You know your doctor's appointment is next week. You think Dr. Childress is going to say, 'Congratulations, Chief, a month of eating meatball sandwiches and fried chicken and French fries did the trick—your cholesterol has plummeted!'"

Lang pushes the empty second glass over toward me and gives me a crosswise look. "Don't think I don't know what you're doing, missy."

"I'm looking out for the well-being of my only living family."

"No, you're *deflecting*. You call me up and tell me you've been to the crime scene, which you know you're not supposed to do, since this isn't your case, so you try to put me on the defensive about my eating habits."

I pour myself a glass of gin. One won't kill me. "Ten gets you twenty that the abrasions on the armoire leg came from a handcuff. He made each of them watch the other die," I say. "He immobilized Zach and he hand-cuffed Melanie to the armoire. He made them watch each other bleed out."

"Jenna—"

"This guy knew what he was doing," I say. "He stabbed Zach in a place where he wouldn't die instantly. I mean, he could have sunk that knife into his heart, or slit his throat. Instead, he stabbed him in a place that would cause incredible pain and a slow death. And when Zach made any feeble attempt to raise himself up, he stomped on his hands. And he did the same thing to

Melanie. Every time she tried to move, he stabbed her. She kicked her legs, and he stabbed her in the calf. She raised her free arm, and he stabbed her in the triceps—"

"Jenna—"

"These were sadistic, brutal torture-murders," I say, "not crimes of passion committed by a jealous lover."

"Crimes of passion can be sadistic, Jen—"

"Do you really think if Noah was in love with Melanie, he'd watch Zach have sex with her first? Why wouldn't he rush in while they were in the heat of it?"

"Hey!" the chief shouts. "Do I get a word in here? I've heard enough. There is protocol, and there is a chain of command, and nobody breaches that in Southampton. If you think just because you're my niece—"

"Of course I don't think that. And I'm just trying to help—"

"You're not helping. You're not helping at all!" The chief coughs into his fist, his face turning red. He needs to take better care of himself. I can make all the heart-healthy meals the culinary world has to offer, but I can't make him eat them. I can tell him to walk a couple of miles a few times a week, but I can't walk them for him.

He ignores every bit of advice I give him. He openly defies me on a daily basis. So why do I love this grouchy old man so much?

"Why am I not helping?" I ask.

Lang polishes off his glass of gin and composes himself. "Because Noah Walker confessed," he says.

I draw back. "He . . . confessed?"

"Ah, the hotshot from NYPD doesn't have all the answers, does she?" Lang pours himself another inch of gin. "He confessed this morning. So don't you go writing up a report that I'll have to show a defense lawyer. Not when this thing is tied up in a bow."

"Noah confessed," I mumble, raising the glass to my lips. "I'll be damned."

"Noah Walker is guilty, and Noah Walker confessed," he says. "So do me a favor and move along."

Chapter 8

THE DIVE BAR is aptly named, dark in every way, from the dim lighting to the oak furnishings, with the Yankees on the big screen, mirrors behind the bar sponsored by various breweries, and nothing but some fried appetizers on the menu for those who dare eat. But the people are friendly and laid-back. It's a place to disappear, and disappearing sounds good to me at the moment. It started as a glass of wine, and then it became three, and I'm thinking it's five now. Once I started, I couldn't think of a good reason to stop.

This place is locals only—tradesmen and laborers and the occasional cop—which I prefer, because it's high season in the Hamptons and all the money's in town. Not that I don't enjoy seeing men with cardigans tied around their necks and women with so much work done on their faces that they've begun to resemble the Joker. Just not on my day off. And not after the day I've had, making a jerk out of myself in front of my uncle, the guy who gave me a second chance.

I should stop drinking. My thoughts are swimming and my mood is darkening. I'm still not sure I made the right move, coming to the Hamptons. I could have found something else to do in Manhattan, or I could have tried to find another big city and start over, even if I had to start at the bottom rung again on patrol. But my uncle the chief made me an offer, and nobody else was knocking down my door.

"Shit," I say, the word slow and heavy on my tongue. I check my watch, and it's nearing six o'clock in the evening. I haven't eaten anything since breakfast, and my stomach is hollowed out and churning. (Some might argue that's an apt summary of my life, too.)

"Whatever, man. Whatever! You know I'm good for it! How long I been comin' here?"

The small outburst comes from the guy at the end of the bar, whom I've managed not to notice since I've been here. Or maybe he just arrived. My brain isn't hitting on all cylinders right now.

He's dressed the same way he was today at Melanie Phillips's funeral, a dark T-shirt that I might otherwise use to wipe my kitchen counter, a green ball cap turned backward, his long, strawlike hair popping out on both sides and covering his ears.

"Jerry," I say to the bartender. That's a good bartender name, *Jerry*. "Put his beer on my tab."

Jerry, a portly guy with a big round head and a green apron, gives me a crosswise look. I nod and he shrugs, pulling on the lever to fill Aiden Willis's mug with a Budweiser he couldn't afford.

Aiden's deep-set eyes move in my direction. He

doesn't say anything. There may be a glint of recognition, if he noticed me at the cemetery. My biggest flaw as a cop is my bright-red hair. When I was undercover for a year and a half and didn't want to be memorable, I dyed it black.

I go back to my Pinot, trying to remind myself that I'm off duty but wondering if Aiden the cemetery caretaker will come over. When I glance back up a few minutes later, Aiden is still looking at me, his beer untouched. He doesn't acknowledge me in any way, just stares with those raccoon eyes. But even his stare isn't really a stare. His eyes move about, wandering aimlessly, always returning to me but never staying on me.

My cell phone buzzes, a text message. Ten mins away. R U at home?, the message reads. My hesitation to respond surprises me, but there it is. *Always trust your gut*, my father used to say. *Sometimes it's all you have.*

Well, Pop, I had a gut feeling about Noah Walker, and look where that got me.

I type in the address of the bar and hit Send. I look back to the corner of the bar, where Aiden's mug remains full of beer, but Aiden himself is gone.

I'm into my next glass, which now puts me at about five too many, if anyone's counting, when the door of the place pops open and a lot of people's chins rise. I don't even need to turn around to know it's Matty, who would stick out in this place like an oil stain on cotton. A moment later, an arm comes over my shoulder and playfully around my neck. His cologne greets me next, before his face is against mine. This is where I'm supposed to swoon with unbridled delight.

"Hey, gorgeous. What's with the depressing-bar thing?"

Matty Queenan is a Wall Street investor with a job I can't really describe because I've never really understood all the financial hocus-pocus these guys pull. All I really understand is that it's a game without rules: You pick a winner for your clients, then bet on them to lose behind their backs, and if everything goes to shit, the little guy will get screwed but the government will bail you out.

"Want a drink?" I ask Matty.

"Here? No. Let's go someplace decent."

I look at Jerry, who pretends he didn't hear what Matty just said.

"Seriously, Murphy. This place is a dump. I'm going to need a tetanus shot—"

"Keep your voice down." I'm standing now, whispering harshly in his ear. "People can hear you. You're being rude."

He takes me by the arm, but I pull away. "Jerry," I say, "I apologize for my rude friend, and please buy everyone a round on me." I slap a fifty on the bar, having already paid for my other drinks, and get some applause for the gesture along with some hard stares in my boyfriend's direction.

I hear my cell phone ring in my purse, but I'm too hacked off to do anything but storm out of the place, Matty not far behind.

Chapter 9

"WHAT'S WITH THE asshole routine?" I say to Matty as soon as I'm back in the sweltering heat outside.

"What's with being half in the bag before I show up? What's with hanging out in a seedy dive like that?"

I turn to look at my boyfriend of eleven months, the first two of which we spent together when I lived in the city, the last nine of which have been long-distance. I probably am a little tipsier than I should be, but he didn't even call and let me know he was coming until a few hours ago, when he was already on his way. That's Matty for you, always on his own schedule, just assuming I'll drop everything and jump into his arms when he shows up.

Okay, to be fair, it's not like I was working on my doctoral thesis or trying to end world hunger when he called.

I turn back to him. Matty looks like a Wall Street guy even when he dresses down, in an Armani sport coat, silk shirt, and expensive trousers, with Ferragamo shoes

47

that would consume an entire paycheck of mine, his long hair slicked back. He's got the looks, no doubt. His confidence, more than anything, drew me to him when we met—guess where—at a bar in Midtown.

"Don't get me wrong," he says, moving to me. "I like you when you're tipsy."

I push his hands away. "Those people in there are nice folks. You insulted them."

He thinks for a moment, then puts a hand on his chest. "Then I will march back in there and give a bar-wide apology. Will that make Jenna happy?" He doesn't wait for an answer, instead raising his arm and checking his watch. "I just decided something," he says.

I guess I'm supposed to ask what. A few one-liners leap to mind.

"I just decided that this place is bad for you. You don't belong here. Just seeing you in the bar seals it. You need the city, kiddo. This place is depressing you."

"Manhattan would depress me," I say, even though in some ways, there's no place I'd rather be. There's no place like it in the world. But I got to know it through a cop's eyes, and seeing it otherwise now would be like a cruel joke every day.

"Well, we need to figure *something* out," he says as we reach his Beemer, fire-engine red with a beige interior. "This commute is a bitch."

"It'll be better after Labor Day, when the Rockefellers and Vanderbilts take off."

"Talk about depressing," he says as he uses his remote to pop the locks. "Summer's the only time this place is interesting. Hey," he says as I open the passenger door.

"Hey what?"

He nods at me. "Are you going to change? We're going to Quist."

For the first time, I take an inventory of myself. I'm wearing a sleeveless white blouse, blue jeans, and low heels. But even the nicest places—and Quist is the nicest, a hotel restaurant opened by some celebrity chef—have a pretty relaxed dress code in the summer.

"Let's swing by your place," he says. "Wear that lavender dress I bought you. Then you'll be turning heads."

"But I won't turn heads in this?"

He chuckles at his faux pas. "C'mon, you know what I mean. We're going to a five-star restaurant. You really want to look like that?"

I hike my purse back over my shoulder and remember my cell phone, the call I missed a moment ago. I pull out my iPhone and see that the call came from "Uncle Langdon," which I really should change to "Chief James" now.

Taking another look at my phone, I see that the chief actually called me twice, once a minute ago and once twenty-four minutes ago.

Still standing outside the car, I dial him back.

"Jenna Rose," he answers, the only person who's ever incorporated my middle name when addressing me. The only one who's lived to tell about it, anyway. "I was about to give up on you."

"How can I help you, Chief? Were you looking for my recipe for grilled asparagus? It's not that hard. Just grill the asparagus."

49

"No, missy, not just now. You wanted to work a homicide, right?"

I spring to attention. "Yes, sir. Absolutely."

"Then get your butt in gear, Detective," he says. "You just got a homicide. One you may never forget."

Chapter 10

"IT'S MY JOB. It's not like I have a choice," I say to Matty, his knuckles white on the leather steering wheel of his Beemer as we drive along the back roads. "A woman was murdered."

"It can't wait until after dinner? She'll still be dead."

I close my eyes. "You didn't really just say that, did you?"

The back roads are narrow and winding and unforgiving, two lanes at best, with no shoulders. Driving them in the dark is even worse. But without the back roads, the locals in Bridgehampton would collectively commit suicide during the tourist season, when the principal artery—Main Street or, if you prefer, Montauk Highway—is clogged like a golf ball in a lower intestine.

"I passed up Yankees tickets on the third-base line," he says. "Sabathia against Beckett in game one."

I know. I watched it in the bar. Sabathia got tagged for six earned runs in five innings. "It's my job," I say again. "What am I sup—"

"No, it's not."

"What do you mean, it's not—"

"Not *tonight* it's not!"

We find our destination, lit up by the STPD like a nighttime construction job, spotlights shining on the scene deep within the woods. The road has been reduced to one lane by traffic cones and flares.

Matty pulls up, puts it in park, and shifts in his seat to face me. "Don't act like you have no choice. There are detectives on duty right now. You're not one of them. You didn't have to take this assignment. You *wanted* it."

I pinch the bridge of my nose. "Sorry about your Yankees tickets."

"Jenna, c'mon."

I step out of the Beemer and flash my badge to the uniform minding the perimeter. I dip under the crime-scene tape and watch my step as I walk through the woods, with their uneven footing and stray branches.

It's a large lot, undeveloped land full of tall trees, with a FOR SALE sign near the road. Whoever did this picked a remote location.

Isaac Marks approaches me. "Bru-tal," he says. "C'mon." I follow him through the brush, my feet crunching leaves and twigs. "The guy who owns this lot found her," he says. "Nice old guy, late seventies. He was stopping by for some routine maintenance and heard a swarm of insects buzzing around."

I slow my approach when I see her. It's hard to miss her, under the garish lighting. She looks artificial, like a museum exhibit—*Woman in Repose,* except in this case, it would be more like *Woman with a tree stump through her midsection.*

"Jesus," I mumble.

The woman is naked, arms and legs splayed out, her head fallen back, as she lies suspended several feet off the ground, impaled on the trunk of a tree that has been shaved down to the point of a thick spear.

Technicians are working her over right now, photographing and gently probing her. The insects buzzing around her are fierce. She's suffered some animal bites, too. That, plus the look of her skin, gives me an approximate window on time of death.

"She died . . . maybe one, two days ago," I say.

Isaac looks at me. "Very good, Detective. At least that's what the ME is saying at first glance. One to two days."

"That's a significant difference, one versus two days."

"Yeah? Why?"

"Two days ago," I say, "Noah Walker was a free man. But one day ago, we took him into custody, and he couldn't have done this."

"You're connecting this with *Noah Walker?*" Isaac gives me a crosswise glance. "This is nothing like those murders."

I move in for a closer look at the victim. This nameless woman, hardened and discolored now, with the ravages of nature having taken their toll, is hard to categorize. I'm thinking she's pretty young, from the bone structure and lithe build. Early twenties, maybe, what appear to be nice features, and beautiful brown hair hanging down inches from the grass.

She was pretty. Before some monster impaled her on a wooden spear like a sacrificial offering to the gods, this woman was pretty. "No ID yet," says Isaac. "But we have a missing-persons from Sag Harbor that we think will check out. If it does, then this is . . ." He flips open a notepad and holds it in the artificial light. "Bonnie Stamos. Age twenty-four. Couple of arrests for take-a-wild-guess."

"She was a working girl." Not terribly surprising. The clients a prostitute serves come in all shapes and sizes, but it's like I felt when I was on patrol, approaching a car I'd just pulled over—you're never really sure what's waiting for you.

"This is totally different than what we found on Ocean Drive," Isaac says. "Those were a bloodbath. This thing is . . . what . . . posed, I guess. Dramatic. Like some ritual thing, some ancient Mayan ceremony. How do you connect these two crimes?"

I squat down next to the tree stump and gesture at it. "See the side of the tree and the surrounding grass and dirt?"

"I see blood everywhere, if that's what you mean."

"Exactly," I say. "Blood everywhere. Her heart was still pumping. *That's* how I connect these crimes."

"Not following."

"She was still alive when he did this, when he impaled her on the tree trunk." I stand back up and feel a wave of nausea. "The symbolism was incidental, a means to an end," I say. "He wanted her to die a slow death, Isaac. He wanted her to suffer."

Chapter 11

THE CHIEF HAS the porch light on for me when I walk up the steps to his house. The squad car that drove me here idles in the driveway. The door is open, and Uncle Lang has a bottle of gin and two glasses on the kitchen table. Dirty dishes are piled high in the sink just as they were earlier today, with evidence of meal choices—remnants of dried catsup or smears of brown gravy, a bit of hamburger. The floor could use a good wash, too. The clock on the wall says it's almost two in the morning.

My uncle doesn't look well. He's gained a lot of weight since Aunt Chloe left him two years ago. His face is splotchy, broken capillaries on his prominent nose, his eyes rimmed with heavy bags. He's wearing a wife-beater T-shirt that accentuates his added poundage, tufts of curly white chest hair peeking over the top.

"You don't look good," he says to me.

I kiss him on the forehead before I turn to the refrigerator. "I was just thinking the same about you. Still drinking, I see." I take another glance into his refrigerator. The fruit container still hasn't been touched, but a second square is missing from the pan of spinach lasagna.

I look back at him with an eyebrow raised.

"See?" he says. "I listen to you."

"Yeah?" I take a seat across from him. "And if I look through your trash, will I find an entire square piece of lasagna, without a bite taken?"

"Now you've insulted me. I'm insulted."

That's not a denial. But I can't spend every waking moment hectoring him.

"I'm serious, though," Uncle Lang says. "You look worn out. Are you still having nightmares?"

I shrug. It's been a thing, since I returned to Bridgehampton. Usually they come at night, the sensation of choking, the terror, the desperate cries. What happened to me today, at 7 Ocean Drive, was the first time it ever happened during daylight.

Lang pours me an inch of gin and slides the glass across the table. "Maybe you never should have come back here."

The thought has crossed my mind. It leads to another thought. "Why did my family stop coming here when I was a kid?" I ask.

The chief shrugs. "A story for another time."

"So there's a *story*. Something happened?"

Lang casts a fleeting glance at me, then deflects. "Did you move the body tonight?"

I nod. "We had to cut the tree from underneath her. Didn't want to separate her from the trunk yet. Never know what forensics might pick up."

"Good. Good that you moved her. I don't need to see photos in the *Patch* tomorrow. This is a dead hooker, Detective. Not a dead hooker who was split in half on a tree stump like some human *shish kebab*. Understand me? A dead hooker, to the media. That's it. Just another hooker *adiosed* in the Hamptons. That's a one-day story."

A one-day story. Appearances. Politics. There's an election coming up, and the town supervisor is already feeling heat from the Zach Stern / Melanie Phillips murders. Another sensational murder would just add pressure. It's good police procedure, too, not mentioning gory details to the press. In Manhattan, that plan never worked; the NYPD leaked like a colander. But here, it might.

"Your case has nothing to do with Noah Walker," Lang says.

Oh, Isaac, you little shit. Talk about leaks. No wonder the chief wanted to meet me tonight. Isaac must have sneaked away from me in a free moment and called him. So now I know where his loyalties lie. That little twerp.

"Too early to tell," I say.

The chief casts his eyes in my direction. He takes a sip of Beefeater and lets out a breath. "A few hours ago, you thought Noah was an innocent man, wrongly accused. Now you like him for the carnage in the woods, too."

"I don't like him or dislike him. Not yet. But it's possible the prostitute was killed while Noah was still a free man, not yet in custody. I'm just playing all the angles. That's what I'm paid to do."

He makes a noise as he finishes another sip. "No, you're paid to do what I *tell* you to do."

"I'm a detective," I say. "Once in a while, I try to detect."

The gin is sharp on my tongue, hot down my throat, leaving a delicious citrus aftertaste. Tastes better than it should. I take the bottle and pour myself another. "Let me ask you a question, Chief."

He shows me a wary look but doesn't speak.

"Why did we go in so hard on the arrest?"

"What do you mean?" He pours himself another drink.

"When we arrested Walker. The SWAT team. The automatic weapons. We were braced for a firefight. Noah didn't have any weapons."

The chief's jaw tightens, but he doesn't make eye contact with me. "Missy, you're lucky you're my favorite niece."

"I'm your only niece."

"Don't fuck with my case, Jenna." He slams down his glass. "I've got Noah Walker dead to rights. I need that solved. I've got orders from on high. You start tying this dead-hooker murder in with it, then we have to turn your report over to Walker's lawyer, and he'll play with that window of time—maybe two days, maybe three, maybe Noah was already in custody when the hooker got hers—and suddenly Clarence Darrow is saying that one person did both murders, and that one person couldn't have been Noah Walker."

"And what if that's true?"

My uncle gives me a look that I remember seeing as

a child, that look an adult gives when a kid is being adorably precocious, a combination of pride and annoyance. But in this case, the annoyance is outweighing the pride.

"Stay away from Noah Walker. Don't make your case something it's not."

"Just 'another hooker *adiosed* in the Hamptons,' right?" I push myself out of the chair. "I'm not going to do it. I'm following the leads wherever they go. You don't like it, relieve me."

The chief looks exhausted. He gestures toward me, the sign of the cross, absolution from a priest. "You are hereby relieved of any responsibility for the dead hooker in the woods."

"That's *bullshit,* Lang!" With the back of my hand, I whack my glass off the table, smashing it against the sink.

"Yeah? You wanna go for a suspension, too?"

"Sure!"

"Great! You're suspended without pay for a week."

"Only a week?" I yell, lost in my rage now, spinning out of control.

"Fine, then, a *month!* How about dismissal? You want me to can you?" The chief rises from his chair, directing a finger at me. "And before you answer that, missy, remember that being a cop is all you know. And I gave you a second chance. You'd think that would buy me just a little bit of loyalty from you, but oh, no!"

I shake my head, fuming. "I can't believe you just said that."

He waves me away with a hand. "One-month suspension, Detective, effective immediately. Now get out of my house."

Chapter 12

FOR THE FIRST time in over a week, he breathes fresh air, he walks in grass, he wears his own clothes, he sees the sun, not over a concrete wall for one hour a day but out in the open. Noah Walker takes a moment to savor it before he steps into the minibus that will transport him to the train station for passage from Riverhead to Bridgehampton.

When he's home, he first takes a shower—no fancy shower-head or immaculate tub, but at least a healthy flow of water, without mold on the fixtures, without raw sewage bubbling from the drain, without having to look over his shoulder to wonder whether he was going to have an unexpected visitor. The biggest problem with Suffolk County Jail in Riverhead was the temporary nature of it all. Nobody in Riverhead had been convicted of a crime—if they had, they'd be in prison. Riverhead was just a pretrial holding facility for people with unaffordable bail or no bail at all, and thus there was nothing in the way of remedial programs or education, no recreational facilities, no pretense of nutritious meals. It was just walls, a handful of books, a chaplain on Sunday, shit for food, and an overpopulation of pissed-off detainees. He met someone inside, a guy named Rufus, who'd been in county lockup for over four years waiting for his trial.

None of that for Noah. He's demanded a speedy trial, his constitutional right. He can't stomach the thought of waiting months, even years, wondering.

Out of the shower, hair dripping wet, feeling warm and refreshed, he picks up his cell phone and hits the speed dial.

"Are you out?" Paige says breathlessly when she answers.

"I'm out," he says, thanks to her, and the checking account that bears only her name, that her husband doesn't control. "I'm home now."

"I can . . . I'll be there as soon as I can."

He feels a rush, a longing for her, tempered with fear. "Are you sure? What about—"

"I don't care. I'll figure something out. I'll tell him something. I don't think he knows about us. He's never said a word—"

"He knows about us," Noah says. Of course her husband knows. That has to be what's going on here. John Sulzman is a man of boundless influence. Influential enough to snap his fingers and have someone thrown in prison? Noah's no expert on backroom deals, but he doesn't doubt it.

"Well, I'm coming. I can't wait to see you!"

"Me too." Noah closes his eyes. "Just . . . be careful," he says.

Chapter 13

NOAH'S TOES CURL into the moist sand. He looks out over the Atlantic, black and restless in the dark, the post-rain breeze brushing his face. *This is what freedom feels like,* he thinks. *This is what I missed the most.*

He hears the familiar hum of the superior engine approaching. He stands and sees her Aston Martin pulling up in the lot. She pops out of the car and forgets to close the door. Noah is already running toward her.

No, he thinks, *she is what I missed the most.*

"I can't believe it," she manages as he scoops her up in his arms; she wraps her legs around him and grips his hair. Their mouths press against each other, more of a smash than a kiss. His body is charged with electricity.

"I didn't . . . kill those people," he whispers.

"You don't need to say that to me. Of course I know that." Paige strokes his face. "What can I do to help? Do you need money for a lawyer? A private detective?"

"You can't do that," Noah says. "John will—"

"I don't care about John. You need someone on your

side. I'll do whatever I have to do. I won't let you go through this alone. Tell me what you need."

"I just need you. That's all I need right now." Noah draws her close, breathes in her fresh-strawberry scent, takes in the warmth of her body. As long as he holds her, which could be five seconds, could be an hour, there is no criminal indictment, there is no prospect of life in prison, there is only Paige, the woman he loves, the woman who loves him.

And then he hears another vehicle approaching.

Noah raises his head. The beach had been empty, thanks in part to the lateness of the hour but more so to the rainfall an hour ago. The approaching SUV is not familiar to him. It stops in the middle of the small parking lot that serves as the end of Ocean Drive, positioned so that its headlights are trained on Noah and Paige.

Noah walks around the Aston Martin to stand between the headlights and Paige, a protective gesture.

"Well, shit, timing sure is everything, isn't it?" says Detective Isaac Marks, getting out of his vehicle. "Another case of coitus interruptus."

"What do you want *now?*" Noah's hands curl into fists. He moves toward Isaac.

"Easy, son, easy."

Son. Noah's always hated how cops talk to him, the condescension. But especially from Isaac Marks, who was the same year as him at Bridgehampton, and their history—and now he's calling Noah *son.* What a difference a badge can make.

"Just stop right there, Noah. I wouldn't want to

interpret your movements as a *threat*. Then I'd have to violate you, wouldn't I? Send you right back where you came from." Isaac nods in Paige's direction. "Of course, I could violate you right now for public indecency."

Noah, fuming, stands his ground. How much he'd love to wipe that smirk off Isaac's face. But that would be giving the cop exactly what he wants, to haul Noah back to Riverhead.

"Who's your friend?" asks Isaac, moving around Noah, shining his Maglite in Paige's direction. "Is that the same little honey from when we busted you?"

What an asshole. He knows very well it's Paige. This whole thing is because of Paige. It has to be. This has to be John Sulzman's doing.

"What do you want, Isaac?"

"That's Detective Marks to you."

"This is harassment!" Paige shouts. "We're not hurting anybody, we're not doing anything indecent at all! The only indecency here is the police harassing an innocent man. Don't you have anything better to do with your time, *Detective*?"

"Lady, let me give you a piece of advice," says Isaac. "I know it's fun to slum it once in a while and fuck the hired help, but your stallion here, turns out he's a vicious killer. Now, I don't know how in glorious hell he came up with the cash to bond himself out, but you better believe we're going to watch every move he makes, and we're not going to let him be alone with another woman after what he did to that waitress—"

"I don't know what's going on here," Paige says, frustration overtaking her composure. "But Noah is innocent, and it would be nice if the police department spent its time searching for a killer instead of following around someone who's out on bail."

"You're a real feisty one, lady, you know that?" Isaac shows her his teeth. "All the same, if we see you two together again, Noah gets violated and heads back to jail." He turns to Noah. "That simple enough for you to understand, Mr. Walker? See, lady, Noah here, he didn't do so well in school—"

"Oh, you want to talk about *school*?" Noah approaches Isaac. For a moment, it's like they're back on the playground, two kids, not a cop and an accused felon. "You want to talk about old times, Isaac? Because I've got a lot of stories. You wanna tell her how you got your nick—"

"That's enough, boy." Isaac raises a finger. "One more word, and it's back to Riverhead. Your choice."

Noah sucks in a breath. There's nothing he can say.

"There, that's better," says Isaac. "Mrs. Sulzman, you should be getting along now. Say good-bye to the Hamptons until next summer. Noah, he'll be at Sing Sing by then, but I'm sure you can find another boy toy, some gutter cleaner to pass the time."

With that, Paige breaks down, into tears and gasping breaths. Isaac swings his SUV in a three-point turn and drives away.

"Don't worry, I'll think of something," Noah says, holding Paige, touching her wet face. "I'll think of something."

And then, just like that, like the snap of a finger, he does.

Chapter 14

NO, PLEASE DON'T make me, I don't wanna—

Childish giggles, pressure on my throat, darkness, then light—

A bird, an angry bird with a hooked nose, standing upright—

Please don't make me—

I wake with a gasp, my head coming off the pillow, sucking in air, the sounds of giggling and desperate cries slowly fading, the pressure removed from my chest, hands no longer gripping my throat.

"Shit." My breathing finally slows. The clock says it's two minutes to seven. Who needs an alarm clock when you have nightmares every day?

I grab my iPhone and scroll through photos, spotting the picture I took of that little monument on the lawn at 7 Ocean Drive, that gray-and-black bird with the hooked beak and long tail feather. Yep, that was it, the same one from the nightmare. Great.

I shower, eat some toast and fruit, and chug two

glasses of water to work off my hangover, courtesy of the two bottles of wine Matty and I had last night as a send-off, my last night of forced vacation before I resume my job. Matty is long gone, having left my apartment around five this morning to head back to Manhattan; I have a brief memory of his aftershave and a kiss good-bye.

I go to work for the first time in thirty days. I feel like a tourist stepping onto foreign soil, the uncertainty of it all, especially of the reception I'll get from the natives when I show my face.

The Southampton Town Police substation in Bridgehampton is not exactly an intimidating place, nestled in the corner of an outdoor shopping mall called Bridgehampton Commons off Main Street, filled with chain shops like the Gap, Staples, Panera, a King Kullen grocery store, Victoria's Secret, and yes, a Dunkin' Donuts (I know, the jokes write themselves). The black patrol vehicles park in the south corner next to a row of tall recycling bins for clothes and shoes.

I park my beater in the back and walk into the substation, my bag over my shoulder and a general wariness in my gut. I get some mock applause from a couple of detectives who welcome me back after my one-month vacation. Isaac Marks isn't there, the weasel. He probably has his nose up the chief's ass right now.

Somebody tidied up my desk during my absence. Not that there's much to it, other than a photograph of my parents, and one of my brother, Ryan. There was a particularly nice shot of the entire family with Uncle Langdon and Aunt Chloe at Coney Island that I used to have on my desk at the NYPD, but I didn't want to emphasize the familial relationship here, with my uncle being the top dog. There's some resentment already, some whispers of nepotism about my hiring, though nobody could accuse the chief of favoritism after my suspension.

"Chief wants to see you, Murph." One of the administrative assistants, Margaret, drops a bunch of papers on my desk, mail and assorted paperwork.

"The chief's here?" Lang doesn't usually spend time at the substation, generally working out of headquarters on Old Riverhead Road.

When I enter his office, he seems to be expecting me, wiggling his fingers for me to come in and pointing to the seat opposite the desk while he finishes up a phone call. He finishes barking out directions to one of his deputies before hanging up and looking me over, a hand straying over his mouth.

"Sit," he says.

"I'm fine standing."

He folds his hands together. "When an uncle tells his niece to sit, she can say she's fine standing. But when the chief tells one of his detectives to sit, she sits. And right now, Detective, I'm your chief."

I look away, biting my tongue. He's right. Whatever else, he's right about this.

I take a seat.

"At least you didn't quit," he says. "I thought you might."

I toss my shoulders, like the statement is irrelevant. I'm not going to quit. That's the one thing I learned from the month I spent in Matty's condo in Greenwich Village, dining out and going for long runs, sleeping in and watching old movies, catching some theater and Yankees games. I love living in Manhattan, but I love being a cop more. And if I lose this job with the STPD, nobody will ever give me another chance.

Lang riffles through some paper on his desk. "There's a joint task force tracking heroin coming out of Montauk. You're joining it today."

My mouth comes open, but I don't speak. Look, it's not like I'm too good to work narcotics. My last assignment with the NYPD was working undercover on a major heroin ring. But I volunteered for that, because undercover work was a new challenge, and I'd come from Robbery-Homicide. Your basic narcotics task force—that's below my experience level. It's a clear step backward. And the chief, my dearest uncle, would know that better than anybody.

"Yes, sir," I say. "Anything else?"

"That's it."

I nod and push myself from the chair. When I reach the doorway, he calls out to me. I turn back and look at him.

"I'm having a salad for lunch today," he says. "And I've been walking a mile and a half every day for the last two weeks."

I don't smile. I'm not going to give him the satisfaction. "Why would a detective care what her chief has for lunch? Or what his exercise regimen is?"

He winks at me without smiling. "You're still my favorite niece."

I'm his only niece. But I won't take the bait.

"Don't worry, your favorite niece still loves you," I say. "But your favorite *detective* still thinks you're a horse's ass."

Chapter 15

"THE SUPREME COURT of Suffolk County is back in session," calls the bailiff. *"People versus Noah Lee Walker."*

Noah shakes his head quietly. He hates it when they announce the case name. It's hard to feel like you have a fighting chance when it's the entire State of New York against you. And his full name—nobody's ever called him Noah Lee. It makes him sound like a presidential assassin or a mass murderer.

He's probably starting to look like one, too. In the three months since his arrest, Noah has not cut his hair, which was on the longer side to begin with. Now it falls in waves around his unshaven face. *USA Today* was the first to use the nickname Surfer Jesus, but now even the *Times* and Nancy Grace have adopted it.

"Mr. Akers?" The judge, an intimidating, steely-faced, silver-haired man named Robert Barnett, looks over his glasses at the prosecutor, Assistant District Attorney Sebastian Akers. Akers is a tall man with thick dark hair and the clean-cut good looks of a varsity quarterback or presidential candidate. But it's not just his looks; his presence, too, the confidence, the performance adrenaline; he's a man who seems to grow a few inches, whose voice lowers an octave, as he stands before a courtroom bursting at the seams with spectators and reporters.

"May it please the court," Akers says, buttoning his suit coat and positioning himself before the jury box. Fifteen sets of eyes—twelve jurors and three alternates—are fixed on the prosecutor. "Melanie Phillips was one of ours, born and raised in Bridgehampton. She didn't graduate at the top of her class and she hadn't yet attended college. But she had dreams. At age twenty, she worked day shifts at a seafood hut and took drama classes at night to realize that dream, the dream of becoming an actress. It may have been unrealistic. Sometimes dreams are. But this is America, and we all have the right to pursue our dreams, don't we? But Melanie—Melanie never got that chance. Her life, her dreams were cut short when she was brutally murdered, stabbed and slashed over and over again in a rental house by the beach three months ago."

Akers sits on that thought a moment, shaking his head with sadness. "Zachary Stern," he says, and the jurors pop to attention again. "Long time ago, Zach had the same dream. He was an actor. Never made it big, but did it for years, a few commercials here, a couple of television appearances there. And when he finally realized that being a movie star wasn't in the cards for him, he decided to help other people fulfill their dreams. He became an agent, one of the most successful in

Hollywood. And one day, while vacationing in the Hamptons, he met Melanie Phillips. He was going to sign her. Would he have made Melanie famous? Maybe. But we'll never know. Because Zach was murdered along with Melanie."

Akers turns sideways, so that the jurors can clearly see Noah at the defense table. Akers turns his head toward Noah and raises his arm. "That man, Noah Lee Walker," says Akers, jabbing his finger at him, "savagely killed Melanie Phillips and Zach Stern in a fit of rage, in the most brutal of ways. He sliced them open and left them for dead."

Noah shakes his head and locks eyes with the jurors. His defense lawyer said not to respond, to look composed and dignified, but he can't listen to that accusation without responding.

"It was a crime of passion, a crime of rage," says Akers. "A crime of jealousy. You see, Noah Walker was in love with Melanie. He didn't want to lose her to Zach Stern or to Hollywood. No, if you try to leave Noah Walker, this is the price you pay."

Akers nods to his assistant, who pushes a button. Noah's lawyer had argued desperately to keep this out of the trial, but the judge ruled against him.

The slide show that pops on the screen shows crime-scene photographs of Melanie, close-ups and full-body shots, her vacant eyes staring into space, her mouth barely open, a dozen cuts from a knife, some of them deeper, some superficial. The photos of Zach Stern aren't much better, perhaps less graphic but still horrific. The jury recoils at them, audibly gasping and murmuring.

Then the screen goes blank. Akers walks over to the witness stand. "You will hear from people who knew Melanie and Noah. They will sit in this chair and they will tell you about that relationship. They will tell you about Noah's obsession. They will tell you that Noah couldn't bear the thought of losing Melanie, that he was insane with jealousy." Akers walks over to the evidence table and lifts a bag. "You will hear expert testimony that this knife was stained with the blood of Zach and Melanie. And you will hear from Chief of Police Langdon James that he found this knife under a heating duct in Noah Walker's kitchen floor, along with a charm necklace that Melanie had worn around her neck every day of her life since she was six years old."

Akers takes a moment, waiting for his conclusion.

"And you will hear something else from Chief James. You will hear testimony that Noah Walker *confessed* to these murders, that when his guard was down, he admitted killing Melanie and Zach and explained exactly how he did it."

Akers turns again and points at Noah. "We will prove all of this to you, ladies and gentlemen, that much I promise you. And when this trial is over, we will ask you to give Melanie and Zach the only thing that you can give them now: justice. We will ask you to return two verdicts of guilty of murder in the first degree against Noah Lee Walker."

In ten minutes, Akers has summarized the whole thing in a way that makes Noah look obviously guilty. Akers has horrified them with the gruesome photos and appealed to their sympathy with the talk of Hollywood dreams dashed. Hell, he's even made that bloodsucker Zach Stern sound like a swell guy.

Noah sees it in the jurors' eyes, the way they follow the prosecutor as he returns to the defense table, the way they stare in Noah's direction with contempt.

He's going to need a miracle.

Chapter 16

"REMY HANDLEMAN," THE bailiff calls out into the hallway, summoning the prosecution's first witness.

Remy Handleman enters the courtroom and takes the witness stand. He is wearing a suit, but not one that he's worn before. The jacket hangs limp over his shoulders and the collar is too wide. Remy's probably never worn a suit in his life.

After he takes his oath, he runs a hand over his oily hair and fidgets in his chair, his hands likewise unable to find a comfortable place to rest. The behavior of a liar, a bad one, at least.

"Mr. Handleman," says the prosecutor, buttoning his coat at the podium, "is your appearance here today pursuant to a subpoena?"

"My appear—" Remy looks down at himself. "Somebody said I should wear a suit. Is that what you mean?"

Despite his predicament, Noah can't help but feel for Remy, who's too dim to understand why everyone's chuckling in the courtroom. Remy first came to Bridgehampton when Noah was a seventh grader. He was one of those needy kids who wanted everyone to like him and could never understand when they didn't, and never stopped trying. Noah tried to befriend him, even defended him a couple of times from playground beatings, but Remy never quite fit in. He smoked a lot of weed and sold some, too. He was known to the STPD long before they first busted him selling Oxy behind a diner off the turnpike about four years ago.

"Mr. Handleman, were you acquainted with the deceased, Melanie Phillips?"

"Yeah, I knew Melanie. I go into Tasty's for steamers, maybe a couple times a week."

"Tasty's was the restaurant where Melanie waitressed?"

"Uh-huh, yes."

"Take us back to the first weekend of June this year, Mr. Handleman," says the prosecutor, Akers. "Thursday, June second. Did you go into Tasty's that day?"

"Yeah, I did. I had lunch there."

"Who waited on you that day?"

"Melanie did."

"Did you see the defendant there on that day, at that time?"

"Yeah." Remy nods at Noah. "Noah was there. He was, like, like following her around."

"Melanie was doing her waitressing duties, and Noah was following her around?"

"Yeah."

"Did you hear them speak?"

"Yeah. Melanie was like, 'Leave me alone.' And Noah was like, 'Give me another chance, I love you,' stuff like that."

"Mmm-hmm." Akers nods with grave importance, as if the witness has just said something brilliant. Remy is anything but. But he's not so stupid that he couldn't recognize a deal when it was offered to him. Three months ago, the STPD busted him for the second time for selling Oxy, and the second bust was likely to mean serious prison time. It was awfully convenient, then, that he just happened to have information that would help the STPD solve one of the biggest murders the region had ever seen. Suddenly an eight-year sentence is pleaded down to twenty months, all because of his testimony today, his assistance in a high-profile double-murder trial.

"The defendant told Melanie he loved her?"

"Yeah."

"And he asked Melanie to give him another chance?"

"Yeah, he said, 'Give me another chance.' And she said it was over."

"She said it was over?" The prosecutor leans in, like the testimony is just getting interesting. "Did the defendant say anything else that you heard?"

"Yeah, he said, 'You don't just walk away from me.' He, like, grabbed her when he said it."

"He . . . grabbed her where?"

"Like, by the arm. She dropped a dish when he done it, too."

"He grabbed her arm and said, 'You don't just walk away from me'?"

"Right."

"And this took place just two days before Melanie was found dead?"

"Yeah, it sure did."

Sebastian Akers shakes his head, as if he's hearing this testimony for the first time and can't believe how damning it is. "No further questions," he says.

Chapter 17

WEEK TWO OF the Noah Walker murder trial. My first day attending, but it's packed wall-to-wall, as it's apparently been every day since it began. The Suffolk County Sheriff's Office has started a lottery for the general public's admission and a separate one for the media, though if you're a reporter, not drawing a lucky ticket just means you go to a spillover room down the hall to watch the trial on a closed-circuit television. Even coppers like me have a hard time getting in, but I know Rusty the bailiff—that's a good name for a bailiff, *Rusty*—so I got a spot in the fourth row, jammed between an older guy and a young woman wearing too much perfume.

I have a couple of days off after we completed our nine-week sting operation on the heroin trafficking, taking down over twenty people throughout Long Island, most notably a school principal at a private school in Montauk. I didn't have anything else to do, so after my five-mile run this morning, I decided to clean up and come see "Surfer Jesus" for myself.

There he is at the defense table, scratching his beard and whispering to his defense lawyer. The press was initially intrigued with the story because Zach Stern was a victim and it happened in the Hamptons, but Noah himself has now become as interesting as anything else to the talking heads on the evening cable channels—his swarthy good looks, for one, and also his rebellious attitude, refusing to wear a suit to court, opting instead for the desert-islander look with a white shirt and blue jeans.

Taking the stand is a man named Dio Cornwall, an African American in his midtwenties with a long skinny neck and braids pulled tight against his head. He's awaiting trial for armed robbery and had the pleasure of sharing a cell with Noah Walker during the week following Noah's arrest, before Noah bonded out.

"It woulda been the second, maybe third night," says Cornwall. "Guy just starts talkin', is all. Didn't need to ask him or nothin'. Just started talkin'."

"And what exactly did he say about it?" asks the prosecutor, Sebastian Akers, who could double as a Ken doll.

"Says she got hers." Cornwall shrugs. "Says the woman got hers."

"Did you ask him what he meant?"

"Yeah. He says, 'No bitch gonna leave me.' He says, 'I cut her up good. Can't be no movie star now.' "

Oof. That's not good for Noah. But then, nothing's gone that well for Noah, from what I've read and heard on TV.

I look at him, huddling with his lawyer, and again feel something swim in my stomach. When I met him, I made him for a guy who'd grown up rough, and who didn't hold the police department in high esteem, and yeah, someone I might like for a B-and-E or maybe an assault-and-battery. But a brutal killer? He just didn't ping my radar that way.

But it doesn't matter what I think anymore. It matters what twelve jurors think. The opening witness had Noah hounding Melanie at the restaurant where she worked, begging her to take him back and threatening her when she wouldn't. The forensics came next. The knife found in Noah's kitchen had traces of both Zach's and Melanie's DNA. A forensic pathologist testified that the knife had a slight jag in the tip that matched some of the cuts found on the victims.

There was no doubt, in other words, that the knife they found in Noah's house was the murder weapon.

And now this guy, Cornwall, the second person to attribute incriminating statements to Noah.

"When he said 'No bitch gonna leave me,' and that she 'can't be no movie star now,' did the defendant identify this woman by name?"

"Melanie," says Cornwall. "He said her name was Melanie."

Sebastian Akers nods and looks over at the jury box. Strong testimony for the prosecution, no doubt, but still—this guy Cornwall is no different than the first witness, a jailhouse snitch who'd probably sell out his grandmother to shave some time off his sentence.

Which makes the final witness all the more crucial

for the case. The witness being my uncle, Chief Langdon James, the one who found the knife in Noah's kitchen, and the one to whom Noah Walker confessed his guilt. Without the chief, there's the knife and two cons who'd say just about anything.

After the chief's done testifying, Noah Walker will be toast.

Chapter 18

LANGDON JAMES TAKES a hit off his joint and squints through the smoke at the cable news show, where four well-dressed lawyers are talking over one another, arguing about the merits of Dio Cornwall's testimony and the overall strength of the prosecution's case against "Surfer Jesus."

"If I'm Noah Walker's lawyer, my argument is that the prosecution's case is bought and paid for," says one. "Remy Handleman and Dio Cornwall are criminals who would say or do anything to save their own necks."

"But the case isn't over, Roger. The chief of police will testify tomorrow—"

With that, the chief sees his image on TV, a stock photograph taken of him over ten years—and forty pounds—ago, walking outside headquarters, his sunglasses on, hands on his hip, head profiled to the right.

God, where did the years go? That was a different time, in so many ways. That was before Chloe left. That was back when the job was still new to Lang, when he still considered it an honor, even a thrill, to wear the badge.

That was back when his niece, Jenna, still looked up to him, following his career path into law enforcement. He remembers all those nights when Jenna was still a young girl, after her father and brother died, when she would sit with Lang, how her eyes would widen as she listened to his tales of cops and robbers, good guys and bad, fighting for truth and justice. He remembers the swell of pride he felt on Jenna's first day at the academy, when he looked at her, eager to one day don a uniform and make the world a safer place.

The chief clicks off the TV and rubs his eyes. She's a good kid, Jenna. He wishes they hadn't clashed over Noah Walker. After all, she did what any good cop should do—pick up a scent and follow it—and he shot her down when she started to question Walker's guilt.

He hated doing it, dousing her flame that way. But as good a cop as she is—she has more instinct in her pinkie finger than most cops will ever have in their whole bodies—she doesn't always see the bigger picture. Noah Walker is guilty. He's sure of it. Rules and procedure and evidence aside, at the end of the day, that's all that matters.

Is the dead hooker's murder in the woods linked to the murders at 7 Ocean Drive? He doubts it. Hell, Jenna didn't even know for sure—it was just a hunch, an itch she was scratching. But he makes himself this promise: He will follow that lead—soon. Just not now. Not when Noah's defense attorney could play with it. After Noah is convicted, he'll personally check it out.

"Oh, Jenna," he mumbles to himself. Maybe she never should have come back here. The nightmares, the drinking—yes, he's noticed how much she drinks—it all kicked in since she came back here. Is that just a coincidence?

No, it can't be a coincidence.

Seven hours. He remembers it well. If there were seven hours in all the world he could remove, erase completely, it would be those seven hours from Jenna's life.

Seven hours of hell.

And her mother never let Jenna set foot in the Hamptons again.

Until she came back as an adult, to be a cop.

And he let her do it. He thought he was helping her, after she got run out of Manhattan. He thought he was doing a good thing.

He pushes away his notes on tomorrow's testimony. He's testified a hundred times in court. He knows the drill, the flow of the questioning, the way to frame his answers, the phrases to avoid, the importance of maintaining the appropriate demeanor. He stamps out the remainder of the joint, feeling a little stoned but not wanting to take it too far tonight, with the big day tomorrow. Seems like these days, he's always seeking some kind of lubricant to get through the evenings.

He kicks his feet off the bed and heads for the kitchen, for a glass of Beefeater. Just one glass tonight, no more, especially after smoking so much—

Something . . . something is wrong.

A shudder runs through him. He reaches the

threshold of the kitchen before he realizes that the *something*—a change in the pressure, a creak in the floor, a foreign heat source—is behind him, not in front.

He turns back just as the figure steps into the hallway from the bathroom. A man wearing a full mask, though Halloween is still weeks away.

"Wait," the chief says as he sees the weapon rising, training on him. "Wait, just hold on, let's—"

He feels the sharp pinch, the pure heat in his left upper thigh, an instant before he hears the *thwip* from the gun's suppressor. He doubles over but keeps his balance, yells, "Wait!" before another bullet tears through his left biceps. The momentum spins him around, and this time he loses his balance, falling to his hands and knees, crawling like a wounded dog away from his predator, who takes slow, deliberate steps behind him, tracking him.

The chief makes it into the kitchen, pushing off with his good arm and good leg. Another bullet blows through the bottom of his foot, ricocheting off the tile, and this time the cry he lets out is gargled, and he collapses to the floor. He tells himself to keep breathing, to avoid shock, and when he finally manages a pushup, his right elbow explodes from another bullet and he's down for good.

The floor is spinning, everything is upside down. The intruder now casts a shadow over the chief, seeming to be in no particular hurry for this ordeal to come to an end. The chief can do nothing but hope—hope that this man just wants to hurt him and not kill him.

The next bullet drills through his right calf. Langdon can no longer bring himself to scream.

Silence follows, a pause. For just that moment, the chief feels a surge of hope. He's been shot in the limbs, not the head or torso, no vital organs. Maybe the man will let him live. Maybe—

The chief feels a foot in his ribs, a gentle nudging. And then he hears the man's voice, slow and deliberate, icy-calm.

"I . . . need a few minutes," the man with the mask says. "Your fireplace . . . is really old."

Chapter 19

I CUP THE badge in one hand and slam through the double doors with the other. There are other officers already in the emergency room, who register who I am and point down the hall with looks of apology, sympathy on their faces. The hallway feels narrow and too bright, full of people in police uniforms or surgical scrubs. Someone tries to stop me and I say, "I'm next of kin."

There are rooms to the left, all covered with gray-blue curtains. A gurney pops through one of them, several doctors and nurses jogging alongside it, holding bags of fluids and calling out stats to one another.

An arm grabs me. Isaac Marks says, "They're taking him to surgery, Murphy. He—"

"Call Aunt Chloe," I tell him.

"I did already."

I pry my arm free and follow the doctors. "I'm his niece," I say when they object, and I position myself between them and the elevator so they can't stop me.

Uncle Langdon looks foreign, ancient, a mask over

his face for oxygen, a bulge in the covers by his lower torso. I take his right hand in mine. "I'm here, Lang," I manage, yelling over the commotion.

His hand squeezes back. The elevator opens and we all go inside. I angle between two medics who don't resist, allowing us as private a moment as they can possibly give us.

"You're going to be fine," I whisper, my face close to his.

Lang slowly raises his arm, like he's doing a difficult biceps curl, his hand finally reaching the oxygen mask. He pulls it down to his chin. "Jenna Rose," he says, the words thin and whispery.

"I'm here," I choke out.

"You're . . . a good cop."

"I learned from the best." I place my hand delicately on the top of his head, tears streaming down my face, my throat hot and full. "I'm so sorry I questioned you and said all—"

"No." His eyelids flutter, and his head turns ever so slightly back and forth. "Don't ever stop . . . questioning . . . look up . . . Chloe . . . look . . ."

"I will—Chloe's on her way—"

"Okay, we have to go!"

The elevator doors part. I press my lips against his forehead. "You're my favorite uncle." I squeeze out the words through a sob.

One side of his mouth curves just for a moment; a tear slides down his temple into his ear. "I'm your . . . only uncle," he whispers.

And then we are separated, a tug on my arm holding

me back, my uncle wheeled off to surgery, my view of him narrowing as the elevator doors move toward each other and then shut.

Not Lang, I think. *Not Lang, too. No. Please, no.*

When the elevator doors open again, I hear Isaac Marks's voice, talking to another cop. "Five gunshot wounds to his extremities," he says. "And then he heated up a fireplace poker and drove it through his kidney."

I turn in Isaac's direction, not looking at him, the words echoing between my ears. *Shot in the extremities and speared with a poker.*

Tortured. Just like Zach Stern. Just like Melanie Phillips. Just like the prostitute impaled on the tree stump in the woods.

"Oh, Murphy." Isaac's hand rests on my shoulder. "You okay?"

I don't answer. I can't speak.

"It's going to be hours before he's out of surgery, Murph. Maybe—maybe get some fresh air. Get away from this place for a while. But take the back exit. The press is gathered out front. The chief was supposed to testify tomorrow against Noah Walker."

Noah Walker.

I stagger toward the rear exit, into the humid night air, where I finish the long hard cry that I started in the elevator. I don't cry much, but when I do, it's a heaving, gasping avalanche. I fall to my hands and knees and let it all out, the images from my childhood rushing back, Langdon holding me in his arms after Dad and Ryan died, showing up on weekends at our house in the Bronx, always with a little toy or gadget for me, always ready with stories about the bad guys he put away.

Not Lang. Please, God, I know I've doubted you, but I'll do anything now, anything at all, just please, please don't take him away.

And then, after some amount of time I can't quantify, it stops. I get up and brush myself off. The soft tide of sorrow running through my chest turns hard. My senses readjust, back to alert, cop-alert. My vision clears. My nose stops running. My muscles tense.

Noah Walker.

I check my magazine for bullets, then reholster the weapon.

Hours, Isaac said. That will be more than enough time. Noah Walker's house is only a half hour away.

I shove my star deep in my pocket. I won't need a badge tonight.

Chapter 20

NOAH WALKER'S HOUSE is dark. If he's home, he's pretending to be asleep. But he won't have to pretend much longer, and this time he'll never wake up.

The night is sticky but peaceful, nothing but some stray insect sounds. I trot gingerly over the gravel driveway on the balls of my feet and cross around to the back of his house. There is a small yard that borders on heavy woods, an afterthought of a concrete slab with a barbecue grill covered by a hood. The back door is less secure than the front, especially after we busted through it during the arrest.

The door comes open with minimal noise. I shine my Maglite into the back room—a couple of motorcycle helmets, an old Corona typewriter, an easel with a canvas of a seascape, boxes stuffed with clothes and knickknacks, an antique desk in the corner, some framed artwork resting against a wall.

I move into the hallway, my flashlight and gun at eye level, moving them in tandem while I shuffle forward along the tile, surveying room after room—the kitchen, the foyer, the living room.

I stop. Listen. The house groans. The wind outside plays with the trees.

Now the attic bedroom. The only room left.

I try my weight on the first stair and it complains to me. I take every other step, crouched low, slowly transferring my weight onto each new stair like a spider approaching prey, keeping the light beam down.

My eyes are now level with the second floor, my body still below it. I listen for any sounds. There is no such thing as silence in a house. But this house, suddenly, is silent.

I take a step up into the attic, a large open space. I throw the beam of light onto a bed right in front of me, with the covers pulled back and a pillow indented in the middle. I swing to my left when something strikes me, sharp and violent, cracking me in the cheek, knocking me sideways to the right, sending fluorescent stars through my eyelids. The Maglite skitters across the floor, sending a crazy pattern of rolling circles of light against the wall. I remain standing but unbalanced, staggering, disoriented, and all I can think is—

Duck.

I drop to a crouch as a force propels itself at me, over me. Noah's lunging tackle misses me, worthy of a *SportsCenter* highlight, but as he sails over me, his knees connect with my shoulder and we fall awkwardly. Noah's momentum carries him to the corner, slamming him against the wall, while I land hard on my back, my head bouncing on hardwood, the gun no longer in my hand.

Everything is dancing, but there's no time. I get to my feet just as he does. He's like a shadow, in a fighter's stance in a dark room, the only illumination coming from the far corner, where the Maglite has rolled to rest and shines a wide yellow circle against the back wall.

My training comes to me by instinct, legs spread, knees bent, weight evenly balanced, fists raised. Noah makes a move toward me, but I jab with my left, connecting with his nose, straightening him up for a moment, then follow with my right hand, my knuckles catching on his teeth. His head snaps to the right, but he recovers quickly—more quickly than I would have thought—and lunges toward me, this time with his head down, not making the same mistake twice. My left leg shoots up for a kick, but I'm off my game, disoriented myself, and he's too fast, too athletic. His shoulder plunges into my midsection and sends me spiraling backward, he along with me. We land hard and I lose my wind.

"Who are you?" he spits, straddling me now, his palms pinning my shoulders. "What the hell are—wait—you're—you're that cop—"

In the moments it takes me to recover my breath, I bring up my right knee and find my backup piece on the ankle holster. I remove it and shove it into his rib cage.

"Get off me now," I say.

The pressure eases off my shoulders. My left arm free, I shove my palm against his chest and knock him backward, until I'm out from under him. I get to my feet with some effort, my gun trained on him, a tidal wave of adrenaline coursing through me.

"I didn't know you were a cop," Noah says, panting, touching the cuts on his face. "Aren't you supposed to announce who you are?"

But I'm not a cop tonight. Tonight, I'm a niece. The niece of a dear, sweet man who was shot five times in the extremities and speared with a hot poker.

"You okay?" he says to me. "I've never hit a woman in my—"

"Shut up!" I hiss. I move a step closer to him. "You killed all of them. Say it. Say it right this second, *right this second,* or I'll shoot."

As my eyes adjust in the semidarkness, I see Noah more clearly, a man in his boxers, crouched at the knees; I see the whites of his eyes.

"I didn't kill anybody," he says.

I drive my shoe into him like I'm kicking a field goal, catching arms and knees and maybe his chin. I see him fall to the floor. I see other things, too. *Uncle Lang, bobbing me up and down on his leg when I was a child. Tearing up at my cadet graduation, telling me how proud my father would have been—*

Tears fill my eyes, screams fill my head, adrenaline fills my chest. I struggle to keep control of my weapon. "Admit you attacked him," I say, "or die right now."

I want him to defy me. I want to kill him. I want to shoot him the same way he shot my uncle, in all the places it hurts, maximizing his suffering, making him beg for his life, before driving a red-hot stake through his kidney—

"I'm not going to admit something I didn't do," Noah says with control, with calm. "You can shoot me if you want. But I don't think you will. Because you're a fair person. And deep down, I think you know—"

"*Shut up!* You . . . you took him from me . . . you took him . . ."

My entire body quivering, my voice choking off, tears rolling down my face, my breath coming in tight gasps, I lower the gun, then raise it back up, the screams in my head drowning out everything else.

"What are you talking about?" he asks.

I shuffle toward him, only steps away from him, both hands desperately clutching my gun. "Say it!" I scream.

But it doesn't matter what he says anymore. *I'm going to do it. I'm going to pull this trigger.*

"I didn't kill anybody," he says.

My breath held tight in my lungs, I pull the trigger once, a single bullet, and then drop the weapon to my side.

Chapter 21

I STAND OVER the grave, the outlines of the freshly dug earth a tangible reminder of the funeral yesterday. It was a nice affair, with the police force in formal dress, a gun salute, the works. It was the very opposite of a private family ceremony, in part because Lang didn't *have* any family besides me, but appropriate, too, because Lang was such a public figure, a giant in this community, the chief law enforcement officer for almost two decades. Lang died in surgery that night at the hospital. The hemorrhaging was too massive, the doctor said. Too many wounds. Too much blood lost for too long.

Chloe Danchisin—Aunt Chloe—slides her arm inside mine and perches her chin on my shoulder. "He always loved this cemetery," she says. "He bought these plots for us when we were first married."

I blow my nose and take a breath. My throat aches from all the crying I've done over the past several days. "I . . . still can't believe he's gone."

Chloe rubs her hand on my back, tiny circles. "It's not fair to you, honey. It seems like just yesterday that Lydia died."

Almost three years to the day, actually, that my mother gave in to the cancer.

"You know how much Lang loved you, don't you?"

I nod but don't speak. My throat is so strained that I don't even sound like myself. My head is filled with a constant ringing.

"Oh, when he hired you to work here—he was so excited. He called me. We hadn't spoken in over a year, but he called me to give me the news. He was like a giddy schoolboy."

Despite the fact that I've shed enough tears over the last few days to fill a small lake, my eyes well up again. "I questioned his judgment," I say. "I doubted his investigation of the Ocean Drive murders. I actually—I actually suggested that Noah Walker might be innocent." I scoff at the notion in hindsight. It's so clear to me now. Noah killed Lang so he couldn't testify, and in much the same way he killed Zach and Melanie, and the prostitute in the woods. Different methods, but the same sociopathic brutality—maximizing their suffering, making sure they would bleed out in painful deaths.

Chloe directs my shoulders away from the grave, south toward the beach, and moves me along. "You were doing your job. I'm sure he was proud of you. Don't confuse his stubbornness with disappointment."

We walk toward the beach. Chloe looks good, notwithstanding the circumstances. Now single again for two years, she has lost about twenty pounds, cut her hair in a stylish bob, and dresses like she doesn't mind being noticed. Sixty is the new forty, and all that.

My head is finally clearing of the hangover, from the extra bottle of wine after I left Chloe last night and went home. The nightly drinking is weighing me down, leaving me off balance and foggy. But right now, foggy feels like the best I can do.

Ocean Drive is teeming with joggers and bicyclists and people heading, like us, toward the beach. The activity, the smell of the ocean—this is precisely what I remember as a kid.

"Chloe," I say, "why did we stop coming here when I was a kid?"

She keeps her head down, strolling along with me.

"Lang said there was a story."

"You don't know?" she asks.

"No."

"If *you* don't know, *I* don't know." She looks up at our surroundings, half-built structures and carved-out foundations. "That's the house, isn't it?"

I focus my eyes and realize that we're passing 7 Ocean Drive, the Murder House. The crime-scene tape has been removed, but the Gothic monstrosity has no trouble looking creepy all by itself. It brings back everything in a rush, my meddling at the crime scene, my argument with Lang, resulting in my thirty-day suspension.

We were never the same after he dinged me. I was sent off to the narcotics task force assignment, and I saw him only sparingly after that. I turned down several offers to get together, for dinner or drinks or an afternoon at the beach. I was resentful. I wanted to punish him. And now he's gone, and I'd do anything to have those weeks back. I'd tell him how much I love him, how he saved my life so many times, in so many different ways.

We arrive at the beach. Chloe lets out a satisfied sigh. Behind her, the beachfront homes stand in marked contrast to the cedar-shingled houses along Ocean Drive. They are gigantic, modern, concrete structures with oversize windows and sharp angles.

"Can I say something to you, sweetheart?"

I take her hand. "Anything."

The breeze plays with the bangs on Chloe's forehead. "Have you thought about going back to Manhattan now?"

I squat down, scoop up a handful of sand, weigh it in my hand. There is an inch-long scar on the palm of my hand that I got—according to my mother—trying to chop a tomato when I was a little girl.

Little things like that, small memories that sting the most.

"Lang called me a couple of weeks ago," she continues. "He said you were having nightmares every night. That you were drinking a lot, too, probably as a coping mechanism."

I look up at her. "He said that?"

"He did. He was concerned. He was glad to have you close, of course. But he wasn't sure this was the right thing for you anymore, working here."

I pick up a shell and send it flying into the ocean. I squint into the wind, the wet mist.

Chloe squats down next to me. "All your life, you've taken care of everyone else," she says. "When your father and Ryan died, your mother . . . Lydia was devastated. I know you were, too, but it always seemed like you were the one doing the consoling. And you were so young. You were, what, twelve?"

"Yes." It was less than a month before my thirteenth birthday.

"I remember just a couple of days after they died, you were supposed to be in bed, and Lydia was crying and Lang was holding her. We were all on the couch. And you walked in. You'd been sleeping. Your hair was all matted and your eyes were sleepy and you were in your pajamas. You opened your arms as wide as they could go and you said, 'Don't worry, Mommy, I have enough love for all of them.' Do you remember that?"

I wipe away a tear. I remember. I remember my mother looking like there was nothing left in the world for her.

"Well." Chloe rubs my arm. "Maybe it's time you took better care of yourself. Go home, Jenna. Your best friends are there. Matty's there. What's left here?"

I stand straight as the wind off the ocean kicks up. I look back at the oceanfront housing, at the endless stretch of beach. This isn't my home. It never will be. But it holds one thing for me that no other place in the world does.

"This is the only place I can be a cop," I say.

Chapter 22

THE ROOM LOOKS more like a maximum-security prison than a court of law. The number of sheriff's deputies has doubled, virtually lining the walls of the courtroom, beefy security guards with jumpy eyes, armed with handguns and cuffs and Tasers. The tension in the room has raised the temperature to something between stuffy and downright unbearable.

As we wait for the judge, I scroll through photos on my iPhone. Nearly all of the recent ones include Lang: in his ridiculous polka-dot swimsuit at the beach; flipping burgers on his Smokey Joe in his backyard, chomping on a cigar; asleep on his lawn chair, his wife-beater T-shirt creeping up to reveal his added poundage (a photo I often used when arguing about his diet). Silly shots, all of them, but so dear to me now, those little things, those frivolous moments that mean so much in hindsight.

And then, amid these pictures, the one from the lawn on 7 Ocean Drive, that crest with that hook-beaked bird, that insipid creature that has taken up permanent residence in my daily nightmares. What's with that stupid bird?

We all rise; then a collective hush falls over the room as the Honorable Robert Barnett, a handsome and deadly serious judge, assumes the bench. "We are back on the record in *People versus Noah Lee Walker,*" he says dryly. "For the record, the court has stood in recess for the last week. Six days ago, the next witness scheduled to testify, Southampton Town Police Department chief Langdon James, was attacked in his home and later died of his injuries. The court granted a recess at the prosecution's request."

I shift in the courtroom pew, a front-row seat granted me by the prosecution. Noah Walker denied any involvement in Lang's murder, but Judge Barnett revoked his bond anyway, out of an abundance of caution, so he's locked up again in Riverhead when he's not here in court.

"For the record, Mr. Akers is present today for the State, and Mr. Brody is present for the defense." The judge removes his glasses. "And of course, Mr. Walker, the defendant, is present as well."

My eyes move to Noah, sitting at the defense table with his hands folded and his eyes cast downward. His feet are crossed, raising the cuffs of his jeans slightly and revealing bare ankles. He didn't even bother to wear socks to the trial. He looks like a hippie islander.

I let you live, you little shit. You could at least show a little respect.

I replay that moment in his attic bedroom, feel the

surge of adrenaline returning. How close I came to doing it. How close I came to putting that bullet between his eyes, instead of firing it over his head.

As if he senses me, Noah turns his head ninety degrees and catches my eyes. He still has the shiner I gave him that night, though it's now a dull-yellow bruise. The split lip has healed and the swelling dissipated. His jaw probably still hurts, but nothing was broken.

As far as I know, Noah hasn't publicly complained about how I treated him that night, sneaking into his house, punching and kicking him, not to mention firing a bullet within inches of his scalp. That should be coming any time now, a police brutality lawsuit, probably a request for ten million dollars for his pain and suffering.

But for now, it's just his eyes locked on mine. Something flutters through my chest as I stare back at him, that nagging feeling that I can't read him, that I don't know him. He is neither antagonistic nor smug in his stare. He is neither enjoying himself nor resentful. He just stares at me as if somehow, in some way, we are discovering each other, we are connecting with each other, something is happening between us.

I snap my head away, breaking eye contact, sweat popping at my hairline. I take a deep breath and brush the hair off my face.

He is the worst kind of creep. He's the kind who can suck you in, the sociopath who can smile at you tenderly while he's devising monstrous ways to torture you. Well, not me, pal. Not anymore. You may have fooled me initially, but no longer.

I turn back, looking in his direction again. He hasn't moved. His eyes are still on me, his long dark hair hanging over his unshaven face. My heartbeat kicks into a higher gear. I uncross my legs and play with my hands. I shake my head slowly, discreetly, unsure of the meaning of what I'm doing, answering no to a question that has not been asked. His eyes narrow to a squint. His jaw rises slightly and his lips part, as if he's going to speak, but surely he won't, not in the middle of a court session while the judge is talking.

He will never speak to me again. And I will never speak to him.

I get to my feet and walk down the courtroom aisle toward the exit, which is guarded by two sheriff's deputies. I'm done with Noah Walker. The next time I see him, it will be at his sentencing, after the judge informs him he'll spend the rest of his life behind bars. *Yeah, let's make eye contact then, pal. Let's see the look on your face then.*

"Mr. Brody," says the judge, "you have a motion?"

"Yes, Judge, I do."

Defense lawyers always have motions. They always have bullshit arguments, smoke and mirrors, misdirection. But the next words coming from the mouth of Noah Walker's lawyer freeze me in my tracks, only a few paces from the courtroom door.

"Your Honor," he says, "the defense moves for a dismissal of all charges."

Chapter 23

THE COURTROOM, ALREADY respectfully silent, is sucked dry of all sound as Joshua Brody, Noah Walker's lawyer, makes his pitch for his client's release.

"There is no competent evidence tying the murder weapon to my client," he says. "There was never a fingerprint on the weapon. And the only evidence that the knife was found at my client's house would have come from Chief James—who obviously cannot testify now."

"Your Honor!" Sebastian Akers jumps to his feet, his perfect-cool persona shaken for the first time. "We will call Detective Isaac Marks—I'm sorry, Acting Chief Isaac Marks—who will testify that the chief showed him the knife after he discovered it under the heating duct in the defendant's kitchen."

"But Mr. Marks didn't *see* it under the heating duct. Only the chief did, allegedly," says Noah's lawyer. "The defense's theory is that Chief James planted that knife. But now we can't cross-examine him to establish that.

The prosecution shouldn't be allowed to suggest that the knife was found in my client's house when we can't cross-examine the person who supposedly 'found' it."

The judge looks at the prosecutor. "Mr. Akers, the defense makes a valid point here. If the defense can't cross-examine the chief about a frame-up, how can I let you put the knife in the defendant's house?"

"Everyone in this courtroom knows the reason why Chief James isn't here to testify," says Akers, his voice wobbling. "Everyone knows who made that happen." He turns and looks at Noah Walker.

"If the State believes my client killed Chief James, they are free to charge him," says the defense lawyer, Brody. "The last I heard, they found no physical evidence at that crime scene. They have no leads on the chief's death, just supposition. And more importantly, Judge, this trial is not about Chief James's murder. This trial is about Zach Stern and Melanie Phillips, and there is no evidence tying my client to the murder weapon, with the chief's untimely passing. And the chief obviously can't testify that my client confessed to him, either." He opens his hands. "So what do they have, without the murder weapon and without a confession to the chief of police? Without any physical evidence whatsoever? They have evidence that my client argued with Melanie Phillips at Tasty's Diner, and they have this ridiculous testimony from a jailhouse snitch that my client confessed to him."

"The jailhouse informant's testimony isn't evidence?" the judge asks.

"It is, Judge, but c'mon. The unreliability of jailhouse snitch testimony is well documented. He got a sweetheart deal in exchange for making up these ridiculous claims against my client. I mean, Judge, really." Brody takes a step toward the bench. "Can any of us say that a man should be convicted of two counts of first-degree murder based on no eyewitnesses, no physical evidence, no forensic evidence, no confession—nothing more than the word of a convicted felon looking to cut a deal? And keep in mind, Judge, that it's our theory that Chief James coerced the snitch into testifying. But now I can't cross-examine him on *that* issue, either. For the same reason the knife shouldn't be considered against my client, neither should the testimony of Dio Cornwall, the snitch."

"My God," I whisper to myself. He's making this sound credible. And the judge—he looks like he's actually considering this. How could this—this couldn't possibly—

No. No, no, no.

"Mr. Akers," says the judge, "I agree with the defense on the murder weapon. The prosecution cannot introduce evidence that the murder weapon was found at the defendant's house. And the testimony of the jailhouse informant is not exactly something you base an entire case around, now, is it?"

The judge puts out a hand. He seems troubled by this, too, as if he doesn't want to toss the charges and is looking for help. "But . . . aside from the knife, there was the defendant's confession to Chief James. Obviously, the chief can't tell us about that now. Is there—I don't suppose anyone else was present at that confession who could testify about it?"

"I . . ." Sebastian Akers shrugs and shakes his head absently.

"My memory, Mr. Akers, is that the chief was going to testify that he was alone with Noah Walker during the alleged confession."

"That may be—it—but Judge, it would be grossly unfair to the administration of justice for Noah Walker to *profit* by murdering the star witness—"

"Mr. Akers," the judge booms. "I know you have your suspicions about Mr. Walker's involvement in the chief's death. But it's been six days and you haven't arrested him, much less sought an indictment. Do you, or do you not, have evidence—*evidence*—that Noah Walker killed Chief James?"

Akers raises his hands helplessly. "As far as I know, the investigation is still in its infancy—"

"I will take that as a no." Now the judge shakes his head. "So I will ask you again, Counsel, am I correct that Chief James was the only one who could testify to Mr. Walker's confession?"

"Judge, I would have to—"

"Mr. Akers, you know your case. Don't stonewall me. Was Chief James the only person present with Noah Walker when he confessed to the murder?"

Sebastian Akers flips through some papers, stalling for time, but he knows the answer as surely as Noah's lawyer does, as surely as I do. The chief was alone with Noah during the confession.

A single thread in the weave has been pulled by the defense, and the entire fabric of the prosecution's case has come apart. Without Uncle Lang to testify, the State can't tie the murder weapon to Noah's house. The State can't say that Noah confessed to a decorated veteran of the Southampton Town Police Department. All Akers can say is that a jailhouse snitch claimed to hear a confession—if the judge doesn't toss out that testimony, too.

The case is over. I can't believe this. The case is over. He killed my uncle and is going to walk away from two other murders because of it.

And I passed on the chance to put a bullet between his eyes.

"We're going to take a thirty-minute recess," says the judge. "Mr. Akers, I'd advise you to use that half hour well. If you can't think of some reason between now and then, this case is over."

Chapter 24

I PUSH SEBASTIAN Akers into the witness room adjacent to the courtroom and close the door. "This can't happen," I say.

"Detective, I know you're upset, but right now I have to—"

"There's a police report," I say. "Lang filled out a report when Noah confessed. Can't you introduce that as evidence?"

Akers, on the verge of coming unglued, lets out a pained sigh. "A police report is hearsay. You can't use it unless the defense can cross-examine the cop who wrote it."

"And Noah *killed* that cop," I protest.

"But we can't prove that, Detective! You know as well as I do that we haven't been able to come up with a hint of physical evidence. His motive is all we have."

I look up at the ceiling, searching for answers in the peeling white paint.

"He told me Noah confessed," I say. "Lang told me."

"Well, sure!" Akers waves his hand, exasperated. "He probably told a lot of people. Hell, he told newspaper reporters. But guess what that is?"

I drop my head. "Hearsay."

"Hearsay. Inadmissible in a court of law."

A long moment passes. I steady myself by placing my hands on the small table. But I sense something in the silence. I look up at Akers, who is studying me carefully.

"Unless," he says.

I straighten up. "Unless what?"

"There are exceptions to every rule," he says carefully. "Including the rule against hearsay."

He gives me a long hard look. Sebastian Akers is a very ambitious man. Undoubtedly, he considers this high-profile case a launching pad for bigger and better things. Or, conversely, a crash landing if he blows it. And five minutes ago, standing before the judge, Akers was on the verge of seeing his case implode before a national audience.

And I was on the verge of watching the man who killed my uncle, and three other people, skip out of court a free man.

"Tell me about the exceptions," I say.

Akers watches me very carefully, wondering if we're on the same page. I'm wondering that myself.

"One exception in particular," he says. "It has to do with when the chief told you about the confession. If he just mentioned it to you casually later that day or something like that, we're out of luck."

"But," I say.

"But if he told you *just after* the confession

happened—let's say, if he walked out of the jail cell, stunned that Noah had confessed, and told you at just that moment, still in a state of excitement and shock—the law considers that statement to be sufficiently reliable to be admissible. It's called an excited utterance."

I sit down in the chair. "An excited utterance."

"Right. If he said it while he was still in the moment."

"Still in a state of excitement and surprise."

"That's right, Detective."

Akers's eyes are wide and intense. He's holding his breath.

"Whether Noah Walker gets justice, or whether he laughs his way out of court, and probably kills again," he says to me evenly, "is riding on your answer."

It's not the only thing riding on my answer. My sworn oath as a police officer is, too. Because I remember now. I remember when Lang told me about Noah's confession. It was on his back porch in the early afternoon; he told me Noah had confessed to him that morning, hours earlier.

I clear my throat, adrenaline buzzing through me. "So if I testify that the chief told me about Noah's confession immediately after it happened—"

"While he was still in a state of excitement . . ."

Time passes. Memories flood through my mind. My stomach churns like the gears of a locomotive. What does it mean to be a cop? Is it about rules, or is it about justice? In the end, what do I stand for?

What would my uncle do for me, if our roles were reversed?

Finally, Sebastian Akers takes the seat across from

me. "We only have a few minutes," he says. "So, Detective Murphy, I have a question for you."

My eyes rise up to meet his.

"When was it, exactly, that the chief told you that Noah Walker confessed?"

A hush falls over the courtroom as Judge Barnett resumes his seat on the bench. There are even more sheriff's deputies present now than earlier, ready to calm the crowd should it be necessary. The energy in the room is suffocating. Or maybe that's just the shortness of breath I'm experiencing, seated in the front row of the courtroom.

The judge looks over his glasses at the prosecution. "Mr. Akers, does the prosecution have any additional evidence to present?" he asks.

The room goes still. Sebastian Akers rises slowly and buttons his coat. He turns and looks in my direction but does not make eye contact.

"The State calls Detective Jenna Murphy," he says.

Chapter 25

THE JUDGE GAVELS the courtroom to order after the lunch break. The morning was spent arguing over the admissibility of my testimony, a bunch of lawyer-speak about the rules of evidence that nobody else in the courtroom understood.

Then I testified for an hour. I told the truth—that my uncle told me that Noah had confessed to him—and then I told a lie. I lied about *when* he told me. Does it really matter if he told me immediately after the confession or several hours later?

That's what I've been telling myself over and over, anyway, that a handful of hours should not be the difference between a killer going to prison and his walking free to kill again.

Joshua Brody gets to his feet eagerly for cross-examination. My adrenaline starts to pump. I know what's coming, and it's something I have to willingly accept, the price I have to pay for testifying.

"Detective Murphy," says Brody, "you once worked

for the New York City Police Department, correct?"

He's not wasting any time. "Yes. I resigned about a year ago."

"At the time you resigned, you were under investigation by the Internal Affairs Division, isn't that true?"

"Yes," I say, the heat rising to my face.

"You were under investigation for skimming money and drugs during the arrest of a drug dealer, true?"

"I was investigated for it. But I was never charged."

"You were never charged because you resigned from the force," he says. "The department couldn't discipline someone who no longer worked for them."

"I was never charged," I reply evenly, "because I did nothing wrong."

"Oh, *I see*." Brody looks away from me toward the jury, then turns his stare back to me. "You just coincidentally decided that it was a good time to move on, at the same time that you were under investigation."

"As a matter of fact, yes," I say. "And I would add—"

"There's no need to *add*," he says, patting the air. "You answered my—"

"*I would add* that the district attorney's office was free to charge me, whether I worked for the NYPD or not. But they didn't."

There is so much more I could say, everything that happened that led up to that bogus charge. But I don't have the energy to fight.

Brody smirks. He's gotten all he can here.

"Detective, you weren't present for this alleged . . . 'conversation' between Chief James and Noah Walker."

"Correct. I was down the hall from the jail cell."

"You have no firsthand knowledge of what was said between them."

"Firsthand? No."

"You took the chief's word for it."

"Yes."

"And this jury," says Brody, gesturing toward the jury box, "they have to take not only the chief's word for it, but yours as well."

"I'm not sure I take your point, Counselor."

"This jury has to believe that *you're* telling the truth about what the chief said, *and* that the chief told the truth about what my client said."

I nod. "I suppose that's right."

"They have to believe you, who resigned while under investigation for being a dirty cop—"

"Objection," says Sebastian Akers, jumping to his feet.

"Sustained."

Brody doesn't break stride. "—and they have to believe the chief, whom they don't get to hear from at all."

I pause a beat, anger surging to the surface. "That's right, they don't get to hear from the chief, Mr. Brody. Because your client killed him before he could testify."

I brace myself for an objection, for Brody to go crazy, for the judge to excuse the jury and give me a thorough dressing-down.

But to my surprise, Brody doesn't object.

"My client hasn't been arrested for that murder, has he?"

"Not yet."

120

"As far as you know, there is no physical evidence implicating my client?"

"Not yet."

"Very good, Detective." I have no idea why he's letting my statement slide. Presumably, he's calculated that every juror—every human being in the Hamptons— has heard about the chief's murder, and most believe that Noah killed him. He must figure it's easier to acknowledge it, so he can make his points about the lack of any arrest or evidence thus far.

Or does he have some other reason?

"Can you tell the jury what happened to you the day after this alleged confession?"

"The . . . following day?"

"Yes, Detective," he says, approaching me, a spark in his eyes. "Isn't it true that the following day, you were *suspended* for one month from active duty?"

The spectators react sufficiently for the judge to call for silence.

"Yes, I guess that was the following day, now that you mention it."

"Why were you suspended?"

Because I doubted the guilt of Noah Walker. Because I thought the murder of the prostitute might be connected to the Ocean Drive murders. But I can't say that. It would be a gift-wrapped present to the defense. And it's not what Lang said in the report he wrote up. That would be the last thing he'd write down.

"Insubordination," I say. "I let our personal relation- ship intrude on our professional relationship. I was disrespectful and I was wrong."

121

"You were disrespectful to him?"

"I was," I answer, feeling a lump in my throat, recalling the moment.

"You and your uncle, you were upset with each other?"

I feel the first hints of emotion creeping in. I'm not going to break down in front of this jury.

"He was certainly upset with me," I say. "And he was right to be."

"You feel . . . I can see that you feel guilty about that."

I don't answer. I don't need to.

"Looking back, it bothers you, doesn't it? That just before his death, you were disrespectful to your uncle."

I know what my answer should be. It should be *Yes, but that doesn't mean I would lie for him*. But that is precisely what I'm doing here today.

"It bothers me," I answer.

"You wish you could make it up to him."

Again, I don't answer. He doesn't wait very long.

"You think my client killed your uncle, correct?"

I nod. "Yes."

"But you'd agree with me that, with the full resources of the STPD on the case for almost a week, there's been no proof thus far to back up your suspicion."

"Not yet."

"So this case here," he says, pointing to the floor, "this case might be your *only chance* to get Noah Walker."

"Objection," says Akers, but the judge overrules him.

"And with the chief unable to testify about this

supposed confession from my client, and with the judge on the verge of dismissing the charges against my client, you now *suddenly* come forth to claim that the chief told you about this confession immediately"—he snaps his finger—"immediately after it happened."

I don't reply. My eyes move along the floor, then upward to the defense attorney.

"What a convenient and unexpected coincidence!" Brody says, waving his hands.

I look at Noah Walker, his chin resting on his fists. He watches me intently, his eyebrows pitched, as if—as if he pities me.

"No further questions," says Brody.

Chapter 26

NOAH WALKER PLACES his head gently against the bars of his holding cell, barely touching Paige Sulzman's head on the other side. His hands come through the bars and interlock with hers.

"I don't like you coming here," he says. "I don't like you seeing me like this."

"I know, baby. Good thing I'm stubborn."

"It's not a good idea. How would John—"

"John's in Europe. Copenhagen, this week, I think. I told you. He'll be gone for another two weeks."

Despite his protests, Noah looks forward to the fifteen-minute visits Paige is allowed every night in lockup. Riverhead is a dank, dark, miserable cesspool, purgatory for the accused in Suffolk County, short on hope and long on desperation and bitterness. Paige, with her freshly cut hair and generous smile, her sympathetic eyes and gentle demeanor, is like a rose sprouting in a swamp of manure.

"You could use a shave and a haircut," she says, trying to keep it light.

He acknowledges the attempt at humor, but it's hard to find anything funny right now. The trial is at its apex. Difficult decisions need to be made.

"Your lawyer did a good job today." The hope in Paige's expression, the tears shimmering in her eyes, reveal her lack of objectivity, but Noah doesn't totally disagree.

"Yeah, he did. But still, babe. The jury heard a cop say I confessed to the murders. What's the jury supposed to think when they hear I confessed?"

"That she made it up," Paige replies. "That she's trying to make it up to her uncle out of guilt. I thought that came through very clearly."

"Yeah, I know." He doesn't sound like he's convinced, because he's not. Yes, his lawyer did a good job cross-examining Detective Murphy, but the jurors seemed to like her regardless, and their opinions are the only ones that matter.

"She just lied," Paige says, spitting out the words. "She just *lied*."

Noah purses his lips. "She thinks I'm guilty. I could see it that night, when she broke into my house. She thinks I killed her uncle, and she thinks I killed Zach and Melanie, too. She thinks she's doing the right thing."

Paige draws back. "You're *defending* her? You must be joking."

Noah almost laughs at the paradox, the fact that he's sticking up for the cop who lied on the witness stand to put him away. "I just . . . understand why she did it."

He wants to be upset with Murphy. She's surely no friend of his. But there's something in the way she handles herself, like she's trying to prove something to somebody but isn't sure what she's proving, or to whom. He feels like he understands her. And regardless of what she did to him today, he can't shake the feeling that . . .

. . . that they understand each other. That she doesn't really believe, deep in her heart, that he's guilty.

"Oh, why is this happening?" Paige says softly.

There's no answer to that question. Noah feels like he's caught in a tornado, unmoored from any reality, whisked away with brutal force and carried through the air against his will. He has lost all control. Forces beyond his reach—the sensationalist media, ambitious prosecutors, crooked cops—have aligned to deem him guilty and deny him any chance of fighting back.

He must focus on this one fact: It doesn't really matter what anybody else thinks. It only matters what twelve jurors believe. He's seen the looks on their faces, their disgusted expressions, their averted eyes. He knows he has an uphill battle. He can only hope that their minds are still open, however slightly, to what he has to say.

He has to testify. His lawyer doesn't want him to. But he has no choice. He has to find some way to convince those jurors that he's not the killer they think he is.

If he fails, his life is over.

Chapter 27

JOSHUA BRODY LETS out a sigh. Almost three hours have passed, Noah testifying in response to Brody's questions, and now it's coming to an end. A pregnant pause by the lawyer, to emphasize these final questions— questions already asked and answered, but important enough to be repeated.

"Let me ask you one last time, Noah," says Joshua Brody. "Did you kill Melanie Phillips?"

Noah leans forward into the microphone on the witness stand. "No, I did not."

"Did you kill Zach Stern?"

"No, I did not."

Joshua Brody casts a glance at the jury. "No further questions."

Noah takes some deep breaths. Halfway done. The easy half, and it wasn't that easy. *It has to feel natural, not rehearsed,* his lawyer kept telling him as they prepared for today, and Noah feels like, all in all, it was convincing. From time to time during Joshua Brody's questioning, he glanced over at the jury. Did he see reasonable doubt on their faces? He doesn't know. This isn't what he does for a living. And he's in the moment, tense and focused. He wouldn't trust his instincts, anyway.

But he can't suppress the surge of hope he feels. He has a chance.

"Cross-examination?" Judge Barnett asks.

The prosecutor, Sebastian Akers, drops a notepad on the lectern between the prosecution and defense tables. This is the kind of moment a guy like Akers lives for. The packed courtroom, the big trial, the cross-examination that will make or break this case.

Keep your composure, his defense attorney told Noah. *Akers wants to paint you as someone who committed murder in a blind rage. He wants you to show the jury that rage. He's going to try to bring it out, get you upset.*

"Mr. Walker," Akers begins, "you have no alibi for the night of the murder, correct?"

Noah clears his throat. "As I told Mr. Brody, I stayed in that night."

Akers makes a face. "What I meant was, nobody can *corroborate* your alibi, correct?"

"Correct."

"The jury has to take your word, and only your word, for it."

"Yeah, I guess so."

"And you admit you were once given a key to the front door of 7 Ocean Drive, correct?"

"Yes. I've done work on that mansion for years. At some point, it made sense for the contractor who used me to just give me my own key."

"And that key has now magically disappeared."

"I don't know about 'magically'—but I don't know where it is."

There was no evidence of forced entry at the mansion on the night of the murders. The fact that Noah had his own key isn't a good fact for him.

"You deny that you confessed to this crime to Chief James. You deny that, right?"

"Yes."

"So when he said you did, he wasn't telling the truth."

"He wasn't."

"And when Detective Murphy testified to what the chief told her about your confession, she wasn't telling the truth, either."

"I don't know if she was or not. Maybe the chief said that to her. Maybe he didn't."

"If he did, then he was lying to her, too."

"Right."

"Or maybe Detective Murphy just made the whole thing up! Right, Mr. Walker?"

Noah feels perspiration on his forehead, his neck. "Could be."

"So maybe she was also lying. Right, Mr. Walker?"

"Maybe."

"Sure," Akers says with no shortage of sarcasm, flipping a hand. "And Dio Cornwall, who shared a cell with you in lockup, who testified that you confessed to killing Melanie, that you said you 'cut her up good' and that she 'couldn't be no movie star now'—Mr. Cornwall was *also* lying. Right, Mr. Walker?"

"He was lying. I never said anything like that to him. I never talked to him about my case at all."

"I see." Akers looks at the jury. "Any idea how Mr. Cornwall would have known the name Melanie, or that she'd wanted to be a movie star, if you didn't tell him anything about your case at all?"

"I—I don't know. Maybe he read it in the newspaper."

"The newspaper? Mr. Walker, Dio Cornwall was in lockup with you. Do you recall ever being given a copy of any newspapers while you were in lockup?"

Noah pauses. He casts his eyes downward.

"If you like, we can bring in the sheriff's deputies who controlled lockup while you were—"

"No, we never got newspapers," Noah concedes. "I don't know how Dio got that information. Maybe Chief James told him."

"Chief James? So now you're saying not only that Chief James lied about your confession, but that he helped Dio Cornwall make up a story, too?"

"I don't know."

"And Chief James isn't here to testify, is he, Mr. Walker? So we'll never be able to ask him, will we?"

Noah fixes a glare on the prosecutor. He feels his blood go cold.

"During your direct testimony, you admitted that you confronted Melanie at her job—at Tasty's Diner— asking her to take you back. You admit that, correct?"

Noah shakes his head, focuses on the change of subject. "Yes, I admit that we argued, and I grabbed her arm, but Remy has the date wrong. He said it happened two days before Melanie was killed. June second. But that's wrong. Melanie broke up with me in April. About seven weeks before she died. *That's* when I talked to her at Tasty's."

He met Paige a week after Melanie dumped him, in April. He'd moved on from Melanie. But he's never told anyone that. He's never publicly acknowledged his affair with Paige. And he won't now. No matter how many times Paige has told him to do so. He won't bring Paige into this.

Akers nods along, his eyes alight. "Pretty big difference between April—seven weeks before the murder—and two *days* before the murder."

"Yes, it is."

"So Remy's lying, too."

"I don't know if he's lying—"

"But he's not telling the truth."

"That's right. He's not."

"So, to summarize," Akers says, strolling along the edge of the jury box, "Chief James, Detective Jenna Murphy, Dio Cornwall, and Remy Handleman—none of them are telling the truth. But you, Mr. Walker, on trial for your life, whom Melanie broke up with so she could start dating Zach Stern—*you* are telling the truth."

Noah feels his pulse ratchet up. The way Akers is stacking up all the evidence . . . nobody's going to believe Noah. It hits him hard, for the first time. *They won't believe me. They're going to convict me.*

"I'm telling the truth," he pleads. "I swear I am. I would never hurt somebody else."

"You'd never hurt anybody?" Akers asks, with mock

innocence. "Well, Mr. Walker, isn't it true that, in 1995, you brought a rifle to Bridgehampton School and opened fire on a number of your classmates?"

Chapter 28

THE COURTROOM ERUPTS at Sebastian Akers's question. Noah's defense lawyer, Joshua Brody, is on his feet, arguing. Judge Barnett stands down from the bench and walks to the far end of the courtroom, away from the jury, for a sidebar with the lawyers. The spectators are all abuzz.

I wasn't in Bridgehampton back in 1995, but I have a memory of Uncle Lang mentioning that someone had brought a BB gun to school and shot a bunch of the kids on their way into school. He never mentioned a name; no reason he would have. This was before Columbine, before zero-tolerance policies cropped up around the country and kids were expelled from school for even bringing toy replicas in their backpacks.

If this was in 1995, Noah would have been young. Eleven, twelve, thirteen, something like that. It would have been a juvie beef. And if it was in juvenile court, it would have been confidential. I wonder if the town even knew who it was who did it. There would be rumors, sure, but I wonder if there was ever an official announcement. Judging from the reaction of the spectators—many of whom are presumably lifelong Bridgehampton residents—it seems like they're hearing this news for the first time.

The lawyers and court reporter and judge resume their positions, and the room goes quiet again.

Noah's lawyer, Joshua Brody, objects. "This is a juvenile offense," he says.

"Your Honor," Sebastian Akers replies, "he just testified he'd never hurt anybody. He opened the door. I'm entitled to impeach him."

"Overruled," says the judge. "Proceed, Mr. Akers."

And the prosecutor does just that, with a vengeance, a gleam in his eye. "You were arrested on Halloween, 1995, for shooting a number of schoolchildren on the south playground of Bridgehampton School, correct, Mr. Walker?"

"I was . . . I was arrested, yes. It was a BB gun."

"Fifteen schoolkids were shot that day, weren't they?"

"I believe . . . that's right."

"One child was hit in the eye, wasn't he?"

Noah nods but doesn't speak.

"That boy was *nine*," says Akers. "He had to have two surgeries to repair the damage, isn't that true?"

Noah's eyes are fixed on the floor now. "That happened, yes."

"Yes, that 'happened.' That '*happened*' because you shot him with a BB gun, correct?"

Noah doesn't speak. Still staring at the floor.

"Is that a yes, Mr. Walker?"

"I didn't shoot him," Noah says, almost in a whisper, though the microphone gives it sufficient volume.

"No? You didn't shoot that boy? You were wrongfully accused then, too, is that it?"

"I didn't shoot him."

"I see. So when school officials said you did, they weren't telling the truth, either, were they?"

Noah's shoulders close in on him, like he's trying to shelter himself from a storm. "I don't want to talk about that anymore," he says.

"Oh." Akers lets out a chuckle. "Well, what do you wanna talk about? The Yankees' chances in the postseason?"

That gets a roar from the spectators. I thought it was clever, too, but I'm watching Noah. His face is turning red. He's practically curled up into a ball. Akers, if he's half the trial lawyer he thinks he is, senses it, too.

By the time the laughter has subsided and the judge has gaveled the room to order, Akers has slowly approached Walker, a tiger stalking prey.

"You shot fifteen people that day, Mr. Walker."

"I—no—I'm not going to—I don't want—"

"But you claim the school officials lied."

"I said I don't—"

"Just like you claim a decorated police chief, Langdon James, lied."

Noah shakes his head.

"Just like Detective Murphy lied."

It's clear now Noah's not going to answer, and that seems to be fine with Akers. He's watching—we're all watching—a defendant smoldering on the witness stand, and Akers is hoping he'll erupt.

"Just like Dio Cornwall lied. Just like Remy Handleman lied."

Noah turns his head away, as if he's done with this examination.

"All of them lied," says Akers. "It's a grand conspiracy, isn't it, Mr. Walker? The whole world against you."

Noah says something, but he's turned away from the mike and it's inaudible.

"Mr. Walker—"

"Yes!" Noah hisses, spinning around, nearly knocking over the microphone. Akers jumps back. The judge reacts, too. Several of the jurors recoil, seeing a new side of Noah Walker.

"Everyone's lying! The chief, that detective, the prison snitch, Remy, who couldn't tie his own shoes without help—they're all lying! They set me up!"

Noah surges to his feet, sweeping his hand, this time knocking the microphone to the floor. "They all set me up! They framed me! They're all liars!"

"Sit down, Mr. Walker, or I'll have you restrained!" the judge commands. "Deputies?" he calls out, and quickly two sheriff's deputies approach Noah.

When Noah doesn't immediately take his seat, one of the deputies grabs his arm. He yanks it free. Both bailiffs reach for their batons, but Noah drops himself back into his chair. The judge calls for order and admonishes Noah. His face has lost all hope now; it's distorted with bitterness.

But when he looks up, his expression breaks, the

scowl changing to despair, and for the briefest of moments, I think he's looking at me. Then I realize he's looking past me. I glance over my shoulder and see the woman he was with when I arrested him—Paige, I think her name was. She's mouthing something to him from across the courtroom, but I can't make out what she's saying.

I look back at Noah, who shakes his head and breaks eye contact.

"Your Honor, I have no further questions," says Sebastian Akers.

Chapter 29

THE FIRST DAY, Noah didn't think much of it. It had been a long trial. There was a lot of information to review. It could just be the simple matter of plowing through all the material, wanting to be thorough.

The second day, he began to wonder. He had no experience with this kind of thing, so he tried not to think too much about it.

The third day of jury deliberations, he began to have hope. Somebody on that jury was doing some heavy thinking about his guilt. *Don't read too much into it,* his lawyer advised him during a visit. *A lot of people have lost a lot of bets trying to guess what a jury is thinking.*

At a quarter after one on the fourth day of jury deliberations, Noah is summoned by the sheriff's deputy. He is heading, as always, toward the side door of the county courthouse, reserved for prisoner transfers, but the transport vehicle slows a block from the courthouse. The crowd has swelled beyond the sidewalks into the street. There are blockades, but they are hopeless against the swarm of onlookers. The transport vehicle moves slowly, and people grudgingly open a path, shouting at the vehicle as it passes, some of them even slapping the hood or one of the side windows.

When the vehicle turns toward the transfer door, Noah sees the trucks from all the national media lined up, faces of reporters he'd seen on television before the trial began and with whom he's now practically on a first-name basis, plus countless other reporters who couldn't get inside the courtroom but are always here, every morning, ready to shoot video footage or snap his picture.

The thousands of locals are here for various reasons, geriatric trial-watchers, concerned citizens, people just interested in the spectacle of it all, friends or family of Melanie Phillips. From time to time in the courtroom or standing outside here by the prisoner transfer, he has seen people who vaguely resemble Melanie and wondered if they were cousins or aunts or uncles. Melanie had a big family, though Noah never met any of them. They were only together for two months before Melanie ended things.

He remembers that day well, the day Melanie broke up with him, her resolve, the firmness of her words. *I'm sorry, but I've made my decision.* That was it. She wouldn't hear his protests. She just made the statement, a second time to be clear, and that was that. Noah always wondered if she'd discussed it with her friends or family ahead of time. He imagines someone advising her, *It's best to do it clean, just break it off, no long explanations or debate.* It bothered him to think that others knew about their breakup before he did.

He lets these thoughts occupy him so he won't think about what's coming as he passes down a long corridor lined with armed deputies, as he enters the courtroom from the side and dozens of heads turn in his direction. The law enforcement presence in this room is also heavy; the wall space is occupied by sheriff's deputies ready to keep order when the verdict is read.

And then it's as if everything is under water, almost dreamlike. His lawyer says something to him, but Noah doesn't really listen; he's gone to another place now, readying himself for what's about to come. Judge Barnett walks in and calls for the jury. The jurors file in and take their seats, one by one. You're supposed to watch them as they come in, looking for clues—*If they make eye contact, they're going to acquit you; if they don't, they're going to convict.* That never made sense to him, why you'd look for clues in the first place, when you're about to find out in a few seconds.

Instead, he turns around and finds Paige in the fourth row by the aisle. She moves her head so they can see each other between the other spectators. She mouths the words *I love you.* He wants to stay there, looking at her, but his lawyer takes his arm and he gets to his feet for the reading of the verdict.

He turns to face forward but doesn't look at the jury. He finds a blank spot on the wall and stares at it, thinking through everything that has happened and wondering, *How did it come to this?*

He hears a woman's voice. It turns out the foreperson of the jury is the single mother of two who has her own graphic design business, the one who sits in the front row of the jury box, three people from the left end. Is it a good thing that a woman is the leader? Another question that doesn't make any difference. All that matters is what she's going to say next.

"On count one, murder in the first degree with special circumstances, to wit the murder of Melanie Phillips, we find the defendant, Noah Lee Walker, guilty."

Noah sucks in his breath.

"On count two, murder in the first degree with special circumstances, to wit the murder of Zachary Stern, we find the defendant, Noah Lee Walker, guilty."

Noah turns and sees Paige. He starts toward her and she runs up the aisle toward him. There are bailiffs covering the gate that cordons off the spectators, and there are other bailiffs assigned specifically to Noah. Both sets of deputies do their jobs. Paige nearly makes it through, coming within a few feet of the defense table. The deputies grasp Noah firmly, gripping his arms, holding down his neck. He goes limp, compliant, before surprising them by breaking free and reaching Paige.

It won't last, but he just wants to touch her one more time. "Oh, baby," she says to him, her face wet.

He puts his hand gently on the back of her neck and kisses her quickly. Then he moves his mouth to her ear. "Don't give up on me," he says as the deputies recover their leverage, pulling him back. When he refuses to go down, they shove a Taser against his neck, electrical current surging through him. His legs and arms go limp just before his mind does. He falls to the floor in a heap, his last memory of this courtroom.

Book II

BRIDGEHAMPTON, 2007–08

Chapter 30

DEDE PARIS AND Annie Church have disappeared. They were last seen leaving their last final exam at Yale on May 9, completing their sophomore years. They said something vague to their friends about backpacking through Europe with the cash they've saved up while waitressing. They told their parents they were going to stay in New Haven for summer school and rent an apartment with their waitressing money. Neither set of parents made any attempt to verify their stories. Since May 9, over three weeks ago, no known acquaintance or family member has seen either woman.

Which is exactly how they want it.

Dede and Annie rush out of the ocean, holding hands, and find their towels and bags and umbrella. They slip into their flip-flops and don their shades. They are two beautiful, tanned twenty-year-olds, euphoric with love, with very few answers in life yet but, fortunately, very few questions, either. They will have the rest of their lives to discover their calling, to do their internships, apply to grad school, and brace for a hard world. This summer, they're going to discover each other, and nothing else.

By the time they reach the place where they're staying, their skin has long dried, and the withering oven-hot sun beats down on them. Fortunately, they don't have to go far. Their place is just a two-minute walk from the beach. They're staying at 7 Ocean Drive.

Well, it's not their place, exactly. But nobody else is staying here, and it would be a shame for it to stay empty all summer, wouldn't it?

"I love how freak-show this house is," Dede says, looking up at the scowling Gothic structure. She is tall and lanky, with bleached-blond hair cropped like a boy's that practically glows against her suntan. "I keep waiting for Elvira to pop out or something."

They turn east, walking along the southern border of the estate, covered by thick shrubbery that is taller than they are. Dede, the more athletic and adventurous of the two, was the first to explore the shrubbery, looking for a point of entry. The coiled-wire fence hidden within the shrubbery was formidable but nothing that a good set of shears couldn't handle, if you had time and patience, and they have plenty of both this summer. Besides, it didn't have to be pretty, just a large enough hole for them to slip through, the slipping made easier by the thick pieces of rubber they've tied over the jagged edges of fence to avoid cuts and scratches during ingress and egress. Sure, they have to squat down and turn sideways to make it through, but it's worth it—rent free and a ten-thousand-square-foot mansion all to themselves.

As they slide through the opening, Annie looks up at the mansion, the faded multicolored limestone, the stained glass and sharply pitched roofs and medieval-style adornments. She remembers the week she spent in the Hamptons as a girl, when she and her sister heard all about this place.

"No one ever leaves alive / The house at 7 Ocean Drive," she says in her best ghoulish horror-movie voice, repeating the poem she'd heard. *"Not friend or foe, not man or mouse / Can e'er survive the Murder House."*

"That creeps me out," Dede says.

They head toward the rear of the house. The ten-foot shrubbery provides good cover on the grounds, but the mansion itself is perched on a hill, and they've decided their entries and exits should be as covert as possible. In the rear there is a door that, once upon a time, was probably reserved for the servants. The door doesn't have a knob, just a latch held closed by a chain, another victim of Dede's shears.

The smell of disinfectant and soap greets them when they open the door. They scrubbed down the rear entrance the first time they came in, clearing out the cobwebs, mopping the floor, scrubbing the walls. The first thing they see is the door to the basement, which is likewise chained. Sure, they thought it was a little odd that an interior door would be locked in such a way, but they haven't bothered to investigate. There's enough house without it, and their tolerance for *creepy* has just about hit its limit. The basement will remain a mystery.

They pass through the foyer, ignoring the museum-like rooms on each side, and climb the winding, creaky stairs. A veranda off a bedroom on the third floor that they found last week has a panoramic view of the ocean.

Annie leans against the railing, sighing with satisfaction. Her hair, up in a ponytail, is the color of cinnamon but has lightened in the sun. Dede comes up behind her and kisses her long bronzed neck. She runs her hands along the outline of Annie's figure. Annie leans back into Dede's arms, gently humming as Dede cups her breasts, caresses the skin on her flat belly. "That tickles," says Annie as she turns to face Dede. They kiss deeply and lie down together on the blanket they've spread out, their legs intertwined.

And then they hear a noise. The hollow *clink* of metal tapping metal, and footsteps, and then a man whistling. Staying low, they inch toward the side of the veranda and peek through the wooden supports.

A man approaches the side of the house with a long ladder held at his side. He is shirtless and looks pretty damn good that way, a V-shaped physique, rippled abs. His curly dark hair falls from a Yankees cap, turned backward.

"Hot tool-belt guy," Annie whispers. "If I liked boys . . ."

The hot tool-belt guy drops the ladder against the side of the house and quickly climbs up. The women don't move, holding their breath, as he reaches their level on the third floor.

"Just behave yourselves, ladies," he says without looking in their direction. "Deal?"

Busted! Neither woman says anything. Neither woman moves.

"Deal?" he repeats.

Dede stands up, leans on the railing. "We have to behave? That's no fun."

Annie stands up, too. "So what's your story, guy?"

The man gestures upward with his chin. "Me, I'm just patching up the flat roof. Not having as much fun as you, looks like."

"That's not fair," Annie says, which sounds close to an invitation. She gets an elbow from Dede. "So what's your name?"

"Noah," he says.

"Are you going to turn us in, Noah?" Dede asks.

He considers them a moment. "Well, that wouldn't be very nice, would it?"

"It sure wouldn't."

"Just don't make a mess while you're here," he says. "I'll have to clean it up."

He starts to climb. Both girls can't help but enjoy the view. Straight or gay, this guy is hard not to admire.

"And one more thing," he says as he reaches the flat roof. "Don't go in the basement."

"Why's that, Noah?"

"Didn't you hear? This house is haunted." The man hauls himself up on the roof and disappears.

Chapter 31

ANNIE'S BEATER VW Bug pulls up to the gate of 7 Ocean Drive. The sun has fallen now at nine o'clock, so all is clear. When they use their car, which isn't very often, they prefer to enter and exit under the cover of darkness.

Dede gets out to push open the massive gate, using all her weight to do so. Once it's open, she turns back, squinting into the car's headlights.

Beyond the beams, across the street, she sees someone, standing flat-footed, looking at her. She does a double take, shields her eyes with a hand—which doesn't really help—and moves away from the blinding beams to get a better look. It seems as if . . . the figure moves along with her, and then disappears—maybe into the shrubbery?—leaving Dede with spots in her vision from the car lights.

Dede rushes back to the car and gets in.

"What's the matter?" Annie asks.

"I thought I . . . saw someone. Across the street. Staring at us. Watching us."

Annie strains to look behind her. "I didn't see anyone when we drove up."

"I know. Me either."

"What did he look like?"

Dede lets out a shudder. "Couldn't really see. A man, looked like. Kind of—you're gonna laugh—like a scarecrow, sort of? Like, his hair was all stringy and sticking out. He had a hat on, too, I think."

"A scarecrow?" Annie looks at Dede with mock horror. "You don't think . . . the Tin Man might be out there, too?"

"Stop."

"Not the Cowardly Lion!" Annie brings a hand to her mouth.

"Just drive the car."

Annie pats Dede's leg. "You're paranoid, girl. We're not supposed to be here, so you think everyone's looking to bust us. I mean, someone walking down Ocean Drive in the summer isn't exactly unusual." She puts the car into gear and drives through the gate. Dede closes the gate behind them, taking another look across the street and seeing nothing.

"That's the thing, though," she says when she reenters the car. "He wasn't walking. He was just watching us. I mean, I think. With the headlights, I couldn't really see. It could just be my eyes playing tricks."

Annie pulls the Beetle onto the grass next to the massive detached garage, hidden from sight. She lets out a sigh. "Good to be home," she says. "There's no place like home. There's no place like—"

"Would you shut up?"

As they walk toward the back entrance, they see the ladder the hot tool-belt guy used yesterday, broken down and lying in the grass. "Noah was cute," Annie says.

"Was he? Was he *cute?*" Dede throws another elbow.

"Now, now, dearest, I only have eyes for you."

Inside, they unpack their groceries. They've found a place in Montauk that sells lobster tails and oysters at nontourist prices, and Dede apparently looks old enough to buy champagne—the cheapest they had. Tonight is an anniversary of sorts, exactly six months from the day they met on campus.

Annie gets the food ready while whistling that *Wizard of Oz* song "If I Only Had a Brain." Dede keeps punching her playfully in the arm, but it only emboldens Annie. As much as it gets under her skin, it's one of the reasons Dede loves her.

Yes, she thinks, *I do love her.* Dede has no trouble opening her heart to Annie. She's accepted her sexual orientation for years now. She came out in high school, and she grew up in Santa Monica, where they practically throw you a parade for doing so. Annie, though, had never been with a woman before meeting Dede. Of course, she *knew,* on some level, but growing up in rural Michigan, she didn't acknowledge her sexual preference to her friends or her devout Catholic parents, or even to herself. You'd think, by 2007, people would have loosened up enough, but Dede knows as well as anyone that discrimination doesn't evaporate overnight but slowly fades over time.

Dinner is great. The dining room is over-the-top ornate, full of all kinds of detail on the walls, little statuettes perched around the room, tall windows with ornamental trim, an enormous chandelier hovering over a big five-sided dark oak table that's surrounded by high-backed chairs with leather cushions. It's like Henry VIII meets Count Dracula.

On their jam box, they play some symphonic music that Annie, the violinist, chose; she plays maestro, conducting the music with her fork. And the lobster and oysters are delicious. The cheap champagne is like Pop Rocks in Dede's mouth. It goes to her head quickly, enhancing her euphoria. *Annie is it,* she thinks. *She is my one and only.*

The window rattles and Dede turns to it. The wind, surely. But still, she walks over and cups her hand over the glass to block the interior reflection, looking out onto Ocean Drive.

"Is the Scarecrow still out there? I'd be more worried about him, if he only had a brain."

"You've been waiting to say that, haven't you?" Dede looks back and finds Annie sitting on the windowsill on the opposite side of the dining room. "What are you doing?"

Annie has her Swiss Army knife open, carving into the wood.

"Annie, you can't do that! This place is, like, three hundred years old. And it's not like you can just erase that."

Dede walks over to get a look at what Annie is doing. As Dede suspected, she is carving their initials in jagged letters:

DP + AC

"I don't want to erase it," Annie says. "I want it to be here forever."

Dede puts her arm around Annie and draws her close, breathing in her shampoo. "Forever?" she says tentatively. Her heart is pounding. This is one of those moments when she feels so vulnerable, her heart laid bare to be embraced or trampled.

"Forever." Annie looks up at Dede. The champagne tastes even better to Dede the second time, on Annie's tongue.

Chapter 32

THE GIRLS STAYING at 7 Ocean Drive are now on the second floor of the mansion, the southwest bedroom. The purple-and-gold bedroom, with the canopy bed and the velvet. The master bedroom where, over two hundred years ago, Winston Dahlquist once slept.

They are naked, and they are doing very fun things to each other. Their young bodies are shapely and athletic and limber, fueled by lust and maybe love—who can say?—and helped mightily by the two bottles of champagne they've drunk. The alcohol has undoubtedly lowered their inhibitions, and also impaired their judgment a bit—which is probably why they've forgotten to pull the bedroom drapes.

Now, to be fair, the bedroom window looks south, toward the beach and ocean, with only one house in between, which is not nearly as tall. A reasonable person would thus believe that, even with the drapes open wide as they are, she would not be visible to anyone.

But a reasonable person might not expect a man to be standing on the beach, peering northward with a pair of binoculars.

The man who thinks of himself as Holden lowers the binoculars and lets them hang around his neck. Wait—no—no, no. He removes the binoculars and throws them into his bag, which he calls his Fun Bag. This time of night, having binoculars is a dead giveaway—no chance of bird-watching or any other legitimate reason for using them, at ten in the evening. You might just as well wear a sign that says PEEPING TOM.

Be more careful, Holden! He likes calling himself that name. It gets him in the mood, in much the same way the alcohol gets those girls feeling more sexually adventurous. He rolls his neck. Stretches his arms. Cracks his knuckles. Jogs in place a moment, some sand kicking up.

He picks up his Fun Bag and climbs the beach onto Ocean Drive. He is happy, almost giddy. The sky is a deep purple and a soft wind plays with his hair. He is healthy and prepared. Tonight, he is Holden, and he can do anything.

He wonders how long they'll stay up in the bedroom. Could be they'll fall asleep, exhausted from the alcohol and sex. It won't matter. He'll be prepared either way.

They probably have the doors locked. They certainly should—there are scary people out there! Not that a lock will stop him.

He has a key to the place, after all.

But the front door isn't an option—too creaky and

noisy. No, he'll use his private entry, his secret way into the house, reserved for special occasions.

Because this has all the makings of a special occasion.

Chapter 33

HOLDEN RESTS IN the room that Winston Dahlquist once called the guest parlor, a waiting room of sorts off the ground-floor living room. It is ridiculously ornate, like all the rooms—candelabra and chandeliers and custom molding, a fireplace and a marble mantel, a Persian area rug.

They are almost directly above him. He closes his eyes and listens to their laughter upstairs. They are in love, he thinks, or at least they sound like it. His heart is pounding. He is here, and they don't know it. That is special all by itself—they think they're sharing something intimate, but he gets to be a part of it.

He opens up a small compact and checks himself over. His hair is smartly combed. His shirt is pressed. His beige trousers are new. His erection is at full mast, pushing against his trousers.

There's no way to describe this. One part forbidden, one part intimate, one part sexual, and one part full of possibilities unknown even to him—he's not sure what he's going to do yet. There should be a word for how he feels.

He thinks of how they'd react if they saw him. What they would say. What they would do. The snappy dialogue that would ensue. The flirtation. They'd be attracted to him, wouldn't they? Of course they would. Maybe a . . . a threesome? Wow. Maybe.

Footsteps overhead. Holden shakes out of his fantasy and listens closely. The footsteps are heading . . . where? Down the hallway toward the staircase?

No. No, she's just walking into the master bedroom. He hears the water turn on now.

He sighs. This is not good enough, not real enough. He thought this was going to be special. This is kind of fun, but not *special*. He's too far away from them, too remote. Should he go up the stairs? No, that would be too risky.

The kitchen, maybe. There will be glasses and dishes they touched. Maybe an article of clothing they left behind? That would help. That would really help.

He has to take a piss. But he can't do that. Even if he used the bathroom near the back, and even if he sat down like a girl to cut down on the noise, he'd either have to flush—which they'd hear—or leave evidence behind. He's not stupid. He's not stupid at all. Stupid? He's the opposite of stupid. He's really smart.

Oh, maybe he should just leave.

But tonight I'm Holden.

Okay. He removes his shoes to minimize his footfalls and drops them in the Fun Bag. He picks it up and pushes through the French doors quietly, into the living room. From there, he walks through the foyer. He stops at the staircase, where he hears them upstairs singing in unison to Justin Timberlake:

"I'll let you whip me if I misbehaaaave!"

He smiles to himself, feels himself relax. Feeling better, he walks into the dining room, where two empty bottles of champagne, an empty bottle of Evian, a bottle of Tabasco, two plates of discarded lobster tails and oyster shells, and a dish of horseradish rest on the pentagonal table beneath a grand chandelier. Winston Dahlquist used to bring the girls in here. They'd feast on duck and lobster and dates and olives. They'd drink the finest French wines. He probably viewed it as fattening them up before the slaughter.

He hikes the Fun Bag over his shoulder, carefully picks up one of the empty champagne bottles and one of the plates, and heads into the kitchen.

He's never liked the kitchen much because it's not original. Back when Winston built this place, the kitchen was for servants only, tiny and functional. Winston's descendants remodeled the kitchen in the seventies, tripling the size, installing cherrywood cabinets, marble countertops, and stainless steel appliances. It just looks like a boring kitchen, no character. But it's safe, and it will have to do.

He opens up the Fun Bag just to be safe, just to be sure, just to be prepared. He thinks of the girls having sex upstairs, and then singing "SexyBack," and it helps him. They'd like him. He's sure of it. They could share so much.

He smells the champagne bottle. Nothing special.

Then he sees lipstick on it, so he touches it with his lips. Not cherry ChapStick, but red and sticky and sweet. Yes. Good. This is getting better now. This was a good idea—

And then it happens in an instant, sneaking up on him, how, *how* it could have happened he isn't sure, because he's so cautious and careful, but he hears footsteps bounding down the stairs and suddenly those footsteps are in the dining room, adjacent to the kitchen, where he is. He moves very quietly toward the opening, hoping, *praying* that nobody heard him, and peeks into the dining room.

It's the blonde, the taller one with the short hair. She's unplugging the stereo resting on the windowsill. She looks good bending over, just wearing a bra and panties. So firm and lean. So . . . so special.

Oh, God, if I could just . . .

He ducks back, just on the off chance that she might cast a glance in his direction. His heartbeat is drumming so loudly that he can't hear, he can't think straight, but he prepares just in case, he's had it planned out just in case, and he recites it to himself now. *I'm the owner. This is my house.* Just in case.

And he reaches into the Fun Bag, also just in case.

He slowly steps back into the recesses of the kitchen and holds his breath.

It'll be okay, he thinks. *This will be better. It will enhance the whole experience, make it more real, more vivid.*

That's what he's telling himself when the blond girl walks into the kitchen.

Chapter 34

THE BLOND GIRL doesn't see him at first. Her head is down and she's balancing the remnants of the meal—the champagne and water bottles, the plates of food and the Tabasco—and turns toward the counter in the center of the kitchen to plop it all down before she even realizes she's not alone.

She recoils in an instant, her breath whisked away in surprise, her hands rising up defensively, everything she'd been holding crashing to the tile floor. Glass shatters everywhere. The sound only amplifies her shock.

Be indignant. This is your house. She's the intruder. Say that. Say that!

"I'm the . . . owner," he manages. He raises a hand in peace.

The girl is too stunned for a moment, but Holden planned this out well. The words did the trick. She doesn't turn and run, not immediately.

"Oh—oh. I—you're the own—"

"Dede? Is everything okay?" It's the other girl. *"Dede?"*

The blonde looks back toward the living room, then back at Holden.

"How . . . many of you are . . . here?" he asks. *Excellent! Just what an indignant owner would say.*

"Just two of—oh. Oh." Her eyes dart downward just as Holden feels the warm stain spreading across his crotch. He just pissed himself. He looks down, and then back up at her.

"We'll leave right now, mister. I'm really sorry."

She spins on her heels to leave. Holden closes the distance between them in an instant. She senses his approach and starts to run and is nearly out the door when he reaches her, stabbing the Taser into the back of her neck. She goes down hard, her body suddenly limp and unable to break her fall, her face smacking against the kitchen wall and landing hard on the ceramic tile.

"Dede?" comes the voice from upstairs.

Holden drags the blond girl—Dede—into the kitchen, away from the view of the dining room, a trail of blood smearing in her wake. Is she . . . dead? The fall was nasty. She's bleeding from the nose and forehead.

What has he done? What's he *going* to do? He's thinking fast, but the adrenaline is catching up with him now and he can't let it paralyze him, he's got to think-think-think—

Hearing the urgent footfalls in the living room, Holden grabs a frying pan from the overhead rack and raises it above his head. The brunette gasps before she's even entered—seeing the bloodstain first, no doubt—and when she rushes in, her eyes are already cast downward at her lover. She lets out a horrific scream as she looks up to meet Holden's eyes, but by then the frying pan is already crashing down on the crown of her skull.

The pan almost bounces out of Holden's hand from the harsh impact. He's never hit anything so hard. The brunette is stunned, reaching for support but unable to find any. She sinks to her knees, still upright but precariously so, and before she falls like a tower tumbling over, Holden raises the pan and cracks it against her skull a second time. When she crumples to the floor, she is lifeless, like a balloon figurine that the air has been let out of. Her eyes are open but still.

Is *she* dead?

Holden bounces on his toes, looking at each of them. The blonde is still breathing. The brunette is not.

"It was a . . . accident," he says. "I didn't . . . I just wanted . . ."

What does he do now? Panic sweeps over him. *Run,* he thinks, but *No, too many clues left behind.* The blonde knows what he looks like.

She moans. Her shoulders move. She's trying to turn over.

Holden watches her. Watches her struggle. Watches her suffer.

But this is their fault. They shouldn't have surprised him. They made him do this.

"No . . . no . . ." The blonde is making noise on the floor. He taps her with his foot. She groans in response. He bends down and rolls her over on her back. Turns her bloodied face to the left, so she can see her girlfriend.

"Look at her," he says. "Look."

Her eyes widen in horror. She manages a low, guttural, garbled wail.

It's the most beautiful sound he's ever heard.

Chapter 35

HOLDEN PUTS A hand on his stomach. It causes a physical pain, a rumble in his stomach like hunger for food, a growl that resembles the angry hum of the motorcycle on which he's riding at the moment.

He needs it again. He needs the thrill of the chase, the anticipation, the climax itself. It's been over a year since Dede and Annie, and he can't decide what was most invigorating: the initial approach, sneaking into the mansion; the physical act; the pain and suffering . . .

. . . so much to choose from. It's kind of like deciding what you like best about pizza, the cheese or the sauce or the toppings; they are inseparable ingredients of a delicious experience. But if he had to choose, it was none of those things. No, it was the aftermath, what's happened every day since, the feeling of invincibility that comes with knowing he got away with it, that he can do whatever he pleases and nobody can catch him, nobody can stop him.

Oh, there was an investigation. Apparently the girls,

Dede Paris and Annie Church, hadn't told anyone where they were spending the summer. They had told their friends one lie, their parents another, but nobody the truth. It was only through cell phone records that authorities were able to place them in the Hamptons at all. But it was over two weeks after he'd killed them that a search even began, and it wasn't much of a search. Nobody had any idea where the girls were staying in the Hamptons. They never even focused on Bridgehampton, much less the house at 7 Ocean Drive. The best guess was that the girls were staying in Montauk, because that was where they found Annie's car, in a tow yard after it had been parked illegally in a church parking lot, stripped of its license plates. (Yes, Holden has congratulated himself for moving her car.) It was when the authorities found the car that they officially determined . . . *drumroll, please* . . . that "foul play" was involved.

Ta-da! They don't have a clue. The lesson: *You can do whatever you want. If you're smart. If you're disciplined. If you take care in choosing your victims. If you don't get greedy.*

He drives by the nightclub again, passing the alley where they congregate in the shadows, waiting for any car that might pull over. He slows his motorcycle to an idle and looks to his right, directly where he knows they are. Several of them step out from the shadows into the light of the streetlamp in their skintight dresses, hiked up to show plenty of leg, their hair teased up, their boobs pushed out, hoping to make eye contact with potential customers. There are a half dozen of them, a nice variety of busty and petite, white and black and Hispanic. A smorgasbord of potential victims.

Victims. It's fun to think of them that way. Not women but prey.

He immediately crosses the tall, leggy blonde off the list, because she is too much like Dede—though Dede ended up being great fun in the end. Still, variety is the spice of life, and, more to the point, an intelligent man like Holden realizes that he cannot leave a pattern of any kind in his wake.

He quickly narrows it down to a busty black woman and a petite blonde.

The blond one it is! Smaller, probably no more than a hundred pounds, and therefore easier to subdue, should any difficulty arise.

But why should any difficulty arise? He has his Fun Bag back at the motel. And unlike last time, when Dede and Annie surprised him, this time he'll have the chance to show off his charm, to gain her trust, lure her in.

She'll have no idea what's coming. She'll probably think the corkscrew is for a bottle of champagne. She'll think the handcuffs are just a kinky sex thing.

She might wonder about the handheld kitchen torch, though.

It's past midnight and there is a healthy stream of people coming and going from the club nearby. Witnesses, potentially—a careful man like Holden thinks of such things—but most are drunk and, in the end, what could they say about him? He's wearing a helmet with a tinted face shield, and he's removed the license plate. All anyone could possibly describe is a guy in a leather jacket wearing a helmet on a black motorcycle.

Anyway, if it was entirely risk-free, it wouldn't be any fun.

Yet he feels a pang of doubt, even as he nods toward the petite blonde. Can he go through with it? He's rusty; it's been over a year. As much as he's been romanticizing it since then, he now remembers how scared he was at the time. Exhilarated, yes, but scared, too.

On his nod, the blonde saunters up to him, wearing a black outfit that covers little more than a bikini would. Her belly is flat, with a piercing through her navel. She has the body of a twenty-year-old, the face of someone older, more seasoned, more worked over. Her heels make her two inches taller, but she's a little thing.

"Hi, handsome. You want some company?"

"I want . . . all night," he says, keeping his helmet on, the face shield down.

"I'm by the hour, hon."

"I want . . . all night." That's Holden being smart. If she's leaving for the night, nobody will expect her back in an hour. Nobody will think to look for her at least until tomorrow. Assuming anybody looks for her, period.

"The whole night? That's two thousand." She runs her hand over his arm, the leather of his jacket. "It's worth it."

"No," he says. See, that's Holden being smart again— make her think this is a real negotiation, that he actually plans on paying her something. "Five hundred."

"Five hundred for this?" she says, running her hands over the outline of her body, moving to the music coming from the nightclub. "C'mon, lover, fifteen hundred. For a night you'll never forget."

He doesn't know what a streetwalker makes in a night, but it can't be anywhere near that. "A . . . thousand," he says.

"Awww, baby. Hang on." The girl walks back to her friends and says something. *See, you were right—she's telling them she's done for the night, not to expect her back. Smart, Holden.*

"Do I need a helmet?" she asks when she hops on the bike.

He turns back to her as she wraps her arms around his waist.

"No," he says. "You're safe with me."

Chapter 36

HOLDEN AND THE blond hooker drive to a motel off Sunrise Highway. He rented the room two days ago, paying in cash and asking for a room in the back away from traffic. He parks within ten feet of the door and brings the girl inside. The room isn't much to look at. The carpet is torn up, the wallpaper is peeling, the lighting is dim, and the mattress is about as thick as a slice of cheese. But it's clean and it doesn't smell. He's seen worse. And he's certain she has, too.

He sets his helmet on the small table where the television sits. He spots the Fun Bag in the corner, just where he left it. He looks in the mirror and fixes his hair.

"We need to take care of business first."

He turns and gets his first look at her in normal lighting. She has a round face, her eyes set slightly too far apart, with a crooked smile that is probably supposed to be sexy. Her dirty-blond hair is teased up in some kind of bun on top of her head. She is very slender, and her skin is pale and freckly. Her breasts are small and her butt is tiny and round.

"Okay." He has a thousand in cash. He peels it out and hands it to her. She stuffs it in her purse. Is that her idea of safekeeping? It must be. Though it's not that safe. She's in a room with a stranger, after all. It's not safe at all. *She's* not safe at all. But that's an occupational hazard. Everything she does is full of risk. That must be hard, having to make a living by meeting strange men and—

Stop it. Stop thinking like that.

"I'm gonna freshen up," she says, and then she spins on her heels and heads to the bathroom, her red purse slung over her shoulder.

He looks at himself in the mirror. *Don't start thinking about her life. Think about what you want. Think about what you're going to do. Think about the handcuffs and the corkscrew and the torch. Don't fuck this up. You've been waiting a year for this—*

She returns looking a little more chipper, her eyes glassy.

She's high. She took something in the bathroom.

He looks over her arms. No signs of needle marks. Cocaine, probably. That's probably how she gets through this job, high as a kite.

Stop it. You don't give a shit about her or how she copes with life.

You don't care.

"So what's your pleasure, guy?" Her tone is less

flirtatious than it was on the street. More businesslike.

"My . . . ?"

"What do you want me to do?" Her eyes bug out, like she's impatient.

"I just . . . can we . . . can we just . . . talk?"

He's trembling. She looks at his hands. She sees it, too.

"Okay, we can talk." She sits down on the bed and looks up at him. "What do you wanna talk about?"

"I . . ." He swallows hard. *What the hell is wrong with you?* "What's your name?"

She shrugs. "What do you want it to be?"

He shakes his head. "No . . . no."

"Okay, my name's Barbie."

Her name isn't Barbie. That's her street name.

"Do you . . . wanna know . . . *my* name?"

"Sure, mister. Lots of guys don't want to tell me their name. It's your money."

He stares at her, unsure of himself.

"Okay, what's your name, guy?"

She's so hardened. Deadened. Drugged out. She'll spread her legs for him or suck him off, she'll twist and turn her body however he asks, but she won't really be here. This isn't real.

It's not supposed to be like this. Dede and Annie, they were real. He thought the one thing missing was that he didn't know them first, didn't get intimate with them, killed them almost at first sight. But that was better. That was better than this—

"Got anything to drink, mister?"

He shakes his head, unable to speak. He should've

thought of that. He should've had a bottle of whiskey or something.

"Got any music?"

Shit. He shakes his head again. He feels everything slipping away, every turn a wrong one . . .

"I . . . can't," he whispers.

"Can't what?"

Sweat has broken out on his forehead. His pulse is racing. He doesn't feel right.

"I can't . . . kill you," he says. His eyes slowly rise to meet hers.

She studies him a moment, lips parted, fear beginning to spread across her face. He feels himself getting hard. He feels the energy suddenly fueling him.

And then her eyes grow big again, when she sees the look on his face.

There. There it is!

She bounces off the bed, rushing for the door.

Yes.

"No!" she cries as he grabs her arm. "No, please!"

He pins her up against the wall, bringing a hand over her mouth. She bites down on his hand, causing a glorious pain, but he pushes back hard, slamming her head against the wall with all the force he can summon. Her eyes roll back and she begins to slide down the wall, unconscious.

He lowers himself, sliding down with her. He drags her over near the bed and lays her out properly.

"Thank you, Barbie," he whispers.

He handled this wrong, but she salvaged it for him, a last-minute save.

He learned something. He won't make this mistake again.

He walks to the corner to get his Fun Bag.

Book III

BRIDGEHAMPTON AND SING SING, 2012

Chapter 37

SING SING CORRECTIONAL Facility, thirty miles north of New York City on the east bank of the Hudson River, houses nearly two thousand inmates over fifty-five acres of property. Up the hill from the lower-level secured facilities is Cell Block A—"Maximum A"—one of the largest max-security cell blocks in the world, with over six hundred inmates packed into six-by-nine-foot cells. They are murderers and rapists and sex traffickers and mob bosses and major drug dealers, divided into fierce factions predominantly by race—the Bloods and the Crips, the Latin Kings and *Trinitarios*, the Aryan Brotherhood. If you belong to one of the gangs, they have your back—you're protected—but even then you're not *really* protected, because the sins of the individual are the sins of the gang, and retaliation in Cell Block A is as common as census counts four times a day. In the last eight days, Cell Block A has been on lock-down four times, as the Latin Kings and the Bloods have worked out their differences the only way they know how. Guns are uncommon; it's by shanks and razors, anything that can be pried loose and sharpened into a weapon, that most of the injuries are inflicted.

The first time Noah Walker walked into Cell Block A, he was overwhelmed. Overwhelmed by the sheer enormity, the cell block extending four stories high and so far from right to left that there seems to be no beginning or end, just an endless wall of steel and chain-link barriers. Overwhelmed by the noise, a deafening clamor of hundreds of caged men shouting, radios playing, gates slamming.

This is his home now, on the top tier of A-Block, Gallery L, seventh cell. He will live in L-7 for the rest of his life. He will live amid a massive series of cages, covered by a concrete-and-brick dome with windows that miraculously let in very little light, sunshine filtered through filth. The polluted air, the noise, the solitude of hour upon hour spent in a cell no bigger than a normal person's closet—in the seventy-three days that Noah has spent here, they have had the effect of deadening him, killing his hope, erasing his dreams, leaving him numb.

Outside the cell—the mess hall, the showers, the machine shop, and the prison yard—it's a different story. Noah is alert at all times, his eyes constantly moving about. Noah is not affiliated. The only real option for a white guy is the Aryan Brotherhood, and he's not going anywhere near those racist morons. That makes him fair game to everyone. Stick a shank into Noah's back, or accost him in the shower, or jump him in the yard, and nobody will retaliate. Noah is alone in every sense of the word.

And with every day that passes, he finds that he cares less and less. There is nothing for him here but the passage of time. He is simply waiting for time to move along until he dies.

His tiny cell is barren of personal effects. He hasn't built up enough in the commissary for a radio, and no television is allowed. He has only two personal items, a photograph of Paige and a copy of his favorite novel, *The Catcher in the Rye*.

In the photograph, Paige is in Noah's attic bedroom, her hand up to shield her face from his camera, a look of embarrassed amusement on her face. Strands of her hair curl around her cheek. He likes this photograph because it touches all of his senses. He hears Paige's voice—*Don't take my picture!* He smells her the way he liked her best, sweaty after sex. He feels her hand on his arm while she tries to keep him from snapping the photo with his phone.

Paige. He will never see her again. He told her not to come here, and to drive the point home, he told her he wouldn't see her if she came. They have no future now, and it's better she remembers him when life was good, to hold that sweet memory close to herself, rather than having her image of him deteriorate slowly over the years as he grows harder, more bitter.

He met yesterday with his lawyer, who told him there would be a one-month delay in getting his appeal on file. Noah told him that was okay. He doesn't have a chance. He knows that. He's in no hurry to find out that his appeal has been rejected.

That's the worst part, worse than the fear in the

prison yard, or the loneliness, or the shame of being convicted of a double homicide. The lack of any hope, of any future, of any meaning to his life, will kill him—if a shank in the neck doesn't.

Which of those will come first, he has no idea.

Chapter 38

THE MACHINE SHOP in Sing Sing is in the former "death room," where the electric chair, "Old Sparky," killed more than six hundred people, including the spies Julius and Ethel Rosenberg, over the course of seventy years. "Old Sparky" has been moved to a museum, and the death penalty has been abolished in New York— Noah now often wishes it hadn't—so instead, Noah works in that space assembling chairs for toddlers, to be used, he assumes, in either an elementary school or a hospital.

If there have been any moments of enjoyment in his two and a half months in Sing Sing, they have come while he's been doing this work, taking care and pride in putting together these chairs. He's always enjoyed working with his hands, knowing that there is something tangible to show for his effort. Someone will sit in this chair. Someone will learn something in this chair. Someone will laugh in this chair.

"On the count!" One of the COs walks in for the

census, taken four times a day to make sure all prisoners are accounted for. The correctional officers cannot, as a practical matter, follow around every inmate all the time, so they move them in groups through the narrow hallways, always staying to the right of the yellow stripe down the center, and even let them walk on their own when going to the yard or the gym.

At the CO's call, Noah stands and keeps his hands at his sides. The CO counts off the inmates aloud. There are eleven in the machine shop, divided among the various rooms for printing, woodwork, and welding. There are only three, Noah included, here in woodworking.

Noah gets back to work, squatting down on one knee. Behind him, he hears the other two inmates—both of them African American, Al and Rafer—abruptly put down their tools and walk out of woodworking. Noah senses something.

He gets to his feet just as three men enter the room. Unlike Al and Rafer, these men aren't black. They are white. He recognizes one of them as Eric Wheaton, the leader of the Aryan Brotherhood here at Sing Sing. His two friends are massive, with shaved heads and skin ink up and down their tree-trunk arms.

Wheaton, himself above average in size but dwarfed by his companions, is the elder statesman of his clan, probably fifty. He shows Noah his teeth. "Well, Noah. Seems like you been avoiding us. My friends have offered to be your friends."

"I don't need friends like you," says Noah. He wishes he had something in hand, like the hammer on the floor.

"You don't need friends? You're the only guy in A don't need friends? How's a guy like you gonna get along in here with all the mongrels?"

The men on each side of Wheaton fan out, forming a semicircle around Noah. Two more men, nearly as big as the first set of goons, also proud members of the Brotherhood, enter the room. Now it's five on one.

"So I'm askin' nice," says Wheaton. "For the last time."

Noah takes a breath, steels himself. "I don't need you or your white-trash racist asshole buddies."

Wheaton's smile widens, showing stained, crooked teeth. "He's too good for us, friends. He's Jesus. Didn't you hear? Surfer Boy Jesus. Someone help me remember, now—what happened to Jesus?"

With that, they close in from both sides. Noah keeps his fist in tight and pops one of the goons in the mouth, snapping his head back, and then spins to his right and connects with a roundhouse left to the jaw of the thug from the other side. It's enough to throw the man off balance but not enough to knock him over. Noah will still have to deal with him and with the other two. He turns back to his left for the oncoming rush, but he's not fast enough; the biggest of the goons barrels into him, three hundred pounds of force, knocking him to the floor. He kicks out his legs and tries to bench-press the man off him before a boot connects with his temple, sending a shock of lightning across his eyes. Then the man on top of him rises up and slams down a fist. Just in time, Noah ducks his head, and the man's fist hits the floor instead of Noah's face. He cries out in pain. Noah lunges up at the midsection like a bucking bronco to topple the man off him.

But they are too many, and too big. After the initial burst of action, it simply comes down to numbers. Five on one. Five men kicking and punching Noah, who is pinned down. Blood flies from his mouth and nose with each kick, each punch, until he can no longer hold his head up. Now he is nothing more than a punching bag. He feels his ribs crack with successive kicks, but he can't offer any response. He is getting the life beaten out of him, and if they want to kill him, he can no longer stop them.

After a while, the pressure comes off his chest, and he is being tugged by all four limbs. Then he is lifted off the ground and thrown down onto one of the large woodworking tables.

"Keep his arms out, boys," one of them says. Noah is hardly conscious as his arms are spread out, palms up. Men climb onto the table and sit on each of his forearms, while two others sit on his shins. He is completely pinned down.

By the time he feels the prick of the nail on the palm of his hand, he is unable to even cry out. He looks through the fog, through the tiny slits of his eyes, and sees Eric Wheaton poising the nail over his right hand, a hammer raised above his head.

When the hammer comes down on the nail, it's like a drilling rig finding oil, blood spurting into the air. Noah lets out an animal cry and his eyes go to the ceiling. They do quick work of it, nailing both hands to the wooden tabletop, while Noah focuses on a single thought.

Let me die, he prays.

Chapter 39

"ALMOST READY, BABE?"

I flip the page, then flip back, reading through police reports and investigation summaries and cross-referencing trial transcripts.

"Babe?"

"Um. Yeah. Almost ready."

Well, not so much. I'm sitting on the bed, feet up, doing work. But I can get ready fast.

Matty pokes his head into the room. He's wearing a new Hugo Boss sport coat and cologne of the same label. His hair is freshly slicked back from his shower.

"What are you doing? You haven't even showered?"

"No, I—sorry," I say. "Just reading."

"Reading what? Christ, Murphy, do you ever stop working? And that comes from someone who works on Wall Street." He walks over to the bed, where I'm sitting with the transcript on my lap. Matty reaches for the stack of paper I'm reading, revealing the solid-gold cuff links on his sleeves.

"This is the guy who killed your uncle? The 'Surfer Jesus' guy?"

"Yeah." I look up at him. "Just checking something."

"Checking what? That guy went down, what, four months ago? What is there to check?"

I shrug. "There was a shooting at Bridgehampton School a long time ago. Halloween of ninety-five."

"And that has what to do with what?"

"Noah was arrested for it."

"Noah," he says. "Now you're on a first-name basis with the guy."

"I pulled the file yesterday," I say. "Let me run this by you, okay?"

"Hurry." Now he's at the bedroom mirror above the dresser, checking himself over, fixing the collar of his new shirt.

"Fifteen people were shot that day in the southern playground," I say. "Noah was on the east end of the yard, by the trees. Of the fifteen shot, about eight of them were hit within thirty feet of where he was standing with his BB gun."

"Uh-huh."

"Another seven were walking up to the school but farther away, farther west."

"Oh. Okay." He smoothes his hair, looks himself over once more, and reaches a favorable conclusion.

"They were more like sixty, seventy feet away. One of the kids on the farther west end, a kid named Darryl Friese, took a BB in his eye."

"Yeah? Wow."

"His *left* eye."

Matty doesn't answer. He walks into the bathroom and runs the water. When he walks back out, wiping his face with a hand towel, he nods at me.

"You still aren't in the shower," he says.

"You're not listening to me."

"Sure I am."

I'm tempted to ask him what I said. But that would embarrass both of us.

"If Darryl Friese was walking north up to the school, and Noah was shooting from the east, how did he hit Darryl on the left side of the face?"

Matty tosses his shoulders. He doesn't know. He doesn't care, either. He finishes with the towel and gives me a sideways glance. "I've seen this guy Noah on TV," he says. "Handsome dude. Should I be jealous?"

"Matty—"

"Who's better-looking, him or me?" he asks.

"Are you kidding me?"

He points at me. "That's a nonanswer. You think that guy's got something on me? He doesn't make seven figures, does he? C'mon, Murphy, give it up," he says, grabbing my ankle. "You like that guy more than me?"

I move my leg, forcing his hand off my ankle. I get off the bed and walk out of the room. He follows me down the hallway.

"What? I was listening. But Murphy, what's your deal? That thing was a lifetime ago. I mean, I know you miss your uncle, and I'm sorry and all that—"

"That's very sweet of you," I deadpan.

"—but seriously, you gotta snap out of this. You're turning into a real drag."

I stop and spin on him. "Am I?"

"Yeah, you wanna know the truth. You are."

I take a step toward him. "This is the guy who killed my uncle. I'm trying to understand him."

"Why? You trying to get closure or something?"

"I don't know. Maybe."

"Well, can you get 'closure' when we don't have reservations at Quist in . . . now it's twenty-four minutes," he says, checking his watch.

"I can still get ready," I say.

"Yeah, you'll wash your hair and tie it into a ponytail and throw on something too casual for where we're going. God forbid you try to look hot when I'm in town. God forbid you put on some makeup and spend more than two minutes on your hair. You're this . . . you're the hottest woman I know, but it's like you don't give a shit about that."

I narrow my eyes to get a better look at this man named Matt Queenan. "I *don't* give a shit about that," I say. "Did you just figure that out?"

"Y'know, I'm gonna let you in on a little secret, princess." He wags a finger at me. "A lot of women would *want* to look hot for me. You think I don't get overtures all the time? Every day? You think there aren't a dozen women who'd jump at the chance to date me?"

"Oh, I'm sure there are *hundreds,*" I say, not hiding my sarcasm. "You're the great Matty Queenan! You make *seven figures* a year! Why don't you go find one of those women tonight?"

I return to the bedroom. As I pass him, he grabs my

arm. "You know what, I think I will," he says through his teeth.

I yank my arm free and give him a forearm shiver to the chest. "Don't grab my arm."

"Don't fucking push me," he says, knocking me back into the wall.

My Irish up now, I lean in and punch him right in the kisser, connecting with his teeth and feeling his jaw crunch. "Is that better?"

He stumbles backward, unprepared, touching his mouth and then checking his fingers, finding blood. "You fucking *bitch*. Nobody hits me."

I shrug. "Hit the road, Matty," I say. "Or I'll hit you again, a lot harder."

"Yeah?"

He moves at me, but I feint toward him and he backs off. He's a lightweight. He knows I could take him. He couldn't handle the embarrassment.

"Have a nice life in this shithole town with your shithole job," he says, turning to leave. "I'll have another date by the time I get back to Manhattan."

Chapter 40

AFTER MATTY DRIVES away, I throw on a baseball cap and head to my car. I don't feel like being around here, smelling his lingering cologne, thinking of him. My nerves are still rattled, but I know, in my heart, that I wasn't going anywhere with him. It was going to happen sooner or later.

I try to avoid the knowledge, also buried deep within, that I'm probably not going anywhere with *any* guy, that I'm not cut out for a relationship. I always rolled my eyes at the cliché of the cop who's married to the job, but now I can see the merits of the stereotype. It's not that I don't care about anything besides my job—it's that the job doesn't let you leave. You see death and misery and suffering, and you don't just click that off when you go home; it doesn't wash off in the shower or vanish with a lover's embrace. You are polluted, toxic, and so you hold back so you don't infect someone else with the poison. You keep part of yourself segregated, hidden.

And as long as I'm being brutally honest with myself:

The truth is I've *always* felt alone, long before I was a cop. Always different. The "red sheep" of my family, I always called myself, because of my shiny red hair contrasted with the blond hair of Ryan and my parents. (I'm told my red locks came from a great-grandmother I never knew; I've only seen a black-and-white photo of her.) I was tall and athletic, while Ryan was stout and bookish. I was a restless troublemaker, while Ryan was calm and content. I was a rebel without a clue, in a loving, happy family, as if I somehow missed out on the one gene that allowed me to just fit in like everyone else.

I drive to Uncle Lang's cottage on North Sea Road. The shrubbery remains well maintained, courtesy of the Realtor who's listing it. The door is locked, but I have a key. The house has been cleaned, the rugs shampooed, the kitchen scrubbed, the fridge emptied of perishables. It feels weird being here without the clothes strewn about, the smell of dirty socks and fried food—the house as it became after Chloe left Lang.

Chloe, Lang said to me, when I saw him before he was wheeled into surgery. *Look up Chloe.* One of his last thoughts was the love of his life. But even *they* couldn't maintain a relationship. What chance do I have?

This is the question I pose as I unscrew the bottle of Beefeater gin. I decide to be an optimist and view the bottle as half full, and thus available for my consumption.

Oh, look at me. I'm a cop with an attitude on her last chance, in a town that gives her sweaty, breathless nightmares almost every night, who drinks too much and can't connect with members of the male species, and with an acting police chief who's no fan of mine, who's probably hoping to run me out by boring me to death with lousy assignments. I'm surprised Matty only *walked* out on me, instead of sprinting.

I find a stray coffee cup in the cupboard, pour myself some gin, and head into Lang's second bedroom, where his remaining effects have been boxed up. A roomful of boxes is so lonely. His desktop computer still sits on a simple wood desk, with the keyboard on a lower shelf that slides out. I boot up the computer and stare at the screen as it requests a password. I feel a pang in my heart as I type the password—JENNAROSE—and watch the computer come to life.

Lang kept copies of his "murder books"—police reports, investigators' notes, crime-scene photos, autopsy reports, interview summaries for a given case—in his home office; they're packed up now and sitting in his garage. He also wrote up summaries of each of these cases in individual word-processing documents, narrative versions of the events from crime to conviction. He'd talked for years about writing his memoirs when he retired, hoping for a boost to his nest egg and also a way of looking back on his tenure, recording it for posterity. *If they made it into a TV series, I could live with that, too,* he used to joke.

There are over fifty files in his CASES folder, going back decades. I look for the one from 1995, the BB gun shooting at Bridgehampton School, but there's no entry for it. I don't know why I want to understand what happened there. Matty, asshole that he is, did have a point. But that's me in a nutshell, the kind of cop I am—I have to fit every piece of the puzzle together. And no matter how minor a detail a school shooting from almost seventeen years ago may have been, it's still a piece that doesn't fit.

I stare at the home screen of the computer, the icons for the antivirus and the recycle bin, the Microsoft Word file folder. One small file sits in the corner, not in any folder, a Word document entitled CHLOE.

Look up Chloe, Lang said to me in the trauma center before he died. "Look up" Chloe? I assumed he meant contact her, let her know what had happened, ask her to come to the hospital.

Look up . . . Chloe, the document?

I double-click on the icon and wait for the document to pop up. A handful of seconds later, it appears. It's a letter, dated two days before his death.

My dearest Chloe, it begins. *I have to tell someone, and even now, with you gone from me forever, I want that someone to be you.*

"Oh my God," I say to the empty room as I read the letter. "Oh my God."

Chapter 41

"L-7." THE GUARD taps on the cell door with his pen. He gets no answer. "L-7," he says again. "I'm doing the go-round."

Noah raises his head out of his hands, blinks into the light.

"Where you gonna be after lunch, L-7?"

Noah shakes his head. He's been back in A-Block for three weeks now, after spending over a month in the prison hospital and having multiple surgeries at Phelps Memorial, where he was kept under heavy security and cuffed at the ankles to his bed. Since returning to A-Block, Gallery L, cell number 7, he has only left his cell for required trips—the mess hall, classes, and the occasional psych visit. He doesn't have a job, still not having regained a sufficient range of motion in his hands to do much of anything, and won't go to the prison yard or the gym. So even though inmates are allowed out of their cells in the afternoon, after lunch, he has stayed within this cramped, dreary space, staring at the walls, for almost the entire day. He sleeps, he supposes, but in the zombie-like daze in which he finds himself, it's hard to distinguish between sleep and wakefulness, between dream and reality. His life has become a meaningless fog. There is no hope or despair, no fear or happiness.

"L-7?" It's one of the "white shirts," the senior correctional officers, joining the other CO. "You in pain, L-7? You know we have meds for you. All you have to do is tell us who did this to you."

The warden cut off pain medication as soon as Noah was released from the prison hospital, trying to get Noah to implicate the Aryan Brotherhood in the attack. Everyone knows who attacked Noah, but they can't prosecute them or even write up a disciplinary ticket without Noah's cooperation.

Noah's no snitch. He'd like nothing more than to stick it to Eric Wheaton and his buddies, but it's just not in him to rat someone out. Growing up with his buddies, that was the one rule you didn't break. You might bend the law or outright fracture it; you might fail to do unto others as you would have them do unto you—but you never snitched.

"That's your choice, L-7." The lieutenant and the other CO leave.

Time passes in slow motion. Noah goes to the mess hall for lunch but doesn't touch his food; he's lost almost twenty pounds since the attack.

Later in the afternoon, another CO shows up at his cell. "Mail, L-7," he says, and he reaches through the bars and drops a single envelope into the small bucket reserved for such things. "Sorry for your troubles."

He's sorry? Noah looks up at the CO, who gives a grim shake of the head and moves down to the next cell. They read the inmates' mail in Sing Sing, unless it bears the seal of an attorney-client communication, so the *sorry* must pertain to the mail he just received.

How, he thinks, *could things possibly get worse?*

Noah's limbs are stiff when he gets up; he's sat in the same position for almost three hours straight. He reaches into the bucket and grabs the envelope, perforated at the top by whoever read it. When he opens it, there is a Post-it that simply says *Sorry* and then a newspaper article, folded up. He unfolds it with a knot in his stomach and reads the headline: MANHATTAN SOCIALITE'S DROWNING RULED SUICIDE. Along with the article is a photo of Paige Sulzman in a sundress at some fancy gala.

"No!" he cries out. "No!" He forces himself to read a bit of the article, enough to know that Paige was found dead in her pool, before he grabs hold of the prison bars and shakes them. "No!" His bandaged hands start to bleed through the gauze and pads, but he doesn't care, doesn't even feel the pain. He screams until he has no voice, hundreds of other inmates hearing his cries and joining in with shouts and catcalls of their own.

Finally, exhausted, Noah crumples to the floor, leaning against the cell door. "Not her," he whispers. "Not Paige." She was supposed to move on. She was supposed to forget about him and get on with her life. She was supposed to leave John Sulzman and start the interior design business she'd always dreamed of having. She was supposed to have a life. She promised him. He made her *promise* she'd do that.

He cries, for the first time that he can remember. The tears pour out until he is gasping for air, coughing and gagging.

And then he has nothing left. He lies flat on his cell floor, oblivious to the dust, to the insect that crawls past his face. He stares into nothingness. He finds consolation in one and only one thing.

That the first chance he gets, he'll see Paige again, this time in another world.

"L-7?" a CO calls out. "Everything okay?"

Noah raises his head, turns to the guard.

"Hey, CO," he says. "I want to go into the yard."

"There's less than an hour left of yard time," the CO replies.

But that's okay. Noah won't need longer than that.

Chapter 42

THE PRISON YARD for A-block is a large swath of concrete and dead grass, plus a full basketball court, all of it surrounded by fence and razor wire. It is unseasonably mild in late February, but most of the inmates still wear the allotted jacket and cap.

Noah Walker moves into the yard with a purpose, turning in the direction of the basketball court. He is not wearing either the jacket or the cap, because he doesn't plan to be out here very long.

Beyond the basketball court, on a set of low wooden bleachers, Eric Wheaton and four of his Aryan brothers sit, smoking cigarettes and engaging in animated banter. They snap to attention when they see Noah Walker heading their way. For a moment, they look amused, even pleased, but the closer Noah gets, his body tensed, his fists closed tightly, the more they sense this is not a social call.

Two of the biggest Aryans—the bodyguards, they call themselves—jump to their feet and approach Noah.

They aren't looking for a fight, but they won't back down from one, either.

"Well, well," says Eric Wheaton, getting to his feet as well.

"How are the hands?" calls out one of the bodyguards.

Noah slows. His hands are not fully healed. A couple of the tendons were damaged badly, and a couple of the fingers on his left hand do not fully close into a grip.

Luckily, Noah is right-handed.

Noah looks to his right, then spins left and lands his right fist on the jaw of one of the bodyguards, feeling a satisfying crunch. The other two goons with Wheaton, plus the other bodyguard, converge on Noah, but he lowers his head and plows through the center of them like a halfback running for daylight. Prepared for a fist-fight, and not expecting his evasive move, the Aryan brothers are unable to stop him.

"No!" Eric Wheaton calls out, raising his arms and trying in vain to move along the bleachers to avoid Noah's charge. Noah bears down on Wheaton and leaves his feet, tackling Wheaton in midair and knocking him over the back of the wood supports. They both fall hard to the ground, but Wheaton gets the worst of it, hitting his head with a wicked thud. Noah turns him over on his back and puts his hands on Wheaton's neck, pressing his thumbs on his throat with all his might. He hears the calls of the other Aryans; the roar of the other inmates enjoying the show; the whistles of the COs; the voice over the loudspeaker calling for the inmates to retreat to the far corner, like a referee moving a boxer during a ten-count.

Someone knocks him off Wheaton with a force that feels like a truck. It could be an Aryan. Could be a CO. He doesn't care. Several bodies fall on top of him. He hears utter chaos around him and closes his eyes and his mind to it. He takes several hits to the back of the head, and then his hands are zip-tied behind his back and he is lifted off his feet, facedown, blood dripping from his nose and mouth. He doesn't care about this, either. He doesn't care if he killed Eric Wheaton or just gave him a very, very sore throat. Either way, the ultimate result will be the same for Noah.

"You're going to the Box, tough guy," one of the COs grunts at him. The Box, officially the Special Housing Unit—solitary confinement—is a short, wide building separated from A-Block. The upper floors are reserved for inmates in protective custody because they are rats or because they are believed to be on the verge of violence, usually attack victims expected to retaliate when they return to general pop. But the bottom floor is where Noah will be sent. In a prison known to house the worst of the worst criminals, the lower level of the Box is for the worst of the worst of the worst—humans by designation, but closer to animals, violent predators, locked in small cells with tiny windows and low ceilings.

Noah is thrown inside one of those cells, the floor sticky and reeking of urine and feces. His fellow inmates howl like hyenas and scratch and claw at their cell bars. Noah's zip-ties are cut, the COs make a hasty retreat, and the door slams him into darkness.

It will come now. It won't take long. A correctional officer, probably, aligned with the Brotherhood. The saying in Sing Sing is *The only difference between an inmate and a CO is the color of the uniform*. But it doesn't matter to Noah. It doesn't matter if it's a shank in the mess hall or an assault in the yard, or a visit from a CO late in the night. It will come soon now.

Time passes. He can't measure it, doesn't even try. But at some point, the outside door to the Box opens, and then he hears footsteps. One, two, three COs, wearing full inmate-extraction gear—hats and bats, they call it: helmets with face shields, heavy boots and gloves, vests, pads on their knees and elbows, thick batons. In the darkness of his cell, he can't see their faces, only their silhouettes from the light streaming in behind them: The men are as big as houses, more muscular than the Aryan bodyguards, and prepared for action.

"On your feet, hands backward through the bars," one of them says. "You give us any trouble and we'll beat you down."

He complies. He won't give them any trouble. They walk him through the open air and he lifts his face up to the stars, feeling the cool air on his skin for the last time, as he takes his final walk—the waltz, they used to call it, when there was an electric chair, the walk from Death Row to the execution chamber.

They take him through another door, walk him down a hall, footsteps echoing on the hard surface. He is disoriented, thinking of Paige, humming symphonic music fit for a waltz, ready now, however it will come.

Then his feet are on carpet, a surface they have not touched for many months. He doesn't understand. He looks up at a door that says WARDEN'S OFFICE.

Two COs see Noah and give him a smirk. Then they open the double doors, and Noah is pushed into the warden's office. So this is how it happens? Right here in the warden's office?

Then he sees the warden, a lean, aging black man. Standing next to him is . . .

No.

"What . . . what is this?" he says.

Detective Jenna Murphy says, "I'm having you transferred, Noah. We're sending you back to Suffolk County Jail, pending a post-conviction hearing."

"A . . . hearing on what?"

"You were framed, Noah," she says. "And I can prove it."

Chapter 43

THE COURTROOM IS wall-to-wall with spectators and media, cops and prosecutors, people from the community, standing room only once again. The room is so quiet that you can actually hear that ringing sound that absolute silence produces, everyone craning forward, eagerly awaiting the next words that will come from the mouth of this witness—even the judge, peering over his glasses at the witness stand, his brow furrowed, his lips pursed.

The news leaked out yesterday—CNN picked it up first—but not the details. The details are for today. For this hearing. For this moment.

Detective Jenna Murphy, dressed in a blue suit, has testified for over an hour thus far, setting the table for what will come next. Noah's defense lawyer, Joshua Brody, has proceeded methodically, establishing her credentials, her minor role in the investigation, and going through a lot of technical questions and answers that the court needs to establish the "authenticity" of the letter found on her uncle's computer. Ultimately, the judge decided that the letter could be admitted into evidence, which paved the way for Brody to cut to the heart of this hearing.

"My uncle was the chief, so he could take over any crime scene he wanted," says Detective Murphy. "He took over the investigation of the crime scene at 7 Ocean Drive, and he removed the bloody knife and Melanie's charm necklace before any investigators arrived. Then he controlled the search of Mr. Walker's house after his arrest." She shrugs. "He could do whatever he wanted. Nobody would know."

Joshua Brody nods. "So you're telling us—"

"I'm telling you that my uncle taped the knife and necklace under the heating duct and pretended to 'discover' them there," she says. "I'm telling you that my uncle planted the evidence in Noah Walker's kitchen."

A release throughout the courtroom, a collective gasp. Behind him, footsteps—reporters, prohibited from using smartphones in the courtroom, rushing out to send off a text message, a tweet, a quick phone call. That courtroom exit is probably like a revolving door right now, journalists stepping out for the breaking news, then returning to hear if there's anything more.

But Noah Walker won't turn back to look. His eyes are forward, on Jenna Murphy. The woman who spin-kicked him in the face the first time they met, who broke into his house and fired a bullet only inches from his head the second time, who provided the crucial testimony, the testimony that led to his conviction, the third. And who now, after reading a letter from her uncle on his computer, is coming forward to stand up for Noah.

"There was testimony at trial," says Brody, "that my client confessed to the murders of Melanie Phillips and Zach Stern."

Murphy nods, blinking slowly, her expression blank. If she is enjoying this, she doesn't show it; if she's conflicted, she hides that as well. Something tells Noah she's good at that, at concealing her thoughts, her feelings.

"That's what the chief told me," Murphy says. "But it was a lie. He lied to me, and I repeated the lie to the jury without realizing it was false."

Another audible reaction from the spectators, another banging of the gavel from the judge. "Anyone who is unable to sit quietly," says the judge, "will be removed."

"Noah didn't confess to Dio Cornwall," Murphy says. "I talked to Dio after I found this letter on my uncle's computer. Chief James told him he would get a better sentence if he lied about Noah confessing to him—and a worse sentence if he didn't. He gave Dio information so Dio could tell a convincing lie to the prosecutors. Everything my uncle admitted to in this letter, Dio confirmed to me."

"I see." Brody nods. "And what about Noah's so-called confession to the chief himself?"

"It never happened." Murphy shakes her head. "He lied to everyone about that. He lied to his lieutenants. He lied to prosecutors. He . . ."

She pauses, clears her throat, the first sign of any emotion at all from her.

"He lied to me," she says.

A thrill courses through Noah, tears filling his eyes. He wouldn't let himself believe it. This roller coaster, this sensation of free-falling through the air, this entire terrifying journey through a system with murky rules and mysterious procedures—he's never been able to trust it. Not even coming here today. He wouldn't allow his hopes to rise, only to crash to the ground again.

But now. Now it's happening.

"If I may ask, Detective," says Brody. "Why did you come forward? This man was your uncle. You could have easily brushed this aside."

Jenna Murphy, eyes cast downward, shakes her head. "Because it's not supposed to be like this," she says. "It's supposed to be about justice, not winning. Because deep down, even my uncle understood that, which is why he wrote that letter."

Noah begins to tremble uncontrollably, the tears streaming down his face. So many times he gave up hope, so often he wanted to die. He thinks of Paige, who can't be here to see this, and squeezes his eyes shut, crying harder than he ever remembers crying.

His lawyer's arm comes around him, while Noah hears the voice of the prosecutor, Sebastian Akers, reminding the court that the prosecution, through Detective Murphy, brought this information to light, that the prosecutor is just as concerned with the proper administration of justice as anyone.

And then someone else is talking. The judge, the

Honorable Robert Barnett, known as one of the county's toughest judges.

"Listen, Noah," his lawyer whispers to him.

Noah raises his eyes, his vision blurred by the tears, the catch in his throat leaving him speechless.

"Based on the material that's been submitted to the court, as well as the testimony today," says the judge, "and the lack of any objection from the State, there is only one conclusion this court can reach. The defendant has been the victim of a blatant miscarriage of justice. The defendant's Article 440 motion is well taken."

The judge removes his glasses and looks at Noah, pausing first, considering his next words.

"Mr. Walker, the State of New York owes you an apology. You have spent nearly a year of your life under this cloud. And I understand you have suffered greatly while incarcerated—incarcerated for a crime that, it is now clear to me, you did not commit. I only hope that you won't let this ordeal consume you with bitterness and anger, that you can find something positive out of this experience. If I could give you back the last year of your life, I would. But I can't. All I can do now is find, as a matter of law, that your convictions cannot stand."

Noah, emotionally overloaded, shaking, manages to nod in response.

"The defendant's motion is granted," says the judge, banging the gavel. "The defendant's convictions for the murders of Melanie Phillips and Zachary Stern are hereby vacated. The defendant shall be discharged from custody immediately."

Chapter 44

THE GATE OPENS, and Noah Walker strides through it, looking around as if he's entering a new world. It may feel that way to him. Prison, from my experience on the other side of the bars, at least, is a universe unto itself, especially for the lifers. The loss of hope is a powerful toxin, like being dead while alive.

I've sent a lot of people to Sing Sing, murderers and rapists and even some drug dealers, but there's nothing fun about doing it. If I could run the world, I'd find another way to treat most of these criminals—most of them, not all of them—but we find widespread solutions to widespread problems in this country, so we just build big prisons and stick everyone inside them and, for the most part, forget about them once they're gone.

Noah stops short when his eyes come to rest on me where I'm leaning against my car. He looks different—not just the short prison haircut, which makes him look younger, but also something in his eyes, more relaxed, even refreshed.

"They said I had a ride," he says.

"That's me."

He looks at me, considering.

"Don't look so happy," I say.

He raises an eyebrow.

"Hey, I'm not putting a gun to your head."

"No, you did that once already." He has a small bag with him, things he brought into the prison. He walks over and gets into the car.

I walk around to the other side and climb in. My ten-year-old Chevy isn't exactly a limousine, but it beats the hell out of a prison transport bus.

"Your own personal copy," I say, dropping a *New York Post* on his lap, the front-page headline NEW YORK OWES YOU AN APOLOGY—quoting the judge—with the text underneath, *Officer's Emotional Testimony Clears "Surfer Jesus" of Murder Charges.*

Noah reads a little of the article, then exhales and gazes out the window. "I didn't think your testimony was emotional," he says. "I couldn't tell *how* you felt."

"That makes two of us."

He looks over at me but doesn't say anything. Pure heat radiates off him, the source of which I can't place. Maybe anger, aggression, bottled-up rage. I kick on the air-conditioning. Must be the unseasonably warm March weather. That must be it. Yeah.

Not a word passes between us as I turn onto the Long Island Expressway. I focus on the road and flip through the radio channels; no kind of music seems right, so I go to talk radio, all about spring training for the Yankees and Mets. It's been so warm in New York this March, I'm not sure the Yankees even needed to travel to Tampa to practice.

All the while, Noah says nothing, just stares at me. Once again, I turn the AC down—or up, whatever, I make it colder—and pull my shirt off my sticky chest. Something flutters through me, some sense of foreboding, danger, anxiety.

"You wanna stop staring at me?" I say.

"Are you gonna arrest me?"

I look over at him, his prison haircut—high and tight—accentuating his thick neck and shoulders, concealed previously by his long hair. The beard is gone, too, but he hasn't shaved in a couple of days.

"You're sweating," he says.

"No, I'm not."

"My mistake." But he's still turned toward me, as if, at any moment, he might lunge at me or something. That wouldn't be a smart move for a guy who's finally tasting freedom again. But maybe he likes doing that, living on the edge, pushing his luck. Or maybe he just wants to make me nervous.

We drive like that for a while. I turn up the radio, as if hearing the speculation over Mariano Rivera—will 2012 be his last year?—at a higher volume will somehow shield me from Noah's stare.

As we're driving through Queens, he breaks the silence. "Do you expect me to thank you?"

"No," I say. "I don't need your gratitude."

"Good. Because you don't have it. You lied at the trial. You're the reason I got locked up to begin with."

I whip the car to the right, swerving across a lane of

traffic, just making the exit for Little Neck Parkway. I find a small park by Horace Harding and pull the car over.

"Get out," I say as I push the car door open. I walk into the park and wait for him to meet me there. He walks toward me briskly. For a moment, I think he's not going to stop, that he's going to knock right into me, or put his hands on my throat. He stops just short of me, close enough that I can see a tiny nick above his lip, that I can smell him, that prison smell of sweat and rage.

"Did you kill them?" I ask.

His eyes narrow and his head tilts slightly, like he doesn't get the question.

"You have double jeopardy now," I say. "No one can ever prosecute you again for Melanie and Zach. So now it's just you and me. Did you kill them?"

He smiles, bemused. "You gotta be kidding."

"You were framed, yes, but that doesn't mean you're innocent. Lang thought you were guilty. He just didn't think he could prove it. You can frame a guilty—"

"No," he spits. "I didn't kill them."

My heart banging against my chest, choking my throat, my hands balling into fists, I ask my next question. "What about my uncle?"

He shakes his head. "You're unbelievable."

"Tell me," I say.

He regards me for a moment. He takes another step forward, leaning into me so close, it's as if he's about to make a pass at me. I hold my breath and steel myself.

"I . . . don't think I have double jeopardy for that murder, now do I, Detective?"

"You might as well," I say. "You're a media darling. We'd look vindictive if we prosecuted you again. Sebastian Akers would sooner swallow his own tongue. So what's it gonna be, cowboy?"

His nose almost touching mine, his breath on my face, his eyes searching mine, that heat radiating off him. "Okay," he says. "I'll answer your question."

His face moves around mine, his razor stubble against my cheek, his lips touching my ear.

"I didn't kill your uncle," he whispers. He draws back, turns, and walks to the car.

Chapter 45

WHEN I ARRIVE at work the next morning, I get a lot of stares, a lot of whispers as I pass. These days at Southampton Town Police Department, I'm about as welcome as a venereal disease. I've given the department a black eye. Oh, there are probably a few people who would admit, if pressed, that I did the right thing, that I prevented a miscarriage of justice, even if I had to tarnish the department, and the memory of a beloved chief, in the process.

But most people just seem to remember that last part—that I've brought shame on the department, that I crossed the thin blue line.

"Chief wants to see you," says one of the assistants, passing me.

More good news: My old partner, Isaac Marks, is now running the show. The town supervisor took the *Acting* off his title two weeks ago, making Isaac the new, permanent chief. You might think I'd benefit from that, that my former partner would look kindly on me, but you'd be wrong. Isaac was at Noah Walker's house during the search, when my uncle planted the incriminating evidence, and since my testimony, Isaac has had to answer questions from reporters and the town supervisor. He's denied any wrongdoing, of course—he had no idea, he says, that Lang planted the knife and necklace—but nobody is completely convinced, so he's beginning his tenure under a dark cloud—thanks to me!

He should feel lucky they gave him the job before all of this came out about Lang; if the decision were made today, he surely wouldn't have received the promotion.

But when I walk into his office, Isaac doesn't look like he feels lucky.

"Morning," I say.

"Sit, Murphy." He throws something across the desk. A folder full of something, with the words SAFE IN SCHOOL INITIATIVE across the top. I have a pretty good idea what's coming.

"After that school shooting in Ohio in February," he says, "the school board here has been anxious to review the safety procedures for the school. Evacuation, prevention, that kind of thing. You're going to run it. You'll be reassigned to Bridgehampton School for a couple of months. It's all in the folder."

I stare at the folder in my hand, dumbfounded. This is not an assignment for a veteran detective. Both of us know it. Isaac can't fire me, because I'm too protected right now—the media would pick up on it, and it would look like exactly what it was, that the STPD was retaliating against me for coming forward with the evidence against Lang—but there are other ways to punish a rogue cop like me, the best of which is to give me shitty assignments, to bore me to death until I quit in disgust.

"Isaac," I say.

"What did you call me?" His head snaps up.

"I'm sorry, *Chief*—Chief, I've been doing some looking into the murders at 7 Ocean Drive, now that they're 'unsolved' again—"

"They're not unsolved. We know who killed them. We let the killer walk free, didn't we, Detective?" A bit of color to those plump cheeks of his.

"I . . . understand," I say. "Could I just tell you what I'm thinking?"

"Tell me what you're thinking, Murphy. I can't wait." He throws up his hand, like he'd rather have a needle stuck in his eye, and leans back in his chair.

"Besides those murders, there's my uncle's murder. And that murder that you and I were looking at, the prostitute in the woods, impaled on the tree stump."

"Yeah?" He scratches his neck. "So?"

"Well, all four of these have one thing in common— they resulted in slow, torturous deaths," I say. "But especially my uncle and the prostitute in the woods. Both of them were impaled. I think that could have meaning. I think they're connected."

"Noah Walker killed Zach and Melanie. He probably killed Lang, too, but now that you've gone and made Noah untouchable, you couldn't get the DA to prosecute him if God came down from heaven and declared Noah guilty. And the prostitute? Who the fuck knows who killed her? Let Sag Harbor worry about that."

Just another hooker adiosed *in the Hamptons,* Uncle Lang had said.

"I don't want you investigating those murders," Isaac says. "I want you at the school. Effective immediately. If you go near those cases, you'll be disciplined. That's all." He flicks his hand at me, a shooing gesture.

Looks like I'm going to have to eat this shit for a while. I return to my desk and start to gather my things.

A woman's voice calls out to me. I turn and see a uniform, a rookie, the only female patrol officer working Bridgehampton, all of six weeks on the force.

"Haven't had the chance to introduce myself," she says. "Officer Ricketts."

We shake hands. Ricketts is probably in her mid-twenties but looks more like she's in her midteens, big wondering eyes and cropped blond hair.

"Nice to meet you, Ricketts. Call me Murphy. Let me know if I can ever help."

"Well," she says as I begin to turn away from her.

"Well, what?"

"I was wondering if I could be any help to *you,*" she says. "I've heard a lot about you. I'd like the chance to work with you."

I remember being that young, being green, being a woman on a male-dominated force. Being hungry. Looking for a chance to prove myself.

And, actually, there is something . . . .

"This would have to be on your own time," I say. "Off the record."

"Sure, no problem," she says, not hiding her eagerness.

Well, what the hell? "Okay, Ricketts," I say. "Get me a list of all unsolved murders on the South Shore over the last decade. Focus on victims of knife attacks, or some spearing instrument."

"Knife . . . or spearing," she repeats, writing it down on a notepad.

"Stabbed, impaled, sliced, diced, whatever," I say. "This guy likes to cut people."

Chapter 46

WHEN I ENTER Bridgehampton School, red brick and white pillars on Main Street—Montauk Highway, if you prefer—I am directed to the school principal, a woman named Paulina Jacoby. She looks like a school principal, conservatively dressed, her gray hair neatly combed, a humorless way about her. Her office is simply decorated, with a nice view of the massive school grounds to the south. Behind her, yearbooks going back to the seventies line an entire bookcase.

We spend a few minutes with small talk—they had a good relationship with the former chief, she tells me; she knows I'm his niece, pretty much everybody knows that by now. "We were . . . pleasantly surprised to hear from Chief Marks," she says.

Chief Marks. It will take a long time before I'm used to hearing that.

"But we're always happy to hear from the STPD. There is no such thing as a school that has too much security."

True—but what she's saying is, we called her, not the other way around. That isn't surprising. Isaac was trying to find the least desirable assignment he possibly could for me, without being too obvious about it. If he assigned me to parking meter duty, it would be blatantly clear that he was punishing me. A school assignment is just perfect, from his perspective. Who can be against school security in this day and age? But that doesn't change the fact that this is an assignment for a much younger cop than me. He's a devious one, Isaac, that little fuck.

"We've been lucky," the principal says, knocking on her wooden desk. "We haven't had a school shooting for sixteen—well, now I guess it's seventeen years."

Right. That's right. "The BB gun shooting in 1995," I say. I point out the window. "Out there on the south grounds."

She nods, looks through the window. "That was Halloween. We banned costumes at the school for over a decade after that."

"It was Noah Walker," I say. "Noah shot those kids with the BB gun."

She looks at me, unsure of how to answer. Because Noah was a juvenile at the time, the criminal proceedings against him would have been sealed. The school would have been prohibited from publicly announcing his name.

"Well," she says, "I guess it's not much of a secret, after it came out last year during his trial."

Not a secret at all. But she's getting a little squirmy, so I don't push the point.

"Well, let me introduce you to our security

personnel," she says, getting out of her chair. "Is there anything else you'll need from me?"

"Maybe just one thing," I say. "Could I take a look at the school yearbook from 1995?"

Once I have some time alone, after meeting with the school security personnel, and once I'm shown to a small office, cramped and windowless, that probably was once a janitor's closet, I crack open the yearbook, heading to the index in the back and finding the name *Walker, Noah.*

I flip to the page and run along the names on the right column until I come to his. Noah would have been, what, twelve or thirteen back then. I admit to a curiosity—and maybe more than curiosity—about how a guy with a ripped physique and rugged good looks would have appeared as an adolescent.

I find his name, but when I look across to the corresponding picture, there is no face staring back, just a NOT PICTURED graphic. Okay, that probably makes sense; he was suspended from school after the Halloween shooting that year, so he probably was gone by the time they were taking yearbook photos. I let out a sigh, disappointed, but then catch myself—why am I disappointed? And why am I thinking about Noah Walker's muscles?

Next to the graphic for Noah: a weaselly-looking kid with straw hair parted down the middle, a skinny face, and eyes too close together. He isn't smiling or frowning; he looks confused, actually, like the invention of the camera was a revelation at that moment.

But I know this guy. I look at the name on the side

and square it up. This is Aiden Willis. Right. Aiden Willis, the raccoon eyes, the squirrelly guy who works at the cemetery—I saw him at Melanie's funeral, then again at the Dive Bar, when I bought him a beer and he disappeared.

Small town. You forget that. The locals all grew up together, know one another.

I flip to the index, then find the page for Isaac Marks. Isaac, my former partner and new boss, asswipe that he may be, was the same age as Noah and Aiden. In his photo, he is wearing a stern expression, like he's trying to look tough. That feels about right. Isaac, back then, probably dreamed of being important, of having the respect he probably didn't receive in school. All speculation, of course, but it fits with the kind of guy he is now—and we don't really change that much, do we?

I look up. Noah, Aiden Willis, and Isaac Marks. Isaac and Noah, the same age, the same class; Aiden, one year older. They all would have known one another back then. A tiny school. Everyone knew everyone.

I pick up my phone and dial the extension for the school principal. After a moment, they put me through.

"Ms. Jacoby?"

"Please, it's Paulina," she says.

"Paulina," I say. "Do you have anyone on staff who was here during that school shooting in 1995?"

Chapter 47

THE SOUTH SIDE of Bridgehampton School is over an acre of open grass, with a baseball diamond closer to the school and a playground next to it for the younger kids. To my right, but a healthy distance away, are the woods, a thick layer of trees providing the eastern border of the school grounds. As I move closer to the school, to my left—northwest—I see the parking lot that bends around from Main Street.

"Here," says Darryl Friese, walking with me. "I was right here. I didn't even know what happened at first. I mean, my first thought? I thought, like, an insect had flown into my eye or something. Dumb, right?"

I shake my head. "There's no such thing as dumb in a situation like that."

Darryl turns to me. He was nine in 1995, which makes him twenty-six, maybe twenty-seven now, but these seventeen years have not been kind to him, his hair receding badly, an unhealthy gut hanging over his slacks. His left eye looks odd because of the color, grayer than his other eye, which is solid blue, but otherwise there's no lingering trace of the BB injury.

"Okay, so let's get this exactly right," I say. "Stand at exactly the same angle, the same position."

He adjusts himself. "It was just like this. I remember because this girl, Angela Krannert—God, haven't thought about her for a long time—anyway, Angie was standing by the back entrance of the school, and I was walking toward her. I remember—the last thing I was thinking, before the BB hit me—I was trying to think of something that would make Angie laugh."

He is facing directly north. If he walked straight forward from this angle, he'd eventually walk right into the school's back door.

He points over by the woods. "You see that little alcove there?" he says. "Kids used to go there to make out or smoke cigarettes. Because you were technically still on school property, but you were hidden."

I nod. I see it. A tree stump, a small clearing. "That's where Noah was set up?"

"Yeah."

I line it up. Noah, from his position, would have been almost directly to Darryl's right.

"So how did he shoot me in the left eye?" Darryl laughs. "Believe me, I've always asked that. They just chalked it up to the pandemonium. I mean, it was chaos. I was out of commission, basically. I was on the ground screaming. But nobody could hear me because they were all screaming, too. Nobody knew it was a BB gun, not at first."

"They said you must have spun around, giving him a clear shot at you."

He laughs. "That's *exactly* what they said. And I get it, I was just a punk kid, nobody believed me. I have a seven-year-old now, and the things that come out of his mouth?" He shakes his head with conviction. "But I'm telling you, I got hit with the BB before anybody knew what was going on. There was no screaming, no chaos, nobody scattering in different directions. I was probably the first one shot. No," he says, "I was walking straight for Angie at the back door."

I survey the place again. The woods, Noah's perch, directly east, to my right.

And to the northwest, the school parking lot.

With a healthy row of shrubbery separating the parking lot from the south grounds. A perfect place to hide.

"Is this part of some investigation?" Darryl asks me. "Are you investigating the Halloween shooting again?"

"No," I tell him. "Nothing like that."

Which is technically true. I'm not investigating the 1995 Halloween shooting per se. I'm just trying to learn more about Noah Walker, and by extension the people with whom he associated. I don't know, yet, who ran with Noah back then, back when they were preteen punks.

But I do know this much: One of them was the second shooter that day.

Chapter 48

"YOU JUST TRY to find something that interests them," says the phys ed teacher, a man named Arnie Cooper, an aging African American man. He's tall and well-built, age adding a few inches to his midsection, but you can still see the remnants of an athlete—the high hurdles, from what I've heard, and what I've seen in glass cases near the gym, in framed photos on the walls. Born and raised in Bridgehampton—"south of Main Street," he is quick to say—state champion in the high hurdles in 1978, a member of the US Olympic team that didn't compete in the 1980 games in Moscow because of the US boycott.

Behind us, the south grounds of the school are littered with multicolored foam archery targets, the bull's-eye yellow, the next ring orange, then powder blue and black. Half of the fourth graders are missing the target altogether, the rubber-suction-cupped arrows sailing in the air and falling harmlessly to the grass.

"Hard to get kids to run around and play anymore," the teacher says. "They got their faces buried in those phones and contraptions. That's all I did when I was a kid. I always remember running." He gestures to an older student out on the yard, some kind of teacher's assistant. "Brendan, I'm gonna be a few minutes, okay?"

Coop, as he demands everyone call him, walks with a limp these days, the years of clearing hurdles and pounding his feet having taken a toll. "I was running okay in my thirties, though," he tells me as we walk along the yard. "And I was definitely running okay the day of the shooting."

He stops and gestures toward the back door of the school. "I was in the gym shooting hoops when I heard the screaming," he says. "At first, it didn't mean anything to me. Just kids shouting, y'know? But then it did. I think it was . . . hearing an adult voice. Some of the parents walk the little kids up to the school. When I heard a parent yelling, I knew something was wrong. So I came out that door."

"And what did you do?" I ask.

"Well, soon as I came out—I mean, it was all wrong. There were kids lying on the ground, there were parents covering up their kids, people were scattering like cockroaches, y'know what I mean? I'm thinking, *These kids have been shot. I mean, really shot. With bullets.* But there wasn't really any blood I could see, so it was confusing." He stops, puts his hands on his hips, shakes his head. "Man, it had been a long time since I was that scared."

"So you—"

"So someone was pointing over by the east side of the school, and someone was saying, 'He went that way, he went that way,' and someone else was saying, 'He's dressed as Spider-Man, he's Spider-Man,' so I started running around the side of the school toward the front, toward Main Street, looking for Spider-Man."

We start following that same route, walking east and then turning north, moving along the immaculately landscaped grass and trees, toward the paved drive off Main Street.

"I practically ran right into the street," he says. "I didn't know where he was." I follow him until we're standing just along the curb on Main Street.

He gestures to his right, down the street to the east. "That's where I found him," he says. "Right next to Small Potato."

A little shack of a nursery stand, painted red with white supports, covered in chicken wire, empty this time of year, its quaint green sign proclaiming it the OLDEST FARM STAND IN THE HAMPTONS. I bought my Christmas tree here after Thanksgiving.

"Back then, they were selling pumpkins," he says. "But they'd pretty much packed up by then. There wasn't anyone there. But Noah, he was sitting on a bench just past the nursery, in a Spider-Man costume with the head part removed. He wasn't moving. He was wearing headphones. He looked—I mean, I know how this sounds—but he looked like he was waiting for a bus."

"Well—was the rifle nearby?"

He raises his shoulders. "I didn't see it. They found it later. He tossed it in the bushes behind him. I just told him he had to come with me, and I gripped him pretty tight and hauled him back toward the school, but he didn't resist me. He didn't fight. All he said was 'What did I do?'"

What did I do? "So," I say, "this kid shoots a couple dozen people with a BB air rifle, runs around to the front of the school, and sits down on a bench like he's . . . like he's waiting for a bus. Like nothing's wrong."

Coop shakes his head, laughs in agreement. "I know. I hear what you're saying. I figure it's one of two things."

I turn and face him.

"Either he didn't do anything wrong," he says, "or he's one cold-blooded son of a bitch. The kind who doesn't feel anything. Who could slice someone open while he's smiling at them, and then look you in the eye and deny it. You know what I mean?"

"I think maybe I do," I say. I drop my eyes and nod slowly. "I think maybe I do."

Chapter 49

I TURN OFF Sag Harbor Turnpike onto the gravel drive, my car crunching over the rocks. I pull up to a small shingled shack with a tent over the entrance and an old, beat-up wooden sign with a single word—TASTY'S—carved into it.

The parking lot is full, and so is the restaurant, when I walk in to the scent of delicious seafood. I love places like this, no-frills dives, simple tables with paper tablecloths, random photos and signs hanging on the walls, food served in paper trays. The menu is on a chalkboard on the wall—both kinds of clam chowder, steamers, shrimp two ways, scallops two ways, oysters on the half shell, mussels, fried clam strips, about four versions of lobster, and hand-cut French fries.

Ricketts, the rookie cop who's off duty today, has a table for us. She's already nursing a bottle of Miller High Life. There's a second bottle on the table, either for her or for me. Either way, I decide I like this kid.

"Hey, rookie."

"I love this place," she says. "Best seafood on the South Fork, and the cheapest. They haven't raised prices in a decade." She's a little looser than the first time I met her, when she was in uniform at the station. She's wearing a sweater and jeans and her short blond hair is tousled.

A man appears with a Mets cap on backward and a gray shirt. Ricketts orders the scallops, so I do the same, along with a couple of waters, and we'll split a cone of fries.

Ricketts reaches down to her purse and removes a file folder. "Your list of unsolved murders over the last decade on the South Shore," she says. "Anything involving a knife or cutting."

I nod. "How many?"

"Eight," she says.

"*Eight?*" I reach out my hand for it. "Gimme."

She pauses. "You, uh . . . might want to eat first. You might not have an appetite afterward."

"That bad, huh?" Okay, fair enough. "But eight?"

"Well, I counted Melanie and Zach as unsolved."

"As you should."

"The prostitute found impaled on the tree trunk last summer, too."

"Definitely." Bonnie Stamos. Some images will never leave your mind, and one of them is that poor girl, her body split in half over that tree stump.

"And I'm including . . . you know—"

"Chief James." I nod. "As you should."

She finishes a swig of beer. "Then that's eight." She

gestures around the place. "You know, this is where Melanie Phillips worked."

I partake of the alcoholic beverage she's offered me, because I don't want to seem rude, or make her feel lonely.

"Oh, you knew that. Of course you did. Sorry. I'm—maybe I'm—"

"Relax, Ricketts. I'm hard to offend."

She takes a deep breath. "I was kind of nervous to meet you, actually. I saw you one other time in the station, but I was intimidated, actually."

"By me?" The beer is tasting good. "You shouldn't be. We girls have to stick together."

"I know, but you're like, this—pretty much everyone's intimidated by you. Y'know, coming from Manhattan, and you're smart and tough and . . . well, beautiful. Most of the men don't know how to handle you. Most of them want to sleep with you, from listening to them. But they also want to see you fall on your face."

That sounds about right, that last part. "Keep your head down and do a good job," I say. "The acclaim will come, if it's deserved. You have to prove yourself to these cavemen by your actions. Let the rest of that stuff slide—the sexist comments, all that crap. It will all fall away if you do a good job as a cop."

"Okay," she says, nodding compliantly like a student.

"Don't sleep with other cops," I say. "Because then it won't matter how good you are. You'll just be the girl that fucks."

She takes a deep breath.

"I didn't say it was fair, rookie. I'm just trying to help

you avoid headaches. You'll be subjected to double standards all over the place. You'll have to be better than the men to be considered equal to them."

"Okay." She nods. "Okay."

"There's a lot of good men on the force. I'm only talking about a few bad apples here. Unfortunately, some of those bad apples are the ones calling the shots. So keep your head down and work your ass off. Always have your partner's back. And call me, anytime, day or night, if you need anything."

Her face lights up. "Yeah?"

"Of course."

"Here you go, guys. Scallops and a cone of fries." A different man, wearing a button-down shirt and blue jeans. Tall and trim, bronzed skin, a nice smile, thick brown hair swept to one side. The kind of guy your parents would want you to bring home. And I thought the scallops looked yummy.

"Hey, Justin, this is Jenna Murphy. Jenna, this is Justin Rivers. This is his place," Ricketts says.

"Here every day," he says. "Great to meet you." He wipes his hand on his jeans and offers it to me, a strong grip when I shake it.

"Likewise," I say. "So you're the guy who hasn't raised prices in a decade."

"Yep, yeah, that's right." He makes eye contact with me, holds it for maybe one meaningful beat longer than normal, but then breaks it off. A shy one. Not a slickster. I like the shy, awkward ones. Why do I always pick the jerks to date instead?

No ring on his finger, either. A girl always looks.

"Well," he says, clapping his hands, "nice meeting you, and enjoy your food."

"I will," I say as he walks away. "I will."

"I know, right?" Ricketts laughs. "Now you know why it's my favorite place."

The scallops are the best I've ever had, cooked just perfectly, a touch of butter and lemon but not overplaying it, letting the seafood speak for itself. The fries are nicely seasoned and the creamy garlic sauce accompanying them is enough to make me change religions. We top it all off with a second round of beer, but I'll stop there.

"Okay," I say, now that we've gotten a peek at the hunky owner of this place, I've dispensed my advice, and I've had some of the best seafood I've ever eaten. "Now it's time to ruin my appetite."

"It will," she says. "It definitely will."

Chapter 50

"OKAY, HERE." RICKETTS removes a piece of paper from her file folder. "Eight victims over the last decade. All unsolved."

"I know about the ones last year, summer of 2011," I say. "Zach and Melanie, Bonnie Stamos, my uncle. Let's start with the older ones, before I came here."

"Good," she says. "That's what I did."

"Dede Paris," I say, reading the first name. "Last seen May 9, 2007."

"The first two go together," says Ricketts. "Dede Paris and Annie Church. Yale sophomores. May ninth was when they left New Haven that summer. They lied to their friends and family about how they were spending their summer. They came here to the Hamptons. That was discovered later, through cell phone records and then their car, which was ultimately found in Montauk after a lengthy search."

She removes two photos from her file folder and

hands them to me. "Dede is the blonde, Annie the brunette."

Dede's photograph is from a volleyball game. She's tall and athletic, with blond hair cropped tight against her head. The photo of Annie is a school photo, probably from high school, a bright smile and warm eyes, her hair past her shoulders, reddish brown.

"So they were killed in Montauk?" I ask.

Ricketts shrugs. "Nobody knows. That's where their car was found. Their bodies were never found. Or, I should say, most of their bodies was never found."

I look at the document she typed, organized and professional. "Her finger," I say, reading her one-line summary for Dede.

"Yeah, they found one of Dede's fingers in the woods near Montauk, two years after they disappeared. We always assumed foul play but didn't know it until somebody's dog found the finger. Then they got a DNA match."

So they were killed in 2007, and a single finger was found in 2009. Two years, and nobody found it. Well, that's possible, sure, but . . .

"Tell me about the finger," I say. "Was it decomposed? Was there anything distinctive about it?"

"No and yes." She opens her folder again and shows me a photograph of the finger. "Not decomposed much at all, well preserved, with a ring on it—a class ring from . . . Santa Monica High School, if I'm reading that right."

"Okay," I say, handing her back the photo. She slides it into her folder. "So after that, we have the third one . . . Brittany Halsted," I say. "July 2008."

"Prostitute," says Ricketts. She hands me another photo. A mug shot. Oh, she's young, not more than eighteen or nineteen in this photo. She is thin, blond, attractive but with a beat-up look about her that most working girls have.

"She used the name Barbie on the street," says Ricketts. "Last seen alive getting on the back of a motorcycle outside a nightclub in Shirley. She told her friends she was going to be gone for the night."

The whole night. Smart of him. Nobody would be expecting her back. It would give the offender some time before anyone would be looking for her.

"Last seen *alive*," I say. "So they found her."

"They found Brittany." She hands me another photograph. "A couple of miles down Sunrise Highway from where she was picked up on the motorcycle."

She is lying facedown in a bed of leaves, her head turned toward the camera, her eyes shut. She has the ghostly mannequin look of a corpse dead for at least a couple of days. A pool of blood surrounds the lower half of her body.

"This photo doesn't show it," says Ricketts. "But he carved her up. He disemboweled her. The ME thought he used a corkscrew."

"Oh, God, a corkscrew?" I say, as if there were a nice way of disemboweling someone.

I look at the remainder of the sheet. "So then, in 2010, we have Sally Pfiester. And then we move up to 2011, to Melanie and Zach, Bonnie Stamos, and my uncle. That's interesting."

"Why's that interesting?"

I look at Ricketts, who is watching me carefully. She's a pup, looking to learn a thing or two, so I explain my thoughts. "We don't know if this is the same offender," I say. "But if it is, look at the timing. He kills in 2007. Then, in 2008, he kills again. Then he doesn't kill again until 2010, with Sally Pfiester."

"So—what does that mean? He didn't do anything in 2009."

"Well, he *did* do something in 2009," I correct. "He planted Dede Paris's finger for us to find. Clearly, he'd preserved that finger, or it would have been badly decomposed. And just in case we had trouble identifying it, he made sure her high school class ring was on it. He might as well have posted a sign saying, 'Look, everyone, this is Dede's finger!'"

"He wanted us to know," she says. "Why?" Ricketts sits quietly, her eyes moving around the room, her mental machinery fully in gear.

"He was struggling," I say. "He didn't want to kill anybody else. But you know what else was bothering him?"

"What?"

"He wasn't getting any attention," I say.

She draws back. "Attention? You think he wants to get caught?"

"Oh, no. This guy does *not* want to get caught. Quite the opposite—this guy gets off on the thrill of getting away with it. Of doing something so terrible and walking away scot-free. I'm sure the stories about Annie and Dede were all over the South Shore papers in 2007. Two Yale undergrads gone missing? It was

240

probably huge news on the South Shore. And the murder of the prostitute in 2008? Well, not as big, but still a gruesome murder, right? So once again, he's getting attention, he's reminded of how powerful he is. Big, newsworthy crimes, crimes that *he* committed, and he's reading about them in his bathrobe with a cup of coffee."

"But his conscience was bothering him," she says.

"Right." I point to her. "So in 2009, he's struggling. He doesn't want to kill again. But he needs the adulation, the feeling of power. So what does he do?"

"He reminds everyone of what he did in 2007."

"Exactly. He plants Dede's finger with the class ring, and *voilà!* There were probably a ton of stories, all over again, this time assuming the Yale students are dead, how tragic, how horrible, how mystified the police are—"

"And how powerful he is."

"How powerful and impressive he is." I sweep a hand. "He gets the thrill of it without the bloodshed or the risk."

"That's fascinating," she says, leaning her head on one hand. "How your mind works."

I wave it off. "I could be all wrong. Might not even be the same person."

Her eyebrow rises slightly. "Well, it makes sense to me. Especially when you see what he did to Sally Pfiester in 2010."

Book IV

THE HAMPTONS, 2010

Chapter 51

HE IS COLD, though the sun beats down on him at this beach café, the temperature nearing ninety degrees.

He has to piss, though he just went twenty minutes ago.

His stomach churns like rusty grinding gears, though he's just eaten.

He sees her through his sunglasses, basking in the white-bright sunlight, a bronzed, lithe body, the backpack over both shoulders, a white tank top and denim shorts, sunglasses perched atop her white-blond hair, as she takes a photo of herself on her smartphone with the Atlantic Ocean in the background.

He watched her. Watched her as she ate at this very café—vegetables and hummus, a glass of Chardonnay—and texted on her smartphone, and told the waitress what she's doing this summer, and got a recommendation for a good beach to "crash on" tonight. She and the server even talked music briefly—she likes the modern pop stuff but prefers classical, cello music mostly, of course Yo-Yo Ma and du Pré but also a newer crop, like Alisa Weilerstein, whoever that is.

He likes the name Alisa. It would be cool to have a girlfriend named Alisa.

He wrote down everything she said. The beach where she will sleep, her musical preferences. And this, too: *Sally*. She told the waitress her name was Sally.

Not quite as exciting a name as Alisa.

He reaches for the check the waitress has left and notices the tremble in his hand. His fingernails chewed down to the point of bloodiness. He shouldn't chew his nails. He knows that. His mother would say it makes him look "unrefined."

But he's got lots of . . . refinement. Is that a word? He'll look it up later.

He feels the pressure building in his bladder, a dam on the verge of bursting.

Sally is exiting the beach now, walking up onto the asphalt parking lot, her hands gripping the shoulder straps of the backpack. The muscles in her legs straining, well defined. Her arms are hard, too—long thin slivers of muscle.

But his favorite part is the backpack. It means she's passing through. Not a native. A loner.

No friend or spouse or lover expecting her home tonight.

Holden is smart. Maybe not school-smart. But he isn't dumb.

And he knows his history well:

A peasant, any peasant will do, and better still a
* stranger;*
Whosoever shall not be missed is welcome in my
* chamber.*

He walks over to his motorcycle and throws on his helmet but keeps the shield up. Climbs onto the bike. Looks over at Sally as she passes. Nods to her.

Too nervous to speak, though. And probably best that he doesn't. His voice might shake. He's still a little nervous. A little rusty.

He drives off, lets time pass, the sun disappearing in a burst of color to the west.

He uses his secret entrance into 7 Ocean Drive, the one specially for him. The one he used when Annie and Dede were staying there. The one he uses when he wants to sleep there himself, which he does from time to time.

It's his house, after all. Even if nobody else knows it.

Once he's inside, down in the basement, he drops his Fun Bag and gets to work. He lays down the tarp, tests the chain's connection to the ceiling, locks and unlocks the handcuffs.

Tonight he's going to feast on duck and pheasant, on grapes and cheese.

And then he's going to find the girl named Sally and bring her back to the chamber.

Chapter 52

SALLY PFIESTER STRETCHES her legs in the cushy sand and rests her head against her soft pack, the water crashing to the shore only ten yards away. She looks up into a purple sky and lets out a satisfied breath. This is just what she needed, this summer. After a soul-killing desk job for two years and a ridiculous decision to accept that marriage proposal, she was starting down a road from which she would not be able to turn aside. Oh, he was a nice enough guy, and he had a terrific smile, a good sense of humor, but he didn't ignite that pilot light inside her.

Isn't life supposed to be exciting? Aren't you supposed to love, not merely tolerate, your job? Aren't you supposed to commit to a man not because it's "time," or because you want kids, or because he'd be a good provider—but because he makes your heart go pitter-pat?

Of course. Yes to all of that. It seems so obvious now. It didn't when she was stuck in that rut, like a hamster on a wheel. But once she opened her eyes and broke off the engagement, quit her shitty job and gathered up her savings for a year of travel, it revealed itself to her so clearly. She wants to explore. She wants to meet people and experience new things. She wants a man who's adventurous, nonjudgmental, not materialistic. She wants a man who is patient and at ease with himself. She wants a man who transports her to a world she's never known. Or fuck it, she'll do without a man altogether.

The decision to travel alone—deemed by her mother insane, by her envious friends awesome—was the best she could have made. She's only nine weeks in thus far, traveling the beaches of Long Island this summer by foot before heading to the West Coast and then Europe, but she's learned so much about herself, about what she wants and needs and expects from life.

And damn, all this walking has restored her triathlon physique from two years ago. She feels like herself again.

She's reaching for her smartphone—because solitude has its limits; she still posts regularly on Facebook and texts with her friends—when she sees something out of the corner of her eye, a figure emerging from the ocean in a wet suit, the glow of moonlight on him. She's a night swimmer, too, but it's a bit chilly this evening, so she took a pass.

The man trudges up the beach in her general direction, but then stops. For the first time, she notices that he's staked out a spot on the beach just like her, about twenty yards to her left. There aren't that many people sleeping on the beach tonight, but then again, she chose this remote beach for that very reason.

A light comes on by the man's spot—a flashlight? No, a battery-charged lantern—and he seems to be settling in for the night. She watches him for a time and then returns her gaze to the sky.

Sometimes she likes company and seeks it out, hangs out at bonfires, shares a bottle of wine or a joint, but other nights, like this, she prefers the quiet of her own company. It's her choice. That's the best part. It's her decision entirely.

And then: Faint at first, and then her hearing adjusts to it, over the sound of rolling waves—music. The soft whine, the dramatic upward lilt to the impossibly high notes, so sweet and despairing.

Cello music, she thinks. *He's listening to cello music.*

Chapter 53

HE CAN SEE why Sally likes this music. It's really good. It can be really loud and it can be really quiet, really fast and really slow. It can be violent. It can be chaotic. And it can be like a lullaby, almost. It makes him feel happy and sad within the same song—except they don't call it a song, they call it a *concerto*. He already knew that. He knew they were called *concertos* before he looked up the cello stuff this afternoon.

This music can do one other thing, too, at least tonight: It can get Sally's attention, up the beach a ways.

"Excuse me."

He pretends to be startled at Sally's voice. It's actually not that hard to pretend, because he's nervous, anyway. So it kinda works double like that.

"Sorry to bother you. Is this—is this Weilerstein?"

"Oh, um . . . is the music too . . . too loud?"

"No, not at all—"

"Sorry."

"No, I love this music. You're a fan?"

"Yeah." He shrugs. "I don't know much about it. I just . . . like it."

See, he planned this out. He knew that if he pretended like he knew all sorts of stuff about the cello, she'd ask him questions he couldn't answer. That's an example that he's maybe not so smart in school, but smart in planning stuff.

She laughs. "That's all you *need* to know. People get so caught up in all the pretentious bullshit."

"Yeah. It's just so . . ." He leans forward. "Like you feel happy and sad at the same time, kinda."

"I totally know what you mean. It can be so emotional, right?"

He can hardly see Sally's face as she stands over him, but he can smell her. Fruit. She smells like fruit.

"I have . . . wine," he says. "If you . . ."

"Yeah, I mean . . . if that's cool."

"Okay, yeah." Still nervous. But that's okay, because it makes him seem harmless to her.

She sits down next to him on the blanket he's laid out, next to the Fun Bag with the wine bottle sticking out.

Through the speaker on his iPod, the cellist bursts out of a lull with a crisp flourish.

Holden pours some wine into a plastic glass and hands it to Sally. "It's not . . . fancy or anything," he says.

"No, that's cool, whatever."

He hopes she doesn't notice his fingernails, all chewed up. But it's dark.

They listen to the music. The smell of the ocean, the

gentle rush of the waves, the berry scent of Sally's shampoo . . .

"Now, *this* is paradise," Sally says. "I mean, what's better than listening to music like this with the waves crashing out here, the stars in the sky, and a glass of wine?"

The wind kicks up, plays with Sally's hair. She has on a sweatshirt, but her legs are bare. He considers offering her a blanket—but better to stay low-key.

One concerto ends, Sally making a comment about the fluidity of the cellist's bow strokes, and before long she has drained her glass. That should be enough.

"I'm Sally, by the way."

"Holden," he says.

She looks over at him. "That's a nice name. Unique. Like *The Catch*—oh. Oh, wow." She puts her hand on her chest, sits upright.

A new concerto. The cellist hits a climax early on, joined by other strings and some percussion.

"I think . . . I think something . . ." Sally lets out a low moan.

He lifts his face to the sky, feels the gentle breeze. "I think . . . it's time," he says.

"I—I feel funny." Sally lets out a moan. She tries to push herself up, but it's like the signals aren't reaching her limbs. She can't make her arms or legs work.

"I finally . . . get it," he says. Warmth spreads through him, like a cup of hot cocoa.

There is a monster inside me. It can sleep for days, for months. But it will never go away.

"Help . . . help me." Sally turns to him, her face tight

with fear, her eyes searching his. He watches her face closely, the trembling lips, the wide eyes, the flaring nostrils, pure horror. So pure. So real.

She's losing her motor functions. She can't move her arms or legs anymore. She'll have trouble speaking, too. But she can still breathe.

"I . . . pl-please . . ." Just a whisper now. Her arms give out and she falls prone on the blanket, the music dropping to a low point. Lots of highs and lows with this cello music. Like a roller coaster. Like his stomach feels sometimes.

Her lips are quivering and her eyes move frantically about. That's going to be the extent of her physical movements until the drug wears off. By then, it will be too late.

He puts himself over her, lowers his face to hers. "Don't be afraid," he whispers, his voice feeling stronger now. "You can't . . . move, but . . . you'll still feel."

Her trembling lips try to form a word.

"You'll feel . . . everything," he says.

Chapter 54

HE RESTS HIS cheek against the concrete wall, sniffing the faint smell of bleach. The chamber is all concrete—floor, walls, ceiling. The acoustics are poor and the lighting is dim; there is no electricity in here and zero sunlight, so he makes do with three kerosene lanterns he has placed strategically. The effect is haunting, the light constantly changing as the small torches flicker inside their containers.

Is this what it used to look like? He imagines it is. The walls were probably padded in some way back then, and of course there were a cage and a long chain—but otherwise, this seems right.

"Let me go, mister . . . I promise I won't say anything. . . ."

Sally: straining in a backward position, suspended in the air like a roasting pig over a fire. Her back arched painfully, her hands cuffed behind her back, her legs bound together likewise, then the hands and feet joined together by yet a third set of cuffs, attached to the chain that loops through a hook in the ceiling and runs to the crank attached to the wall. A crude pulley system. Not so crude, really, in fact quite well constructed and in fair working order, despite decades of nonuse. They don't make 'em like they used to.

The metal pole, built into the floor, protruding upward five feet with a steel tip, only two or three feet below Sally's straining, suspended body, lined up almost precisely with the lowest point of her body, near her belly button, her intestines, allowing gravity to do its work when the time comes.

He turns the crank one full rotation. Sally's body free-falls downward a foot or so, the chain shaking but holding. Her head bobs from the impact, but her body hardly moves, bound up as tightly as it is. She lets out a squeal, more animal than human.

He walks over to her to measure things up, her terrified eyes, in the flickering light, like something primeval. She is so beautiful. Fear is so raw, so pure.

She tries to wiggle free. Admirable, but useless. She is basically hog-tied in midair, and even if she were somehow able to free herself of the various steel handcuffs—to pull a stunt beyond even Houdini—it would only mean a quicker and more violent death on the spear.

Maybe that's what she wants now. Maybe she's given up. Dede and Annie didn't. They fought. The prostitute, Barbie, though—she gave up. That was the best, watching her eyes surrender all hope, waiting, praying for the end to come.

He touches Sally's face and she snaps her head away violently.

That wasn't very nice.

"Let me down from here, mister, please! I have money!"

He can't let her go. He realizes that now.

I can no longer resist it, any more than I can resist my very existence.

Shaken, he returns to the wall and grabs hold of the crank.

There is a monster inside me. It can sleep for days, for months.

He turns the crank another full rotation.

But it will never go away.

It will feast on me, prey on me, until the day I die.

Book V

BRIDGEHAMPTON, 2012

Chapter 55

"YOU SHOULDN'T BE doing this," I say as I walk along the side of the road down Ocean Drive toward the Atlantic, the wind calm and the sun beating down on us.

"Roger that," says Ricketts, my rookie companion.

"I'm a dead-ender," I tell her. "You know what that is?"

"I think so. Your career's hit a wall?"

"Roger *that*." Without realizing it, I find that my stride has slowed as I near the end of the road, as I approach 7 Ocean Drive.

"Point being, I've got nothing to lose," I explain. "Chief's going to stick me in one dead end after another until I quit. So I figure I might as well solve a crime or two in my free time. But you, Ricketts? You've got a whole career ahead of you."

Ricketts is wearing a Red Sox T-shirt with running shorts and Nikes. She has the same build as me, lean and hard, but she gets it from genetics, not from working out like I do. "Dad always said I had an attitude problem."

"The Red Sox shirt being one example," I note.

I feel my heartbeat escalate, a banging drum against my chest. My breathing tightens up as well.

"Are you okay, Murphy?"

I stop and take a breath. Something about this damn house, every time I get close to it. Like my nightmares, only while awake. Put claustrophobia and panic in a bowl and stir for two minutes.

"I'm fine. Let's go." I trudge forward on shaky legs, not eager to share my sob story of scary dreams and panic attacks with the rookie.

"Why are we going to the house?" she asks me, a welcome question, allowing me to focus on the case, and not on this feeling overcoming me.

"The hooker, Brittany Halsted," I say. "He stuck a corkscrew so far inside her it almost came out the other side. Sally Pfiester, that backpacker? He used some kind of spear and drove it almost all the way through her midsection, right?"

"And somehow managed to drain all the blood out of her body," Ricketts says. "By the time they found her on an East Hampton beach, she was white as a bedsheet."

"Right. And last year, the other prostitute, Bonnie Stamos—impaled on a tree stump. And then my uncle Lang . . ."

I can't bring myself to finish the sentence, but she gets it. The killer drove a heated poker through Lang's kidney and into the kitchen floor.

"He likes to do more than just cut them," says Ricketts. "He likes to stick it in deep. You think maybe this is a sexual thing with him?"

Murder House

We stop at the grand wrought-iron gates of 7 Ocean Drive. All at once, it's like the temperature has been turned up, the loss of breath, the pressure on my chest. I close my eyes and take a deep breath.

"Jesus, Murphy, are you having a heart attack or something?"

Something. I shake it off, slide between the gates, and look back at her through the bars. "Nobody invited us here," I say. "And we're cops."

"Right," she says.

"As in, we're not supposed to do this."

"Roger that."

"You can turn back now, Ricketts."

"I could."

"You *should* turn back now."

"I probably should." She slips through the small space between the gates, joining me on the other side. "But I'm not. I'm going where you're going. Tell me why we're at the Murder House."

I nod, take another breath, and move up the driveway until it curves off toward the carriage house up the hill. At that point, I take the stone path that, after a healthy hike, will lead to the front door of this grandiose monstrosity of a house.

"This place always gives me the creeps," says Ricketts. "It's like a multiheaded monster. All the different-color limestone, the different rooflines, all those gargoyles and ornamental spears pointed up at the sky."

"Yeah, it's a real fun place." I divert from the stone path onto the enormous expanse of grass before the slope upward toward the mansion. I stop at the stone fountain with the monument bearing the family crest and inscription. "This is why we're here," I say.

"Because of a fountain?"

I point at the small stone tablet, the crest featuring the bird with the hooked beak and long tail feather, the circle of tiny daggers surrounding it. "That," I say. "That fucking bird."

She doesn't get the context. She doesn't know that this miserable little winged creature has been haunting my dreams.

"Looks like an ordinary bird," she says, moving closer. "An ugly one. But it looks harmless. Why would you have a little bird like this on your family crest? You'd think it would be a falcon or an eagle or some scary, majestic bird."

I've spent the last two days researching that animal, trying to identify it among hundreds of species of birds in a catalog. When I matched it up, some things started to make more sense.

"It's a shrike," I say. "A small bird, yes. No large talons, no great wingspan. Not what you'd think of as a bird of prey. You're right, it looks harmless. But guess how it kills its food?"

Ricketts looks upward, thinking. "I'm going to use my powers of deductive reasoning and say . . . it spears them somehow."

"Close," I say. "It impales them."

She draws back. "Really?"

"Really. It scoops up insects, rodents, whatever, and carries them to the nearest sharp point—a thorn, the spikes of a barbed-wire fence, whatever it can find—and shish-kebabs them. Then it tears at them with that hooked beak."

Ricketts slowly nods. "Most of our victims suffered some version of impalement."

I wag my finger at that monument, the crest and the shrike. "This isn't a coincidence. Our psychopath has a real hard-on for this family, maybe for this house," I say. "So I want you to find out everything you can about 7 Ocean Drive. And this note under the crest—*Cecilia, O Cecilia / Life was death disguised* —find out what that means, too."

"I will," she says, not hiding her excitement. "Right away."

"Great. Now it's time for you to go home, Ricketts."

"Why? What are you gonna do?"

I nod toward the house. "I'm going inside."

"I'll come with you."

"No." I shake my head. "Walking into the yard is one thing. Breaking into the house is another. I don't want to be responsible for you."

"I'll take my chances."

"Get lost—that's an order," I say. "Besides, you have a lot of work to do."

Chapter 56

I HOLD MY breath and push open the front door. When I walk in, I immediately feel a weight pressing down on me, my movements slowing, an impossible wave of heat spreading through me.

Fight through it. You have work to do. So do it!

I stagger forward, feeling disoriented, light-headed, as if drugged.

So, so hot, like a fireplace inside my chest.

The dramatic Old Testament frescoes on the ceiling. The gold-framed portraits of men in formal eighteenth-century dress, mocking me.

Feeling my oxygen depleting, taking shallow breaths and keeping my chin up, my wits about me, as the childish cackling and taunting echo through my ears.

Please, don't make me go there
Please, don't do this
I wanna go home

The anteroom angling sideways, the lighting in front

of me spotty, but I'm not turning back, there's got to be something here and I'm going to find it—

Into the foyer, the staircase to the second floor before me, a parlor of some kind to my right, antique furniture and custom molding and chandeliers, an ornate fireplace. I turn toward the parlor but can't move toward it, as if a gravitational pull is drawing me in the opposite direction, and suddenly I'm staggering to my left instead, nearly losing my balance—

The dining room. Elaborate carvings on the walls, tall windows with fancy trim, a chandelier hanging over a pentagonal oak table with high-backed chairs. I reach for one of the chairs and grip it as if holding on for my life.

"I can't do this," I whisper, the childish taunts still banging between my ears, drowning out even my own voice. *I need to be here, but I can't be here*.

I push myself off the chair and start across the dining room, headed toward what must be the kitchen, my nerves scattered about, my vision unfocused, oxygen coming as if I'm taking breaths through a straw.

I draw my sidearm, for no reason that makes sense.

Get out of here

Stay and investigate

My legs finally give out, and I fall to my knees as if in prayer.

Let me go

Don't make me do this

Someone please help me

Let me out of here

I put my hand on the windowsill for support, push

myself up with my free hand, my Glock held forward with the other hand, trembling.

Then I look down.

On the windowsill, jagged letters carved into the wood.

DP + AC

Black spots before my eyes, my body turning, my legs like gelatin, moving in slow motion, like my feet are wading through thick sand, I can't breathe, I can't breathe—

Let me out of here

Bam-bam-bam

Let me out of here

Bam-bam-bam

The ornate patterned tile floor, then my hand on the door, pushing it, pushing it, why won't it—then turning the handle and *pulling,* fresh air on my face, sunlight—

I take a deep, greedy breath of fresh air and slam the door behind me.

I fall to a knee on the porch and gather myself. I don't know what just happened, why it always happens, why I'm having these dreams, why it all seems to be getting worse, and suddenly tears are falling off my cheeks, my body is trembling uncontrollably, my breath seizing, and I don't understand any of this, I don't know why something inside me seems to be breaking and I don't know how to stop it.

I only know one thing I didn't know before.

"They were here," I say to nobody.

Dede Paris and Annie Church were in this house.

Chapter 57

THE MOTORCYCLE TAKES a left off the turnpike onto the gravel drive, and I keep driving north, but the first chance I get, I turn left into a side street, do a quick U-turn, and head south. I pull into the parking lot a few minutes later, my car bouncing over the uneven gravel.

When I push the door open and walk into Tasty's, Noah Walker is at a corner table, just getting started on a beer. He's halfway to raising the bottle to his lips when he sees me. I see the hunky, clean-cut owner, Justin Rivers, behind the counter. He gives me a soldier's salute—kind of dorky; he's a looker but sort of a nerd—and I nod back.

"If it isn't Bridgehampton's finest," Noah says, taking a swig as I approach. He wears the grunge look well—T-shirt, cargo shorts, and sandals. Since his hair was cut tight while he was at Sing Sing, he looks less like Matthew McConaughey and more like a muscle-head weight lifter. A thick vein runs along his rippled biceps as he lowers the beer bottle to the table.

Not that I'm looking at his rippled biceps.

I stand near his table in the near-empty shack of a restaurant, hands on my hips. "Y'know something, Walker, I can't decide if you're the smartest criminal I've ever met, or a guy with a lot of really bad luck."

He sets down the bottle and finishes his swallow. "Good evening to you, too, Detective."

I look around the place. Only two other customers this time of night, past the dinner rush, and they're at the other end of the shack.

I drop two photographs on the table, next to his beer. "You know those women?"

Noah looks at the photos casually at first, then with what looks to me like a glint of recognition in his eyes, and he lifts the photos, peering at them. His eyes drift off them, like he's recalling something. After a long moment, he looks at me.

"Why?"

"It's a simple question, Noah. If you have nothing to hide, *why* shouldn't matter."

"They look familiar, but I don't know why." He drops the photos back on the table. "Okay?"

"You've worked for years at 7 Ocean Drive," I say.

He shakes his head, bemused. "That house again? Yeah, I think everyone in the world knows by now that I did work on that house."

"Those two girls," I say, "were staying in that house in 2007. They went missing afterward. They were Yale undergrads who came to the Hamptons and were never seen again. Nobody was even looking for them in Bridgehampton, and definitely not in that house. But now we know they were there. So that's two couples who stayed in that house, two couples dead—"

"So now you're accusing me of *that,* too?" He gets up from his chair, kicking it back violently. "You know something, Detective? I can't figure *you* out, either. First you ruin my life by lying on the witness stand and sending me to prison. Then you tell the judge I was framed, and I start to think you might be a human being. And now you're back accusing me of everything that's ever happened in this town. I mean, I can't even have dinner . . ."

I narrow my eyes, appraising him. The same read as always—I'm not getting *killer* from his vibe. I'm not sure what I'm getting.

He keeps his eyes on me, challenging me, a twinkle of a dare in his eyes. The smell of his sweat coming off him.

"There's a lot of coincidences involving you, Noah." I back away from the table. "But for now, I'll leave you to your dinner."

The other diners in the restaurant, getting a good eyeful, return to their meals as I pass them. I wave to Justin on my way out.

"Hey," Noah says as I'm ready to push through the door.

I turn, and he's walking up to me.

He looks me over, works his unshaven jaw.

Heat across my chest.

"Lemme ask you something," he says. "You're an experienced cop, right? You've stared down all sorts of bad people, cold-blooded killers?"

"I've seen my share."

"Do I really seem like a killer to you?" He opens his arms, as if to give me a clear view. The thick scarring on his palms, from the crucifixion at Sing Sing.

That's been my problem all along. Even when certain evidence points to him, when the facts line up against him—every time I look him in the eye, I just don't see it. There is anger behind his eyes, and he's lived rough, no doubt. But is there rage? The capacity for horrific sadism? That mental switch that flips on and allows him to turn into a monster?

I tell him the truth.

I say, "I'm not sure."

Chapter 58

MIDNIGHT. THE TEMPERATURE fallen to the low fifties, the wind coming hard off the ocean, less than a mile to the south, carrying some hint of the rain that just stopped an hour ago, with me unprepared in my short sleeves. I left the bar in a fog, not drunk exactly, not on alcohol at least, my emotions swirling, my thoughts consumed by the murders, by Uncle Lang, by my shipwreck of a life, and somehow instead of driving home I found myself at the cemetery on Main Street.

The lighting from the street is dim, casting the cemetery in almost complete darkness. I can't even read the tombstone, but I know it, of course, by heart.

LANGDON TRAVIS JAMES, it reads. HE KEPT US SAFE. That's what he told Chloe he wanted said about him, when it was all over, that he devoted his life to protecting people. And he did. Sure, he cut some corners with the Ocean Drive murders, but he thought Noah was his guy—he thought he was framing a killer whom he otherwise couldn't catch. Wrong methods, but right reasons.

And I, of all people, exposed him. I didn't have a choice. I hope he knows that. Aunt Chloe promised me that he does, wherever he is now. Aunt Chloe, whose blank tombstone rests next to Lang's. He bought these tombstones early in their marriage, Chloe said, so they'd be together forever.

He was broken when she left him. She surely had her reasons, but he lost the love of his life. He was never the same person again. My mother was never the same after my father and Ryan died in that car accident, either. Losing your soul mate, by death or divorce—is it better than never having one in the first place? Better to have loved and lost, as they say, than never to have loved at all?

I drop to my haunches, suddenly exhausted. Chloe's right. I have to leave this place. It's doing something to me. But that means I'll have to give up being a cop. Nobody will give me another chance. The job's my love, probably the only one I'll ever have. But I'll have to leave. I don't think I can survive many more of these night terrors, these panic attacks or whatever they are.

But first things first.

"I'm not leaving," I say to Lang's stone, "until I figure out who killed you."

The winds die down.

A noise. A shuffling movement.

I get to my feet and spin around. I look south into darkness, my eyes not fully adjusted.

A beam of light, twenty yards away, a small yellow circle on the ground.

I draw my sidearm.

"Who's there?" I call out.

The light swings in my direction until it passes across my face, then returning to me, blinding me.

"Town police!" I call out, shutting my eyes.

The light on my face disappears. I open my eyes, unable to see much of anything from the overload to my retinas; I squint and drop low.

"Identify yourself!" I yell.

I hear something, feet adjusting in wet grass, think maybe I see a figure moving. The flashlight beam has disappeared, nothing but spotty darkness. I break into a run, the gun at my side, my eyes still off-kilter after the blinding light, dodging tombstones as best I can. As I race farther south, some faint light off the side street helps me navigate.

The figure up ahead, in a full-out sprint.

"Stop! Town police!"

I pick up my pace, feeling like I'm closing the gap, a faint mist hitting my face, but it's not far from the street, and then the woods, plenty of places to hide. I'm running full-speed, but I'm running out of time.

I fire a round into the earth, the gunshot's echo piercing, and the sloshing sound of feet running on wet grass suddenly stops.

"Don't move! Town police!"

I shuffle forward, both hands on the gun trained ahead of me, though I can't really make out the figure yet. "Hands out where I can see them!" I order, as if I could possibly see them.

As I get closer and my eyes readjust, I make him. He has turned to face me. His arms are extended upward.

A mousy face, hair jutting out from beneath a baseball cap flipped backward.

"Who are you?" I ask, but I think I know the answer.

"Who are *you*?" he says.

"Detective Murphy, STPD. Tell me who you are, and don't move!"

"Aiden Willis."

I shuffle toward him, closing the gap, less than ten yards away. The wind picks a lousy time to kick back up, carrying mist and some stray leaves.

"You in the habit of running from cops, Aiden?"

"I didn't know you were a cop."

"I announced myself." Moving closer still. Gun still held high. Adrenaline still pumping.

"So? How do I know it's true?"

A fair point, I guess. This time of night, in a cemetery.

"Where's that flashlight?" I ask.

"In my hand."

"Shine it under your chin," I say. "And move slowly, Aiden. Don't make a cop with a gun nervous."

He complies. The light goes on, and there he is, illuminated by a haunting, ghost-story-around-the-campfire light under his face, those raccoon eyes that constantly flitter about.

"What are you doing here, Aiden?" Moving closer, under five yards now.

"What are *you* doin' here?"

"Hey, pal, you wanna stop asking me the same question I ask you?"

"I work here."

True enough, that. Isaac told me he did maintenance here.

"You're working at midnight, are you?"

"It rained. We got an open site for burial tomorrow. Sometimes the rain messes it up. I'm just checkin'."

"Who's getting buried?"

"How should *I* know?"

I feel my adrenaline decelerating. "You scared the shit out of me," I say.

"You scared the shit out of *me*."

What's with this guy repeating everything I say? But I have no basis to detain him, and now that my heart has stopped racing, and the wind's finding its way under my shirt and licking my sweat-covered face and neck—I'm reminded how freaking cold it is out here.

"I remember you now," he mumbles, or at least that's what I think he said.

"What?"

Did he say he *remembers me?*

He double-blinks. "Can I go now?"

I let out a breath. "Yeah."

The light goes off under Aiden's face.

Bathing him in darkness again.

Chapter 59

LET ME OUT
> *Bam-bam-bam*
> *Let me out*
> *Bam-bam-bam*
> *I can't see can't breathe*
> *Darkness, then penetrating light from above, a shadow blocking it*
> *A face coming into focus, backlit by blinding yellow*
> *A boy, long hair, a hand*
> *Don't touch me, please don't touch—*

I lurch forward in bed, sucking in air, my heartbeat rattling. The same nightmare, but different.

Closed in, dark, *let me out,* suffocating—

But a boy. This time, a boy.

I squeeze my eyes shut and try to re-create it, to make out a face, but it's like trying to grasp vapor in your hand. You can't pull back a dream from the netherworld of the subconscious.

It comes when it wants to, and it vanishes at will.

I climb out from under the covers, wipe thick sweat off my forehead, splash cold water on my face in the bathroom. A quarter to five. Slept for four hours.

I throw on a shirt and shorts, lace up my New Balance shoes, and hit the pavement for ten miles.

The Hamptons, at their most charming at sunrise, the tranquil bays and deserted beaches and open roads, the smell of recent rain. I run over sand and grass and asphalt, working out the kinks, exorcising the night demons.

Later, I'm in my car, heading toward the school, my thrilling assignment. I dial information on my cell phone and get the number for the church.

"Presbyterian church." An elderly woman's cheery voice.

"Hi," I say, "I was wondering if you could tell me if there's a burial today."

"Today? Hold on, sweetie." Muffled conversation in the background. "Today? No, ma'am. We don't have any burials scheduled for the rest of this week. What's the name of the deceased?"

No burials today. Aiden Willis lied to me.

"I must have the wrong cemetery, my apologies. Thank you very much."

Why would Aiden lie about his reason for being at the cemetery last night?

My cell phone buzzes in my hand. It's from the substation.

"Murphy," I say.

"Detective, it's Margaret at the substation. Chief Marks wants to see you."

"I'm on my way to my assignment," I say.

"He said right now."

I blow out air.

"He didn't say it very nicely, either," she adds in a quieter voice.

Chapter 60

I TURN MY car around and drive to the substation. What assignment is Chief Marks going to give me now— school crossing guard?

By the time I enter his office, I've worked up a little attitude. How much worse can it get for me here?

Isaac takes his time reading a report, making me wait—purposeful, a show of authority—and starts talking to me without looking up. "Detective Murphy," he says, "why are you asking people at the school about the Halloween BB gun shooting from seventeen years ago?"

I should have seen this coming. "I'm trying to figure out more about Noah Walker," I say. "Who he hung around with. Who helped him shoot all those kids."

"*Helped him* shoot those kids?" The chief drops his report. "Nobody helped Walker shoot those kids. He did it all by himself."

I shake my head. "There was a second shooter."

"No, there wasn't. I was there. I was the same age as Noah. Same school."

I'm well aware of that fact, Isaac.

"The angles of the shots fired," I say. "And why was Noah just sitting on a bench by the school, waiting to get caught?"

"Are you kidding me? Because he's a psychopath, Murphy. The kind that could slaughter a family and then sit next to you on a bus and engage in polite conversation. He had no remorse, no guilt, no sense that he'd even done anything wrong." He leans forward in his chair. "And why are we even having this conversation? Why are you looking into this?"

"Because if Noah didn't kill those people at 7 Ocean Drive, or my uncle, then someone sure made it look like he did."

"Someone set him up . . . and someone set him up seventeen years ago, the school shooting, too? You're actually trying to tie those two things together?"

I shrug. "Call it a hunch. But yeah. This is a really small town. It's possible. Look, I'm doing the assignment you gave me. I'm doing this other stuff on my free time."

"I don't want you doing it on *any* time," he says. "No more questions about a second shooter. No more investigations into 7 Ocean Drive or your uncle. Can I be any clearer?"

"No, you're very clear, Chief," I reply. "In fact, I'd like to compliment you on how clear you're being, *Chief*. May I be excused, *Chief*?"

Isaac stares me down, his tongue rolling inside his cheek. He gets out of his seat and comes around the desk. I stand, too, so we're face-to-face.

"Let's go off the record," he says.

"Let's."

"Nothing leaves this room."

"Agreed."

"What is this fascination with Noah Walker?"

"I don't have a fas—"

"You want to fuck him, don't you?"

I draw back. "*What* did you just say?"

Isaac throws up a hand in disgust. "Always the same with that guy. A juvenile fucking delinquent since the day I met him, but every girl in school fantasized about him. The kid's never been anything but bad. Believe me, I know him a lot better than you, Murphy. Don't be fooled by the movie-star good looks. That guy's nothing but a bad seed."

For a moment, I'm speechless. Isaac's chest is heaving, his cheeks crimson. It's like we're replaying middle school here.

"Did he steal your girlfriend or something, Isaac?"

His eyes flare. He drives a finger into my chest. "Noah Walker killed those people at 7 Ocean Drive and Noah Walker killed your uncle. Noah Walker shot up that school all by himself. You will stop trying to prove otherwise. You will stop right now, or I'm pulling your badge."

I hold my breath, willing myself to calm down. "You're pathetic," I say. "I mean, since we're off the record."

He nods, grins at me, coffee breath and stained teeth. "You think you're untouchable, but you're not. I'm going to run you out of here sooner or later."

"Yeah? Good." I turn and head for the door.

"Oh, and Murphy? Since we're off the record?" He takes a breath and composes himself. "I thought your uncle was a worthless prick."

Chapter 61

THE MAN WHO thinks of himself as Holden is getting restless. No, it's not summer yet, but this March has been one of the warmest on record—is that close enough?

Maybe. For right now, he'll enjoy the sights and sounds at Tasty's. So many people to choose from, men and women both. He'll have to make a list and plan this out. He's good at planning them.

Hell, look at last summer, the summer of 2011. Four victims! In one summer, he doubled what he'd done up until then. Zach and Melanie, that hooker named Bonnie, and the good ol' police chief. The police chief!

And is he in prison?

Nope, he sure isn't. How's that for smart? You kill the chief of police and nobody can lay a glove on you.

His eyes wander beyond the crowded restaurant to the window, where he recognizes someone getting out of a car in the parking lot.

Detective Jenna Murphy, the sexy redhead detective.

Blue jacket over a white blouse, tight-fitting jeans, low heels.

She thinks she's smart. She thinks she's smarter than everyone.

But she's not that smart.

If she's so smart, why doesn't she remember me?

From all those years ago.

It might be fun to remind her one of these days.

Chapter 62

OFFICER RICKETTS AND I are out of luck when we enter Tasty's for lunch—no open tables. We take seats at the counter, with its view of the kitchen, where cooks in aprons and white hats are chopping and broiling and frying, reading orders off slips of paper clipped above them. The smells of garlic and tomato sauce and fried food fill the air.

Aiden Willis is sitting alone at a middle table, always that cap turned backward, the strawlike hair jutting out, those beady, meandering eyes. He's reading something while he eats fried fish out of a paper tray. Time will come, I'll ask him how that "burial" went yesterday, to see if he'll keep lying about it, but I don't want to tip my hand yet.

We both order scallops. Ricketts orders one of those iced-tea drinks served in those giant, colorful cans; ice water for me.

Over my shoulder, I see Chief Isaac Marks, wearing a bib and dipping lobster into butter sauce. Another table for one. He must see me, but after our words yesterday, there isn't much left to say.

"Careful," I tell Ricketts. "Chief's sitting over there. Let's not be too obvious."

She leans into me. "How 'bout I just talk quietly, then? I won't pull out my notes." She taps her head. "It's all up here, anyway."

It's pretty loud in here, so that would probably work.

"Give me the *Reader's Digest*," I say.

She takes a deep breath. A waiter serves us our drinks, mine in a plastic cup. "The *Reader's Digest*," she says, "is cree-py."

A ripple of boisterous laughter behind us. I turn back and see a group of guys—construction workers, a testosterone fest—in the corner.

One of them: Noah Walker. T-shirt stretched tight over his chest, dirty jeans, work boots.

I feel my temperature rise and pull my shirt off my suddenly sticky chest.

Something about that guy. I can't deny it. Can't understand it, either.

I have my back to the crowd, but when I'm turned toward Ricketts, I have a good sight line to both Noah and Aiden Willis. Isaac is behind me.

Three men, all about the same age, all at Bridgehampton School.

Ricketts says, "The house at 7 Ocean Drive was built by a Dutch settler named Winston Dahlquist in the late 1700s. He had, like, this massive potato farm on Long Island and was crazy rich. He had a wife, Cecilia, and one son."

Cecilia, O Cecilia / Life was death disguised.

"Cecilia died in 1813. They said she jumped out of her bedroom window. She landed on the spiked fence."

"She . . . *landed* on it?"

"Oh, yeah, they found her impaled on the fence, twenty feet off the ground. Her body was almost cut in half. But the author of the book I read on this—she had someone diagram everything, the angles, the distances. She concluded that if Cecilia had jumped from her bedroom, she would've landed several yards short of the fence."

"So the wife was pushed."

Ricketts nods.

"Tell me about the son," I say.

"His name was Holden. Holden Dahlquist."

Noah's eyes break away from his conversation and catch mine. He does a double take; then he fixes on me, his expression easing, his eyes narrowing.

"Holden was basically insane," she says. "Erratic. Violent. Couldn't be in school. The author of the book thinks Holden's the one who killed Cecilia. He would've been seventeen at the time."

"He killed his mother." I nod along, casually, like she's telling me about a new pair of heels she bought.

"Apparently, after Cecilia died, Winston was never the same. As time went on, Winston started going batty, too. He wrote in a letter—I remember this—he wrote, 'I hesitate to declare what is more alarming, the extent to which my son is beginning to resemble a wild animal, or the extent to which I am beginning to resemble him.'"

Aiden Willis stands up and fishes in his pocket for

money, drops it on the table. Under his arm is a paperback—Steinbeck, *Of Mice and Men*.

A little deeper reading than I might have expected from our Aiden.

"Apparently, after Cecilia's death, a string of murders and disappearances began," Ricketts continues. "Over two dozen people died over the next twenty years."

I turn back to Ricketts. "Tell me about the victims."

"They were hookers or immigrants. They'd go missing in the summer and then they'd be found dead with some kind of hole in their body, usually a through-and-through."

"Impaled," I say, my heartbeat responding.

"Yeah. Always some kind of spear or cutting instrument. And sometimes with all the blood drained out of their bodies."

"Jesus." I draw back. "And they never put this on Winston? Or his kid, Holden?"

My eye catches Aiden Willis, stuffing his hands in his pockets, checking me out with a sidelong glance on his way out, the paperback still tucked under his arm.

Then I look back at Noah, who's watching me while he drinks a bottle of beer, still with his friends at the table.

Then Noah's expression changes, goes cold, hard, and his eyes move away from mine to . . .

. . . Isaac, approaching him, the entire table freezing up. Isaac, with that cop bravado, saying something to Noah that elicits a frown, and I see something in Noah's eyes that makes me think there's going to be violence between them. But then Isaac moves along, heading toward the exit, catching my eye as well, smirking at me.

"They never charged either Winston or Holden," says Ricketts. "Legend has it, Winston had the local constable in his pocket. He was one of the wealthiest people on Long Island."

I watch Isaac leave and think over what Ricketts has told me. "He chose prostitutes and immigrants," I say. "Drifters. People—"

"—who wouldn't be missed. Yeah, there's a saying attributed to Winston. I think I have this right: 'A peasant, any peasant will do, and better still a stranger. Whosoever shall not be missed is welcome in my chamber.'"

Our scallops arrive, with a delicious buttery aroma, but I've lost my appetite.

"Sounds like a fun family," I say.

"Oh, but it gets better," Ricketts says, trying to keep her voice down. "Every generation left a single son, each of them named Holden. Holden Junior, Holden the Third, etc., all the way to Holden the Sixth. All of them suffering some mental illness, most of them suspected of violence. One of them killed his wife. Several committed suicide."

"Where's the most recent Holden?" I ask.

Ricketts spears a scallop with her fork.

"In the ground," she says. "The last Holden died almost twenty years ago, without any children."

Chapter 63

I CHECK MY sidearm for ammunition and holster it.

My head is buzzing after spending hours poring over a copy of the book that Ricketts used for her research, *Winston's Heirs: A Haunted House in the Hamptons,* chronicling the Dahlquists from the time when Winston came to Long Island in the late 1700s until recent years, the many generations of Holdens.

The original Holden, who these days would have been in an institution for the criminally insane, who may have murdered as many as two dozen women.

Holden Junior, who had three kids of whom only one survived, the only boy.

Holden III, who decapitated his wife on their fifth anniversary before jumping out of the same bedroom window from which Cecilia fell.

Holden IV, who went through four wives and a lot of booze before hanging himself at age fifty-two.

Holden V, who married and divorced three times and

overdosed on a combination of amphetamines and alcohol, just days after four vacationers were stabbed to death on the beach not fifty yards from his home at 7 Ocean Drive.

And Holden VI, described by his mother as a "simpleton with violent tendencies and the empathy of a rattlesnake, but other than that a dear boy." Known for his philanthropy publicly, but suspected of multiple rapes and assaults, none of which ever stuck. Holden was found dead in his bedroom in 1994; he slashed his own throat and tossed the knife out the window before dying, thus ending the ignominious reign of the Dahlquist clan.

My sidearm in place, I leave the house, a chill in the midnight air.

I start up my car and put it into gear. The roads are all but empty at this hour, in late March, before the summer vacationers have begun to arrive.

A gray pall hangs over the lonely streets.

I kill the headlights as I approach and let my foot off the gas. I pull my car over on Main Street and kill the engine. I'll walk the rest of the way. One hand on my sidearm. The other clutching my Maglite.

I approach the cemetery from the west. The air is thick, promising rain, but none has yet fallen. As I get closer, the street lighting dims considerably, leaving the cemetery in sleepy black.

This time, I'm more prepared. A sweater instead of short sleeves. Running shoes, not flats. A flashlight.

I pass through the gate quietly and drop down low in the grass among the tombstones. It may take a while, if it happens at all. But just to be sure, I'm not signaling my presence.

The wind kicks up off the ocean, making me wish I'd worn a second layer. Standing still, crouched down, it's not easy to stay warm. My eyes begin to adjust to the darkness, but the effect isn't helpful—it's still too dark to see much of anything, but now the darkness is filled with dancing shadows and fleeting movements.

Keep it together, Murphy.

The sleep deprivation doesn't help. My eyes feel heavy these days, my movements lumbering, my brain fueled by adrenaline but unfocused, sloppy.

A noise. Something soft but persistent. At first, I think it's wind rustling through the trees, but it stays consistent when the breeze ebbs, grows stronger as it draws closer.

Footfalls. Someone walking over the soft earth, heading toward the cemetery.

But no flashlight beam. Nothing illuminating his path.

I steel myself but don't dare move. I can't see anything in the blackness, but the sound is unmistakable now—someone walking into the cemetery.

He's walking in pitch dark without the aid of a flashlight, and without hesitation. He knows exactly where he's going.

Knows it by heart.

And then the footsteps stop.

I look up but can't see anything. Close enough for me to hear, too far away for me to see. Maybe a hood—a sweatshirt with a hood—

Murder House

A beam of light pops on. Startling me—I almost fall backward in my crouch.

I try to gauge his location from the flashlight beam. But then the light disappears, almost as quickly as it appeared.

Darkness again, and silence. What is—

A new sound. Spray of some kind, a thin stream of liquid slapping against stone.

Sounds like . . .

No, I decide. *Couldn't be.*

Chapter 64

I STAY FIXED in my position until the sound stops; then the footsteps begin again, but now moving away from me. He's leaving the cemetery, same way he came, disappearing into the void of black.

Should I accost him? I'm assuming it's Aiden Willis, as before, but I can't see shit out here. And if I confront him, I might be giving up an advantage.

No. Better I let him leave and try to figure out what he does here at night.

I wait until I can't hear him anymore, then wait another ten minutes for good measure. I keep my eyes focused on where I saw that momentary flashlight beam, trying to use it as a beacon to guide me in the pitch dark.

Once I'm ready to move, I shine my Maglite at that destination point and start walking toward it. It's not perfect, but it should get me where I'm going. Especially if that sound was what I think it was.

Something big up ahead. Something tall. The cemetery has all kinds of tombstones, large and elaborate, small and simple, many variations in between. This one is of the big-and-fancy variety. I run the light over the monument until I hit the name.

Dahlquist

A large stone monument bearing that same family crest with the bird, the shrike. The whole plot surrounded by an iron bar, no more than three feet off the ground, supported by small stone pillars.

My heart skips a beat. I move closer, sweep the beam of light around.

Three tombstones at the monument's base: Winston, Cecilia, Holden. The first Dahlquists. Then, just below them, five more tombstones, presumably for the successive generations of Dahlquists, all males named Holden.

I shine my light over each Holden tombstone, the earliest ones in not nearly as good shape as the more recent ones. Finally, I hit the last generation—Holden VI, buried here since 1994.

There it is.

I bend down to get a closer look at the tombstone. Fresh liquid splattered all over it. I don't dare taste it, but I lower my face close enough to confirm with my nose what I thought I heard with my ears.

Urine.

Whoever crept into this cemetery just took a piss all over Holden VI's grave.

Good thing I looked up Aiden's address.

Maybe it's time to pay him a visit.

Chapter 65

I KILL THE headlights so Aiden won't see my car approaching his house. But he might hear it bouncing over the bumpy, unforgiving roads just north of Main Street.

His house is obscured by trees until I reach his driveway. I pass it and pull the car over on the sloping shoulder of the road.

Only a quarter mile away, last summer, the prostitute, Bonnie Stamos, was found impaled on that tree stump.

The house is dark as I walk up the driveway. It's a dilapidated shingled ranch that almost sags at its sides, a beater Chevy parked in the driveway. I step up onto a cracked concrete porch and can't find a doorbell.

I open the screen door, which is on the verge of falling off, and bang my fist on the door.

"Open up, Aiden. Town police!"

Nothing at first. I bang again. Announce my office once more.

Nothing.

He couldn't have beaten me here by much. Fifteen minutes, tops.

No way he's asleep.

It was Aiden I saw, wasn't it?

"Open up, Aiden!" I pound on the door until my fist hurts.

I check my watch. Half past midnight.

Either he's not home or he's ignoring me.

Either way, I'm out of luck. It's not like I can kick in the door. I don't have probable cause or anything close to it.

But nothing says I can't check the back of the house.

No outdoor lighting on the house, the property surrounded by trees that block any neighboring light, so I use my Maglite to move around the narrow side of the house.

The backyard is equally dark and tree lined. A bicycle lies in the grass. No back porch or patio.

Something moving—

A squirrel or some small animal, sprinting through my beam of light.

I take a breath. Shine the light on the house.

A window well, into the basement. I shine my light inside. Just enough room for me to fit in there.

The window's been unlatched, pulled inward.

I squat down. The window's filthy. I wipe the muck with the sleeve of my sweater, but the light combines with the smears to block any view, like high beams in fog.

I push on the window to open it farther, as far as it will go, to a sixty-degree angle inward.

A noise in the woods behind me, something moving across fallen branches and dead leaves. I shine my light over the woods.

Dry grass moving gently with the breeze. Long, naked trees like skeletons waving at me.

An animal, probably.

The open window gives me, maybe, an inch or two of space. I shine my light directly into the basement and peek inside.

Looking right at me is a woman, sitting in a chair.

Chapter 66

I JUMP AT the sight, fall against the back of the window well. Shine the light through the crack in the window again, make sure I actually saw what I think I saw.

The small circle of light, cutting through the darkness, searching for her—

There.

The woman, seated in a chair, wearing an old-fashioned shawl over her shoulders, her hair pulled back tightly in a bun, her hands resting quietly in her lap. A relaxed expression on her face. Her mouth closed. Her eyes glazed, immobile.

"Town police!" I call out, just to be sure. "Ma'am, can you hear me? Ma'am, are you okay?"

My pulse in overdrive, I draw back, brace my hands against the window well, raise my leg into kicking position.

Wait. Something about that . . .

I lean back in, shine the light once more, find her again.

No movement. Her eyes don't respond to the light. She's dead.

I move the light slowly, probing as best I can the quality of her skin. Hard to do from a distance, with a flashlight.

But little decomposition.

Actually, *no* sign of decomp. None. Her skin looks flawless, even . . .

Inhuman.

I look around her. Next to the rocking chair in which she's seated is a—

"Oh, Jesus—"

My hand jerks, and the beam of light shoots to the ceiling. Hands shaking, I sweep the light through the darkness again, past the woman—

A man. Wearing some kind of coat, tweed. Hair greased back. A thin face, eyes open and vacant. Sitting on a love seat, legs crossed.

Same deal with the glossy skin, the immobile eyes, unresponsive to light.

Not dead people. Not people at all.

Wax figures.

I exhale with the realization. I was two seconds away from kicking in this window to rescue a couple of wax mannequins.

I keep the light moving.

An area rug on the floor. A battered coffee table with a vase and flowers—fresh flowers, not fake.

Against the wall, a faux fireplace—something painted on the wall, complete with logs and a spirited flame.

A television set. I can only see its back, but a soft, flickering glow emanates from it, the only occasional illumination in this basement, other than my flashlight.

A picture over the fake fireplace. A blown-up photograph.

Aiden as a boy, that scarecrow hair and scrawny face, next to a woman.

"What the hell?" I say, repositioning my feet on the bed of rocks.

Which is why I don't hear the footsteps, approaching me from behind on the soft grass.

But I *do* hear the pump action of a shotgun.

Chapter 67

"DON'T MOVE!" A voice calls out.

Startled, I lose my flashlight on the rocks, bathing myself in a little circle of light inside the window well. I turn my head for a look back, but it's no use. I'm below him and lit up; he's above me in the dark.

"I said *don't move!* Put up your hands!"

If I raise my hands right now, squatted down as I am, I'll probably fall over.

"I'm with—"

"Hands up or I shoot!"

"Listen to me, I'm a po—"

"Now!"

"Okay, okay. Easy." I do my best, like a tightrope walker struggling for balance, rising from my crouch and bringing my hands out, leaving my Maglite on the floor of rocks. I'm half turned toward him, so he can see my profile, but I can't see him.

"I'm a cop," I say. "Southampton Town Po—"

"Who sent ya?"

"I'm a *cop*."

"Whatchoo doin' here? What right you got?"

I take a breath. "Aiden—"

"Don't move!"

"I'm not moving. I'm not moving."

Aiden's breath, raspy and heavy.

"Mr. Willis, I just identified myself as a police officer. You don't want to be pointing a shotgun at a cop, do you?"

He doesn't answer.

"The correct answer," I say, "is no, you don't. You know me, Aiden. I'm Detective Jenna Murphy. You saw me the other night at the cemetery."

At which time, I note, the roles were reversed—I had a gun trained on him. Turns out, it's more fun when you're the one holding the weapon.

"Put the gun down, Aiden. I'm not telling you again."

He moves around so he's behind me again, my six o'clock.

"You come ta kill me," he says.

"No, Aiden. I'm a cop. I'm—"

"You comin' ta *kill* me! You been followin' me. You think cuz—"

"No, Aiden."

"Why'd ya have to come back? Ya shouldn'ta come back—"

"Aiden!" I crank up the volume this time, trying to gain the upper hand. "Aiden, I'm a cop. You know me. Now, I'm going to climb out of this window well and you're going to put down that shotgun."

I move slowly, putting my hands on the top of the aluminum well.

"I'll shoot." He shuffles backward as he speaks, feet rustling in the grass.

"No, you won't." I jump and use my arms to push myself onto the grass.

"Don't you move!"

I show my palms, though he probably can't make me out very well.

"Now put down that damn shotgun," I say. I rise to my feet.

I get a little bit of a bead on him, an outline, the hair sticking out, the shotgun in his hand.

"Self-defense," he says, raising the shotgun.

I lose my breath, brace myself, consider my options. If I go for my sidearm, it's a long shot. If I dive, I'm unlikely to miss the wide blast from his gun. Something out of a movie—drop and roll and come up shooting?

"You were at the cemetery tonight," I say.

"No, I wasn't."

I'm calculating how well Aiden can see me now, standing as I am on solid ground in the darkness. Hoping he can't see very well.

"You sure about that?" I put my hands on my hips, as if demanding an answer.

My right hand sliding down to my sidearm.

My fingers fitting into the grooves of the grip.

"Why did you take a piss on the Dahlquist grave, Aiden?"

"I didn't. You're just makin' excuses so you can come here and kill me."

306

My finger caressing the trigger.

If I draw my weapon, one of us dies.

"Aiden, drop the weapon," I say.

"No." One leg moves back, like he's bracing himself for a shot. "You're gonna kill me," he says.

Maybe both of us die.

"No, Aiden—"

And then we both hear it, footsteps to the west. The beam of a flashlight, coming into the backyard.

"Aiden Willis, put down that goddamn gun."

The chief's voice. Isaac.

Chapter 68

ISAAC SWAGGERS INTO his office and stands behind his desk. He crosses his arms and leans against the wall, next to the American flag and the flag of the Town of Southampton, blue and maize with a pilgrim in the center. He stares at me for a long time in his police jacket, a sweater underneath and blue jeans.

I've been here a good half hour, stewing in my juices, after Isaac ordered me to the substation.

"Is Aiden in lockup?" I ask.

His eyes narrow. "Aiden's probably in bed now, fast asleep."

"You didn't arrest him?"

He stares back at me, his eyes shiny with venom. "Are you carrying?"

Am I carrying? "*Yeah*, I'm carrying."

"Hand over your piece."

"Why?"

Isaac lets out a heavy breath. "Detective, your

commanding officer has ordered you to surrender your weapon."

I blink. Something flutters through my chest.

I reach for my sidearm.

"Slowly," he says.

"Isaac, what the fuck?" I set my Glock, grip first, on his desk.

He picks up the gun, ejects the magazine, catches it in his hand. "You been drinking, Murphy?"

"No. I haven't. What's the chief of police doing out on patrol past midnight?" I ask. "And why are we letting Aiden Willis walk when he was about to shoot me?"

He plays with his goatee, stares at me, almost amused. Having the upper hand is fun for him.

"The better question, Murphy, is what the fuck were *you* doing?"

Not such a good question for me, though. He told me to stay away from the Ocean Drive murders, my uncle's murder, anything other than safety issues at Bridgehampton School. So there's no answer remotely resembling the truth that will exonerate me. I give him most of the cemetery story, only I make it seem like I was simply visiting Uncle Lang's grave, not lying in wait for Aiden.

"You actually saw Aiden take a piss on a tombstone?"

Well, no, I didn't—couldn't make out the actual act; couldn't even make out that it was Aiden. But I'm not going to admit that. "So I went to his house to ask him about it. And yeah, I looked around his place when he didn't answer. There are no lights outside, so I used my Maglite. I just walked the perimeter, Isaac."

He watches me closely. "You were shining a light into his basement?"

"Yeah, and you wanna know what I found?"

"What does Aiden Willis's basement have to do with him taking a piss on a grave? I mean, assuming he even did that, like you claim. You figured, what, you'd find evidence to support a public urination charge by searching his *basement?* No. You're up to something else."

I pause. But he has me. What possible bullshit story could I conjure up?

And besides, I shouldn't have to bullshit. I'm a cop, investigating a series of murders. When did that become a wrong thing? When did following up on a hunch, just to see where it led, become a capital offense?

"It was the Dahlquist grave," I say. "The family that owned the house where Melanie and Zach were—"

"No. No." He shakes his head presumptively, like he's had enough.

"Some strange shit is going on in this town," I say, trying to salvage the conversation. "And there's something about Aiden—"

"Aiden Willis couldn't spell his own name if you gave him all the letters," says Isaac. "And he couldn't hurt a june bug with a sledgehammer. I've known that kid my whole life. That boy is harmless."

"He pulled a gun on me tonight, Isaac."

"Yeah, and you know what? He had every goddamn right to. A prowler on his property, sneaking into his basement? Landowner's got that right."

"I announced my office."

310

"And maybe he didn't believe you. What's he supposed to think, Murphy? Lucky for us, Aiden's a reasonable man. He's going to let this be water under the bridge."

"Bullshit," I say, getting my Irish up, getting to my feet. "He knows me. Even if he didn't at first. I identified myself. Yeah, okay, maybe at first, I can't blame him. But he knows me, Isaac. I told him who I was and I posed no threat to him at all. And he was *still* going to shoot me. You're gonna let him walk?"

"Hell, yes, I am. A cop of mine, without anything close to probable cause, is looking into a private citizen's basement window? That's a lawsuit right there. The department doesn't need *another* black eye courtesy of you."

I shake my head. "I can't believe this."

"You're behaving in an erratic, irrational manner, Detective Murphy."

My blood goes cold. Magic words, those. The police union's collective bargaining agreement allows the chief to strip a cop whose behavior is "erratic or irrational."

A hint of a smile on Isaac's face. Oh, he's been waiting for this moment.

"Just hear me out first, Isaac, I'm beg—"

"Detective, turn over your badge."

"Isaac, no—"

"You're suspended indefinitely," he says. "I'm stripping you of your police powers. You're no longer a cop. You come back tomorrow, I'll give you thirty minutes to clean out your desk."

He leans over his desk, his eyes boring into mine, a snarl across his mouth.

"Now get the fuck out of my police station."

Chapter 69

THE DIVE BAR'S liquor license cuts off the service of alcohol at two in the morning. That means they have to stop pouring when the little hand hits two, and they can't let in any new customers.

It doesn't mean they can't hand over a bottle to me at 1:55 a.m. and then watch me drink it for an hour, as they close down the place, turn out most of the lights, turn over the chairs and put them on top of the tables, and mop the floors and wipe down the counters.

The good news for me is that I'm a regular, so I get this special treatment from Jerry, the bartender and owner.

The bad news, I suppose, is that I'm a regular.

"I don't like to speak ill of my fellow man," Jerry says to me as he sprays the counter. "But I never much liked Isaac. Worst thing that ever happened to him was getting that badge. Give a guy with an inferiority complex some power and watch out."

I look over at him, my eyes heavy and slow, almost

dreamy. Almost as if, an hour ago, I didn't lose the only thing that mattered to me in this world. Almost like that.

"Fuck Isaac." My tongue thick, numb. All of me feeling numb.

"Okay, three a.m.," Jerry says. "I'm gonna turn into a pumpkin." He lifts the bottle of Jim Beam, three-quarters empty. "I'll hold on to the rest for you, Murph. Your private stash. Let me give you a ride home."

I surrender the bottle but shake my head.

"You can't drive, Murph."

"Not gonna drive. I'll walk. Pick up . . . pick up my car tomorrow." I step off the barstool gingerly, get my balance. "Not like I'll have anything else to do."

"Let me give you a ride, Jenna. C'mon."

"I'm good. I'm good."

The walk will do me good. Or so I think. I'm about a half hour from here, and the cool air helps clear out some of the fog. My hand brushes against my side for my piece, which of course I had to surrender. Because I'm no longer a cop.

I'm no longer a cop. It still hasn't sunk in.

I'm dizzy and unfocused, my emotions careening wildly from utter despair to bitterness to hot rage, grabbing at clues that don't add up, like I'm trying to put together a puzzle that's missing half the pieces.

The start of a massive headache is pressing against my forehead, between my eyes.

By the time I approach my street, the inside of my head is screaming at me. But the blood is flowing again, and much of the alcohol's effect is waning.

All except the emotional part. With the numbness

wearing off, all that's left is my fear of what's to come, a life without a badge.

And sleep, which will end as it always does, with a breathless nightmare.

I rent the bottom floor of a two-flat, all of four rooms inside—living room with tiny kitchenette, bathroom, and bedroom. Always planned to buy a place once I "settled in," but I never really settled in, did I? I never got around to making anything about my apartment feel like a real home, nor did I buy an actual home.

Probably for the best, now.

When I approach the apartment, I see something underneath the porch light. A figure. A man?

I draw closer, feel my hand, by instinct, sweep my side for a gun that isn't there.

A man, sitting up, resting against the outside wall.

"Noah?" I say.

Chapter 70

WHEN I TAKE my first step onto the porch, Noah Walker stirs. He was sleeping.

"Oh, yeah." He pushes himself up, shakes out the cobwebs. Sweatshirt, jeans, sandals.

"Why are you here?"

"Waiting for you," he says.

"Same question," I say, "second time."

"I wanted to tell you something."

"So tell me."

He nods. "I remember now," he says. "Those girls."

"Dede and Annie."

"I saw them. I remember them now. They were at the house, 7 Ocean Drive. I think they were squatting there. I was doing some work. I think . . . patching the lower flat roof. I'm pretty sure it was them. It was five or six years ago, so I'm not positive. They seemed like nice girls. If something happened to them, and I can help . . ."

So that's confirmation. I was pretty sure they'd been

staying there—hard to imagine the initials AC and DP scratched on the windowsill were a coincidence—but it's nice to know for sure.

He looks up at me. He didn't have to tell me any of that. His lawyer, in fact, would have told him to keep his mouth shut.

"It doesn't matter anymore," I say. "Go home."

He steps in front of me. "It *does* matter. You're asking because you think it's connected. Whoever it was who killed those girls might have killed Melanie."

Melanie. Right. He had a relationship with her.

"I loved her. Yeah, she broke up with me and it hurt. And I moved on. But you don't stop caring about someone." He takes a long breath, looks out in the distance. "Y'know, after she died—you guys arrested me right away, and all of a sudden I'm on trial for my life. I never had a chance to . . . I don't know."

To grieve. To mourn her loss.

"And then Paige's suicide . . ."

I didn't even know about that. The woman he was with after Melanie.

"That happened after I went to prison," he says. He slowly nods, gains some steam. "Whoever killed Melanie—in my mind? He's responsible for Paige, too. And a lot of other people, it sounds like. Like those two girls. And your uncle."

This is not the time for me to be thinking about that. The fog may have cleared from my head, but my emotions are on the verge of bursting. It's over for me here in Bridgehampton. Over. I didn't solve the cases, and I'll never be a sworn officer again.

"Let me help you," he says. "Let me help you find him."

"I'm not a cop anymore," I say. "I've lost my badge. I lost everything," I add, for some reason—whiskey-induced self-pity.

"You didn't lose as much as me. And you don't see me running."

I look at him. Still standing tall, after what he's been through. Wrongly accused of a crime—yes, I believe that in my gut—crucified at Sing Sing by white supremacists he refused to join; losing two women he loved; and still being harassed by our police force. And here he is, volunteering for duty. If it were me, I'd have run from this town as soon as I left prison.

No, you wouldn't have. You're too stubborn.

Just like Noah.

That shield that has stood between us, suddenly gone.

I start to say something but don't. Everything swimming through me now, all the regret and anger and yearning, that familiar heat filling my body whenever I see him, but none of the typical restraints, all washed away by the alcohol and emotion, and I don't know if I'm going to burst into tears or—

Or—

"I can help you," Noah says. "I'm not as dumb as I look."

"I'm not a cop anymore."

He shrugs.

"Then what do we have to lose?" he says.

Chapter 71

"THE KEY TO all this," says Noah, "is someone who's been dead for twenty years?"

"Eighteen," I say. "And yes."

We're walking the next morning along Main Street, the sun blistering overhead. I skipped my morning run and pounded aspirin and water to ward off my hangover. The adrenaline helps, too. Funny that I feel almost reborn after the pep talk Noah gave me last night—that losing my badge actually has the effect of motivating me to work harder.

That's the thing: I may have lost my official authority, not to mention my gun, but I have gained some freedom—now Isaac can't prevent me from asking questions and probing where I wish.

I'd just better be careful. Because without said authority, and without said gun, there are limits to how far I can push things.

Noah follows me into the cemetery, all the way up to the Dahlquist plot.

"A family of violent, mentally deranged, suicidal men named Holden," I say. "The first Holden killed, like, twenty or thirty women."

"According to that book." Noah read most of the book after I gave it to him last night. He must not have slept at all. The dark circles under his eyes attest to that fact. "It may not be true."

"Doesn't matter if it's true. All that matters is that he believes it."

"Who?"

"Our suspect," I say. "Our killer."

Noah looks at the plot, the large memorial, then back at me. "He's mimicking what the first Holden did a couple hundred years ago? He has some kind of obsession with the family or something?"

"Very good," I say. "You're smarter than you look."

"Well, dagnabbit, Ms. Murphy—that makes me happier'n a puppy with two peters. I been a-hankerin' for your say-so—"

"All right, enough."

"Yes'm, I'm as pleased as a goat in a briar patch, I am."

I shake my head. "If it's okay with you, can we get back to the point now?"

Noah looks pleased enough with himself, but he turns it off and gets serious again. "Okay, so this guy has a thing for the Dahlquist family. Okay, I get that. But you said this is about the last Holden. The guy who died twenty years ago."

"Eighteen."

"Okay, whatever, eighteen—you're talking about Holden the Sixth."

"Right. Holden the Sixth."

"The guy who died without any heirs," says Noah. "The guy who said—let me find this." He reaches into his satchel and pulls out the book, opens to a page he has dog-eared. "The guy who said, 'The greatest gift I can bequeath mankind is to avoid procreation at all costs.' "

"Yes, that guy."

"The guy who killed himself by downing two fifths of Jack Daniel's, popping some pills, then slitting his own throat and tossing the knife out the window."

"Yes, that guy," I agree.

"The guy who was suspected of raping and assaulting a bunch of women, but the charges never stuck."

"Yes, that guy."

"The guy who, as far as we know, never committed a single murder."

"Yes, that guy."

"Not one murder that we know of."

"Correct," I say. "That guy."

Noah closes the book. "It all starts with *that* guy? He had no children, he committed no murders. I mean, he was a bad guy—he raped women, they think—but the guy running around right now isn't raping anybody. He's killing them in violent ways."

I smirk at him.

"Am I missing something?" Noah asks.

"I think you are," I say. "Our killer is mimicking what the original Holden did. And he's pretty damn good at it. But the question is why."

Noah stares at me, then shrugs. "I have no idea."

"I think he feels a sort of obligation," I say. "He thinks it's his destiny."

Noah opens his hands. "But . . . why would it be his destiny—"

His jaw drops.

I smile at him.

"Oh," says Noah. "You think?"

"I do," I say. "I think, no matter how much he didn't want to, Holden the Sixth left behind a son. A son who wants to restart the family tradition."

Chapter 72

I LEAVE NOAH at the cemetery with a research assignment and continue walking up to the turnpike. It's a little before eleven, so Tasty's is probably not even open for business yet, which is how I prefer it. Because I'm not here for the delicious scallops.

The gravel parking lot is almost empty when I walk up to the door. It's open, so I push through and enter the restaurant. In the back, chefs and servers are busy preparing for the lunch rush, boiling and steaming and chopping, wiping down counters, filling out the chalkboard with today's selections, shouting to one another in English and Spanish. The smells of garlic and butter make me reconsider whether I'm here for business only.

Seated in the dining area, alone, is Justin Rivers, wearing a flannel shirt that he fills out very well, thank you very much, and blue jeans. He's got a pencil poised over a section of newspaper—a crossword puzzle.

Must be nice, being the owner, relaxing while the employees bust a move to get the diner open.

He glances up at me with those boy-next-door looks and smiles widely.

"Detective!"

It's like a punch in the stomach. But I don't correct him. I'm not going to lie if he asks, but if he wants to think I'm still a cop, all the better.

"Hi, Justin. How're you doing?"

"Great, great." He looks down at his watch.

"I'm not here for lunch," I say. "I was hoping to speak with you a moment."

"With me? Okay." He stands up. "You wanna . . ."

"Maybe we could step outside?"

"Sure. I'll be right back," he calls out to his staff, though nobody seems to notice.

He follows me outside and faces me, beaming, clean-cut and handsome.

"Good to see you," he says. The million-dollar smile, the hair swept to one side, the broad shoulders.

"Um—thanks. You too. Listen, I was hoping to ask you a few questions."

"Oh, you mean, official stuff?" His face dropping a bit, like he's disappointed.

I nod. "If that's okay. Did you think there was some . . . other reason?"

"Oh, uh." His face turns red. "Now I'm embarrassed. Oh, I feel stupid."

It sometimes takes me a while, but I get there. He thought I was going to ask him out.

"A guy can hope," he says.

Now we're both embarrassed.

"Oh, Justin, I'm sort of—I mean it's not that I wouldn't—"

He raises his hands. "No explanation required. My fault. My fault totally. God, this is embarrassing." All the blood has reached his face at this point. "Go right ahead and ask, Detective." He nods for emphasis.

"Okay," I say, hoping that if I get down to business, both of us will feel less awkward. "Melanie Phillips. Your waitress."

"Sure." The mention of her name is enough to sober him up. "Great kid. Everyone loved her."

"Well, I'm wondering if anyone seemed to take an interest in her while she worked here."

He looks at the sky, thinks it over. I'm tempted to prompt him with a name, but I want to see if he comes up with it himself.

"Well, I mean, she was very pretty, so lots of guys would stare and stuff. But, like, obsess over her?"

"Yes, obsess."

He runs his hand over his mouth. "Mmm . . . nah, not really. I mean, she and Noah had that breakup, like everybody knows."

Noah. Not the name I was looking for, but since he mentioned it, I might as well see where that goes.

"What did you think about Noah for a suspect?"

"Me? Oh, jeez, I'm no cop. I always liked Noah, tell you the truth."

"I noticed he still eats here, since he's been out."

"Yeah, sure. We get a lot of blue-collar types. Probably because we're cheap."

"But . . . I assume if you thought he did harm to Melanie—"

"Oh, right."

"—you wouldn't let him back in."

"Definitely. I never thought Noah would do something like that. He always seemed like a good guy."

"Okay." I scribble a note in my little pad. "Change of subject. What can you tell me about Aiden Willis?"

"Aiden?" He smiles, shakes his head. "Well, he's a good guy. He's one of a kind, but a good guy."

"Could you be more specific?"

"I mean, he's . . . unusual, I guess. I don't know. Maybe we all are. Good man, though. Good man."

This guy's Mr. Sunshine. *Never speaks ill of his fellow man,* as my favorite bartender would say.

"You said he was unusual."

"Well, I mean—he comes in alone. Sits there and reads some book. Doesn't talk much. Comes in for beers at night sometimes but pretty much keeps to himself. Grew up here. Went to Bridgehampton School. I think Noah did, too."

"What about you?" I ask.

"Me? I grew up in Sag Harbor. Not far."

"You didn't go to school with Aiden and Noah?"

"No, I went to Lanier Academy in East Hampton."

Oh, a private school. A rich kid. I was hoping to talk to someone who went to school with Aiden and Noah.

"You didn't know them growing up?"

"Aiden and Noah? Nope. Hey, Aiden's not some kind of suspect, is he?"

I give a noncommittal shrug. "Just basic questions, at this point."

"I mean, he's kinda odd, but not like that. Odd, but in a funny way, not scary."

That seems to be the prevailing sentiment. I don't remember laughing last night, when he had a shotgun aimed at my head.

"Well, anyway," says Justin, "Aiden didn't kill Melanie."

I snap my focus off my pad to him. "How could you know that?"

"Because he was with me, here," says Justin. "We have a liquor license until two a.m. I was pouring, and Aiden closed down the place with me."

I feel some air deflate from my lungs. "You're sure? You're positive you have those dates lined up? It was a long time ago."

"I'm positive," he says. "The next day, Melanie missed work. We were calling her cell phone, even sent someone over to her condo. Then the cops showed up and told us she was killed the night before at the house on Ocean Drive. They asked me who was here that night. I gave them a list. It wasn't that hard. It was just me and Aiden."

I scribble a note, trying to hide my disappointment.

My biggest lead has just swirled down the drain.

Chapter 73

OFFICER RICKETTS, STILL in patrol uniform, shakes her head as we look out over the Atlantic Ocean. "I still can't believe they did this to you, Murphy."

"You should take my advice and stay away from me."

Ricketts nods and looks over at me, looking younger than her age, her cropped blond hair just long enough to show a hint of curl on the ends. "I'm not so good at taking advice," she says.

"If Isaac ever knew—"

"I'd be fired. I get it."

We are quiet. The sky is darkening and the ocean is reacting in kind. A storm on the way.

"We're supposed to catch the bad guys," Ricketts says. "The day I'm not supposed to do that is the day I look for another job."

I like this girl. She's way more poised and mature than I was as a rookie. And just as stubborn.

I look at her. "Are you sure?"

"Don't ask me that again, Murphy. Just tell me what you need."

"The last Holden was suspected in a number of rapes, right?"

"That's what the book said."

"So let's see if we can find out if anyone filed a criminal charge. Someone must have. Maybe one of his victims got pregnant."

"Okay. What else?"

I shrug. "That's it."

"That's not it," Ricketts says. "We should see what else may have been going on back then, in the early nineties. Missing-persons reports, unsolved murders. The last time you had me do that, I only went back ten years. Now I'll go back to the early nineties."

"To what end?" I ask.

"Who knows? Let's just do it. See what shakes loose."

I let out a long breath. "Ricketts, you're going to make a good detective someday."

"If I don't get fired first."

I take her hand. "That can't happen. I wouldn't be able to live with myself if you got canned for helping me."

She waves me off. "I just want you back on the force. We solve this thing, maybe I'll have my mentor back."

"Let's not get too optimistic."

She looks at me. "You know what you need, Murphy? If I may be so bold."

"Shoot. Be bold."

"You need to get laid."

I let out a laugh. It feels good.

"I was thinking Justin," she says.

I hem and haw. "Yeah, I mean, he's . . ."

"He's really cute. And I saw the way he was looking at you."

I've already told Ricketts about my conversation with Justin today, the substantive part. Now I tell her the personal part.

"He actually said 'A guy can hope'?" She pushes my shoulder. "What do you need, a written invitation?"

"Yeah, I know." I let out a low moan. "Honestly, I mean—he's a really nice guy, but I don't know."

"What, he's too nice?"

I sigh. "Something like that."

"You like the bad boys, don't you? The guys with an edge? The dangerous types?"

"That's my curse."

"Murphy." She puts her hands on my shoulders. "He's a super-nice guy. He runs a diner with incredible food and he could double the prices and still fill the place, but he doesn't. I mean, c'mon. He's hot and he's sweet and he has a crush on you. You're gonna pass on that guy because he's *too nice?*"

I just . . . I just can't see it.

"I don't have time for romance," I say. "I have too much to do."

"I didn't say romance. I said *sex.* Just have dinner one time with the guy and then fuck his lights out. And then, of course, tell me all about it."

"The dinner or the sex?"

"Both."

I shake my head. I just . . .

"You know what you are? You're afraid to be happy," she says.

"Thank you, Doctor."

She hits me on the arm. "I'll get you that research," she says.

"Hey, Ricketts?" I call out to her as she's halfway up the beach. "I don't even know your first name."

She smiles. "It's Lauren."

"Well, thanks, Lauren. Seriously. Thank you."

She nods back at me. "One more piece of advice?" she says. "Get some sleep. You look like crap."

Chapter 74

TWO IN THE morning. The promise of a violent storm no longer just a promise. The windows rattling from the wind and rain, the sky a deep purple.

Pages and pages of notes, all over my desk, pinned up on the wall. I take a sip of wine and arch my back, roll my neck. My head aching, my eyelids heavy.

The answer has to be here. There has to be something. Just keep shaking trees and something will come loose. Keep connecting different dots and you'll find it.

You're getting closer.

Just keep telling myself that.

I'm getting closer . . .

Getting closer . . .

Closer . . .

Let me out

Bam-bam-bam

Let me out

Bam-bam-bam

I can't see can't breathe

Murder House

Darkness, then penetrating light from above, a shadow
blocking it
   A face coming into focus, backlit by blinding yellow
   A boy, long hair, a hand
   Don't touch me, please don't touch
   Get away, please don't hurt me
   I wanna go home

My head snaps upward, my hands shooting out across the desk, sweeping off papers, knocking the wineglass to the floor with a hollow *clink*. I take a long breath and shake out the cobwebs.

The boy. The long hair. The hand reaching for me into the darkness.

And the face. This time, I saw his face.

A face I've seen before.

The boy in my nightmare is Aiden Willis.

Chapter 75

NOAH WALKER PULLS his Harley up to the curb outside Jenna Murphy's apartment. The streets are still slick from the heavy downpour last night. His sandals squish in the grass on his way up to the door.

He raps on the door and waits, adjusting the satchel over his shoulder.

When the door opens, he sees the face of a ghost.

Jenna's hair is matted and unkempt, her face drawn and pale, her eyes deep-set and dark. A black Yankees T-shirt and men's boxers are all she's wearing.

She squints in the sunlight, doesn't make eye contact with Noah. "You sure about Aiden?" she says as she turns back into her apartment.

"Good morning to you, too." He wishes he'd brought coffee. She looks like she could use some.

The main room of the apartment looks more like an office than residential quarters. Papers everywhere—on the desk perched in the corner, covering the floor, lining the walls. Newspaper clippings, copies of police files scribbled over with notes in Magic Marker, Post-its haphazardly stuck everywhere. Organized in columns for the various victims, Annie Church and Dede Paris, Brittany Halsted, Sally Pfiester, Melanie and Zach, Bonnie Stamos—and Chief Langdon James, her uncle.

"You sure about Aiden?" she asks again, pacing the room, disappearing into her bedroom and coming out again.

"Am I sure Aiden's not a killer? Yes, I'm sure. Why?"

She shakes her head absently, still pacing. "I've been having these . . . nightmares. Ever since I came here."

"What kind of nightmares?"

She throws up her hands. "Like I'm trapped. Enclosed. Pleading to get out. And there's someone above me, a boy, reaching down for me, going to hurt me. And I'm begging, *Please, let me go, don't hurt me,* that kind of thing."

That explains the sleep deprivation he's noticed since he met her. She must have had a doozy of a nightmare last night, because it looks like she didn't sleep much at all.

"Last night, Aiden showed up in the dream."

"Aiden was the boy?" Noah nods. "That's because you have Aiden on the brain, Murphy. You think there's some meaning to your dream? Like, you're assuming the role of one of the victims? Or you're . . . seeing the future or something?"

"How the hell should I know?" She's still pacing; then she stops and puts her hands on the wall. "Sorry. I don't know. I . . . there's probably no meaning to it. I don't know. It's just . . ."

It's just making you crazy, he thinks.

She turns and looks at Noah, sizes him up, narrows her eyes.

"What?" he asks.

"The BB gun shooting at the school," she says. "Back when you were a kid."

"Oh, come *on,* Murphy."

"I'm shaking trees," she says.

"You're what?"

"Tell me." She walks toward him, then stops short, her hands on her hips. She could practically fall over. "Someone did it with you. A second shooter. And then set you up to take the fall. And you let him get away with it. Some kind of . . . code with you. Never rat out your friends or something."

Noah looks down, pinches the bridge of his nose. All these years, all the investigation that took place back when it happened—everyone was sure it was Noah and Noah alone. Nobody ever questioned that. Any evidence to the contrary was swept aside, and the unanimous conclusion was that Noah shot all those kids on the playground, all by his lonesome self.

Not until sixteen, almost seventeen years later, when Detective Jenna Murphy from Manhattan came along and patched together a couple of interviews and some dry reports and reached a different conclusion.

"If you're right," he says, "and I live by the code that you don't rat out your friends, why would I rat them out now?"

She works her jaw, her deep-set eyes burrowing into him.

"What's it matter, Murphy? It doesn't have anything to do with—"

"You were set up," she says. "You were set up for Melanie's and Zach's murders. You were set up for the murder in the woods, the hooker, Bonnie Stamos. You were set up for my uncle's—"

Her voice falters. Her whole body is trembling now.

She clears her throat hard, like an engine struggling to start. "And you were set up to take the fall with the BB gun shooting."

Noah shakes his head. What happened in that school yard doesn't have anything to do with the murders. It was close to seventeen years ago now. She doesn't need to know this.

"This guy is smart," she says. "He's careful. He might be deranged, he might be schizophrenic or a psychopath, but he does *not* make mistakes. He handed you to us as a suspect. Shit, I almost shot you myself, I was so sure you were guilty."

That's true. Something he'll never forget, when she broke into his house after her uncle was attacked.

"Look, I'm grasping at straws, I'm looking for anything I can," she says. "You said you wanted to help. You gave me this bullshit pep talk about—"

"I do want to help." Noah slings his bag off his shoulder. "You didn't even ask me why I'm here. Remember the research assignment you gave me?"

Jenna's eyes move to the satchel.

"You found something," she says.

Chapter 76

"IT'S NOT MUCH," Noah tells me, opening his satchel. "I searched all the public records. Turns out I knew one of the clerks there, someone who grew up down the street from me. She helped."

He removes a manila folder from his bag. "Holden the Sixth was part of three lawsuits in Suffolk County that we know of," he says.

"Anything on paternity?" I ask.

"No, but my friend at the clerk's office said, a lot of times, paternity lawsuits are filed under seal. She said that means the—"

"The names are redacted from the lawsuit," I say. "Kept out of the public domain. So it's possible there was a paternity suit, but we wouldn't know it."

"Yeah. I made copies of the three lawsuits I *did* find. They aren't criminal cases. They're civil. One is a property dispute and one is a defamation suit, whatever that means, and the last one is a lawsuit for assault and battery brought by a neighbor, some guy who said Holden punched him at a party."

He hands me copies of the three civil complaints. He's no lawyer, and neither am I, though a cop knows a thing or two about the legal system.

"Nobody claiming rape, nobody claiming paternity," I say. "So we don't know anything."

"We know one thing." Noah takes the papers and flips through each of them to a particular page.

He hands them to me. Each of these lawsuits has a sheet attached to the front of it, with the names of the attorneys representing the plaintiff and defendant.

"We know the name of Holden's lawyer," Noah says.

Chapter 77

THE WAITER opens the bottle of wine and hands the cork to Justin, who defers to me. The waiter pours an inch of Pinot into my glass and I swirl it, sniff it, taste it, and nod my approval.

"Cheers," says Justin, looking very nice in a white shirt with an open collar, and a blue sport coat. We clink our glasses.

It's a nice place near the intersection of Main Street and the turnpike—not very far, really, from Justin's own restaurant, Tasty's. But this is more than a slight step up from his diner—dark oak and caramel leather, dim lighting, people dressed as formally as it gets in the Hamptons.

"What made you change your mind?" he asks me.

I shrug. "My friend told me I should have dinner with you."

That, and I've gone about seventy-two hours straight obsessing about the case. A little battery recharging may be in order.

"Well, I'm glad." He takes a drink of the wine. "Hey, this is good."

"It *is* good." If I saw the price correctly on the menu, this bottle was over two hundred dollars, a 2011 Pinot from the Russian River Valley. All I know about wine is what I learned from Matty, who would always line up the year it was bottled with the vintage and location to find the "perfect" bottle to pair with our meal.

"I gotta say, I don't know anything about wine," says Justin. "I'm the kind of guy who picks based on the label." He laughs at himself.

"Me too."

An awkward silence follows. He seems a little nervous. Not so adept at small talk, that's for sure. But that part, I like. I've had enough of the smooth talkers.

Still, with two people who aren't good at chatter, there is a palpable sense of relief when the appetizers arrive—chilled zucchini soup for me, burrata with peaches for him.

"So what brought you to the Hamptons?" he asks.

I stop on that one. "I thought everyone knew about that," I say.

"Well, I remember the trial," he says. "Some trouble you had with the NYPD. But I always figure, there's two sides to every story. I mean, if you want."

An initial buzz is kicking in from the wine, maybe loosening me up a little.

"I was working undercover," I say. "Going after meth dealers. High up on the chain. I got close to the top guy."

"How'd you do that? Get close to him." He settles his elbows on the table.

"I slept with him," I say. "I became his girlfriend."

"Wow." He leans back. "Wow."

"Yeah, it was pretty intense. Only way to do it, though. These guys are wired tight. They don't trust anybody. But when it comes to sex, they don't use their brains so much."

"That's—that's pretty—wow."

"So anyway," I say, "I came to find out that some of the people helping the boss were cops. There was a whole ring set up. The cops were running protection for the dealers. So I sent that information back to head-quarters. I reported it. I made a big mistake, though."

"What?"

"I didn't report it to IAD. Internal Affairs."

"Who'd you report it to?"

"My boss, my lieutenant."

"Why was that a mistake?"

I gesture with my wineglass, take a sip. "Two days later, totally out of the blue, three cops are suddenly claiming that I skimmed off the top of a drug raid before I went undercover."

"Skimmed off the . . ."

"They said I stole money and drugs from drug dealers. That I arrested them and only turned in some of the money and some of the drugs—kept the rest for myself."

"That kind of thing happens?"

"It happens if you're a dirty cop," I say. "The drug dealers aren't going to complain, right? If you're busted, would you rather be busted with a thousand grams of cocaine and a hundred thousand dollars, or with ten grams and ten thousand bucks? Either way, you're not getting any of it back. But you get a lesser sentence this way. It's a pretty classic shakedown. If you're a dirty cop."

He nods slowly.

"Which I am not," I say. "I touched a nerve in the department, I told the wrong person, and they wanted to silence me. So they trumped up these charges and gave me a choice—resign or go to prison."

We don't speak for a while. I drain my first glass of the Pinot. *Easy, Murphy. Don't let the emotions bubble to the surface.*

"Do you regret it?" he asks.

I let out air. "Do I regret not staying and fighting for my job? Every single day."

"But it was three cops against one," he says.

I nod. "That's what Lang said. He said I couldn't beat those odds. He said, 'Get out while you still have your badge, come work for me.' So I did."

"Well, I'm glad you did. Hope you like it here."

I shrug. "I won't be here much longer," I say. "I'm just staying until I figure out who killed my uncle."

His smile loses a few degrees of wattage. It seems he might have had some ideas about me. I figured I should let him know, up front, that I'm not in his long-term plans.

For the main course, I have scallops with sweet corn and shishito peppers. They are absolutely delicious—but really no better than the ones at Tasty's.

"They get their seafood from the same place we do," Justin says.

"Really? You guys and this restaurant?"

"Yeah," he says, cocking his head, surprised at my surprise.

I put down my fork. "Your food is as good as this place's," I say. "But you can't be operating Tasty's at a profit with the prices you're charging."

"Who said I was operating at a profit?" He smiles and takes the last sip of his wine. He calls over the waiter and orders a second bottle.

"Okay, so what's your angle?" I ask. "This whole man-of-the-people thing about not raising prices for ten years."

"Angle? Why does there have to be an angle?"

I look him over. Good looks, private schools growing up, an expensive dinner tonight, a restaurant that loses money . . .

"I'm no saint," he says. "We come close to breaking even some years. It's . . . fun to have a place where everyone comes and enjoys themselves. It's fun for me, too."

"There's gotta be something wrong with you," I say. "Are you sure you're not a serial killer or something?"

"I never said I wasn't." He smiles and wipes his mouth with his napkin. "You've been a cop too long, Jenna. You only see bad people. There are lots of good people in the world, too."

Maybe he's right. Maybe not everyone in this world has an angle. Maybe I've been so closed off in the cocoon of crime and punishment that I've lost sight of some things. Maybe losing my badge is a good thing.

Maybe there's hope for me yet.

Chapter 78

"I'LL WALK YOU to the door," Justin says, pulling his Jaguar up to the curb. It's a nice ride, this car.

Nice dinner. Nice car. Nice guy.

"This was fun," he says as he steps up onto the porch.

My cell phone vibrates in my purse.

I stand at my door, fishing for my keys.

"So listen." Justin claps his hands together. "I had a great time. I had a . . . great time. It was a . . ."

"Great time?" I rise up on my toes and kiss him softly on the lips. He responds, but awkwardly, his hand touching my arm, unsure whether he should open his mouth.

Shy and clumsy.

"It was fun for me, too," I say as we draw back. His face has lost a bit of color.

Very shy.

"Call me," I say.

He nods, then cocks his head. "Why would I call you?"

I draw back. "Oh, I mean, if you want to . . . have dinner again."

"We already had dinner. Why would we do it again?"

I stare at him, at a loss for words.

"Gotcha." He breaks into laughter. "You should see the look on your face."

Score one for him. He did get me. A little corny . . . but he got me.

"I will call you, Jenna. For sure."

He pauses, like he's thinking about another kiss, but he steps off the porch and heads to his car, whistling. I don't know very many people who whistle. I don't know anybody who whistles.

Snap assessment: nice guy, but not a lot of sparks.

Then again, that's always been my problem. I look for chemistry right away and if I don't feel it, I walk. Maybe that can develop over time. Maybe if I just let someone in . . . someone really nice . . .

Someone without an angle . . .

Justin drives away with a brief toot of his horn.

Yeah, I don't know . . . maybe . . .

I walk inside my tornado of an apartment and fish my cell phone out of my purse.

The call was from Lauren Ricketts. I punch her up and she answers on the second ring.

"Murphy," she says.

"Ricketts. What's up?"

Suddenly my enjoyable Saturday night with Justin is over, and I'm slipping back into the darkness, the quagmire, slogging through evidence and driving myself crazy.

"I finished going through criminal complaints and missing-persons reports," she says. "I went back to the eighties and got through the mid-nineties."

"And?" I say, my heartbeat kicking up. "Did you find any criminal complaints?"

"No. Nobody ever filed a criminal charge against Holden the Sixth."

"Shit." I really thought that was promising. "And what about unsolveds or missing-persons bulletins?"

"No unsolveds that look interesting, not from that time period."

"And no missing-persons reports that looked interesting?"

"Just one from 1994," she says. "I guess it would go under the category of interesting. I wish you'd prepared me for it."

"Prepared you for what?" I ask. "Who was the missing person?"

A pause on the other end of the line.

"You don't know?" she asks.

"Ricketts, just freakin' tell me," I say. "Who went missing?"

Another pause. As if she's debating. As if she's thrown for a loss. And then, finally, she speaks.

She says, "*You* did, Murphy. You were the missing person."

Chapter 79

SUNDAY NIGHT, 7 p.m. The sun almost completely fallen now, a blanket of darkness, the air mild and pleasant.

April Fools' Day, which feels appropriate. I was a fool ever to have returned to this place.

I pull my car into Uncle Langdon's driveway just as Aunt Chloe is locking the house up. Some final boxes to remove, some papers to sign, before the sale of the house goes through this month.

"I was so glad you called," she says. "We could grab a quick bite . . ."

She has a big smile on her face, until she gets a look at mine.

I stop short in front of her, no hug, no nothing.

"What happened to me here in 1994?" I ask. "When I was eight years old."

Her face falls. Her mouth works, but no words come out.

"I asked Lang why my family stopped coming to the

Hamptons when I was a kid," I say. "He never told me. 'A story for another time,' he said. And then I asked you, and you said, 'If you don't know, I don't know.' Whatever that cryptic bullshit is supposed to mean."

"It means just what I said." Chloe looks me over. "I don't know what happened. Nobody knows. Apparently, not even you."

"I saw a missing-persons report, Chloe. From July of 1994. It ended seven hours after it began."

Chloe slowly nods. "That's right. 'Seven hours of hell,' your mother called it. You went missing. You were playing down the street, just right down this street. And then you were gone. Nobody could find you." She places a hand at the base of her throat. "It still gives me a sickening feeling when I remember it. We looked everywhere. Lang had the entire Southampton Town Police Department searching for you. Your mother and I searched for you. Your father and Ryan searched for you. Everyone searched for you."

"And then?"

"And then . . . we found you." Her eyes shine with brimming tears. "Seven hours later. We found you on the beach. You were just . . . sitting there, looking peacefully out at the ocean."

I roll my hand impatiently, like I want her to continue.

"I don't know what else to tell you," she says. "You wouldn't tell us anything. Lang said you were in shock. We took you to the hospital and they checked you out. Nobody had . . . done anything . . . or hurt you—"

"No evidence of any assault," I say, "sexual or otherwise."

"No, nothing like that," she says. "Just this."

She takes my hand, turns it over, palm up, and traces the small scar on my hand, about an inch long.

"You had that cut on your hand."

"That's how I got that cut?" I look at Chloe. "Mom always said I got it chopping a tomato when I was little."

Chloe nods. "Sometimes we tell our children little white lies to protect them," she says. "Anyway, your family left the island that day and never came back to the Hamptons. They asked you about it for a while afterward. Days, weeks. But you wouldn't talk about it. Or couldn't. And then . . . life went on. Finally, they just dropped it. The nightmare with a happy ending."

I don't remember any of this. Or at least, I thought I didn't remember.

"I was at the beach the whole time?"

Chloe looks at me like she's unsure of the answer.

"For God's sake, Chloe, speak."

She breathes out. "No. That's the thing. The spot where they found you—I had personally looked there with your mother. It was one of the first places we checked. I'm sure of it. You weren't there at first."

"So I wasn't at the beach, and then seven hours later, I was."

She nods.

"But you don't know where I was for those seven hours."

She shakes her head, her expression grim. "Seven hours of hell."

I look over her shoulder at Lang's house, now empty, soon to be sold to a young couple with a baby. A new life in a new town. New memories, new dreams.

"Get in the car," I say.

"Jenna—"

"Get in the car, Chloe."

"Why?"

"You're going to show me."

The drive doesn't take long. She directs me, but I'm beyond being surprised at this point. There are any number of roads that lead to the sweeping beach, but I know which one before she says it.

I drive down Ocean Drive and park in the parking lot and make her get out and walk onto the beach until she shows me the exact spot where I was found.

"Right here," she says. "I'll never forget the sound your mother made when she saw you sitting here."

Those nightmares—they aren't random spooky dreams. They aren't some glimpse into the future. They aren't telepathic visions of other victims' experiences.

They're my memories. Repressed memories.

I look out over the ocean, then turn my back to it, looking north.

Looking at the second house from the end, looming over the coastline. The house at 7 Ocean Drive. The Gothic facade, the spears aimed at the sky.

The memories, the flashbacks are at their most intense when I'm inside that house. Paralyzing panic attacks, every time I set foot inside that mansion.

That's where I was for seven hours, when I was a little girl.

I was inside the Murder House.

Chapter 80

MY CAR BUMPS violently over the rough road, sending my head banging against the roof. I stop on the shoulder, not wanting to pull into his driveway—not wanting to announce myself in advance.

I remember you now, he said to me when I accosted him at the cemetery.

I find his driveway, walk up to the front porch, and reach the door.

"Open up, Aiden!" Pounding the door so hard that my knuckles start to bleed.

Nothing.

You shouldn't have come back, he said to me when he caught me looking into his basement.

My chest heaving, my emotions skittering about, I move to the window closest to the front door and look inside.

The window is open, a screen letting in fresh air. I lean in, kick the screen off, push it into the house, and get one leg and my body through the window.

Just as Aiden is rushing past me, panic on his face.

He cries out in surprise and tries to avoid me, but I grab hold of his arm, getting a poor grip, enough to spin him slightly before he wrests his arm free. I'm off balance, my back leg just coming through the open window, and I fall to the floor as he continues to run.

"What did you do to me?" I shout as I get to my feet and race after him.

He reaches a door—looks like a bedroom door—and opens it and closes it quickly. I reach it a moment later, just as I hear the *click* of the dead bolt.

I pound on the door.

"What did you do to me? What did you do to me when I was a little girl?"

Punching the door like it's his face, the blood from my knuckles smeared across the white wood.

I rear back and give the door a kick. An interior door, not as substantial as an outside door. And it's been a while, but once upon a time when I was training, I had a pretty good kick.

I kick at the doorknob and the adjacent wood. After three furious blows, it splinters, and then my foot breaks through. I reach inside and unlock the dead bolt and the button on the knob.

He could have anything inside there. He could have the shotgun. He could have a knife. Nothing I've done so far is smart, fueled as I am by insatiable rage—but I charge through, anyway.

A dark room, but fresh air sweeping in.

The window, open.

He escaped out the back window.

I climb through the window and run into the backyard, into a vacuum of blackness.

He's gone. This is his home turf. He probably knows every nook and cranny of those woods behind his house. He's long gone.

The darkness, suddenly interrupted by colored, flashing lights.

A car engine, tires crunching over gravel.

A patrol car, pulling into Aiden's driveway.

I move to the side of the house and peek around to the front. I hear a car door open and close. I hear footsteps, but not coming my way. Moving into the house.

I place myself flat against the house, not moving an inch. The only sound the gentle swaying of the trees in the wind.

Then a light comes on in the bedroom, where I just came from. I hear the footsteps inside.

A head pops out of the window, looking outside. I hold my breath.

It's our beloved chief of police, Isaac Marks, illuminated by the light of the room. He's only twenty feet or so away from me, but I'm bathed in darkness and far to his right—I don't think he can make me.

"Shit," he says into the darkness.

A noise; then I hear beeps. He's dialing a cell phone.

"You okay?" Isaac says. "Where are you? No, she's gone. I don't know, do you? She said what? Okay. Don't worry about her. I'll take care of her. I said I'll take care of this. You gotta relax. Listen to me . . ."

His voice fading as he leaves the room, as he moves into the interior of the house.

Chapter 81

AFTER WAITING OVER an hour in Aiden's backyard, I head back to my car. Aiden's not coming back, and Isaac left long ago.

My car is tucked away on the shoulder of the road down the street. Did Isaac spot it? I don't see an ambush awaiting me. No doubt there's an APB out, possibly a warrant for my arrest.

I don't know what Isaac has planned. I don't know what he meant when he told Aiden he would "take care" of me.

And I'm not anxious to find out.

I have to get my car out of sight. I have to get *myself* out of sight.

I pull my car into his driveway and ring the doorbell. Nobody likes unannounced visitors at midnight.

"Who's there?" he calls through the door.

"It's Murphy."

When he opens the door, Noah Walker is wearing an undershirt and sweat pants. He's clutching a hand towel, his face still dripping with water.

As always—that heat across my chest.

There. That's the difference. That's the spark. That's what's missing with Justin.

No time for that now, Murphy.

"You okay?" Noah asks.

"No," I say. "I can't go home. The police are looking for me."

"The pol— Well, come in." He moves out of the way to let me in. "So what happened?" he asks.

"I broke into Aiden's house," I say. "I know it was him."

"What, that dream again?" Noah closes the door and locks it.

"He did something to me," I say. "A long time ago. Back in ninety-four. The dream is a flashback, Noah. It's a memory. I saw the police report myself."

"Then why wasn't Aiden arrested or—"

"Aiden's not in the report. I didn't tell anybody anything. I couldn't. But now I know."

"Look, Aiden's a strange bird," he says, "but he's a sweet kid."

"That's what everyone says. That's what *everyone* says." I grip my hair as if I'm going to yank it out at the roots, feeling a buzz of nervous energy. "What happened to me was in 1994," I say. "And in 1995, there was the school shooting. I know Aiden was involved in the first of those. Was he involved in the second?"

Noah's head drops. "Murphy—"

"Tell me, Noah. Tell me what happened in that school yard."

"Let me make you some coffee or—"

"Fuck coffee," I spit. "I don't give a shit about some stupid code or promise you made seventeen years ago. People we care about have died. More will die. Was Aiden a part of that school shooting or wasn't he?"

Flustered, Noah puts his hands on his head. Looking off in the distance. Probably pondering the importance of a promise made, or maybe just reliving what happened back then.

Finally, he drops his arms, clears his throat.

"I always met Aiden by that bench before school," he says. "Back then, people used to pick on him. I tried to help him out. So we'd meet at that bench and walk into school together."

I suck in a breath. *Aiden*. I knew it.

"So that day, I sat on the bench, listening to music on my headphones. Then all of a sudden, a gym teacher, Coach Cooper, is running up to me and telling me I have to come with him, I'm in big trouble."

I stare at him, waiting for more.

"You didn't participate?" I ask. "You had nothing do with the school shooting?"

He shrugs. "I didn't even know it was happening. I was on the other side of the school, down the road, blasting music in my ears."

I step closer to him. "What about the rifle they found in the bushes behind you?"

"Don't know anything about it. Never saw it."

"And—what did Aiden say to you afterward?"

"Nothing." Noah raises his hands. "I was suspended for the rest of the year. I didn't see Aiden for months.

When I did—I mean, what was there to say? I don't rat people out. And it's not like I knew Aiden had something to do with it. I *still* don't know that. I just know I didn't."

I start pacing. "Reports said the shooter—the one they saw, over by the woods—was wearing a Spider-Man costume. Just like you were."

"Yeah."

"Did Aiden know you were going to wear a Spider-Man costume to school?"

Noah thinks about that. "Probably. Yeah, he probably did."

"And it never occurred to you that Aiden set you up?"

"It crossed my mind. But I didn't know. And I'm not a rat."

I bring a hand to my forehead, push my hair off my face.

"The second shooter," I mumble.

"Yeah, you keep going on about that," says Noah. "You're sure two people did this?"

I nod. "That's the only way it could've happened. So if you didn't do it . . ."

"Then someone else helped Aiden," says Noah.

And after tonight, I think I know who. I think I know who was working with Aiden, who's been working with him all along.

The man who was in Noah's house with my uncle when Lang planted the incriminating evidence to frame Noah.

The man who always seems to show up conveniently to rush to Aiden's rescue.

The man who demanded that I stop investigating the school shooting, my uncle's murder, all of it.

The man who told Aiden tonight, *I'll take care of this.*

"I have to go," I say.

"No, don't." Noah puts a hand on my shoulder. "You said yourself, you can't go home."

"I can't stay here."

"You could, actually," he says, his voice quieter.

I look at him, his eyes peering directly into mine.

He puts his hand on my face and moves in for a kiss.

Like a surge of electricity through my body. Realizing that I've always wanted this. His hands in my hair, my hand cupped around his neck, letting myself surrender—

"No," I say, breaking away. "I have to go. They'll look for me here. It might not be the first place Isaac looks, but he'll get here eventually."

"So let him."

"Why?" I gather myself, fix my hair. "So we both get in trouble?"

He concedes that. "Where will you go?"

I don't know. Hotel, not an option—no cash to my name, and using a credit card would be the same as handing the address to Isaac. Ricketts's house, negative. Uncle Lang's house, nope, I already gave back my keys.

Someone I can trust, but close by, so I don't have to drive the streets very long.

"Justin," I say.

"Justin . . . Rivers? The guy who owns Tasty's?"

I nod, suddenly feeling awkward admitting that to someone I just kissed.

"I . . . didn't know," says Noah, taking a step back.

"No, it's not like that," I say. "I mean, we went on one date."

Noah's eyes trail away. "Okay. I understand. He's a nice guy."

"Hey," I say, and when he looks back at me, I grab his shirt and draw him in and kiss him hard.

Then I pull away and leave his house.

Chapter 82

I PULL MY car into the lot at Tasty's Diner and park around the back, out of sight. There's only one other car in the lot, Justin's Jaguar. I walk in and find him behind the bar, reading something on his laptop.

I admit—one of the reasons I came here tonight was the small chance that I might run into Aiden Willis, who apparently spends a lot of nights at Tasty's drinking. But no luck. Justin is here alone.

"Hey there," he says when he looks up, not unhappy to see me.

"Slow night?" I ask.

"It picks up in the summer," he says. He looks me over. "You doing okay?"

I take a long breath.

"You must not be," he says, coming around the counter, walking up to me, unsure of how close to get, whether to touch me—the whole awkward thing again.

I give him the short version of my lovely evening,

that in the course of investigating my uncle's murder, I may have bent the law tonight and found myself on the wrong end of an arrest warrant.

"I don't know for a fact that I'm wanted for questioning," I say. "Or that an arrest warrant was issued. But my guess is they're looking for me."

"You need a place to stay," he says. "You can't go home."

"Well . . ."

"That's no problem. You can stay at my place. I have plenty of room."

"If you're sure it's not a bother," I say. "Technically, you wouldn't be harboring a fugitive. But you might want to give this some thought."

He thinks about it for a moment. "I've always wanted to harbor a fugitive."

I laugh, in spite of the circumstances.

He looks at the clock on the wall. It's half past one in the morning. "Let's go," he says. "Nobody's coming at this point."

We take our own cars. I follow him into East Hampton, checking my mirrors at all times, feeling very conspicuous out here on Main Street at this hour.

But I don't see any patrol cars.

Justin has a house by the ocean, a beautiful two-story cedar A-frame. I park my car next to his in the garage and he lowers the door, shielding my car from any inquisitive law enforcement.

Inside, he leads me to a family room. What a place. Clean and spacious and updated. He directs me to a couch that's more comfortable than my bed, perched next to a floor-to-ceiling window overlooking a large backyard.

I sink into the couch, exhausted. Next to me, on a side table, are two framed photographs of Justin as a child. The first with his mother and father, at a Yankees game. Justin must have been, what, four or five? All of them wearing Yankees caps, smiling for the camera. Justin looking like a miniature version of his father.

The second, just the boy and his mother, when Justin is older, probably ten or so, on the beach, the Atlantic Ocean as a backdrop.

"Nice family," I say.

"Yeah." Justin nods at the photographs. "That's the last photo I have of my father. He died two days later. Crazy, right?"

"Gosh, I'm sorry," I say. "How did he die? Not to pry."

"No, that's okay." He waves me off. "He had a brain aneurysm. Healthy as a horse, worked out regularly. Then all of a sudden, he dropped dead. He just dropped."

"I'm . . . so sorry."

"Yeah." Justin puts his hands on his hips. "The truth? I don't even remember him. I was only four. That's why I keep the photograph around." He waves his hand around the room. "And that's how I have money. A healthy life insurance policy."

"Sure."

He works his jaw. "I'd give it all back to have a father." He claps his hands, shakes himself free of the memory. "Now, Miss Murphy, have you eaten?"

"Have I—oh, listen, that's not—"

"Did you eat, ma'am? It's a simple yes-or-no question."

I chuckle again. "No."

He nods in the direction of his kitchen. "I have cold cuts and some cheese and crackers. Maybe even some fruit. I'd like some myself."

"That sounds great," I concede.

He starts to leave but turns and spins. "And what are we drinking? I can't tell if you need coffee or wine."

I look at him.

"Wine," we say together.

He returns first with two glasses of Chardonnay. "Cheers," he says. "Our second date."

I realize my hands are shaking as I clink glasses with him. "You're trembling," he says. He puts his hand on my free one.

"You're safe here, Jenna. Just relax."

I nod and take a sip. It's on the sweeter side, but alcohol feels good right now, a little numbing of the anxiety.

"I'll get the snacks." He pops off the couch and heads into the kitchen.

Justin's right. Isaac would never look for me here. I'm safe for tonight.

But so much to do. I have to reach out to Ricketts to see what my status is. I need to find out more about Holden VI. I have his lawyer's name, but—

No. Justin's right about that, too. I have to slow down. If I don't get some sleep, I'm going to fall apart.

I look over the room. Picture windows on two sides. Expensive leather furniture. A big-screen TV mounted on one wall. An oak bookcase lining another wall.

A nice, handsome, rich guy. Yeah, run away from this one, Murphy. You wouldn't want to be happy and comfortable, would you?

"You look more relaxed now," he says. He's carrying a tray of cheese and salami, some sliced tomatoes and grapes, a small fancy knife, the Chardonnay bottle tucked under one arm.

He sets it all down and sits next to me on the couch.

"Now eat," he says. "And drink. And be merry."

I pick a couple of grapes off the bunch and pop them in my mouth.

"You're spoiling me," I say. "I show up unannounced, with the cops on my tail, and you spoil me."

When he doesn't respond right away, I turn to him. He's watching me.

"Maybe I like spoiling you," he says, touching my hair.

Is this guy for real? Are there actually guys like this out there? In that other world, I mean, the one Justin mentioned, where people are truly decent and honest?

And handsome, too.

He leans into me slowly, giving me the chance to decide, and I lean into him as well. This kiss is better than last time, less inhibited, more natural, each of us more at ease.

He pulls back. "You can stay here as long as you need to," he says. "You're safe here."

And then we both hear it, footsteps from a distance. From behind us, outside.

And then a piercing smash, as something—or someone—comes crashing through the picture window.

Chapter 83

SHARDS OF GLASS everywhere, something hard striking my head, and Justin and I are thrown from the couch as another body sails into us.

All three of us hit the hardwood floor.

Darkness.

Chaos and shouting and thumping and grunting and smashing.

Darkness.

I open my eyes, my head reeling, my vision blurred.

Justin and . . .

Aiden.

Struggling on the floor. Aiden on top, with the knife raised. Justin grabbing his arm to hold him off.

Telling myself to move, begging my arms and legs to work, the room angled sideways, spinning—

Move.

I lunge forward, both hands aiming for the knife. The knife, the most important thing, disarm the suspect, disable the weapon.

All my body weight, plowing into Aiden, both hands gripping his wrist, sending Aiden and me over Justin to the floor. I hit the floor again, hard, colorful bursts dancing around my eyes.

But I have the knife.

Behind me, the shuffling of feet. With everything I can muster, I manage to crane my neck around.

Just as Aiden Willis is climbing up on the couch and jumping out through the window, the same way he came.

Justin moans. Blood coming from his forehead, his breathing shallow.

Around us, chaos. A piece of lawn furniture, the one that helped Aiden break through the window, the one that smacked me in the temple, lying by the bookcase. The glass table overturned. Food everywhere. Broken glass littering the couch and floor.

And blood. Justin's blood. And mine, some of which is spilling into my eyes right now from the head wound.

"Are you . . . okay?" I ask.

"Yeah," he says, short of breath. He props himself up on his elbows. Several cuts across his cheeks and forehead from the glass. Nothing too serious, nothing life-threatening. "How about you?"

"Were you cut?" I crawl toward him. "By the knife, I mean."

He shakes his head. He looks about as stunned as I am. "What the hell just happened?"

The wind gusting through the open, shattered window.

"We have to call the police," I say, just now catching my breath.

"But . . ." Justin forces himself to sit up, grimacing. "If there's a warrant for your arrest, you can't be—"

"It doesn't matter. We have to report this."

He reaches over and grabs my hand. I squeeze back. After a moment, we help each other to our feet. He brings me close, hugging me, our chests heaving, our hearts pounding in tandem.

"I'm . . . so sorry, Justin," I say into his chest. "I brought this to you. I never should have come here."

"No, no." He cradles my head with his hand. "I want you here."

"I think . . . you just saved my life," I say.

"I'm just glad you're okay. And here I told you . . . you were safe."

I close my eyes and nestle in the comfort of his arms.

I *was* safe. Or at least, I should have been safe. How did Aiden even know I was here? I wasn't followed in my car. I checked the rearview mirror the whole time for patrol cars. The streets were deserted. Nobody followed me by car.

So how did Aiden know?

Nobody knew I was coming here.

Then my eyes pop open.

A chill courses through me.

One person knew.

Chapter 84

THE EAST HAMPTON Town Police respond to Justin's call. I know some members of that force from working on the multijurisdictional drug task force, but I don't know any of the ones who arrive at the scene. It's clear the officers know who I am when I give them my name, thanks to the Noah Walker trial. They are respectful and courteous as they scribble their notes and take photographs and scan the living room and backyard for evidence.

I sit quietly for hours, letting them do their work, waiting for one of them to inform me that there's a warrant outstanding for my arrest, or an APB, from the STPD. But it doesn't happen. No handcuffs come out. No perp walk. They just promise to keep us updated on their investigation and leave.

An armed invasion in East Hampton is something the cops take seriously, so I know they're going to be looking hard for Aiden now.

Which also means that, if Aiden has a single

functioning brain cell in his head, he's in the wind now. Gone. Skedaddled.

"I'm sorry about this," I say to Justin. "He was after me, not you. I brought him to your house."

"He brought himself." Justin touches my arm. "You're the good guy, remember?"

Not sure about that. I'd say *Justin's* the good guy. And dammit, I really wish my feelings for him went deeper than that. I wish I could manufacture some chemistry, a spark between us.

The wind whips up, straining the large pieces of cardboard that we used to cover the shattered window.

"I have to go," I say.

"Stay. It's after four in the morning. And you can't go home."

I probably *can* go home, actually. Apparently, Isaac's plan to "take care of" me doesn't include issuing a warrant for my arrest for breaking into Aiden's house.

So yeah, I can probably go home. But I won't. Not yet.

Aiden's surely not home, after all. What better time to visit his house again?

Chapter 85

I PARK MY car on the shoulder of the road, just as I did last night, and I approach his house with caution, just as before.

First blush, I see nothing different about Aiden's house. The front window through which I climbed, almost grabbing Aiden as he raced past me to his bedroom, is still open. If Aiden had come back, surely he would have closed it.

Same deal in the backyard. His bedroom window still open.

Isaac didn't close up the house? Not his job, I suppose. And he was probably distracted.

Or maybe not. Maybe he knew I'd come back. Maybe I'm walking into a trap.

The front window would be an easier entry point, but the backyard is more private, nothing but a sloping yard and swaying trees, and total darkness.

I climb into the bedroom and stand for a moment, silent. Hard to hear much of anything inside the house.

Wind coming in from windows in the front and back, simultaneously, like the entire house is whistling to me.

Daylight will come in an hour. I want to be home by then.

Start with the bedroom. A battered dresser with a framed photograph on top, one of those side-by-side frames. On the left, a beautiful young woman, probably in her late teens, with strawberry-blond hair and elegant features. On the right, the same woman, propped up against pillows in a hospital bed, her face pale, her hair unkempt, no makeup, but a radiant, beaming smile as she holds a newborn. Pretty much a standard postbirth hospital photo.

I remove the hospital photo and flip it over. On the back, handwritten in cheap blue ink:

Aiden and Mommy, 6-8-81

Aiden as a baby. And this very attractive woman, his mother. He doesn't look a thing like her.

Then again, I haven't seen the father yet.

I replace the photos and open some drawers, having no interest in his clothes or underwear but hoping for anything else that might be tucked away in here.

When I get to the final drawer, I don't find clothes at all. I find a small photo album, a cheap one you'd get at a convenience store with plastic sleeves to hold the photos.

Most of them are of his mother, going back as far as the hospital photo. Little Aiden, with those raccoon eyes even as an infant, appears once or twice. And I get the first shot of the father, his cheek pressed against Aiden's, smiling for the camera. A strong resemblance to Aiden, deep-set eyes and straw-colored hair, not by any means a handsome man.

But the mother dominates these photos. About twenty photos in all. Starting with the hospital and moving forward, chronologically I assume, but—

But she looks different as time moves on in these photos. Not older, but different. Hard to tell how much she has aged—not too much, a year or two, at most—but a definite change. Her eyes darker, deeper. Looking more gaunt, more tired.

Sick? Can't tell, but—darker, for sure. More troubled, more weary, as the photos progress, like I'm watching the story of her decline in time-lapse photography.

And then the last photo, her head turned from the camera, her hand raised in a *stop* gesture, as if she didn't want to be photographed.

And a baby bump, unmistakable, protruding from her belly, beneath her black T-shirt.

My heartbeat kicks up. A second child?

The last page doesn't contain photos. It contains two news clippings, one of them a vertical column, the other merely a headline and photo. Old articles, each of them, faded, with the crispy texture of aged newspaper.

The vertical column, stapled to the album page, has this headline:

Hit-and-Run Kills BH Woman

They're talking about Aiden's mother. Gloria Willis,

age thirty, of Bridgehampton, pronounced dead at Southampton Hospital after being hit by a car on Sugar Hill Road the previous night. The article claims she had several priors for prostitution and drug possession. Her blood analysis revealed the presence of narcotics and alcohol in her system at the time of her death.

The article is cut out of the bottom quarter of a newspaper page, so there's no date. But it can't be that hard to find out when Aiden's mother died.

Gloria Willis was a drug addict and a prostitute?

Holden VI liked prostitutes. It seemed to be a family trait, in fact.

The other news clipping isn't even an article. It's a photo, likewise ripped from the center of the newspaper and thus undated.

The photo shows Uncle Lang, in his chief's uniform, holding a child swaddled in blankets.

Beneath it, this caption:

Newborn Abandoned at Police Station

Southampton Town Police Chief Langdon James holds a newborn child, left abandoned at the entrance to the Bridgehampton substation last night. The infant will be turned over to the Suffolk County Division of Child Protective Services.

What does this all mean? Is this abandoned child Aiden? No. No, of course not. There are photographs of Gloria and Aiden in the hospital at birth.

The baby bump. The second child.

I close the photo album and leave the bedroom. In the kitchen, there is a door that could possibly be a door to a pantry, but my money says it's a door to the basement.

The basement with those wax figures, arranged perfectly, like a family portrait.

It's time I got a better look at them.

Chapter 86

I OPEN THE basement door, flip on the switch, and head downstairs.

The basement is unfinished, with an aging washer and dryer, an unused sink.

I walk toward the back of the basement, the part I saw through the open window last time. But this time, the lights are on.

The creepy wax figures, the Norman Rockwell setting around a coffee table, the faux fireplace.

On the love seat, the wax figure of the man, in a tweed coat, hair greased back, beady eyes, looking a lot like the man in the photo album.

In the rocking chair, the woman, seated and wearing a shawl over her shoulders—a dead ringer for Aiden's mother.

A third chair, empty. For Aiden?

For Aiden to sit down here and play "let's pretend" with his family?

Weird. Creepy.

Sad, actually.

I get a closer look at the woman and see, for the first time, something I didn't notice when I was shining a flashlight in here from the backyard.

On the floor, next to the woman's chair.

A tiny toy crib, for an infant.

Not a wax figure this time, just a doll—a naked doll, a tiny, bald newborn, swaddled in blankets.

A newborn.

Trying to connect it now.

Aiden at the cemetery, urinating on the tombstone of Holden VI.

Holden VI, the man notorious for frequenting prostitutes.

Gloria Willis, a prostitute—in that photo, pregnant with a second child.

The caption from that photograph in the paper: NEWBORN ABANDONED AT POLICE STATION.

"Shit," I mumble. "That's it."

Gloria Willis had two children. Aiden first, then a child she gave up at birth, abandoned anonymously at the police station.

And why would she abandon her son at the police station anonymously?

Because she didn't want him? Because she didn't want a child whose father was a monster? Because she didn't want the father to ruin the son?

I don't know. There are still some questions.

But at last, finally, I might have a few answers.

Aiden Willis had a brother. Or more accurately, a half brother.

Whose biological father was Holden Dahlquist VI. And somehow, in some way, that abandoned boy found his way back into dear old Dad's life.

Book VI

BRIDGEHAMPTON, 1993–94

Chapter 87

TONIGHT IT WILL be the beach. Sometimes it's a park, sometimes one of the taverns as it's closing and drunk patrons are stumbling out. The beach is always the best. Because there's always someone there, and they're asleep, unaware—easy prey.

His trombone case feels heavy. The boy alternates hands as he carries it along Ocean Drive toward the Atlantic, the beach, just past two in the morning.

The wind coming sharply off the ocean. Darkness, and roiling, chaotic waves.

And light.

Three small beacons of light. Lanterns, or some form of them, for the beach bums, the ones not comfortable sleeping in pitch darkness. He knows how they feel—he slept with the closet light on for years, his mother yanking on the shoestring to turn it on, then sliding closed the closet door, leaving it open just a crack. He'd beg for another inch, for additional light, and they'd negotiate it every night. She usually let him win.

Kind of funny, though, that they'd sleep out here on the beach, in a natural setting, and still require the comfort of artificial light.

What are they afraid of, scary monsters?

What scares you? Dr. Conway always asks him. *Scary monsters, things like that? Or does something else scare you?*

The boy climbs to the small perch where the parking lot meets the sand. He opens the trombone case and removes the BB rifle, fully loaded.

Safely enveloped in darkness, further shielded by the wild grass on his perch, he closes his left eye and nestles his right eye against the rifle's scope, slowly moving the barrel of the air gun through the deep blackness, through the dark, until he finds the small glow of light.

You wanna know how I feel, Doctor?

When the rifle's sight is perfectly aligned with the lantern, when the circular scope is filled with nothing but the yellow-orange glow, he pulls the trigger.

A quick, hollow *clink* as the glass breaks, and the light disappears.

Over the wind, over the rush of the crashing waves, he hears it, ever so faintly. Movement. Rustling. Someone jarred awake.

He imagines that person's reaction: disoriented. Confused. Alarmed. And worse—not knowing. Not knowing whether he should be scared. Not knowing whether he's safe. Not knowing whether something really bad is about to happen.

That's how I feel, Doc. That's how I feel, all the time.

The boy places the rifle back in the trombone

case and slides down from the sandy perch. He steps back onto the pavement of the parking lot and heads north.

The house, the Murder House, on his right, just two houses from the beach.

He knows the house. His mother comes here once a week for her job.

He stops at the iron gate. Looks up at the sad monster of a mansion, at the gargoyles and the spears on the roof, aimed at the sky, as if angrily threatening the gods—

A loud, sudden noise, the slap of doors flying open, wood hitting wood.

The boy crouches down, fear swirling inside.

A man's mumbling, angry voice carrying in the wind.

The house, still dark. But the boy finds it. The second floor, south end.

His eyes adjust. He makes out a bedroom. A balcony that wraps around the west and south sides. Double doors, flung wide open.

A man—*the* man, it must be him. *Six,* they call him, or *Number Six,* or just *The Sixth*. But it's him. Holden Dahlquist VI.

Shirtless, hair blowing in the wind, leaning over the balcony, looking down.

Trying to get his leg up on the top of the railing that borders the balcony. Trying to stand on top of it?

The boy gently places his trombone case on the ground.

Unlocks the latches.

Removes the air gun.

Looks through his scope, moving through darkness

until he finds the man, illuminated by the bedroom light behind him.

With a final thrust, the man pushes himself onto the top of the railing. He rises, wobbly, standing on a narrow perch, a tightrope walker getting his balance.

He's only on the second story, but this is no ordinary house. The man must be thirty, forty feet up. No way he'd survive a fall, especially when his landing would most likely be on the spiked fence below him.

The man arches his back, raises his arms as if beseeching the heavens. As if preparing to jump, as if preparing to fly off the balcony to another world.

The boy watches all of this through the rifle's scope.

He pulls the trigger.

The man takes the blow, staggers, flutters on his perch, his arms doing tiny circles, his legs buckling, before he falls backward onto the balcony.

Aim-fire-click. The boy can do it well. He fires two, three pellets at the man. The man, injured from his fall, confused, reacts to each shot, jumping with surprise before scurrying back into the bedroom, out of sight.

The boy smiles. Then he packs up his rifle and runs back to his house.

Chapter 88

THE BOY RETURNS the next day. An itch he has to scratch. He hasn't stopped thinking about the man. Can't get the images from last night out of his head.

No trombone case this time. And this time, during the day. No school today, and Mom says dinner isn't until two.

Ocean Drive is empty. The beach is empty. Even the beach bums, the drifters, have found someplace else to be today. It seems like everybody has someplace else to be on Thanksgiving.

The boy slips through the iron gates. It takes some effort, but he's small enough.

He walks into the front yard, which slopes upward to the house. Colorful leaves dancing all around him, the air brittle with cold, the wind coming off the ocean downright treacherous.

He's staring at the monument by the fountain—*Cecilia, O Cecilia / Life was death disguised*—when he hears the noise in the back.

He rushes to the back of the house, his feet crunching the blanket of leaves.

The first thing he sees: a rope, dangling from a tree branch, knotted in such a way that an oval circle hangs down, bobbing in the wind.

A noose. He knows the word for it. That's a noose.

A ladder. A man—the man, it's him—standing on the top rung, reaching for the noose, struggling to fit it over his head. Crying, sobbing, cursing.

And then suddenly noticing him, a trespasser, a boy, having just come around the corner.

"Get . . . get outta . . . get outta here . . . kid." His words thick and slurred. The noose in his hands, not yet around his neck.

He is so terrified, he can't respond to Mr. Dahlquist.

"I said . . . get out . . . get—" The man swaying, the ladder rocking, the man losing his grip on the noose as the ladder topples over, the man falling with the ladder to the blanket of leaves below with a muted *thump*.

The man cursing, then sobbing, his shoulders heaving. Punching the ground, swatting leaves, gripping his hair, grunting and screaming, like something inside him is trying to get out.

Then he stops. He's worn himself out. He looks around and he finds the bottle, half-filled with some brown liquid, obscured by the leaves. He unscrews the top and takes a long guzzle, empties most of the bottle, wipes his mouth with his sleeve.

Then he turns and looks at the boy.

"It was . . . you . . . last . . . last night," says Holden

Dahlquist VI. The words struggling to escape his mouth, heavy and blurry.

The boy doesn't answer. Doesn't confirm, doesn't deny.

But he walks toward the man.

"You my . . . guardian angel . . . or some . . . something?"

The boy stops short in front of him.

Mr. Dahlquist, dressed in a flannel shirt and pajama bottoms, yanks open the right side of his shirt, ripping off a button, revealing a small, deep-red wound.

"You . . . shot . . . shot me . . . last night." His eyes red and heavy and unfocused, his face unshaven but handsome. Thick auburn hair. Tall and lean.

And then the boy sees the handgun, nestled in the leaves, three feet from him, and three feet from Mr. Dahlquist.

The boy reaches down and picks it up.

It is tiny, and light. Gold and silver. A short barrel. A big looping circle in the middle of the brass grip. Nothing like the guns that cops have, or that you see on TV.

"My great . . . grandfather's revolver," says Mr. Dahlquist. "Over a . . . a hundred . . . years old. A knuckle . . . knuckle duster."

The boy wraps his fingers in the circle. Can't even fire the trigger.

"I'm a good shot," the boy says.

The man's eyes grow wide for a moment, his lips parting. His eyes shift from the gun to the boy. "That gun's . . . loaded," he says. "It has . . . bullets—"

"I know what *loaded* means."

Mr. Dahlquist stares at the gun, as if lost in a deep dream, his body swaying slightly, his chest heaving. "Give it . . . to me, kid."

The boy doesn't move. He cocks the gun, which produces the trigger, protruding against his index finger.

"What . . . are you . . . doing?" Mr. Dahlquist reaches out with his hand, palm open. "Gimme it." He lets out a noise, air whooshing out of him, and pushes himself to his feet, unsteady.

The boy doesn't move. Holding the gun, aiming it at the man. The sensation it brings, the feeling of power, control, over another person.

The boy isn't scared anymore. For the first time he can remember, he isn't scared or confused. He feels . . . in control. For the first time in his life, he's composed, in command.

He relishes that feeling. He doesn't ever want to lose that feeling. He wants to remember that feeling forever.

He doesn't ever want to go back to those other feelings he has.

He puts the barrel of the gun against his temple.

Mr. Dahlquist raises his hands, palms out. "No . . ."

The boy pulls the trigger.

Nothing but a loud *click* against his temple.

He cocks the gun again, pulls the trigger again.

Nothing again. The boy hurls the gun like a tomahawk across the yard. Adrenaline swirling inside him, his heartbeat rattling against his chest.

Mr. Dahlquist, chest heaving, eyes bugged out, looks at the boy, then at the gun in the grass, then back at the boy.

"You . . . think about . . . about doing that . . . a lot? Kill . . . killing yourself?"

The boy doesn't answer.

Every day, he thinks. *I think about it every day, every hour, every minute.*

"Me too," says Mr. Dahlquist.

Like the man can read his thoughts. Like he's the first person who understands him.

"Good thing . . . that gun's a . . . hundred years old." And then Mr. Dahlquist starts laughing. He laughs for a long time, wiping at his eyes.

The boy doesn't know what's so funny.

"We're quite a . . . pair. Can't even . . . kill ourselves . . . right."

Holden Dahlquist VI brushes himself off. "I'm cold. Are you . . . cold, kid?"

He picks up his bottle, drinks the remaining liquid, and staggers toward the house.

The boy follows him inside.

Chapter 89

A SECRET. THAT'S part of what has made these last six months so fun. It's a secret, the two of them. Nobody knows he comes over every day after school. Not his mother, not his friends—nobody knows about his new and special friend, Holden.

Well, six days a week, not seven. His mom comes here once a week. The boy doesn't come on that day.

But all the other days, the boy slips through the gate and comes around the back.

"Did you kill yourself today?" he asks Mr. Dahlquist.

"Nope. Did you?"

"Nope."

Their running joke.

"I won't . . . if you won't," Holden always says at the end. "Prom . . . promise?"

Sometimes Holden looks happy to see him. Most days, he doesn't look happy about anything else. Always unsteady on his feet, always reeking of alcohol—"my medicine," he calls it—always slurring his words, forcing them out in small spurts.

Every day there is a chore, and the reward of ten dollars. Usually the task is really small, like raking a meager pile of leaves or shoveling snow off the front walk or washing a few dishes. The boy can tell that most of this work has already been done by someone else, and only a small portion of the project has been reserved for him.

Most days they talk. The boy, mostly. He tells Holden stories about his life, or his day at school, or the things that bother him. Holden doesn't like to talk about himself, or even his family, for some reason. He likes to listen more than talk.

The boy watches Holden sometimes, even when he doesn't come in for a visit, standing outside the gate and just watching. Holden doesn't leave the house very much. He lives alone, save for the servant who comes in every other day to clean and cook and run errands.

He doesn't have any other visitors, except the pretty women who come by once in a while and stay for a few hours, looking disheveled and sometimes bruised, sometimes limping, when they leave. Holden doesn't like to talk about them, either.

Sometimes Holden paints. Sometimes he reads. Always, he drinks.

Canvases fill his upstairs, nearly all of the artwork dark, macabre. Storms ravaging houses, angry oceans, portraits of people dying, sometimes in bloody, grisly fashion, spears protruding through their midsections, gaping wounds in their chests. Anguished, tortured faces, death and destruction.

"You don't . . . have to come here . . . every day," Holden tells him one day.

"I want to."

"You have . . . friends . . . friends your . . . age? Kids in . . . school?"

"Not really," he says, when the true answer is a hard *no*. "I'm not really—" The boy isn't sure how to finish the sentence. "They're not . . . like me."

Holden turns away from his artwork and looks at him, appraises him.

"I'm not like them," the boy says.

Holden nods.

I'm like you, the boy does not say.

His other secret—the one he hasn't even told Holden: the journal.

Or diary, whatever you call it. The thick book, bound in red leather, more than two hundred years old, which the boy found around Christmastime in Holden's parlor. Wrapped in plastic for preservation.

He doesn't understand every word of what's written in that journal. Some of the words he has to look up in a dictionary. But he gets the gist of it. Some passages he reads and rereads. He doesn't dare dog-ear the pages, but he slips makeshift bookmarks into those pages.

From Winston, the patriarch:

I've come to surrender my inhibitions and any pretense of civility. I may be able to fool the authorities, but I'm far too advanced in age to fool myself. There is a monster inside me. It can sleep for days, for months. But it will never go away. It will feast on me, prey on me, until the day I die.

From Holden III, Winston's great-grandson:

The lust has taken up permanent residence within me. I can no longer resist it, any more than I can resist my very existence. Blessing or curse, it is now my identity. I will use an axe, and I will watch Anna bleed, and then I will pray for death.

Holden VI:

Like Winston before me, I have surrendered. I can say that I'm filled with remorse over the four dead tourists, but in fact what swims inside me is neither dread nor sadness, but relief.

They can't help it. That's what they're saying. It's not their fault. They can't stop it. It's a part of them. It's outside their control.

They don't want to do it. They *have* to do it.

He reads it every day. It makes him feel different. It makes him feel better. As if something inside him is blossoming, something changing, like a drug releasing its contents into his bloodstream.

He's not the only one.

He's not the only one who feels like there's a monster inside him.

And he knows that Holden's just like him, too. No matter how hard he tries to resist it, Holden's no different from him, no different from his ancestors.

So he will wait. It may take months. It may take years.

He will wait for the moment when Holden is ready to show everyone what lies inside him.

Book VII

BRIDGEHAMPTON, 2012

Chapter 90

IT'S LATE, SO late that now it's technically called early. Predawn, nearly five in the morning.

The man who sometimes thinks of himself as Holden positions the note card carefully on the desk, his fingers covered in rubber gloves. He considers cutting the words out of a magazine or newspaper, like an old-fashioned ransom note, but there is no time for that. So he will write with his nondominant hand, to avoid detection by any handwriting expert.

Again, this is him being smart.

The words come out wobbly—especially the words *bodies* and *Aiden,* for some reason—but they're legible, which is all that matters.

He closes up the envelope but, of course, does not lick the adhesive. That would be something, wouldn't it? After all this time, to make a mistake like that, leaving his DNA on the envelope?

On his way, he makes a detour and turns down Ocean Drive. It's still dark, and nobody will see him. He likes to visit this time of the day.

When he reaches 7 Ocean Drive, he steps out of his car and crosses the street to the magnificent wrought-iron gates, leans against them, pokes his nose between the bars.

He can't fit between the bars anymore.

"Bet you never expected this, did you, Holden?" he whispers.

Who could have expected this turn of events? But it's happening.

He pushes himself off the gate and returns to his car. It's not far from dawn, and he wants to deliver the note under the cover of darkness. He throws the car into drive and heads back toward town.

It isn't difficult to find the car, parked on the street, and nobody is out at this hour. He tucks the note on the windshield, safely and securely beneath the wiper blade, like a flyer advertising a liquidation sale at a sporting goods store or a buy-one, get-one-free at some fast-food restaurant.

This note, of course, has a bit more gravity to it than a coupon.

This note's going to turn everything on its head.

Chapter 91

I LEAVE AIDEN'S house and get home before dawn. My apartment is a slum, papers strewn about, the bed unmade, unwashed glasses in the kitchen sink, a musty smell.

I'm exhausted but propped up by the hum of adrenaline. I look again at the newspaper photo I pilfered from Aiden's scrapbook, with the caption NEWBORN ABANDONED AT POLICE STATION.

I must be right. It makes everything fit. Aiden's mother, a prostitute, had a second child, one fathered by Holden VI. She gave the boy up for some reason— because she didn't want a child fathered by Holden, or because she didn't want Holden to have any influence over him. But in some way I can't possibly know, father and son were reunited.

But then—why is Aiden a part of this? How does he figure in?

And more importantly—who is that second child, Aiden's half brother?

Is it Isaac Marks? He seems to be working with Aiden against me.

Is it Noah? He's the one who must have tipped off Aiden that I'd be with Justin last night, when Aiden came through the window and tried to kill me.

Isaac and Noah. Each of them a grade younger than Aiden.

Three kids who grew up together, who went to school together. Did they learn more than reading, writing, and 'rithmetic while they were in school together?

I'm buzzed but exhausted at first light. Everyone else is just beginning to waken, to start a new day, and I'm about to collapse. My brain is fuzzy from sleep deprivation. I have a lot to do, but I can't function without sleep. . . .

Bam bam bam

Let me out

Buzz buzz buzz

Please let me out

Buzz buzz buzz

My eyes pop open, mid-dream, adrenaline swirling. My cell phone vibrating. I pat the bed until I find it, pick it up, stare at it through foggy eyes.

The caller ID says NOAH WALKER.

A flutter through my chest. I'm not ready to answer it. I wait until the buzzing ends. A NEW VOICE MAIL message pops up.

I look at the clock. It's one in the afternoon. Wow. I slept for almost six hours. It felt like six minutes.

Then I play the voice mail.

Murphy, it's Noah. Just want to make sure you're okay. I have an idea I wanna run by you. Give me a call.

I punch out the phone and drop it on the bed. He has an idea he wants to run by me? *Yeah, I have something to run by you, too, Noah—why don't you explain to me who told Aiden Willis that I'd be at Justin's house last night?*

And by chance, were you adopted? Were you left abandoned at the police station as a child? Did you later discover that your biological father was part of a family line of deranged killers going back centuries?

Did you decide to pick up the mantle where they left off?

And was I, Detective Jenna Murphy, the dumb shit who sprang you from prison?

I move slowly, as if I'd been drugged last night, as if I'm recovering from a hangover. I eat some toast and drink some coffee and sit under a cascade of scalding shower water until the hot water runs out—which, in my apartment, doesn't take very long.

My cell phone rings again. I find it in the bathroom through the steam. Noah, again. I ignore it, again.

Somehow, it's four in the afternoon now.

I have to find Holden Dahlquist's son. If that baby was abandoned at the police station, he would have been turned over to Child Protective Services, like the news clipping said. He would have entered the system—he would have been adopted, or placed in a foster home. Something that would have generated a paper trail.

Did the child trace that paper trail back to Holden? Or did Holden trace that paper trail back to the boy?

I don't know. And I don't care.

Because however it happened—a paternity suit, an

adoption, whatever—Holden would have involved his attorney. And I have his lawyer's name, thanks to Noah.

So how do I get this information from Holden's lawyer, who will assert his attorney-client privilege?

No clue. All I know is that I'm getting closer, shaking some trees, and people are getting nervous.

Maybe all I can do is wait for their next move.

My phone rings again. It's Lauren Ricketts.

"Hey there," I say.

"Murphy!" Her voice excited, breathless.

"What's going on?"

"You're not going to believe this."

I push my laptop computer aside. "Try me."

"Annie Church and Dede Paris," she says. "We just found their bodies."

I close my eyes. Somebody—Aiden, Isaac, Noah — just made their next move.

Chapter 92

MY THIRD TIME in two days driving in this neighborhood. But this time, it's not directly to Aiden Willis's house. And this time, traffic is at a standstill, log-jammed as far as the eye can see, traffic down to a single, narrow lane on the turnpike.

I inch forward until I reach the barricades blocking access to the very road on which Aiden Willis lives. TV crews have lined up their vans and satellite feeds, well-coiffed reporters taking their turns before the cameras with their microphones. Once past the barricade, the turnpike opens up again, so I head north another quarter mile to Tasty's, where I park in the lot and head back to the scene on foot.

Two bodies discovered in the woods, almost directly behind Aiden Willis's property line in the backyard, buried ten feet belowground.

That was all I got from Lauren Ricketts, one of the officers on the scene. She didn't have much time to talk to me; I was lucky to get as much as she gave me.

I walk down to the barricaded street. A reporter from one of the local stations, a guy with hair so brittle from hair spray that he could weaponize it, recognizes me. He probably doesn't know I've lost my badge. Either way, he allows me inside the van and shows me the feed his station's helicopter is getting, an overhead shot.

The overhead view: A lot of the work has already been completed. A bulldozer has already excavated the dirt, and a crane has somehow lifted the bodies out of the crater. The team is on the ground, officers and forensic investigators and medical examiners.

Two gurneys are loaded into a hearse and driven off the property. I step out of the news van. Five minutes later, I see the hearse approaching the turnpike barricade, officers removing the barriers to allow it to leave.

Annie and Dede. Why now? And how did it happen?

I send a text message to Ricketts: I'm here on the scene when you have a minute. It will be a while, I expect, before her work is done.

But thirty seconds later, I get a reply: Where?

I text back, then wait. Ricketts, looking the worse for wear—dusty and dirty, like a soldier emerging from battle—but excited, too, approaches the barricade.

"It's Annie and Dede?" I ask.

She nods. "I think so. One of the fingers was missing."

Right. He cut off one of Dede's fingers and left it for the cops to find, a few years ago.

"The knife was there, too," she says. "The murder weapon."

Wow. He left the murder weapon with the girls? Our

killer was probably too careful to leave fingerprints on the knife, but you never know.

"I found the bodies," Ricketts says. "It was me."

I put my hand on her shoulder. "How the heck did *that* happen?"

"Well, that's the thing—someone put a note on my windshield this morning."

I draw back. "What?"

Ricketts looks around at the bedlam, the reporters and onlookers, practically shutting down the turnpike. "A note said I could find their bodies back here. By the large elm tree with the *X* in red spray paint." She shrugs. "Why would someone do that? Why would someone write *me* a note?"

I think about that. But she knows the answer, same as I do. The note was written to her because she was working on this case with me.

"Whoever did this—he wants you to know," she says. "Since I'm the responding officer, it's my case. I have access to all the data. He wants you to have the information, Murphy. He knows I'll tell you."

She's right. It makes sense.

"Aiden didn't work alone," I say. "There are at least two people doing this. Aiden and someone else, maybe two somebody elses. Someone who knows we're working on this case together."

She thinks about it, nods. "So what do we do now?"

"Do your job," I say. "Find out all you can. And then, when it's safe, you and I should work through this."

"Okay. Right. Okay."

Ricketts takes a deep breath. This is a big moment

for her. It's not every day a rookie patrol officer breaks a major unsolved case.

"Watch your back, Officer," I say. "They may be trying to communicate with me, but they're using you to do it."

I walk back to my car as a light mist begins to fall, my mind racing with questions. He's messing with me now, telling me something, sending me in a certain direction. But which direction? And why? How does showing me Dede's and Annie's bodies help him?

My head starts to ache. Another new piece of evidence, yielding nothing but more questions.

When I reach my car, Noah Walker is leaning against it, his arms crossed.

"Hello, stranger," he says to me.

Chapter 93

"I'VE BEEN CALLING you," Noah says. He pushes himself off my car. He's in his construction gear, jeans and T-shirt, boots, protective vest. Off work now, catching dinner at Tasty's.

I feel something between us, always that radiating heat, but this time more penetrating, turning my stomach sour.

"I guess you heard about Annie and Dede," I say.

"Yeah. You have any information?"

"None," I say. "I'm not on the inside anymore."

"But you have that friend, that young cop. What's her name again?"

Playing dumb. I'm not going to play back. "What do you want, Noah?"

He opens his hands. "Same thing you want," he says, like it's obvious. "I thought we were a team."

So did I. Before you tried to help Aiden kill me.

"What's wrong?" he says.

Ask him. Just ask him and see what he says.

"Were you adopted, Noah?"

He gives me a funny look. "Adopted? No."

"You sure?"

"Am I sure I wasn't adopted? I think I'd be sure about that."

I look him over, try to read him. I'm not getting a solid hit either way.

"It's public information," I say. "I can find out."

"I don't think so," he answers. "I don't think adoptions are public information."

"For a guy who wasn't adopted, you seem to know a lot about them."

"Murphy, what the hell?" He steps toward me. "What's with this bizarre interrogation? I've been leaving you messages—"

"By the way," I say, getting my Irish up now, "I went to Justin's last night, like I told you I would. And guess who paid me a visit?"

He shakes his head. Playing dumb again.

"Aiden," I say. "He came through a window at me. With a knife."

"He *what*? Are you okay?"

"I wonder how he knew I'd be there, Noah. Got any ideas?"

He waves his hand, like he's erasing something. "Wait a second, wait a second. You don't think it was *me*—"

"Oh, no, of course not. It was probably the long list of *other* people who knew I was going to be at Justin's last night. Oh, wait—*nobody* else knew."

"Murphy, just hold on a second."

He reaches for me, but I pull back.

"Don't you touch me," I say. "Don't come near me ever again. Just know something, Noah—I *will* figure this out. You tell your buddies, whoever's a part of this: I'm close. I'm going to nail all of you. Or die trying."

Noah steps between me and my car.

"Okay, you got to talk," he says. "Now I get to talk."

"Get out of my way, or you'll be sorry."

"Hey!"

Noah and I both turn. Justin is jogging toward us, from the restaurant.

"Is there a problem?" he asks.

Noah glares at him. Something primitive in his eyes. These two are casual acquaintances—each has said a kind word about the other—but something passed between Noah and me last night, until I mentioned Justin. I remember the look on his face, the blow he suffered, even though I insisted Justin and I are just friends.

"Nothing that concerns you," Noah says to Justin.

Justin stops short of us, looks at me. "Jenna?"

"It's none of your business," Noah says.

"You're on my property, Noah. And you're bothering my friend. So I think it *is* my business."

"Stay out of this, Justin." Noah squares off on Justin. "This is a private conversation."

Two men, the macho thing, battling over the damsel's honor. Only this damsel ain't interested.

"Uh, guys? Over here?" I wave my hand. "I'm leaving. I'll call you later, Justin. And Noah? Stay away from me."

I climb into my car and slam the door. I start up the engine and throw it into reverse, gravel flying in my wake, then head north on the turnpike, unsure of my destination, only certain that wherever I'm going, I'm going alone.

Chapter 94

I DRIVE HOME as darkness sweeps over Bridgehampton.

Aiden's still out there, and while I seriously doubt he'd be dumb enough to hang around the Hamptons to take another shot at me, I take simple precautions. I lock the dead bolt and prop a chair against the door, and I move the dresser against the small window. It's not much of a deterrent, but at least it will keep Aiden from doing another nose dive through a plate of glass.

I have almost nothing in my cupboard but some noodles, so I boil some water and drop them in.

Eat and sleep, Murphy. Or you'll crumble like a stale cookie.

But I have no appetite. My stomach is a pool of nerves and chaos.

You're getting closer, Murphy.

I push the plate of noodles aside.

But you're not there yet.

Then two things happen at once, causing me to jump from my seat.

My cell phone buzzes, and my doorbell rings.

The phone is Ricketts. I punch it on while I move to the door.

I look through the peephole at the man standing at my door.

It's Isaac Marks, our beloved chief of police.

"Ricketts, let me call you back," I say into the phone. "Your boss is at the door."

"No, Jenna, wait—"

I punch the phone off, release the dead bolt, and open the door.

And stare at the man who just might be responsible for the murder of eight people. Including the man he replaced as chief.

"Murphy," Isaac says, nodding. Wearing his uniform. Probably did some press today on Annie and Dede.

"Need you to come down to the substation," he says.

"You can talk to me right here."

He takes a deep breath, grimaces. "Don't make this difficult. Come down with me voluntarily. Make a good decision for once in your life."

"You don't have anything better to do?" I ask. "After finding two dead bodies today?"

He gives me a funny look.

"The two dead bodies," he says, "are the reason I'm here."

Chapter 95

I SIT IN the same interview room where I've sat many times, only on the other side of the table. I used to be good at this, questioning witnesses, sizing them up, reading them, making them sweat, gaining their trust, taking them on a roller-coaster ride from fright to horror to despondence to remorse to confession.

The door opens, and in walks Isaac Marks. He stands against the wall, arms crossed.

What is he capable of? Did he kill all those people, with Aiden as his accomplice? And maybe Noah, too?

Did he do something to me, along with Aiden, at 7 Ocean Drive when I was a little girl?

I've never had a bead on the guy. I was his partner for less than a year, and he was a phone-it-in cop, a guy who liked to strut around with the badge, enjoyed the power more than the responsibility. Never one to put in the extra hours necessary. Never one to go the extra mile.

But a killer? If it's true, I missed it. Never saw it.

Then again, I wasn't looking for it.

"I want some answers, Murphy," he says. "Some straight answers."

"So do I."

He shakes his head. "Doesn't work that way. Maybe you forgot."

"It does now. Or I take Five."

Most people are afraid to invoke their Fifth Amendment rights. They think it makes them look guilty. They're right, but they're wrong. Yeah, you look bad if you won't talk. But how you appear at that moment to a cop pales in comparison to the damage you do by answering detailed questions, locking yourself in.

Maybe I should be heeding that advice right now.

"The bodies were Annie and Dede?" I ask.

Isaac closes his eyes, nods. "We have a rush on DNA. We won't have it for another day or so. But there was a missing finger, and some personal articles on the bodies that the families confirmed. It's not official, but unofficially? There's no doubt."

"How did you make the discovery?" I ask.

Still planted against the wall, still stoic, but now with a gleam in his eye. He knows Ricketts and I are friends. He knows I know.

"Anonymous tip," he says.

"How convenient."

He cocks his head. "Convenient? How so?"

I shrug. "Maybe someone was getting too close to solving this whole thing. Maybe Aiden's being given up as a sacrificial lamb. A scapegoat."

"A scapegoat." Isaac's eyes narrow. "Meaning he's innocent."

"Meaning," I say, "that he wasn't the only one. He has a partner."

Isaac doesn't move. Expression doesn't break. Tough to read, because interrogators are playing a role, acting out a scene, so it could be just him doing his job. Or it could be he's sweating bullets underneath that uniform.

"A partner," he says. "Two people?"

"At least two," I say, "and the partner just fucked Aiden."

Isaac pushes himself off the wall and pulls out the chair across from me. He takes his time getting seated, settling in, training his stare on me.

"How did the partner fuck Aiden?" he asks.

My heartbeat ratcheting up. He has me in an enclosed room, in his custody. But it's a police station. There are witnesses, other cops watching through the one-way. It's not like he can silence me.

Do I want to do this? Right here, right now?

Hell yes, I do. With other cops as witnesses.

"Let's say Aiden was getting nervous," I say. "He talks to his partner. He says, 'They're getting close.' So his partner tells Aiden to leave town. Get out of Dodge for a while. Let things settle down."

Isaac nods, listening intently.

"Maybe the partner tells Aiden, 'Don't worry, I'll take care of this.' "

Isaac does a double blink with his eyes. I've just quoted what he said to Aiden on the phone last night—when he didn't see me hiding outside.

"Go on," he says, his voice flat and cold.

"But once Aiden scrams, his partner makes an

anonymous tip to the cops. Bodies are discovered a stone's throw from Aiden's property line. And ten gets you twenty there's incriminating evidence found at that burial scene, evidence that implicates Aiden and Aiden alone. My guess? Aiden's fingerprints on the murder weapon."

Isaac is silent, his eyes deadened.

"So now Aiden's an obvious suspect," I say. "Gift-wrapped, practically. And his partner walks away scot-free."

Isaac takes a breath, leans back in his chair.

"Cat got your tongue, Chief?"

His fingers tap the table. "You think Aiden's a part of this."

"Yes. I've suspected him for a while now. In fact, I tried to confront him last night at his house. He ran from me before I could question him. But . . . you already know that, don't you, Isaac?"

The dam has burst. I've all but accused him now. I don't know if this is the smart move here, but I'm running out of options. Smart or not, it's time to move.

Isaac tries to smile. It doesn't work very well.

"Tell me more about this second killer," he says.

I shrug. "He's lasted this long, eight murders over five years, so he's smart, and he's able to function in society as a normal person. A classic psychopath. He could be anyone. He could be a construction worker. He could be a ditch-digger."

I look Isaac squarely in the eye.

"He could be a cop," I say.

"A cop? Interesting." Isaac purses his lips. "Well,

Murphy, it turns out we *did* find Aiden's fingerprints on the murder weapon."

"You have Aiden's prints on file?"

"He was arrested once, long time ago, for retail theft. Shoplifting. His prints are in the database."

"Did you run *all* the databases, Chief? Even the government employees' database? Every cop in our department has their prints in that database. Did you remember to check that database, too? Or did it . . . slip your mind?"

My blood is boiling now. But the cops who are watching this interview need to hear this, all of it.

"You figure," says Isaac, "that if we found another set of prints, we'd have the second person—Aiden's partner."

"Worth a shot."

"Someone who can act perfectly normal in society. Like a construction worker."

"Or a cop," I say again.

"Yeah, you said that before," he says. "A cop?"

"Why not? It's the perfect cover. He could manipulate the evidence. He could influence the investigation."

"True," says Isaac. "That's true."

I open my hands. "What are you afraid of, Isaac? Check the government database. Or . . . are you worried that maybe your hand slipped, and your prints accidentally got on that knife?"

Now his smile comes on, full glow. He shakes his head.

"We did run the prints on the murder weapon through the government database," he says. "And we got a match."

He rises out of his chair and leans over the table, so he can whisper his next words.

"Aiden's prints weren't the only ones on that murder weapon," he says. "We found yours, too, Jenna Murphy."

Chapter 96

I SPRING OUT of my chair. A slow burn through my chest.

"No," I say. "No way."

Chief Isaac Marks is suddenly enjoying himself very much. He sits back in his chair, crosses a leg. "I suppose now you're going to claim that I manipulated the process somehow. Planted your fingerprints. Right?"

My mind racing, my throat full, everything moving too fast.

"Well, let me put you at ease, Murphy. I had no part in the gathering of the evidence or in running the prints. If you don't believe me, you can ask your bestest buddy, Officer Ricketts."

The walls closing in. The heat turned way up. This isn't right.

It can't be right.

"You can't possibly think . . ." My throat closes before I can finish the sentence.

"I can't possibly think what?" he says whimsically.

"That you had something to do with Annie's and Dede's murders? Well, let's think about that. Have a seat, if you would."

I put my hand against the wall to brace myself. My prints are on the murder weapon? That can't possibly be right. Somebody, somehow, must have—

"I said sit the fuck down, Murphy."

My legs unsteady, I find the seat and plant myself.

"So let's think this through," he says. "You have very persuasively argued that there were two killers—Aiden Willis and another person. You have also persuaded me that the second killer could be a police officer, that it would be the perfect cover for a psychopath."

"I didn't mean me—"

"So we have two girls who were murdered in the summer of 2007. Since we don't know the exact day, or even the exact month of their death, it's impossible to know your whereabouts at the time. You were a cop in Manhattan, but how easy would it have been to drive out here and do the deed, then drive back without anyone knowing? *Very* easy, I'd say."

"No. No." I push myself out of the chair, knocking it over with a clatter. "You can't actually believe that. No."

My pulse soaring. Sweat covering my brow. This is like a bad dream. This can't be happening.

"You did this, Isaac. You think I don't know what's going on?"

"Oh, Murphy, I think you know *exactly* what's going on."

Two officers, uniforms whose names I've forgotten,

step into the room. Isaac nods to them. Cool and collected, he is having the time of his life.

"Jenna Murphy," he says, "you're under arrest for the murders of Annie Church and Dede Paris."

Chapter 97

NOAH WATCHES. And waits. Two hours pass, while the midnight air moves from brisk to cold. He's underdressed in his black sweatshirt and black baseball cap and black jeans. They may not keep him warm, but they serve another purpose.

Nobody can see him in the dark.

He hears a noise—probably just the wind—and scrapes his cheek against one of the shrubs. He's been crouched low for a long time, so he stretches out, kicking out one leg at a time, like a sprinter preparing for a race, so he'll be loose when the time comes.

No police, no security.

Probably a burglar alarm on the outside door. But on the window?

Well, let's find out.

He steps out into the clearing, a small expanse of grass behind the building, but still outside the reach of the overhanging lights. Still in the dark. Still invisible.

The window has iron bars over it. He'll deal with the bars if necessary, but first he wants to see if the window has an alarm.

He raises his tire iron to eye level, angles it through the bars, and jams it against the glass. The glass shatters, an unmistakable sound, but not a very loud one, especially with a light wind. And really, nobody should be around right now, past midnight in an empty industrial park.

After shattering the glass, Noah steps back, ready to retreat into the darkness.

He hears no glass-shatter alarm. No police sirens.

But there could be an alarm on the window itself, triggered when it's opened.

So he tries that next, slipping his hand between the iron bars, carefully through the half-shattered window, until he finds the interior latch. He unlocks the window. Then, with both hands, he pushes it up from the bottom frame.

A few more shards of glass fall onto the floor inside.

But no alarm sounds. The window is not armed.

They must have figured the iron bars were enough.

They figured wrong.

Noah shines his flashlight on the screws. They are deeply embedded, some of them rusted. They won't be easy to unscrew. But his cordless drill will get the job done, sooner or later.

It will make some noise, but nothing too loud, and he's out here alone.

He just needs to hurry.

Noah puts on his rubber gloves. Then he fits the drill bit into the first screw and gets to work.

Chapter 98

"HEY THERE."

I'm sitting upright, against the wall in a holding cell beneath the substation, on a mattress about as thick and comfortable as a piece of paper, my thoughts scattering about.

My head turns toward the cell bars, toward the voice.

Lauren Ricketts, in uniform, giving me a sympathetic smile.

"Had to wait until the chief went home," she says. "He didn't want anyone visiting you. Least of all me."

I push myself off the wall, pain running down my neck and back.

"What the hell's going on, Murphy?" she asks. "How can this be right?"

That's all I've been thinking about.

"No clue," I say. "No freakin' clue. These girls were murdered in 2007. I wasn't even *here* in 2007. I didn't come here until last year—four years later."

"But you can't prove that," she says.

"How can I prove I never came here?" I throw up my hands. "Like Isaac said, nobody knows when, specifically, those two girls were murdered. June? July? August? There's no specific day or even month that the murders happened. So how can I produce an alibi? Am I supposed to have an alibi for every single day of the entire summer of 2007? It's impossible."

"Oh, Murphy. What a clusterfuck."

"And this hunting knife they found, the murder weapon? I haven't so much as touched a hunting knife since I came back here. I'm not sure I've ever held one in my life. I mean, it's not physically possible."

Ricketts doesn't have an answer for that. Neither of us does.

"What about Aiden?" I ask. "They're looking for him?"

"Oh, yeah. His prints on the weapon, the bodies behind his property—and we heard from East Hampton PD about what happened at Justin's house last night, the attack. There's a manhunt."

"We have to find him, Lauren," I say. "We have to find Aiden."

"Believe me, we're trying—"

"No, I mean, *we* have to find him. *Isaac* doesn't want Aiden found. He's the one who told Aiden to leave. And if he *does* find Aiden, he'll kill him. Y'know, make it look like a shootout with a suspect or something. He wants Aiden gone or dead. So Aiden will take the fall all by himself."

Ricketts looks at me, doubt creeping into her eyes. "Jenna . . ."

"You think I'm wrong?"

She lifts her shoulders. "I'm not sure. Are you? Are you so sure it's Isaac? That Isaac's a killer? That he framed you for this?"

I'm not sure of anything anymore. Aiden, Isaac, Noah—or some combination thereof. My fingerprints magically appearing on murder weapons without my knowledge. I feel like I'm in the Twilight Zone.

"The fingerprint match was clean," Ricketts says. "I found the murder weapon, that hunting knife, myself. And I delivered it directly to our forensics team. I watched the guy run the analysis, Murph. Isaac didn't tamper with that. So how could Isaac get your fingerprints on the knife?"

"How could anybody? But somebody did. Probably easier for him than anybody else."

Ricketts steps back from the cell bars, her focus dropping to the floor.

"You don't believe me," I say.

She shakes her head slowly. "I'm not ready to believe our chief of police is a serial killer. No."

I stare at her. She looks suddenly uncomfortable, shifting her weight from one foot to the other.

"He got to you," I say. "He told you what a great job you're doing. How a big promotion could be in the works. A bright future. 'But just watch out for Jenna Murphy! Don't believe anything she says. She's bad news. She'll take you down.' Is that about it, Officer Ricketts?"

"No, that's *not* it." Some steam in her voice, color to her face. "I'm following the facts wherever they lead."

"Including my prints being found on that hunting knife."

"Yeah, including that." Her eyes rise to meet mine.

A gulf between us, suddenly, the cop on the one side, the suspect on the other.

"So we're done?" I say. "You and me?"

"I told you, Murphy. I'll follow the facts wherever they lead."

Another one bites the dust. First Noah, now Ricketts. My "team" has been reduced to a team of me, myself, and I.

"Then I have some facts for you to follow," I say. "Aiden's mother. Gloria Willis."

"Yeah?"

"She was killed in a hit-and-run," I say. "Find out when."

She thinks about that, nods. "I can do that."

"And while you're at it," I say, "find out whether Isaac or Noah Walker was adopted."

Chapter 99

JOSHUA BRODY, ONCE Noah Walker's attorney and now mine, walks into my holding cell as Lauren Ricketts leaves. He looks around and then looks at me.

"Thanks for coming in the middle of the night," I say.

"Part of the job." He scratches the back of his neck, his eyelids heavy. He looks around again. "So is this the cell where Noah supposedly confessed to Chief James?"

I shake my head. I'm not in the mood. Joshua beat me up pretty good over that during the cross-examination.

"Talk to me," I say.

"The arrest is solid," he says. "Your prints on the murder weapon are sufficient for probable cause."

"We don't know it's the murder weapon," I counter. "They don't have DNA back yet. We don't know that it's Annie's and Dede's blood on the knife."

Brody looks at me like he would look at a child who

just doesn't get it. "The hunting knife was covered in blood and was found with the bodies," he says. "You're right. They haven't conclusively tied the knife to the dead girls, but c'mon. Dead women with stab wounds, a bloody knife found inside . . ."

"Did they die of stab wounds? I thought their skulls were crushed."

"I don't know," he says. "Autopsy's tomorrow. But whatever the cause of death, they have sufficient evidence for an arrest. Remember, they don't have to show guilt beyond a reasonable doubt until trial."

The trial. I can't believe it. I'm going to be tried for murder?

"You have to get me out of here," I say.

"Best I can do is try to get a reasonable bond," Brody says. "The hearing's tomorrow. But on two counts of murder? It will be hard. If you get bond at all, it will be a million dollars. Maybe two million. Which means you'll need to come up with ten percent. A hundred thousand, two hundred thousand, whatever."

"Noah Walker bonded out. He was charged with a double murder."

"Noah Walker had a girlfriend for whom a million dollars was pocket change. I don't suppose you have a trust fund or anything like that?"

I let out a bitter laugh. I have a little bit of money saved up, but nowhere near that kind of scratch.

"I'll come back tomorrow," Brody says. "Unless there's anything else I can do."

I drop my head against the wall. But then it comes to me. There is one thing.

Murder House

"You're a lawyer," I say.

"Last I checked, yeah."

"Maybe you can help me with something," I say.

Chapter 100

JOSHUA BRODY RUBS his unshaven face, mulling over everything I've just told him.

"So you think the sixth and last Holden Dahlquist had a son. A son who's running around killing people."

"That's my theory, yes. A pretty good one, I think."

"And you think this boy is the younger half brother of Aiden Willis, the other person whose prints were found on the knife."

"Yes. The half brother was abandoned at birth. But somehow, in some way, he was able to discover his biological father, or vice versa."

"So you figure there might be some records of this? Maybe the biological mother filed a paternity suit. Or there'd be adoption records. Or both."

"Something," I say. "But whatever it may be, I'm pretty sure—"

"It would involve his attorney," Brody says. "Yes, I agree with that much. If a guy like Holden Dahlquist had a problem like that, his first call would be to his lawyer. Sure."

"So that's why I'm asking about his attorney," I say.

"Okay. Well, to answer your question: These days, most files are stored electronically. But Holden the Sixth, as you call him, he died . . . when, again?"

"He died sometime in 1994," I say.

"Okay." Brody nods. "So any records would be no later than ninety-four. And back then, nobody was creating the kind of electronic files we have today. There would be hard copies."

Hard copies. That's what I thought. That's what I was hoping.

"Where would those hard copies be?"

"Something that old, they would be in off-site storage," he says. "But it's not like you have access to them. These are attorney-client documents. You'd need a court order."

"Then let's get one."

"On what grounds? Your hunch?"

"Yes, my hunch."

He shakes his head. "It would be hard. Nearly impossible."

"How long would it take?"

"Very long. Months. There'd be a vicious court battle."

"I don't have months, Mr. Brody. I have to know this *now*."

"Murphy," he says, "you haven't even been indicted yet. When you are, there will be a court case, and maybe we can explore that. But now? Right now? No chance. Zero."

I deflate. He's making sense, I know it. It would take months to get court-approved access to those files, if they even exist at all.

Unless . . .

"Just out of curiosity," I say, "where would the law firm keep its old hard copies of files?"

"Oh." Brody shrugs. "Most law firms around here use a place out in Riverhead called Dunbar Professional Storage."

Dunbar Professional Storage in Riverhead.

"I know the name of Holden the Sixth's lawyer," I say. "A guy named Finneus Rucker. Do you know him?"

"I *knew* him," says Brody. "He died a few years ago. Cancer, I think."

I deflate. "But I looked up his law firm online. Rucker, Rice and Spong."

"Yeah, his firm still exists. But he doesn't."

"But—his firm would still have the records."

Brody nods. "I'm sure they do."

"Well, do you have any idea if his firm uses that storage facility?"

Brody's eyes narrow. "No, I have no idea. But like I said, wherever they keep those records, you'd have to go through a judge."

"Absolutely," I say.

"Don't get any dumb ideas. You're in enough trouble already."

"Of course."

Murder House

Dunbar Professional Storage in Riverhead.
Remember that.
That's my next stop. If I ever get out of this jail cell.

Chapter 101

NOAH REMOVES THE third iron bar from the window and decides it's enough.

He tosses his cable cutters in through the open window.

He stuffs the flashlight into his front pocket.

Using the remaining iron bar as a brace, he hauls himself up and onto the window ledge.

His head through the open window, his body dangling outside, he looks around. It's dark, but he can see enough to get the drift.

An office. A desk covered in paper, a chair, file cabinets.

He has no choice but to fall in headfirst. He can't see the floor, but he knows it's littered with broken glass now.

He lunges forward and catches the chair to break his fall, but fall, and fall hard, he does. An awkward landing, his jeans doing enough to protect him from the glass. Could have been a lot worse.

He brushes himself off and turns on his flashlight just for a second. Then he opens the locked office door, looks beyond it.

Darkness, until he finds the light switch.

And then: a warehouse, a wide and long and high expanse of space, filled with nothing but rows and rows of shelving, a rolling ladder in each row to reach the higher shelves. He looks around long enough to get his bearings. Then he kills the lights. Those overhead lights are no good. Someone could detect an intruder from a mile away.

With his flashlight, he roots around the office and finds the index. He leafs through it until he finds what he's looking for.

Then he walks into the warehouse, his footsteps echoing, the space pitch-dark except for the beam from his flashlight.

He finds the right row, and then the right shelf. He's ready to break a lock with the cable cutters, but there aren't any locks on the doors.

Even better.

He riffles through the files, the flashlight in his mouth. It takes him longer than expected, the risk of detection growing with each moment that passes.

When he finds it, he flips through the pages briefly—time does not permit a thorough review—shining his flashlight over each page, before he closes it up, the story from the newspaper on top:

Newborn Abandoned at Police Station

He takes the news clipping and the other documents, stuffs them back in the file folder, and places the folder under his arm. Then he closes the doors and climbs down the ladder.

He retraces his steps, closing the office door, climbing back out the window, falling into the grass.

He scrambles back to his hiding spot in the shrubs and looks over his handiwork. If he had all the time in the world, he could replace the iron bars. But he doesn't. And there's no replacing a shattered window.

But that's okay. He didn't leave any prints. He didn't even have to break any locks. The file doors he opened are now closed up, like before, with no evidence that Noah looked inside that door versus any of the other hundreds of doors in the facility.

So tomorrow, when the employees of Dunbar Professional Storage arrive at work, they'll know someone broke one of their windows and got inside, but that's all they'll know.

They won't know who broke in. They won't know where he looked.

And they'll have no idea which files he took.

Chapter 102

THE COURTROOM, FILLED with media and spectators. The discovery of the Yale students, plus the ex-cop who starred prominently in the Noah Walker case—too much for the reporters to stay away. I've become tabloid fodder.

Justin, sitting in the front row, trying to give me an upbeat expression when I walk into court. I can't bear to make eye contact with him.

The lawyers make their arguments. Joshua Brody argues that the evidence against me is weak—the fingerprints on the knife, but that's all. No motive. No evidence that I even set foot on Long Island during the summer of 2007.

Sebastian Akers rises for the prosecution. Oh, how he must savor the opportunity to prosecute me. He's never forgiven me for blowing his conviction against Noah Walker.

"Of course she's a flight risk," he says. "These women were stabbed, and her prints are on the knife. It's hard to

441

imagine more direct evidence of guilt, short of capturing the whole thing on video."

The judge, an old guy I've never met named Corrigan, raises his hand.

"Bond will be set at two million dollars," he says. "In the event bond is made, the defendant will surrender her passport and will submit to electronic monitoring. She will be restricted to home confinement with waivers for work, attorney or medical visits, religious observation, and household errands under the supervision of the sheriff's office."

The judge bangs his gavel.

We won, but we lost.

Two million dollars? That means I have to come up with two hundred thousand to get out of here. I don't think I have *ten* thousand to my name, and what little I have is going to Joshua Brody as a retainer to defend me.

"I'll pay it," Justin calls out to me as the courtroom grows noisy. "It'll take me a day or two, but I have it."

"I—can't ask you to do that," I say.

He looks at me, almost wounded. "You didn't ask," he says.

I don't know how to respond. I absolutely hate being dependent on someone else for anything. But I don't have any other options.

Before the deputies escort me from the courtroom, my lawyer asks for a moment.

"We're lucky to get bond at all," he says. "Whoever that guy is in the front row, if he's offering to pay it, you should say yes."

"But I have to wear an electronic ankle monitor? And home confinement?"

"It's pretty standard these days," he says.

I know—but then I can't do what I need to do. I'll be trapped.

"And Jenna," he says. "I called that facility, that off-site storage place I use. Dunbar Professional Storage?"

"Yes?" I perk up.

"I know someone there. I'm a longtime client. Anyway—Holden's lawyer, Finn Rucker? His firm *does* use that facility."

I nod. "Okay, good."

"But you should know something. Someone broke into their facility last night."

"What?" I draw back from him.

"Yeah. Broke through a window. Removed the iron bars. Had the run of the place. So just in case you were getting a dumb idea like breaking into that warehouse—which we both know you were thinking—you should know that they've doubled down on security. They're posting guards around the clock now."

"What—what was taken?" I ask.

"They don't know. Practically impossible to tell. I think they're doing an inventory, but it's so hard to know. There are literally millions of files there." He looks at me, cocks his head. "Why? You think this is related to your—"

"Of *course* it's related," I whisper harshly. "Whoever broke in there—he did it so I wouldn't find those files."

"*Jenna.*" He squeezes my arm. "You're watching too many conspiracy shows."

"He took it so I wouldn't find it," I say. Realizing that I probably sound paranoid to him, just another irrational client.

The guards intervene, place me in handcuffs, and escort me out.

I glance back at Brody, who looks like he's never felt sorrier for anyone.

Then I glance at Justin, who looks like he's just lost his best friend.

Chapter 103

BOND WAS SET at two million dollars this morning for Jenna Murphy, the former Southampton police detective arrested for the murders of Dede Paris and Annie Church, the Yale sophomores whose disappearance in the Hamptons five years ago sparked a massive manhunt. . . .

Noah Walker paces back and forth in his living room as the newscast—*News at Noon*—talks about Murphy and the murders of the Yale sophomores.

Noah is exhausted, not having slept last night, after breaking into the storage facility and removing those files. He needs to sleep, he needs to shower—but he can't do anything but think about his next move.

He passes the couch, the pile of documents he took from the warehouse.

The news clipping with the catchy headline, NEWBORN ABANDONED AT POLICE STATION, which tells most of the story right there.

And the letter, aged and dusty, having sat in a file inside that storage facility for the better part of twenty years now. The nice stationery, the fancy letterhead bearing the name of the private investigator hired by Holden VI, with tabs behind the letter, supporting documentation:

Mr. Dahlquist:

This private investigation was undertaken on your behalf, at the direction of Mr. Finneus Rucker, Esq., your attorney. This investigation is thus covered by the attorney-client privilege and will remain confidential.

You asked us to determine whether a woman named Gloria Willis, of Bridgehampton, mother of Aiden Willis, gave birth to a second child approximately eight years ago.

Noah looks away from the documents, thinks of the things Jenna Murphy has said to him over the last few weeks.

At the cemetery, when she told him her theory for the first time: *Holden the Sixth left behind a son,* she said. *A son who wants to restart the family tradition.*

And yesterday, in the parking lot at Tasty's: *Were you adopted, Noah?*

Holden left behind a son. Were you adopted, Noah?

He looks back down at the letter:

The answer to your question is yes. Eight years ago, Ms. Willis did give birth to a second child at Southampton Hospital but left the hospital with her

child only hours later, without filling out any
paperwork. We believe that she abandoned this
child later that evening at the Bridgehampton Police
Substation (see attached news headline).

He reads through the packet of information behind
the letter—the hospital records, the county adoption
records, the photographs.

Noah goes upstairs to his bedroom loft, finds the
handgun he hasn't held in years. Checks it for
ammunition. Stuffs it in his pants. Puts on a clean shirt,
pulls it down over the gun.

He grabs his leather jacket on the way out and hops
on his Harley.

Her apartment isn't far. And she's definitely not
home. She's in jail, stuck on a two-million-dollar bond.

He parks his Harley outside her apartment and
approaches it. It's broad daylight, and cars occasionally
whisk by on Main Street. But no pedestrians approach.

His heartbeat speeds up. Should he do it?

Yes.

He slams against the door, four times, five times,
violent thrusts, wood splintering, sharp pain in his
shoulder, until enough of the door frame has been
compromised that he can reach inside and unlock the
dead bolt and open the knob from the inside.

He pushes open the battered door and he's inside
Jenna Murphy's apartment.

A mess. A train wreck.

A timeline, on her wall, covering all of the murders.
Right. He's seen that before.

But there's something he hasn't seen before. On her desk, beneath the timeline. A newspaper clipping, jagged edges, still with tape attached to all four corners, as if she removed it from something:

Newborn Abandoned at Police Station

Noah's heart skips a beat.

She knows, he thinks. *She already knows.*

Knowing what he has to do now. Wishing it hadn't come to this.

He was really starting to like Jenna Murphy.

Chapter 104

ANOTHER DAY IN this cramped, drafty jail cell. A special kind of torture for me, listening to the hustle and bustle one floor above me, hearing the police department at work, reminding me of how far I've fallen in such a short time.

Isaac wanted it that way. He normally would transfer me to the Suffolk County Jail after my bond hearing, where I'd be placed in administrative segregation because I'm a former cop, who can't be put in with ordinary inmates. But the jail is over-crowded, which gave Isaac the excuse to keep me here, so close and yet so far from the job I once had, the job I loved.

Footsteps. Somebody approaching my cell. It's not lunch. I ate a half hour ago. Tea and crumpets, maybe? A complimentary massage?

No, and no.

It's Isaac, staring at me, looking . . . not so happy. I mean, he's not Mr. Sunshine on a good day, but . . . why shouldn't he be happy? He should be dancing a jig, the way things are going.

He produces a key from behind his back and opens the door. He walks in and sizes me up. I try to put on a brave front, to look like I'm holding up much better than I really am. But I can't hide the dark circles under my eyes, and I haven't showered in two days; my hair is flat and oily. My clothes look exactly as they should—like I've slept in them for two nights.

He doesn't just look unhappy. He looks like he just swallowed a bug.

Why the long face, Isaac?

"You have the right to remain silent," he says to me. And then he runs through the rest of the Miranda warnings. I could say them backward by now.

"Why are you Mirandizing me?" I ask.

"I want you to acknowledge I've made you aware of your rights," he says.

"Fine. Done."

But fresh Miranda warnings? Only one reason for that.

He wants to question me on a new topic.

"What happened in 1994?" he asks.

I draw back. Why is he asking me about 1994? When I was just a kid. The year that thing happened, when I disappeared, only to be found on the beach by 7 Ocean Drive. The day my parents whisked me away from the Hamptons, never to return during my childhood.

Seven hours of hell, Aunt Chloe called it.

"There was a missing-persons report that summer," he says. "It lasted less than a day. I saw it myself. July—"

"I have nothing to say to you, Isaac. Zilch."

Isaac steps back. He can't be surprised that I'd clam up. His face turns tomato red.

"I just want you to know," he says, "that I know you're behind this. I don't know what kind of crap you're pulling here, but I'm going to figure it out. You may have won this battle, but you won't win the war."

What the hell is he talking about? What battle did *I* win? As far as I can tell, right now I'm getting the royal crap beaten out of me.

He opens his hand. "You're free to leave," he says.

Oh. Justin came through with the money that quickly? Quicker than he thought he could.

But this doesn't seem right. Isaac doesn't have any handcuffs.

There's a protocol when you bond out. You're transported to the sheriff, who makes arrangements for your home confinement, gets a list of addresses for doctors and lawyers and grocery stores so they can input the coordinates into the GPS. Then someone fits the ankle bracelet on you.

But until then, you're still locked up. You're handcuffed and transported.

"I said you're free to leave," he says. "You're being released."

"I don't understand."

Isaac shoots me a look. He thinks I *do* understand. He thinks I've pulled some kind of fast one, that I'm just playing dumb.

"You're no longer under arrest for the murders of Dede Paris and Annie Church," he says.

My head spins, some strange version of hope floating through me.

"The DNA came back on the murder weapon," he says. "None of the blood on the knife matches those girls. Their stab wounds don't match up with the knife blade, either. That knife wasn't used to kill Dede and Annie."

I stand up for the first time, unsteady, certain I'm not hearing this correctly. A bloody knife, with both Aiden's and my fingerprints on it, but . . .

"We did get matches on the blood, though," says Isaac. "Not Dede or Annie, but two matches. One of the matches was you, Murphy."

Like the floor has dropped out from beneath me, like I'm spinning, falling . . .

"My . . . blood?"

My blood on the knife? My prints and my blood?

"And . . . who else's blood?" I manage. "You said . . . two matches."

"You know," says Isaac, fuming. "You damn well know. Tell me, Murphy. Tell me everything."

But I can't. I *don't* know. I don't know what the hell is going on.

"That knife wasn't used to kill Annie and Dede," says Isaac. "It was the knife used to kill Holden Dahlquist the Sixth, on July 13, 1994. The same day that you went missing for seven hours."

Chapter 105

I STUMBLE OUT of the police station with a bag holding my cell phone, wallet, keys.

I don't know what to do.

I don't know where to go.

I look at my hand, at the inch-long scar across my palm. The only injury they found on me, Aunt Chloe said, after I went missing for seven hours and then was found on the beach, otherwise unharmed.

That scar must have come from the knife. The knife that had my fingerprints on it. It cut my hand. I must have touched it, too.

My prints, my blood.

On the knife that Holden VI used to kill himself.

On July 13, 1994.

I was there. I was there when it happened.

What the hell happened that day?

Aiden, I think. I need to find Aiden.

But how? And whom can I trust at this point? Not Noah. Not Ricketts, not anymore.

Only one person I can think of.

I make the call, and not fifteen minutes later, Justin's Jaguar pulls up in front of the substation.

He pops out. "What happened? How did you get out?"

I shake my head. It's a long story. A story I don't even understand.

"Justin," I say, "I need someone I can trust. That's a rapidly dwindling population, I'm afraid."

Justin nods, a look of concern on his face.

"Can I trust you?" I ask.

"Only one way to find out." He smiles, then realizes the comment fell flat. He touches my arm. "Hey, listen. You know how I feel about you. I haven't made a secret of that. And I know . . . I know you don't feel quite the same way about me. I know I'm not your type."

"No, it's not—"

"I'm not dumb, Jenna. And I'm not blind, either. But I'm here for you if you need me. Maybe—maybe I'll grow on you. Maybe not. But either way, if you need something, you know all you have to do is ask."

I hate this. I hate having to rely on someone else. Especially for this.

"Aiden already tried to kill me once," I say. "He'd do it again. And someone's working with him. There are people in this town who don't want me to figure this out, and they'll kill to stop me."

Justin takes a deep breath, then nods.

"I'm in," he says. "Let's do it."

Chapter 106

JUSTIN DRIVES HIS Jaguar toward his house, having just gotten an earful from me.

"Okay," he says, glancing at me. "So something happened to you here in July of 1994, and you think Aiden had something to do with it."

"Yes. And someone else did, too."

"Okay," he says. "And you think this 'someone else' is Aiden's younger half brother."

"Yes. And his father is Holden Dahlquist the Sixth."

Justin takes a deep breath. "You think Holden the Sixth, and his newfound son, and Aiden, tried to kill you when you were a little girl."

"Something like that," I say. "I don't have it all figured out. Maybe—maybe I was their first. Maybe I was a dry run, a test, to see if they could pull it off. Whatever it was, something must have gone wrong, because *Holden* ended up dead, not me."

"Wow. And now the son is carrying on the legacy."

"I think so," I say. "So the key is, who is Holden's

son? Who is the baby abandoned at the police station? Isaac? Noah?"

Justin shrugs. "Can you ask them?"

"They wouldn't admit it. I asked Noah if he was adopted and he said no. But that doesn't mean he's telling the truth."

"Or maybe he doesn't know," says Justin. "Maybe his parents never told him."

"Oh, come on."

"No, seriously, Jenna—how do any of us know that our parents are our biological parents? We take our parents' word for it, right?"

"There are birth certificates," I say.

"Those are just records. They can be doctored."

"Or there's a strong physical resemblance."

Justin makes a face. "Maybe. But not always. I'm not adopted, but I don't look a whole lot like either of my parents. I'm kind of a blend of them. Do you look like your parents?"

I think about that. "Actually, I got my looks and red hair from my Irish great-grandmother." I turn to Justin. "Okay, point taken. So you think there might be someone running around with Holden the Sixth's genes, and he doesn't even *know* it?"

"Possibly. Do you think there's some kind of serial-killer gene that can be passed down from generation to generation? Even without your knowledge?"

That one is definitely above my pay grade.

"We have to find Aiden," I say. "Aiden's the key to all of this."

"Okay, so how do we do that?"

"I have no idea."

Justin touches my arm. "Don't say that. Think."

Think. He's right, think.

"If I'm Aiden," I say, "I don't have much money. I don't have a car. I can't go to airports or train or bus stations. I can't use a credit card for a rental car or a hotel. How do I run? I could hitchhike."

"Have you gotten a good look at Aiden?" Justin asks. "Would you pick him up?"

"Stranger things have happened. But okay. What else? He could boost a car, I suppose. But I don't have access to that kind of information right now, recent auto thefts or anything else. I don't have any resources at all."

"I'll try not to take that as an insult," says Justin.

"You know what I mean."

If I'm Aiden, what do I do? If I'm Aiden . . .

If I'm Aiden . . .

Wait.

"Maybe he didn't run at all," I say. I turn to Justin. "Maybe he's right here in town. He's lived here his whole life, right? If he could find a place to hide for a while, it would beat the hell out of traveling somewhere with no money, no resources."

Justin shakes his head.

I slap my hand on the dashboard. Could it be that simple?

"I can't believe this," I say, "but I think I might know where he is."

Chapter 107

NOAH JUMPS ONTO his motorcycle, his heartbeat racing faster than the bike's engine as he heads across town.

He parks his Harley and removes the gun from his pants, placing it inside the saddlebag on his bike. Cops don't like it when you walk into a police station with a handgun.

Noah enters the police substation. Someone at the front desk, behind a plate of bulletproof glass.

"I'm here to see one of the people in the holding cell," he says.

"Are you a lawyer?" the man asks, though he doesn't seem to think Noah fits that bill.

"No, but this is important," he says. "Jenna Murphy is—"

"Jenna Murphy isn't here," the man says.

"Oh—where are you holding her?"

"We're not. She was released half an hour ago."

"She was *released*? On bond?"

The officer on duty looks over his glasses at Noah. "Sir, whoever you are, I can't give that information to you."

He looks outside. She was released half an hour ago? But . . . he saw her car at her house just now. How did she leave? She wouldn't have walked—

Justin, he thinks. *She must be with Justin.*

"I need to speak with Isaac," he says. "I need to speak with the chief."

"Sir," says the duty officer, "you can't just waltz in here and demand to speak with the chief."

"It's important."

"Sir, the chief isn't—"

"Listen!" Noah slaps his hand against the plate of glass. "I need to speak with him and I need to speak with him now!"

"Hey."

Noah turns at the sound of the voice. A uniformed officer approaching him, a young woman—Murphy's friend, the rookie cop, Lauren Ricketts.

"What's going on, Noah?" she says.

"I have to talk to Isaac," he says. "Right now."

"Why? Tell me what's going on."

Noah thinks it over. He doesn't know Ricketts. He has no idea what she knows and what she doesn't know.

"No," he says. "I'll only talk to Isaac."

Chapter 108

JUSTIN PULLS HIS car into his garage in East Hampton. The garage door grinds to a close behind us.

"So tell me," he says. "Tell me where you think Aiden is."

"Later," I say.

"Later? Why later?"

My cell phone buzzes. Caller ID says it's Lauren Ricketts. I don't dare answer. I let the call go to voice mail and then play the message on my speakerphone:

Murphy, it's Ricketts. I'm not sure what's going on, and I probably shouldn't be calling you, but—but whatever, I'm calling you. Listen, about twenty minutes ago, Noah Walker had a private conversation with the chief, and the next thing I know, Isaac has issued an APB for you. They think you're with Justin.

I look over at Justin, whose face has gone pale.

He mobilized the SWAT teams, Murphy. We're coming after you with everything we have. You should surrender at the station before something bad happens. I can coordinate it with you. Please, call me before this gets out of hand.

Justin turns and looks at me, the gravity of what we've just heard sinking in. "He just released you, and now he's after you again?"

After talking to Noah, apparently. And here I thought Noah didn't get along so well with the chief.

I get out of the car, and Justin follows suit. We go into his house, his beautiful, spacious kitchen.

"You said you have a gun," I say.

"Um—yeah, I do," he says, still distracted. "Hang on."

"And a flashlight," I call out to him as he leaves the kitchen.

I take a breath. Isaac and Noah got together, had a nice little chat, and now the STPD is after me with full force.

Isaac and Noah. They've made a very public show of not getting along so well. An act? An act I fell for hook, line, and sinker?

"Okay." Justin returns to the kitchen with not one gun but two, holding each of them with two fingers, the barrels dangling down.

"A regular arsenal," I say.

But not really. One is a shiny, polished revolver, new and, from the looks of it, unused. The other is a beat-up revolver with a pearl handle, a vintage piece, a .38 special with a very short, maybe two-inch barrel that is probably thirty or forty years old.

"Take your pick," he says, placing them gently on the kitchen table.

I laugh. "Take my pick? How old is that thirty-eight special?"

Justin shrugs. "My dad bought it years ago—probably the seventies. This new one, I bought. I assume it works."

"You assume?"

He shakes his head. "Never used it. Bought it for home protection. Some silly notion that I'm safer with it. I have a feeling if I ever had to use it, I'd end up shooting myself in the foot or something."

"You're probably right." I choose the shiny new revolver, hold the gun toward the floor, pop open the cylinder, and confirm the presence of rounds in all six chambers.

Justin looks at all of this like he's scared to death of guns.

He probably is. This isn't his thing. He isn't cut out for this. He's a nice guy, a wonderful guy, but he lives in a world where people are decent and gracious. He doesn't live in a world full of bad guys. That's where we differ. That's where we'll always differ.

"And the flashlight," I say.

"Oh—right," he says. He removes one from a kitchen drawer and hands it to me.

Then he claps his hands, as if ready for action, but the paleness of his face suggests otherwise. "Where to?" he asks. "Where do you think Aiden is hiding out?"

I stuff the revolver in the back of my pants. "I have to go now," I say.

He looks at me. "Don't you mean *we* have to go?"

"No, I mean I have to go. This is my problem, not yours."

"Jenna—"

"You've done enough. You've given me your gun and a flashlight, and a ride. But I can't ask for anything else."

"For the last time, you *didn't ask,*" he says. He puts his hands on my shoulders. "You can't do this by yourself. I may not be a veteran police officer or some Navy SEAL—shit, I wasn't even an athlete—but you can trust me. I'd do anything for you, Detective Murphy. Haven't you figured that out by now?"

I look into his eyes. Yes, there's something there, something more than gratitude for all his attempts to help me. Maybe what I feel for him is enough. Maybe. But now is not the time to be gauging my emotions.

I have to do this, and I have to do it alone.

"I'll just follow you," he says.

"Not if I shoot you in the leg."

He laughs, in spite of the circumstances.

Then the doorbell rings. We both turn our heads toward the front door. Justin takes a couple of cautious steps backward and peeks beyond the kitchen, presumably through a window.

"Police car," he says.

"East Hampton PD?"

"Southampton," he says. "That's Isaac Marks at my front door."

Chapter 109

"SHIT," I SAY, panic swirling inside me. "*Shit.*"

Justin puts out a hand for caution. "I'll take care of it. Stay here."

"I should hide."

"No place to hide. He'd see you running through the kitchen. Sit tight."

Justin walks out of the kitchen. A moment later, I hear him opening the front door. I steel myself, close my eyes, listen carefully.

"Isaac," he says.

My blood goes cold.

"Hello, Justin. I'm looking for Jenna Murphy. Is she here?"

"Here? No. No, she's not here. Why?"

"Do you know where she is?"

"No idea," says Justin. "Is everything okay?"

"It's a police matter. When did you last see her?"

"I dropped her off at her house earlier today. After she was released from custody."

"And?"

"And nothing. That's it. I dropped her off and I drove here."

"You drove here? Why not to the restaurant?"

A pause. "I'm the boss, Isaac. I come and go as I please. I didn't think I had to get the police department's permission."

"You come and go as you please." A pause, this time from Isaac. "You wouldn't be lying to me, would you, Justin? Because you know it's a crime to lie to a law enforcement officer, don't you?"

"I think I've heard that somewhere," Justin says. "Oh, I know—it was on TV."

I smile but don't dare laugh.

"You think this is funny? Listen to me, and listen to me very closely. We are actively seeking to bring Jenna Murphy into custody. She's not who you think she is."

"I think she's an honorable and decent person."

"Well, she isn't. I'm gonna take her down. The easy way or the hard way, I'm gonna do it. I prefer the easy way. The safe way. But if you're helping her evade us, you become an accessory. You ever heard *that* term from TV? It means you're just as guilty as she is."

Justin doesn't respond.

"I've known you a long time, Justin. Never had a beef with you. You've always been a good egg. And you make the best damn barbecue shrimp on Long Island. So I'm going to give you one more chance. And think about what I said. You can help us find a dangerous person who's committed some very serious crimes. Or you could lie to me and spend a very long time in prison. And I will personally see to it that you do."

My heart is sinking as Justin himself sinks deeper and deeper into my problems.

"I understand." Justin's tone is cold and flat.

"Do you know where Jenna Murphy is?"

I hold my breath. I'd come out right now and show myself, and spare Justin any further trouble. But if I do, it's game over. I'll never know the truth.

"I have no idea where she is," Justin tells Isaac.

Justin returns to the kitchen, his face ashen, after Isaac drives away.

"Well, that was fun," he says, trying to maintain a brave front, but he can't even bring himself to smile.

"I'm so sorry," I say. "I'm going to leave now."

"I'm going with you."

"No. I leave now, you have plausible deniability. I'll scrape the serial number off your gun so it can't be traced back to you. No one will ever know you helped me. But if you go with me, you spend the next decade in prison. Assuming you don't get killed."

"I don't care." He touches my arm. "I understand the risks. But you need help, and the risk of losing you is worse than . . ." He swallows hard. His eyes fill. "I don't usually—I've never responded to anyone like I do to you."

I step away from him. "Justin, you know I can't reciprocate those feelings. I just don't know—"

"Yeah, I know. But I don't care. You just haven't figured out what a wonderful guy I am yet. You will, someday."

I drop my eyes and smile. Still trying to make this

easier for me. Maybe he's right. Maybe someday I'll feel about him the same way he does about me. If there is a *someday* in my future.

"At least tell me where you're going," he says.

"No, Justin."

"Then take my car."

"No. They find your car and that's the same thing as you coming with me. You're aiding and abetting. I'll walk. Better I stay off the roads, anyway. And I'm in no hurry. I need the sun to go down before I make my move. I'll wait until midnight, probably."

"Call me on your cell, then. At least tell me you're okay."

"Turning my cell phone off right now," I say. "So they can't track me."

Justin lets out air, shaking his head. "Oh, Jenna. Don't say good-bye to me. Just—tell me this isn't good-bye."

I walk up to him and plant a soft kiss on his cheek. "This isn't good-bye," I say, before I head out his back door.

Chapter 110

MY THOUGHTS ZIGZAGGING in every direction, trying to make sense of it all—Noah, Isaac, Aiden—not to mention the entire Southampton Town Police Department after me, heavily armed and prepared for combat. But something is telling me that the key to this is Aiden Willis. If I can get hold of him tonight, if I can surprise him and subdue him, I can finally put an end to this.

The walk from East Hampton isn't bad. It's about seven miles, which under different circumstances would be a typical day's jog for me, and it's safer than driving. When you're on foot, you're nimble. You can escape into crowds, cut corners, hide among foliage—you can obscure yourself in any number of ways.

The sky overhead is threatening rain, which will royally suck if it happens, but the good news is that in the meantime, it darkens the sky and brings the rough equivalent of nightfall prematurely.

I make it to the beach and kick off my shoes and

tromp along the sand, the restless Atlantic Ocean to the south, the carefree breeze playing with my hair. I don't look like a fugitive, and unless the police are conducting beach patrol, I'm practically invisible to them.

So I sit in the sand, less than a mile from my destination, watching the foamy tide crash ashore and recede, waiting for the moment to arrive. If my guess about Aiden is right, he's settling in right now, nestled in his hiding spot, his guard slowly lowering.

Somewhere in the house at 7 Ocean Drive.

At midnight, I make the decision—it's time. Hopefully, he's asleep, or at least close to it. Not expecting company, in any event.

I step out of the sand onto the parking lot and look up at the mansion. No lights are on. No visible sign of life. Not that I expected Aiden to be hosting a party.

I walk along Ocean Drive until I reach the front of the house, my nervous system catching up now, sending warning signals to me, filling my chest. Justin's revolver in my right hand, the flashlight in my left.

I try the driveway entrance, expecting resistance, planning to push it open and squeeze myself between the twin gates. But it's not locked. I push one side open and enter, then close it back up, without allowing my imagination to wonder why the gate would be open.

My breathing erratic, my legs heavy, I walk up the driveway to the fork—to the right, the walk heading up the hill to the house; to the left, the driveway continuing on to the carriage house or whatever it is.

For some reason, I don't take the familiar path, the

one I've traveled several times during my investigation, up the sidewalk toward the house.

This time, I stay left, remaining on the driveway, walking toward that oversize carriage house.

Not knowing why. Unable to place it in my brain, but feeling something inside me growing, spreading like poison.

And then a flash through my brain like lightning.

Walking, shoved from behind, forced forward, wondering what it is, a stable, a garage, a separate house, where is it he's taking me?

Walk. Move! Walk faster, you stupid girl!

I suck in a breath. I should turn around now. I know that. If I had any sense, I'd turn and run. Instead, I shine my light forward, just briefly, to see if there's anything in front of me, up the driveway toward the structure.

I move slowly—

Faster! Walk faster!

—as I approach it. Tall double doors for an entrance. On the ground, at my feet, a long chain with a broken lock.

Somebody unlocked this door recently.

He's here. Aiden is here.

I put my flashlight in my mouth and raise my gun. With my free hand, I pull on the door handle and yank it open.

In one motion, I drop to a knee, remove the flashlight from my mouth, and click it on, sweeping it over the space inside.

Open air. Two stories tall. Big, yes, but empty.

Empty.

Stains on the concrete floor from automobiles, once upon a time. A rack on the wall for tools, though none are present right now. A carpenter's desk, too, a wooden top with steel legs, with an old saw and a vise on top.

Empty. But a different kind of empty.

I shine my light along the floor by the desk. There are circles on the floor, dust markings, from where the legs of the tool desk rested not long ago.

"Someone moved that desk," I mumble to myself. Recently. Very recently.

Why move it?

I shine the light along the floor.

In the area where the desk once stood, before being moved, there is a break in the concrete. An outline. A square. Lying on top of it, a short length of rope.

I squat down for a closer look. Same color paint, but the surface of the square looks different.

I try to pick up the rope, but it's stuck to the floor, attached somehow.

And the surface is . . . wood, not concrete.

A wooden square with a rope attached to it.

I grab the rope and, this time, pull on it hard.

The wooden square jars loose.

"What the hell . . ."

I pull harder, and the piece of wood pops upward.

A burst of cool air escaping from beneath it.

"A hidden door," I whisper.

There's something underneath this floor.

Chapter 111

MY GUN POISED, I pull the trapdoor fully open. I turn on the flashlight, dust particles floating in the beam, aiming it down into the darkness below.

A ladder, a wooden ladder, leading down several steps to a floor.

My lungs thirsting for air, my head spinning. A small tremor spreads through my limbs, immediately turning into a full-scale tremble, my hand shaking so hard I can hardly hold my gun. I don't dare cock the revolver's hammer, putting the gun in ready position, for fear I'll start shooting, maybe even hitting myself.

The ladder so wobbly
I don't know how far down it will go
The boy yelling at me, "Move! Move!"

I drop to my knees and suck in air, desperately seeking breath while my lungs seize up.

I was here. I was in this carriage house. I went down this ladder.

Sweat stinging my eyes, my shirt stuck to my back,

my vision spotty, my heart pounding so fiercely I can hardly move.

"Move, Murphy," I whisper. "Move."

I tuck the gun into the back of my pants. I fish around the open space with one leg until my foot finds a rung on the ladder.

I move slowly, hoping to minimize the noise, praying I don't lose my grip, the ladder itself quaking along with my hands, my arms and legs.

Darker, the lower I climb.

Colder.

White noise filling my ears, bits and pieces of memories, the sounds of the boy's voice taunting me—

Move! Keep moving, stupid girl

—my body shivering so violently, my feet hitting the floor, something hard like marble. I remove my gun and aim it in all directions, spinning, somehow keeping my balance, as I shine the flashlight all around.

A tunnel. I'm at one end. The other end, I can't see. High ceilings, width sufficient for two, maybe three people to stand side-by-side.

The lightning bolts between my eyes, the fragments coming back.

Wearing sandals and the bathing suit Mommy just bought me, a Lion King *T-shirt over it. So hard to walk in these sandals, especially when the boy pushes me, afraid that if I fall he'll get mad, afraid of what he might do to me—*

Stepping forward gingerly, every forward advance an effort, half blind from the sweat burning my eyes, electricity filling my body—

I don't understand what is happening, why this boy is

making me go down here, where are we going, where are we going—

The beam of my flashlight dancing along the floor, the walls, the ceiling, and then I see it.

A wall. The end of the tunnel.

A doorknob.

I tuck the flashlight under my left arm, my left hand holding a wobbly gun. With my right, I reach for the knob.

I steel myself. "You can do this," I tell myself.

I turn the knob slowly, then whip the door open.

Chapter 112

I POINT THE gun inside the room, my pulse pounding against my temples.

The smell of bleach and burning oil. A square, windowless room, a single kerosene lamp on one side casting flickering orange light about. Next to the lamp, a sleeping bag, unfolded, but nobody inside it. Nobody in this room, period. No chairs or furniture or anything except—except something near the back—

A spear. Protruding from the floor, a long narrow missile with a sharp top—

"No," I say. "No." Hot tears blurring my vision, running down my cheeks into my mouth.

I step into the room, my words echoing between my ears, the walls moving, the room spinning, the cries, the horrific, ghoulish screams from all directions filling my head, my legs unsteady as I move forward—

—as I move toward the other end of this square room—

—because somehow I know, some internal compass

is directing me, some force is moving me toward a door at the other end of the room, a door I can't see but that I know, somehow I know is there.

Everything slowing down, like I'm moving through quicksand, but *I must reach the door,* I have to reach it for some reason, but my legs are suddenly numb, up is down, down is up, the floor is suddenly rising up to meet my face with a violent smack, sending shock waves through my skull, jarring the roots of my teeth.

The revolver bounces out of my hand on impact with the floor.

Everything fuzz and fog, but I can't let go now, can't let go now.

The flashlight underneath me—I fell on it—but the gun . . .

I need the gun.

My head lifting off the floor, searing pain over my right eye, nausea rising to the surface; I'm woozy and disoriented. Patting the floor around me. Forcing myself to my knees, light flickering in and out from the glow of the kerosene lamp, the gash over my eye making me pay a severe price every time I whip my head from one side to the other, but I need the gun—

Words screaming at me, but I can't make them out, so loud that I can't hear them, echoing through my head with such force that I can't understand them, what is he saying, what is he—

Come with me

Footsteps, coming from the other side of the room, near the door I can't see, footsteps, someone's coming—

Come with me

Murder House

Come with me
The gun, I need the gun—
Where is that gun?
The click of a doorknob, the groan of a door opening.
And Aiden Willis walks in.

Chapter 113

AIDEN, THE SCARECROW hair sticking out from his baseball cap turned backward, his features lit up with the flickering orange light, holding something in his hand, a thermos, closing the door behind him.

I hold my breath, hold my body still, searching for the gun only with my eyes.

There. I spot it. Justin's revolver, over by the wall.

"Oh—" Aiden jumps upon seeing me on the floor to his left. The thermos falls from his hand, clanging and bouncing on the ground. He falls against the wall and struggles to keep his balance.

I slide my body toward the far wall and grab the revolver, cock the hammer.

"What—how—what do you—"

I grip the gun with both hands, trembling so fiercely that I couldn't possibly aim properly.

My insides on fire, my head ringing, nausea and bile at my throat, oxygen coming in tiny, thirsty gulps—

The door opens

Bright light streaming in, and a boy, a boy with scarecrow hair

With some reserve energy I didn't know existed, as if I'm watching someone else perform the task, I rise to my knees and aim the gun toward Aiden.

Aiden's eyes go wide; he looks ghoulish in the intermittent orange light, pinned against the wall, watching me.

Lightning, thunder between my ears.

Come with me

Come with me

The gun so unsteady in my hand, rising and falling, swaying back and forth.

Aiden watching me, watching the gun bob up and down, back and forth.

Tears filling my eyes again, my chest heaving, my throat so full I can't speak—

Come with me

Sobbing and shaking, the gun moving all over the place—

Aiden watching me, watching the gun.

Come with me

The gun dropping to my side. I can't do it. I know it and Aiden knows it.

Aiden pushes himself off the wall, straightens himself.

Looks at me, just for a single moment, those darting eyes making contact with mine.

Come with me

Then he walks toward me. No sudden movement, just slowly approaching me.

Come with me

The boy with the scarecrow hair

Aiden places a hand over my gun hand, then carefully removes the revolver from it.

I look up at him, on my knees, helpless.

He uncocks the revolver, points it upward, pops open the cylinder, and empties all six rounds from the chamber into his cupped hand. He locks the cylinder back in place and hands the unloaded gun back to me.

"Aiden, wait," I manage, my throat full, my words garbled.

Then Aiden Willis disappears through the door from which he entered.

"Please, wait," I say as I get to my feet, the synapses not firing properly, but I manage to stumble and stagger toward the door.

Chapter 114

NOAH WALKER SITS on his idling Harley, down the street from Justin's house in East Hampton. He's logged a lot of miles tonight looking for Jenna Murphy, driving loops around Bridgehampton, hitting some familiar spots like Murphy's apartment, Tasty's, the Dive Bar, even Aiden's house, but always doubling back here to Justin's place.

Because Justin's the best bet for finding her. Jenna was last seen, according to Isaac, being picked up outside the police station by someone driving a Jaguar, which almost assuredly means Justin. And it would make sense she'd call him.

They aren't together right now, apparently, because all Justin has done for the last couple of hours is pace back and forth in his living room.

There he is right now, standing close enough to the window on the west side of his property that Noah can see him. Checking his watch. Pacing. Running his hands through his hair. Nervous. Anxious.

Maybe it's time to drive around some more, do another loop.

He jumps at the sight of Justin's garage door lifting. A moment later, the Jaguar pulls out of the driveway, backing up not far from where Noah rests on his Harley.

This is it. He's sure of it.

He waits until Justin has turned off his street before he starts up his bike and drives. He turns in the same direction as Justin and follows him from a distance, only a small amount of traffic on the roads but sufficient to hide his presence.

Justin travels west on Main Street toward Bridgehampton. Noah keeps his distance, considers even killing his lights, but he sees no indication that Justin knows he's being followed.

If only he knew where Justin was going. If he knew that, he could—

Justin's car slows near the cemetery. He puts on his signal for a right turn.

Wait.

Wait a second.

He's heading for Ocean Drive. Sure. Of course. He's going to that house.

And I know a shortcut. I can beat him there.

Noah veers off Main Street and drives his bike across the open field of the cemetery, taking a straight line instead of the right angle Justin is forced to take by driving on the streets.

Noah crosses through the south end of the cemetery and hits Ocean Drive before Justin has even turned off Main Street. With a good two blocks' lead on Justin, he kills the lights on his bike and guns it forward, making sure he'll arrive at the mansion at least a full minute before Justin.

He stops at a group of trees just off the street, very close to the mansion. He looks back, seeing the headlights of a car in the distance, heading his way.

He removes his gun and flashlight from his saddlebag. Then he ducks into the shrubbery across the street from the mansion and waits. Only moments later, the Jaguar pulls up in front of the mansion.

Justin gets out of his car without any sense that Noah is nearby, or that he's been followed, jogging up to the mammoth gate blocking the driveway. He grabs it, then pushes it open and heads onto the driveway.

Noah creeps closer, obscured by darkness, in soft grass, watching Justin.

Justin jogs slowly up toward the dark house, looking at it. Looking, as well, at the old carriage house at the end of the driveway.

Noah crosses the street and hides behind the Jaguar.

Justin, at a crossroads, decides to head up the driveway, toward the carriage house. Noah slinks up to the gate by the curb and pushes it open as softly as he can.

A flashlight comes on, Justin illuminating the space in front of him.

Noah sees what Justin saw, the reason he chose to head up the driveway.

The door of the carriage house is wide open.

Justin starts jogging toward it, while Noah follows, moving at a slightly faster clip, closing the distance but taking care not to announce himself.

"Jenna!" Justin calls out in a harsh whisper. "Jenna?" He approaches the carriage house with caution, slowing his pace.

Then Justin disappears inside.

Noah reaches the doors and readies himself.

Chapter 115

NOAH PEEKS INSIDE the carriage house.

Justin is shining his flashlight around. "Shit," he says.

You don't know what shit is, Justin.

But you're about to find out.

Noah springs forward into the room. Before Justin can do anything more than turn around, Noah plows into him, sending him sprawling, crashing into the wall. Noah grabs Justin and throws him facedown on the cement floor, gripping his hair, shoving the gun into the back of Justin's neck.

"Where is she?" Noah growls.

"Noah?" Justin manages, catching his breath. "Is that . . . you?"

"Tell me where she is, Justin, or I'll kill you right now."

His fingers tightly gripping Justin's hair, Noah jerks Justin's head upward and then down, hard, onto the cement floor.

"That's me being nice, Justin. You wanna see me when I'm mean? This is your last chance," says Noah. "Where is Jenna Murphy?"

"I don't—I'm looking for her, too. I thought she might've . . . come here."

Cool air to Noah's right. He looks over, shines his flashlight over the trapdoor, wide open.

"Did she go down there?"

"I'm telling you, I don't know."

"Don't bullshit me."

"I'm not bullshitting you." Justin's voice weaker from the blow to his head. "What . . . what are you going to do to her?"

Noah presses the gun into the soft space beneath Justin's skull. "You should be worried about what I'm going to do to *you*."

"Don't hurt her," Justin says. "Please, Noah, just . . . don't hurt her."

Noah leans down, close to Justin's face. "Justin, I can't tell if you're a liar or a fool."

He cracks Justin's head against the floor again. Justin goes limp with an abrupt groan.

Noah stands and shines his flashlight along the walls, over the carpenter's desk. Some things hanging on the walls that could be helpful.

Then he shines the light back down on Justin, unconscious but still breathing.

He pats Justin down and feels something in the front pocket of his trousers. He removes a tiny gun, one of those old Saturday-night specials, a beat-up vintage .38 with a pearl handle.

"I think I'll take this, Justin," he says. He stuffs the little gun into his pants pocket, a nice complement to his own gun.

"I haven't decided what I'm gonna do to you yet," he says. "Let's see how I feel after my nice, friendly chat with Jenna Murphy."

Chapter 116

I STUMBLE THROUGH the door, the door through which Aiden Willis just escaped, away from the smooth marble onto something different, the floor broken and dirty. Once I'm clear of the doorway, I slam the door behind me.

And take a deep, delicious breath of oxygen.

The air is dry and stale, but I don't care. I'm breathing again, on two feet again. I'm out of that awful room.

Come with me

I put one foot in front of the other, my legs unsteady but better, feeling better now.

"Aiden," I try to call out, my throat and mouth so dry I can hardly speak.

A small room, it feels like, not open air. I'm reaching out for the walls when something slithers across my face—

I jump back and wave my hand around, connect with it again.

A string, dangling in the air.

I reach out, making my hand still, and the string falls

back against my hand. I grip it and pull down.

A light, a single naked overhead light, comes on.

Hanging from the walls, medieval weapons. Lances, stars, battle-axes, cat-o'-nine-tails, maces. A full menu of torture devices.

I shudder but shake it off. I need to figure out a way out of here.

Three of the four walls are covered with this weaponry, but one wall is naked. Nothing hanging on it. Nothing but smooth wood.

Immediately next to it on the adjoining wall, a small button.

A buzzer?

With a trembling hand, I press the button.

I know, somehow, what will happen next: The wall slides open.

I drop to a knee, my weapon useless now without any bullets, and click on the flashlight.

A corridor. Naked walls, concrete floor.

The basement of 7 Ocean Drive.

Follow me

C'mon

"Aiden!" I call out, but I get no response. The hallway turns a sharp left into a giant room, just as dark as everywhere else in the basement. I shine my flashlight over the room, though the beam is weakening and I need to preserve the battery.

"Aiden!"

Boxes, old furniture, photographs and artwork—the kind of stuff in any basement.

And a staircase, leading up.

C'mon
Follow me
Be quiet

I approach the staircase slowly, not trusting my rubbery legs, my head throbbing like I have a hangover from being inside that room.

I take the stairs just as carefully, lightly touching each step before transferring my weight, unsure of the stability of this staircase.

When I reach the top of the stairs, the door is ajar.

Aiden must have blown through here a few minutes ago.

I take a breath and push the door open.

I turn the corner and shine the flashlight, the dwindling beam, over the open foyer of the house. The front door is straight ahead of me, across the foyer and the two ornate anterooms.

The words coming at me so fleetingly, like smoke, whispers—

Run go get out of here
Run!

"Aiden!" I call out again, my voice shakier this time, echoing upward, nothing in response but a groan from this haunted mansion.

I hear something upstairs, an elongated sigh. A house sound or a human sound?

I take a step up the stairs.

You don't wanna go up there

Squeezing my eyes shut, as if it will lock out the whispers between my ears.

Don't come up here

490

Go, leave, don't come up here

"Aiden, please talk to me!" I cry.

The pressure mounting inside my chest again, the momentary reprieve I felt after leaving that room vanishing in the snap of a finger, everything returning like an avalanche, my heart pounding again, sweat on my face once more.

Every step an effort, every instinct telling me to turn back, run out the front door, there's danger upstairs, but I move forward regardless, because I have to know, I have to finally know.

Even if it kills me.

I reach the landing on the second floor, the double doors open onto the second-floor hallway. I walk through like I'm in slow motion, like I'm wading upstream, but I'm not stopping now, so I turn left and head toward the master bedroom, the bedroom where Melanie Phillips and Zach Stern were brutally tortured, where various Holdens over the years committed brutal acts on others and on themselves.

"Aiden Willis!" I call, forcing the words out. "Aiden, I was wrong about you! I know that now! You—you saved my life that day. I remember now. You got me out of this house. Just—just please, *please* talk to me!"

One foot in front of the other down the ornate red-and-gold hallway, shining my dwindling flashlight beam in front of me, until I reach the threshold of the master bedroom.

"Aiden, are you in here?"

I shine my light over the room. Empty. Nobody here. But near the bed, a lamp—another kerosene lamp, the liquid full in the hourglass-shaped clear bowl, a short wick protruding from atop the metal dome. Next to it, a book of matches. I tuck my gun in the back of my pants and pin the flashlight between my arm and body. I strike the match and light the wick, producing a healthy orange glow about the room.

Light, precious light, as my flashlight is on the verge of dying.

I head to the corner of the room, to the French doors and the wraparound corner balcony outside. I push open the French doors, cool air hitting my face, the wind swirling, and look out over Ocean Drive to the west.

I see a glimpse of him, the signature straw hair, the slight hunch to his posture—Aiden Willis running north on Ocean Drive, away from the Atlantic, from this house, from me and my questions, and disappearing into the woods.

I lean against the railing, the wind playing with my hair, my eyes fixed on that point where Aiden ducked into the woods. I'll never catch up with him. He's too far ahead, and much more familiar with every nook and cranny of this town.

Come here, he said to me as a boy. *Follow me.*

I'm trying to pull more from that memory, but the more I reach for it, the farther away it gets. I shake my head. It's no use trying to force it. It's like turning on high beams to see through fog; it only muddies it up more.

I remember his face, remember his words, remember the relief sweeping through me when he guided me out of that basement and up those stairs.

"But then what?" I whisper.

And why—why did Aiden come through Justin's window the other night and try to attack me with that knife?

Deflated, defeated, I push myself off the railing. I curve around the corner to enter the bedroom from the south.

Where Noah Walker stands, training a gun on me.

Chapter 117

"DON'T MOVE, MURPHY. Don't move or I'll shoot."

I show him my empty hands. The flashlight left behind, on the bed. Justin's revolver stuffed in the back of my pants, which he can't see.

Focus, Murphy.

Assess—assess the situation.

I'm on the balcony by the railing. Noah is maybe eight, ten feet away, inside the room but just at the entrance to the balcony. The lamp, behind him, is sufficient to give me a decent look at his features—his eyes narrowed from the wind licking his face, stinging his eyes, his face crumpled up in anger, the gun trembling in front of him.

Anger—at me? For screwing up his plans? I guess he was having a pretty easy time killing people before I came along.

"I should kill you right now," he hisses.

"What's stopping you?" I say. My eyes cast about for options, but it's pitch-black out here on the balcony.

494

About my only option is jumping from the balcony and hoping I avoid the spiked fence, hoping I survive with just some broken bones.

Or charging him. He doesn't look that comfortable holding that gun. Most of the people he killed were cut or stabbed or impaled. Maybe firearms aren't his thing.

Still, he's so close to me. He couldn't miss me if he tried.

"I have a few questions," he says.

"And you think I'm going to answer them?"

"Yeah, I do," he says, "because I still haven't decided whether I'm going to kill your boyfriend Justin."

Justin. Roped into this because of me.

"Justin has nothing to do with this, Noah. Leave him out of it."

Noah pauses. "He doesn't know anything?"

"Nothing."

"Nothing?" he asks.

"Nothing."

"Don't fuck with me, Murphy. I'm done with you screwing with my head. You know I actually started to *care* about you? What a freakin' joke."

Emotion in his voice with these last words, choking on them. Shifting his weight from one foot to the other. He's upset, coming unraveled.

Something I can use, maybe.

"I started to care about you, too," I say.

"*Shut up!* I don't wanna hear that!"

He takes another step closer to me. I can almost feel the bitterness radiating off him. His chest heaving now.

Shaking his head. "Why?" he asks. "Why did you do all this?"

"Do all what?" I ask as calmly as I can. "Try to catch a killer? Because it's—"

"Stop it! Is that how you wanna play this? Even now, when there's nobody else here to hear your lies? Do you *want* me to put a bullet through your head? Because I'll do it. I swear I will."

The gun bobbing slightly. Do I have a move here?

Dive to the ground and make him shoot wildly in the dark? Then I see it, over Noah's shoulder, at the far end of the bedroom, where the hallway meets the doorway.

The beam of a flashlight, searching along the floor.

Justin, limping forward down the hallway.

The swirling wind drowning out any noise he's making, at least for me, and probably for Noah, too—at least I hope so.

Stall. Stall for time, Murphy.

"You're the one who broke into the warehouse and stole those attorney files, aren't you?" I ask.

"Damn straight I am," he says. "Guess I beat you to them."

Justin drawing closer. I'm willing myself not to look too closely at him, not to signal Noah.

Keep that flashlight beam down, Justin, or Noah will see it.

The flashlight turns off—Justin is at the threshold of the bedroom now, and the glow from the kerosene lamp is sufficient.

But the closer he gets, the more likely it is Noah will

hear him, no matter how violently the wind swirls through this balcony and into the bedroom.

No matter how quietly Justin approaches, with long tiptoe strides.

Keep Noah talking.

"That was a nice move," I say. "Getting those lawyer files before I could."

Something in Justin's hand, something long and thin—a golf club?

A golf club.

"Are those the last remaining copies?" I ask.

"You tell me, Murphy."

Justin raising the golf club, holding it with two hands.

"How the hell should I know?" I ask.

"Shut up," Noah spits. "Just stop with all your bullshit."

Justin is only a few steps away now. It's all I can do to pretend I don't see him, not to tense up, not to give away his presence.

"What bullshit?" I ask.

"I said *shut up!* I'm done with this, Murphy. You know what's in those lawyer files. You've known all along."

Justin stops, the club poised like a baseball bat, ready for the most important swing of his life.

"I have no idea what's in those files," I say.

Noah does a double take, his head cocked, a hint of doubt crossing his face.

Then his eyes suddenly become alert, and he spins to his right just as Justin swings the golf club.

Chapter 118

ALL AT ONCE—

Noah spins to his right and instinctively ducks—

The violent swing of the golf club, grazing the top of Noah's head before continuing its momentum and splintering the wood on the balcony doorway—

Noah's gun, hitting the other side of the doorway during his spin, falling from his hand onto the balcony floor.

I lunge for the gun as Noah, stunned, falls against the opposite side of the doorway.

I scoop up the gun in my hands and fall forward into the bedroom.

"Don't move, Noah," I say, jumping to my feet.

Noah, dazed, has managed to remain upright. His woozy eyes drift over to me and his gun, his Glock, now in my hands, now pointed at him.

"Shit," he says. He touches the top of his head and finds blood on his fingers.

"Hands where I can see them," I say. "Show me your palms."

"Or what? You'll shoot me?"

"He has my gun," Justin says, still clutching the golf club with two hands, like a weapon.

He doesn't mean the revolver he lent me—that's stuffed in the back of my pants.

"That old thirty-eight I showed you at my house," Justin says. "Noah has it. He jumped me and took it off me."

I look Noah over. In one jeans pocket, something— some papers rolled up and shoved inside, the edges protruding. The other front pocket, unclear, but a slight bulge, which could be the .38 special.

"What are those papers in your pocket?" I ask him.

"The lawyer papers," he snarls. "In case you didn't believe I had them."

"And the other pocket?"

He shakes his head. "Nothing. I threw Justin's gun in the front yard."

"Show me your palms," I say. "The first second you don't, I shoot."

Noah, his brows curled in a frown, shakes his head, a bemused laugh escaping from him as his eyes bore into me. "You're good, Murphy. You're very good. I gotta give you that. But guess what?"

He takes a step toward me.

"Don't, Noah."

"Isaac's preparing warrants for your arrest as we speak," he goes on. "For all of the murders. All of them.

Did you know that, Justin?" Noah nods in Justin's direction. "Does he know everything?"

"Shut up, Noah. It's not going to work. And you take one more step, I start shooting."

He takes another step toward me, but slowly, still showing his palms.

Pushing me, but not pushing me too far. Testing me.

"Why didn't you kill me when you had the chance?" he asks. "That night you broke into my house? You buzzed a bullet right past my ear, but you couldn't finish me off."

"That's enough, Noah."

"Why'd you get me out of prison?" he says.

"Because your trial was unfair," I say, my voice shaking. My hands are shaking, too.

"My *trial* was unfair?" He lets out a bitter laugh. "You kill, what, eight people but suddenly you care about the justice system?"

He takes another step.

I fire a round into the floor near his feet. Noah jumps back, startled for a moment. But he quickly recovers.

"That's the second time you deliberately missed me," he says. "Why, Murphy? Why not kill me?" Heat coming to his face now, the snarl returning. "Why? So you could kill everyone I ever cared about and watch me suffer?"

His eyes are filling with tears now, his shoulders trembling.

"I don't know who you think you're fooling," I say. "I didn't kill anybody."

My mind racing. Signals flying in all directions. *He's screwing with you, Murphy. He always does this. Anyone who could be this good, for this long, made a living out of mind-fucking people.*

He takes another step toward me.

This time, I take a step back.

"Jenna, what are you doing?" Justin says.

"Yeah, Murphy, what are you doing?" Noah says, tears falling down his cheeks, his hands clenched in fists. "Aren't you going to kill me?"

"I'm taking you in."

"Jenna, you heard what he said," says Justin. "Isaac's gonna arrest *you*. We know that's true. You heard Isaac say it himself at my house. Noah's gonna walk away from this!"

Noah takes another step toward me, his eyes searching mine, pure bitterness in his expression.

I take another step back, an earthquake inside my head.

"You can't let him get away with this!" Justin cries. "He killed Melanie! He killed your uncle! He sent Aiden to my house to kill *you!*"

Aiden.

Aiden at Justin's house with a knife, coming through the window.

Noah shakes his head slowly, his eyes still on mine.

Aiden.

And then it happens. It comes to me, all at once, just with the mention of Aiden's name.

I can't be sure. I couldn't prove it in a court of law.

But I think I finally figured it out.

I fire another round into the floor. Noah jumps back again.

His momentum temporarily stopped, I reach into the back of my pants and remove the revolver Justin lent me.

"Justin, catch," I say.

Justin drops the golf club. I toss him his revolver, which he catches in both hands.

Noah steadies himself, looks to his right; Justin is now pointing his revolver at Noah.

Then Noah turns again and looks into my eyes, the odds against him mounting now, me holding Noah's Glock, Justin holding his own revolver. Two people, two guns, two different angles.

I search his eyes for an answer. Every time I've looked into those eyes, I've received mixed messages, a series of crisscrossing signals, heat and passion and rage and lust and pure hatred.

My gun wavers as I replay everything in my head, sorting through it all, trying to make the puzzle pieces fit, everything flying at me at once like a tornado.

"Justin," I say.

"Yeah?"

"Aiden didn't come through your window to kill me."

"What—what do you mean?" he asks.

"He came through that window to *protect* me," I say. "To protect me from you."

Chapter 119

STILL FACING NOAH, the Glock in my hand still trained on him, I see, in my peripheral vision, Justin move the gun away from Noah, toward me.

"I'm so tired," I say. "I'm so tired of all of this."

"You're not thinking clearly," Justin says. "But all the same—keep that gun aimed at Noah. If it moves one inch toward me, it's a bad outcome for you."

"It was you," I say. "You're the one who brought me to this house when I was a little girl. You and Holden the Sixth were going to kill me. Your first murder together, your initiation into the family or something, I don't know. But I *do* know that Aiden rescued me. For some reason, Aiden never told anyone about you. Maybe you held something over him. That bloody knife, I'd guess— the one with Aiden's and my fingerprints on it. The one that killed Holden the Sixth?"

Justin doesn't say anything. I keep my eyes on Noah, who returns an intense stare.

"If I'm guessing," I continue, "Aiden came here that

day out of revenge, after Holden the Sixth killed his mother. He got his revenge. He killed Holden with that knife. And somehow you got hold of the knife, the murder weapon, and you held it over his head all these years. You threatened him, blackmailed him, whatever. Aiden would be easy to intimidate. He's practically a kid even now."

"Jenna—"

"And then you grew up. The boy who tried to kill me that day became the man who's killed eight people. Then, when I started getting close, when it became convenient to pin all these murders on Aiden, you tipped off Officer Ricketts about the whereabouts of the knife. How'm I doing so far?"

"You're doing quite well, Detective. *Quite* well." Justin moves a few steps closer. "Now lower the gun and drop it, Jenna. Slowly, or I'll get nervous."

Noah remains motionless, save for the drop of his jaw, as I do what Justin says. I lower the Glock to my side and let it fall from my hand.

"You must have *just* figured this out," he says. "Or you wouldn't have tossed me the gun."

"You mentioned Aiden," I say. "He wouldn't hurt me. I know that now. And you just confirmed it."

"I guess I did. Quite true about Aiden. He's your hero, after all, the young lad who rescued the damsel in distress all those many years ago. Too bad you realized it after you tossed me this gun. Life's a game of inches, isn't it? If it had come to you just a few seconds earlier, I wouldn't be holding this gun. That's gotta sting."

Justin moves behind me, keeping both Noah and me

in his sight and positioning himself beyond our reach. The right move, strategically. He didn't get this far, for this long, without being smart.

"For what it's worth," Justin says, "I'd hoped that tonight would end differently."

"You wanted me to kill Aiden when I came here looking for him. You knew this was where I'd come to look for him. You wanted me to kill him, to keep you clean. But you followed behind me, with your other gun, just in case it didn't work out that way."

"But I sure didn't expect Noah," he says. "The best-laid plans and all."

Noah's jaw clenches. I look at his left front pocket—was Justin right? Does Noah have Justin's other gun, the .38 special?

"By the way, Noah," Justin says. "In the future, if you think you've knocked someone unconscious, be sure they're not faking. Stick 'em with a pin or something. And if you're going to tie someone up with a rope, don't just bind their hands behind their back. Bind their feet, too, and then bind the feet and hands together. It makes it a lot harder to get out."

Footsteps behind me as Justin presses the revolver into the base of my skull.

"Not that it matters now," he says, "but for the record, Jenna, I didn't want anything to happen to you. You may find this hard to believe, but I really did want us to be together."

I let out a bitter laugh.

"I did. Think of how good we'd have been together. Think of our children! Holden's grandchildren."

505

I stifle the urge to vomit, the bile at my throat. "You're sick," I say.

"Everyone's *sick*," he spits, pushing the muzzle of his gun into the base of my skull, forcing my head forward. "Everyone has it inside them. Some of us are a little more liberal about releasing it, that's all."

Noah is trembling, his eyes smoldering with pure hatred. "You killed Melanie," he growls. "Right here in this room."

"But that's not even the best part," says Justin. "The best part is *you* took the fall for it! Just like old times, with the school yard shooting. You've always been a reliable fall guy, Noah. I've never properly thanked you for that. How have those hands healed up, by the way, from your fun at Sing Sing?"

A furious, tortured smile plays on Noah's face. "You're gonna find out," he says, "when I put them on your throat."

"No, I think your hands are going on top of your head. And you're going to move back toward the balcony. I know you have my thirty-eight special on you. If you make me nervous, this gun goes off. You'll be wearing Jenna's face on your shirt."

Noah blinks, snaps out of his fury, looks at me, the gun shoved against my skull.

He backpedals from us, puts his hands on his head.

"You'll never get away with this," I say.

"Sure I will. *Sure* I will. The happy-go-lucky millionaire philanthropist who serves low-cost food to the middle class? Everyone loves me. Oh, and Jenna?" he says.

"Yes, Justin," I say evenly.

He says it in a whisper. "After I kill you and Noah, I'm going to find your aunt Chloe and kill her, too. She's going to *love* our little fun room downstairs. I'm thinking *shish kebab.*"

And then I feel the vibration against the back of my skull as Justin pulls the trigger.

Chapter 120

CLICK.

Justin pulls the trigger again.

Another hollow *click*.

I dive for the Glock I just dropped, sliding to the floor, then spinning back, faster than Justin can say *Damn, this revolver must not be loaded.*

Thank you, Aiden, for emptying the bullets.

Justin looks at the gun, then me. A bitter smile on his face, then he shakes his head and throws the gun to the floor.

"No one will believe it," he says. "Like Noah said, Chief Marks already has arrest warrants out with your name on it. So the only way you'll get that *justice* you so richly seek is to shoot me."

I get to my feet, the gun steady now, aimed at Justin's chest.

He raises his arms in surrender. "How about it, Detective? Are you gonna shoot an unarmed man? Please, please," he says in a mocking plea, dropping to his knees, "don't shoot me, Ms. Murphy! Don't shoot me!"

Sirens, in the distance, but not that distant. A 911 call, no doubt, after the gunshots I fired. Once Isaac heard that the shots came from the house on 7 Ocean Drive, he'd send the whole force.

I lower the gun slightly—not so low as to give Justin any ideas, but not pointing it directly at him.

"You're not gonna do it," says Justin, as if disappointed. "You're really not." His chest rises and falls, his face locked in a grimace.

It hits me then—he wants to die. He doesn't want to spend his life in prison. Not one member of the Dahlquist clan ever spent a day in prison. He doesn't want to break the streak.

"My favorite was your uncle," he says. "Heating up that poker in the fireplace and driving it through his kidney."

I shake my head. I'm not going to let him bait me.

"Do you wanna know what he said before I did it?"

The sirens getting closer. Multiple squad cars approaching.

"He said, 'Help me, Jenna.' He was begging."

I close the distance between us, the gun aimed at his head.

"He was in so much pain," Justin says.

I rear back, then drive my foot into his ribs, kicking him as hard as I can.

He doubles over on the floor.

"Pain like that?" I say.

He lets out a noise—pain, yes, but also amusement. "That's the spirit," he manages. "I knew you had it in you."

"You're gonna rot in prison, Justin," I say. "You don't get to go out in a blaze of glory, some dramatic suicide, like all your ancestors."

Justin focuses on me with a hint of amusement. He gets himself to his hands and knees. "*My* ancestors?" he says.

"Shut up, Justin," Noah says, suddenly stepping forward.

"*My* ancestors?"

Noah pulls the .38 special from his pocket and aims it at Justin. "I'm warning you, Justin, *shut up*."

Justin lets out a wicked laugh. "Oh, Jenna, you think Holden is *my* father?"

I look at Noah. "What's he talking about?"

"Nothing," Noah says. "We'll talk about it later, when everything's calmed down."

I step back, instinctively, separating myself from both of them. "We'll talk about it now, Noah. And put down that gun!"

"Murphy—"

"Drop the gun, Noah! Now! Slide it over to me."

The sound of tires squealing outside as the squad cars pull up to the mansion.

"Tell her, Noah," says Justin, regaining an upright position, still on his knees. "Or better yet, show her those papers in your—"

Noah throws an uppercut, a violent left fist, connecting just under Justin's chin, sending Justin off his knees and sprawling backward. Justin's head smacks the floor, and this time he's truly unconscious, no faking about it.

Noah with his back to me. The gun in his right hand.

"Don't move, Noah. Don't make a move."

The sounds outside: officers rushing through the gate, up the walk, the front door of the mansion slamming open, footfalls downstairs, their voices, announcing their office, clearing each room on the lower level.

My mind races, thoughts bouncing every which way, trying to make it fit. Noah—Noah—it was Noah all along? Noah is Holden's son? Everything spun upside down, everything unraveled, like a fist coming down on a jigsaw puzzle, scattering the pieces in all directions.

"Tell me, Noah," I say, my voice shaking.

Noah slowly bends down and places the gun on the floor. Though Justin is no longer a threat, he kicks the gun across the room for good measure.

"I want to see those papers," I say.

His back still to me, Noah removes the papers from his pocket, rolled up like an ancient scroll, and turns to face me.

"Put the gun down first," he says.

"No chance. Toss them over."

Noah drops his head, then starts walking over to me.

"Stop, now," I say. "Keep your distance and toss them to me."

He looks up at me, not breaking stride. "Jenna," he says.

"Stop, Noah, or I'll shoot!" My gun is aimed at his face, my feet spread.

"No," he says.

He draws closer to me. Five steps. Three steps.

Footfalls on the stairs as officers race up to the second floor.

"I'll shoot," I say through my teeth.

"You're not gonna shoot me, Jenna."

My finger is on the trigger as Noah's eyes lock on mine, as I feel the familiar heat of his approach.

And I can't. I can't pull the trigger. I don't know why. I don't know anything anymore.

I just know I can't shoot him.

Noah puts his hand over the barrel of my gun—his Glock—and pushes it down.

He puts his forehead against mine.

"It's okay now," he says. "It's gonna be okay."

"Tell me it wasn't you," I whisper. "Tell me you aren't his son."

Noah removes the gun from my hand. He replaces it with the scroll of papers, pressing them firmly into my palm.

His mouth moves to my ear.

"Holden didn't have a son," he says. "He had a daughter."

Chapter 121

"HERE. IT SUCKS, but it's hot."

Officer Lauren Ricketts places the Styrofoam cup of coffee in front of me in the interview room at the substation. When I look up to thank her, I see black spots, and I feel the weight under my eyes.

"Rough night," she says, rubbing my back. "Tomorrow will be better."

Tomorrow is today. It's past five in the morning. And no amount of tomorrows will change it.

I look down again at the documents, still curved along the edges from having been rolled up in Noah's pocket for several hours. I read through them again, for at least the twentieth time. The first page, a piece of stationery bearing the name Lincoln Investigative Services. A letter to Holden Dahlquist VI.

You asked us to determine whether a woman named Gloria Willis, of Bridgehampton, mother of Aiden

Willis, gave birth to a second child approximately eight years ago.

Holden knew, or at least suspected, that he'd impregnated Aiden's mother.

The answer to your question is yes. Eight years ago, Ms. Willis did give birth to a second child at Southampton Hospital but left the hospital with her child only hours later, without filling out any paperwork. We believe that she abandoned this child later that evening at the Bridgehampton Police Substation (see attached news headline).

I flip the page. The news clipping I saw myself, at Aiden's house:

Newborn Abandoned at Police Station

The photo of Uncle Lang, holding the baby at the substation in Bridgehampton.

The next page, a photocopy of a handwritten note, the penmanship poor but legible:

Please find my daughter a good home. She is in danger. Don't ever let her know about me. Don't ever let her try to find me or the father. He will kill her.

My pulse banging like a gong, no matter how many times I read this note, a note from a terrified mother

514

trying to protect her newborn daughter the only way she knew how—by abandoning her.

I flip to the next page, a court document:

> At a Term of the Family Court of the State of
> New York, held in and for the County of Suffolk,
> at Riverhead, New York
> **In the Matter of the Adoption of a Child Known as**
> **Baby Girl X**

I skip a bunch of the middle pages because they are legalese, just a bunch of lawyers' words. The punch line at the final page:

> IT IS HEREBY ORDERED that the petition of
> Gary and Lydia Murphy, for the adoption of Baby
> Girl X, a person born on a date unknown, at a
> location unknown, is allowed and approved; and
> it is further
> ORDERED that the name of the adoptive
> child shall be JENNA ROSE MURPHY, and that
> the adoptive child shall hereafter be known by
> that name.

I can picture her. Of course I can't in reality, but my brain isn't tracking reality now—I can picture my mother, visiting Uncle Lang like they did every summer, taking me from Lang, holding me in her arms and saying, *I'll love her. I'll love this child.*

A single tear, falling onto the page, a thick circular stain in the corner.

Still unable to believe it, though it makes all the sense in the world.

My physical differences from my parents and brother, especially the red hair. My nickname, *the red sheep of the family*.

Never quite feeling like I fit in.

Sometimes we tell our children little white lies, Chloe said to me.

She didn't tell me—none of them told me, not Mom, not Dad, not Lang, not Chloe. They kept me in the dark to protect me. Protect me from whom, they didn't know.

A little white lie.

And here I thought it was random—I thought I was a random victim at that house that day. When in reality, Holden was trying to kill me to end the Dahlquist bloodline. First he ran down Aiden's mother—my mother—with a car, then he had Justin scoop me up and bring me to the house to finish the job.

I would've died in that house if it weren't for Aiden, coming to avenge his mother's death.

Chief Isaac Marks pops his head in the door, measuring the look on my face before deeming it safe to enter.

"Murphy," he says. "We're done with Noah's interview. So you two are free to leave."

I nod and push myself out of the chair, my legs uncertain.

"Murphy, I—I'm sorry," he says. "I was a jerk. And I had you all wrong. I thought you were a loose cannon hassling poor Aiden for no reason. And then I—well, I admit for a time there, I—"

"You thought I was a serial killer."

He throws up a hand.

"That's okay," I say, "for a time there, I thought you were, too."

He laughs, which might, under the circumstances, be the best response of all.

"When Noah showed me those investigative records," he says, "and it turned out you were the daughter of—I mean, I thought you'd been playing me all along."

That's what Noah thought, too.

"Plus, your fingerprints on that knife—"

"I got it," I say. I may not like it, but I have so much emotion stirred up inside me right now, I don't have room for anger.

"Justin's spilling like a volcano," he says. "Now that we have him in custody, he won't shut up. He's proud of it. He says he's part of the legacy now, he'll go down in history, et cetera."

"I'm sure he feels that way."

"He told us about everything in 1994, too. Apparently, Holden saw you and your family walking to the beach one day, right past his house. He got one look at you and—I guess there's a strong resemblance to your biological mother. He followed you around the beach all day, then he hired an investigator, and—well, you know the rest. You got the investigator's file right there. Then he had Justin snatch you up and bring you to the house—"

"Isaac," I say, raising a hand. "I don't want to know the details. I don't remember and I don't *want* to remember."

"Sure. Yeah, sure, Murphy. Well, I'll see you next week, then. If you're ready."

I shake my head. "You need me to testify at the prelim?"

"That's not what I meant."

He places my badge and my gun on the table.

"You don't think I'm going to lose my best cop, do you?" he says. "I may be a horse's ass on occasion, but I'm not stupid."

Chapter 122

I WALK TO the cemetery on Main Street, the cemetery where Winston Dahlquist and his descendants are buried. The afternoon air is mild and smells of the rain this morning.

Just down from the Dahlquist plot, Aiden Willis is busy planting flowers in a vase by some tombstone. Back at work already. Always the same, the raggedy shirt, the baseball cap turned backward, the scarecrow hair. He surely takes after his father, not his mother.

Yesterday, the DA's office officially announced that it had no basis to proceed with murder charges against Aiden for the death of Holden VI. Aiden was too young at the time to have been charged as an adult, and the circumstances, they said, "strongly suggest that his use of force was justified."

That might be the understatement of the year.

Aiden stops what he's doing when he sees me approach, squints at me.

I don't really know what to say to him. I have no

sense of family with him. We couldn't be less alike. We've never known each other. We've never shared a single thing, other than a mother.

"Hey," I say.

His eyes scatter about, as always, never holding a gaze.

"You doin' okay?" he asks me.

"Me? Yeah, sure. Listen, Aiden, I'm sorry for the way I treated you. I thought—I thought you were a part of this. I had no idea it was Justin."

He nods, his eyes roaming around the ground at my feet.

"Did you?" I ask, uncertain if I should even ask. "All these murders? Did you know it was him?"

His eyes go blank a moment, as if he's lost in a thought—more accurate, probably, to say lost in a feeling. "Didn't know for sure," he says. "Couldn'ta ever proved nothin'. Who'd believe me, anyhow? I'm just a ditch-digger. He's got all that money and shit."

"And he had the knife you tossed out the window," I add.

For a moment, Aiden's eyes focus, though not on me, looking off in the distance, his mouth forming a small o. "He said he kept it somewheres for safekeepin'. Case I ever got any ideas, he said."

A not-so-subtle threat. *Don't mess with me,* Justin was saying to Aiden, *or the cops will suddenly find this bloody knife. Fuck with me and I'll send you to prison.*

He tortured Aiden. He made Aiden shoot up the school yard with him a year after Holden's death—one of the many things Justin has bragged about to the police—and who knows what else he said and did to him over the years.

"What about me?" I ask. "Did you know who I was?"

His eyes are still darting around, but a sheen of tears covers them. He shakes his head. "When you first came back to town, first time I saw you—you looked familiar, but I couldn't figure it. Then I finally 'membered where I'd seen you, from all that time ago when we was kids, that day at the Dahlquist house. I didn't know why you'd come back. Couldn't figure. But I didn't know that you were my—that we was—"

The flowers, halfway in the vase, start to tip over. Aiden reaches for them.

"You should probably get back to your work," I say.

Aiden fixes up the flowers, sets them down firmly, turns to me in his indirect, no-eye-contact way. "I's too young to know 'bout you at the time. I'da been only little when you was born. One time, when I's older, I saw a picture of her, with her belly."

I saw it, too. The photo from the scrapbook, with the baby bump.

"She said the baby didn't live. She got real sad."

Probably the same thing that she told Holden VI, that I didn't live, that I was stillborn.

A little white lie. To protect me, so Aiden wouldn't look for me. So Holden wouldn't look for me. So nobody would ever look for me.

His darting eyes, just for a single moment, make contact with mine before skittering away again. "You look like her," he says. "A good bit like her."

"I'm lucky. She was very pretty. And courageous. She

did a brave thing for me. So did you, Aiden. If there's anything I can—"

"You wanna see her grave?" he asks.

I start to speak, but a lump fills my throat. I nod and follow him.

It's a simple grave, farther to the south of the cemetery, an ordinary headstone kept up pristinely.

Gloria Jane Willis
March 5, 1964 – July 12, 1994
Our Beloved Mother

Our beloved mother. Even though, for all practical purposes, Aiden was an only child. Even though, as far as he knew, I didn't survive the birth. Still, he included me, the sibling he never really had, the sibling he never knew.

My—*our*—biological mother. The woman who gave me up to save me. A prostitute who surely wanted something better for herself, and for her son.

And for her daughter.

July 12, 1994—the day Gloria was killed in a hit-and-run. The day before the seven hours of hell, when I was plucked off the street and taken to 7 Ocean Drive, so Holden could take my life, too, and end any vestige of the tortured, maniacal Dahlquist bloodline.

I look over at Aiden, whose eyes have filled with tears.

"I still miss her," he says, his voice quaking. "You'da—you'da liked her."

Murder House

"I know I would have." I take Aiden's hand in mine. "But you still have family. You still have me. You're my hero, Aiden. And you're my brother."

I lean over and kiss him on the cheek. He recoils slightly. I don't get the sense that a lot of women have kissed him in his life.

"Okay," he says awkwardly. His face brightens just a bit. "That'd be okay."

Chapter 123

I NESTLE MY feet into the sand and let out a long sigh. The beach is utter chaos in mid-August, kids running everywhere, boats and parasails and sand castles, but to me it feels like complete and total peace.

Four months, almost to the day, since it all happened.

Four months since Justin's murderous ways were exposed and he was taken into custody, a now-infamous killer who will go down in history with the legions of others. Someone told me they did a Google search on his name and got over ten thousand hits.

Hooray for him.

"Let's go watch," says Noah, sitting next to me.

"Not sure I want to."

"Oh, c'mon. Come *on*. You don't wanna watch?"

I relent, pushing myself out of the sand, fitting my toes into my sandals, my fingers intertwined with Noah's.

"Your hair's getting long again," I say. "Are you going back to Surfer Jesus?"

"Hey, be nice to me," he says, squeezing my hand. "I've been through a lot. I've been shot at by a cop two times."

"But she intended to miss each time," I add.

"So she says. So she says."

We climb onto the pavement of the parking lot and walk up Ocean Drive.

A thick crowd is gathered at the gate of 7 Ocean Drive. A couple of news crews as well. It's been like that ever since everything happened. They say there was a spike in tourism this summer due to all the people who wanted to come see this house.

So there will be a few people, some shop owners, who might be sorry to see what's about to happen. But I think most people will approve.

"Just in time," Noah says.

The wrecking ball slams into the roof first, crushing the slate inward, the spears and ornamental gargoyles disappearing in a satisfying rush, a collective gasp of awe from the crowd. They told me it will take hours to knock down the entire mansion. I told them I didn't care how long it took, I just wanted everything gone. The house. The tunnel and dungeon beneath. The carriage house.

It's my property, after all. That's what all the lawyers concluded after reviewing the trust documents. The property went into trust because nobody knew that Holden VI had left behind any offspring. So now it's mine.

It won't be for long. I wish I could open a museum or a shelter for battered women or something on this property, but this is prime real estate, and there are zoning laws designed to protect its value.

So I've put this massive lot up for sale, hopefully to a nice family who will build a nice new house with a very different future. The Realtors quoted me an estimate that's more money than I'd make in my lifetime, and far more money than I'll ever need. So I'll keep a fraction for myself and give the rest of the proceeds to Aiden Willis.

Another whack from the wrecking ball, this time taking out the wraparound balcony, the master bedroom where so many people lost, or took, their lives—centuries of horror gone with one crushing boom.

"I'm gonna miss that house," says Noah.

I laugh. It feels good to laugh. Odd, unusual, but good.

"But speaking of houses," he says, "those rooms aren't going to paint themselves."

Our new place, he means. Not far down the road from Uncle Lang's old house. A three-bedroom, two-bathroom in a nice, quiet spot. *Quiet* sounds good right about now. We cosigned the loan, on the salaries of a newly promoted detective, first grade, and the owner of a new handyman business.

Seeing this house, even in its deliciously beaten and battered form now, brings back everything from that final night.

I lean into Noah. "You were *that* sure I wouldn't shoot you?" I ask.

He cradles me with an arm. "Oh, yeah," he says. "It was clear that you were madly in love with me."

I smile to myself. I am, in fact, madly in love with this man.

I watch the wrecking ball do its work. I said I didn't want to watch, but now I'm fixated. Now I have to see it. I have to see every single piece of limestone battered and knocked to the ground. I need to see every inch of earth turned over—

Noah looks at me, sees the intensity in my face.

"Y'know what?" he says. "I changed my mind. This is boring. This house is old news. I wanna go to our new house."

This man understands me, sometimes better than I understand myself.

"Me too," I say.

We walk off, hand in hand, leaning against each other, the sun beating down on us.

Behind us, another boom, the sound of crushing rocks, another awed gasp from the crowd, but neither of us looks back.

ALL'S FAIR IN LOVE, WAR,
AND ESPIONAGE.

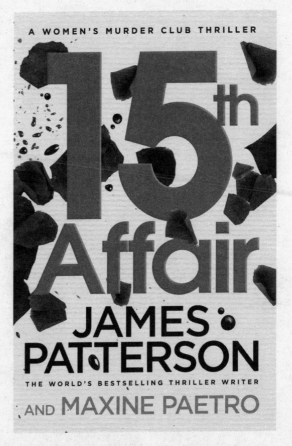

FOR AN EXCERPT, TURN THE PAGE.

ALISON MULLER WASN'T classically beautiful, but she was striking, with swinging blonde hair and peekaboo bangs brushing the frames of her wraparound shades. Her black leather coat flared above the knees of her skinny jeans, and her purposeful stride was punctuated by the staccato clacking of her high-heeled boots.

That afternoon, as she cut through the golden-hued lobby of San Francisco's Four Seasons Hotel, Ali checked out every man, woman, and child crossing the floor, on the queue at reception, slouched in chairs in front of the fireplace. She noted and labeled the tourists and business-people, deflecting the stares of the men who couldn't look away, while on the phone with her husband and their younger daughter, Mitzi.

"I didn't actually forget, Mitz," Ali said to her five-year old. "More like I lost track."

"You *did* forget," her daughter insisted.

"Not completely. I thought your big day was tomorrow."

"Everyone wanted to know where you were," her daughter complained.

"I'll make it up to you, sweetheart," Ali said.

"When? With what?"

Ali's thoughts ran ahead to the man waiting for her in a room on the fourteenth floor.

"Let me speak to Daddy," Ali said.

She passed the stunning exhibition of modern art and reached the elevator bank at the northwest end of the lobby. She stood behind the couple in front of the doors. They were French, discussing their dinner plans, agreeing that they had enough time to shower and change.

Ali thumbed her phone, checked her e-mail and the *Investors Business Daily* headlines and the text from Michael asking if she'd gotten lost. Ali's husband came back on the line.

"I did my best," he said. "She's inconsolable."

"You can handle her, dear. I'm sure you can do it. I'll order her something online when I get home."

"Which will be when?" her husband asked.

God. The questions. The never-ending questions.

"After dinner," Ali said. "I'm sorry. I wouldn't blow you off if it wasn't important."

The elevator doors opened.

"Gotta go."

Her husband said, "Say good-bye to Mitzi."

Shit.

She said, "Hang on a minute. I'm losing reception."

Ali stepped into the elevator and stood with her back to the corner, her jacket parting to reveal the butt of a gun tucked into her waistband. The doors closed and the car rose swiftly and quietly upward.

When Ali got out at the fourteenth floor, she spoke to her daughter as she walked along the plush carpeted hallway.

"Miss Mitzi?"

She reached room 1420 and rapped on the door, and it opened.

Ali said into the phone, "Happy birthday. See you soon. Kiss, kiss. Bye-bye."

She clicked off, stepped inside the room, and kicked the door closed behind her as she went into Michael's arms.

"You're late," he said.

MICHAEL CHAN TOOK off Ali's glasses and sucked in his breath. He couldn't get over this woman—and he had tried. She smiled at him and he put his hands on both sides of her face and kissed the smile right off her.

One kiss ignited a string of them: deep, telling, momentous. Michael lifted Ali and she hooked her legs around his hips and he walked her into the luxurious blue-and-bronze suite backlit by the watercolor sunset over San Francisco.

Chan didn't notice the view. Ali smelled like orchids or some exotic musk, and she had her tongue at his ear.

"Too much," he muttered. "You're too damned much."

She was panting as he lowered her to the bed. "Wait," she said.

"Of course. I'm a patient man," he said. His blood was surging, narrowing his focus. He put his hands on his hips and watched to see what she would do.

She looked up at him, her warm gaze flicking over his body and his strong features as if she were memorizing him. They met infrequently, but when they did, they pretended they were strangers. It was a game.

"At least tell me your name," she said.

"You first."

He pulled off her boots, tossed them aside. She sat up, shrugged off her coat, and shoved it over the edge of the bed. He plucked the gun from her waistband, looked through the sight, smelled the muzzle, and put it on the nightstand.

"Interesting," he said. "Hand-tooled."

He sat on the bed next to her and told her to lie down, and he lay next to her. He moved her bangs away from her eyes.

"Your name."

She reached down and ran her hand across the front of his pants. He grabbed her wrist.

She said, "Ummmm, I'm Renata."

"Giovanni," he said. "Prince of Gorgonzola."

She laughed. It was a terrific laugh. "Finally, I meet the Prince of Cheese."

Michael kept a straight face. "Correct. And you should never keep royalty waiting."

He stroked her cheek, then dipped his fingers beneath the neckline of her blouse.

"I think I may have met you once before," she said.

He freed the pearl buttons from their loops.

"I don't think so," he said. "I would have remembered."

He ran his hand over the tops of her breasts, then gathered up her hair, wrapped it around his left hand, and pulled her head back.

She moaned and said, "You paid me with three gold coins. I came to your room in the hotel overlooking"—she sighed—"the Trevi Fountain."

"I've never stayed in Rome," he said.

He turned her so that she faced away from him. He stroked the long side of her body down to her haunch and back. He enjoyed the soft sounds coming from her throat as she tried to twist away from him.

"Did you tell your husband?"

"Why would you ask me that?" she said.

"Because I want him to throw you out."

He undid the closure at the waist of her jeans, pulled down the zipper, got to his feet, and removed her jeans and all of his clothes.

He didn't hear the sound at the door.

This was unlike him. He had superior senses, but they were engaged. Ali was looking up at him with—what was that look in her eyes?

She said, "I heard a card in the lock."

A voice called out, "Housekeeping."

Chan said, "I didn't lock the door. You?"

Ali said, "Hell no."

Chan shouted, "Come back later," but the door was already opening and the cart was bumping over the threshold. He grabbed his pants from the floor and, holding them in front of him, he went toward the foyer.

He shouted, *"No! Wait!"*

The three shots were muffled by a suppressor. If Michael Chan had known his killer, it didn't matter now.

Lights out.

Game over.

Michael Chan was gone.

IT HAD BEEN a rough week, and it was only Monday.

My partner, Rich Conklin, and I had just testified against Edward "Ted" Swanson, a cop who had, over time, left eighteen people dead before the shootout with a predatory drug lord called Kingfisher took Swanson out of the game.

All of the SFPD had known Swanson as a great cop. We had liked him. Respected him. So when my partner and I exposed him as a psychopath with a badge, we were stunned and outraged.

During Swanson's lethal crime spree, he had stolen over five million in drugs and money from Kingfisher, and this drug boss with a murderous reputation up and down the West Coast hadn't taken this loss as the cost of doing business.

After the shootout, while Swanson lay comatose in the ICU, Kingfisher figured that his best chance of getting his property back was to turn his death threats on the lead investigator on the case.

That investigator was me.

His phone calls were irrational, untraceable, and absolutely *terrifying*.

Then, about the time Swanson was released from the hospital and indicted on multiple charges of drug trafficking and murder, Kingfisher's phone calls stopped. A week later, Mexican authorities turned up the King's body in a shallow grave in Baja. Was it really over?

Sometimes terrifying events leave aftershocks when you realize how bad things could have become. Kingfisher's threats had embedded themselves inside me on a visceral level, and now that I was free of them, something inside me unclenched.

On the other hand, events that seem innocuous at the time can flip you right over the edge into the dark side.

And that was the case with Swanson.

A dirty cop shakes up everything: friendships, public trust, and belief in your own ability to read people. I thought I had done a good job testifying against Swanson today. I hoped so. Richie had been terrific, for sure, and now the decision as to Swanson's guilt or innocence was up to his jury.

My partner said, "We're done with this, Lindsay. Time to move on."

I was checking out of the Hall of Justice at just after six when my husband texted me to say that he would be home late, and that there was a roasted chicken in the fridge.

Damn.

I was disappointed not to see Joe, but as I stepped outside the gray granite building into a luminous summer evening, I formulated a new plan. Rather than chicken for three, I would have a quiet dinner with my baby daughter, followed by Dreamland in about three hours, tops.

I fired up my old Explorer and had just cleared the rush-hour snarl on Bryant when the boss called me.

Against my better judgment, I picked up.

"Boxer," Brady said, "a bad scene just went down at the Four Seasons. I need you there."

The only scene I wanted to see was my little girl in clean onesies, and me with a glass of Chardonnay in my hand. But Homicide was understaffed, my partner and I had a fresh gap in our caseload, and Brady was a good lieutenant.

I said, "Were you able to catch Conklin?"

"He's on the way," said Brady.

I made a U-turn on Geary, and twenty minutes later, I met up with my partner in the sumptuous lobby of the Four Seasons Hotel. Conklin was as tired as I was, but it looked good on him.

"Overtime pay, Lindsay."

"Yahoo," I said with an appropriate lack of enthusiasm. "What did Brady tell you?"

"To be smart, thorough, and quick."

"Instead of what? Stupid, sloppy, and slow?"

Richie laughed. "He said the Four Seasons wants their hotel back."

We took the elevator to the fourteenth floor, and when the doors opened, we saw that the hallway was cordoned off and law enforcement personnel were standing at the exit doors, leaning against walls, waiting for us.

Conklin and I ducked under the tape and nodded to uniforms we knew, finally pulling up to the open door marked 1420.

The cop at the door signed us into the log, and I asked him, "Who called it in?"

"Hotel's head of security. He responded to complaints of gunshots."

"How bad is it?"

"Bad enough," he said.

"Let's see," I said.

THE FIRST OFFICER stepped aside, revealing a naked male body lying faceup, about fifteen feet inside the deluxe hotel suite. He had been shot once in the forehead, once through the right eye, and had taken another bullet to his chest for good measure.

I said to Conklin, "What do you think? Midthirties? Asian?"

Conklin nodded and said, "That's an expensive watch. He's wearing a wedding ring. We're probably not looking at a robbery."

Someone called my name.

Charlie Clapper, director of San Francisco's forensic unit, came around a corner in the suite. "Boxer," Clapper said. "Conklin. Welcome to the

Four Seasons. How can we make your stay here more enjoyable?"

I said, "Tell me you've ID'd the victim and have the shooter in custody. And that by the way, the shooter confessed."

Clapper is a former homicide cop, a pro who knows what he's doing and never has to prove it. He laughed and said, "I guess miracles happen—but not here. Not today."

I peered behind Clapper. Lights had been set up and CSIs were processing the expensively furnished suite, which had soundproof windows and a high city view. There was a lot of blood around and under the victim, but the room behind him looked spotless.

I took in the silvery-blue carpeting and upholstery, the lightly rumpled bed, bedspread still in place. I saw no wine bottles or remains of a room service meal, and the TV was off.

It looked like room 1420 had only been used for a short time before what happened here went down.

Conklin asked Clapper to run what he knew so far.

Clapper said, "To start with, it looks like our

victim had company. We found fresh lipstick and a few long blonde hairs on a pillowcase. There's no wallet, no suitcase, no papers, no clothes, no shoes."

"Perfect score," said Conklin.

Clapper went on. "This gentleman checked in under the name Gregory Wang. He used a credit card with that name and the charge went through, but there is no Gregory Wang at the address on the card or anywhere.

"Also notable, the room has been thoroughly wiped down. No prints old or new. Entry was by a key card that was traced to a Maria Silva in housekeeping. Ms. Silva is now off duty, not answering her phone. A patrol car has gone to her address."

"What about *his* prints?" Conklin asked, indicating the victim.

"We ran the victim's prints and came up with nothing. He's not in the system, has never been in the military, or taught grade school, or been arrested. And wait. There's more," said Clapper. "There's a whole other crime scene right next door. Can't be a coincidence, but right now, I don't see the connection."

JAMES PATTERSON
BOOK**SHOTS**

stories at the speed of life

BOOK**SHOTS** are page-turning stories by James Patterson and other writers that can be read in one sitting.

Each and every one is fast-paced, 100% story-driven; a shot of pure entertainment guaranteed to satisfy.

Under 150 pages
Under £3

Available as new, compact paperbacks, ebooks and audio, everywhere books are sold.

For more details, visit: **www.bookshots.com**

BOOK**SHOTS**
THE ULTIMATE FORM OF STORYTELLING.
FROM THE ULTIMATE STORYTELLER.

Also by James Patterson

ALEX CROSS NOVELS

Along Came a Spider • Kiss the Girls • Jack and Jill •
Cat and Mouse • Pop Goes the Weasel • Roses are Red •
Violets are Blue • Four Blind Mice • The Big Bad Wolf •
London Bridges • Mary, Mary • Cross • Double Cross •
Cross Country • Alex Cross's Trial (*with Richard
DiLallo*) • I, Alex Cross • Cross Fire • Kill Alex Cross •
Merry Christmas, Alex Cross • Alex Cross, Run •
Cross My Heart • Hope to Die • Cross Justice

THE WOMEN'S MURDER CLUB SERIES

1st to Die • 2nd Chance (*with Andrew Gross*) •
3rd Degree (*with Andrew Gross*) • 4th of July (*with Maxine
Paetro*) • The 5th Horseman (*with Maxine Paetro*) •
The 6th Target (*with Maxine Paetro*) • 7th Heaven (*with Maxine
Paetro*) • 8th Confession (*with Maxine Paetro*) •
9th Judgement (*with Maxine Paetro*) • 10th Anniversary (*with
Maxine Paetro*) • 11th Hour (*with Maxine Paetro*) •
12th of Never (*with Maxine Paetro*) • Unlucky 13 (*with Maxine
Paetro*) • 14th Deadly Sin (*with Maxine Paetro*) •
15th Affair (*with Maxine Paetro*)

DETECTIVE MICHAEL BENNETT SERIES

Step on a Crack (*with Michael Ledwidge*) • Run for Your Life
(*with Michael Ledwidge*) • Worst Case (*with Michael Ledwidge*) •
Tick Tock (*with Michael Ledwidge*) • I, Michael Bennett (*with
Michael Ledwidge*) • Gone (*with Michael Ledwidge*) •
Burn (*with Michael Ledwidge*) • Alert (*with Michael Ledwidge*) •
Bullseye (*with Michael Ledwidge*)

PRIVATE NOVELS

Private (*with Maxine Paetro*) • Private London (*with Mark Pearson*) • Private Games (*with Mark Sullivan*) • Private: No. 1 Suspect (*with Maxine Paetro*) • Private Berlin (*with Mark Sullivan*) • Private Down Under (*with Michael White*) • Private L.A. (*with Mark Sullivan*) • Private India (*with Ashwin Sanghi*) • Private Vegas (*with Maxine Paetro*) • Private Sydney (*with Kathryn Fox*) • Private Paris (*with Mark Sullivan*) • The Games (*with Mark Sullivan*)

NYPD RED SERIES

NYPD Red (*with Marshall Karp*) • NYPD Red 2 (*with Marshall Karp*) • NYPD Red 3 (*with Marshall Karp*) • NYPD Red 4 (*with Marshall Karp*)

NON-FICTION

Torn Apart (*with Hal and Cory Friedman*) • The Murder of King Tut (*with Martin Dugard*)

ROMANCE

Sundays at Tiffany's (*with Gabrielle Charbonnet*) • The Christmas Wedding (*with Richard DiLallo*) • First Love (*with Emily Raymond*)

OTHER TITLES

Miracle at Augusta (*with Peter de Jonge*)

FAMILY OF PAGE-TURNERS

MIDDLE SCHOOL BOOKS

The Worst Years of My Life (*with Chris Tebbetts*) • Get Me Out of Here! (*with Chris Tebbetts*) • My Brother Is a Big, Fat Liar (*with Lisa Papademetriou*) • How I Survived Bullies, Broccoli, and Snake Hill (*with Chris Tebbetts*) • Ultimate Showdown (*with Julia Bergen*) • Save Rafe! (*with Chris Tebbetts*) • Just My Rotten Luck (*with Chris Tebbetts*)

I FUNNY SERIES

I Funny (*with Chris Grabenstein*) •
I Even Funnier (*with Chris Grabenstein*) •
I Totally Funniest (*with Chris Grabenstein*) •
I Funny TV (*with Chris Grabenstein*)

TREASURE HUNTERS SERIES

Treasure Hunters (*with Chris Grabenstein*) •
Danger Down the Nile (*with Chris Grabenstein*) •
Secret of the Forbidden City (*with Chris Grabenstein*)

HOUSE OF ROBOTS SERIES

House of Robots (*with Chris Grabenstein*) •
Robots Go Wild! (*with Chris Grabenstein*)

OTHER ILLUSTRATED NOVELS

Kenny Wright: Superhero (*with Chris Tebbetts*)
Homeroom Diaries (*with Lisa Papademetriou*)

For more information about James Patterson's novels, visit
www.jamespatterson.co.uk

Or become a fan on Facebook

By the same author

NOVELS

The Grass is Singing
The Golden Notebook
Briefing for a Descent into Hell
The Summer Before the Dark
Memoirs of a Survivor
Diary of a Good Neighbour
If the Old Could . . .
The Good Terrorist
The Fifth Child
Playing the Game
    (illustrated by Charlie Adlard)
Love, Again
Mara and Dann
The Fifth Child
Ben, in the World
The Sweetest Dream
The Story of General Dann and Mara's
    Daughter, Griot and the Snow Dog
The Cleft

'Canopus in Argos: Archives' series
Re: Colonised Planet 5, Shikasta
The Marriages Between Zones
    Three, Four, and Five
The Sirian Experiments
The Making of the Representative for
    Planet 8
Documents Relating to the Sentimental
    Agents in the Volyen Empire

'Children of Violence' novel-sequence
Martha Quest
A Proper Marriage
A Ripple from the Storm
Landlocked
The Four-Gated City

OPERAS

The Marriages Between Zones Three,
    Four and Five (Music by Philip Glass)
The Making of the representative for
    Planet 8 (Music by Philip Glass)

SHORT STORIES

Five
The Habit of Loving
A Man and Two Women
The Story of a Non-Marrying Man
    and Other Stories
Winter in July
The Black Madonna
This Was the Old Chief's Country
    (Collected African Stories, Vol. 1)
The Sun Between Their Feet
    (Collected African Stories, Vol. 2)
To Room Nineteen
    (Collected Stories, Vol. 1)
The Temptation of Jack Orkney
    (Collected Stories, Vol. 2)
London Observed
The Old Age of El Magnifico
Particularly Cats
Rufus the Survivor
On Cats
The Grandmothers

POETRY
Fourteen Poems

DRAMA
Each His Own Wilderness
Play with a Tiger
The Singing Door

NON-FICTION
In Pursuit of the English
Going Home
A Small Personal Voice
Prisons We Choose to Live Inside
The Wind Blows Away Our Words
African Laughter
Time Bites

AUTOBIOGRAPHY
Under My Skin: Volume 1
Walking in the Shade: Volume 2

Praise for *The Sweetest Dream*:

'She has an extraordinary feeling for the peculiar vulnerabilities of the young, elderly and mentally unstable. And her portraits of sympathetic human relationships are of quite staggering beauty. Lessing illuminates the passing of the 20th century's anti-capitalist dream: looking back, it seems extraordinary that the dream went on for so long: and looking forward, it is far too early to tell what its failure really means.'

RUTH SCURR, *The Times*

'Thank goodness for Doris Lessing. While the rest of us flounder about noisily in the muddy waters of life, she never fails to expose with startling clarity the essential folly of our dreams and good intentions. Despite Lessing's scathing exposé of pompous self-interest and futile idealism, her book is pervaded by what she would describe as "a layer of energetic optimism."'

KATE CHISHOLM, *Evening Standard*

'This book brings with it a rare kind of literary pleasure – the kind you might have in suddenly coming upon a long lost novel by George Eliot or Balzac. Six pages in, and you know that you have entered a fictional world which is already indelibly imprinted on your imagination, and which has in some measure shaped you. The characters are your familiars. You recognise their terrors and desires, the houses, landscape and politics they inhabit. Simultaneously, everything has shifted and is new. The haunting brilliance of her characters, whom one feels one knows rather better than one's friend, the passion of her ideas and vision, remain undiminished. She's up there in the pantheon with Balzac and George Eliot. We're lucky she's still writing.'

LISA APPIGNANESI, *Independent*

'A startling, burningly committed book which contains a marvellous sense of possibilities opening as the fiction progresses, an enriching and absorbing conviction of change and growth.'

PHILIP HENSHER, *Spectator*

'Lessing demonstrates that the realist novel is still possessed of a range and authority that makes all the clever antics of post-modernism seem like the giggling of naughty schoolchildren . . . Because Lessing is a humanist, in the end – though she spares us no revelation of selfishness, nastiness and stupidity – goodness prevails. She is one of the few writers who does not hesitate to offer up some characters for admiration, and who has no time for those who are cheap.' ALLAN MASSIE, *Scotsman*

'Lessing has always been a generous writer, and one who is determined to get to the bottom of things, and she effortlessly captures what is quintessential in each of her charming characters. She has claimed that her quest for the truth propelled her into becoming a writer. No doubt it is the same impetus that has produced a volume that speaks so loudly to the present. In its critique of mass-produced thinking and the long-term personal effects of war, *The Sweetest Dream* approaches a universal truth: both damage people's capacity to give and receive love. Something to mull over in these troubled times.'

JUSTINE ETTLER, *Observer*

'Lessing's power is in her awareness of detail, commitment to truth and human dignity, strengths that hold the book together. The fate of her characters and the indignation of the author towards unfeeling humanity keep the work gripping and rewarding.'

JOHN F DEANE *Irish Independent*

'Comrade Johnny, a figure of near-Dickensian hypocrisy, pomposity and selfishness, is the comic masterpiece of the novel, a flawless carica- ture of the career revolutionary, who speaks in formulas and clichés, lives parasitically and well on others, and blithely abandons his wives and children with the motto that "the struggle must come before family obligations."' ELAINE SHOWALTER, *TLS*

'Doris Lessing appears more and more as some Olympian figure, sur- veying from her mountain-top the chaotic, fumbling, ludicrous human panorama beneath. Here her panoramic sweep is worthy of a 19th century doorstopper: she casts her cool eye over whole decades (1960s to 1990s); entire ideological systems (shiny new Marxism, second-hand feminism, rusty old family values); large messy families, complete with neurotic ex-spouses and teenagers other people seem to have mislaid; drugs; anorexia; big chunks of Africa; Aids, Catholicism. It's a beauti- fully made novel, with full-blooded virtues, both fictional and moral. Her portrait of Africa's miseries, although devastatingly vivid, still manages to allow a few rather feeble rays of goodness to glimmer through.' JAN DALLEY, *Financial Times*

THE
SWEETEST
DREAM

DORIS LESSING

HARPER PERENNIAL

Harper Perennial
An imprint of HarperCollins*Publishers*
77–85 Fulham Palace Road
Hammersmith
London W6 8JB

www.harperperennial.co.uk

This edition published by Harper Perennial 2004
7

Previously published in paperback by Flamingo 2002

First published in Great Britain by Flamingo 2001

This novel is entirely a work of fiction.
The names, characters and incidents portrayed in it
are the work of the author's imagination.
Any resemblance to actual persons, living or dead,
events or localities, is entirely coincidental.

A catalogue record for this book is available
from the British Library

ISBN 0 00 655230 7

Set in PostScript Monotype Bembo with Medici Script display
by Rowland Phototypesetting Ltd,
Bury St Edmunds, Suffolk

Printed and bound in Great Britain by
Clays Ltd, St Ives plc

With gratitude to my editor at Flamingo, Philip Gwyn Jones, and to my agent Jonathan Clowes, for good advice and criticism, and to Antony Chennells, for help with the Roman Catholic parts of the book.

'And people leave who were warm children.'

Author's Note

I am not writing volume three of my autobiography because of possible hurt to vulnerable people. Which does not mean I have novelised autobiography. There are no parallels here to actual people, except for one, a very minor character. I hope I have managed to recapture the spirit of, particularly, the Sixties, that contradictory time which, looking back and comparing it with what came later, seems surprisingly innocent. There was little of the nastiness of the Seventies, or the cold greed of the Eighties.

Some events described as taking place at the end of the Seventies and early Eighties in fact happened later, by a decade. The Campaign for Nuclear Disarmament took a stand against the government doing anything at all to protect the population against the results of nuclear attack or accident, even fall-out, though surely protection of its citizens should be any government's first responsibility. People who believed that the population should be protected were treated as if they were enemies, attacked with verbal abuse, *fascists* being the least of it, and sometimes physically. Death threats . . . unpleasant substances pushed through letterboxes – the whole gamut of mob abuse. There has never been a more hysterical, noisy and irrational campaign. Students of the dynamics of mass movements will find it all in the newspaper archives, and I have had letters from them on the lines of, 'But that was crazy. Just what was it all about?'

*A*N EARLY EVENING in autumn, and the street below was a scene of small yellow lights that suggested intimacy, and people already bundled up for winter. Behind her the room was filling with a chilly dark, but nothing could dismay her: she was floating, as high as a summer cloud, as happy as a child who had just learned to walk. The reason for this uncharacteristic lightness of heart was a telegram from her former husband, Johnny Lennox – Comrade Johnny – three days ago. SIGNED CONTRACT FOR FIDEL FILM ALL ARREARS AND CURRENT PAYMENT TO YOU SUNDAY. Today was Sunday. The 'all arrears' had been due, she knew, to something like the fever of elation she was feeling now: there was no question of his paying 'all' which by now must amount to so much money she no longer bothered to keep an account. But he surely must be expecting a really big sum to sound so confident. Here a little breeze – apprehension? – did reach her. Confidence was his – no, she must *not* say stock-in-trade, even if she had often in her life felt that, but could she remember him ever being outfaced by circumstances, even discomfited?

On a desk behind her two letters lay side by side, like a lesson in life's improbable but so frequent dramatic juxtapositions. One offered her a part in a play. Frances Lennox was a minor, steady, reliable actress, and had never been asked for anything more. This part was in a brilliant new play, a two-hander, and the male part would be taken by Tony Wilde who until now had seemed so

I

far above her she would never have had the ambition to think of her name and his side by side on a poster. And *he* had asked for her to be offered the part. Two years ago they had been in the same play, she as usual in a serviceable smaller role. At the end of a short run – the play had not been a success – she had heard on the closing night as they tripped back and forth taking curtain calls, 'Well done, that was very good.' Smiles from Olympus, she had thought that, while knowing he had shown signs of being interested in her. But now she had been watching herself burst into all kinds of feverish dreams, not exactly taking herself by surprise, since she knew only too well how battened down she was, how well under control was her erotic self, but she could not prevent herself imagining her talent for fun (she supposed she still had it?) even for reckless enjoyment, being given room, while at the same time showing what she could do on the stage, if given a chance. But she would not be earning much money, in a small theatre, with a play that was a gamble. Without that telegram from Johnny she could not have afforded to say yes.

The other letter offered her a niche as Agony Aunt (name still to be chosen) on *The Defender*, well paid, and safe. This would be a continuation of the other strand of her professional life as a freelance journalist, which is where she earned money.

She had been writing on all kinds of subjects for years. At first she had tried her wings in local papers and broadsheets, any place that would pay her a little money. Then she found she was doing research for serious articles, and they were in the national newspapers. She had a name for solid balanced articles that often shone an unexpected and original light on a current scene.

She would do it well. What else had her experience fitted her for, if not to cast a cool eye on the problems of others? But saying yes to that work would have no pleasure in it, no feeling she would be trying new wings. Rather, she would have to steady her shoulders with the inner stiffening of resolve that is like a suppressed yawn.

How weary she was of all the problems, the bruised souls, the waifs and strays, how delightful it would be to say, 'Right, you can look after yourselves for a bit, I am going to be in the theatre every evening and most of the day too.' (Here was another little cold nudge: have you taken leave of your senses? Yes, and she was loving every minute.)

The top of a tree still in its summer leaf, but a bit ragged now, was glistening: light from two storeys up, from the old woman's rooms, had snatched it from dark into lively movement, almost green: colour was implied. Julia was in, then. Readmitting her mother-in-law – her ex-mother-in-law – to her mind brought a familiar apprehension, because of the weight of disapproval sifting down through the house to reach her, but there was something else she had only recently become aware of. Julia had had to go to hospital, could have died, and Frances had to acknowledge at last how much she relied on her. Suppose there was no Julia, what would she do, what would they all do?

Meanwhile, everyone referred to her as *the old woman*, she too until recently. Not Andrew, though. And she had noticed that Colin had begun to call her Julia. The three rooms above hers, over where she stood now, below Julia's, were inhabited by Andrew the elder son, and Colin the younger, her and Johnny Lennox's sons.

She had three rooms, bedroom and study and another, always needed for someone staying the night, and she had heard Rose Trimble say, 'What does she need three rooms for, she's just selfish.'

No one said, Why does Julia need four rooms? The house was hers. This rackety over-full house, people coming and going, sleeping on floors, bringing friends whose names she often did not know, had at its top an alien zone, which was all order, where the air seemed gently mauve, scented with violets, with cupboards holding decades-old hats that had veils and rhinestones and flowers, and suits of a cut and material not to be bought anywhere now. Julia Lennox descended the stairs, walked down the street, her back straight, her hands in gloves – there were drawers of them – wore perfect shoes, hats, coats, in violet or grey or mauve,

3

and around her was an aura of flower essences. 'Where does she *get* those clothes?' Rose had demanded before she had taken in that truth from the past, that clothes could be kept for years, and not discarded a week after buying them.

Below Frances's slice of the house was a sitting-room that went from back to front of the house, and there, usually on a huge red sofa, took place the intense confidences of teenagers, two by two; or if she opened the door cautiously, she might see on it anything up to half a dozen of 'the kids', cuddled together like a litter of puppies.

The room was not used enough to justify taking such a big slice out of the centre of the house. The life of the house went on in the kitchen. Only if there was a party did this room come into its own, but parties were few because the youngsters went to discos and pop concerts; though it seemed hard for them to tear themselves away from the kitchen, and from a very large table that Julia had once used, one leaf folded down, for dinner parties when she had 'entertained'. As she put it.

Now the table was always at full stretch with sometimes sixteen or twenty chairs and stools around it.

The basement flat was large and often Frances did not know who was camping out there. Sleeping bags and duvets littered the floor like detritus after a storm. She felt like a spy going down there. Apart from insisting they kept it clean and tidy – they were taken by occasional fits of 'tidying up' which it was hard to see made much difference – she did not interfere. Julia had no such inhibitions, and would descend the little stairs and stand surveying the scene of sleepers, sometimes still in their beds at midday or later, the dirty cups on the floors, the piles of records, the radios, clothes lying about in tangles, and then turn herself around slowly, a severe figure in spite of the little veils and gloves that might have a rose pinned at a wrist, and, having seen from the rigidity of a back, or a nervously raised head that her presence had been noted, she would go slowly up the stairs, leaving behind her on the stale air the odours of flowers and expensive face powder.

Frances leaned out of the window to see if light was spilling down the steps from the kitchen: yes, they were all there then, and waiting for supper. Who, tonight? She would soon find out. At that moment Johnny's little Beetle appeared from around the corner, parked itself neatly, and out stepped Johnny. And, at once, three days of foolish dreams dissolved, while she thought, I've been mad, I've been crazy. What made me imagine anything was going to change? If there was in fact a film, then there wouldn't be any money for her and the boys, as usual . . . but he had *said* the contract was signed?

In the time it took her to walk slowly, stopping at the desk to look at the two fateful letters, reaching the door, still taking her time, beginning to descend the stairs, it was as if the last three days had not happened. She was not going to be in the play, not enjoy the dangerous intimacy of the theatre with Tony Wilde, and she was pretty sure that tomorrow she would write to *The Defender* and accept their job.

Slowly, collecting herself, down the stairs, and then, smiling, she stood in the open door of the kitchen. Against the window, standing with his arms spread to take his weight on the sill, stood Johnny, all bravado and – though he was not aware of that – apology. Around the table sat an assortment of youngsters, and Andrew and Colin were both there. All were looking towards Johnny, who had been holding forth about something, and all admiringly, except for his sons. They smiled, like the others, but the smiles were anxious. They, like herself, knew that the money promised for today had vanished into the land of dreams. (Why on earth had she told them? Surely she knew better!) It had all happened before. And they knew, like her, that he had come here now, when the kitchen would be full of young people, so he could not be greeted by rage, tears, reproaches – but that was the past, long ago.

Johnny spread out his arms, palms towards her, smiling painfully, and said, 'The film's off . . . the CIA . . .' At her look he desisted, and was silent, looking nervously at his two boys.

'Don't bother,' said Frances. 'I really didn't expect anything else.' At which the boys turned their eyes to her; their concern for her made her even more self-reproachful.

She stood by the oven where various dishes were shortly to reach their moments of truth. Johnny, as if her back absolved him, began an old speech about the CIA whose machinations this time had been responsible for the film falling through.

Colin, needing some sort of anchor of fact, interrupted to ask, 'But, Dad, I thought the contract . . .'

Johnny said quickly, 'Too many hassles. You wouldn't understand . . . what the CIA wants, the CIA gets.'

A cautious glance over her shoulder showed Colin's face a knot of anger, bewilderment, resentment. Andrew, as always, seemed insouciant, even amused, though she knew how very far he was from that. This scene or something like it had been repeated throughout their childhoods.

In the year the war began, 1939, two youngsters, hopeful and ignorant – like those around the table tonight – had fallen in love, like millions of others in the warring countries, and put their arms around each other for comfort in the cruel world. But there was excitement in it too, war's most dangerous symptom. Johnny Lennox introduced her to the Young Communist League just as he was leaving it to be a grown-up, if not yet a soldier. He was a bit of a star, Comrade Johnny, and needed her to know it. She had sat in the back rows of crowded halls to hear him explain that it was an imperialist war, and the progressive and democratic forces should boycott it. Soon, however, he was in uniform and in the same halls, to the same audiences, exhorting them to do their bit, for now it was a war against fascism, because the attack by the Germans on the Soviet Union had made it so. There were barrackers and protesters, as well as the faithful; there were boos and loud raucous laughter. Johnny was mocked for standing up there tranquilly explaining the new Party Line just as if he had not been saying the exact opposite until recently. Frances was impressed by his calm; accepting – even provoking – hostility by his pose, arms out, palms forward, suffering for the hard necessities of the times. He was in the RAF uniform. He had wanted to be a pilot, but his eyes were not up to it, so he was a corporal, having refused on ideological grounds to be an officer. He would be in administration.

So that had been Frances's introduction to politics, or rather, to Johnny's politics. Something of an achievement, perhaps, to be young in the late Thirties and to care nothing about politics, but so it was. She was a solicitor's daughter from Kent. The theatre had been her window into glamour, adventure, the great world, first in school plays, then in amateur dramatics. She had always played leading roles, but was typecast for her English-rose looks. But now she was in uniform too, one of the young women attached to the War Ministry, mostly driving senior officers around. Attractive young women in uniform in her kind of job had a good time, though this aspect of war tends to be played down from tact, and perhaps even shame, towards the dead. She danced a good deal, she dined, she mildly lost her heart to glamorous Frenchmen, Poles, Americans, but did not forget Johnny, or their anguished passionate nights of love that rehearsed their later longing for each other.

Meanwhile he was in Canada attending to the RAF fliers being trained there. By now he was an officer, and doing well, as his letters made clear; then he came home, an aide to some bigwig, and he was a captain. He was so handsome in his uniform, and she so attractive in hers. In that week they married and Andrew was conceived, and that was the end of her good times, because she was in a room with a baby and was lonely, and frightened, because of the bombing. She had acquired a mother-in-law, the fearsome Julia, who, looking like a society lady in a nineteen-thirties fashion magazine, descended from her house in Hampstead – this house – to show shock at what Frances was

7

living in, and to offer her space in her house. Frances refused. She may not have been political, but with every fibre she shared her generation's fervent desire for independence. When she left her home, it was for a furnished room. And now, having been reduced to little more than Johnny's wife and a baby's mother, she was independent, and could define herself with that thought, holding on to it. Not much, but her own.

And the days and nights dragged by, and she was as far from the glamorous life she had been enjoying as if she had never left her parents' home in Kent. The last two years of the war were hard, poor, frightening. The food was bad. Bombs that seemed to have been designed to wreck people's nerves affected hers. Clothes were hard to find, and ugly. She had no friends, only met other mothers of small children. She was afraid above all that when Johnny came home he would be disappointed in her, an overweight tired young mother, nothing like the smart girl in uniform he had been madly in love with. And that is what happened.

Johnny had done well in the war, and had been noticed. No one could say he wasn't clever and quick, and his politics were unremarkable for that time. He was offered good jobs in the London reshaping itself after the war. He refused them. He wasn't going to be bought by the capitalist system: not by an iota had he changed his mind, his faith. Comrade Johnny Lennox, back in civvies, was preoccupied only by The Revolution.

Colin was born in 1945. Two small children, in a wretched flat in Notting Hill, then a run-down and poor part of London. Johnny was not often at home. He was working for the Party. By now it is necessary to explain that by the Party was meant the Communist Party, and what was meant to be heard was THE PARTY. When two strangers met it might go like this: 'Are you in the Party too?' 'Yes, of course.' I thought you must be.' Meaning: You are a good person, I like you, and so you must, like me, be in the Party.

Frances did not join the Party, though Johnny told her to. It was bad for him, he said, to have a wife who would not join.

'But who would know?' enquired Frances, adding to his contempt for her, because she had no feeling for politics and never would.

'The Party knows,' said Johnny.

'Too bad,' said Frances.

They were definitely not getting on, and the Party was the least of it, though a great irritation for Frances. They were living in real hardship, not to say squalor. He saw this as a sign of inner grace. Returning from a weekend seminar, 'Johnny Lennox on the Threat of American Aggression', he would find her hanging up the children's clothes to dry on rickety arrangements of pulleys and racks screwed precariously to the wall outside the kitchen window, or returning, one child dragging on her hand, the other in a pushchair, from the park. The well of the chair would be full of groceries, and tucked behind the child was a book she had been hoping to read while the children played. 'You are a real working woman, Fran,' he would compliment her.

If he was delighted, his mother was not. When she came, always having written first, on thick white paper you could cut yourself with, she sat with distaste on the edge of a chair which probably had residues of smeared biscuit or orange on it. She would announce, 'Johnny, this cannot go on.'

'And why not, Mutti?'

He called her Mutti because she hated it.

'Your grandchildren,' he would instruct her, 'will be a credit to the People's Britain.'

Frances would not let her eyes meet Julia's at such moments, because she was not going to be disloyal. She felt that her life, all of it, and herself in it, was dowdy, ugly, exhausting, and Johnny's nonsense was just a part of it. It would all end, she was sure of it. It would have to.

And it did, because Johnny announced that he had fallen in love with a real comrade, a Party member, and he was moving in with her.

'And how am I going to live?' asked Frances, already knowing what to expect.

'I'll pay maintenance, of course,' said Johnny, but never did.

She found a council nursery, and got a small job in a business making theatre sets and costumes. It was badly paid, but she managed. Julia arrived to complain that the children were being neglected and their clothes were a disgrace.

'Perhaps you should talk to your son?' said Frances. 'He owes me a year's maintenance.' Then it was two years, three years.

Julia asked whether if she got a decent allowance from the family would she give up her job and look after the boys?

Frances said no.

'But I wouldn't interfere with you,' said Julia. 'I promise you that.'

'You don't understand,' said Frances.

'No, I do not. And perhaps you would explain it to me?'

Johnny left Comrade Maureen and returned to her, Frances, saying that he had made a mistake. She took him back. She was lonely, knew the boys needed a father, was sex-starved.

He left again for another real, genuine comrade. When he again returned to Frances, she said to him: 'Out.'

She was working full time in a theatre, earning not much but enough. The boys were by then ten and eight. There was trouble all the time at the schools, and they were not doing well.

'What do you expect?' said Julia.

'I never expect anything,' said Frances.

Then things changed, dramatically. Frances was amazed to hear that Comrade Johnny had agreed that Andrew should go to a good school. Julia said Eton, because her husband had gone there. Frances was waiting to hear that Johnny had refused Eton, and then was told that Johnny had been there, and had managed to conceal this damaging fact all these years. Julia did not mention it because his Eton career had hardly covered him or them with glory. He had gone for three years, but dropped out to go to the Spanish Civil War.

'You mean to say you are happy for Andrew to go to that school?' Frances said to him, on the telephone.

'Well, you at least get a good education,' said Johnny airily, and she could hear the unspoken: Look what it did for me.

So – Julia paying – Andrew took off from the poor rooms his mother and brother were living in, for Eton, and spent his holidays with schoolfriends, and became a polite stranger.

Frances went to an end-of-term at Eton, in an outfit bought to fit what she imagined would suit the occasion, and the first hat she had ever worn. She did all right, she thought, and could see Andrew was relieved when he saw her.

Then people came to ask after Julia, Philip's widow, and the daughter-in-law of Philip's father: an old man remembered him, as a small boy. It seemed the Lennoxes went to Eton as a matter of course. Johnny, or Jolyon, was enquired after. 'Interesting . . .' said a man who had been Johnny's teacher. 'An interesting choice of career.'

Thereafter Julia went to the formal occasions, where she was made much of, and was surprised at it: visiting Eton in those brief three years of Jolyon's attendance there, she had seen herself as Philip's wife, and of not much account.

Colin refused Eton, because of a deep, complicated loyalty to his mother whom he had watched struggling all these years. This did not mean he did not quarrel with her, fight her, argue, and did so badly at school Frances was secretly convinced he was doing it on purpose to hurt her. But he was cold and angry with his father, when Johnny did blow in to say that he was so terribly sorry, but he really did not have the money to give them. He agreed to go to a progressive school, St Joseph's, Julia paying for everything.

Johnny then came up with a suggestion that Frances at last did not refuse. Julia would let her and the boys have the lower part of her house. She did not need all that room, it was ridiculous . . .

Frances thought of Andrew, returning to various squalid addresses, or not returning, certainly never bringing friends home.

She thought of Colin who made no secret of how much he hated how they were living. She said yes to Johnny, yes to Julia, and found herself in the great house that was Julia's and always would be.

Only she knew what it cost her. She had kept her independence all this time, paid for herself and the boys, and not accepted money from Julia, nor from her parents who would have been happy to help. Now here she was, and it was a final capitulation: what to other people was 'such a sensible arrangement' was defeat. She was no longer herself, she was an appendage of the Lennox family.

As far as Johnny was concerned, he had done as much as could be expected of him. When his mother told him he should support his sons, get a job that paid him a salary, he shouted at her that she was a typical member of an exploiting class, thinking only of money, while he was working for the future of the whole world. They quarrelled, frequently and noisily. Listening, Colin would go white, silent, and leave the house for hours or for days. Andrew preserved his airy, amused smile, his poise. He was often at home these days, and even brought friends.

Meanwhile Johnny and Frances had divorced because he had married properly, and formally, with a wedding that the comrades attended, and Julia too. Her name was Phyllida, and she was not a comrade, but he said she was good material and he would make a communist of her.

This little history was the reason why Frances was keeping her back to the others, stirring a stew that didn't really need a stir. Delayed reaction: her knees trembled, her mouth seemed full of acid, for now her body was taking in the bad news, rather later than her mind. She was angry, she knew, and had the right to be, but she was angrier with herself than with Johnny. If she had allowed herself to spend three days inside a lunatic dream, fair enough – but how could she have involved the boys? Yet it was

Andrew who had brought the telegram, waited until she showed it to him, and said, 'Frances, your errant husband is at last going to do the right thing.' He had sat lightly on the edge of a chair, a fair, attractive youth, looking more than ever like a bird just about to take off. He was tall and that made him seem even thinner, his jeans loose on long legs, and with long elegant bony hands lying palms up on his knees. He was smiling at her, and she knew it was meant kindly. They were trying hard to get on, but she was still nervous of him, because of those years of him rejecting her. He had said 'your husband', he had not said 'my father'. He was friendly with Johnny's new wife, Phyllida, while reporting back that she was on the whole a bit of a drag.

He had congratulated her on her part in the new play and had made graceful fun of agony aunts.

And Colin, too, had been affectionate, a rare thing for him, and had telephoned friends about the new play.

It was all so bad for them both, it was all *terrible*, but after all only another little blow in years and years of them – as she was telling herself, waiting for her knees to get back their strength, while she gripped the edge of a drawer with one hand and stirred with the other, eyes closed.

Behind her Johnny was holding forth about the capitalist press and its lies about the Soviet Union, about Fidel Castro, and how he was being misrepresented.

That Frances had been scarcely touched by years of Johnny's strictures, or his lexicon, was shown by the way, after a recent lecture, she had murmured, 'He seems quite an interesting person.' Johnny had snapped at her, 'I don't think I've managed to teach you anything, Frances, you are unteachable.'

'Yes, I know, I'm stupid.' That had been a repetition of the great, primal, but at the same time final, moment, when Johnny had returned to her for the second time, expecting her to take him in: he had shouted that she was a political cretin, a lumpen petite bourgeois, a class enemy, and she had said, 'That's right, I'm stupid, now get out.'

She could not go on standing here, knowing that the boys were watching her, nervously, hurt because of her, even if the others were gazing at Johnny with eyes shining with love and admiration.

She said, 'Sophie, give me a hand.'

At once willing hands appeared, Sophie's and, it seemed, everyone's, and dishes were being set down the centre of the table. There were wonderful smells as the covers came off.

They sat down at the head of the table, glad to sit, not looking at Johnny. All the chairs were full, but others stood by the wall, and, if he wanted, he could bring one up and sit down himself. Was he going to do this? He often did, infuriating her, though he believed, it was obvious, that it was a compliment. No, tonight, having made an impression, and got his fill of admiration (if he ever did) he was going to leave – surely? He was not leaving. The wine glasses were full, all around the table. Johnny had brought two bottles of wine: open-handed Johnny, who never entered a room without offerings of wine . . . she was unable to prevent this bile, these bitter words, arriving unwanted on her tongue. Just go away, she was mentally urging him. Just leave.

She had cooked a large, filling, winter stew of beef and chest-nuts, from a recipe of Elizabeth David, whose *French Country Cooking* was lying open somewhere in the kitchen. (Years later she would say, Good Lord, I was part of a culinary revolution and didn't know it.) She was convinced that these youngsters did not eat 'properly' unless it was at this table. Andrew was dispensing mashed potatoes flavoured with celeriac. Sophie ladled out stew. Creamed spinach and buttered carrots were being allotted by Colin. Johnny stood watching, silenced for the moment because no one was looking at him.

Why didn't he leave?

Around the table this evening were what she thought of as the regulars: or at least some of them. On her left was Andrew, who had served himself generously, but now sat looking down at the food as if he didn't recognise it. Next to him was Geoffrey

Bone, Colin's schoolfriend, who had spent all his holidays with them since she could remember. He did not get on with his parents, Colin said. (But who did, after all?) Beside him Colin had already turned his round flushed face towards his father, all accusing anguish, while his knife and fork rested in his hands. Next to Colin, was Rose Trimble, who had been Andrew's girlfriend, if briefly: an obligatory flutter with Marxism had taken him to a weekend seminar entitled, 'Africa Bursts Its Chains!', and there Rose had been. Their affair (had it been that? – she was sixteen) had ended, but Rose still came here, seemed in fact to have moved in. Opposite Rose was Sophie, a Jewish girl in the full bloom of her beauty, slender, black gleaming eyes, black gleaming hair, and people seeing her had to be afflicted with thoughts of the intrinsic unfairness of Fate, and then of the imperatives of Beauty and its claims. Colin was in love with her. So was Andrew. So was Geoffrey. Next to Sophie, and the very opposite, in every way, of Geoffrey, who was so correctly good-looking, English, polite, well-behaved, was stormy and suffering Daniel, who had just been threatened with expulsion from St Joseph's for shoplifting. He was deputy head boy, and Geoffrey was head boy, and had had to convey to Daniel that he must reform or else – an empty threat, certainly, made for the sake of impressing the others with the seriousness of what they all did. This little event, ironically discussed by these worldly-wise children, was confirmation, if any was needed, of the inherent unfairness of the world, since Geoffrey shoplifted all the time, but it was hard to associate that open eagerly-polite face with wrongdoing. And there was another ingredient here: Daniel worshipped Geoffrey, always had, and to be admonished by his hero was more than he could bear.

Next to Daniel was a girl Frances had not seen before, but she expected to be enlightened in good time. She was a fair well-washed well-presented girl whose name appeared to be Jill. On Frances's right was Lucy, not from St Joseph's: she was Daniel's girlfriend from Dartington, often here. Lucy, who at an ordinary school would certainly have been prefect, being decisive, clever, responsible and born to rule, said that progressive schools, or at least Dartington, suited some people well, but others needed discipline, and she wished she was at an ordinary school with rules and regulations and exams one had to work for. Daniel said that St Joseph's was hypocritical shit, preaching freedom but when it came to the point clamping down with morality. 'I wouldn't say clamping down,' explained Geoffrey pleasantly to everyone, protecting his acolyte, 'it was more indicating the limits.' 'For some,' said Daniel. 'Unfair, I'll grant you,' said Geoffrey.

Sophie said she adored St Joseph's and adored Sam (the headmaster). The boys tried to look indifferent at this news.

Colin continued to do so badly at exams that his unthreatened life was a tribute to the school's famous tolerance.

Of Rose's many grievances against life, she complained most that she had not been sent to a progressive school, and when their virtues or otherwise were discussed, which happened frequently and noisily, she would sit silent, her always rubicund face ever redder with anger. Her shitty horrible parents had sent her to a normal girls' school in Sheffield, but though she had apparently 'dropped out', and appeared to be living here, her accusations against it did not lessen, and she tended to burst into tears, crying out that they didn't know how lucky they were. Andrew had actually met Rose's parents, who were both officials in the local council. 'And what is wrong with them?' Frances had enquired, hoping to hear well of them, because she wanted Rose to go, since she did not like the girl. (And why did she not tell Rose to leave? That would not have been in the spirit of the times.) 'I am afraid they are just ordinary,' replied Andrew, smiling. 'They are conventional small-town people, and I do think they are a bit out of their depth with Rose.'

'Ah,' said Frances, seeing the possibility of Rose's returning home recede. And there was something else here too. Had she not said of her parents that they were boring and conventional? Not that they were shitty fascists, but perhaps she would have described them thus had the epithets been as available to her as they were to Rose. How could she criticise the girl for wanting to leave parents *who did not understand her*?

Second helpings were already being piled on to plates – all except Andrew's. He had hardly touched his food. Frances pretended not to notice.

Andrew was in trouble, but how bad it was hard to say.

He had done pretty well at Eton, had made friends, which she gathered was what they were meant to do, and was going to Cambridge next year. This year, he said, he was loafing. And he certainly was. He slept sometimes until four or five in the afternoon, looked ill, and concealed – what? – behind his charm, his social competence.

Frances knew he was unhappy – but it was not news that her sons were unhappy. Something should be done. It was Julia who came down to her layer of the house to say, 'Frances, have you been inside Andrew's room?'

'I wouldn't dare go into his room without asking.'

'You are his mother, I believe.'

The gulfs between them illumined by this exchange caused Frances, as always, to stare helplessly at her mother-in-law. She did not know what to say. Julia, an immaculate figure, stood there like Judgement, waiting, and Frances felt herself to be a schoolgirl, wanting to shift from foot to foot.

'You can hardly see across the room for the smoke,' said Julia.

'Oh, I see, you mean pot – marijuana? But Julia, a lot of them smoke it.' She did not dare say she had tried it herself.

'So, to you it's nothing? It's not important?'

'I didn't say that.'

'He sleeps all day, he fuddles himself with that smoke, he doesn't eat.'

'Julia, what do you want me to do?'

'Talk to him.'

'I can't . . . I couldn't . . . he wouldn't listen to me.'

'Then I will talk to him.' And Julia went, turning on a crisp little heel, leaving the scent of roses behind her.

Julia and Andrew did talk. Soon Andrew took to visiting Julia in her rooms, which no one had dared to do, and returned often with information meant to smooth paths and oil wheels.

'She's not as bad as you think. In fact, she's rather a poppet.'

'Not the word that would immediately come to my mind.'

'Well, I like her.'

'I wish she'd come downstairs sometimes. She might eat with us?'

'She wouldn't come. She doesn't approve of us,' said Colin.

'She might reform us,' – Frances attempted humour.

'Ha! Ha! But why don't you invite her?'

'I'm scared of Julia,' said Frances, admitting it for the first time.

'She's frightened of you!' said Andrew.

'Oh, but that's absurd. I am sure she's never been frightened of anyone.'

'Look, mother, you don't understand. She has had such a sheltered life. She's not used to our rackety ways. You forget that until grandfather died I don't think she boiled an egg for herself. And you cope with hungry hordes and speak their language. Don't you see?' He had said *their* not *our*.

'All I know is she sits up there eating a finger of smoked herring and two inches of bread and drinking one glass of wine while we sit down here guzzling great meals. We could send up a tray, perhaps.'

'I'll ask her,' Andrew said, and presumably did, but nothing changed.

Frances made herself go up the stairs to his room. Six o'clock, and already getting dark. This had been a couple of weeks ago. She knocked, though her legs had nearly taken her downstairs again.

After quite a wait, she heard, 'Come in.'

Frances went in. Andrew lay dressed on the bed, smoking. The window beyond him showed a blur of cold rain.

'It's six o'clock,' she said.

'I know it is six o'clock.'

Frances sat down, without the invitation she needed. The room was a big one, furnished with old solid furniture and some beautiful Chinese lamps. Andrew seemed the wrong inhabitant for it, and Frances could not help bringing to mind Julia's husband, the diplomat, who would certainly be at home here.

'Have you come to lecture me? Don't bother, Julia already has done her bit.'

'I'm worried,' said Frances, her voice trembled; years, decades of worry were crowding into her throat.

Andrew lifted his head off the pillow to inspect her. Not with enmity, but rather with weariness. 'I alarm myself,' he said. 'But I think I am about to take myself in hand.'

'Are you, Andrew? Are you?'

'After all, it is not as if it were heroin, or coke, or . . . after all, there are no caches of empty bottles rolling about under the bed.'

There were in fact some little blue pills scattered there.

'What are those little blue pills then?'

'Ah, the little blue pills. Amphetamines. Don't worry about them.'

'And,' said Frances, quoting, meaning to sound ironical and failing, 'it's non-addictive, and you can give it up at any time.'

'I don't know about that. I think I'm addicted – to pot, though. It certainly takes the edge off reality. Why don't you try it?'

'I did try it. It doesn't do anything for me.'

'Too bad,' said Andrew. 'I would say that you have more reality than you can cope with.'

He did not say anything more, and so she waited a little, and got up to leave and heard as she closed the door on him, 'Thanks for coming, Mother. Drop in again.'

Was it possible he wanted her 'interference' – had been waiting for her to visit him, wanted to talk?

On this particular evening she could feel the bonds between herself and her two sons, but it was all terrible – the three of them were close tonight because of disappointment, a blow falling where it had before.

Sophie was talking. 'Did you know about Frances's wonderful new part?' she said to Johnny. 'She's going to be a star. It's so *wonderful*. Have you read the play?'

'Sophie,' said Frances, 'I'm not doing the play after all.'

Sophie stared at her, her great eyes already full of tears. 'What do you mean? You can't . . . it's not . . . it *can't* be true.'

'I'm not doing it, Sophie.'

Both sons were looking at Sophie, probably even kicking her under the table: *shut up*.

'Oh,' gasped the lovely girl, and buried her face in her hands.

'Things have changed,' said Frances. 'I can't explain.'

Now both boys were looking, full of accusation, at their father. He shifted a bit, seemed to shrug, suppressed that, smiled and then suddenly came out with: 'There's something else I've come to say, Frances.'

And so that was why he hadn't left, but had stood uncomfortably there, not sitting down: he had something more to say.

Frances braced herself and saw that Colin and Andrew did the same.

'I have a big favour to ask of you,' said Johnny, direct to his betrayed wife.

'And what is that?'

'You know about Tilly, of course . . . you know, Phyllida's girl?'

'Of course I know about her.'

Andrew, visiting Phyllida, had allowed it to be understood that it was not a harmonious household and that the child was giving a lot of trouble.

'Phyllida doesn't seem able to cope with Tilly.'

At this, Frances laughed loudly, for she already knew what

20

was bound to come. She said, 'No, it's simply not possible, it isn't *on*.'

'Yes, Frances, think about it. They don't get on. Phyllida's at her wit's end. And so am I. I want you to have Tilly here. You are so good with . . .'

Frances was breathless with anger, saw that the two boys were white with it; the three were sitting silent, looking at each other.

Sophie was exclaiming, 'Oh, Frances, and you are so kind, it's so wonderful.'

Geoffrey, who had after all been so long visiting this house that he could with justice be described as a member of the household, followed Sophie with, 'What a groovy idea.'

'Just a minute, Johnny,' said Frances. 'You are asking me to take on your second wife's daughter because you two can't cope with her?'

'That's about it,' admitted Johnny, smiling.

There was a long, long pause. It had occurred to enthusiastic Sophie and Geoffrey that Frances was not taking this in the spirit of universal liberal idealism they had at first assumed she would: that spirit of *everything is for the best in the best of all possible worlds*, which would one day be shorthand for 'The Sixties'.

Frances managed to bring out: 'You are perhaps planning to contribute something to her support?' – and realised that, saying this, she was agreeing.

At this Johnny glanced around the young faces, judging if they were as shocked by her pettiness as he was. 'Money,' he said loftily, 'is really not the point here.'

Frances was again silenced. She got up, went to the working surface near the stove, stood with her back to the room.

'I want to bring Tilly here,' said Johnny. 'And in fact she's here. She's in the car.'

Colin and Andrew both got up and went to their mother, standing on either side of her. This enabled her to turn around and face Johnny across the room. She could not speak. And

Johnny, seeing his former wife flanked by their sons, three angry people with white accusing faces, was also, but just for the moment, silenced.

Then he rallied, stretched out his arms, palms towards them, and said, 'From each according to their capacity, to each according to their need.' And let his arms drop.

'Oh, that is so beautiful,' said Rose.

'Groovy,' said Geoffrey.

The newcomer, Jill, breathed, 'Oh, it's lovely.'

All eyes were now on Johnny, a situation he was well used to. He stood, receiving rays of criticism, beams of love, and smiled at them. He was a tall man, Comrade Johnny, with already greying hair cut like a Roman's, *at your service always*, and he wore tight black jeans, a black leather Mao jacket especially made for him by an admiring comrade in the rag trade. Severity was his preferred style, smiling or not, for a smile could never be more than a temporary concession, but he was smiling boldly now.

'Do you mean to say,' said Andrew, 'that Tilly's been out there in the car waiting, all this time?'

'Good God,' said Colin. 'Typical.'

'I'll go and bring her in,' said Johnny, and marched out, brushing past his ex-wife and Colin and Andrew, not looking at them.

No one moved. Frances thought if her sons had not been so close, enveloping her with their support, she would have fallen. All the faces around the table were turned towards them: that this was a very bad moment, they had at last understood.

They heard the front door open – Johnny of course had a key to his mother's house – and then in the doorway to this room, the kitchen, stood a little frightened figure, in a big duffel-coat, trembling with cold, trying to smile, but instead out of her burst a great wail, as she looked at Frances, who she had been told was kind and would look after her, 'until we get things straightened out'. She was a little bird blown by a storm, and Frances was across the room to her, and had her arms round her, saying, 'It's all right, shhh, it's all right.' Then she remembered this was not a child, but a girl of fourteen or so, and her impulse, to sit down and hold this waif on her lap was out of order. Meanwhile Johnny, just behind the girl, was saying, 'I think bed is indicated,' and then, generally around the room, 'I'll be off.' But did not go.

The girl was looking in appeal at Andrew, whom after all she did know, among all these strangers.

'Don't worry, I'll deal with it.' He put his arm round Tilly, and turned to go out of the room.

'I'll put her down in the basement,' he said. 'It's nice and warm down there.'

'Oh, no, no, no, please,' cried the girl. 'Don't, I cannot be alone, I can't, don't make me.'

'Of course not, if you don't want to,' said Andrew. Then, to his mother, 'I'll put a bed in with me for tonight.' And he led her out. They all sat quiet, listening to how he coaxed her up the stairs.

Johnny was face to face with Frances, who said to him, low, hoping it would not be heard by the others, 'Go away, Johnny. Just get out.'

He tried an appealing smile around, caught Rose's eyes, who did smile back, but she was doubtful, withstood passionate reproach from Sophie, nodded sternly at Geoffrey, whom he had known for years. And left. The front door shut. The car door slammed.

Now Colin was hovering behind Frances, touching her arm, her shoulder, not knowing what to do.

'Come on,' he said, 'come on upstairs.' They went out together. Frances began swearing as she climbed the stairs, first softly, so as not to be heard by the young, then loudly, 'Fuck him, fuck him, fuck, the shit, the absolute *shit*.' In her sitting-room she sat crying, while Colin, at a loss, at last thought of getting her tissues and then a glass of water.

Meanwhile Julia had been told by Andrew what was going

on. She came down, opened Frances's door without knocking, and marched in. 'Please explain it to me,' she said. 'I don't understand. Why do you let him behave like this?'

Julia von Arne was born in a particularly charming part of Germany, near Stuttgart, a region of hills, streams and vineyards. She was the only girl, the third child in a genial gentle family. Her father was a diplomat, her mother a musician. In July 1914 came visiting Philip Lennox, a promising Third Secretary from the embassy in Berlin. That fourteen-year-old Julia should fall in love with handsome Philip – he was twenty-five – was not surprising, but he fell in love with her. She was pretty, tiny, with golden ringlets, and wore frocks the romantic man told her were like flowers. She had been brought up strictly, by governesses, English and French, and to him it seemed that every gesture she made, every smile, every turn of her head, was formal, prescribed, as if she moved in a dance. Like all girls taught to be conscious of their bodies, because of the frightful dangers of immodesty, her eyes spoke for her, could strike to the heart with a glance, and when she lowered delicate eyelids over blue invitations to love he felt he was being rejected. He had sisters, whom he had seen a few days ago in Sussex, jolly tomboys enjoying the exemplary summer that has been celebrated in so many memoirs and novels. A sister's friend, Betty, had been teased because she came to supper with solid brown arms where white scratches showed how she had been playing in the hay with the dogs. His family had watched him to see if he fancied this girl, who would make a suitable wife, and he had been prepared to consider her. This little German miss seemed to him as glamorous as a beauty glimpsed in a harem, all promise and hidden bliss, and he fancied that if a sunbeam did strike her she would melt like a snowflake. She gave him a red rose from the garden, and he knew she was offering him her heart. He declared his love in the moonlight, and next day spoke to her father. Yes, he knew that fourteen was too young, but he was asking for formal permission to propose when she was sixteen. And so they parted, in 1914, while war was coming to a boil, but like many liberal well-adjusted people it seemed to both the von Arnes and the Lennoxes that it was ridiculous Germany and England could go to war. When war was declared, Philip had left his love in tears just two weeks before. In those days governments seemed compelled to announce that wars must be over by Christmas, and the lovers were sure they would see each other soon.

Almost at once xenophobia was poisoning Julia's love. Her family did not mind her loving her Englishman – did not their respective Emperors call themselves cousins? – but the neighbours commented, and servants whispered and gossiped. During the years of the war rumours followed Julia and her family too. Her three brothers were fighting in the Trenches, her father was in the War Office, and her mother did war work, but those few days of fever in July 1914 marked them all for comment and suspicion. Julia never lost her faith in her love and in Philip. He was wounded, twice, and in devious ways she heard about it and wept for him. It did not matter, cried Julia's heart, how badly he was wounded, she would love him for ever. He was demobbed in 1919. She was waiting for him, knowing he was coming to claim her, when into the room where five years before they had flirted came a man she felt she ought to know. An empty sleeve was pinned up on his chest, and his face was taut and lined. She was now nearly twenty. He saw a tall young woman – she had grown some inches – with fair hair piled on top of her head, held with a big jet arrow, and wearing heavy black for two dead brothers. A third brother, a boy – he was not yet twenty – had been wounded and sat, still in his uniform, a stiff leg propped before him on a stool. The two so recent enemies, stared at each other. Then Philip, not smiling, went forward with an outstretched hand. The youth made an involuntary movement of turning away, with a grimace, but he recovered himself and civilisation was reinstated as he smiled, and the two men shook hands.

This scene, which after all has repeated itself in various forms since then, did not then have as much weight on it as it would now. Irony, which celebrates that element which we persist in excluding from our vision of things, would have been too much for them to bear: we have become coarser-fibred.

And now these two lovers who would not have recognised each other passing in a street, had to decide whether their dreams of each other for all those terrible years were strong enough to carry them through into marriage. Nothing was left of the enchanting prim little girl, nor of the sentimental man who had, until it crumbled away, carried a dead red rose next to his heart. The great blue eyes were sad, and he tended to lapse into silences, just like her younger brother, when remembering things that could be understood only by other soldiers.

These two married quietly: hardly the time for a big German–English wedding. In London war fever was abating, though people still talked about the Boche and the Hun. People were polite to Julia. For the first time she wondered if choosing Philip had not been a mistake, yet she believed they loved each other, and both were pretending they were serious people by nature and not saddened beyond curing. And yet the war did recede and the worst of the war hatreds passed. Julia, who had suffered in Germany for her English love, now tried to become English, in an act of will. She had spoken English well enough, but took lessons again, and soon spoke as no English person ever did, an exquisite perfect English, every word separate. She knew her manners were formal, and tried to become more casual. Her clothes: they were perfect too, but after all, she was a diplomat's wife and had to keep up appearances. As the English put it.

They started married life in a little house in Mayfair, and there she entertained, as was expected of her, with the aid of a cook and a maid, and achieved something like the standards she remembered from her home. Meanwhile Philip had discovered that to marry a German woman had not been the best prescription for an unclouded career. Discussions with his superiors revealed that certain posts would be barred to him, in Germany, for instance, and he might find himself edged out of the straight highway to the top, and find himself in places like South Africa or Argentina. He decided to avoid disappointments, and switched to administration. He would have a fine career, but nothing of the glamour of foreign ministries. Sometimes he met in a sister's house the Betty whom he could have married – and who was still unwed, because of so many men being killed – and wondered how different life could have been.

When Jolyon Meredith Wilhelm Lennox was born in 1920 he had a nurse and then a nanny. He was a long thin child, with golden curls and combative critical blue eyes, often directed at his mother. He had soon learned from his nanny that he was a German: he had a little tantrum and was difficult for a few days. He was taken to visit his German family, but this was not a success: he disliked the place, and the different manners – he was expected to sit at mealtimes with his hands beside him on either side of his plate when not actually eating, speak when spoken to, and to click his heels when he made a request. He refused to go back. Julia argued with Philip about her child being sent off at seven to school. This is not unusual now, but then Julia was being brave. Philip told her that everyone of their class did this, and anyway look at him! – he had gone to boarding school at seven. Yes, he did remember he had been a bit homesick . . . never mind, it wore off. That argument, 'Look at me!', expected to cast down opposition because of the speaker's conviction of his superiority or at least rightness, did not convince Julia. In Philip there was a place forever barred to her, a reserve, a coldness, which at first she ascribed to the war, the trenches, the soldier's hidden psychological scars. But then she had begun to doubt: she had never achieved intimacy enough with the wives of her husband's colleagues to ask if they too experienced this forbidden place in their men, the area marked VERBOTEN, No Entrance – but she did observe, she noticed a good deal. No, she thought, if you are going to take a child from its mother so young . . . She lost the fight, and lost her son; who thereafter was polite, affable, if often impatient.

As far as she could see he did well in his first school, but Eton did not go well. His reports were not good. 'He does not make friends easily.' 'A bit of a loner.'

She asked him one holidays, manoeuvring him into a position where he could not escape easily, for he did evade direct questions and situations, 'Tell me, Jolyon, has my being German made problems for you?'

His eyes seemed to flicker, wanted to evade, but he faced her with his wide polite smile, and said, 'No, mother, why should it?'

'I wondered, that's all.'

She asked Philip if he would 'talk' to Jolyon, meaning, of course, Please change him, he's breaking my heart.

'He plays his cards pretty close to his chest,' was her husband's reply.

Her worries were in fact soothed by the mere fact of Eton, the fact and the weight of it, a purveyor of excellence and a guarantee of success. She had surrendered her son – her only child – to the English educational system, and expected a quid pro quo, that Jolyon would turn out well, like his father. and in due course walk in his footsteps, probably as a diplomat.

When Philip's father died, and then, soon after, his mother, he wanted to move into the big house in Hampstead. It was the family house, and he, the son, would live in it. Julia liked the little house in Mayfair, so easy to run and keep clean and did not want to live in the big house with its many rooms. But that was what she found herself doing. She did not ever set her will against Philip's. They did not quarrel. They got along because she did not insist on her preferences. She behaved as she had seen her mother do, giving way to her father. Well, one side had to give way, the way Julia saw it, and it did not much matter which. Peace in the family was the important thing.

The furniture of the little house, most of it from the home

in Germany, was absorbed quite easily into the Hampstead house where in fact Julia did not seem to do nearly as much entertaining, though there was so much space for everything. For one thing, Philip was not really a sociable man: he had one or two close friends and saw them, often by himself. And Julia supposed she must be getting old and boring, because she did not enjoy parties as much as she had. But there were dinner parties and, often, important people, and she was pleased she did it all so well, and that Philip was proud of her.

She went home to Germany for visits. Her parents, who were getting old, were so glad to see their daughter, and she liked her brother, now her only brother. But going home was troubling, even frightening. Poverty and unemployment, and the communists and then the Nazis were everywhere, and gangs roamed the streets. Then there was Hitler. The von Arnes despised in equal measure the communists and Hitler, and believed that both unpleasant phenomena would simply go away. This was not their Germany, they said. It was certainly not what Julia remembered as her Germany, that is, of course, if she forgot the vicious rumour-mongering during the war. A spy, they had said she was. Not serious people, of course, not educated people . . . well, yes, there were one or two. She decided she did not much like visiting Germany these days, and it was easier not to, when her parents died.

The English were sensible people, after all, she had to agree to that. One couldn't imagine allowing battles between communists and fascists in the streets – well, there were some scuffles, but one mustn't exaggerate, there was nothing like Hitler.

A letter arrived from Eton saying that Jolyon had disappeared, leaving behind a note saying that he was off to the Spanish Civil War, signed, Comrade Johnny Lennox.

Philip used every influence to find out where their son was. The International Brigade? Madrid? Catalonia? No one seemed to know. Julia tended to sympathise with her son, for she had been shocked at the treatment of the elected government in Spain, by Britain and the French. Her husband, who was a diplomat after all, defended his government and his country but alone with her said he was ashamed. He did not admire the policies he was defending and conducting.

Months passed. Then a telegram arrived from their son, asking for money: address, a house in the East End of London. Julia at once saw this meant he was wanting them to visit him, otherwise he would have designated a bank where he could pick up the money. Together she and Philip went to a house in a poor street, and found Jolyon being nursed by a decent sort of woman of the kind Julia at once thought of as a possible servant. He was in an upstairs room, ill with hepatitis, caught, presumably, in Spain. Then talking with this woman, who called herself Comrade Mary, it slowly became evident she knew nothing of Spain, and then that Jolyon had not been in Spain, but had been here, in this house, ill.

'Took me a bit of time to see he was having a bit of a breakdown,' said Comrade Mary.

These were poor people. Philip wrote out a fair-sized cheque, and was told, politely enough, that they did not have a bank account, with the only just sarcastic implication that bank accounts were for the well off. Since they did not have that kind of money on them, Philip said that money would be delivered, next day, and it was. Jolyon, but he was insisting on being called Johnny, was so thin the bones of his face suggested the skeleton, and while he kept saying that Comrade Mary and her family were the salt of the earth, easily agreed to come home.

That was the last his parents heard of Spain, but in the Young Communist League, where he now became a star, he was a Spanish Civil War hero.

Johnny had a room, and then a floor, in the big house, and there many people came who disturbed the parents, and made Julia actively miserable. They were all communists, usually very young, and always taking Johnny off to meetings, rallies, weekend schools, marches. She said to Johnny that if he had seen the streets in Germany full of rival gangs he would have nothing to do with such people, and as a result of the quarrel that followed he simply left. He anticipated later patterns of behaviour by living in comrades' houses, sleeping on floors or anywhere there was a corner for him, and asked his parents for money. 'After all, I suppose you don't want me to starve even if I am a communist.'

Julia and Philip did not know about Frances, not until Johnny married her when he came on leave, though Julia was familiar enough with what she described as 'that type of girl'. She had been observing the smart cheeky flirty girls who looked after the senior officials – some were attached to her husband's department. She had asked herself, 'Is it right to be having such a good time in the middle of this terrible war?' Well, at least no one could say they were hypocrites. (An ancient lady, standing to spray white curls with a fixative and peering at herself mournfully in a mirror, said, decades later: 'Oh, we had such a good time, such a good time – it was so *glamorous* – do you understand?')

Julia's war could have been really terrible. Her name had been on a list of those Germans who were sent off to the internment camp on the Isle of Man. Philip told her: 'There was never a question of your being interned, it was just an administrative error.' But error or not, it had taken Philip's intervention to get her name removed. This war afflicted Julia with memories of the last one, and she could not believe that yet again countries meant to be friends should be at war. She was not well, slept badly, wept. Philip was kind – he was always a kind man. He held Julia in his arms and rocked her, 'There now, my dear, there now.' He was able to hold Julia because he had one of the new clever artificial arms, which could do everything. Well, nearly everything. At night he took the arm off and hung it on its stand. Now he could only partially hold Julia, and she tended to hold him.

The parent Lennoxes were not asked to the wedding of their son Jolyon with Frances. They were told about it, in a telegram, just as he was off again to Canada. At first Julia could not believe he was treating them like this. Philip held her and said, 'You

31

don't understand, Julia.' 'No, I don't, I don't understand anything.' With humour that made his voice grate, he said, 'We're class enemies, don't you see? No, don't cry Julia, he'll grow up, I expect.' But he was staring over her shoulder with a face set in the dismay that was what she felt – and felt more often and more strongly every day. A weeping, generalised, drizzling dismay, and she could not shake it off.

They knew that Johnny was 'doing well' in Canada. What did doing well mean in this context? Soon after he had returned there, a letter arrived with a photograph of him and Frances on the steps of the register office. They were both in uniform, hers as tight as a corset, and she was a bright, apparently giggling, blonde. 'Silly girl,' judged Julia, putting the letter and photograph away. The letter had a censor's stamp on it, as if it were out of bounds – which is what she felt. Then Johnny wrote a note to say, 'You might drop in to see how Frances is doing. She is pregnant.'

Julia did not go. Then came an airletter, saying a baby had been born, a boy, and he felt the least Julia could do was to visit her. 'His name is Andrew,' said the postscript, an afterthought, apparently; and Julia remembered the announcements of Jolyon's birth, sent out in a large white thick envelopes, on a card like thin china, and the elegant black script that said, *Jolyon Meredith Wilhelm Lennox*. None of the recipients could have doubted that here was an important new addition to the human race.

She supposed she should go and see her daughter-in-law, put it off, and when she reached the address Johnny had provided, found Frances gone. It was a dreary street that had a house sagging to its knees in ruins, because of a bomb. Julia was glad she did not have to enter any house there, but she was directed to another that seemed even worse. It was in Notting Hill; she was let in by a slatternly woman who did not smile, and she was told to knock on that door there, the one with the cracked skylight.

She knocked, and an irritated voice called, 'Wait a minute, okay, come in.' The room was large, badly lit, and the windows were dirty. Faded green sateen curtains and frayed rugs. In the greenish half-dark sat a large young woman, her unstockinged legs apart, and her baby sprawled across her chest. She held a book in her hand, above the baby's head; a rhythmically working little head, the spread-out hands opening and shutting on naked flesh. The exposed breast, large and lolling, exuded milk in sympathy.

Julia's first thought was that she had come to the wrong house, because this young woman could not be the one in the photograph. While she stood there forcing herself to admit that she was indeed looking at Frances, Jolyon Meredith Wilhelm's wife, the young woman said, 'Do sit down.' She sounded as if having to say this, even to contemplate Julia's being there, was the last straw. She frowned as she eased her breast out of a discomfort, the baby's mouth popped off the nipple, and milky liquid ran down over the breast to a sagging waist. Frances eased the nipple back, the infant let out a choking cry and then fastened itself again on the nipple with a little shaking movement of its head Julia had observed in puppies ranged along the teats of a nursing bitch, her little pet dachshund, from long ago. Frances put a piece of cloth Julia could swear was a nappy over the resting breast.

The women stared at each other, with dislike.

Julia did not sit. There was a chair, but the seat was suspiciously stained. She could sit on the bed, which was unmade, but did not care to. She said, 'Johnny wrote to ask me to find out how you are.'

The cool, light, almost drawling voice, modulated according to some measure or scale known only to Julia, caused the young woman to stare again, and then she laughed.

'I am as you see, Julia,' said Frances.

Julia was filling with panic. She thought this place horrible, a lower depth of squalor. The house she and Philip had found Johnny in at the time of the Spanish Civil War misadventure had been a poor one, thin-walled, temporary in feel, but it had been clean, and Mary the landlady was a decent sort of woman. In this place Julia felt trapped in a nightmare. That shameless young

33

woman half-naked there, with her great oozing breasts, the baby's noisy sucking, a faint smell of sick, or of nappies . . . Julia felt that Frances was forcing her, most brutally, to look directly at an unclean unseemly fount of life that she had never had to acknowledge. Her own baby had been presented to her as a well-washed bundle after he had been fed by the nurse. Julia had refused to breastfeed; too near the animal, she felt, but did not dare say. Doctors and nurses had tactfully agreed that she was not able to nurse . . . her health . . . Julia had often played with the little boy who arrived in the drawing-room with toys, and she actually sat on the floor with him, and enjoyed a play hour, measured by the nanny to the minute. She remembered the smell of soap, and baby powder. She remembered sniffing at Jolyon's little head with such pleasure . . .

Frances was thinking, It's unbelievable. *She* is unbelievable, and derision was in danger of making her burst out in raucous laughter.

Julia stood there in the middle of the room, in her neat wool crêpe grey suit, that had not a wrinkle, not a bulge. It was buttoned up to her throat where a silk scarf provided a hint of mauve. Her hands were in dove-grey kid gloves, and even though thoroughly protected from the unwashed surfaces around her, were making anxious little movements of rejection, and fussy disapproval. Her shoes were like shiny blackbirds, with brass buckles that seemed to Frances to be locks, as if making sure those feet couldn't fly off, or even to begin to try out a few prim dance steps. Her grey hat was fenced with a little net veil that did not conceal her horrified eyes, and it, too, was caught with a metal buckle. She was a woman in a cage, and to Frances, under such pressures of loneliness, poverty, anxiety, her appearance in that room, which she loathed, and wished only to escape from, was like a deliberate taunting, an insult.

'What am I to tell Jolyon?'

'Who? – oh, yes. But . . .' And now Frances energetically sat herself up, one hand cupping the baby's head, the other holding the cloth over her exposed breast. 'Don't tell me Johnny asked you to come here?'

'Well, yes, he did.'

Now the two women shared a moment: it was incredulity, and their eyes actually did engage, in a query. When Julia had read the letter which commanded her to visit his wife, she said to Philip, 'But I thought he hated us? If we weren't good enough to see him married, then why is he ordering me to visit Frances?'

Philip replied, dry enough, but remote too, because as always he was absorbed in his duties with the war, 'I see that you are expecting consistency. Usually a mistake, in my view.'

As for Frances, she had never heard Johnny refer to his parents as anything other than fascists, exploiters, at the best reactionaries. Then how could he be . . .

'Frances, I would like very much to help you with some money.' An envelope appeared from her handbag.

'Oh, no, I am sure Johnny wouldn't like that. He'd never take money from . . .'

'I think you'll find that he can and he will.'

'Oh, no, no, Julia, please not.'

'Very well then, goodbye.'

Julia did not set eyes on Frances again until after Johnny had returned from the war, and Philip, who was by then ill and would shortly die, said he was worried about Frances and the children. Her memories of that visit caused Julia to protest that she was sure Frances did not want to see her, but Philip said, 'Please, Julia. To set my mind at rest.'

Julia went to the flat in Notting Hill, which she was convinced had been chosen because of the area's seediness and ugliness. There were two children now. The one she had seen before, Andrew, was a noisy and energetic toddler, and there was a baby, Colin. Again, Frances was breastfeeding. She was large, shapeless, slatternly, and the flat, Julia was convinced, was a health hazard. On the wall was a food safe, and in it could be glimpsed a bottle of milk and some cheese. The wire net of the safe had been painted, the paint had clogged: air therefore could not circulate properly. Babies' clothes were strung on fragile wooden contraptions that seemed about to collapse. No, Frances said, in a voice cold with hostility and criticism. No, she didn't want any money, no, thank you.

Julia stood there unconsciously all appeal, hands a-flutter, eyes full of tears.

'But, Frances, think of the children.'

It was as if Julia had deliberately touched an already sore place with acid. Oh, yes, Frances thought often enough of how her own parents, let alone Johnny's, must see her and how she lived, with the children. She said in a voice stiff with anger, 'It seems to me that I never think of anything else but the children.' Her tone said, *How dare you!*

'Please let me help you, please – Johnny's always so wrong-headed, he always has been, and it's not fair on the children.'

The trouble was, by now Frances agreed unreservedly about Johnny's wrong-headedness. Any shreds of illusion had dissolved away, leaving a residue of unresolvable exasperation about him, the comrades, the Revolution, Stalin, Uncle Tom Cobbleigh and all. But what was in question here was not Johnny, it was herself, a small, threatened sense of identity and of independence. That was why Julia's *Think of the children* went home like a poisoned bullet. What right did she, Frances, have to fight for her independence, her own self at the cost of . . . but they were not suffering, they were not. She knew they were not.

Julia went away, reported back to Philip, and tried not to think of those rooms in Notting Hill.

Later, when Julia heard that Frances had gone to work in a theatre, Julia thought, A theatre! Of course, it would be! Then Frances was acting and Julia thought, Is she acting servants' parts then?

She went to the theatre, sat well back where she could not be seen, she hoped, and watched Frances in a small part in a quite nice little comedy. Frances was thinner, though still solid, and her fair hair was in frilly waves. She was a hotel owner, in Brighton. Julia could not see anything of that pre-war giggler in her tight uniform, but still, she was doing the part well enough, and Julia felt encouraged. Frances knew that Julia had been to watch her, because it was a small theatre, and Julia was wearing one of her inimitable hats, with a veil, and her gloved hands were on her lap. Not another woman in the audience wore a hat. Those gloves, oh those gloves, what a laugh.

All through the war, particularly at bad moments, Philip had kept the memory of a certain little glove, in Swiss muslin, and those dots, white on white, and the tiny frill at the wrist, seemed to him a delicious frivolity, laughing at itself, and a promise that civilisation would return.

Soon Philip died of a heart attack, and Julia was not surprised. The war had been hard on him. He had worked to all hours and brought home work at nights. She knew he had been involved in all kinds of daring and dangerous ventures, and that he grieved for men he had sent into danger, sometimes to their deaths. He had become an old man, during the war. And, like her, this war was forcing him to relive the last one: she knew this, from the small dry remarks he did allow himself to drop. These two people, who had been so fatally in love, had lived always in patient tenderness, as if they had decided to protect their memories, like a bruise, from any harsh touch, refusing ever to look too closely at them.

Now there was Julia alone in the big house, and Johnny came and said he wanted the house, and she should move out into a flat. For the first time in her life Julia stood her ground and said No. She was going to live here, and she did not expect Johnny or anyone else to understand her. Her own home, the von Arne house, had been lost. Her young brother had been killed in the Second World War. The house had been sold and the proceeds had come to her. This house, where she had been so reluctant to live, was now her home, the only link with that Julia who had a home, who expected to have one, who was defined by a place, with memories. She was Julia Lennox, and this was her home.

'You are selfish and greedy, like all your class,' said Johnny.

'You and Frances may come and live here, but I shall be here.'

'Thank you so much, Mutti, but we shall decline.'

'Why Mutti? You never called me that when you were a child.'

'Are you trying to conceal the fact that you are a German, Mutti?'

'No, I don't think I am doing that.'

'I do. Hypocritical. It's what we expect from people like you.'

He was really furious. His father had not left him anything, it had all gone to Julia. He had planned to live in this house and to fill it with comrades needing a home. Everyone was poor, living from hand to mouth, after the war, and he was subsisting on the proceeds of work for the Party, some of it illegal. He had been furious with Frances for refusing to accept an allowance from Julia. When Frances had said, 'But, Johnny, I don't understand, how can you want to take money from the class enemy?' Johnny had hit her, for the only time in their lives. She hit him back, harder. She had not meant her question as a taunt or a criticism, she genuinely wanted to have it explained to her.

Julia was well off, but not rich. Paying for the two lots of school fees, Andrew's and Colin's, was within her scope, but if Frances had not agreed to move in, she had planned to let part of the house. Now she was economising in ways that would have made Frances laugh, if she had known. Julia did not buy new clothes. She dismissed the housekeeper who had been living in the basement, depended on a woman who came in twice a week, and did a good bit of her own housework. (This woman, Mrs Philby, had to be coaxed and flattered and given presents to go on working when Frances and her ill-bred ways arrived.) She no longer bought food at Fortnum's, but she discovered now, when Philip was dead, that her own tastes were frugal, and that the standards required of a wife married to a Foreign Office official had never really been hers.

When Frances arrived, to take over all the house except for

Julia's top floor, it was a relief to Julia. She still did not like Frances, who seemed determined to shock her, but she loved the boys, and intended to shield them from their parents. In fact, they were afraid of her, at least to start with, but she never found this out. She thought Frances was keeping her from them, did not know that Frances urged them to visit their grandmother. 'Please, she's so good to us. And she'd love it if you did.' 'Oh, *no*, it's *too* much, do we have to?'

Frances visited the newspaper to establish her job, and she knew how right she had been to prefer the theatre. As a freelance she had had little experience of institutions, and did not look forward to a communal working life. As soon as she set foot in the building that housed *The Defender*, she recognised there an atmosphere: this was an *esprit de corps* all right. *The Defender*'s venerable history, going back into the nineteenth century, as a fighter for any number of good causes, was being continued, so it was generally felt, and most particularly by the people who worked for it; this period, the Sixties, was able to stand up to any of the great times of the past. Frances was being welcomed into the fold by one Julie Hackett. She was a soft, not to say womanly woman, with bundles of strong black hair fastened here and there with a variety of combs and pins, a resolutely unfashionable figure, because she saw fashion as an enslaver of women. She observed everything around her with a view to correcting errors of fact and belief, and she criticised men in every sentence, taking it for granted, as believers tend to do, that Frances agreed with her in everything. She had been keeping an eye on Frances, had seen articles by her here and there, and in *The Defender* too, but one article had decided her to get her on to the staff. It was a satirical, but good-natured piece about Carnaby Street, which was in the process of becoming a symbol for trendy Britain, and attracting youngsters, not to mention the young in heart, from all over the world. Frances had said that they must all be suffering from some sort of collective hallucination, since the street was grubby, tatty, and if the clothes were attractive – some of them – they were no better than others in streets that did not have the magic syllables *Carnaby* attached to them. Heresy! A brave heresy, judged Julie Hackett, seeing Frances as a kindred soul.

Frances was shown an office where a secretary was sorting through letters addressed to Aunt Vera, and putting them in heaps, since even the nastiest predicaments of humanity must fall into easily recognised categories. My husband is unfaithful, an alcoholic, beats me, won't give me enough money, is leaving me for his secretary, prefers his mates in the pub to me. My son is alcoholic, a druggie, has got a girl pregnant, won't leave home, is living rough in London, earns money but won't contribute to the household. My daughter . . . Pensions, benefits, the behaviour of officials, medical problems . . . but a doctor answered those. These more common letters were dealt with by this secretary, signing Aunt Vera, and it was a flourishing new department of *The Defender*. Frances's job was to scan these letters, and find a theme or concern that predominated, and then use it for a serious article, a long one, which would have a prominent place in the paper. Frances could write her articles and do her research at home. She would be of *The Defender* but not in it, and for this she was grateful.

When she got out of the Underground, coming home from the newspaper, she bought food, and walked down the hill, laden.

Julia was standing at her high window, looking down, when she saw Frances approaching. At least this smart coat was an improvement, not the usual duffel-coat: perhaps one could look forward to her wearing something other than the eternal jeans and jerseys? She was walking heavily, making Julia think of a donkey with panniers. Near the house she stopped, and Julia could see that Frances's hair had been done, the blondeish hair falling straight as straw on either side of a parting, as was the mode.

From some of the houses she had passed, the music pounded

and beat, as loud as an angry heart, but Julia had said she would not tolerate loud music, she could not bear it, so while music was played, it was soft. From Andrew's room usually came the muted tones of Palestrina or Vivaldi, from Colin's traditional jazz, from the sitting-room where the television was, broken music and voices, from the basement, the throb, throb, throb, that 'the kids' needed.

The whole big house was lit up, not a dark window, and it seemed to shed light from walls as well as windows: it exuded light and music.

Frances saw Johnny's shadow on the kitchen curtains, and at once her spirits took a fall. He was in the middle of a harangue, she could see, from gesticulating arms, and when she reached the kitchen, he was in full flood. Cuba, again. Around the table was an assortment of youngsters, but she did not have time to see who was there. Andrew, yes, Rose, yes . . . the telephone was ringing. She dropped the heavy bags, took up the receiver, and it was Colin from his school. 'Mother, have you heard the news?' 'No, what news, are you all right, Colin, you just went off this morning . . .' 'Yes, yes, listen, we've just heard, it's on the news. Kennedy's dead.' '*Who?*' 'President Kennedy.' 'Are you sure?' 'They shot him. Switch on the telly.'

Over her shoulder she said, 'President Kennedy is dead. He's been shot.' A silence, while she reached for the radio, switched it on. Nothing on the radio. She turned to see every face blank with shock, Johnny's too. He was being kept silent by the need to find *a correct formulation*, and in a moment was able to bring out, 'We must evaluate the situation . . .' but could not go on.

'The television,' said Geoffrey Bone, and as one 'the kids' rose from the table and went out of the room and up the stairs to the sitting-room.

Andrew said, calling after them, 'Careful, Tilly's watching.' Then he ran after them.

Frances and Johnny were alone, facing each other.

'I take it you came to enquire after your stepdaughter?' she asked.

Johnny fidgeted: he wanted badly to go up and watch the *Six O'clock News*, but he planned to say something, and she stood, leaning back against the shelves by the stove, thinking, Well now, let me guess . . . And as she had expected, he came out with, 'It's Phyllida, I am afraid.'

'Yes?'

'She's not well.'

'So I heard from Andrew.'

'I'm going to Cuba in a couple of days.'

'Best if you take her with you, then.'

'I am afraid the funds wouldn't run to it and . . .'

'Who is paying?'

Here appeared the irritated what-can-you-expect look from which she was always able to judge her degree of stupidity.

'You should know better than to ask, comrade.'

Once she would have collapsed into a morass of inadequacy and guilt – how easily, then, he had been able to make her feel an idiot.

'I am asking. You seem to forget, I've got reason to be interested in your finances.'

'And how much are you being paid in this new job of yours?'

She smiled at him. 'Not enough to support your sons and now your stepdaughter as well.'

'And feed Uncle Tom Cobbleigh and anyone who turns up expecting a free meal.'

'What? You wouldn't have me turn away potential material for the Revolution?'

'They're layabouts and junkies,' he said. 'Riff-raff.' But he decided not to go on, and changed his tune to a comradely appeal to her better nature. 'Phyllida really isn't well.'

'And what am I expected to do about it?'

'I want you to keep an eye on her.'

'No, Johnny.'

'Then Andrew can. He's got nothing better to do.'

'He's busy looking after Tilly. She is really ill, you know.'

'A lot of it is just playing for sympathy.'

'Then why did you dump her on us?'

'Oh . . . fuck it,' said Comrade Johnny. 'Psychological disorders are not my line, they're yours.'

'She's ill. She's really ill. And how long are you going for?'

He looked down, frowned. 'I said I'd go for six weeks. But with this new crisis . . .' Reminded of the crisis, he said, 'I'm going to catch the news.' And he ran out of the kitchen.

Frances heated soup, a chicken stew, garlic bread, made a salad, piled fruit on a dish, arranged cheeses. She was thinking about the poor child, Tilly. The day after the girl had arrived, Andrew had come to where she was working in her study, and said, 'Mother, can I put Tilly into the spare room? She really can't sleep in my room, even though that's what I think she'd like.'

Frances had been expecting this: her floor really had four rooms, her bedroom, her study, a sitting-room, and a small room which, when Julia ran the house, had been a spare room. Frances felt that this floor was hers, a safe place, where she was free from all the pressures, all the people. Now Tilly and her illness would be across a small landing. And the bathroom . . . 'Very well, Andrew. But I can't look after her. Not the way she needs.'

'No. I'll look after her. I'll clear the room for her.' Then, as he turned to run up the stairs, he said quietly, urgently, 'She really is in a bad way.'

'Yes, I know she is.'

'She's afraid we are going to put her in a loony bin.'

'But of course not, she's not crazy.'

'No,' he said, with a twisted smile, more of an appeal than he knew, 'But perhaps I am?'

'I don't think so.'

She heard Andrew bring the girl down from his room, and the two went into the spare room. Silence. She knew what was happening. The girl was lying curled on the bed, or on the floor, and Andrew was cradling her, soothing her, even singing to her – she had heard him do that.

And that morning, she had observed this scene. She was preparing food for this evening, while Andrew sat at the table with Tilly, who was wrapped in a baby's shawl, which she had found in a chest, and appropriated. In front of her was a bowl of milk and cornflakes, and another was before Andrew. He was playing the nursery game. 'One for Andrew . . . now one for Tilly . . . one for Andrew . . .'

At 'one for Tilly' she opened her mouth, while the great anguished blue eyes stared at Andrew. It seemed she did not know how to blink. Andrew tilted in the spoon, and she sat with her lips closed, but not swallowing. Andrew made himself swallow his mouthful, and started again. 'One for Tilly . . . one for Andrew . . .' Minute amounts of food arrived in Tilly's mouth, but at least Andrew was getting something down him.

Andrew said to her, 'Tilly doesn't eat. No, no, it's much worse than me. She doesn't eat at all.'

That was before anorexia was a household word, like sex, and AIDS.

'Why doesn't she? Do you know?' Meaning, please tell me why you find it so hard to eat.

'In her case I would say it's her mother.'

'Not in your case, then?'

'No, I would say that in my case it's my father.' The humorous deprecation, the winning ways of that personality that Eton had created in him, seemed at this moment to have slipped out of alignment with his real self, and become a series of grotesqueries, like out-of-place masks. His eyes stared, sombre, anxious, all appeal.

'What are we going to do?' said Frances, as desperate as he was.

'Just wait, wait a bit, that's all, it'll be all right.'

When 'the kids' – she really must stop using the phrase – came crowding down to sit around the table, waiting for food,

Johnny was not with them. Everyone sat listening to the quarrel that was going on at the top of the house. Shouts, imprecations – words could not be distinguished.

Andrew said, 'He wants Julia to go and live in his flat and look after Phyllida while he is in Cuba.'

They looked at her, to see her reaction. She was laughing. 'Oh, my God,' she said. 'He's really not possible.'

Now they glanced at each other – disapproval. All, that is, except Andrew. They admired him, and thought Frances bitter. Andrew said to them, seriously, 'It simply isn't on. It's not fair to ask Julia.'

The top of the house, where Julia had her being, was often a subject for mockery, and Julia had been referred to as 'the old woman'. But since Andrew had been home, and had become friends with Julia, they were having to take their cue from him.

'Why should she look after Phyllida?' said Andrew. 'She's got her hands full with us.'

This new view of the situation caused a thoughtful silence.

'She doesn't like Phyllida,' said Frances, supporting Andrew. And she suppressed: and she doesn't like me. She has never liked Johnny's women.

'Who could?' said Geoffrey, and Frances looked at him enquiringly: there was something new here.

'Phyllida came here this afternoon,' said Geoffrey.

'She was looking for you,' said Andrew.

'Here? Phyllida?'

'She's nuts,' said Rose. 'I was here. She's bonkers. Round the twist.' And she giggled.

'What did she want?' said Frances.

'I sent her off,' said Andrew. 'I told her she shouldn't be here.'

Upstairs doors were slamming, Johnny was shouting, and he came leaping down the stairs followed by the single word from Julia, 'Imbecile!'

He arrived, sparking off anger.

'Old bitch,' he said, 'fascist bitch.'

'The kids' looked for guidance to Andrew. He was pale, seemed ill. Loud voices – quarrelling – too much for him.

'Too *much*,' said Rose, in admiration of the general unpleasantness.

Andrew said, 'Tilly'll be upset again.' He half rose and Frances appealed, afraid that he would find this an excuse not to eat, 'Please sit down, Andrew.' He did, and she was surprised that he obeyed her.

'Did you know that your . . . that Phyllida was here?' said Rose to Johnny, giggling. Her face was flushed, her little black eyes sparkled.

'*What?*' said Johnny, sharp, with a quick glance at Frances. 'She was here?'

No one said anything.

'I'll speak to her,' said Johnny.

'Has she got parents?' asked Frances. 'She could go home while you're in Cuba.'

'She hates them. With good reason. They're lumpen scum.'

Rose had the back of her hand against her mouth, pressing back more hilarity.

Meanwhile Frances was looking around, taking in who was here this evening. Apart from Geoffrey – well, of course, and Andrew, and Rose, there was Jill, there was Sophie, and she was crying. There was also a boy unknown to her.

At this moment the telephone rang and it was Colin again. 'I've been thinking,' he said. 'Is Sophie there? She must be terribly upset. Let me speak to her.'

This reminded everyone that Sophie had to be upset, because her father had died of cancer last year, and the reason why she was here most evenings was because in her own home her mother wept, and claimed Sophie for grief. Kennedy's death would of course . . .

At the telephone Sophie sobbed, and they heard, 'Oh, Colin, thank you, oh, thank you, you understand, Colin, oh, I knew you would, oh, you are coming, oh, thank you, thank you.'

She returned to her place at the table, saying, 'Colin'll catch the last train tonight.' She buried her face in her hands, long elegant hands pink-tipped in the shade prescribed that week by the fashion arbiters of St Joseph's, of whom she was one. Long glistening black hair fell to the table, like the thought made visible that she would never ever have to sorrow alone for long.

Rose said sourly, 'We're all sorry about Kennedy, aren't we?'

Shouldn't Jill be at school? But from St Joseph's pupils came and went, with little regard for time, tables or exams. When teachers suggested a more disciplined approach, they might be reminded of the principles that had established the school, self-development being the main one. Colin had gone off to school this morning, and was on his way back. Geoffrey had said he might go tomorrow: yes, he was remembering he was head boy. Had Sophie 'dropped out' altogether? She certainly seemed to be more often here than there. Jill had been down in the basement with her sleeping bag, coming up for meals. She had told Colin who had told Frances that she needed a break. Daniel had gone back to school, but could be expected to return, if Colin did: any excuse would do. She knew they believed that the moment they turned their backs all kinds of delightfully dramatic events occurred.

There was a new face, at the end of the table, smiling placatingly at her, waiting for her to say, 'Who are you? What are you doing here?' But she only put a plate of soup in front of him, and smiled. 'I'm James,' he said, flushing. 'Well, hello James,' she said. 'Help yourself to bread – or anything else.' A large embarrassed hand reached out to take a thick hunk of (healthy) wholemeal. He sat with it in his hand, staring about him with evident delight.

'James is my friend, well he's my cousin actually,' said Rose, managing to be both nervous and aggressive. 'I said it would be all right if he came . . . I mean, for supper, I mean . . .'

Frances saw that here was another refugee from a shitty family, and was mentally checking food she would need to buy tomorrow.

Tonight there were only seven at the table, with herself. Johnny was standing, as stiff as a soldier, at the window. He wanted to be asked to sit down. There was an empty place. She was damned if she was going to ask him, did not care that her reputation with 'the kids' would suffer.

'Before you go,' she said, 'tell us, who killed Kennedy.'

Johnny shrugged, for once at a loss.

'Perhaps it was the Soviets?' suggested the newcomer, daring to claim his place with them.

'That is nonsense,' said Johnny. 'The Soviet comrades do not go in for terrorism.'

Poor James was abashed.

'Perhaps it was Castro?' said Jill. Johnny was already staring coldly at her. 'I mean, the Bay of Pigs, I mean . . .'

'He doesn't go in for terrorism either,' said Johnny.

'Do give me a ring before you leave,' said Frances. 'A couple of days, you said?'

But he still wasn't leaving.

'It was a loony,' said Rose. 'Some loony shot him.'

'Who paid the loony?' said James, having recovered again, though he was flushed with the effort of asserting himself.

'We should not rule out the CIA,' said Johnny.

'We should never rule them out,' said James, and earned approval from Johnny in a smile and a nod. He was a large young man, bulky, and surely older than Rose, older than any of them, except perhaps Andrew? Rose saw Frances's inspection of James, and reacted at once: she was always on the alert for criticism. She said, 'James is into politics. He is my elder brother's friend. He is a drop-out.'

'Well blow me down,' said Frances, 'what a surprise.'

'What do you *mean*?' said Rose, frantic, angry. 'Why did you say that?'

'Oh, Rose, it's just a joke.'

'She makes jokes,' said Andrew, interpreting his mother, as it were vouching for her.

'And talking about jokes,' said Frances. When they had all run upstairs to watch the television news, she had seen on the floor two large carrier bags filled with books. She now indicated these to Geoffrey, who could not suppress a proud smile. 'A good haul today I see?' she said.

Everyone laughed. Most of them shoplifted in an impulsive way, but Geoffrey made a business of it. He went regularly around bookshops, pilfering. School textbooks when he could, but anything he could get away with. He called it 'liberating' them. It was a Second World War joke, and a wistful link with his father, who had been a bomber pilot. Geoffrey had told Colin that he thought his father had not really noticed anything since the end of that war. 'Certainly not my mother or me.' His father might just as well have died in that war for all the good his family got of him. 'Join the club,' was what Colin had said. 'The War, the Revolution, what's the difference?'

'God bless Foyle's,' said Geoffrey. 'I've liberated more there than anywhere else in London. A benefactor to humankind, is Foyle's.' But he was glancing nervously at Frances. He said, 'Frances doesn't approve.'

They knew Frances didn't approve. She often said, 'It's my unfortunate upbringing. I was brought up to think stealing is wrong.' Now, whenever she or anyone else criticised or did not go along with the others, they would chant, 'It's your unfortunate upbringing.' Then Andrew had said, 'That joke's getting a bit tired.'

There had been a wild half-hour of variations on tired jokes with unfortunate upbringings.

Now Johnny began on his familiar lecture, 'That's right, you take anything you can get from the capitalists. They've stolen it all from you in the first place.'

'Surely not from us?' – Andrew challenged his father.

'Stolen from the working people. The ordinary people. Take them for what you can get, the bastards.'

Andrew had never shoplifted, thought it inferior behaviour

49

fit only for oiks, and said in a direct challenge, 'Shouldn't you be getting back to Phyllida?'

Frances could be ignored, but his son's rebuke took Johnny to the door. 'Never forget,' he admonished them generally, 'you should be checking everything you do, every word, every thought, against the needs of the Revolution.'

'So what did you get today?' Rose asked Geoffrey. She admired him almost as much as she did Johnny.

Geoffrey took books out of the carrier bags and made a tower of them on the table.

They clapped. Not Frances, not Andrew.

Frances took from her briefcase one of the letters to the newspaper which she had brought home. She read out, '"Dear Aunt Vera" ... that's me ..."Dear Aunt Vera, I have three children, all at school. Every evening they come home with stolen stuff, mostly sweets and biscuits ..."' Here the company groaned. '"But it can be anything, school books too ..."' They clapped. '"But today my oldest, the boy, came back with a very expensive pair of jeans."' They clapped again. '"I don't know what to do. When the door bell rings I think, That's the police."' Frances gave them time for a groan. '"And I am afraid for them. I would very much value your advice, Aunt Vera. I am at my wits' end."'

She inserted the letter back in its place.

'And what are you going to advise?' enquired Andrew.

'Perhaps you should tell me what to say, Geoffrey. After all, a head boy should be well up in these things.'

'Oh, don't be like that, Frances,' said Rose.

'Oh,' groaned Geoffrey, his head in his hands, making his shoulders heave as if with sobs, 'she takes it seriously.'

'I do take it seriously,' said Frances. 'It's stealing. You are thieves,' she said to Geoffrey, with the freedom licensed by his practically living with them, for years. 'You are a thief. That's all. I'm not Johnny,' she said.

Now a real dismayed silence. Rose giggled. The newcomer's, James's, scarlet face was as good as a confession.

Sophie cried out, 'But, Frances, I didn't know you disapproved of us so much.'

'Well, I do,' said Frances, her face and voice softening, because it was Sophie. 'So now you know.'

'It's her unfortunate upbringing . . .' began Rose, but desisted, on a look from Andrew.

'And now I'm going to catch the news, and I have to work.' She went out, saying, 'Sleep well, everyone.' Giving permission, in this way, to anyone, James for instance, who might be hoping to stay the night.

She did catch the news, briefly. It seemed that some madman had shot Kennedy. As far as she was concerned, another public man was dead. He probably deserved it. She would never have allowed herself to voice this thought, so very far from the spirit of the times. It sometimes seemed to her that the one useful thing she had learned in her long association with Johnny, was how to keep quiet about what she thought.

Before settling down to work which, this evening, would be going through a hundred or so letters she had brought home, she opened the door to the spare room. Silence and dark. She tiptoed to the bed and bent over a shape under the bedclothes that could have been a child's. And, yes, Tilly had her thumb in her mouth.

'I'm not asleep,' said a little voice.

'I'm worried about you,' said Frances, and heard her voice shake: she had promised herself not to get emotionally involved, because what good would that do? 'If I made you a cup of hot chocolate, would you like that?'

'I'll try.'

Frances made chocolate in her study, where she had a kettle and basic supplies, and took it to the girl, who said, 'I don't want you to think I'm not grateful.'

'Shall I put the light on? Do you want to try drinking it now?'

'Put it on the floor.'

Frances did so, knowing that most likely the cup would be there, untouched, in the morning.

She worked until late. She heard Colin come in, and then he and Sophie went to the big sofa, where they sat talking – she could hear them, or at least their voices, just below hers: the old red sofa was immediately under her desk. Immediately over it was Colin's bed. She heard their lowered voices, and then careful footsteps just above her. Well, she was sure Colin knew how to be careful: he had said so, loudly, to his brother, who lectured him on these matters.

Sophie was sixteen. Frances wanted to put her arms around the girl and protect her. Well, she never felt anything like that about Rose, Jill, Lucy, or the other young females who drifted in and out of this house. So why Sophie? She was so beautiful, that was it: that was what she wanted to guard and keep safe. And what nonsense *that* was – she, Frances, should be ashamed. She was ashamed about a good deal, this evening. She opened the door, and listened. Down in the kitchen, there seemed to be more than Andrew, Rose, James . . . she would find out tomorrow.

She slept restlessly, twice went across the landing to see how Tilly was doing; on one occasion found a very dark room, stillness, and the faint stuffy smell of chocolate. Once she saw Andrew retreating upstairs from a similar mission, and went back to bed. She lay awake. The trouble was, the shoplifting. When Colin first went to St Joseph's after his not very good comprehensive, articles she knew were not his began appearing, nothing much, a T-shirt, packets of biros, a record. She remembered being impressed that he had stolen an anthology of verse. She remonstrated. He complained that everyone did it and she was a square. Do not imagine the issue rested there. This was a progressive school! One of the first wave of schoolfriends, who came and went, but much less freely, since after all they were younger, a girl called Petula, informed Frances that Colin was stealing love: the housemaster had said so. This was discussed noisily at the supper table. No, not the love of her parents, but that of the headmaster, who had ticked off Colin for something or other. Geoffrey, already more or less a fixture then, five years ago, more, was proud of what he garnered from the shops. She had been shocked, but had not said more than, Well, then, don't get caught. If she had not said, Don't do it, that was because she would not have been obeyed, but also because she had no idea then of how prevalent it would become, shoplifting. And, too, and that was what now kept her awake, she had liked being one of them, the trendy youngsters who were the new arbiters of modes and morals. There was – had been – undoubtedly a feeling of *we against them*. Petula, that sparky girl (now in a school for diplomats' children in Hong Kong) had said that stealing without being caught was an initiation rite, and adults should understand that.

Today Frances was going to have to write a solid, long, and balanced article on this very subject. She was actually regretting she had ever said yes to this new job. She was going to have to take a stand on any number of issues, and it was her nature to see opposing points of view, and refuse to say more than, 'Yes, it's all very difficult.'

Recently she had come to see stealing as very definitely wrong, and not because of her unfortunate upbringing, but because of listening for years to Johnny urging all kinds of anti-social behaviour, rather like a guerilla leader: hit and run. One day a simple truth had arrived in her mind. He wanted to pull everything down about his ears, like Samson. That was what it was all about. 'The Revolution' which he and his mates never stopped talking about would be like directing a flame-thrower over everything, leaving scorched earth, and then – well, simple – he and the mates would rebuild the world in their image. Once seen it was obvious, but the thought then had to be faced: how could people unable to organise their own lives, who lived in permanent disarray, build anything worthwhile? This seditious thought – and it was years in advance of its time, at least in any circles she had been introduced to – lived side by side with an emotion she hardly knew was there. She thought Johnny was . . . no need to spell that out . . . she had become very clear about what she thought, but at the same time she relied on an aura of hopeful optimism that surrounded him, the comrades, everything they did. She did believe – but hardly knew she did – that the world was going to get better and better, that they were all on an escalator of Progress, and that present ills would slowly dissolve away, and everyone in the world would find themselves in a happy healthy time. And when she stood in the kitchen, producing dishes of food for 'the kids', seeing all those young faces, listening to their irreverent confident voices, she felt that she was guaranteeing this future for them, in a silent promise. Where had this promise originated? From Johnny, she had absorbed it from Comrade Johnny, and while her mind was set in criticising him, more and more every day, she relied emotionally without knowing it on Johnny and his brave sweet new worlds.

In a few hours she would sit down and write her article and say what?

If she had not taken a stand against stealing, in her own home, and even when she had come most strongly to disapprove, then what right had she to tell other people what to do?

And how confused these poor children were. As she had left the kitchen last night she had heard them laughing, but uneasily; had heard James's voice louder than the others, because he wanted so much to be accepted by all these free spirits. Poor boy, he had fled from boringly provincial parents (as she had) to the delights of Swinging London, and a house described by Rose as Freedom Hall – she loved the phrase – where he had heard exactly the same condemnation – he was bound to be stealing, they all did – as he had from his parents.

It was nine o'clock by now, late for her. She must get up. She opened the door on to the landing and saw Andrew sitting on the floor where he could look across at the door of the room where the girl was. It was open. He mouthed up at her: Look, just look.

Pale November sun fell into the room opposite, where a slight erect figure with an aureole of fair hair, in an old-fashioned pink garment – a housecoat? – was perched on a high stool. If Philip were to see this vision now, how easily he could have been persuaded that this was the girl Julia, his long-ago love. On the bed, wrapped tight in her baby's shawl, Tilly was held up by pillows, and staring with her unblinking gaze at the old woman.

'No,' came Julia's cool precise voice, 'no, your name is not Tilly. That is a very foolish name. What is your real name?'

'Sylvia,' lisped the girl.

'So, why do you call yourself Tilly?'

'I couldn't say Sylvia when I was little, so I said Tilly.' These were more words than any of them had heard from her, at one time.

'Very well. I shall call you Sylvia.'

Julia had in her hand a mug of something with a spoon in it. Now she carefully, beautifully, caused an appropriate amount of the mug's contents – there was a smell of soup – to fill the spoon, which she held to Tilly's, or Sylvia's, lips. Which were tight shut.

'Now, listen carefully to me. I am not going to let you kill yourself because you are foolish. I won't allow it. And now you must open your mouth and begin eating.'

The pale lips trembled a little, but opened, and all the while the girl was staring at Julia, apparently hypnotised. The spoon was inserted, and its contents disappeared. The watchers waited, breathless, to see if there was a swallowing movement. There was.

Frances glanced down at her son and saw that he was swallowing in sympathy.

'You see,' Julia was going on, while the spoon was again being recharged, 'I am your step-grandmother. I do not allow my children and grandchildren to behave so foolishly. You must understand me, Sylvia . . .' In went the spoon – a swallow. And again Andrew made a swallowing movement. 'You are a very pretty clever girl . . .'

'I'm horrible,' came from the pillows.

'I don't think you are. But if you have decided to be horrible then you will be, and I won't allow that.'

The spoon went in, a swallow.

'First, I shall make you well again, and then you will go to school and take your examinations. After that you will go to university and be a doctor. Now I am sorry I wasn't a doctor, but you can be a doctor in my place.'

'I can't. I can't. I can't go back to school.'

'Why can't you? Andrew has told me that you were clever at your lessons, before you became foolish. And now take this cup and drink the rest by yourself.'

The observers hardly breathed, at this moment of – surely? – crisis. Suppose Tilly–Sylvia refused the cup with its life-giving soup, and put that thumb back in her mouth? Suppose she shut her lips tight? Julia was holding the mug against the hand that was not clutching the shawl around her. 'Take it.' The hand trembled, but opened. Julia put the mug carefully into the hand, and held the hand around the cup. The hand did lift, the cup reached the lips and over it came the whisper, 'But it's so hard.'

'I know it's hard.'

The trembling hand was holding the cup to her lips, while Julia steadied it. The girl took a sip, swallowed. 'I'm going to be sick,' she whispered.

'No, you are not. Stop it, Sylvia.'

Again Frances and her son waited, holding their breaths. Sylvia wasn't sick, though she had to conquer retching, when Julia said, 'Stop it.'

Meanwhile, down the stairs from the 'boys' floor' came Colin, and behind him, Sophie. The two stopped. Colin was blushing bright red, and Sophie was half laughing, half crying, and seemed about to run back upstairs, but instead came to Frances, put her arms around her, and said, 'Dear, dear Frances,' and ran off down the stairs, laughing.

'It's not what you think,' said Colin.

'I'm not thinking anything,' said Frances.

Andrew merely smiled, keeping his counsel.

Now Colin saw the little scene through the door, took it in, and said, 'Good for Grandma,' and went off down the stairs in big leaps.

Julia who had taken no notice of her audience, got down from the stool, and smoothed down her skirts. She took the mug from the girl. 'I'm going to come back in an hour and see how you are,' she said. 'And then I'll take you up to my bathroom, and you can put on clean clothes. You'll be better in no time, you'll see.'

She picked up the cup of cold chocolate left last night by Frances, and came out of the room and handed it to her. 'I think this is yours,' she said. And then, to Andrew, 'And you can stop being foolish too.' She left the door into the room open, and went up the stairs, holding up her pink skirt, which rustled, with one hand.

'So that's all right,' said Andrew to his mother. 'Well done, Sylvia,' he called to the girl, who smiled, if weakly. He ran upstairs. Frances heard one door shut, Julia's and then another, Andrew's. In the room opposite a blotch of sunlight lay on a pillow, and Sylvia, for there is no doubt that this was who she was now, held her hand in it, turning it back and forth, examining it.

At this moment there was a banging on the front door, the bell rang repeatedly, and a woman's voice was shouting. The girl sitting in the sun on her bed let out a cry, and dived under the bedclothes.

As the door opened, the shout of 'Let me in' could be heard through the house. A hoarse hysterical voice, 'Let me in, let me in.'

Andrew's door opened with a bang, and he came leaping down the stairs saying, 'Leave this to me, oh, *Christ*, shut Tilly's door.' Frances shut the door, as Julia called down, 'What is it, who is it?' Andrew called up to her, but softly, 'Her mother, Tilly's mother.'

'Then I am sorry to say that Sylvia will have a setback,' said Julia, and continued to stand there, on guard.

Frances was still in her nightdress, and she went into her room, and dragged on jeans and a jersey and ran down the stairs towards voices in altercation.

'Where is she? I want Frances,' shouted Phyllida, while Andrew was saying quietly, 'Hush, don't shout, I'll get her.'

'I'm here,' said Frances.

Phyllida was a tall woman, thin as a bone, with a mass of badly dyed reddish hair, and long needle nails, painted bright purple. She pointed a large angry hand at Frances and said, 'I want my daughter. You have stolen my daughter.'

'Don't be silly,' said Andrew, hovering about the hysterical woman like an insect trying to decide where it should dart in. He laid a calming hand on Phyllida's shoulder but she shook it off, and Andrew shouted at her, suddenly out of control and surprised at himself. 'Stop it.' He leaned back against a wall, composing himself. He was trembling.

'And what about me?' demanded Phyllida. 'Who is going to look after me?'

Frances found that she was trembling too; her heart thumped, her breathing was tight: she and Andrew were being affected by this dynamo of emotional energy. And in fact Phyllida, whose eyes stared blankly like a ship's figurehead's, who stood there erect and triumphant, seemed calmer than they were.

'It's not fair,' announced Phyllida, pointing her purple talons at Frances. 'Why should she come to live here and not me?'

Andrew had recovered. 'Now, Phyllida,' he said, and the humorous smile that protected him was back in place, 'Phyllida, you really can't do this, you know.'

'Why shouldn't I? she asked, turning her attention to him. 'Why should she have a home and not me?'

'But you have a home,' said Andrew. 'I've visited you there, don't you remember?'

'But he's going away and leaving me.' Then, shrieking, 'He's going away and leaving me alone.' Then, more calmly, to Frances,

'Did you know that? Well, did you? He's going to leave me the way he left you.'

This rational remark seemed to prove to Frances how thoroughly the hysteria had transferred itself to her: she was shaking and her knees were weak.

'Well, why don't you say something?'

'I don't know what to say,' Frances brought out. 'I don't know why you are here.'

'Why? You actually have the nerve to ask why?' And she began shouting, 'Tilly, Tilly, where are you?'

'Leave her alone,' said Andrew. 'You always complain you can't handle her, so let us have a shot at it.'

'But she's here. *She's* here. And what about me? Who is going to look after me?'

This cycle was likely to continue.

Andrew said quietly, but his voice was shaking, 'You can't expect Frances to look after you. Why should she?'

'But what about me? What about me?' Now it was more of a grumble, and for the first time those angry eyes seemed actually to see Frances. 'It's not as if you're Brigitte Bardot, are you? So why does he come here all the time?'

This threw an unexpected light on things. Frances was unable to speak.

Andrew said, 'He comes here because we are here, Phyllida. We are his sons, remember? Colin and I – have you forgotten us?'

It seemed she had. And suddenly, having stood there for a few moments, she lowered that outstretched accusing finger, and stood blinking, apparently coming awake. Then she turned and slammed out of the door.

Frances felt her whole self go loose. She was shaking so she had to lean against the wall. Andrew stood limply there, pitifully smiling. She thought, But he's too young to cope with this sort of thing. She staggered to the kitchen door, held on to it while she went in, and saw Colin and Sophie at the table, eating toast.

Colin, she could see, was in his mood of disapproving of her. Sophie had been crying again.

'Well,' said Colin, coldly furious, 'what do you expect?'

'What do you mean?' said Frances, absurdly, but she was trying to gain time. She slid into her chair and sat with her head in her arms. She knew what he meant. It was a general accusation: that she and his father had screwed things up, that she was not a conventional comfortable mother, like other mothers, and there was this bohemian household, which he had moods of violently resenting, while admitting he enjoyed it.

'She just comes here,' said Colin, 'she just turns up and makes a scene and now we have to look after Tilly.'

'She wants to be called Sylvia,' said Andrew, who had come in and was at the table.

'I don't care what she's called,' said Colin. 'Why is she here?'

And now he was tearful, and looked like a ruffled little owl, with his black-rimmed spectacles. If Andrew was all length and leanness, then Colin was round, with a soft open face, which was at this moment puffy with crying. Now Frances understood that all last night these two, Colin and Sophie, had probably lain in each other's arms weeping, she for her dead father, and he for his misery over – well, everything.

Andrew, who like Frances was still cold and shaking, said, 'But why take it out on Mother? It's not her fault.'

If something were not done the brothers would start quarrelling; they often did, always because Andrew took Frances's side, while Colin accused her.

Frances said, 'Sophie, please make me a cup of tea – and I am sure Andrew could do with one.'

'God, could I,' said Andrew.

Sophie jumped up, pleased at being asked. Colin, having lost the support of her being there, just opposite him, sat blinking vaguely about, so unhappy that Frances wanted to take him in her arms . . . but he would never tolerate that.

Andrew said, 'I'll go and see Phyllida later. She'll have calmed down. She's not so bad when she's not in a state.' And then he jumped up. '*Christ*, I'd forgotten Tilly, I mean Sylvia, and she'll have heard. She goes to pieces when her mother starts in on her.'

'And I am certainly in pieces,' said Frances. 'I can't stop shaking.'

Andrew ran out of the room, but did not return. Julia had descended to sit with Sylvia, who hid beneath the clothes, wailing, 'Keep her away, keep her away,' while Julia said over and over again, 'Shhhh, be quiet. She'll go in a minute.'

Frances drank tea in silence while her shaking subsided. If she had read in a book that hysteria was contagious she would have said, Well, yes, that makes sense! But she had not experienced it. She was thinking, If that's what Tilly has been living with, no wonder she's in a mess.

Sophie had sat down beside Colin and the pair had their arms around each other, like orphans. Soon they went off to catch a train back to school, and Colin gave her an apologetic smile before he left. Sophie embraced her. 'Oh, Frances, I don't know what I'd do if I couldn't come here.'

And now Frances had to write her article.

She put aside the letters about shoplifting and took up another theme, 'Dear Aunt Vera, I am so worried I don't know what to do.' Her daughter, aged fifteen, was having sex with a boy of eighteen. 'These young people they think they are the Virgin Mary and it can't happen to them.' She advised the anxious mother to get contraception for her daughter. 'Go to the family doctor,' she wrote. 'Young people are beginning sexual relations much earlier than we did. You could ask about the new contraceptive pill. There will be problems. Not all teenagers are responsible beings, and this new pill must be taken regularly, every day.'

Thus it was that Frances's first article evoked storms of moral outrage. Letters arrived in bundles from frightened parents, and Frances expected the sack, but Julie Hackett was pleased. Frances was doing what she had been hired to do, as could have been expected from a being brave enough to say that Carnaby Street was a shoddy illusion.

The waves of refugees who washed into London, escaping from Hitler, and then from Stalin, were bone-poor, often threadbare, and lived as they could on a translation here, a book review, language lessons. They worked as hospital porters, on building sites, did housework. There were a few cafés and restaurants as poor as they were, catering for their nostalgic need to sit and drink coffee and talk politics and literature. They were from universities all over Europe, and were intellectuals, a word guaranteed to incite waves of suspicion in the breasts of the xenophobic philistine British, who did not necessarily think it a commendation when they admitted that these newcomers were so much better educated than they were. One café in particular served goulash and dumplings and heavy soups and other filling items to these storm-tossed immigrants who would soon would be adding value and lustre in so many ways to native culture. By the late Fifties, early Sixties, they were editors, writers, journalists, artists, a Nobel Prize winner, and a stranger walking into the Cosmo would judge that this must be the trendiest place in north London, for everyone was in the current uniform of non-conformity, polo necks and expensive jeans, Mao jackets and leather jackets, shaggy hair or the ever-popular Roman Emperor haircut. There were women there, a few, in mini-skirts, mostly girlfriends, absorbing attractive foreign ways as they drank the best coffee in London and ate cream cakes inspired by Vienna.

Frances had taken to dropping in to the Cosmo, to work. In the layer of the house she had thought of as hers, safe from invasion, she now sat listening for Julia's footsteps, or Andrew's, for they both visited Sylvia, to give her cups of this or that, and insisted that her door must be kept open because the girl feared a door that was shut on her. And Rose crept about the house. Once Frances had found her nosing through papers on her desk, and Rose had giggled and said brightly, 'Oh, Frances,' and run out. She had been caught in Julia's rooms, by Julia. She did not steal, or not much, but she was by nature a spy. Julia told Andrew that Rose should be asked to leave; Andrew told Frances that this was what Julia had said; and Frances, relieved, because she disliked the girl, told Rose that it was time she returned to her family. Collapse of Rose. Reports were brought up from the basement where Rose hung out ('It's my *pad*') that Rose was in bed crying, and that she seemed to be ill. Things had drifted, and Rose appeared again at the supper table, defiant, angry, and placatory.

It could be argued that to complain about these minor disruptions at home, and then choose to sit in a corner at the Cosmo, which always reverberated with debate and discussion was – surely – a little perverse. Particularly as the overheard talk was bound to be revolutionary. All these people were types of revolutionary, even if the results of revolution were what they had fled from. They were mostly representatives of some phase of the Dream, and might argue for hours about what happened in such and such a meeting in 1905 in Russia, or in 1917, or in Berchtesgaden, or when German troops invaded the Soviet Union, or the state of affairs in the Rumanian oilfields in 1940. They argued about Freud, and Jung, about Trotsky, Bukarin, about Arthur Koestler and the Spanish Civil War. And Frances, whose ears shut tight when Johnny began on one of his harangues, found it all rather restful, though she did not actively listen. It is true that a noisy café full of cigarette smoke (then an indispensable accompaniment to intellectual activity) is more private than a home where individuals drop in for a chat. Andrew liked it there. So did Colin: they said it had good energy, not to mention positive vibes.

Johnny used it a lot, but then he was in Cuba, so she was safe.

Frances was not the only one from *The Defender*. A man was there who wrote political articles, to whom she had been introduced by Julie Hackett thus, 'This is our chief politico, Rupert Boland. He's an egghead but he's not a bad sort of person, even if he is a man.'

He was not a person you would notice at once, normally, but here he did stand out, because he wore a rather dull brown suit and a tie. He had a pleasant face. He was writing, or making notes, with a biro, just as she was. They smiled and nodded, and at that moment she saw a tall man in a Mao jacket stand up to leave. Good Lord, it was Johnny. He shrugged on a long Afghan coat, dyed blue, the last word in Carnaby Street, and went out. And there a few tables away, in a corner, obviously trying not to be seen (probably by Johnny) was Julia. She was in conversation with . . . he was certainly an intimate friend. Her boyfriend? Frances had recently been acknowledging that Julia was not much over sixty. But no, Julia could not have an affair (the word she would use was probably *liaison*) in a house crammed with ever-watching youngsters. It was as ludicrous as that Frances could.

Giving up the theatre, which probably she had done for ever, Frances had felt she was slamming a door on romance, or serious love.

And Julia . . . Frances was thinking that Julia must be pretty lonely, by herself at the top of that crammed noisy house, where the young ones called her the old woman or, even, the old fascist. She listened to classical music on the radio, and read. But she did go out sometimes, and it seemed she came here.

Julia was wearing a misty-blue costume and a mauveish hat with – of course – a tiny net veil. Her gloves lay on the table. Her gentleman friend, grey haired, well-kept, was as elegant and old-fashioned as she was. He got up, bent over Julia's hand, where his lips met in the air over it. She smiled, and nodded, and he went out. Her face, when he left, composed itself into a look Frances understood was stoicism. Julia had enjoyed an hour off her leash, and would now go home, or perhaps do some frugal shopping. Who was keeping an eye on Sylvia? That meant Andrew must be at home. Frances had not again been in his room, but she believed that he was spending long hours alone there, smoking and reading.

It was Friday. That evening she could expect the supper table to have chairs fitted close all around it. It would be an occasion and everyone knew it, the St Joseph crowd too, because Frances had telephoned Colin to say Sylvia was coming down to supper, and could he make sure everyone called her Sylvia. 'And ask them to be tactful, Colin.' 'Thanks for having so little confidence in us,' he had replied.

Meanwhile his protective care of Sophie had become love, and the two were acknowledged as a couple at St Joseph's. 'A couple of lovebirds,' Geoffrey had said, being magnanimous, since he was bound to be jealous. Of Geoffrey one could expect gentle-manly behaviour, even if he did shoplift . . . even if he was a thief. Which was more than one could say of Rose, whose jealousy of Sophie shone from her eyes and spiteful face.

Dear Aunt Vera. Our two children say they won't go back to school. Our son is fifteen. The girl is sixteen. They were playing truant for months before we knew it. Then the police told us they were spending the time with some bad types. Now they hardly come home at all. What shall we do?

Sophie had said she wasn't going back to school after Christmas, but perhaps she would change her mind to be with Colin. But he said he was doing badly, and didn't want to take his final exams, due this coming summer. He was eighteen. He said exams were stupid, and he was too old for school. Rose – *not* her responsi-bility – had 'dropped out'. So had James. Sylvia hadn't been to school in months. Geoffrey did well, always had, and it looked as if he would be the only one who would actually sit the exams. Daniel would because Geoffrey did, but he wasn't clever, like his idol. Jill was more often here than at school. Lucy, from Darting-ton, would sit exams and do brilliantly, that was evident.

Frances herself, obedient girl, had gone to school, was punctual, sat exams, and would have gone to university if the war and Johnny had not intervened. She could not understand what the problem was. She had not much enjoyed school, but had seen the process as something that had to be undergone. She would have to earn her living, that was the point. These youngsters never seemed to think about that.

Now she wrote down the letter she would like to send, but of course would not.

Dear Mrs Jackson, I haven't the faintest idea what to advise. We seem to have bred a generation that expects food simply to fall into their mouths without their working for it. With sincere regrets, Aunt Vera.

Julia was getting up. She gathered up her bag, her gloves, a newspaper, and as she came past Frances, nodded. Frances, too late, got up to push a chair towards her, but Julia was already gone. If she had handled it properly, Julia would have sat down – there had been a little moment of hesitation. And then at last she might have become friends with her mother-in-law.

Frances sat on, ordered more coffee, then soup. Andrew had said that if one was lucky with one's timing and ordered goulash soup, you got the thick part at the bottom of the pot, like stew, very good. Her goulash when it came was evidently from the middle of the pot.

She did not know what to write for her third piece. The second had been on marijuana, and it was easy. The article had been cool and informative, that was all, and many letters came in response.

What an attractive crowd this was, the Cosmo crowd, these people from all over Europe, and of course, by now, the kind of British attracted by them. Many of them Jews. Not all.

Julia had remarked, in front of 'the kids' when one of them asked if she had been a refugee, 'I am in the unfortunate situation of being a German who is not a Jew.'

Shock and outrage. Julia's fascist status had been confirmed: though they all used the word fascist as easily as they said fuck,

or shit, not necessarily meaning much more than this was somebody they disapproved of.

Sophie had wailed that Julia gave her the creeps, all Germans
did.

Of Sophie, Julia had remarked, 'She has the Jewish young
girl's beauty, but she'll end up an old hag, just like the rest of us.'

If Sylvia—Tilly was coming down to supper then the food had
to be right for her. She could not be given a dish different from
the others, and yet she did not eat anything but potato. Very well,
Frances would cook a big shepherd's pie, and the girls who were
slimming could leave the mash and eat the rest. There would
be vegetables. Rose would not eat vegetables, but would salad.
Geoffrey never ate fish or vegetables: she had been worrying
about Geoffrey's diet for years, and he was not even her child.
What did his parents think, when he hardly ever went home, was
always coming to them – rather, to Colin? She asked him and he
said that they were quite pleased he had somewhere to go. It
seemed they both worked hard. Quakers. Religious. A dull
household, it seemed. She had become fond of Geoffrey but was
damned if she was going to spend time worrying about Rose.
Careful, Frances: if there was one thing she had learned, it was
not to say what one will accept or refuse from Fate, which had
its own ideas.

But perhaps one's fate is just one's temperament, invisibly
attracting people and events. There are people who (probably
unconsciously, when young, until it is forced on them that this
is their character) use a certain passivity towards life, watching to
see what will arrive on their plate, or drop in their lap, or stare
them in the face – 'What's wrong with you? Are you blind?' –
and then, try not so much to grasp it as wait, allowing the thing
to develop, show itself. Then the task is to do your best with it,
do what you can.

Would she have believed, aged nineteen, marrying Johnny
when there was no reason to expect anything ever but war and
bad times, that she would find herself a kind of house-mother –

but 'earth-mother' was the current term. Where along the road should she have said (if she had been determined to avert this fate) 'No, I won't.' She had fought against Julia's house, but probably it would have been better if she had succumbed much earlier, saying yes, yes, to what was happening, and consciously saying it, accepting what had arrived in front of her, as was now her philosophy. Saying no is often like those people who divorce one partner only to marry another exactly the same in looks and character: we carry invisible templates as ineluctably ourselves as fingerprints, but we don't know about them until we look around us and see them mirrored.

'We know what we are . . .' (Oh, no, we don't!) '. . . but not what we may be.'

Once she would have found it hard to believe that she could live chaste, without a man in prospect . . . but she still cherished fantasies about a man in her life who would not be a mad egotist, like Johnny. But what man would want to take on a tribe of youngsters all 'disturbed' for one reason or another. Here they were, congratulated on living in Swinging London, promised everything the advertisers of at least two continents could think up, yet if 'the kids' did swing – and they did, they were off to the big jazz concert on Saturday, tomorrow – then they were screwed up, and two of them, her sons, because of her and Johnny. And the war, of course.

Frances took up her burden, heavily loaded carrier bags, paid her bill, went home up the hill.

A pearly post-Clean Air Act fog floated outside the windows and bedewed the hair and eyelashes of 'the kids' who came into the house laughing and embracing each other like survivors. Damp duffel-coats loaded the banisters, and all the chairs around the table except two on Frances's left, were occupied. Colin had sat down by Sophie, saw that he would be next to his brother in the third empty chair, and quickly moved to the end where he stood by Geoffrey, who sat opposite Frances, and now Colin claimed the important chair by pushing Geoffrey out with a thrust of his buttocks. A schoolboy moment, rough and raw, too young for their almost adult status. Geoffrey then came to sit on Frances's right, without looking at Colin. Sophie suffered from any discord, and she got up to go to Colin, bent to slide an arm around him, and kissed his cheek. He did not permit himself to smile, but then could not prevent a weak and loving smile at her which then included everyone. They all laughed. Rose . . . James . . . Jill – these three seemed to be ensconced in the basement; Daniel was next to Geoffrey, head boy and his deputy. Lucy was next to Daniel, having come up from Dartington to spend the weekend with him, here. Twelve places. They were all waiting, ravenously eating bread, sniffing the smells that came from the stove. At last Andrew came in, his arm around Sylvia. She was still inside the baby shawl, but wore clean jeans, that were loose on her, and a jersey of Andrew's. Her pale wispy hair had been brushed up, making her look even more infantile. But she was smiling, though her lips trembled.

Colin, who resented her being here at all, got up, smiling, and made her a little bow. 'Welcome, Sylvia,' he said, and tears came into her eyes at their chorus of 'Hello, Sylvia.'

She sat down next to Frances, and Andrew was next to her. The meal could begin. In a moment dishes filled all the space down the table. Colin got up to pour wine, forestalling Geoffrey, who was about to do it, while Frances put food on to plates. A moment of crisis: she had reached Andrew, and next would be Sylvia. Andrew said, 'Let me,' and there began a little play. On to his plate he put a single carrot, and on to Sylvia's, a carrot. He was solemn, frowning, judicious, and already Sylvia was beginning to laugh, though her lips still made nervous painful little movements. On to his plate, a little spoon of cabbage, and one for her, ignoring the hand that had gone up instinctively to stop him. For him, a mere sample of the mince, and the same for her. And then, with an air of recklessness, a rather big lump of potato for her, and for him. They were all laughing. Sylvia sat looking at her plate, but Andrew, with a determined let's-get-this-over look, had taken up a spoon of potato and waited for her to do the same. She did — and swallowed.

Now, trying not to watch what went on, as Andrew and Sylvia fought with themselves, Frances raised her glass of Rioja — seven shillings a bottle, for this pleasant wine had yet to be 'discovered' — and drank a toast to Progressive Education, an old joke which they all enjoyed.

'Where's Julia?' came Sylvia's little voice.

An anxious silence. Then Andrew said, 'She doesn't come to meals with us.'

'Why doesn't she? Why not? It's so lovely with you.'

This was a moment of real breakthrough, as Andrew described it later to Julia — 'We've won, Julia, yes, we really have.' Frances was gratified: she actually had tears in her eyes. Andrew put his arm around Sylvia and, smiling at his mother, said, 'Yes, it is. But Julia prefers to be up there by herself.'

Having unwittingly created a picture of what must be loneliness, it struck him, and he jumped up and said, 'I'll go and ask her again.' This was partly to relieve him of the burden and the challenge of his still scarcely touched plate. As he went out and up the stairs, Sylvia put down her spoon.

In a moment Andrew returned, and sat down with, 'She says perhaps she'll drop in later.'

This caused a moment not far from panic. In spite of Andrew's efforts on his grandmother's behalf, they all tended to see Julia as a kind of old witch, to be laughed at. The St Joseph's contingent could not know how Julia had wrestled for a week, two, with Sylvia's illness, sitting with her, bathing her, making her take mouthfuls of this and sips of that. Julia had hardly slept. And here was her reward, Sylvia, picking up her spoon again, watching Andrew lift his, as if she had forgotten how to use one.

The difficult moment passed, the kids appeased their teenage appetites, and Frances ate more than she usually would, to be an example to the two on her left. It was a wonderful evening, with an undertone of tenderness because of Sylvia and their concern for her. It was as if they were collectively putting their arms around her, while she got down one mouthful after another. Andrew too.

And then they saw she had gone white and was shaking. 'My father . . .' she whispered. 'I mean, it's my stepfather . . .'

'Oh, no,' said Colin, 'it's all right, he's gone to Cuba.'

'I'm afraid not,' said Andrew, and leaped up to intercept Johnny, who was in the hall outside the kitchen. Andrew shut the door, but everyone could hear Johnny's bluff, reasonable, confident voice, and Andrew: 'No, father, no, you can't come in, I'll explain later.'

Voices loud, then low, and Andrew returned, leaving the door open, and slid down again beside Sylvia. He was red and angry, and he clutched his fork like a weapon.

'But why isn't he in Cuba?' asked Colin, petulantly, like a child.

The brothers looked at each other, suddenly as one, exchanging understandings.

Andrew said, 'He hasn't left, but I expect he will.' He added, still angry, 'Actually, I think he's going to Zanzibar – or Kenya.' A pause, while the brothers communed, with their eyes and angry smiles. 'He's not alone, he's got a black man . . . a man from there . . . an African comrade.' These adjustments to the spirit of the times were followed carefully by the company. They had taken Africa into their hearts and consciences, the progressive schools had seen to that, and even Rose at a far from progressive school chose her words with, 'We've got to be nice to dark-skinned people, that's what I think.'

Sylvia had not recovered. Her spoon hung listless in her thin hand.

And now James, who was understandably at a loss, said, 'Why is he going to Africa instead of Cuba?'

At this the brothers laughed, together, and it was not pleasant, while Frances prevented herself from joining in, though she would have liked to. She had always tried never to criticise Johnny in public.

Colin said, like an orator, 'Keep them guessing,' and Frances, hearing the quote, had to laugh. 'That's it,' said Andrew, 'keep them guessing.'

'Why are you laughing?' asked Sylvia, 'what's funny?'

Andrew at once stopped his mockery, and picked up his spoon again. But it was over, their meal, his and Sylvia's. 'Johnny's coming,' he said to her. 'He's just getting something from the car. If you want to get out of the way . . .'

'Oh, yes, I do, yes, please,' said Johnny's stepdaughter, and up she got, supported by Andrew's arm. The two went out. At least they had both eaten something.

Frances called after them, 'Tell Julia not to come down, otherwise they'll quarrel again.'

The meal continued, subdued.

The St Joseph contingent were talking about a book Daniel had stolen from a secondhand bookstall, *The Ordeal of Richard Feverel*. He had read it, said it was groovy, and the tyrannical father was just like his. He recommended it to Geoffrey who pleased him by saying it was great, and then the novel migrated to Sophie who said it was the best book she had ever read, it made her cry. Now Colin was reading it. Rose said, 'Why can't I read it? It isn't fair.'

'It's not the only copy in the world,' said Colin.

'I've got a copy, I'll lend it to you,' said Frances.

'Oh, Frances, thank you, you're so sweet to me.'

This meant, as everyone knew, I hope you are going to go on being sweet to me.

Frances said, 'I'll get it,' to have an excuse to go out of that room which so soon would swirl with discordant currents. And everything had been so nice until now . . . She went up to the room just over the kitchen, the sitting-room, found *The Ordeal of Richard Feverel* in a wall of books, turned and saw that Julia was sitting there alone in the half dark. Not since Frances had taken over the lower part of the house had she found Julia in this room. Now, ideally, she should sit down and try to make friends with Julia, but as always, she was in a hurry.

'I was on my way down to you all,' said Julia, 'but I hear Johnny has arrived.'

'I don't see how I can stop him coming,' said Frances. She was listening downwards, to the kitchen – were they all right there, no quarrels? Upwards . . . was Sylvia all right?

Julia said, 'He has a home. It seems to me that he is not often in it.'

'Well,' said Frances, 'if Phyllida is in it, who can blame him?'

She had hoped that this might make Julia at least smile, but instead she was going on, 'I must say this . . .' And Frances waited for what she was sure would be a dose of disapproval. 'You are so weak with Johnny. He has treated you abominably.'

Frances was thinking, Then why give him the key to the house? – though she knew the mother could hardly say to the son that he couldn't have a key to a house he thought of as his own. Besides, what about the boys? She said, trying to joke a little, 'Perhaps we could have the locks changed?'

But Julia took it seriously with, 'I would see to it if I did not think you would at once give him a new key.' She got up, and Frances, who had been planning to sit down, saw another opportunity slide away.

'Julia,' said Frances, 'you always criticise me, but you don't support me.' And what did she mean by that, except that Julia made her feel like a schoolgirl deficient in everything.

'What are you saying?' said Julia. 'I do not understand.' She was furious, and hurt.

'I don't mean . . . you have been so good . . . you are always so generous . . . no, all I meant was . . .'

'I do not believe that I have been lacking in my responsibilities to the family,' said Julia, and Frances heard, incredulously, that Julia might easily cry. She had hurt Julia, and it was the fact that this was possible that made her stammer, 'Julia . . . but Julia . . .

you are wrong, I didn't mean . . .' And then, 'Oh, *Julia*,' in a different tone, which made Julia stop on her way out of the room to examine her, as if she was prepared to be touched, reached: even to reach out herself.

But downstairs a door slammed, and Frances exclaimed, in despair, 'There he is, it's Johnny.'

'Yes, it's Comrade Johnny,' said Julia, departing upstairs.

Frances went down into the kitchen and found Johnny in his usual position, standing back to the window, and with him was a handsome black man wearing clothes more expensive than anyone else's, smiling as Johnny introduced him, 'This is Comrade Mo, from East Africa.'

Frances sat, pushing the novel across the table at Rose, but she was staring in admiration at Comrade Mo, and at Johnny, who resumed his lecture to impress Comrade Mo, on the history of East Africa and the Arabs.

And now Frances was in a dilemma. She did not want to ask Johnny to sit down. She had asked him – though Julia would never believe this – not to drop in at mealtimes, and to telephone before he came. But here was this guest and of course she must . . .

'Would you like something to eat?' she asked, and Comrade Mo rubbed his hands together and laughed and said he was starving, and at once sat down in the chair next to her. Johnny, invited to sit, said he would just have a glass of wine – he had brought a bottle. Where Andrew and Sylvia had sat, minutes before, now sat Comrades Mo and Johnny, and the two men put on their plates all that was left of the pie, and the vegetables.

Frances was angry to the point where one is dispirited with it: what was the point, ever, of being angry with Johnny? It was obvious he had not eaten for days, he was cramming in bread, taking great mouthfuls of wine, refilling his glass and Comrade Mo's, in between forkfuls from his plate. The youngsters were seeing appetites even greater than their own.

'I'll serve the pudding,' said Frances, her voice dull with rage.

On to the table now went plates of sticky delights from the

Cypriot shops, concoctions of honey and nuts and filo pastry, and dishes of fruit, and her chocolate pudding, made especially for 'the kids'.

Colin, having stared at his father, and then at his mother: *Why did you let him sit down? Why do you let him . . . ?* now got up, scraping back his chair, and pushing it back against the wall with a bang. He went out.

'I feel this is a real home from home,' said Comrade Mo, consuming chocolate pudding. 'And I do not know these cakes? Are they like some cakes we have from the Arab cuisine?'

'Cypriot,' said Johnny, 'almost certainly influenced from the East . . .' and began a lecture on the cuisines of the Mediterranean.

They were all listening, fascinated: no one could say that Johnny was dull when not talking about politics, but it was too good to last. Soon he was on to Kennedy's murder, and the probable roles of the CIA and the FBI. From there he went on to the American plans to take over Africa, and in proof told them that Comrade Mo had been propositioned by the CIA offering vast sums of money. All his teeth and gums showing, Comrade Mo confirmed this, with pride. An agent of the CIA in Nairobi had approached him with offers to finance his party, in return for information. 'And how did you know he was CIA?' James wanted to know, and Comrade Mo said that 'everyone knew' the CIA roamed around Africa, like a lion seeking its prey. He laughed, delightedly, looking around for approval. 'You should all come and visit us. Come and see for yourself and have a good time,' he said, having little idea he was describing a glorious future. 'Johnny has promised to come.'

'Oh, I thought he was going now – at once?' said James, and now Comrade Mo's eyes rolled in enquiry to Johnny, while he said, 'Comrade Johnny's welcome any time.'

'So, you didn't tell Andrew you were going to Africa?' asked Frances, to elicit the reply, 'Keep them guessing.' And Johnny smiled and offered them the aphorism, 'Always keep them guessing.'

'Who?' Rose wanted to know.

'Obviously, Rose, the CIA,' said Frances.

'Oh, yes, the CIA,' said James, 'of course.' He was absorbing information, as was his talent and his intention.

'Keep them guessing,' said Johnny. And, in his severest manner to his willing disciple, James, 'In politics you should never let your left hand know what your right hand does.'

'Or perhaps,' said Frances, 'what your left hand does.'

Ignoring her: 'You should always cover your tracks, Comrade James. You should never make things easy for the enemy.'

'Perhaps I shall come to Cuba too?' said Mo. 'Comrade Fidel is encouraging links with the liberated African countries.'

'And even the non-liberated ones,' said Johnny, letting them all in on secrets of policy.

'What are you going to Cuba for?' asked Daniel, really wanting to know, confronting Johnny across the table with his inflammatory red hair, his freckles, and eyes always strained by the knowledge that he was not worthy to lick the boots of – for instance, Geoffrey. Or Johnny.

James said to him, 'One should not ask that kind of question,' and looked to Johnny for approval.

'Exactly,' said Johnny. He got up, and resumed his lecturer's position, back to the window, at ease, but on the alert.

'I want to see a country that has known only slavery and subjection build freedom, build a new society. Fidel has done miracles in five years, but the next five years will show a real change. I am looking forward to taking Andrew and Colin, taking my sons, to see for themselves . . . Where are they, by the way?' For he had not noticed their absence until now.

'Andrew is with Sylvia,' said Frances. 'We are going to have to call her that now.'

'Why, has she changed her name?'

'That *is* her name,' said Rose, sullen: she continually said she hated her name and wanted to be called Marilyn.

'I have only really known her as Tilly,' said Johnny, with a whimsical air that momentarily recalled Andrew. 'Well, then, where's Colin?'

'Doing homework,' said Frances. A likely story, though Johnny would not know that.

Johnny was fidgeting. His sons were his favourite audience, and he did not know what a critical one it was.

'Can you go to Cuba, just like that, as a tourist?' asked James, evidently disapproving of tourists and their frivolity.

'He's not going as a tourist,' said Comrade Mo. Feeling out of place at the table, while his comrade-in-arms stood in front of them, he got up and lounged there by Johnny. 'Fidel invited him.'

This was the first Frances had heard of it.

'And he invited you too,' said Comrade Mo.

Johnny was clearly displeased: he had not wanted this to be revealed.

Comrade Mo said, 'A friend of Fidel's is in Kenya for the Independence celebrations, and he told me that Fidel wants to invite Johnny and Johnny's wife.'

'He must mean Phyllida.'

'No, it was you. He said Comrade Johnny and Comrade Frances.'

Johnny was furious. 'Comrade Fidel is clearly unaware of Frances's indifference to world affairs.'

'No,' said Comrade Mo, not noticing apparently that Johnny was about to explode, just at his elbow. 'He said he had heard she is a famous actress, and she is welcome to start a theatre group in Havana. And I'll add our invitation to that. You could start a revolutionary theatre in Nairobi.'

'Oh, Frances,' breathed Sophie, clasping her hands together, her eyes melting with pleasure, 'how wonderful, how absolutely *wonderful*.'

'Frances's line seems rather more to be advice on family problems,' said Johnny, and, firmly putting an end to this nonsense, raised his voice, addressing the young ones, 'You are a fortunate generation,' he told them. 'You will be building a new world, you young comrades. You have the capacity to see through all the old shams, the lies, the delusions – you can overturn the past, destroy it, build anew . . . this country has two main aspects. On the one hand it is rich, with a solid and established infrastructure, while on the other, it is full of old-fashioned and stultifying attitudes. That will be the problem. Your problem. I can see the Britain of the future, free, rich, poverty gone, injustice a memory . . .'

He went on like this for some time, repeating the exhortations that sounded like promises. *You* will transform the world . . . it is *your* generation on whose shoulders the responsibility will fall . . . the future is in *your* hands . . . *you* will live to see the world a better place, a glorious place, and know that it was *your* efforts . . . what a wonderful thing to be *your* age, now, with everything in *your* hands . . .

Young faces, young eyes, shone, adored him and what he was saying. Johnny was in his element, absorbing admiration. He was standing like Lenin, one hand pointing forward into the future, while the other was clenched on his heart.

'He is a great man,' he concluded in a soft, reverential voice, gazing severely at them. 'Fidel is a genuinely great man. He is pointing us all the way into the future.'

One face there showed an incorrect alignment to Johnny: James, who admired Johnny as much as Johnny could possibly wish, was in the grip of a need for instruction.

'But, Comrade Johnny . . .' he said, raising his hand as if in class.

'And now goodnight,' said Johnny. 'I have a meeting. And so has Comrade Mo here.'

His unsmiling but comradely nod excluded Frances, to whom he directed a cold glance. Out he went, followed by Comrade Mo, who said to Frances, 'Thanks, Comrade. You've saved my life. I was really hungry. And now it seems I have a meeting.'

They sat silent, listening to Johnny's Beetle start up, and leave.

'Perhaps you could all do the washing-up,' said Frances. 'I've got to work. Goodnight.'

She lingered to see who would take up this invitation. Geoffrey of course, the good little boy; Jill, who was clearly in love with handsome Geoffrey; Daniel because he was in love with Geoffrey but probably didn't know it; Lucy . . . well, all of them, really. Rose?

Rose sat on: she was fucked if she was going to be made use of.

The influences of Christmas Day, that contumacious festival, were spreading dismay as early as the evening of the 12th of December when, to Frances's surprise, she found she was drinking to the independence of Kenya. James lifted his glass, brimming with Rioja, and said, 'To Kenyatta, to Kenya, to Freedom.' As always, his warm friendly, if public, face under the tumbling locks of black hair, sent messages all around of unlimited reservoirs of largesse of feeling. Excited eyes, fervent faces: Johnny's recent harangues were still reverberating in them.

A vast meal had been consumed, a little of it by Sylvia, who was as always by Frances's left elbow. In her glass was a stain of red: Andrew had said she must drink a little, it was good for her, and Julia had supported him. The cigarette smoke was denser than usual; it seemed that everyone was smoking tonight, because of the liberation of Kenya. Not Colin, he was batting away waves of smoke as they reached his face. 'Your lungs will rot,' he said. 'Well, it's just tonight,' said Andrew.

'I'm going to Nairobi for Christmas,' James announced, looking around, proud but uneasy.

'Oh, are your parents going?' Frances unthinkingly asked, and a silence rebuked her.

'Is it likely?' sneered Rose, stubbing out her cigarette and furiously lighting another.

James rebuked her with, 'My father was fighting in Kenya. He was a soldier. He says it's a good place.'

'Oh, so your parents are living there? Or planning to? Are you visiting them?'

'No, they aren't living there,' said Rose. 'His father is an income tax inspector in Leeds.'

'So, is that a crime?' enquired Geoffrey.

'They are such squares,' said Rose. 'You wouldn't believe it.'

'They aren't so bad,' said James, not liking this. 'But we have to make allowances for people who are not yet politically conscious.'

'Oh, so you are going to make your parents politically conscious – don't make me laugh,' said Rose.

'I didn't say so,' said James, turning away from his cousin, and towards Frances. 'I've seen Dad's photographs of Nairobi. It's groovy. That's why I'm going.'

Frances understood that there was no need to say anything as crass as, Have you got a passport? A visa? How are you going to pay for it? And you are only seventeen.

James was floating in the arms of a teenage dream, which was not underpinned by boring realities. He would find himself as if by magic in Nairobi's main street . . . there he would run into Comrade Mo . . . be one of a group of loving comrades where he would soon be a leader, making fiery speeches. And, since he was seventeen, there would be a girl. How did he imagine this girl? Black? White? She had no idea. James went on talking about his father's memories of Kenya. The grim truths of war had been erased, and all that remained were high blue skies, and all that space and a good chap (corrected to a *good type*) who had saved his father's life. A black man. An Askari, risking his life for the British soldier.

What had been Frances's equivalent dream at, not sixteen, she had been a busy schoolgirl; but nineteen? Yes, she was pretty sure she had had fantasies, because of Johnny's immersion in the Spanish Civil War, of nursing soldiers. Where? In a rocky landscape, with wine, and olives. But where? Teenage dreams do not need map points.

'You can't go to Kenya,' said Rose. 'Your parents will stop you.'

Brought down, James reached for his glass and emptied it.

'Since the subject has come up,' said Frances, 'I want to talk about Christmas?' Faced with already apprehensive faces, Frances found herself unable to go on. They knew what they were going to hear, because Andrew had already warned them.

Now he said, 'You see, there isn't going to be a Christmas here this year. I am going to Phyllida for Christmas lunch. She rang me and said she hasn't heard from my . . . from Johnny, and she says she dreads Christmas.'

'Who doesn't?' said Colin.

'Oh, Colin,' said Sophie, 'don't be like that.'

Colin said, not looking at anyone, 'I am going to Sophie's because of her mother. She can't be alone on Christmas Day.'

'But I thought you were Jewish,' said Rose to Sophie.

'We have always done Christmas,' said Sophie. 'When Daddy was alive . . .' She went silent, biting her lips, her eyes filling.

'And Sylvia here is going with Julia to Julia's friend,' said Andrew.

'And I,' said Frances, 'propose to ignore Christmas altogether.'

'But, Frances,' said Sophie, 'that's awful, you can't.'

'Not awful. Wonderful,' said Frances. 'And now, Geoffrey, don't you think you should go home for Christmas? You really should, you know.'

Geoffrey's polite face, ever attentive to what might be expected of him, smiled agreement. 'Yes, Frances. I know. You are right. I will go home. And my grandmother is dying,' he added, in the same tone.

'Then, I'll go home too,' said Daniel. His red hair flamed, and his face went even redder, as he said, 'I'll come and visit you, then.'

'As you like,' said Geoffrey revealing by this ungraciousness that perhaps he had been looking forward to a Daniel-free hols.

'James,' said Frances, 'please go home.'

'Are you throwing me out?' he said, good-humouredly. 'I don't blame you. Have I outstayed my welcome?'

'For now, yes,' said Frances, who was by nature unable to throw anyone out permanently. 'But what about school, James? Aren't you going to finish school?'

'Of course he is,' said Andrew, revealing that admonitions must have occurred. His four years seniority gave him the right. 'It's ridiculous, James,' he went on, talking direct to James. 'You've only got a year to go to A-levels. It won't kill you.'

'You don't know my school,' said James, but desperation had entered the equation. 'If you did . . .'

'Anyone can suffer for a year,' said Andrew. 'Or even three. Or four,' he said, glancing guiltily at his mother: he was making revelations.

'Okay,' said James. 'I will. But . . .' and here he looked at Frances, 'without the liberating airs of Frances's house I don't think I could survive.'

'You can visit,' said Frances. 'There's always weekends.'

There were left now Rose and the dark horse Jill, the always well-brushed, well-washed, polite, blonde girl, who hardly ever spoke, but listened, how she did listen.

'I'm not going home,' said Rose. 'I won't go.'

Frances said, 'You do realise that your parents could sue me for alienating your affections – well, that kind of thing.'

'They don't care about me,' declared Rose. 'They don't give a fuck.'

'That's not true,' said Andrew. 'You may not like them but they certainly care about you. They wrote to me. They seem to think I am a good influence.'

'That's a joke,' said Rose.

The hinterlands behind this tiny exchange were acknowledged as glances were exchanged among the others.

'I said I am not going,' said Rose. She was darting trapped glances around at them all: they might have been her enemies.

'Listen, Rose,' said Frances, with the intention of keeping her dislike of the girl out of her voice, 'Liberty Hall is closing down over Christmas.' She had not specified for how long.

'I can stay in the basement flat, can't I? I won't be in the way.'

'And how are you going to . . .' but Frances stopped.

Andrew had an allowance and he had been giving money to Rose. 'She could claim that I treated her badly,' said Andrew. 'Well, she does complain, she tells everyone how I wronged her. Like the wicked squire and the milkmaid. The trouble was, she was all for me, but I wasn't for her.' Frances had thought, Or all for the glamorous Eton boy and his connections? Andrew had said, 'I think that coming here was what did it. It was such a revelation to her. It's a pretty limited set-up – her parents are very nice . . .'

'And are you – and Julia – going to keep her indefinitely?'

'No,' said Andrew. 'I've said, enough. After all, she's done very well out of a kiss or two in the moonlight.'

But now they were faced with a guest who would not leave.

Rose looked as if she were being threatened with imprisonment, with torture. An animal in a too small cage could look like that, glaring out, glaring around.

It was all out of proportion, ridiculous . . . Frances persisted, though the girl's violence was making her own heart beat, 'Rose, just go home for Christmas, that's all. Just do that. They must be worried sick about you. And you have to talk to them about school . . .' At this Rose exploded up out of the chair, and said, 'Oh, shit, it just needed that . . .' and she ran out of the room, howling, tears scattering. They listened to her thud down the stairs to the basement flat.

'Well,' said Geoffrey gracefully, 'what a carry-on.'

Sylvia said, 'But her school must be horrible if she hates it so much.' She had agreed to go back to school, while she lived here, 'with Julia,' as she put it. And she had said yes, she would stick it out and study to be a doctor.

What was burning Rose up, consuming her with the acid of envy, was that Sylvia – 'And she isn't even related, she's just Johnny's stepchild' – was in this house, as a right, and that Julia was paying for her. It seemed Rose believed that justice would make Julia pay for her, Rose, to go to a progressive school, and keep her here for as long as she liked.

Colin had said to her, 'Do you think my grandmother's made of money? It's a lot for her to take on Sylvia. She's already paying for me and for Andrew.'

'It isn't fair,' had been Rose's answer. 'I don't see why she should have everything.'

There now remained Jill, who had not said a word. Finding them all looking at her, she said, 'I'm not going home. But I'll go to my cousin in Exeter for Christmas.'

Next morning Frances found Jill in the kitchen, boiling a kettle for tea. Since there was plenty of everything in the basement kitchen, this might mean Jill had hoped for a chat.

'Let's sit down and have tea,' said Frances, and sat down.

Jill joined her, at the end of the table. This was obviously not going to be like an encounter with Rose. The girl was watching Frances, not with hostility, but was sad, serious, and sat holding her arms around herself, as if she were cold.

Frances said, 'Jill, you do see that I am in an impossible position with your parents.'

The girl said, 'Oh, I thought you were going to say you didn't see why you should keep me. Fair enough. But . . .'

'I wasn't going to say that. But don't you really see that your parents must be going mad with worry?'

'I told them where I was. I said I was here.'

'Are you thinking of not going back to school?'

'I don't see the point of it.'

She wasn't doing well at school, but at St Joseph's this was not a final argument.

'And don't you see that I must be worrying about you?'

At this the girl seemed to come alive, leave behind her cold apprehension, and she leaned forward and said, 'Oh, Frances, no, you mustn't. It's so nice here. I feel so safe.'

'And don't you feel safe at home?'

'It's not that. They just . . . don't like me.' And she retreated back inside her shell, hugging herself, rubbing her arms as if she were really cold.

Frances noted that this morning Jill had painted great black lines around her eyes. A new thing, on this neat little girl. And she was wearing one of Rose's mini-dresses.

Frances would have liked to put her arms around the child and hold her. She had never had such an impulse with Rose: she wished Rose would simply take herself off. So, she liked Jill, but did not like Rose. And so what difference could that make, when she treated them exactly the same?

Frances sat alone in the kitchen, and the table which she had wiped and waxed shone like a pool. Really, it was a very nice table, she thought, now that you can see it. Not a plate or a cup, and no people. It was Christmas Day and she had shouted goodbye to Colin and Sophie first, both dressed for Christmas lunch, even Colin, who despised clothes. Then it was Julia, in a grey velvet suit and a sort of bonnety thing with a rose on it, and a blueish veil. Sylvia was wearing a dress bought for her by Julia, which made Frances glad the jeans and T-shirt wearers had not seen it: she didn't want them laughing at Sylvia, who could have gone to church fifty years ago in that blue dress. She had refused to wear a hat, though. Then off went Andrew, to console Phyllida. He had put his head around the door to say, 'We all envy you, Frances. Well, all except Julia, she's upset that you will be alone. And you must expect a little present. She was too shy to tell you.'

Frances sat alone. All over this country women laboured over the stove, basting several million turkeys, while Christmas puddings steamed. Brussels sprouts sent out sulphuric fumes. Fields of potatoes were jammed around the birds. Bad temper reigned, but she, Frances, was sitting like a queen, alone. Only people who have known the pressure of exorbitant teenagers, or emotional dependants who suck and feed and demand, can know the pure pleasure of being free, even for an hour. Frances felt herself relax, all through her body, she was like a balloon ready to float up and away. And it was quiet. In other houses Christmas music exulted or pounded, but here, in this house, no television, not even a radio . . . but wait, was that something downstairs – was that Rose down there? But she had said she was going with Jill to the cousins. The music must be coming from next door.

So, on the whole, silence. She breathed in, she breathed out, oh happiness, she had absolutely nothing to worry about, even think about, for several hours. The doorbell rang. Cursing, she went to find a smiling young man, in decorative gear, red, for Christmas, and he handed her, with a bow, a tray enclosed in white muslin, that was twisted up in the centre and held with a red bow. 'Merry Christmas,' he said, and then 'Bon appetit.' Off he went, whistling 'Good King Wenceslas'.

Frances put the tray in the centre of the table. It had a card on it announcing it was from an elegant restaurant, of the serious kind, and when the muslin was opened, there was revealed a little feast, with another card, 'Best wishes from Julia.' *Best wishes*. It was clearly Frances's fault that Julia could not say *With Love*, but never mind, she was not going to worry about that today.

It was all so pretty she did not want to disturb it.

A white china bowl held a green soup, very cold, with shaved ice on it, that a testing finger announced was a blend of velvety unctuousness and tartness – what was it? Sorrel? A blue plate decorated with frills of bright green lettuce pretending to be seaweed held scallop shells and in them sliced scallops, with mushrooms. Two quails sat side by side on a bed of sauteed celery. By it a card said, 'Please heat for ten minutes.' A little Christmas pudding was made of chocolate and decorated with holly. There was a dish of fruit Frances had not tasted and scarcely knew the

names of, Cape gooseberries, lychees, passion fruit, guavas. There
was a slice of Stilton. Little bottles of champagne, burgundy and
port fenced the feast. These days there would be nothing remarkable in the witty little spread, which paid homage to the Christmas
meal, while it mocked, but then it was a glimpse of a vision from
celestial fields, a swallow visiting from the plenitudes of the future.
Frances could not eat it, it would be a crime. She sat down and
looked at it and thought that Julia must care for her, after all.

Frances wept. At Christmas one weeps. It is obligatory. She
wept because of her mother-in-law's kindness to her and to her
sons, and because of the charm of the meal, sparking off its invitations, and because of her incredulity at what she had managed
to live through, and then, really getting down to it, she wept at
the miseries of Christmases past. Oh my God, those Christmases
when the boys were small, and they were in those dreadful rooms,
and everything so ugly, and they were often cold.

Then she dried her eyes and sat on, alone. An hour, two
hours. Not a soul in the house . . . that radio was downstairs, not
next door, but she chose to ignore it. It might have been left on,
after all. Four o'clock. The gas boards and electricity would be
relieved that once again they had coped with the national Christmas lunch. Tired and cross women from Land's End to the
Orkneys would be sitting down and saying, 'Now, *you* wash up.'
Well, good luck to them.

In armchairs and in sofas people would be dozing off and the
Queen's speech would be intermittently heard, interrupted by the
results of over-eating. It was getting dark. Frances got up, pulled
the curtains tight shut, switched on lights. She sat down again.
She was getting hungry but could not bring herself to spoil the
pretty feast. She ate a piece of bread and butter. She poured herself
a glass of Tio Pepe. In Cuba Johnny would be lecturing whoever
he was with on something: probably conditions in Britain.

She might go upstairs and have a nap, after all, she didn't often
get the chance of one. The door into the hall from outside opened,
and then the door into the kitchen and in came Andrew.

'You've been crying,' he announced, sitting down, near her.

'Yes, I have. A little. It was nice.'

'I don't like crying,' he remarked. 'It scares me, because I am afraid I might never stop.'

Now he went red, and said, 'Oh my God . . .'

'Oh, Andrew,' said Frances, 'I'm so sorry.'

'What for? Damn it, how could you think . . .'

'Everything could have been done differently, I suppose.'

'What? What could? Oh, *God*.'

He poured out wine, he sat hunched into himself, not unlike Jill, a few days ago.

'It's Christmas,' said Frances. 'That's all. The great provoker of miserable memories.'

He as it were warded this thought off, with a hand that said, Enough, don't go on. And leaned forward to inspect Julia's present. As Frances had done, he dipped a finger into the soup: an appreciative grimace. He sampled a slice of scallop.

'I'm feeling a terrible hypocrite, Andrew. I've sent everyone off, like good children, but I hardly went home after I left it. I'd go home for Christmas Day and leave the next morning or even that afternoon.'

'I wonder if they went home for Christmas – your parents?'

'Your grandparents.'

'Oh, yes, I suppose they must be. Have been.'

'I don't know. I know so little about them. There was the war, like a sort of chasm across my life, and on the other side, that life. And now they are dead. When I left home I thought about them as little as I could. I simply couldn't cope with them. And so I didn't see them and now I'm hard on Rose when she doesn't want to go home.'

'I take it you weren't fifteen when you left home?'

'No, eighteen.'

'There you are, you're in the clear.'

This absurdity made them laugh. A wonderful understanding: how well she was getting on with her elder son. Well, this had been true since he grew up – not all that long ago, in fact. What a pleasure it was, what a consolation for . . .

'And Julia, she didn't do much going home for Christmas, did she?'

'But how could she, when she was here?'

'How old was she when she came to London?'

'Twenty, I think.'

'*What?*' He actually brought his hands up to cover his mouth and lower face, and let them drop to say, 'Twenty. That's what I am. And sometimes I think I haven't learned to tie my shoelaces yet.'

In silence they contemplated a very young Julia.

She said, 'There's a photograph. I've seen it. A wedding photo. She's wearing a hat so loaded with flowers you can hardly see her face.'

'No veil?'

'No veil.'

'My God, coming over here, all by herself to us cold English. What was grandfather like?'

'I didn't meet him. They weren't approving of Johnny much. And certainly not of me.' Trying to find reasons for the enormity of it all, she went on, 'You see, it was the Cold War.'

He now had his arms folded on the table, supporting him, and he was frowning, staring at her, trying to understand. 'The Cold War,' he said.

'Good Lord,' she said, struck, 'of course, I'd forgotten, my parents didn't approve of Johnny. They actually wrote me a letter saying that I was an enemy of my country. A traitor – yes, I think they said that. Then they had second thoughts and came to see me – you and Colin were tiny then. Johnny was there and he called them rejects of history.' She seemed on the verge of tears, but it was from remembered exasperation.

Up went his brows, his face struggled with laughter, lost and he sat waving his arms about, as if to cancel the laughter. 'It's so funny,' he tried to apologise.

'I suppose it's funny, yes.'

He dropped his head on his arms, sighed, stayed there a long minute. Through his arms came the words, 'I just don't think I've got the energy for . . .'

'What? Energy for what?'

'Where did you lot get it from, all that confidence? Believe me, I'm a very frail thing in comparison. Perhaps I am a reject of history?'

'What? What do you mean?'

He lifted up his face. It was red, and there were tears. 'Well, never mind.' He waved his hands again, dispersing bad thoughts. 'Do you know, I might easily have a little taste of your feast.'

'Didn't you get any Christmas dinner?'

'Phyllida was in a state. She was crying and screaming and fainting in coils. You know she really is rather mad. I mean, really.'

'Well, yes.'

'Julia says it was because they sent her off – Phyllida – to Canada, at the beginning of the war. Apparently she was unlucky, it wasn't a very nice family. She hated it all. And when she got home she was a changeling, her parents said. They hardly recognised each other. She was ten when she left. Nearly fifteen when she got back.'

'Then I suppose, poor Phyllida.'

'I think so. And look what a bargain she's got with Comrade Johnny.' He pulled the tray towards him, got up to fetch a spoon, knife and fork, sat down, and had just dipped the spoon into the soup when the outer door banged, and the door behind them noisily opened and Colin came in, bringing cold air with him, a sense of the dark outside, and, like an accusation against them both, his unhappy face.

'Do I see food? Actually, food?'

He sat down, and using the spoon Andrew had just brought, began on the soup.

'Didn't you get any Christmas lunch?'

'No. Sophie's ma has gone all Jewish on her and says what has Christmas got to do with her? But they've always had Christmas.' He had finished the soup. 'Why don't you cook food like this?' he accused Frances. 'Now that's a soup.'

'How many quails do you think I'd have to cook for each of you, with your appetites?'

'Hang on a minute,' said Andrew. 'Fair's fair.' He brought a plate to the table, then another, for Colin, and another knife and fork. He put a quail on to his plate.

'You are supposed to heat those up for ten minutes,' said Frances.

'Who cares? Delicious.'

They were eating in competition with each other. And having reached the end of the quails, their spoons hovered together over the pudding. And that vanished, in a couple of mouthfuls.

'No Christmas pudding?' said Colin. 'No Christmas pudding at Christmas?'

Frances got up, fetched a can of Christmas pudding from the high shelf where it had been quietly maturing, and in a moment had it steaming on the stove.

'How long will that take?' asked Colin.

'An hour.'

She put loaves of bread on the table, then butter, cheese, plates. They polished off the Stilton, and began serious eating, the vandalised tray pushed aside.

'Mother,' said Colin, 'we've got to ask Sophie to come and live here.'

'But she is practically living here.'

'No – properly. It's got nothing to do with me . . . I mean, I'm not saying Sophie and me are a fixture, that isn't it. She can't go on at home. You wouldn't believe what she's like, Sophie's mother. She cries and grabs Sophie and says they must jump off a bridge together, or take poison. Imagine living with that?' It sounded as if he were accusing her, Frances, and, hearing that he did, said differently, even apologetically, 'If you could just get a taste of that house, it's like walking into the Black Hole of Calcutta.'

'You know how much I like Sophie. But I don't really see Sophie going down into the basement to share with Rose and whoever turns up. I take it you aren't expecting her to move in with you?'

'Well . . . no, it's not . . . that's not *on*. But she could camp in the living-room, we hardly ever use it.'

'If you've packed up with Sophie, do I have your permission to take my chance?' enquired Andrew. 'I'm madly in love with Sophie, as everyone must know.'

'I didn't say . . .'

And now these two young men reverted to the condition *schoolboy*, began jostling each other, elbow to elbow, knee to knee.

'Happy Christmas,' said Frances, and they desisted.

'Talking of Rose, where is she?' said Andrew. 'Did she go home.'

'Of course not,' said Colin. 'She's downstairs, alternately sobbing her heart out and making up her face.'

'How do you know?' asked Andrew.

'You forget the advantages of a progressive school. I know all about women.'

'I wish I did. While my education is in every way better than yours, I fail continually in the human department.'

'You're doing pretty well with Sylvia,' said Frances.

'Yes, but she isn't a woman, is she? More the ghost of a little child someone has murdered.'

'That's *awful*,' said Frances.

'But how true,' said Colin.

'If Rose is really downstairs, I suppose we had better ask her up,' said Frances.

'Do we have to?' said Andrew. 'It's so nice *en famille* for once.'

'I'll ask her,' said Colin, 'or she'll be taking an overdose and then saying it's our fault.'

He leaped up and off down the stairs. The two who remained said nothing, only looked at each other, as they heard the wail from beneath, presumably of welcome, Colin's loud common-sensical voice, and then Rose came in, propelled by Colin.

She was heavily made up, her eyes pencilled in black, false black eyelashes, purple eye-shadow. She was angry, accusing, appealing, and was evidently about to cry.

'There'll be some Christmas pudding,' said Frances.

But Rose had seen the fruit on the tray and was picking it over. 'What's this?' she demanded aggressively, 'What is it?' She held up a lychee.

'You must have tasted that, you get it after a Chinese meal, for pudding,' said Andrew.

'What Chinese meal? I never get Chinese meals.'

'Let me.' Colin peeled the lychee, the crisp fragments of deli-cately indented shell exposing the pearly, lucent fruit, like a little moon egg, which, having removed the shiny black pip he handed to Rose who swallowed it, and said, 'That's nothing much, it's not worth the fuss.'

'You should let it lie on your tongue, you should let its inwardness speak to your inwardness,' said Colin. He allowed himself his most owlish expression, and looked like an apprentice judge who lacked only the wig, as he cracked open another lychee, and handed it to Rose, delicately, between forefinger and thumb. She sat with it in her mouth, like a child refusing to swallow, then did, and said, 'It's a con.'

At once the brothers swept the plate of fruit towards them, and divided it between them. Rose sat with her mouth open, staring, and now she really was going to cry. 'Ohhhhh,' she wailed, 'you are so horrible. It's not my fault I've never had a Chinese meal.'

'Well, you've had Christmas pudding and that's what you are going to get next,' said Frances.

'I'm so hungry,' wept Rose.

'Then eat some bread and cheese.'

'Bread and cheese at Christmas?'

'That's all I had,' said Frances. 'Now shut up, Rose.'

Rose stopped mid-wail, stared incredulously at Frances, and allowed to develop the full gamut of the adolescent misunderstood: flashing eyes and pouting lips, and heaving bosom.

Andrew cut a piece of bread, loaded it with butter, then cheese. 'Here,' he said.

'I'll get fat, eating all that butter.'

Andrew took his offering back and began eating it himself. Rose sat swelling with outrage and tears. No one looked at her. Then she reached for the loaf, cut a thin slice, smeared on a little butter, put on a few crumbs of cheese. She didn't eat however, but sat staring at it: *Look at my Christmas dinner.*

'I shall sing a Christmas carol,' said Andrew, 'to fill in the time before the pudding.'

He began on 'Silent Night', and Colin said, 'Shut up, Andrew, it's more than I can bear, it really is.'

'The pudding is probably eatable already,' said Frances.

The great glistening dark mass of pudding was set on a very fine blue plate. She put out plates, spoons, and poured more wine. She stuck the sprig of holly from Julia's offering on to the pudding. She found a tin of custard.

They ate.

Soon the telephone rang. Sophie, in tears, and so Colin went up a floor to talk to her, at length, at very great length, and then came down to say he would return to Sophie's, to stay the night there, poor Sophie couldn't cope. Or perhaps he would bring her back here.

Then Julia's taxi was heard outside, and in came Sylvia, flushed, smiling, a pretty girl: who would have thought that possible, a few weeks ago? She dropped a curtsy to them in her good-girl's dress, both liking it and amused at the lace collar, lace cuffs and embroidery. Julia came in behind her. Frances said, 'Oh, Julia, do please sit down.'

But Julia had seen Rose, who was like a clown now that her

make-up had smeared with crying, and was cramming in Christmas pudding.

'Another time,' said Julia.

It could be seen that Sylvia would have stayed with Andrew, but she went up after Julia.

'Stupid dress,' said Rose.

'You're right,' said Andrew. 'Not your style at all.'

Then Frances remembered she had not thanked Julia and, shocked at herself, ran up the stairs. She caught Julia up on the top landing. Now she should embrace Julia. She should simply put her arms around this stiff, critical old woman and kiss her. She could not, her arms simply would not lift, would not go out to hold Julia.

'Thank you,' said Frances. 'That was such a lovely thing to do. You have no idea what it did for me . . .'

'I am glad you liked it,' said Julia, turning to go in her door, and Frances said after her, feeling futile, ridiculous, 'Thank you, thank you so much.' Sylvia had no difficulty in kissing Julia, allowing herself to be kissed and held, and she even sat on Julia's knee.

It was May, and the windows were open on to a jolly spring evening, the birds hard at it, louder than the traffic. A light rain sparkled on leaves and spring flowers.

The company around the table looked like a chorus for a musical, because they were all wearing tunics striped horizontally in blue and white, over tight black legs. Frances wore black and white stripes, feeling that this might do something to assert a difference. The boys wore the same stripes over jeans. Their hair was, had to be, well below their ears, a statement of their independence, and the girls all had Evansky haircuts. An Evansky haircut, that was the heart's desire of every with-it girl, and by hook, or most likely by crook, they had achieved it. This cut was between a 1920s bob, and the shingle, with a fringe to the eyebrows. Straight, it went without saying. Curly hair *out*. Even Rose's hair, the mass of crinkly black, was Evansky. Little neat heads, little-ickle cutesy girls, little bitsey things and the boys like shaggy ponies, and all in the blue and white stripes that had originated in matelot shirts, matching the blue and white mugs they used for breakfast. When the *geist* speaks, the *zeit* must obey. Here they were, the girls and the boys of the sexual revolution, though they didn't know yet that was what they would be famed for.

There was one exception to the Evansky imperative, every bit as strong as Vidal Sassoon's. Mrs Evansky, a decided lady, had refused to cut Sophie's hair. She had stood behind the girl, lifting those satiny black masses, letting them slide through her fingers, and then had pronounced: 'I am sorry, I can't do it.' And then, as Sophie protested, 'Besides you've a long face. It wouldn't do anything for you.' Sophie had sat, rejected, cast out, and then Mrs Evansky had said, 'Go away and think about it, and if you insist – but it would kill me: cutting this off.'

And so, alone among the girls, Sophie sat with her sparkling black tresses intact, and felt she was some kind of freak.

The whirligigs of the time had done pretty well for four months. What was four months? – nothing, and yet everything had changed.

First, Sylvia. She too had achieved full uniformity. Her haircut, begged from Julia, did not really suit her, but everyone knew it was important for her to feel normal and like the others. She was eating, if not well, and obeyed Julia in everything. The old woman and the very young girl would sit together for hours in Julia's sitting-room, while Julia made Sylvia little treats, fed her chocolates given her by her admirer Wilhelm Stein, and told her stories about pre-war Germany – pre-First-World-War Germany. Sylvia did once ask, gently, for she would have died rather than hurt Julia, 'Didn't anything bad ever happen, then?' Julia was taken aback and then she laughed. 'I'm not going to admit it, even if bad things did happen.' But she genuinely could not remember bad things. Her girlhood seemed to her, in that house full of music and kind people, like a paradise. And was there anything like that now, anywhere?

Andrew had promised his mother and his grandmother that he would go to Cambridge in the autumn, but meanwhile he hardly left the house. He loafed about and read, and smoked in his room. Sylvia visited him, knocking formally, and tidied his room, and scolded him. 'If I can do it, so can you.' Meaning, now, smoking pot. For her, who had frayed so badly apart, and come together with such difficulty, anything was a threat – alcohol, tobacco, pot, loud voices, and people quarrelling sent her back under her bedclothes with her fingers in her ears. She was going to school, and already doing well. Julia sat with her over her homework every evening.

Geoffrey, who was clever, would do well in his exams, and then go to the London School of Economics to do – well, of course – Politics and Economics. He said he wouldn't bother with Philosophy. Daniel, Geoffrey's shadow, said he would go to the LSE too, and take the same.

Jill had had an abortion, and was in her usual place, apparently untouched by the experience. The impressive thing was that 'the kids' had managed it all, without the adults. Neither Frances nor Julia had been told, and not Andrew, who was apparently considered too adult and a possible enemy. It was Colin who had gone to the girl's parents – she was afraid to go – and told them she was pregnant. They believed that Colin was the father, and would not accept his denials. Who was? No one knew, or would ever know, though Geoffrey was accused: he was always blamed for broken hearts and broken faith, being so good-looking.

Colin got the money for the abortion out of Jill's parents, and he went to the family doctor, who did at last suggest an appropriate telephone number. Afterwards, when Jill was safely back in the basement flat, Julia, Frances and Andrew were told. But the parents said Jill could not return to St Joseph's, if that was the kind of thing that could happen there.

Sophie and Colin had separated. Sophie, who would never in her life do anything by halves, had been too much for Colin: she loved him to death, or at least into something like an illness. 'Go away,' he had actually shouted at her at last, 'leave me alone.' And would not come out of his room for some days. Then he went to Sophie's house and said he was sorry, it was all his fault, he was just 'a little screwed up', and please come back to our house, please, we all miss you, and Frances keeps saying, Where's Sophie? And when Sophie did return, all apology, as if it were her fault, Frances hugged her and said, 'Sophie, you and Colin is one thing, but your coming here when you like is another.'

At weekends Sophie came down to London with the St Joseph's contingent, spent Friday evenings with them, went home to her mother whom she claimed was better. 'Though she doesn't look it. She just slumps around and looks *awful*.' Depression, let alone clinical depression, had not entered the general vocabulary and consciousness. People were still saying, 'Oh, God, I'm so depressed,' meaning they were in a bad mood. Sophie, a good daughter as far as she could bear to be, went home for Saturday nights but was not there in the daytime. Saturday and Sunday evenings she was in her place at the big table.

Something wonderful had happened to her. She often walked down the hill to Primrose Hill and then through Regent's Park, to dancing and singing lessons. There in a grassy glade full of flowerbeds is a statue of a young woman, with a little goat, and it is called 'The Protector of the Defenceless'. This girl in stone drew Sophie to her. She found herself laying a leaf on the pedestal, then a flower, then a little posy. Soon she would bring a bit of biscuit, and stood back to watch sparrows or a blackbird fly up to the statue's feet to carry off crumbs. Once she put a wreath around the little goat's head. Then, one day on the pedestal, was a booklet called *The Language of Flowers*, and tied to it with a ribbon was a bouquet of lilac and red roses. She could not see anyone likely nearby, only some people strolling in the garden.

She was alarmed, knowing she had been watched. At the supper table she told the story, laughing at herself because of her love for the stone girl, and produced *The Language of Flowers* for everyone to pass around and look at. Lilac meant First Emotions of Love, and a red rose, Love.

'You're not going to answer him?' demanded Rose, furious.

'Lovely Rose,' said Colin, 'of course she's going to answer.'

And they all pored over the book to work out a suitable message. But what Sophie wanted to say was, 'Yes, I am interested but don't jump to conclusions.' Nothing in the book seemed suitable. In the end they all decided on snowdrops, for Hope – but they had already come and gone, and periwinkle, Early Friendship. Sophie said she thought there were some in her mother's garden. And what else?

'Oh, go on,' said Geoffrey. 'Live dangerously. Lily of the valley – Return of Happiness. And phlox – Agreement.'

Sophie put her posy on the pedestal, and lingered; went away, came back, and found her flowers gone. But someone else might have taken them? No, for when she went there the next day there was a young man who said he had been watching her 'for ages' and had been too shy to approach her without the language of flowers. A likely story, for shy he was not. He was an actor, studying at the Academy where she planned to go in the autumn. This was Roland Shattock, haggardly handsome and dramatic in everything and he was some kind of Trotskyist. He came often to the supper table and was here tonight. Older than the others, a year older even than Andrew, he wore a worldly-wise look, and a suede jacket dyed purple with fringes, and his presence was felt as a visitation from the adult world, and something like an entrance ticket to it. If *he* did not regard them as 'kids', then . . . It never crossed their idealistic minds that he was often in need of a good meal.

When Roland was there Colin tended to be silent, and even went upstairs early, particularly when Johnny dropped in, for the arguments between the young Trotskyist and the old Stalinist were loud, and fierce and often ugly. Sylvia fled upstairs too, and went to Julia.

Johnny had been in Cuba, and had arranged to make a little film. 'But it won't bring in much money, I am afraid, Frances.' Meanwhile he had gone to visit independent Zambia, with Comrade Mo.

Now Rose: there were difficulties all the way, for what seemed like every day of the four months. She would not go back to her school, and she would not go home. She was prepared to go to St Joseph's, if she could base herself here, in this house. Andrew travelled to see her parents again. They believed that this charming, and so upper-class young man had plans for their daughter, and this made it easier for them to agree, not to St Joseph's, which was beyond their means, but to a day school in London. They would pay the fees for that and give her an allowance for clothes. But they would not pay for Rose's board and keep. They allowed it to be understood that it was Andrew's responsibility to pay for her. That meant Frances, in effect.

Perhaps she could be asked to do something in return, like housework – for there were always problems with keeping the place clean, in spite of Julia's Mrs Philby, who would never do much more than vacuum floors. 'Don't be silly,' said Andrew. 'Can you imagine Rose lifting a finger?'

A school of a progressive kind was found in London, and Rose agreed to everything. 'If she could just stay here, she wouldn't be any trouble.' Then Andrew came to Frances to say there was a big problem. Rose was afraid to tell Frances. And it was Jill, too. The girls had been caught without tickets on the Underground, and it was the third time for both of them. They were summoned to see the juvenile delinquency officer, in the office of the Transport Police. There would certainly be fines, and Borstal was a real possibility. Frances was too angry, in her all too familiar way with Rose, a dull dispirited emotion, like chronic indigestion, to confront her, but asked Andrew to tell the girls she would go with them to their interview. On the appointed morning she came down to find the two sullen girls united in hatred for the world, in the kitchen, smoking. They were both made up to look like pandas, with their white eye-paint and black-circled eyes and black painted nails. They wore little mini-dresses from Biba's, stolen of course. They could not have found an appearance more likely to prejudice Authority against them.

Frances said, 'If you do really care about getting off with just a lecture, you could wash your faces.' She was wondering if the girls were determined to make things as difficult as they could, perhaps even that they were harbouring ambitions to be sent to Borstal. This would of course serve Frances right: one is not *in loco parentis* without at some point taking punishment that is in fact aimed at delinquent parents.

Rose at once said, 'I don't see why I should.'

Frances waited, curious, for what Jill might reply. This formerly quiet, good, conforming girl, who might sit through a whole evening saying nothing, only smiling, was hardly discernible behind her paint and her anger.

Taking her cue from Rose: 'I don't see why either.'

They went by Underground, Frances buying tickets for them all, and noting their sarcastic smiles as she did so. They were soon in the office where non-payers of fares, juveniles, met their fate in the person of Mrs Kent, who wore a navy-blue uniform of a generic kind that suggested the majesty of officialdom. Her face, however, was kindly, while she kept up a severe look, to inspire respect.

'Please sit down,' she said, and Frances sat to one side, while the girls, having stood, like obstinate horses, for long enough to make a point, slumped, in a way that was meant to suggest they had been pushed.

'It's very simple,' said Mrs Kent, though her sigh, of which she was certainly unaware, suggested otherwise. 'You have both been warned twice. You knew the third time would be the last time. I could send you to the magistrate, and it would be up to him if you are taken into care or not, but if you will give guarantees of good behaviour, you will be let off with a fine, but your parents, or parent, or guardian will have to take responsibility for you.' She said this, or something like it, so often that her biro expressed boredom and exasperation, doodling jagged patterns on a notepad. Having ended, she smiled at Frances.

'Are you the parent of either of these two girls?'

'No. I am not.'

'A guardian? In some kind of legal capacity?'

'No, but they are living with me – in our house, and they will be going to school from there.' While she knew Rose would be, she didn't know about Jill, and so she was telling a lie.

Mrs Kent was taking a long look at the girls, who sat sulking, their legs apart, their legs crossed high, knees raised, showing black tights to the crotch. Frances noted that Jill was trembling: she would not have believed this cool girl capable of it.

'Could I have a word with you in private?' Mrs Kent said to Frances. She got up and said to the girls, 'We won't be one minute.' She showed Frances to the door, and followed her in to a little private room, evidently her refuge from the strain of these interviews.

She went to the window, and so did Frances. They looked down over a little garden where two lovers licked at one ice-cream cone. Mrs Kent said, 'I liked your article about Juvenile Crime. I cut it out.'

'Thank you.'

'It's beyond me, why they do it. We understand when poor kids do it, and there's a policy of leniency in hard cases, but they come in here, boys and girls, dressed up to the nines, and I don't get it. One of them said the other day – he was at a good school, mind you – that not paying fares was a question of principle; I asked what principle and he said he was a Marxist. He wants to destroy capitalism, he said.'

'Now that sounds familiar.'

'What sort of guarantee can you give me that I won't have these girls up in front of me in a week or so?'

'I can't,' said Frances. 'No guarantee. Both are quarrelling with parents and they've landed on me. Both are school drop-outs, but I expect they will go back.'

'I understand. A friend of my son's – a schoolfriend – is with us more often than he goes home.'

'Does he say his parents are shits?'

'They don't understand him, he says. But I don't either. Tell me, did you have to do a lot of research for your article?'

'A good bit.'

'But you didn't provide any answers.'

'I don't know the answers. Can you tell me why a girl – I'm referring to the dark girl out there, Rose Trimble – who has just had all her difficulties sorted out, should choose just that moment to do something she knows might spoil everything?'

'I call it brink-walking,' said Mrs Kent. 'They like to test limits. They walk out on a tightrope but hope someone'll catch them. And you are catching them, aren't you?'

'I suppose so.'

'You'd be surprised how often I hear the same story.'

The two women stood close together at the window, linked by a sort of despair.

'I wish I knew what was going on,' said Mrs Kent.

'Don't we all.'

They went back into the office where the girls, who had been giggling and laughing at the older women's expense, resumed their silence and their sulky looks.

Mrs Kent said, 'I'm going to give you another chance. Mrs Lennox says she will help you. But in fact I am exceeding my brief; I hope you both understand that you have had a very narrow escape. You are both fortunate girls, to have a friend in Mrs Lennox.' This last remark was a mistake, though Mrs Kent could not know that. Frances could positively hear the seethe of resentment in the girls, in Rose at least, that they could owe anyone anything.

Outside the building, on the pavement, they said they would go off shopping.

'If I told you not to shoplift,' said Frances, 'would you take any notice?'

But they went off without looking at her.

That night they announced at supper that they had nicked the two Biba, or Biba-type dresses they were wearing, both so short they could only have been chosen with the intention of inviting shock or criticism.

And Sylvia did say she thought they were too short, in an effort that cost her a good deal to assert herself.

'Too short for what?' jeered Rose. She had not looked at Frances once, all evening, and this morning's crisis might never have happened. Jill, though, did say in a hurried mutter that combined politeness with aggression, 'Thanks, Frances, thanks a million.'

Andrew told the girls they were bloody lucky to have got off, and Geoffrey, the accomplished shoplifter, told them it was easy not to get caught if you were careful.

'You can't be careful on the Underground,' said Daniel, who did not buy tickets, in emulation of his idol, Geoffrey. 'It's luck. You either get caught or you don't.'

'Then don't travel on the Underground without a ticket,' said Geoffrey. 'Not more than twice. It's stupid.'

Daniel, publicly criticised by Geoffrey, went red and said he had travelled 'for years' without a ticket and had only been caught twice.

'And the third time?' said Geoffrey, instructing him.

'Third time unlucky,' chorused the company.

That was the week that Jill allowed herself to get pregnant, no, invited it.

All these dramas had played themselves out in the four months since Christmas and, as if nothing had happened, here were the protagonists, here were the boys and girls, sitting around the table on that spring evening making plans for the summer.

Geoffrey said he would go to the States and join the fighters for racial equality 'on the barricades'. A useful experience for Politics and Economics at the LSE.

Andrew said he would stay here and read.

'Not *The Ordeal of Richard Feverel*,' said Rose. 'What crap.'

'That too,' said Andrew.

Sylvia, invited to go with Jill to her cousins in Exeter ('It's a groovy place, they've got horses') said no, she would stay here and read too. 'Julia says I should read more. I did read some of Johnny's books. You'd never believe it, but until I got to this house I didn't know there were books that weren't about politics.' This meant, as everyone knew, that Sylvia could not leave Julia: she felt too frail to stand on her own.

Colin said he might go and pick grapes in France, or perhaps try his hand at a novel: at this there was a general groan.

'Why shouldn't he write a novel?' said Sophie, who always stuck up for Colin because he had hurt her so terribly.

'Perhaps I shall write a novel about St Joseph's,' said Colin. 'I shall put us all in.'

'That isn't fair,' said Rose at once. 'You can't put me in because I'm not at St Joseph's.'

'How very true that is,' said Andrew.

'Or perhaps I could write a novel all about you,' said Colin. '"The Ordeals of a Rose." How about that?'

Rose stared at him, then, suspiciously around. They all stared solemnly at her. Baiting Rose had become a far too frequent sport, and Frances tried to defuse the moment, which threatened tears, by asking, 'And what are your plans, Rose?'

'I'll go and stay with Jill's cousin. Or I might hitchhike in Devon. Or I might stay here,' she added, facing Frances with a challenge. She knew Frances would be pleased to have her gone, but did not believe this was because of any unpleasant qualities in herself. She did not know she was unlikeable. She was usually disliked, and thought that this was because of the general unfairness of the world: not that she would have used the word *dislike* or even have thought it: people picked on her, they put their shit on her. People who are kind or good-looking or charming or all three; people who trust others, never have any idea of the little hells inhabited by someone like Rose.

James said he was going to a summer camp, recommended by Johnny, to study the senescence of capitalism and the inner contradictions of imperialism.

Daniel said forlornly that he supposed he would have to go home, and Geoffrey said kindly, 'Never mind, the summer won't be for ever.'

'Yes, it will,' said Daniel, his face flaming with misery.

Roland Shattock said he was going to take Sophie on a walking tour in Cornwall. Noting signs of misgiving on certain faces – Frances's, Andrew's – he said, 'Oh, don't panic, she'll be safe with me, I think I'm gay.'

This announcement which now would be met by nothing much more than, 'Really?', or perhaps sighs from the women, was too casual then to be tactful, and there was general discomfort.

Sophie at once cried out that she didn't care about that, she just liked being with Roland. Andrew looked gracefully rueful, and could almost be heard thinking that *he* wasn't queer.

'Oh, well, perhaps I'm not,' amended Roland. 'After all, Sophie, I'm crazy about you. But have no fear, Frances, I'm not one to abduct minors.'

'I'm nearly sixteen,' said Sophie indignantly.

'I thought you were much older when I saw you dreaming so beautifully in the park.'

'I am much older,' said Sophie, truthfully: she meant her mother's illness, her father's death, and then Colin's ill-treatment of her.

'Beautiful dreamer,' said Roland, kissing her hand, but in a parody of the continental hand kiss that salutes the air above a glove, or, as in this case, knuckles ever so slightly odorous from the chicken stew she had been stirring, to help Frances. 'But if I do go to prison, it will have been worth it.'

As for Frances, she expected peaceful and productive weeks.

The incendiary letter came addressed to 'J . . . indecipherable . . . Lennox', and was opened by Julia, who, having seen it was for Johnny, *Dear Comrade Johnny Lennox*, and that the first sentence was, '*I want you to help me open people's eyes to the truth*', read it, then again, and, having let her thoughts settle, telephoned her son.

'I have a letter here from Israel, a man called Reuben Sachs, for you.'

'A good type,' said Johnny. 'He has maintained a consistently progressive position as a non-aligned Marxist, advocating peaceful relations with the Soviet Union.'

'However that is, he wants you to call a gathering of your friends and comrades to hear him speak about his experiences in a Czech prison.'

'There must have been a good reason for him to be there.'

'He was arrested as a Zionist spy for American imperialism.' Johnny was silent. 'He was inside for four years, tortured and brutally treated and finally released . . . I would take it as a favour if you did not say, *Unfortunately mistakes have sometimes been made*.'

'What do you want, Mutti?'

'I think you should do as he asks. He says he would like to open people's eyes to the truth about the methods used by the Soviet Union. Please do not say that he is some kind of pro-vocateur.'

'I am afraid I don't see why it would be useful.'

'In that case I shall call a meeting myself. After all, Johnny, I am in the happy position of knowing who your associates are.'

'Why do you think they would come to a meeting called by you, Mutti?'

'I shall send everyone a copy of his letter. Shall I read it to you?'

'No, I know the kind of lies that are being spread.'

'He will be here in two weeks' time, and he is coming to London just for that – to address the comrades. He is also going to Paris. Shall I suggest a date?'

'If you like.'

'But it must be one convenient for you. I don't think he would be pleased if you didn't attend.'

'I'll telephone you with a date. But I must make it clear that I shall disassociate myself from any anti-Soviet propaganda.'

On the evening in question the big sitting-room received an unusual collection of guests. Johnny had invited colleagues and comrades, and Julia had asked people that she thought Johnny should have invited, but had not. There were people still in the Party, some who had left over various crisis points – the Hitler–Stalin Pact, the Berlin Rising, Prague, Hungary, even one or two who went back to the attack on Finland. About fifty people; and the room was crammed tight with chairs, and people standing around the walls. All described themselves as Marxists.

Andrew and Colin were present, having first complained that it was all so boring. 'Why are you doing this?' Colin asked his grandmother. 'It's not your kind of thing, is it?'

'I am hoping, though I am probably just a foolish old woman, that Johnny might be made to see some sense.'

The St Joseph's contingent were taking exams. James had left for America. The girls downstairs had made a point of going to a disco: politics were just shit.

Reuben Sachs had supper with Julia, alone: Frances could have agreed with the girls, and even their choice of language. He was a round little man, desperate, and earnest and could not stop talking about what had happened to him, and the meeting, when it began, was only a continuation of what he had been telling Julia, who having informed him that she had never been a communist and did not need his persuasions, kept quiet, since it was evident that what he needed was to talk while she – or anyone at all – listened.

He had maintained for years a difficult political position in Israel, as a socialist, but rejecting communism and asking that the non-aligned socialists of the world should support peaceful relations with the Soviet Union: this meant that they would necessarily be in an unhappy situation with their own governments. He had been reviled as a communist throughout the Cold War. His temperament was not suited by nature to being permanently out on a limb, being shot at from all sides. This could be seen by his agitated, fervent discourses, his pleading and angry eyes, while the words that repeated themselves like a refrain were, 'I have never compromised with my beliefs.'

He had been on a fraternal visit to Prague, on a Peace and Goodwill Mission, when he had been arrested as a Cosmopolitan Zionist spy for American Imperialism. In the police car he addressed his captors thus, 'How can you, representatives of a Workers' State, sully your hands with such work as this?' and when they hit him and went on hitting him, he continued to use these words. As he did in prison. The warders were brutes, and the interrogators too, but he continued to address them as civilised beings. He knew six languages, but they insisted on interrogating him in a language he did not know, Romanian, which meant that at first he did not know what he was being accused of, which was every sort of anti-Soviet and anti-Czech activity. But: 'I am good at languages, I have to explain . . .' He learned enough Romanian during the interrogation to follow, and then to argue his case. For days, months, years, he was beaten up, reviled, kept for long periods without food, kept without sleep – tortured in all the ways beloved by sadists. For four years. And he went on insisting on his innocence, and explained to his interrogators and his jailers that in doing this kind of work they were dirtying the honour of the people, of the Workers' State. It took a long time for him to realise that his case was not unique, and that the prison was full of people like him, who tapped out messages on the walls to say they were as surprised to find themselves in prison as he was. They also explained that, 'Idealism is not appropriate in these circumstances, comrade.' The scales fell from his eyes, as he said. Just about the time he stopped appealing to the better natures and class situation of his tormentors, having lost faith in the long-term possibilities of the Soviet Revolution, he was released in one of the new dawns in the Soviet Empire. And found he was still a man with a mission, but now it was to open the eyes of the comrades who were still deluded about the nature of communism.

Frances had decided she did not want to listen to 'revelations' that she had absorbed decades ago, but crept into the back of the room when it was full, and found herself sitting next to a man she did seem to remember but who obviously remembered her well, from his greeting. Johnny was in a corner, listening without prejudice. His sons sat with Julia across the room, and did not look at their father. On their faces was the strained unhappy look she had been seeing there for years now. If they avoided their father's eyes, they did send supportive smiles to her, which were too miserable to be convincing as irony, which is what they had intended. In that room were people who had been around through their early childhoods, some whose children they had played with.

When Reuben began his tale with, 'I have come to tell you the truth of the situation, as it is my duty to do . . .' the room was silent, and he could not have complained that his audience was not attentive. But those faces . . . they were not the expressions usually seen at a meeting, responding to what is said, with smiles, nods, agreement, dissent. They were polite, kept blank. Some were still communists, had been communists all their lives and would never change: there are people who cannot change once their minds are made up. Some had been communists, might criticise the Soviet Union, and even passionately, but all were socialists, and kept a belief in progress, the ever-upwards-reaching escalator to a happier world. And the Soviet Union had been so strongly a symbol of this faith, that – as it was put decades later by people who had been immersed in dreams – 'The Soviet Union is our mother, and we do not insult our mothers.'

They were sitting here listening to a man who had done four years' hard labour in a communist prison, been brutally treated, a painfully emotional tale, so that at times Reuben Sachs wept, explaining that it was because of 'the sullying and dirtying of the great dream of humankind', but what was being appealed to was their reason.

And that was why the faces of the people who had come to this evening's meeting, 'to hear the truth', were expressionless, or even stunned, listening as if the tale did not concern them. For an hour and a half the emissary from 'the truth of the situation' talked, and then ended with a passionate appeal for questions, but no one said anything. As if nothing at all had been said, the meeting ended because people were getting up and having thanked Frances, under the impression that she was the hostess, and nodded to Johnny, drifted out. Nothing was said. And when they began talking to each other it was on other subjects.

Reuben Sachs sat on, waiting for what he had come to London for, but he might have been talking about conditions in medieval Europe or even Stone Age Man. He could not believe what he was seeing, what had happened.

Julia continued to sit in her place, watching, sardonic, a little bitter, and Andrew and Colin were openly derisive. Johnny went off, with some others, not looking at his sons or his mother.

The man next to Frances had not moved. She felt she had been right not to have wanted to come: she was being attacked by ancient unhappinesses, and needed to compose herself.

'Frances,' he said, trying to get her attention, 'that was not pleasant hearing.'

She smiled more vaguely than he liked, but then saw his face and thought that there was one person there at least who had taken in what had been said.

'I'm Harold Holman,' he said. 'But you don't seem to remember me? I was around a lot with Johnny in the old days . . . I came to your place when all our kids were small – I was married to Jane then.'

'I seem to have blocked it all off.'

Meanwhile Andrew and Colin were watching: the room was nearly empty now, and Julia was taking the miserably disappointed truth-bringer out and up to her rooms.

'Can I ring you?' Harold asked.

'Why not? But better ring me at *The Defender*.' And she lowered her voice, because of her sons. 'I'll be there tomorrow afternoon.'

'Right,' he said, and off he went. This had been so casual that she was only just taking it in that he was interested in her as a woman, for she had got out of the habit of expecting it. And now Colin came to ask, 'Who's that man?'

'An old friend of Johnny's – from the old days.'

'What is he telephoning you about?'

'I don't know. Perhaps we'll go and have a cup of coffee, for old times' sake,' she said, lying casually, for already that aspect of her self was re-emerging.

'I'll get back to school,' said Colin, abrupt, suspicious, and he did not say goodbye as he went off to catch his train.

As for Andrew, he said, 'I'll go and help Julia with our guest, poor man,' and left her with a smile that was both complicit and a warning, though it was doubtful he was aware of this.

A woman who has shut a door on her amorous self as thoroughly as Frances had, has to be surprised when suddenly it opens. She liked Harold, that was obvious, from the way she was coming to life, pulses stirring, animation seizing hold of her.

And yet why? Why him? He had got under her guard, all right. How very extraordinary. The occasion had been extraordinary, who could believe such a thing, if they hadn't seen it? She wouldn't be at all surprised if this Harold was the only person there who had allowed himself to *take in* what Reuben Sachs had said. A good phrase, take in. You can sit for an hour and a half listening to information that should shoot your precious citadel of faith to fragments, or that doesn't match easily with what is already in your brain, but you don't *take it in*. You can take a horse to water . . .

Frances did not sleep well that night, and it was because she was allowing herself to dream like a girl in love.

He telephoned next afternoon, and asked her to go with him for a weekend to a certain little town in Warwickshire, and she said she would, as easily as if she did this often. And she had to wonder again what it was about this man who could turn a key so easily in a door that she had kept shut. He was a solid, smiling, fairish man, whose characteristic look was of cool, humorous assessment. He was, or had been, an official in some educational organisation. A trade union official?

She supposed the usual assortment of kids would arrive for the weekend, and went up to Julia to say that she would like to take the weekend off. Using those words.

Julia seemed to smile a little. Was that a smile? Not an unkind one . . . 'Poor Frances,' she said, surprising her daughter-in-law. 'You live a dull sort of life.'

'Do I?'

'I think you do. And the young ones can look after themselves for once.'

And, as Frances went out she heard the low, 'Come back to us, Frances,' and this surprised her so much she turned, but found that Julia had already picked up her book.

Come back to us . . . oh, that was perceptive of her, uncomfortably so. For she had been seized with a rebellion against her life, the relentless slog of it, and had wandered into a landscape of feverish dreams, where she would lose herself – and never return to Julia's house.

And there were her sons, and that was no joke. Told that their mother would be away that weekend, both reacted as if she had said she was off for a six-month jaunt.

Colin, from school, said on the telephone, 'Where are you going? Who are you going with?'

'A friend,' said Frances, and there was a suspicious silence.

And Andrew gave her the bleakest smile, which was full of fear, but he certainly did not know that.

She was the stable thing in their lives, always had been, and it was no use saying both were old enough to allow her some freedom. But at what age do such insecurely-based children no longer need a parent to be there, always? This was their mother, taking off for the weekend with a man, and they knew it. If she had ever done anything like it before . . . but how obedient she had always been to their situation, their needs, as if she was making up for Johnny's lacks. 'As if'? – she *had* tried to make up for Johnny.

On the Saturday Frances crept out of the house knowing that Andrew would be on the look-out, for he was a restless sleeper, and Colin might have decided to wake earlier than his usual mid-morning. She glanced up at the front of the house, dreading to see Andrew's face, Colin's – but there were no faces at the windows. It was seven in the morning of a wonderful summer's day, and her spirits, in spite of her guilt, were threatening to shoot her up into an empyrean of irresponsibility, and here he was, her beau, her date, smiling, obviously enjoying what he saw, this blonde woman (she had had her hair done) in her green linen dress, settling herself beside him, and turning to him to share a laugh at this adventure.

They drove comfortably through the suburbs of London, and were in the country, and she was enjoying his enjoyment of her, and her pleasure in him, this handsome sandy man, and meanwhile she combated thoughts of the helpless unhappy faces of her sons.

Dear Aunt Vera, I am divorced and I bring up two boys. I am tempted to have an affair but I am afraid of upsetting my sons. They watch me like hawks. What shall I do? I'd like to have some fun. Don't I have any rights?

Well, if she, Frances, was in line for *some fun* then do it: and she shut her sons firmly out of her thoughts. Either that, or say to this man, Turn around and go back, I have made a mistake.

They stopped by the river near Maidenhead and had breakfast, rested later in a town whose public gardens looked inviting, drove on, were invited by an attractive pub, and had lunch in another garden while sparrows hopped about them in the dust.

He said once, 'Are you having difficulty suspending disbelief?'

'Yes,' and stopped herself saying, It's the boys, you see.

'I thought so. As for me, I am having no difficulty at all.' And his laughter had enough triumph in it to make her examine him for the reason. There was something in all this she was not understanding – but never mind. She was quite recklessly happy. What a dull life she did lead: Julia was right. They drove up side roads to avoid the motorways, got themselves lost, and all the time their looks and smiles promised, Tonight we are going to lie in each other's arms. The day continued warm, with a silky golden haze, and in the late afternoon they sat in another garden, by a river, observed by blackbirds, a thrush, and a large friendly dog who sat by them, until it gained its bit of cake from both of them, and wandered off, its tail slowly swinging.

'A fat dog,' said Harold Holman, 'and that's what I shall be, after this weekend.' Replete, yes, he looked that, but as well there was this other ingredient, a pleasure in her, in the situation, which made her say, without planning to, 'Just what are you so pleased with yourself about?' He at once understood, so that the aggressiveness of it, which she regretted, for it contradicted the radiant content she felt, was annulled as he said, 'Ah, yes, you are right, you are right,' and gave her a laughing look, and she thought that he looked like a lazy lion, his paws crossed in front of him, lifting a commanding head in a slow lazy yawn. 'I'll tell you, I'll tell you everything. But first, I want to get somewhere when the light is like this.' And off they drove again, into Warwickshire, and he parked outside their hotel, and came to open the door for her. 'Come and look at this.' Across the street were trees, gravestones, shrubs, an old yew. 'I was looking forward to showing you this – no, you're wrong, I've not brought a woman here before, but I had to stop in this town, months ago, and I thought, it's magic, this place. But I was alone.'

They crossed the street hand in hand and stood in the old graveyard where the yew seemed almost as tall as the little church. It was an early summer dusk, and a moon was emerging bright into a darkening sky. The pale gravestones leaned about and seemed to want to speak to them. Breaths of warm summer air, wisps of cool mist, brushed their faces, and they stood in each other's arms, and kissed and then were close for a long time, listening to the messages from each other's bodies. And then the pressure of unshareable emotions made them step back from each other, though they still held hands, and he said, 'Yes,' with a quiet regret she did not need to have explained. She was thinking, 'I could have married somebody like this, instead of . . .' Julia called him an imbecile. Since Johnny did not telephone Julia after that little meeting, 'so that everyone could hear the truth', Julia had rung him to find out what he thought, or rather, what he was prepared to say. 'Well?' she had enquired. 'Surely that was worth thinking about . . . what that Israeli said?' 'You must learn to take a long-term perspective, Mutti.' '*Imbecile.*'

The graveyard filled with dark, as the sky lightened, and the gravestones shone bright and ghostly, and they leaned against the yew in the blackness under it, and looked out, watching the moonlight strengthen. Then they walked through the graves, all old ones, no one here younger than the century, and soon were in the room in the old-fashioned hotel where they had registered as Harold Holman and Frances Holman.

She was actually thinking, Oh, why not, I could marry this man, we could be happy, after all people do marry and are happy – but the thought of the weight and complexity of Julia's house pushed aside this nonsense, and she banished that thought too, in her intention to be happy for this one night.

And so she was, so they were. 'Made for each other,' he

breathed in her ear, and then exclaimed it aloud, exulting. They lay side by side, enlaced, while outside the brief night hurried past towards a dawn that was not going to be delayed by cloud: the moonlight glittered on the panes. 'I've been in love with you for years,' he said, 'years. Ever since I saw you first with those little boys of yours. Johnny's wife. You don't know how often I fantasised about ringing you up and asking you to sneak around the corner for a drink. But you were Johnny's wife, and I was so in awe of him.'

Frances's spirits were taking a fall, and she wished that he would not go on: but he would have to, that was obvious, for here was the sad face of the truth. 'That must have been in that dreadful flat in Notting Hill.'

'Was it dreadful? But we didn't go in for gracious living in those days.' And he laughed loudly, from an excess of everything, and said, 'Oh, Frances, if you've ever had a dream you thought would never come true, then tonight is that, for me.'

She was thinking of herself then, overweight and worried, with the small children always at her or on her, clutching her, climbing up her, competing for her lap. 'Just what did you see in me then, I'd like to know?'

He was silent for a while. 'It was everything. Johnny – he was such a hero to me then. And you were Johnny's wife. You were such a couple, I envied you both and I envied Johnny. And the little boys – I hadn't had children then. I wanted to be like you.'

'Like Johnny.'

'I can't explain. You were such – a holy family,' he laughed and flung his limbs about, and then sat on the edge of the bed, stretching up his arms into the moony light of the room and said, 'You were wonderful. Calm . . . serene . . . nothing phased you. And I did realise that Johnny wasn't necessarily the easiest . . . I'm not criticising him.'

'Why not? I do.' Was she really going to demolish this dream – she couldn't. Oh, yes, she could. 'Did you have any idea how much I hated Johnny then?'

'Well, of course we hate our dear loved ones sometimes. Jane – she was a pain.'

'Johnny was consistently a pain.'

'But what a hero!'

She was sitting with her arm around his neck, as close as she could, to be near that exulting vitality. Her breasts were against his arm. How much she did like her body tonight, because he did. Smooth heavy breasts, and her arms – she could grant that they were beautiful. 'When I saw Johnny in that room the other night, I wondered if you two still . . .'

'Good God, no,' and she withdrew from him, body, mind, and even liking, for just that moment. 'How could you think that?' Well, why shouldn't he . . . 'Never mind Johnny,' she said. 'Come back here.' She lay down and he came to lie by her, smiling.

'I admired that man more than anyone in my life. For me he was a sort of god. Comrade Johnny. He was much older than I was . . .' He lifted his head to look at her.

'That means I am much older than you are.'

'Not tonight you aren't. I was in a bit of a mess when I first met Johnny – at a meeting, it was. I was a green boy. I had failed my exams. My parents said, "If you are a communist don't darken our doors." And Johnny was kind to me. A father figure. I decided to be worthy of him.'

Here she controlled the muscles of her diaphragm, but whether to forestall laughter or tears, it was hard to say.

'I found a room in a comrade's house. I took my exams again. I was a teacher for a bit, I was in the Union then . . . but the point is, I owe it all to Johnny.'

'Well, what can I say? Good for him. But surely, good for you?'

'If I had believed then that I could be with you tonight, hold you in my arms, I think I'd have gone mad with joy. Johnny's wife, in my arms.'

They made love again. Yes, it was love, a friendly, even

amorous love, while laughter bubbled in the cauldron, well out of his hearing, but not out of hers.

They slept. They woke. And then it seemed he had bad dreams, for he started awake and lay on his back, holding her, but in a way that said *Wait*. At last he said unhappily, 'That was a bad blow, you know, what that man Sachs said.'

She decided to let it go.

'You can't say it wasn't a shock.'

She decided she would speak. 'Newspapers,' she spelled it out. 'Newspaper reports for years. Television. Radio. The Purges, the camps. The laagers, the murders. For years.'

A long silence. 'Yes,' he said at last, 'but I didn't believe it. Well, some of it of course . . . but nothing like – what he told us.'

'How could you not have believed it?'

'I didn't want to, I suppose.'

'Exactly.' And then she heard herself say, 'And I bet we haven't heard the half of it yet.'

'Why do you say that? It sounds as if you are quite pleased with yourself.'

'I suppose I am. It is something to have been proved right, after years of having been put down and – trampled on. Of being put down *now*,' she said.

And now he was dismayed. But she went on, 'I didn't agree with him. Not after the very first days . . .' She suppressed, *When he came back from the Spanish Civil War*. Since after all, he hadn't. She suppressed, *When I saw what a dishonest hypocrite he was*. Because after all, how could he be called dishonest? He believed every word of it.

'I fell for all that glamour,' she said. 'I was nineteen. But it didn't last.'

He didn't like that, no, he didn't like it all, and she lay there silent by him, enough at one with him to be hurt because he was.

There was a long drowsing silence: outside it was already a full hot day, and the traffic had begun.

'It seems it was all for nothing,' he said at last. 'It was all . . . lies and nonsense.' She could hear the tears in his voice. 'What a waste. All that effort . . . people killed for nothing. Good people. No one is going to tell me they weren't.' A silence. 'I don't want to make a thing of it, but I did make such sacrifices for the Party. And it was all for nothing.'

'Except that Comrade Johnny inspired you to great things.'

'Don't mock.'

'I'm not. I'm going to allot Johnny one good mark. At least he was good to you.'

'I haven't taken it in yet. I haven't begun to take it all in.'

And so they lay side by side, and if he was letting go dreams, such dreams, such sweet sweet dreams, she was thinking, Obviously I'm a very selfish person, just as Johnny always said. Harold is thinking about the golden future of the human race, postponed indefinitely, but I am thinking what I have shut out of my life. She could hardly bear the pain of it. The sweet warm weight of a man sleeping in her arms, his mouth on her cheek, the tender heaviness of a man's balls in her hand, the delicious slipperiness of . . .

'Let's go down to breakfast,' he said. 'I think I'm going to cry otherwise.'

They breakfasted soberly, in a decorous little room, and left the hotel, noting that this morning the graveyard seemed neglected and shabby, and the magic of last night was going to seem like bathos if they did not remove themselves. Which they did, and went off to a place where lying on a grassy hill he told her that here, where they were, landscapes rolling away in all directions, that this was the very heart of England. And then, and she understood it absolutely, he wept, this big man, face on his arm, on the grass, he wept for his lost dream, and she thought, We suit each other so well, but we won't be together again. It was the ending of something. For him. And for her too: what am I doing prancing around the heart of England with a man heartbroken because of – well, not because of me?

In the late afternoon she asked him to set her down where she could take a taxi, because she could not face being seen with him, outside the house with its jealous hungry eyes. They kissed, full of regrets. He saw her step into a taxi, and they drove off in different directions. Up the steps ran Frances, lightly, full of the energy of love-making, and went straight to her bathroom, afraid she smelled too much of sex. Then she went up to Julia's, and knocked, and waited for the close cool inspection – which she got. Then, because it was not unfriendly, but kind, she sat and said nothing, only smiled at Julia, her lips trembling.

'It's hard,' said Julia, and she sounded as if she knew how hard. She went to a cupboard, full of interesting bottles, poured a cognac, and brought it to Frances.

'I shall stink of alcohol,' said Frances.

'Never mind,' said Julia, and lit the flame of her little coffee-maker. She stood by it, with her back to Frances, who knew it was tact, because of how much Frances needed to cry. Then a cup of strong black coffee arrived beside the cognac.

The door opened – no knock; Sylvia ran in. 'Oh, Frances,' she said. 'I didn't know you were here. I didn't know she was here, Julia.' She stood hesitating, smiling, then rushed to Frances and put her arms around her, her cheek against Frances's hair. 'Oh, Frances, we didn't know where you were. You went away. You left us. We thought you'd got fed up with us all and left us.'

'Of course I couldn't,' said Frances.

'Yes,' said Julia. 'Frances has to be here, I think.'

The summer lengthened and loosened, breathed slow, then slower, and time seemed to lie all around like shallow lakes where one could float and dawdle: all this would end when 'the kids' came back. The two already here took up little space in the big house. Frances caught glimpses of Sylvia, across the landing, lying on her bed with a book, from where she waved, 'Oh, Frances, this is such a lovely book,' or running up the stairs to Julia. Or the two could be seen progressing down the street to go shopping – Julia with her little friend Sylvia. Andrew also lay on his bed, reading. Frances had – guiltily, it goes without saying – knocked on his door, heard 'Come in,' had gone in, and no, the room was clear of smoke. 'There you are, mother,' he drawled, for everything about him had slowed too, like her own pulses, 'you should have more confidence in me. I am no longer a hophead on his way to perdition.'

Frances was not cooking. She might meet Andrew in the kitchen, making himself a sandwich, and he would offer to make her one. Or she, him. They sat at opposite ends of the great table and contemplated plenty: tomatoes that came from the Cypriot shops in Camden Town, dense with real sunlight, knobbly and even misshapen, but as the knife cut into them the rank and barbarous magnificence of their smell filled the kitchen. They ate tomatoes with Greek bread and olives, and sometimes spoke. He did remark that he supposed it was all right, his doing Law. 'Why are you having doubts about it?' 'I think I'll make it International Law. The clash of nations. But I must confess I'd be happy to spend my life lying on my bed and reading.' 'And sometimes eating tomatoes.' 'Julia says her uncle sat in his library all his life reading. And I suppose adjusting his investments.'

'How much money does Julia have, I wonder?'

'I'll ask her one of these days.'

A rude little incident interrupted this peace. One night when Frances had gone up to bed Andrew opened the door to two French lads who said they were friends of Colin's, who had told them they could stay the night. One spoke excellent English, Andrew spoke good French. They sat at the table till late, drinking wine and eating whatever could be found, while that game went on when both sides want to practise the other's language. The semi-silent one smiled and listened. It seemed Colin and they had become friends while picking grapes, then Colin had gone home with them, in the Dordogne, and now he was hitching in Spain. He had asked them to say hello to his family.

They went up to Colin's room where they spread sleeping bags, not using the bed, so as to make as little disruption as possible. Nothing could have been more amiable and civilised than these two brothers, but in the morning a misunderstanding had taken them to Julia's bathroom. They were larking about, complaining that there was no shower, admiring the plenitude of hot water, enjoying bath salts and the violet-scented soap, and making a lot of noise. It was about eight: they planned to be off early on their travels. Julia heard splashing and loud young voices, knocked, knocked again. They did not hear her. She opened the door on two naked boys, one wallowing in her bath and blowing soap bubbles, the other shaving. There followed a volley of appropriate exclamations, *merde* being the loudest and most frequent. They then found themselves being addressed by an old woman, her hair in curlers, wearing a pink chiffon negligée, in the French she had learned in her schoolroom from a succession of mademoiselles fifty years ago. One boy leaped out of the bath, not even snatching up a towel to cover himself, while the other turned, razor in hand, mouth open. As it was evident the two were too stunned by her to respond, Julia retreated, and they picked up their things and fled downstairs where Andrew heard the tale and laughed. 'But where did she get that French?' they demanded. 'Ancient regime, at least.' 'No, Louis Quartorze.' So they jested, while they had coffee, and then the brothers departed to hitchhike around Devon, which in the mid-Sixties was *the* grooviest place after Swinging London.

But Frances could not laugh. She went to Julia's, and found the old woman not in her sitting-room dressed and exquisite, but on her bed, in tears. Julia saw Frances, and stood up, but unsteadily. Now Frances's arms of their own accord embraced Julia, and what had seemed until then an impossibility was the most natural thing in the world. The frail old thing laid her head on the younger woman's shoulder, and said, 'I don't understand. I have learned that I understand nothing.' She wailed, in a way that Frances would not have believed possible, from her, and she flung herself out of Frances's arms on to her bed. There Frances lay beside her and held her, while she sobbed and wailed. Evidently this was not any longer an affair of a bathroom being desecrated. When Julia was quieter she managed, 'You just let in anybody,' and Frances said, 'But Colin has been staying with them.' And Julia said, 'Anybody can say that. And the next thing will be raga-muffins'll turn up from America, and say they are friends of Geoffrey's.' 'Yes, that seems to me more than likely. Julia, don't you think it's rather nice, the way these young things just travel about – like troubadours . . .' though this was perhaps not the best simile, for Julia laughed angrily and said, 'I am sure they had better manners.' And then she started crying again, and again said, 'You just let in anybody.'

Frances asked if Wilhelm Stein should be asked to come, and Julia agreed.

Meanwhile Mrs Philby was in the house, and wanted to know, like the bears in the story, 'Who has been sleeping in Colin's room?' She was told. The old woman was the same vintage as Julia, as elegant and upright in her poor neat clean clothes, black hat, black skirt and print blouse, with an expression that refused any truck with this world that had come into being without any assistance from her. 'Then they are pigs,' she said. Up ran Andrew, and found that an orange had rolled from a backpack, and there were some croissant crumbs. If this amount of piggishness was enough to disorientate Mrs Philby – though surely by now she must have become used to it? – then what was she going to say about the bathroom which Sylvia and Julia left scarcely disturbed. 'Christ!' said Andrew, and rushed up to survey a stormy scene of spilled water and discarded towels. He did a preliminary tidying and informed Mrs Philby that she could go in now, and it's only water.

Andrew and Frances were sitting at the table when appeared Wilhelm Stein, Doctor of Philosophy and dealer in serious books. He went straight up to Julia, without coming into the kitchen, then descended, and stood in the doorway smiling, very slightly deferential, charming, an elderly gent as perfect in his way as Julia.

'I don't think it can be easy for you to understand the upbringing that Julia was victim of – yes, I can put it like that, because
I believe it has severely incapacitated her for the world she now
finds herself in.' He, like Julia, spoke a perfect idiomatic English,
and Andrew was contrasting it with the exclamatory, expletory,
excited French he had been listening to last night.

'Do sit down, Doctor Stein,' said Frances.

'Do we not know each other well enough for Frances and
Wilhelm? I think we do, Frances. But I shall not sit down now,
I shall fetch the doctor. I have my car.' He was about to leave, but
turned back to say, feeling, evidently, that he had not adequately
explained himself, 'The young people in this house – I except
you, Andrew – are sometimes rather . . .'

'Rough,' said Andrew. 'I agree. Shocking types.' He spoke
severely, and Doctor Stein acknowledged his small jest with a
bow, and a smile.

'I must tell you that when I was your age I was a shocking
type. I was – rowdy. And I was rough.' He grimaced at what he
was remembering. 'You might not think so to look at me now.'
And he smiled again, in amusement at the picture he knew he
was presenting – and he was presenting it consciously, a hand
resting on the silver knob of his cane, his other spread out as if
to say Yes, you must take in all of me. 'To look at me it would
be hard to see me as . . . I was running around with the communists
in Berlin, with all that that implies. With *all* it implies,' he insisted.
'Yes, it was so.' He sighed. 'I think no one could disagree that
we Germans run to extremes? Or we can do? Well, then, Julia
von Arne was one extreme and I was another. I sometimes amuse
myself by imagining what my twenty-one-year-old self would
have said of Julia, as a girl. And we laugh about it together. And
so, I have a key and I will let myself and the doctor in.'

★   ★   ★

In August there came to the house one Jake Miller, who had read a piece by Frances where she mocked the current fad for alien excitements like Yoga, and I-Ching, the Maharishi, Subud. The editor had said a funny piece was needed for the silly season, and it was that that had caused Jake Miller to telephone *The Defender* and ask Frances if he might visit. Curiosity said yes for her, and here he was in the sitting-room, a large infinitely smiling man, with gifts of mystic books. The smiles of unlimited love, peace, good-will, were soon to be obligatory on the faces of the good, perhaps one should say the young and the good, and Jake was a harbinger, though he was not young, he was in his forties. He was here dodging the Vietnam War. Frances resigned herself to a speech, but politics were not his interest. He was claiming her as a fellow conspirator in the fields of mystic experience. 'But I wrote it as a joke,' she protested, while he smiled and said, 'But I knew you were only writing like that because you had to, you were communicating with those of us who can understand.'

Jake claimed all kinds of special powers, for instance, that he could dissolve clouds by staring at them, and in fact, standing at the window looking up at a fast-moving sky, she watched clouds tumbling past and dissipating. 'It's easy,' said he, 'even for quite undeveloped people.' He could understand the language of birds, he said, and communicated with fellow minds through ESP. Frances might have protested that she was clearly no fellow mind, because he had had to telephone her, but this scene, mildly entertaining, mildly irritating, was ended by Sylvia coming in with a message from Julia – but Frances was never to hear the message. Sylvia was wearing a cotton jacket with the signs of the zodiac on it, bought because it fitted, and she was so small it was hard to find clothes: the jacket was in fact from Junior Miss. Her hair was in two thin pigtails on either side of her smiling face. His smiles and hers met and melded, and in a moment Sylvia was chatting with this new kind warm friend, who enlightened her about her sun sign, the I-Ching and her probable aura. In a moment the amiable American was on the floor casting the yarrow stalks for her, and the resulting reading so wowed her that she promised to go out and get the book for herself. Perspectives and possibilities she had never suspected filled her whole being, as if it had been quite empty before, and this girl who had hardly been able to go out of the house without Julia, now confidently went off with Jake from Illinois, to buy enlightening tracts. She did not return until late for her; it was past ten when she rushed up the stairs to Julia, who received her with arms held out for an embrace, but then let them fall, as she sat heavily down to stare at this girl who was in a state of vivacity she would not have thought possible for her. Julia heard Sylvia's chattering in a silence that became so heavy and disapproving that Sylvia stopped.

'Well, Sylvia, my poor child,' said Julia, 'where did you get all that nonsense?'

'But, Julia, it isn't nonsense, it really isn't. I'll explain, listen . . .'

'It is nonsense,' said Julia, getting up and turning her back. It was to make coffee, but Sylvia saw a cold excluding back, and began to cry. And she did not know it, but Julia's eyes were full, and she was fighting with herself not to weep. That this child, *her* child, could so betray her – that was how she felt. Between the two of them, the old woman and her little love, the child to whom she had given her heart unreservedly and for the first time in her life – so she felt now – were only suspicion and hurt.

'But, Julia; but, Julia . . .' Julia did not turn around, and Sylvia ran down the stairs, flung herself on her bed, and cried so loudly that Andrew heard and went to her. She told him her story and he said, 'Now stop. There is no point in that. I'll go up to grandmother and talk to her.'

He did.

'And who is this man? Why did Frances let him in?'

'But you talk as if he's a thief or a conman.'

'A conman is what he is. He has conned poor Sylvia out of her senses.'

'You know, grandmother, this kind of thing, the Yoga and all that, it's around – you lead a bit of a sheltered life, or you'd know that.' He spoke whimsically, but was dismayed by the old unhappy face. He knew very well what the real trouble was, but decided to persist on the level of simple causes. 'She's bound to come up against this sort of thing at school, you can't protect her from it.' And meanwhile Andrew was thinking that he read his horoscope every morning, though of course he didn't believe in it, and had toyed with the idea of having his fortune told. 'I think you are making too much of it,' he dared to say, and saw her at last nod, and then sigh.

'Very well,' she said. 'But how is it that this . . . this . . . disgraceful thing is everywhere suddenly?'

'A good question,' said Andrew, embracing her, but she was a lump in his arms.

Julia and Sylvia made it up. 'We've made it up,' the girl told Andrew, as if a heavy unhappy thing had become light and harmless.

But Julia would not listen to Sylvia's new discoveries, would not throw the stalks for the I-Ching, nor talk about Buddhism, and so their perfect intimacy, the intimacy possible only between an adult and a child, confiding and trustful, and as easy as breathing, had come to an end. It has to end, for this young one to grow up, but even when the adult knows this and expects it, hearts must bleed and break. But Julia had never had this kind of love with a child, certainly not with Johnny, did not know that a child growing – and Sylvia had gone through a rapid process of growing up, with her – would become a stranger. Sylvia, suddenly, was no longer the maiden trotting happily around after Julia and afraid to be out of her sight. She was mature enough to interpret the yarrow stalks – which had been asked for advice – to mean that she must go and see her mother. She did, by herself, and found Phyllida not shrieking and hysterical, but calm, withdrawn and even dignified. She was alone: Johnny was at a meeting.

Sylvia was waiting for the reproaches and accusations she could not bear: she knew she would have to run away, but Phyllida said, 'You must do what you think is best. I know it must be better for you there, with other young people. And your grand-mother has taken to you, so I hear.'

'Yes. I love her,' said the girl simply, and then trembled for fear of her mother's jealousy.

'Love is easy enough if you're rich,' said Phyllida, but that was the nearest she got to criticism. Her determination to behave well, not let loose the demons that tore and howled inside her, made her slow and apparently stupid. She repeated: 'It's better for you, I know that.' And, 'You must decide for yourself.' As if it had not all been decided long ago. She did not offer the girl tea, or a soft drink, but sat clutching the arms of a chair and staring at her daughter, blinking unevenly, and then, when it was all going to explode out of her, she said hurriedly, 'You'd better run along, Tilly. Yes, I know you're Sylvia now but you're Tilly to me.'

And Sylvia went off, knowing it had been touch and go whether she was screamed at.

Colin returned first: he said it had been great, and that was all he said. He was a good deal in his room, reading.

Sophie came to say she was starting at her acting school, and would make her home her base, because her mother still needed her. 'But please can I come often – I do so love our suppers, Frances, I do so love our evenings.' Frances reassured her, embraced her and knew from that touch the girl was troubled.

'What's wrong?' she asked. 'Is it Roland? Didn't you have a good time with him?'

Sophie said, not intending to be humorous, 'I don't think I am old enough for him.'

'Ah, I see. Did he say that?'

'He said that if I had more experience I'd understand. It's a funny thing, Frances. Sometimes I feel that he's not there at all – he's with me but . . . and yet he does love me, Frances, he says he does . . .'

'Well, there you are.'

'We did some lovely things. We walked for miles, we went

to the theatre, we joined in with some other people and we had a groovy time.'

Geoffrey was starting at the LSE. He dropped in to say that he felt he was a big boy now and it was time he had his own place. He was going to share with some Americans he had met demonstrating in Georgia; it was a pity Colin was a year younger than he was, or he could come and share too. He said he wanted to come here 'like the old days', he felt leaving this house was more like leaving home than if he was leaving his parents.

Daniel, a year younger than Geoffrey, had another year at school, a year without Geoffrey.

James was going to the LSE.

Jill continued to be the dark horse. She did not return with Rose, who never told them where she had been but who did say that Jill had been in Bristol with a lover. But she said she would be back.

Rose was in the basement and announced that she was going to stick it out at school. No one believed her and they were wrong. In fact she was clever, knew it, and was determined 'to show them'. Show who? Frances would have to be first on that list, but it was all of them really. 'I'll show them,' she muttered, and it was like a mantra repeated when it was time for homework, and when the school's progressiveness seemed less than she had hoped, as when she was asked please not to smoke in class.

Sylvia's determination to do well at school was not only for Julia, but for Andrew too, who continued to be elder-brotherly, affectionate, and kind: when he was there, and not at Cambridge.

Financial problems . . . when Frances had come to this house the arrangement was that Julia would pay the rates for the whole house, but Frances would be responsible for the rest: gas, electricity, water, telephones. Also for Mrs Philby, and the auxiliary she brought in to help her when 'the kids' got too much. 'Kids?

Pigs, more like it.' Frances also bought food, generally supplied the house with what it needed, and, in short, needed a lot of money. She was earning it. The bill for Cambridge had arrived weeks before, and Julia had paid: she said that Andrew's year off from education had been a great help. The school bill for Sylvia was paid, by Julia. Then came Colin's bill, and Frances took it up to the little table on the landing at the top of the house where Julia's mail was put, with considerable foreboding, which was confirmed when Julia came down with the St Joseph's bill in her hand. Julia was nervous too. Since the barriers between the women had gone down, Julia had been more affectionate with Frances, but also more testy and critical.

'Do sit down, Julia.'

Julia sat, first removing a pair of Frances's tights.

'Oh, sorry,' said Frances, and Julia accepted the apology with a tight little smile.

'What is all this about Colin and psychoanalysis?'

This is what Frances had dreaded: conversations had already taken place between the school and herself and between Colin and herself, and Sophie, too, had been involved. 'Oh, *lovely*, Colin, that'd be so *good*.'

'It was described to me by the headmaster as Colin having someone to talk to.'

'They can call it what they like. It would cost thousands, thousands, every year.'

'Look, Julia, I know you don't approve of any of these psycho things. But have you thought, he'll have a man to talk to. Well, I hope it's a man. This is such a female house, and Johnny . . .'

'He has a brother, he has Andrew.'

'But they don't get on.'

'Get on? What's that?' And now there was a pause, while Julia stretched out and then clenched the fingers that lay on her knees. 'My older brothers, they quarrelled sometimes. It is normal for brothers to quarrel.'

Now, Frances did know that Julia had had brothers, and that

they had been killed in that old war. Julia's painfully working fingers brought them into this room, Julia's past . . . dead brothers. Julia's eyes had tears in them, Frances could swear, though she sat with her back to the light.

'I said yes to Colin talking to someone because . . . he's very unhappy, Julia.'

Frances was still not sure whether Colin would say yes. What he had actually said was, 'Yes, I know, Sam told me.' The headmaster. 'I said to him it's my father who should be analysed.' 'That would be the day,' Frances had said. He said, 'Yes, and why not you? I am sure you could do with a good talking to.' 'Talking *with*.' 'I don't see that I'm madder than anyone else.' 'I'd agree with that.'

Now Julia got up and said, 'I think that there are some things we are not likely to agree on. But that is not what I came to say. Even without the stupid analysis I can't pay for Colin. I thought he would be leaving school now, and then I hear he's going on for another year.'

'He agreed to try for the exams again.'

'But I cannot pay for him and for Andrew, and for Sylvia too. I will see them both through university until they are independent. But Colin – I am not able to do it. And you are earning money now, I hope it will be enough.'

'Don't worry, Julia. I'm so sorry all this has fallen on you.'

'And I suppose it is no use asking Johnny. He must have money, he's always on some trip somewhere.'

'He gets paid for.'

'Why is that? Why do they pay for him?'

'Oh, Comrade Johnny, you know. He's a bit of a star, Julia.'

'He's a fool,' said Johnny's mother. 'Why is that? I do not think I am a fool. And his father was certainly not a fool. But Johnny is an idiot.' Julia stood by the door, giving an expert glance around the room which had once been her own private little sitting-room. She knew Frances did not care for this furniture – such good furniture; nor the curtains, which would last another fifty years, if properly looked after. Julia suspected the curtains harboured dust and probably moths. The old carpet, which had come from the house in Germany, was threadbare in patches.

'And I suppose you are going to defend Johnny, you always do.'

'I defend him? When have I ever *ever* defended his politics?'

'His politics! That's not politics, that's such – stupidity.'

'The politics of half the world, Julia.'

'It's still stupidity. Well, Frances, I do not like to see you more worried, with so much on your back, but I cannot help it. If you really are unable to pay for Colin then we could mortgage the house.'

'*No*, no, no . . . absolutely *not*.'

'Well, tell me if there are difficulties.' She went out.

There would be difficulties. Colin's school was very expensive, and he had agreed to do the full year. He was too old, nearly nineteen, and that was an embarrassment. The bill for the May-stock Clinic, the 'talking to' – it would be thousands. She would have to find more work. She would ask for a rise. She knew her articles had raised the circulation of *The Defender*. She could write for other newspapers, but under another name. These problems had been discussed with, of all people, Rupert Boland, in the Cosmo. He had financial problems too, unspecified. He would have liked to leave *The Defender*, which he claimed was no place for a man, but he was paid well. He was earning extra by doing research for television and radio: she could too. Even so, she would need more, she would need a lot. Johnny: she could perhaps ask him again? Julia was right, he lived the life of a – today's equivalent of a rajah, he went on delegations and good-will missions, always in the best hotels, all expenses paid, conveying comradely greetings from one part of the world to another. He must be getting money from somewhere: who was paying his rent? He didn't actually work, ever.

With that autumn began a bizarre situation. Colin came up by train twice a week from St Joseph's to go to the Maystock

Clinic, where he had appointments with a Doctor David. A man: Frances was delighted. Colin would have a man to talk to, a man outside his family situation. ('If that's what he needs,' said Julia, 'why not Wilhelm? He likes Colin.' 'But Julia, don't you see, he's too close, he's part of our world.' 'No, I don't see.') The trouble was that pursuing some psychoanalytic theory or other, Doctor David did not speak at all. He said good afternoon, sat himself in his chair, after a brisk handshake, and thereafter spoke not one word for the whole hour. Not a word. 'He just smiles,' reported Colin. 'I say something and he smiles. And then he says, The time is up, I'll see you on Thursday.'

Colin came straight home after the Maystock, and to wherever his mother was in the house. There he addressed to her all that he had not been able to say to Doctor David. It came pouring out, the complaints, the miseries, the angers that Frances had hoped he was at last able to unload on to the professional shoulders of Doctor David. Who only sat silent, so Colin sat silent, frustrated and angry. He shouted at his mother that Doctor David was torturing him, and it was all the school's fault for making him go to the Maystock Clinic. And it was her fault he was in such a mess. Why had she married Johnny? – he shouted at her. That communist, everyone knew about communism but she had married him, Johnny was just a fascist commissar, and she, Frances, had married him and all that shit was landed on him and on Andrew. So he shouted, as he stood in the middle of her room, but it was at Doctor David he was shouting, because it was all pent up in him, it had to come out somewhere. All the way up to London in the little slow train, he rehearsed his accusations of life, his father, his mother, to tell Doctor David, but Doctor David only smiled. And so it had to come bursting out, and it was focused on his mother. And look, he shouted, on visit after visit, look at this house, full of people who have no right to be here. Why was Sylvia here? She wasn't their family. She took everything, they all took everything and Geoffrey had been leeching off them for years. Had Frances ever actually worked out what had been spent on Geoffrey over the years? They could have bought another house the size of Julia's with it. Why had Geoffrey always been here? Everyone said Geoffrey was his friend, but he had never liked Geoffrey much, the school had decided Geoffrey was his friend, Sam had decided they were complementary, in other words they didn't have a fucking thing in common, but it would be good for them, well it hadn't been good for him, Colin, and Frances connived with the school, she always had, sometimes he thought Geoffrey was more Frances's son than he was, and look at Andrew, he had lain on his bed for a whole year and smoked pot, and did Frances know, he had tried cocaine, well, she didn't know that? If not, why not? Frances never knew about anything, she just let everything go on, and how about Rose, what was Rose doing in this house at all, living at our expense, taking everything, he didn't want Rose here, he hated Rose, did Frances know that no one liked Rose, yet here she was downstairs and she had taken over the flat and if anyone else even put their heads around the door she shouted at them to get out. It was all Frances's fault, sometimes he thought he was the only sane person in the house, but it was he who had to go to the Maystock to be tortured by Doctor David.

Listening to Colin, as he stood and orated, taking his heavy black-rimmed glasses off, putting them back on, waving his hands about, stamping around, she was hearing what no human being should ever have to hear – another person's uncensored thoughts. (No one except Doctor David and his ilk, that is.) They were thoughts not dissimilar probably to many people's, when hot and lava-like. Just as well people were not able to hear what people thought of them, as she now had to, with Colin. The tirade of misery went on for an hour, the time he would have spent with Doctor David. Then he would say, in a quite friendly, normal voice, 'Now I have to go and catch my train.' Or, 'I'll stay the night and catch the first train in the morning.' And the Colin she knew was back, even smiling, though in a puzzled, frustrated sort of way. He must be absolutely exhausted after that outpouring.

'You don't have to go to the Maystock,' she reminded him. 'You can say no. Do you want me to tell them you've decided not to?'

But Colin did not want to stop coming to London twice a week, to the Maystock Clinic, to *her*, she knew, because without the frustration of the hour with the analyst he would not be able to shout and rave at her, to say what he had been thinking so long but had not said, never been able to let out.

After an hour of being shouted at, Frances was so tired that she went off to bed, or sat slumped in a chair. One evening, sitting there in the dark, Julia knocked, opened the door, saw the room was dark, and then that Frances was there. Julia turned on the light. She had heard Colin shouting at his mother, and had been disturbed by it but that was not what had brought her down.

'Did you know that Sylvia has not come home?'

'It's only ten o'clock.'

'May I sit down?' And Julia sat, her hands demolishing the little handkerchief in her lap. 'She's too young to be out so late, with a bad crowd of people.'

Sylvia sometimes after school went to a certain flat in Camden Town where Jake and his cronies were most afternoons and evenings. They were all fortune tellers, one or two professionally, or wrote horoscopes for newspapers, were initiates of rites, mostly invented by themselves, went in for table-turning, evoked spirits, and drank mysterious substances called Soul Balm, or Mind Mix, or Essence of Truth – usually not much more than herbal blends, or spices, and generally lived in a world of meaning and significance far removed from most people's. Sylvia was a great success with them. She was their pet, the neophyte those possessed with knowledge yearn for, and she was duly entrusted with secrets of higher meaning. She liked these people because they liked her, and she was always welcome. She never behaved irresponsibly, always telephoned to say she would be back later than usual, and if she stayed with them longer than she had said, telephoned Julia again.

'If you must be with such people, Sylvia, what can I say?'

Frances did not like it, but knew the girl would grow out of it.

For Julia it was a tragedy, her little lamb lost to her, enticed away by sick lunatics.

'These people are not normal, Frances,' she said tonight, distressed and ready to cry.

Frances did not jest, 'Who is?' – Julia would have embarked on definitions. Frances knew Julia had come down for more than her anxiety over Sylvia, and waited.

'And how is it that a son may talk to his mother as Colin does to you?'

'He has to say it to someone.'

'But it is ridiculous, the things he says . . . I can hear it all, the whole house can hear.'

'He can't say it to Johnny, and so he says it to me.'

'It is so astonishing to me,' said Julia, 'that they are allowed to behave like this? Why are they?'

'They're screwed up,' said Frances. 'Isn't it odd, Julia, don't you think it is strange?'

'It is very strange how they behave,' said Julia.

'No, listen, I think about this. They are all so privileged, they have everything, they have more than any of us ever had – well, you might have been different.'

'No, I did not have a new dress every week. And I did not steal.' Julia's voice rose. 'That thieves' kitchen of yours, Frances, they are all thieves and they have no morals. If they want something they go and steal it.'

'Andrew doesn't. Colin doesn't. I don't think Sophie ever did.'

'The house is full of . . . you allow them here, they take advantage of you and they are thieves and liars. This was an honourable house. Our family was honourable, and we were respected by everyone.'

'Yes, and I wonder why they are like that. They all have so

much, they have more than any generation ever had, and yet they are all . . .'

'They are screwed up,' said Julia, getting up to go. Then she stood in front of Frances, hands apart, as if holding there an invisible thing – a person? – which she was wringing, like a cloth. 'It's a good expression, that: *screwed up*. I know why they are. Disturbed, did you say Colin was? They're all war children, that is why. Two terrible wars and this is the result. They are children of war. Do you think there can be wars like that, terrible terrible wars and then you can say, All right, that's over, now back to normal. Nothing's normal now. The children aren't normal. And you too . . .' but she stopped herself, and Frances was not to hear what Julia thought of her. 'And now Sylvia, with those spiritualists, they call themselves, did you know they turn out the lights and sit holding hands and some idiot woman pretends to be talking to a ghost?'

'Yes, I know.'

'And yet you sit there, you always just listen, but you don't stop them.'

Frances said, as the old woman went out, 'Julia, we can't stop them.'

'I shall stop Sylvia. I shall tell her she can go back home to her mother, if she wants to run around with those people.'

The door shut and Frances said aloud into the empty room, 'No, Julia, you will not do that, you are merely muttering to yourself like an old witch, to let off steam.'

On that same evening, when Julia's 'This was an honourable house' still sounded in Frances's ears, the doorbell rang, late, and Frances went down. On the doorstep were two girls, of about fifteen, and their hostile but demanding looks warned Frances of what she would hear which was, 'Let us in. Rose is expecting us.'

'I wasn't expecting you. Who are you?'

'Rose says we can live here,' said one, apparently about to push her way in past Frances.

'It isn't for Rose to say who can live here and who can't,' said Frances, quite amazed at herself for standing her ground. Then, as the girls stood hesitating, she said, 'If you want to see Rose then come tomorrow at a reasonable time. I think she'll be asleep by now.'

'No, she isn't.' And Frances looked down to the window of the basement flat, to see Rose energetically gesticulating to her friends. She heard, 'I told you she's an old cow.'

The girls went off, with *what can you expect* gestures to Rose. One said loudly over her shoulder, 'When we've won the Revolution you'll be laughing on the other side of your face.'

Frances went straight down to Rose, who stood waiting, quivering with rage. Her black hair, no longer tamed by the Evansky haircut, seemed to bristle, her face was red, and she actually seemed to be on the point of physically attacking Frances.

'What the hell do you mean by telling people they can come and live here?'

'It's my flat, isn't it? I can do what I like in my own flat.'

'It's not your flat. We are allowing you to stay in it until you've finished school. But if there are other people who need it, they'll be using the second room.'

'I'm going to let that room,' said Rose.

And now Frances was startled into silence, because of the impossibility of what was happening, hardly an unfamiliar situation with Rose. Then she saw that Rose stood triumphant, because she had not been contradicted, and she said, 'We're not charging you to live here. You live here absolutely free, so how can you imagine for a moment that you could let out a room?'

'I have to,' shouted Rose. 'I can't live on what my parents are giving me. It's just peanuts. They're so mean.'

'Why should you need more when you're not paying anything at all for living here, and you eat with us, and your school's all paid for?'

But now Rose was on a roll of rage, out of control. 'Shits, all of you, that's all you are. And you don't care about my friends.

They have nowhere to go. They've been sleeping on a bench at King's Cross. I suppose that's what you want me to do.'

'If that's what you want, then off you go,' said Frances. 'I'm not stopping you.'

Rose shouted, 'Your precious Andrew knocks me up and then you throw me out like a dog.'

This did take Frances aback, but she reminded herself it was not true . . . and then she had to remember that Jill's abortion had been arranged without her knowing anything about it. This hesitation gave Rose the advantage, and she screamed, 'And look at Jill, you made her have an abortion when she didn't want one.'

'I didn't know she was pregnant. I didn't know anything about it,' said Frances, and understood she was arguing with Rose, which no sane person would do.

'And I suppose you didn't know about me either? All this lovey-dovey be nice to Rose, but you're covering up for Andrew.'

Frances said, 'You are lying. I know when you are lying.' And then was shocked again: Colin said she never knew anything that went on: suppose Rose had been pregnant? But, no, Andrew would have told her.

'And I'm not going to go on living here when you're so horrible to me. I know when I'm not wanted.'

The grotesqueness of this last statement actually made Frances laugh but it was also from relief at the thought that Rose might actually go. The degree of relief told her just how great a burden the presence of Rose was. 'Good,' she said. 'Well, Rose, I agree with you. It is obviously better for you to leave, when you feel like that.'

And she went up the stairs, in a silence like the one they say lies at the heart of a storm. A glance showed Rose's face lifted up in what seemed to be a prayer – but then she howled.

Frances shut the door on her, ran up to her room, and flung herself on her bed. Oh, my God, to get rid of Rose, just to get rid of Rose: but commonsense crept back with, But of course she won't go.

She heard Rose thundering past up the stairs, heard the hammering on Andrew's door. She was up there a good long time. Frances — indeed, the whole house — could hear the sobs, the cries, the threats.

Then, well past midnight, she crept back down past Frances's rooms, and there was silence.

A knock on the door: there was Andrew. He was white with exhaustion.

'May I sit down?' He sat. 'You have no idea how diverting it always is,' he said, preserving his poise in spite of everything, 'to see you in this improbable setting.'

Frances saw herself in well-worn jeans, an old jersey, with bare feet, and then Julia's furniture which probably should be in a museum. She managed a smile and a shake of her head which meant, It's all too much.

'She says you are throwing her out.'

'If only we could. She says she is leaving.'

'I'm afraid no such luck.'

'She says you got her pregnant.'

'What?'

'So she claims.'

'Penetration did not take place,' he said. 'We snogged — more of a lark than anything. Perhaps for an hour. It is amazing how these left-wing summer schools seem to . . .' He hummed, '. . . every little breeze seems to whisper, Please, sex, sex, sex.'

'What are we going to do? Why don't we just throw her out, my God, why don't we?'

'But if we do she'll be on the streets. She won't go home.'

'I suppose so.'

'It's only a year. We'll have to stick it out.'

'Colin is very angry because she's here.'

'I know. You forget we can all hear his complaints about life. And about Sylvia. Probably me as well.'

'Me, most of all.'

'And now I'm going right down to tell her that if she ever

again says I made her pregnant . . . wait, I suppose I got her an abortion too?'

'She didn't say so, but I expect she will.'

'God, what a little bitch.'

'But how effective, being a bitch. No one can stand up to her.'

'You just watch me.'

'So what are you going to do? Call the police? And by the way, where's Jill? She seems to have disappeared.'

'She and Jill quarrelled. I expect Rose just got rid of her.'

'So where is she? Does anyone know? I'm suppose to be *in loco parentis*.'

'Loco's a good word in this context.' He departed.

But Frances was learning that while she was seen by 'the kids' as a sort of benevolent freak of Nature, and they lucky enough to benefit, she was far from the only one *in loco parentis*. A letter had come from Spain after the summer, from an Englishwoman living in Seville, saying she had so much enjoyed Colin, Frances's charming son. (Colin, charming? Well, not in this house he wasn't.) 'A very nice crowd this summer. It's not always such plain sailing. Sometimes they have such problems! I do feel it is an extraordinary thing, the way they go off to other people's parents. My daughter makes excuses not to come home. She's got an alternative home in Hampshire with an ex-boyfriend. I suppose we must admit that that is what it amounts to.'

A letter from North Carolina. 'Hi there, Frances Lennox! I feel I know you so well. Your Geoffrey Bone was here for weeks, with others from various parts of the world, all to take part in the Struggle for Civic Rights. They come knocking at my door, waifs and strays of the world – no, no, I don't mean Geoffrey, I've never known a cooler young man. But I collect them and so do you, and so does my sister Fran in California. My son Pete will be in Britain this coming summer and I am sure he'll drop in.' From Scotland, From Ireland. From France . . . letters that went into a file of similar ones that had been coming for years, from the time when she hardly saw Andrew.

Thus did the house-mothers, the earth-mothers, who prolifer-
ated everywhere in the Sixties slowly become aware of each other's
presence out there, and understand that they were part of a
phenomenon: the *geist* was at it again. They networked, before
the term had become part of the language. They were a network
of nurturers. Of *neurotic* nurturers. As 'the kids' had explained,
Frances was working out some guilt or other, rooted in her childhood. (Frances had said she wouldn't be at all surprised.) As for
Sylvia, she had a different 'line'. (Origin of 'line' – jargon of the
Party.) Sylvia had learned from her groovy mystical mates that
Frances was working on her karma, damaged in a previous life.

On one of Colin's visits home to shout at his mother, he brought
with him Franklin Tichafa, from Zimlia, a British colony that, so
Johnny said, was about to go the way of Kenya. All the newspapers
were saying it too. Franklin was a round, smiling black boy. Colin
told his mother that one could not use the word *boy* because of
its bad connotations, but Frances said, 'He's not a young man, is
he. If a sixteen-year-old can't be described as a boy, who can?'

'She does it on purpose,' said Andrew. 'She does it to annoy.'

This was partly true. Johnny had long ago complained that
Frances was sometimes deliberately politically obtuse, to embarrass
him in front of the comrades, and indeed she had sometimes done
it on purpose, and did now.

Everyone liked Franklin, who was named after Franklin
Roosevelt, 'taking' literature at St Joseph's to please his parents,
but planning to study economics and politics at university.

'That's what you are all studying,' said Frances. 'Politics and
economics. What is so extraordinary is that anyone should want
to, when they never get it right, particularly the economists.'

This remark was so far in advance of its time that it was
allowed to pass, was probably not even heard.

The evening when Franklin first came, Colin did not drop

down to Frances's rooms for the usual session of accusations: he had not gone to the Maystock. Franklin was in his room on the floor in a sleeping bag. Frances could hear them just over her head, talking, laughing . . . her much-overused heart seemed to breathe easier, and she felt that all Colin really needed was a good friend, someone who laughed a lot: they larked about and as young men (or boys) will, went in for a lot of buffeting, pummelling and horseplay.

Franklin came again, and again, and Colin said he was fed up with the Maystock. He had actually caught Doctor David asleep, while he sat fidgeting in his patient's chair, hoping that the great man would at last say something.

'What's he being paid?' he asked.

Frances told him.

'Nice work if you can get it,' said Colin. But was he bottling everything up again? Had he spent all his anger in those evenings of accusation with her? She had no idea. But he was doing badly at school still, and wanted to leave.

It was Franklin who told him it was silly. 'That would be a bad move,' said he, at the supper table. 'You'll be sorry when you're older.'

This last was a direct quote. In any company of young people, sayings, admonition, advice, that have emanated from the mouths of parents can be heard coming from theirs, in joke, in mockery, or in seriousness. 'You'll be sorry when you're older,' had been said by Franklin's grandmother, in firelight – a log burned in the centre of the hut – in a village where a goat might push into open doorways hoping to find something to steal. An anxious black woman, whom Franklin had told he did not want to take up his scholarship to St Joseph's – he was in a funk – had said, 'You'll be sorry when you're older.'

'I am older,' said Colin.

★　　★　　★

It was November again, dark with drizzle. Because it was a weekend, everyone was here. At Frances's left sat Sylvia, and the others were careful not to notice that she was struggling with her food. She had left the magic circle of people who could never say anything without meaningful looks and voices heavy with import, saying, just as Julia might have done, 'They aren't very nice people.' Jake had turned up, asked to see Frances, and was clearly anxious. 'There's a problem here, Frances. It's cultural. I think we're more uninhibited in the States than you are here.'

'I'm afraid you have me at a disadvantage,' said Frances. 'Sylvia has said nothing to us about why she . . .'

'But there was nothing to tell, you must believe me.'

Sylvia confided to Andrew that what had 'upset' her was not wild Satanic rites that the others had imagined and even joked about, while she told them they were just silly, or seances that had gone wrong – or right, depending on how you looked at it, bringing noisy apparitions with something urgent to impart, such as that Sylvia should always wear blue and a turquoise amulet, but that Jake had kissed her and told her she was too old to be a virgin. She had slapped him, hard, and told him he was a dirty old man. To Andrew it was clear that Jake had been offering arcane sexual delights, but Sylvia said, 'He's old enough to be my grandfather.' He was, too. Just.

Andrew was here for the weekend, because Colin had telephoned to say that Sylvia was having a setback. It was Colin who rang: so what did his wild ravings about Sylvia's being here at all amount to, then? 'You've got to come, Andrew. You always know what to do.' And Julia? – did she not know what to do? Apparently not any longer. Julia, hearing that Sylvia was in her room again, and not out night after night, had said in the heavily sorrowful voice that now seemed to be permanently hers, 'Yes, Sylvia, and that's what you can expect when you mix with such people.'

'But nothing happened, Julia,' Sylvia had whispered, and had tried to embrace her. Julia's arms, that had so recently easily embraced her, did hold her, but not as they had, and Sylvia cried in her room, because of those stiff old arms, that reproached her.

Sylvia was sitting, fork in hand, turning over a fragment of potato done in cream, cooked because she liked it.

Andrew was next to Sylvia. Colin was next to Andrew, and beside him, Rose. Not a word or a look did they exchange. James was there from his school, and he would also sleep on the living-room floor. Opposite Rose was Franklin, who had had a little too much to drink. Bottles of wine stood about the table brought by Johnny who was at his post by the window. Next to Franklin was Geoffrey, in his first term at the LSE. He looked like a guerilla fighter, in army surplus. He was there because he had run into Johnny at the Cosmo, had heard that he would be coming that evening. Sophie was not here, but she had visited that afternoon, to see darling Frances. She was finding life hard, not because of acting school where she was doing brilliantly, but because of Roland Shattock. Tonight she was with him at a disco. Next to Frances was Jill, who had reappeared that afternoon. She asked timidly if she could stay to supper. She had a bandage on her left wrist and looked pretty bad. Rose had greeted her with, 'Oh, so what do you think you're doing here?' Jill waited until there was laughter and noise enough, and said to Frances, 'Can I come and live in the other room downstairs? It's for you to say who can be there, isn't it?' The trouble was, Colin had said that he wanted Franklin to have the use of that room, and to be invited for Christmas. And, obviously, Jill and Rose could not be together.

'Are you planning to go back to school?' asked Frances.

'I don't know if they'll have me,' said Jill, with a timid pleading look at Frances, that meant, Will you ask them if they'll have me back?

But where was she going to live?

'Have you been in hospital?'

The girl nodded. Then, still in a whisper, 'I've been in there a month.' That meant, a psychiatric ward, and Frances was intended to understand this. 'Couldn't I just sleep in the sitting-room?'

Andrew, apparently absorbed in Sylvia, encouraging her, laughing with her when she made a joke about her difficulties, was also listening to the exchange between his mother and Jill; and now he caught Frances's eye and shook his head. The thumbs-down could not have been more clear, though it was only a little *no*, meant to be unobserved. But Jill had seen it. She sat silent, eyes kept down, lips trembling.

'The trouble is, where are we going to put you?' Frances said. And Jill probably would not be able to cope with school, even if Frances could get her admitted. What was to be done?

This sad little drama was going on at Frances's end of the table; at the other it was all noisy good humour. Johnny was telling them about his trip with a delegation of librarians to the Soviet Union, and the jokes were at the expense of the non-Party members, who had made one gaffe after another. One had demanded to be reassured – at a meeting in the Union of Soviet Writers – that there was no censorship in the Soviet Union. Another had wanted to know if the Soviet Union, 'like the Vatican', kept an index of forbidden books. 'I mean,' said Johnny, 'that is really an unforgivable level of political naivety.'

Then, there was the recent election that had returned the Labour Party. Johnny had been active: a tricky business, because while on the one hand obviously the Labour Party was a greater threat to the working masses than the Tories (confusing minds with incorrect formulations), on the other, tactical considerations had ordained that it should be supported. James was listening to the ins and outs of this as if to favourite music. Johnny had greeted him with a comradely nod and a hand laid on his shoulder, but now he was concentrating on the newcomer, still to be won, Franklin. He delivered a short history of the colonial policy towards Zimlia, recounted the crimes of colonial policy in Kenya, with particular relish for whenever Britain had behaved badly, and began exhorting Franklin to fight for the freedom of Zimlia.

'The nationalist movements of Zimlia are not as developed as the Mau Mau, but it is up to young people like you to free your people from oppression.' Johnny had a glass in one hand, the left, and was leaning forward, eyes holding Franklin's, while he shook the forefinger of his right hand at him, as if targeting him with a revolver. Franklin was shifting about, smiling uncomfortably, and then he said, 'Excuse me,' and went out – to the toilet as it happened, but it looked like running away, and when he came back he smiled, and handed his plate to Frances for a second helping, and did not look at Johnny, who had been waiting for him to return. 'Your generation in Africa has more responsibility laid on your shoulders by history than any other has had. How I wish I was young again, how I wish I had it all in front of me.'

And for once his features, usually set into a martial authority, were softened into wistfulness. Johnny was getting on, an ageing fighter now, and how he must hate it, Frances thought, for with every day came news of new younger avatars of the Revolution. Poor Johnny was on the shelf. At the same moment Franklin lifted his glass, in a wild gesture that looked like parody, and said, 'To the Revolution in Africa,' and fell forward on to the table, out, while Jill got up from the table and said, 'Excuse me, excuse me, I'll go now.'

'Do you want to sleep here tonight? There's the sitting-room. James and you can keep each other company.'

Jill stood shaking her head, supporting herself with a hand – as it happened – on Frances's arm, and then fainted away, at Frances's feet.

'Here's a carry-on,' said Johnny heartily, and watched while Geoffrey and Colin roused Franklin, and held a glass of water to his lips, and Frances lifted up Jill. Rose sat on, eating as if nothing was happening. Sylvia whispered that she wanted to go to bed, and Andrew took her up.

Franklin was assisted downstairs to the second room in the basement flat, and Jill was put into a sleeping bag in the sitting-room. James said he would look after her, but he went straight off to sleep. Frances came down in the night to have a look at Jill, and found them both asleep. In the dim light from the door on to the landing, Jill looked terrible. She needed looking after. Obviously the girl's parents must be rung and told the situation: they probably did not know it. And in the morning Jill must be asked to go home.

But in the morning Jill had gone, had disappeared into wild and dangerous London. And Rose, when asked where she thought Jill might be, replied that she was not Jill's keeper.

Nervousness on Franklin's account was in order, sharing space with Rose. They were afraid she harboured racial prejudices, 'coming from that background' – Andrew's evasion of the class situation. But it turned out otherwise: Rose was 'nice' to Franklin. 'She's being really nice,' reported Colin. 'He thinks she's great.'

He did. She was. An apparently improbable friendship was growing between the good-humoured kindly black youth and the rancorous girl, whose rage bubbled and boiled as reliably as the red spot on Jupiter.

Frances, her sons, marvelled that one could not think of two more different people, but in fact they inhabited a similar moral landscape. Rose and Franklin were never to know how much they had in common.

Since Rose had first come into this house she had been possessed by a quiet fury that these people could call it theirs, as of a right. This great house, its furnishings, like something out of a film, their money . . . but all that was only the foundation for a deeper anguish, for it was that, a bitter burning that never left her. It was their ease with it all, what they took for granted, what they knew. Never had she mentioned a book – and she had a period of testing them out with books no sane person could have heard of – that they hadn't read, or hadn't heard of. She would stand in that sitting-room, with two walls all books from ceiling to floor, and know that they had read them. 'Frances,' she challenged, being found there, hands on hips, glaring at the books, 'have you actually read all these books?' 'Well, yes, yes, I believe I have.'

'When did you? Did you have books in your house when you were growing up?' 'Yes, we had the classics. I think everyone did in those days.' 'Everybody, everybody! Who's everybody?' 'The middle classes,' said Frances, determined not to be bullied. 'And a good proportion of the working class as well.' 'Oh! Who said so?' 'Check it,' said Frances. 'Not difficult to find out this sort of thing.' 'And when did you have time to read?' 'Let me see . . .' Frances was remembering herself, mostly alone, with two small children, her boredom alleviated by reading. She remembered Johnny nagging at her to read this, read that . . . 'Johnny was a good influence,' she told Rose, insisting to herself that one must be fair. 'He's very well read, you know. The communists usually are, it's funny isn't it, but they are. He made me read.'

'All these books,' Rose said. 'Well, we didn't have books.'

'Easy enough to catch up if you want to,' said Frances. 'Borrow what you like.'

But the casualness of it made Rose clench her fists. Anything mentioned, they seemed to know it; an idea, or a bit of history. They were in possession of some bank of knowledge: it didn't matter what one asked, they knew it all.

Rose had taken books off the shelves, but she did not enjoy them. It was not that she read slowly, she did: but she was nothing if not persevering, and she stuck at it. A kind of rage filled her as she read, getting between her and the story or the facts she was trying to absorb. It was because these people had all this as a kind of inheritance, and she, Rose . . .

When Franklin had arrived, and found himself in the complex richnesses of London, he had had days of panic, wishing he had said no to the scholarship. It was too much to expect of him. His father had been a teacher of the lower grades in a Catholic mission school. The priests, seeing that the boy was clever, had encouraged and supported, and the point came when they asked a rich person – Franklin would never know who it was – if he would add this promising boy to his list of beneficiaries. An expensive undertaking: two years at St Joseph's and then, with luck, university.

When Franklin went from his mission school back to the village, he was secretly ashamed of what his parents' background had been. Still was. A few grass huts in the bush, no electricity, no telephone, no running water, no toilet. The shop was five miles away. In comparison the mission school with its amenities had seemed a rich place. Now, in London, there was a violent dislocation: he was surrounded by such wealth, such wonders, that the mission had to seem paltry, poor. He had stayed for the first days in London with a kindly priest, a friend of those at the mission, who knew that the boy would be in a state of shock, and took him on buses, on the Underground, to the parks, to the markets, to the big shops, the supermarkets, the bank, to eat in restaurants. All this to accustom him, but then he had to go to St Joseph's, a place that seemed like heaven, buildings like illustrations in a picture book scattered about in green fields, and the boys and girls, all white except for two Nigerians who were as strange to him as the whites were, and the teachers, quite different from the Catholic fathers, all so friendly, so kind . . . he had not had kindness from white people outside the mission school. Colin was in a room along the corridor two doors from his own. To Franklin the little room was fitted out with everything anyone could wish for, including a telephone. It was a little paradise, but he had heard Colin complaining that it was too small. The food – the variety of it, the plenty, every meal like a feast, but he had heard grumbles that the food was monotonous. At the mission he had had little to eat but maize porridge and relishes.

Slowly grew inside him a powerful feeling that sometimes threatened to come hot out of his mouth in insults and accusations, while he smiled and was pleasant and compliant. It's not fair, it's not right, why do you have so much *and you take it all for granted*. It was that which ached in him, hurt, stung: they had no idea at all of their good fortune. And when he came home with Colin to the big house that seemed to him must be a palace (so he thought at first), it was crammed with beautiful things, and he found himself sitting in silence while they all joked and teased.

He watched the older brother, Andrew, and his tenderness to the girl who had been sick, and in his mind he was in her place, sitting there between Frances and Andrew, both so kind to her, so gentle. After that first visit it was the same as when he first heard about the scholarship. He couldn't cope with it, he was not up to it, half the time he didn't even know what things were for – a bit of kitchen equipment, or furniture. But he did go back and back, and found himself being treated like a son in that house. Johnny was a difficulty, at first. Franklin had been exposed to Johnny's doctrines, his kind of talk, before, and he had resolved he did not want to have anything to do with these politics, that frightened him. Politicos had exhorted him to kill all the whites, but his experience of good had been through the white priests at the mission even though they were stern, and through an unknown white protector, and now these kindly people at the new school and in this house. And yet he burned, he ached, he suffered: it was envy and it was poisoning him. *I want. I want it. I want. I want . . .*

He knew that most of what he thought he could not say. The thoughts that crammed his head were dangerous and could not be allowed out. And with Rose they were not let out either. Neither Rose nor Franklin ever let the other into the lurid poisonous scenes in their minds. But they liked to be with each other.

It took him a long time to sort out what people were to each other, their relationships, and if they were related. It was not surprising to him that so many sat around that table to eat, though he had to go back for a comparison, to his village, where he was familiar with people being made welcome, expecting to be fed, given a place to sleep. In his father's and mother's little house at the mission, not much more than a meagre room and a kitchen, there was no room for the kind of casual hospitality of the village. When Franklin stayed with his grandparents for the school holidays, around the great log that smouldered all night in the middle of the hut, people lay wrapped in blankets to sleep whom he had not known before and might never see again: distant relatives passing through. Or relations down on their luck came for refuge. Yet this kindly warmth went with a poverty that he was ashamed of and – worse – could no longer understand. When he went back home after all this, would he be able to bear it? – he thought, seeing Rose's clothes heaped on her bed, seeing what the children at school had: there was no end to what they possessed, what they expected to have. And he had a few carefully guarded clothes, which had cost his parents so much to buy for him.

And then, the books upstairs. At the mission were a Bible and prayer books and *The Pilgrim's Progress*, which he read over and over again. He had read newspapers weeks old that he found stacked for lining shelves or drawers in the mission pantry. He treasured an *Arthur Mee Children's Encyclopaedia* that he had found thrown on to a rubbish heap – discarded by a white family. Now he felt as if dreams that had been with him since childhood had come to life in those walls of books in the sitting-room. He took down this book, turned over the pages, and the precious thing pulsed in his hands. He sneaked books down to his room, hoping Rose would not see, for she had shocked him with, 'They only pretend to read those books, you know. It's all just a sham.'

But he laughed, because she wanted him to: she was his friend. He told her that he thought of her as his sister: he missed his sisters.

Christmas was going to be a real one this year because Colin and Andrew would both be home. Sophie's mother had told her she didn't want to spoil her fun, and she herself would go to her sister's. She was more cheerful, no longer cried all day and night, and was taking a course in Grief Counselling.

Since Johnny was home between trips, Phyllida presumably would be looked after, and Andrew would not have to.

When Frances said there would be Christmas, a spirit of frivolity at once appeared in faces, eyes, and in jokes mocking the festival, though these last had to be subdued because of Franklin's joy. He felt he could not wait for the time to pass till the day of feasting, which he read about in every newspaper, saw heralded on television, and was filling the shops with bright colours. He was secretly unhappy because there would be present-giving, and he had so little money. Frances had seen that his jacket was of thin cloth, that he had no warm jersey, and gave him money to fit himself out, as a Christmas present. He kept the money in a drawer, and would sit on his bed, turning it over and over like a sitting hen on its eggs. That this sum of money was in his hands, *his* hands, was part of the miracle Christmas seemed to him. But Rose opened his door to check on him, saw him leaning over the drawer with the money, pounced, and counted it. 'Where did you steal this?'

This was so much what he had learned to expect from white people that he stammered, 'But missus, missus . . .' Rose did not know the word, and insisted, 'Where did you get it?'

'Frances gave it to me, to buy clothes.'

The girl's face flamed with anger. Frances had not given her so much, only enough for a Biba dress, and another visit to Mrs Evansky. Then she said, 'You don't need to buy clothes.' She was sitting on the bed close to him, the money in her hand, so close that any suspicion by Franklin of prejudice had to be abandoned. No white person in the whole colony, not even the white priests, would sit so close to a black person in casual friendliness.

'There are better things to do with that money,' said Rose, and reluctantly gave it back to him. She watched him return it to the drawer.

Geoffrey dropped in for an evening, and he joined Rose in a plan for outfitting Franklin. When he had arrived at the LSE he was delighted that to steal clothes, books, anything one fancied, as a means of undermining the capitalist system was taken for granted. To actually pay for something, well, how politically naive can one get? No, one 'liberated' it: the old Second World War word was having a new lease of life.

Geoffrey would come for Christmas – 'One has to be home for Christmas' – and did not even hear what he had said.

James said he was sure his parents would not mind his absence: he would visit them for New Year.

Lucy from Dartington would come: her parents were off to China on a good-will mission of some kind.

Daniel said he had to go home, he hoped they would keep a piece of cake for him.

A sad little letter had come from Jill. She thought of them all. They were her only friends. 'Please write to me. Please send some money.' But no address.

Frances wrote to Jill's parents, asking if they had seen her. She had written earlier confessing failure to keep her at school. The letter she got back then had said, 'Please don't blame yourself, Mrs Lennox. We've never been able to do anything with her.' The letter this time said, 'No, she has not seen fit to contact us. We would be grateful if you would inform us if she turns up at your place. St Joseph's has heard nothing. No one has.'

Frances wrote to Rose's parents saying that Rose had done well in the autumn term. The letter from her parents said, 'You probably don't know this but we have heard nothing from our girl, and we are grateful for news of her. The school sent us a copy of the report. One went to you, we gather. We were surprised. She used to pride herself – or so I am afraid it seemed to us – on showing us how badly she could do.'

Sylvia had also done well. This had partly been due to Julia's coaching, but it had slackened off recently. Sylvia had again gone up to Julia, and, her voice quavering with love and tears, had said, 'Please, Julia, don't go on being so cross with me. I can't bear it.' The two had melted into each other's arms, and almost, but not quite, the same degree of intimacy had been restored. There was the tiniest fly in Julia's ointment: Sylvia had said that 'she wanted to be religious'. Hearing Franklin's accounts of how the Jesuit fathers had rescued him, touched her somewhere deep, and she was going to take instruction and become a Roman Catholic. Julia said that she herself had been expected to go to mass on Sundays, 'but that was really as far as it went'. She supposed she could still call herself a Catholic.

Sylvia and Sophie and Lucy spent Christmas Eve decorating a tiny tree to set in the window, and helped Frances with preparatory cooking. They were allowing themselves to be little girls again. Frances could have sworn these giggling happy creatures were about ten or eleven. The usually heavy business of preparing food became an affair of jokes and yes, even fun. Up came Franklin, drawn by the noise. Geoffrey, James – they were going to sleep in the sitting-room – then Colin and Andrew, were happy to shell chestnuts and mix stuffing. Then the great bird was smeared with butter and oil, and displayed on the baking tin, to cheers.

It all went on, then it was late, and Sophie said she needn't go home, her mother was all right now, she had brought her dress for tomorrow with her. When Frances went to bed she could hear all the young ones in the sitting-room just below her, having a preliminary party of their own. She was thinking of Julia two floors up, alone, as she was, and knowing that her Sylvia was with the others, not with her . . . Julia had said she would not come to Christmas lunch, but she invited everyone to a real Christmas tea in the sitting-room, which was now full of youngsters getting drunk.

On Christmas morning, like millions of other women throughout the land, Frances descended to the kitchen alone. The sitting-room door, left open presumably for the sake of ventilation, showed huddled outlines.

Frances sat at the table, cigarette in hand, a cup of strong tea sending out rumours of hillsides where underpaid women picked leaves for that exotic place, the West. The house was silent – but no, feet sounded, and Franklin appeared from below, beaming. He was wearing the new jacket, a thick jersey, and lifted his feet one after another to show new shoes, socks; he raised his jersey to show a tartan shirt, and lifted that to display a bright blue singlet. They embraced. She felt she was holding the embodiment of Christmas, for he was so happy he began a little jig, and clapped his hands, 'Frances, Frances, Mother Frances, you are our mother, you are a mother to me.'

Meanwhile Frances noted that mingled with his exuberance of happiness was unmistakable guilt: these clothes had been liberated.

She made him tea, offered him toast – but he was saving space for the Christmas feast, and when he was seated, smiling still, at the end of the table opposite her, she decided that she had to dim this happiness, Christmas or no. 'Franklin,' she said, 'I want you to know that we are not all thieves in this country.'

At once his face became solemn, then puckered with doubt, and he began darting glances around as if at possible accusers.

'Don't say anything,' she said. 'There's no need. I'm not blaming you – do you understand? I just want you to know that we don't all steal what we want.'

'I'll take the clothes back,' he said, all joy gone.

'No, of course you won't. Do you want to go to prison? Just listen to what I've said, that's all. Don't think that everyone is like . . .' But she didn't want to name the culprits, and fell back on the joke: 'Not everyone *liberates* goodies.'

He sat looking down, biting his lip. That joyous expedition into the riches of Oxford Street, the three of them, in such companionship, where warm clothes, bright clothes, things he needed so badly, arrived in Rose's hands, in Geoffrey's, to be stowed away in a big shopping bag – he was not doing the liberating, only marvelling at their dexterity. It had been a trip into a magic land of possibilities, like going to the cinema and then, instead of watching marvels, becoming part of it. Just as yesterday Sylvia, Sophie and Lucy had become little girls, 'a giggle of girls', Colin had called them, so now Franklin became a little boy remembering how far he was from home, a stranger mocked by riches he could never have.

In came Sylvia who, having decided Evansky was not for her, wore red ribbons in her two golden plaits. She embraced Frances, embraced Franklin who was so grateful for what he was experiencing as forgiveness, that he smiled again, but sat shaking his head at himself, rueful, sending sorrowing glances at Frances; but because of Sylvia, the girl's grace, her kindness, soon things were back to normal – well, almost.

The kitchen filled with youngsters already hung-over and needing more to drink, and by the time everyone sat around the great table and the vast bird sat before them ready to carve, the company had already slipped into that state of excess that means sleep is imminent. And in fact James nodded over his plate and had to be roused. Franklin, smiling again, looked down at his heaped plate, thought of his poor village, silently said grace, and ate. And ate. The girls, and even Sylvia, did well, and the noise was incredible, for 'the kids' had returned to being adolescents, though Andrew, 'the old man', remained his age, and so did Colin, though he tried hard to get into the spirit of it all. But Colin would always be on the outside looking in, or on, no matter how much he attempted to clown, to be one of them – and he knew it.

The Christmas pudding arrived in its brandy flames into a room darkened for it, and by then it was four o'clock and Frances said that the room upstairs must be aired and clean for Julia's tea. Tea? Who could eat another mouthful? Groans as hands went out to gather in just another crumb or two of pudding, a lick of custard, a mince pie.

The girls went up to the sitting-room, and piled sleeping bags in a corner. They opened every window, because the room in fact stank. They carried down empty bottles that had spent the night under chairs or in corners, and suggested that perhaps Julia could be persuaded to have her party an hour later, let's say, at six? But that was out of the question.

And now James was sitting with his head in his hands, half asleep, and Geoffrey said that if he didn't have a nap he'd die. At this Rose and Franklin offered beds downstairs, and the company would have dispersed but there was a bang on the front door, and then the door into the kitchen opened, and there was Johnny, permitting himself a Christmas relaxation of his features, his arms full of bottles, accompanied by his new crony, a recently arrived in London working-class playwright from Hull, Derek Carey. Derek was as jovial as Father Christmas, and with good reason, for he was still intoxicated by the cornucopia that is London. Bliss had begun on his very first evening, two weeks ago. At an after-theatre party, he had watched from afar, in wonder, two gorgeous fair women, with posh accents, that at first he had thought were put on. He thought they were prostitutes. But no, they were upper-class escapes into the swampy beds and pungent groves of Swinging London. 'Oh, my God,' he stammered to one of them, 'if I could be in bed with you, if I could sleep with you I'd be as near Paradise as I ever hope to get.' He had stood sheepishly, awaiting chastisement, physical or verbal, but instead he heard, 'And so you shall, dear heart, and so you shall.' Then the other gave him a tongue kiss of the kind he would have had to work hard for, for weeks, or months, back home. Things had gone on from there, ending with the three of them in bed, and with every new place he went he expected and found fresh delights. Tonight he was drunk: he had hardly been sober for the two weeks. Now he stood by the carcass of the turkey, where Johnny was already energetically picking, and joined in. Johnny's sons sat silent, not looking at their father.

'I take it you'd like some turkey?' said Frances to the men, handing them plates. Derek at once replied, 'Oh, yes, that'd be grand,' and filled his, while Johnny stacked his, and sat down. Colin and Andrew went upstairs. They really seemed to be no point in asking, 'And Phyllida? Is she having something?'

The presence of the two men had banished enjoyment, and the young ones crept upstairs to the sitting-room where they found Julia had spread a white lace cloth, and a display of exquisite china, plates of German stollen, and English Christmas cake.

Frances was left with the two men. She sat watching them eat.

'Frances, I have to talk to you about Phyllida.'

'Don't mind me,' said the playwright. 'I won't listen. But believe you me, I'm only too familiar with marital situations. For my sins.'

Johnny had cleared his plate, and now put Christmas pudding into a bowl, doused it with cream, and stood with the bowl in his hand, in his usual place, back to the window. 'I'll come to the point.'

'Yes, do.'

'Now, now, children,' said the playwright. 'You're not married any longer. You don't have to snap and snarl.' He poured himself wine.

'Phyllida and I are washed up,' said Johnny. 'To come to the point . . .' he repeated. 'I want to marry again. Or perhaps we'll dispense with the formalities – bourgeois nonsense anyway. I've found a real comrade, she is Stella Linch, you might remember her from the past – Korean War, that time.'

'No,' said Frances. 'And so what are you going to do with Phyllida? No, don't tell me, you aren't going to suggest she comes here?'

'Yes, I am. I want her to come and live in the basement flat. There's plenty of room in this house. And it is my house, you seem to forget.'

'Not Julia's?'

'Morally, it's mine.'

'But you already have one discarded family in it.'

'Now, now,' said the playwright again. And he hiccupped. 'God bless. Sorry.'

'The answer is no, Johnny. The house is full up, and there is one thing you don't seem to get. If her mother comes here Sylvia will leave at once.'

'Tilly will do as she's told.'

'You forget Sylvia is over sixteen.'

'She is old enough to visit her mother, then. She never comes near Phyllida.'

'You know as well as I do that Phyllida'll start shouting at her. And anyway, surely you ought to be asking Julia.'

'The old bitch. She's gaga.'

'No, Johnny, she's not gaga. And you'd better be quick, because there's going to be a tea-party.'

'Tea-party?' said the comrade from Leeds. 'Oh, goody. Goody, goody gumdrops.' He sat swaying, poured out some wine into a glass already half full, and said, 'Excuse me.' He fell asleep, as he sat, his mouth falling open.

Above her, in the sitting-room, Frances could hear voices – Johnny's, his mother's. 'Stupid fool,' she heard, from Julia, and Johnny came down the stairs, several at a time, and into the kitchen. For once he was off centre, and flustered. 'I have a right to a woman who is a real comrade,' he said to Frances. 'For once in my life I am going to have a woman who is my equal.'

'That is what you said about Maureen, do you remember? Not to mention Phyllida.'

'Absurd,' said Johnny. 'I couldn't have done.'

Here the playwright came to himself, said, 'Seconds out of the ring,' – and fell asleep again.

Sophie appeared to say the party had begun.

'I shall leave you two to wrestle with the sins of the world,' said Frances, and left them.

Before joining the tea-party she went to her room, and put on a new dress, and combed her hair, which transformation enabled her to remember, looking into the mirror, that in her time she had been described as a handsome blonde. And on the stage, more than once she had been beautiful. And with Harold Holman during that weekend which now seemed such an age ago, she had certainly been beautiful.

At the beginning of December Julia had descended to Frances's rooms, and she was looking embarrassed: that was not her style at all. 'Frances, I don't want you to be offended with me . . .' She was holding out one of her thick white envelopes, that had *Frances* on it, in her beautiful handwriting. In it were banknotes. 'I could

not think of a nice way to do this . . . but it would make me so
happy . . . do go to a hairdresser, and buy yourself a good dress
for Christmas.'

Frances tended to comb her hair flat on either side of a parting,
but the hairdresser (certainly not Evansky or Vidal Sassoon, who
could only tolerate the current style) was able to make this look
the last word in chic. And she had paid more for a dress than she
had ever done in her life. No point in putting it on for Christmas
lunch, with all that cooking to do, but now she entered the
sitting-room, as self-conscious as a girl. At once there were compliments, and even, from Colin, a little bow as he rose to offer her
his chair. Clothes makyth manners. And someone else was making
a point of admiring her. Julia's distinguished Wilhelm rose, bent
over her hand – unfortunately it probably still smelled of the
kitchen – and kissed the air just above it.

Julia nodded and smiled congratulations.

'You spoil me, Julia,' said Frances, and her mother-in-law
replied, 'My dear, I wish you could know what it really means
to be loved and spoiled.'

And now Julia poured tea from a silver teapot, and Sylvia, her
handmaid, handed around slices of the stollen, and the heavy
Christmas cake. On their chairs Geoffrey and James, Colin and
Andrew fought to keep awake. Franklin was watching Sylvia trip
about as if she had appeared magically from thin air. Conversation
was being made by Wilhelm, Frances, Julia, and the three girls,
Sophie, Lucy, Sylvia.

A problem: the windows were still open, and it was after all
mid-winter. A fresh cold dark lay outside the polluted room where
Julia sat remembering, and they knew she did, how she had entertained ambassadors and politicians here. 'And even once the Prime
Minister.' And in a corner lay a tangle of sleeping bags, an overlooked empty wine bottle.

Julia wore a grey velveteen suit, with lace, and garnets in her
ears and at her throat, which flashed and reproached them. She
was telling them about Christmases long ago, when she was a girl,

in her home in Germany, a sprightly, even formal recital, as if she was reading it from a book of old tales, while Wilhelm Stein listened, nodding to confirm what she was saying.

'Yes,' he said into a silence. 'Yes, yes. Well, Julia my dear, we have to agree that times have changed.'

Downstairs could be heard Johnny's voice in energetic debate with the playwright. Geoffrey, who had nearly toppled forward, asleep, got up, and with an apology, left the room, followed by James. Frances was overwhelmed with shame, but was pleased they had gone, for at least the girls could be trusted not to nod off while sitting and holding pretty teacups as if they had never done anything else. Not Rose, of course, she was in a corner, apart.

Julia said, 'I think the windows . . .' Sylvia at once went to close them, and drew the heavy curtains, lined and interlined brocade, which had faded after sixty years to a greenish blue that made Frances's blue look crude. Rose had threatened to pull down the curtains and make herself a dress 'like Scarlet O'Hara's', and when Sylvia had said, 'But, Rose, I am sure Julia wouldn't like that,' said, 'You can't take a joke, you've got no sense of humour.' Which was certainly true.

Andrew now said that he knew they were all besotted barbarians but if she could have seen the meal they had just put away Julia would forgive them.

Her stollen, her cake, lay in untouched slices on the tiny green plates, that had pink rosebuds on them.

A burst of laughter from downstairs. Julia smiled ironically. She did smile but there were tears in her eyes. 'Oh, Julia,' crooned Sylvia, going to her, putting her arms around her, so that her cheek lay on the silvery cap of waves and little curls, 'We do love your lovely tea, we do, but if you only knew . . .'

'Yes, yes, yes,' said Julia. 'Yes, I know.' She got up. Wilhelm Stein got up and put his arm around her, patting her hand. The two distinguished people stood together in the middle of the room which made such a frame for them, and then Julia said, 'Well, my children, and now I think that is enough.'

She exited, on Wilhelm's arm.

No one moved, then Andrew and Colin stretched their arms out and yawned. Sylvia and Sophie began gathering up the tea things. Rose, Franklin and Lucy went off to join the lively group in the kitchen. Frances did not move.

Johnny and Derek were seated at either end of the table, conducting a kind of seminar. Johnny was reading passages from *A Revolution Handbook* which he had written and had published by a respectable publisher. It was making some money: as a reviewer had said, 'This has the makings of a perennial bestseller.'

Derek Carey's contribution to the welfare of nations was to exhort young people, at meeting after meeting, to fill in census forms wrongly, to destroy any official letters that came their way, to take jobs in the post offices as postmen and destroy letters, and to shoplift as much as possible. Every little bit helped to bring down the structure of an oppressive state such as Britain. In the recent election they had been advised to spoil voting forms and write insulting remarks on them, such as Fascist! Rose and Geoffrey, needing to distinguish themselves in this exhilarating company, now described their recent shopping expedition. Then Rose ran downstairs and came back with carrier bags full of stolen presents, and began handing them out: soft toys mostly, plushy tigers and pandas and bears but there was a bottle of brandy – handed to Johnny – and one of Armagnac, given to Derek. 'That's the stuff, comrade,' said Derek, with a comradely wink that reached Rose's soul, parched for compliments; it was like a medal for achievement. And Johnny gave her a clenched fist salute. No one had seen her so happy.

Franklin was distressed, because he had wanted so much to give Frances a present, and had expected that some of this 'liberated' stuff would find its way to him, but he saw now this wouldn't happen. Rose said, 'And this is for Frances.' It was a kangaroo, with a baby in its pouch. She held it up, grinning around, waiting for applause, but Geoffrey took it from her, offended at the criticism of Frances. Franklin admired the kangaroo, and thought it a wonderful compliment to Frances, a mother to them all; he had not understood Geoffrey's reaction, and now he reached out for the kangaroo. Geoffrey gave it to him. Franklin sat taking the baby from its pouch and putting it back again.

'You could introduce a few kangaroos into Zimlia,' said Johnny. He raised his glass. 'To the liberation of Zimlia.'

Franklin looked among the debris on the table for a glass, held it out to Rose to be filled, and drank 'To the liberation of Zimlia'.

This kind of joke both excited Franklin and scared him. He knew all about the terrible war in Kenya: they had 'done' it in class, and he could not see why Johnny – or for that matter the teachers at St Joseph's – were so keen on Zimlia's going through a war. But now, happy with food and drink and the kangaroo, he drank again to Derek's toast, 'To the Revolution', while wondering which Revolution and where.

Then he said, 'I'm going to give this to Frances,' and was halfway up the stairs with it when he remembered that it was stolen and that Frances had ticked him off that morning. But he didn't want to return to the kitchen with it, and that was how it found its way to Sylvia, who was carrying a big loaded tray up to Julia's.

'Oh, how lovely,' she said as Franklin tucked the kangaroo under her arm, her hands being full. But she put the tray down on the landing, and admired the kangaroo. 'Oh, Franklin, it's so nice.' And she kissed him, with the warm close hug that made him expand with happiness.

In the sitting-room were now Andrew, asleep in a chair, stretched out, his hands on his stomach, and Colin, with Sophie on the divan, arms around each other, both asleep.

Franklin stood looking at them while his heart took a dive again, and he remembered how puzzled he was by everything. He knew that Colin and Sophie had been 'friends' but were not friends now, and that Sophie had a 'friend' who had gone to his own family for Christmas. Why then were these two in each other's arms, Sophie's head on Colin's shoulder? Franklin had not slept with a girl yet. At the mission there were no girls, and the boys were watched by the Fathers who knew everything that went on. At home with his parents it was the same. Visiting his grandparents he had teased the girls and joked with them, but no more than that.

Like so many newcomers to Britain, Franklin had been confused from the start about what went on. At first he had thought there were no morals at all, but soon suspected that there must be. But what were they? At St Joseph's, girls and boys slept with each other, he knew: at least that's what it seemed like. In the meadow behind the school, couples lay together in the grass, and Franklin, solitary, listened to their laughter, and, worse, their silences. He felt that the females of this island were available to everyone, available to him, if only he could find the right words. Yet he had seen a Nigerian boy, just arrived at St Joseph's, go up to a girl and say, 'Can I come into your bed tonight if I give you a nice present?' She had slapped him so hard that he fell down. Franklin had been turning over in his mind similar words, to try his luck. Yet the same girl who had done the slapping cuddled on the bed with a boy who had a room in the same corridor, leaving the door open so everyone could see what went on. No one took any notice.

He went back down the stairs, stopping to listen at the door to the kitchen, where Johnny's lecture on guerilla tactics to destroy the military imperialistic complex was similar to Derek's: shoplifting was apparently considered a major weapon. He went down to his room, and to the drawer where his money was. It looked less: he counted it: there was less than half. He was standing there counting when he heard Rose behind him.

'Half my money's gone,' he said wildly.

'I took half. I deserve it, don't I? You got all the clothes for nothing. If you had bought clothes you couldn't have got anything as nice for that money. So you've gained, haven't you? You've got new clothes and half the money.'

He stared at her, his face puckered up with suspicion, sullen, angry. That money, to him, was more than a gift from Frances, who was a mother to him. It was like a welcome into this family, making him part of it.

Rose was cold, and full of contempt. 'You don't understand anything,' she said. 'I deserve it, don't you see?'

He gave a helpless shrug, and she stood there for a moment, staring him out and then went up the stairs.

He looked for a place to hide the money in this room that had no place where one could hide anything. At home you could slide forbidden things into thatch or bury them in the earth floor, or in the bush. At his parents' house were bricks that could be loosened and fitted back. In the end he put the money back into the drawer. He sat on the edge of his bed and cried, from homesickness, for shame because Frances was angry with him, and because he did not feel at home with those revolutionaries upstairs and yet they treated him as one of themselves. In the end he slept a little, and went up to the kitchen to find the two men gone, and everyone doing the washing-up. In this he joined, with relief, and with pleasure, one of them. It seemed there was going to be supper, though everyone joked it would be impossible to eat a thing. Rather late, about ten, the turkey carcass appeared again, and all kinds of stuffings and relishes, and there was a big tray of roast potatoes. They were all sitting around, drinking, tired, pleased with themselves and with Christmas, when there was a knock on the front door. Frances peered through the window, and saw a woman on the pavement, uncertain whether to knock again or go off. Colin came to stand by his mother. Both were afraid that it might be Phyllida.

'I'll go,' said Colin, and went out, and Frances saw him talking to the stranger, who was swaying a little. He put his hand on her shoulder to steady her, and then brought her in, with an arm right around her.

She had been wandering in the dark or half-lit streets and now stood blinking at the bright hall light. Frances appeared. The stranger said to her, 'Are you the darling of my heart?' She seemed middle-aged, but it was hard to say, because her face was grimy, so were the rather beautiful white hands that clutched at Colin. She looked like someone rescued from a fire or a catastrophe. Colin's face was wrenched with pain, the tender-hearted youth was in tears. 'Mother,' he said in appeal, and Frances went to the other side, and together she and Colin took the poor stray up the stairs and into the living-room, which was empty now, and tidy.

'What a lovely room,' said the woman, and nearly fell. Colin and Frances laid her down on the big sofa, and at once she lifted her soiled hand and kept time while she sang ... what was it? – yes, an old music-hall song, 'I dillied and I dallied, I dallied and I dillied and I ... yes, I did dilly, darlings, I did, and now I'm far from home.' She had a light clear voice, accurate, sweet. The clothes she wore were not poor, and she did not seem to be poor, though she was certainly ill. There was no smell of alcohol on her breath. Now began another song, 'Sally ... Sally ...' The sweet voice rose true to the high note and held it. 'Yes, darling, yes,' she said to Colin, 'you've a kind heart, I can see that.' Big blue eyes, innocent eyes, even babyish eyes, were turned to Colin. She was ignoring Frances. 'Kind, but be careful. Kind hearts get you into trouble, and who knows that better than Marlene?'

'What's your name, Marlene?' asked Frances, holding a grubby hand which was too cold, and lacked vitality. It lay weakly trembling, in hers.

'My name is lost, dear. It's lost and gone, but Marlene will do.' And now she spoke German, endearments, in German. Then more singing, fragments of songs. World War Two songs, with Lili Marlene again and then again, and more German. '*Ich liebe dich*,' she told them, 'Yes, I do.'

Frances said, 'I'll get Julia.' Up she went and found Julia having supper with Wilhelm, on either side of a small table set with silver and bright glass. She explained, and Julia said, meaning to be jocular, but it was a complaint, 'I see this house has acquired another waif. There are limits to hospitality, Frances. Who is this lady?'

'No lady,' said Frances. 'But a waif, certainly.'

When she got back to the sitting-room, Andrew had arrived, with a glass of water, which he held to the unknown's lips.

'I'm not much of one for the water,' she said, and lay back and sang that another little drink wouldn't do her any harm. And then, again, it was German. Julia stood listening. She gestured to Wilhelm, and the two sat in chairs, side by side, prepared to give judgement.

Wilhelm said, 'May I call you Marlene?'

'Call me what you like, dear, call me what you fancy. Sticks and stones may break my bones. They did once but it was a long time ago.' And now she wept a little, with gulping sobs, like a child's. 'It hurt,' she informed them. 'It hurt when they did that. But the Germans were gentlemen. They were nice boys.'

'Marlene, have you come from hospital?' asked Julia.

'Yes, darling. I'm an escapee from hospital, you could say that, but they'll take poor Molly back, they are good to poor Molly.' And she sang, 'There's none like pretty Sally. She is the darling of my heart . . .' And then high and sweet, 'Sally, Sally . . .'

Julia got up, signed to Wilhelm to stay where he was, and gestured Frances out to the landing. Colin came too. He said, 'I think we should take her in here. She's ill, isn't she?'

'Ill and mad,' said Julia. Then, with delicacy softening her sternness, she addressed Colin, 'Do you know what she is – what she was?'

'Not a clue,' said Colin.

'She was entertaining the Germans in Paris during the last war. She's a whore.'

Colin groaned, 'But it's not her fault.'

The Spirit of the Sixties, with passionate eyes, a trembling voice, and outstretched pleading hands, was confronting the whole past of the human race, responsible for all injustice, embodied in Julia, who said, 'Oh, you foolish boy, her fault, our fault, their fault, what does it matter? Who is going to look after her?'

Frances said, 'What's an English girl doing working as a whore in Paris under the Germans?'

And suddenly, in a tone neither of them had heard from her before, Julia said, 'Whores don't have any problems with passports, they're always welcome.'

Frances looked at Colin, Colin at Frances: what was that all about? But often with the old these moments arrive, in a change of voice, a painful grimace, a harshness – as now – which is all that is left of some hurt or disappointment . . . and then, that's that, it's over, it's gone. No one will ever know.

'I shall telephone Friern Barnet,' said Julia.

'Oh, no, no, no,' said Colin.

Julia went back into the room, interrupted *Sally*, and bent over to ask, 'Molly? You are Molly? Tell me are you from Friern Barnet?'

'Yes, I ran away for Christmas. I ran away to see my friends but where are they, I don't know. But Friern is kind and Barnet is kinder, they'll take poor Molly Marlene back.'

'Go and telephone,' said Julia to Andrew. He went out.

'I'm not going to forgive anyone,' said Colin, fierce, forlorn and rejected.

'Poor boy,' said Wilhelm.

'Sending her back to . . . to . . .'

'To a loony bin, that's what you wanted to say, darling, but it's all right, don't be sad. Don't be mad either,' and she laughed.

Andrew came back from telephoning. They all sat and waited, Colin with wet eyes, and they listened to the mad woman lying on the divan singing her *Sally*, over and over, and that high sweet clear note broke their hearts, not only Colin's.

Downstairs, the supper table was quietened by the crisis, which had been discussed, and had divided the company to the point where it had had to disperse.

The doorbell rang. Andrew went down. He returned with a tired middle-aged woman in a grey garment like an overall, and over her arm was – yes, it was a straitjacket.

'Now, Molly,' said this woman reproachfully, to the wanderer.

'What a time to do this to us. You know we are always short-staffed at Christmas.'

'Bad Molly,' said the sick woman, getting up, supported by Frances. And she actually smacked herself on the hand. 'Naughty Molly Marlene.'

The official examined her charge, and decided there was no need for force. She put her arm around Molly, or Marlene, and walked her to the door, and down the stairs, all but Julia following.

'Goodbyeeee . . . don't cryeeee . . .' She turned in the hall to face them. 'Those were good times,' she said. 'That was my happiest time. They always asked for me. They called me Marlene . . . that's my war name really. They always wanted me to sing my Sally,' and, singing her Sally she went out first, on the arm of her minder, who turned to say to them, 'It's Christmas, you see. They all of them get upset at Christmas time.'

Colin, tears streaming, said to his mother, 'How could we do that? We wouldn't throw a dog out on a night like this,' and went upstairs, Sophie, who was still in the kitchen, following him, to comfort and console. It was quite a mild night: as if that were the point.

The next afternoon Colin took the bus to the mental hospital. All he knew about it was that it served north London. Vast, a mansion, its associations making it seem like the setting for a Gothic novel, it admitted Colin into a corridor that seemed a quarter of a mile long, painted a shiny vomit green. At its end he found stairs, and on them the woman who had come to take away poor mad Molly-Marlene last night. She told him that Molly Smith was in Room 23, and that he mustn't be upset if she didn't know him. She wore a plastic overall, had towels over her arm and a strong-smelling soap in her hand. Room 23 was large, with big windows, light and airy, but it needed painting. Bits of Christmas holly were stuck on the walls, by sellotape. Men and women of various ages were sitting about on shabby chairs, some not looking at anything, some making the restless movements that were the visible expressions of dreams of being elsewhere, and a group of ten or so people sat as if at a tea-party, holding mugs of tea, passing biscuits, and conversing. One was Molly, or Marlene. Awkward and embarrassed, as helpless as a child in a room full of grown-ups, Colin said, 'Hello, do you remember me? You were in our house last night.'

'Oh, was I, dear? Oh, dear, I don't remember. Was I wandering, then? Sometimes I do go wandering and then . . . but sit down, dear. What's your name?'

Colin sat in an empty chair, near her, with the eyes of every person in the room on him: they all longed for something interesting to happen. He was trying to make conversation when the attendant, or nurse, or wardress, from last night, came in and said, 'The bathroom's free.' A middle-aged man got up and went out.

'Me next,' said Molly, smiling with a vague but eager intent at Colin, who blurted, 'How long – I mean, have you been here a long time?'

'Oh, yes, dear, a long, long time.'

The attendant, still wielding towels and soap, but standing at the door as if on guard, said to Colin, 'This is her home. It is Molly's home.'

'Well, I don't have another,' said Molly, laughing merrily. 'Sometimes I go wandering and then I come back again.'

'Yes, you do wander and you don't always come back and we have to find you,' said the attendant, smiling away.

Colin stuck it out, an hour of it, and then as he was thinking he must leave, he couldn't bear it, in came a girl as confused as he was. It seemed that her home was one of those on whose doors Molly had knocked, not last night, but on Christmas Eve.

The girl, a pretty, fresh little thing, her face showing all the dismay Colin felt, sat by Colin and told them all about her school, one of the good girls' schools, chat to which Molly and her friends listened as if to news from far Tartary. Then the attendant said it was time for Molly's bath.

Relief all round. Up got Molly, and went off to her bath, the attendant or wardress with her. 'Now, Molly, you be a good girl.'

Those that were left began squabbling about who was to go next: no one wanted to, because Molly left the bathroom a swamp.

'It's a swamp when she's done,' said an old wild woman, earnestly, to the youngsters. 'You'd think a hippopotamus had been in it.'

'What do you know about hippopotamuses?' scorned an old wild man, clearly a sparring partner. 'You're always having your say out of turn.'

'I do know all about hippos,' said the angry crone. 'I used to watch them from the verandah of our house on the banks of the Limpopo.'

'Anyone can say they had a house by the Limpopo or the blue Danube,' he said. 'When no one can prove otherwise.'

Colin and the girl, who was Mandy, left the hospital, and Colin took her home for supper, where they all wanted to know about the dreaded mental hospital and its inmates.

'They're just like us,' said Colin, and Mandy said eagerly, 'Yes, I don't see why they have to be there.'

Later Colin tackled Julia, then his mother. It is hard, very, for the older ones, world-whipped, when they have to listen while the idealistic young demand explanations for the sadness of the world. 'Why, but *why*?' Colin wanted to know, and it was not the end of it, for he did go back to the hospital, but found himself defeated since Molly had forgotten his visit to her. At last he left her his address and his telephone number, 'In case you ever want anything' – to someone who wanted everything, above all, her wits. Mandy did the same.

'That was a very foolish thing to do,' Julia said.

'That was very kind,' said Frances.

Mandy became for a time one of 'the kids' at the supper table, easy for her, since both her parents worked. She did not say they were shits but that they did their best. She was an only child. Then they whisked her off to New York. She and Colin wrote to each other for years.

And twenty years were to pass before they met.

In the Eighties, at the behest of another ideological imperative, all the mental hospitals and asylums were closed, and their inmates turned out to sink or swim. Colin got a letter in faint straggly writing: *Colin* – just that, and the address. He went down to Brighton where he found her in one of the lodging houses run by the philanthropists who were taking in former mental hospital patients and charging them every penny of their benefit, for conditions Dickens would have recognised.

She was a sick old woman, whom he did not recognise, but she seemed to know him. 'He had such a kind face,' said Molly-Marlene Smith – if Smith was indeed her name. 'Tell him, he has such a nice face, that boy. Do you know Colin?'

She was dying of the drink. Well, of what else? . . . And, visiting her again, Colin found Mandy, a smart American matron now, with a child or two and a husband or two, and they met again at the funeral and then Mandy flew back to Washington, and out of his life.

There was another event on that Christmas night.

Late, long after midnight, Franklin crept up the stairs, listening for Rose, who seemed to be asleep. The kitchen was dark. Up he went, past the sitting-room, where Geoffrey and James were in their sleeping bags. Up to the next floor where he knew Sylvia had her room. There was a light on the landing. He knocked, not louder than a hen's peck, on Sylvia's door. Not a sound. He tried again, the gentlest knock: he didn't dare knock louder. And then just above him, Andrew appeared.

'What are you doing? Are you lost? That's Sylvia's room.'

'Oh, oh, I'm so sorry. I thought . . .'

'It's late,' said Andrew. 'Go back to bed.'

Franklin went down the stairs far enough to be out of Andrew's sight, where he collapsed, bending over, head on his knees. He cried, softly though, not to be heard.

Then he felt an arm across his shoulder, and Colin said, 'Poor old Franklin. Never mind. Don't you get upset about Andrew. He's just one of the world's natural prefects.'

'I love her,' sobbed Franklin. 'I love Sylvia.'

Colin increased the pressure of his arm and let his cheek lie against Franklin's head. He rubbed it on the springy mat which seemed to send a message of health and strength, like heather. 'You don't really,' he said. 'She's still a little girl, you know – yes, she may be sixteen or seventeen or whatever she is but she's . . . not mature, you know? It's all the fault of her parents. They've screwed her up.' Here rather to his own surprise he felt laughter bubbling up: absurdity was confronting him. But he persevered: 'They're all shits,' he informed Franklin, and turned a laugh into a cough.

Franklin was more bewildered than ever. 'I think your mother is so nice. She is so kind to me.'

'Oh, yes, I suppose so. But it's no good, Sylvia, I mean. You'll have to fall in love with someone else. What about . . .' And he began on a list of girl's names from school, chanting them, like a song. 'There's Jilly and there's – Jolly. There's Milly and there's Molly. There's Elizabeth and Margaret, there's Caroline and Roberta.' He said in his usual voice, and with an ugly laugh, 'No one could say they're immature.'

But I do love her, Franklin was saying to himself. That delicate pale girl, with her golden fluffy hair, she enchanted him, to hold her in his arms would be . . . He turned his face away from Colin, and was silent. Colin felt the shoulders under his arm hot and miserable. How well he identified with that misery, how well he did know that nothing he said would make Franklin feel better. He began rocking Franklin gently. Franklin was thinking that all he wanted was to go back to Africa tonight, go for ever, it was all too much, but he knew Colin was kind. And he did like sitting here, with the kind boy's arms around him.

'Would you like to bring your sleeping bag up to my room? Better than the company of Rose, and we can sleep as long as we like.'

'Yes . . . no, no, it's all right. I'll go down now. Thanks, Colin.' But I do love her, he was repeating to himself.

'All right, then,' said Colin. He got up, went up.

And Franklin went down. He was thinking, I'm going to get it in the morning – meaning, from Andrew. But Andrew never mentioned it nor referred to it. And Sylvia never knew that Franklin had been forced by his longing to go up the stairs to knock on her door.

When Franklin reached the bottom of the stairs into the basement flat, there was Rose, her hands on her hips, her face twisted with suspicion.

'If you think you're going to sleep with Sophie, then think again. Colin's mad for her, even if Roland Shattock isn't.'

'Sophie?' stammered Franklin.

'Oh, yes, you all have the hots for Sophie.'

'It was a mistake,' said Franklin. 'A mistake, that's all.'

'Really?' said Rose. 'You could have fooled me.' And she turned her back on him and went to her bed.

She certainly wasn't in love with Franklin, or even fancied him, but she would have liked him to try. A sister, well she'd show him sister. She couldn't say no to a black boy, could she, it would hurt his feelings.

And Franklin in his bed was curled up and clenched, like a fist, weeping most bitterly.

That tumultuous year, 1968, was peaceful enough in Julia's house, which for a long time had not been crammed with 'the kids' but rather with sober adults.

Four years: it is a long time – that is, it is if you are young.

Sylvia had turned out to be almost unnaturally brilliant, crammed two years' work into one, took exams as if they were pleasurable challenges, seemed to have no friends. She had become a Roman Catholic, often saw a magnetic Jesuit priest called Father Jack, at Farm Street, and went every Sunday to Westminster Cathedral. She was on her way to becoming a doctor.

Andrew had done well, too. He was home from Cambridge often. Why didn't he have a girlfriend? worried his mother. But he said his teeth had been set on edge by all the sour grapes he had had to watch being consumed 'by you lot'.

Colin had agreed to take his final exams at school but dropped out. For weeks he stayed in bed shouting 'go away' to anyone who knocked on his door. One day he got up, as if nothing at all had happened, saying he was going to see the world. 'It's time I saw a bit of the world, Mother.' And off he went, postcards arriving from Italy, Germany, the United States, Cuba. 'You can tell Johnny from me he is barking mad. This place is a sink.' Brazil, Ecuador. He would come back between trips, was polite but uninformative.

Sophie had finished drama school and was getting small parts. She came to Frances to complain that she was cast according to her looks. Frances did not say, 'Don't worry, time will cure that.' She was living with Roland Shattock, who already had a name and had played Hamlet. She told Frances that she was not happy, and knew she should leave him.

Frances had almost gone back to the theatre. She had actually said yes to a tempting part, but then again had to refuse. Money, it was money, again. Colin's school fees were no longer an item, and Julia had said she could manage Sylvia and Andrew, but then Sylvia came to ask if Phyllida could live in the downstairs flat. This is what had happened. Johnny had telephoned Sylvia to say she must visit her mother. 'And don't say no, Tilly, it isn't good enough.'

Sylvia had found her mother waiting for her, dressed to make an impression of competence, but looking ill. There was nothing to eat in the place, not so much as a loaf of bread. Johnny had moved out to live with Stella Linch, and was not giving Phyllida money, nor paying the rent. 'Get a job,' he had said to her.

'How can I get a job, Tilly?' Phyllida had said to her daughter. 'I am not well.'

That was evident.

'Why don't you call me Sylvia?'

'Oh, I can't. I can always hear my little girl saying, "I'm Tilly." Little Tilly, that's how I remember you.'

'*You* gave me the name Sylvia.'

'Oh, Tilly, I will try.' And before the real conversation had begun, Phyllida was dabbing her eyes with tissues. 'If I could come and live in that flat then I could manage. I do sometimes get money from your father.'

'I don't want to hear about him,' said Sylvia. 'He was never a father to me. I hardly remember him.'

Her father was Comrade Alan Johnson, as famous as Comrade Johnny. He had fought in the Spanish Civil War – he really had – and was wounded. He was described by Julia who had watched his emergence into stardom as a 'roving Eminence Rouge – like Johnny'.

'Johnny thinks I get more money than I do from Alan. I haven't had a penny from him for over two years.'

'I said, I don't want to know.'

They were sitting in a room almost bare of furniture, for Johnny had taken nearly everything for his new life with Stella. There was a small table, two chairs, an old settee.

'I've had such a hard life,' Phyllida began, on such a familiar note that Sylvia actually got up – no ruse, or tactic, this: she was impelled away from her mother, by fear. She was already feeling the beginning of the inner trembling that in the past had left her helpless, limp, hysterical.

'It's not my fault,' said Sylvia.

'It's not *my* fault,' said Phyllida, in the heavy see-sawing voice of her litany of complaint. 'I've never done anything to deserve the way I've been treated. She now noticed that Sylvia stood across the room from her, as far as she could get, hand to her mouth and staring over it at her as if afraid she was going to be sick.

'I'm sorry,' she said. 'Please don't go. Sit down, Tilly – Sylvia.'

The girl returned, pulled the chair well away, sat down, and with a cold face, waited.

'If I came to live in that flat I could manage. I'd ask Julia, but I'm afraid of Frances, she'd say no. Please ask her for me.'

'Can you blame her?' snapped Sylvia. People who knew and loved the delightful creature who, as Julia said, 'lights up this old house like a little bird', would not recognise that adamant face.

'But it's not my fault . . .' Phyllida was off again, and then, seeing that Sylvia had sprung up to go, said, 'Oh, stop, stop. I'm sorry.'

'I can't stand it when you complain and accuse me,' said Sylvia. 'Don't you understand? *I can't bear it*, Mother.'

Phyllida tried to smile, and said, 'I won't do it, I promise.'

'Do you really promise? I want to finish my exams and be a doctor. If you're in the house getting at me all the time, I'll simply run away. *I can't bear it*.'

Phyllida was shocked by this vehemence. She sighed, and said, 'Oh, dear, was I really so bad?'

'Yes, you are. And even when I was tiny you were always telling me it's all your fault, without you I'd be doing this or that. Once you said you were going to make me put my head into the gas oven, with you, and die.'

'Did I? I expect I had good cause.'

'*Mother*.' Sylvia got up. 'I'm going. I'll talk to Julia and Frances. But I'm not going to look after you. Don't expect me to. You'll only get at me all the time.'

And so just as Frances had joyfully decided to give up journalism and Aunt Vera for ever, and the serious sociological articles, not to mention the odd bits of work she did with Rupert Boland, Julia said that she was going to have to give Phyllida an allowance and 'generally look after her. She's not like you, Frances. She can't look after herself. But I've told her she must be self-contained, and not bother you.'

'And, surely more important, not bother Sylvia.'

'Sylvia says she believes she can cope with it.'

'I do hope she can.'

'But if I give Phyllida an allowance . . . can you do Andrew's fees? Are you earning enough?'

'Of course I am.' And so there went the theatre again. All this had happened in the autumn of 1964, and so had this: Rose had gone. She knew she had done well in her exams: she did not need the results to tell her that. She came up at a time when Frances, Colin and Andrew were together to say, 'And now I've got super news. I'm leaving. So you'll be rid of me now. I'm off for good. I'm going to university.' And she ran off down the stairs. Suddenly she wasn't around. They waited for her to ring, write – but nothing. The flat had been left in a mess, clothes on the floor, bits of sandwich on a chair, in the bathroom tights hanging up to dry. But that was the general style of 'the kids' and need not mean anything.

Frances rang Rose's parents. No, they had heard nothing. 'She says she is going to university.' 'Did she now? Well, I expect she'll enlighten us in her own good time.'

Should the police be told? But this did not seem appropriate for Rose. Going to the police over Rose, Jill, and over Daniel who had disappeared once for weeks, had always been discussed at length and on the basis of principles suitable for the Sixties, and had been rejected. The Fuzz, the Pigs, Old Bill, the upholders of fascist tyranny (Britain) could not be approached. July . . . August . . . Geoffrey had heard through the grapevine that then united the young continent to continent that Rose was in Greece with an American revolutionary.

In August Phyllida had made her appeal, and took up residence in the downstairs flat. In September Rose had turned up, hitching over her shoulder a great black sack, which she dumped on the kitchen floor.

'I'm back,' said Rose, 'with all my worldly goods.'

'I hope you had a good time,' said Frances.

'Putrid,' said Rose. 'The Greeks are shits. Well, I'll just get fixed up downstairs.'

'You can't. Why didn't you let us know? The flat's being lived in.'

Rose subsided into a chair, for once shocked into defence-lessness. 'But . . . why? . . . I said . . . it isn't fair!'

'You told us that you were off. For good, we thought. And you didn't try to get in touch and tell us what your plans were.'

'But it's my flat.'

'Rose, I'm sorry.'

'I can doss down in the sitting-room.'

'No, Rose, you can't.'

'I've had my results. All As.'

'Congratulations.'

'I'm going to university. I'm going to the LSE.'

'But have you actually done something about being accepted?'

'Oh, shit.'

'Your parents don't know anything about it.'

'I see, there's a conspiracy against me.'

Rose sat in a heap, that pudgy little face for once showing vulnerability. She was confronting – perhaps for the first time, but certainly not the last – her real nature, which was bound to land her in this kind of – 'Shit,' she said again. 'Shit.' Then, '*I've got four As.*'

'My advice is to ask your parents if they'll pay. If so, go to your school and ask them to put in a word for you, then ask the LSE. But it's very late for this year.'

'Fuck you all,' she said.

She got up, rather the way a shot bird labours up, picked up her great black sack, dragged herself and it to the door, went out, and there was a long silence from the hall. She was recovering herself? She was having second thoughts? Then the front door slammed. She did not go to the school, nor to her parents, but was seen about in London in the clubs and at demonstrations and political meetings.

No sooner was Phyllida installed than Jill arrived. It was a weekend, and Andrew was there. Frances and he were eating supper and they invited Jill to join them.

They did not ask what she had been doing. There were scars

on both wrists now, and she was unhealthily fat. She had been a slim neat sleek blonde, but now she was too big for her clothes, and her features were lumpy. They did not ask but she told them. She had been in a psychiatric hospital, had run away, had gone back voluntarily, where she found herself helping the nurses with the other patients. She decided she was cured and they agreed. 'Do you think you could get the school to take me back? If I can just take my exams – I'm sure I could. I was even doing a bit of study in the bin.'

Again Frances said that it was a bit late for that year. 'If you could just ask them?' said Jill, and Frances did, and an exception was made for Jill, who was expected to pass her A-levels, if she worked.

And where was she to live? They asked Phyllida if Jill could have the room that Franklin had used, and Phyllida said, 'Beggars can't be choosers.'

No sooner was Jill in than Phyllida began on her accusations, using her as a target. From the kitchen above they could hear the heavy complaining swing of Phyllida's voice, and on and on, and after only a day Jill had appealed to Sylvia, and the two girls had gone together to Frances and Andrew.

'No one could stand it,' said Sylvia. 'Don't blame her.'

'I'm not,' said Frances. 'We're not,' said Andrew.

'I could camp in the sitting-room,' said Jill.

'You could use our bathroom,' said Andrew.

What had been impossible for Rose, was accepted for Jill, who would not fill the centre of the house with thunderclouds of rage and suspicion. And Julia said, 'I knew it. I always knew it. And now at last this beautiful house is a doss-house. I'm surprised it didn't happen before.'

'We hardly ever use the sitting-room,' said Andrew.

'That isn't the point, Andrew.'

'I know it isn't, Grandmother.'

And so that had been the situation, from the autumn of 1964, Andrew coming and going from Cambridge, Jill, studying hard, being responsible and good, Sylvia working so hard Julia wept and said the girl would be ill, Colin sometimes at home and sometimes not. Frances was working from home, and more and more on attractive enterprises with Rupert Boland, and often from the Cosmo. Phyllida was downstairs, behaving well, not tormenting Sylvia, who kept well away from her.

In 1965 Jill made friends with her parents and went to the LSE 'to be with all my mates'. She said she would never forget the kindness that had rescued her. 'You rescued me,' she said earnestly. 'I'd have been done for, without you.' Thereafter they heard about her from other people: she was in the thick of all the new wave of politics and saw a lot of Johnny and his comrades.

And so now it was the summer of 1968, and four years had passed.

It was a weekend. Neither Andrew nor Sylvia had gone off for a holiday, they were studying. Colin had come home and said he was going to write a novel. Julia had said, not in his hearing, though it had been reported to him: 'Of course! The occupation for failures!' – so that first requisite for beginning novelists, discouragement from their nearest and dearest, had been provided, though Frances was careful to be non-committal, and Andrew whimsical.

Johnny telephoned to say he was going to drop in. 'No, don't bother to cook, we will have eaten.' This astounding bit of cheek was, Frances decided – while her blood pressure shot up, and subsided – probably merely Johnny's idea of being ingratiating. Intriguing, that 'they'. He could not mean Stella, who was in the States. She had gone off to join in the great battles that would end the worst of discrimination against black people in the South, and had become known for her bravery and her organisational skills. Threatened with the end of her visitor's visa, she had married an American, ringing up Johnny to say it was only for form's sake, he must understand it was her revolutionary duty. She would be back when the battle had been won. Meanwhile, rumours flowing from across the Atlantic said that this marriage for form's sake was going along well, better than her sojourn with Johnny, which had been a bit of a disaster. She was much younger than Johnny, at first had been in awe of him, but had soon learned to see with her own eyes. She had had plenty of time for reflection, because she had found herself alone while he went to meetings and off on delegations to comradely countries.

Johnny would have liked to join the big American battles, he yearned after them like a child not invited to a party, but he could not get a visa. He allowed it to be understood that was because of his Spanish Civil War record. But soon there was France, and he was on each battlefront as it came into the news. But the events of '68 were in fact chastening for him. Everywhere were new young heroes, and their bibles were new ones too. Johnny had had to do a lot of reading.

He was not the only Old Guard who found himself returning to refresh himself at the pages of the *Communist Manifesto*. 'Now *that's* revolutionary writing,' he might murmur.

In France every hero had a group of girls who served him, they were all sleeping together, because of the new plank in the revolutionary platform – sexual freedom. There were no girls courting Johnny. He was seen not only as English, but as elderly. Nineteen sixty-eight, which would be remembered by hundreds of thousands of politicos who had taken part in the street fighting, the confrontations with the police, the stone-throwing, the running battles, the building of barricades, the sexual free-for-all, as the glittering peak of their youthful achievements, was not a year that Johnny was going to enjoy thinking about.

Seeing that Stella had no intention of coming back to him, he had returned to the flat vacated by Phyllida, which became a kind of commune, home for revolutionaries from everywhere, some dodging the Vietnam War, many from South America, and he usually had African politicians staying with him.

When Johnny arrived, the kitchen at once seemed over-full, and the three sitting at the table eating their supper felt themselves as dull and lacking in colour, for the newcomers were elated and full of vigour, having just come from a meeting. Comrade Mo and Johnny were enjoying a joke, and now Comrade Mo said to Frances, embracing her, 'Danny Cohn-Bendit has said that we won't have socialism until the last capitalist has been hanged with the guts of the last bureaucrat.'

Franklin – she had not immediately recognised this large young man in a good suit – said to the black man with him, 'This is Frances, I told you about her, she was a mother to me. This is Comrade Matthew, Frances. He is our leader.'

'I am honoured to meet you,' said Comrade Matthew, unsmiling, formal, in the older style of the comrades, when Lenin-like severity had been the mode. (And would be again, quite soon.) It was easy to see he was ill at ease, and didn't like being here. He stood unsmiling, and even glanced at his watch, while Franklin was being greeted by 'the kids', now grown up. He stood in front of Sylvia, who had risen, hesitating, then she opened her arms for a hug, and he closed his eyes in the embrace, and when he opened them they were full of tears.

'Sit down,' said Andrew, and pulled up chairs from where they were stacked around the wall. Comrade Matthew sat down, frowning: he looked at his watch again.

Comrade Mo, who since he had been here last had gone to China to bless the Cultural Revolution (as he had the Great Leap Forward and Let Every Flower Bloom), was now lecturing at universities around the world on its benefits for China and all humanity. Now he sat down, and reached for some bread.

Franklin said to Frances, 'Comrade Matthew is my cousin.'

'We are of the same tribe,' said the older man, correcting him.

'Ah, but you must understand, tribe sounds backward,' said Franklin. He was evidently a little frightened of confronting the leader.

'I am aware that cousin is the English term.'

They were all seated now except Johnny, who said to his sons,

'Did you hear, Danny Cohn-Bendit has just said that . . .' This threatened to send Comrade Mo off again into his fits of Ho, ho, ho, and Frances said, 'We heard the first time. Poor boy, he had a terrible childhood. German father . . . French mother . . . no money . . . he was a war baby . . . she had to bring up the children alone.' Yes, she was definitely doing it on purpose, while she smiled amiably, and first Andrew, then Colin, laughed, and Johnny said, annoyed, 'I am afraid my wife has never had even the beginnings of an understanding of politics.'

'Your ex-wife,' said Frances. 'Many times removed.'

'These are my sons,' said Johnny, and Andrew picked up his wine glass and emptied it, while Colin said, 'We have that privilege.'

The three black men seemed discommoded, but then Comrade Mo, who had been at large in the wide world for a decade or so, laughed heartily and said, 'My wife blames me too. She does not understand that the Struggle must come before family obligations.'

'Does she ever see you, I wonder?' enquired Frances.

'And is she pleased when she does?' enquired Colin.

Comrade Mo looked hard at Colin but saw only a smiling face. 'It is my children,' he said, shaking his head. 'That is so hard for me – When I see them sometimes I hardly recognise them.'

Meanwhile Sylvia was making coffee and placing cake and biscuits on the table. It was clear that the guests had expected more. As she had done so often, Frances fetched out everything there was in the fridge, and the remains of their own meal, and put it all on the table.

'Oh, do sit down,' she said to Johnny. He sat, with dignity, and began serving himself.

'You haven't asked after Phyllida,' said Sylvia. 'You didn't ask how my mother is.'

'Yes,' said Frances, 'I was wondering about that too.'

'I'm coming to that in a minute,' said Johnny.

Franklin said, 'When Johnny said he was coming to see you tonight, I had to see you all again. I'll never forget your kindness to me.'

'Have you been back home?' Frances asked. 'You didn't go to university after all.'

'The university of life,' said Franklin.

Johnny said, 'Frances, you do not ask the black leadership what they are doing, not now. Even you must see that.'

'No,' said Comrade Matthew. 'This is not the time to ask that.' Then he said, 'We must not forget that I am to address a meeting in an hour.'

Comrades Johnny and Franklin and Mo began pushing in their food, as fast as they could, but Comrade Matthew had finished: he was a frugal eater, one of those who eat because one must.

Johnny said, 'Before we go, I have a message from Geoffrey. He has been on the barricades with me in Paris. He sends greetings.'

'Good God,' said Colin, 'our little Geoffrey with his nice clean face, on the barricades.'

'He is a very serious, very worthwhile comrade,' said Johnny. 'He has a corner in my place.'

'You sound like an old Russian novel,' said Andrew. 'A corner, what's that translated into English?'

'He and Daniel. They often doss down for a night or two with me. I keep a couple of sleeping bags for them. And now, before we go, I have to ask if you know what Phyllida is up to?'

'And what is she up to?' asked Sylvia, with such dislike of him that they all saw that other Sylvia. A shock. They were shocked. Franklin laughed, with nervousness. Johnny made himself confront her, and said, 'Your mother is doing fortune telling. She's advertising on the newsagents' boards as a fortune teller, from this address.'

Andrew laughed. Colin laughed. Then, Frances.

'What's funny?' enquired Sylvia.

Comrade Mo, finding this *culture clash* getting out of hand, said, 'I'll nip in one of these days and she can tell my fortune.'

Franklin said, 'If she has the gift, then the ancestors must like her. My grandmother was a wise woman. You people say witch doctor. She was an *n'ganga*.'

'A shaman,' Johnny instructed them all.

Comrade Matthew said, 'I agree with Comrade Johnny. This kind of superstition is reactionary and must be forbidden.' He got up to leave.

'If she's earning a bit of money, then you should expect me to be pleased,' said Frances to Johnny, who also got up.

'Come on, comrades,' said Johnny, 'it is time we set off.'

Before he left he hesitated, then said, to regain command of the situation, 'Tell Julia to tell Phyllida she can't do this kind of thing.'

But Frances found she was feeling sorry for Johnny. He was looking so much older – well, they were both nearly fifty. The Mao jacket seemed loose on him. By his dejected air she knew things were not going well for him in Paris. He's past it, she thought. And so am I.

She was wrong about both of them.

Just ahead lay the Seventies, which from one end of the world to the other (the non-communist world) bred a race of Che Guavara clones, and the universities, particularly the London ones, were an almost continuous celebration of Revolution, with demonstrations, riots, sit-ins, lock-outs, battles of all kinds. Everywhere you looked were these young heroes, and Johnny had become a grand old man, and the fact that he was an almost entirely unrepentant Stalinist had a certain limited chic among these youngsters who mostly believed that if Trotsky had won the battle for power with Stalin then communism would have worn a beatific face. And he had another disability, which meant that his entourage was usually young men, and not eager girls. His style was all wrong. The right one was when Comrade Tommy or Billy or Jimmy summoned some girl with a contemptuous flick of the

fingers, and said to her, 'You are bourgeois scum.' And, by implication, *leave all you have and come with me.* (Rather, *give* all you
have to me.) And this goes on to this day. Irresistible. And
there was worse. If cleanliness had once been next to Godliness,
then dirt and smelliness was now as good as a Party card.
Smelly embraces: these Johnny could not provide, having been
brought up by Julia or, rather, her servants. The vocabulary – yes,
he could swing along with that. Shit and fuck, sell-out and fascist,
a good part of any political speech had to be composed of such
words.

But these fumy delights were still ahead.

Wilhelm Stein who so often ascended the stairs on his way to
Julia, nodding gravely at whomever he encountered, this evening
knocked on the kitchen door, waited till he heard, 'Come in',
and entered, with a little bow. Silvery white hair and beard, his
silver-topped cane, his suit, the very set of his spectacles, rebuked
the kitchen and the three sitting at the table, having supper.

Invited to sit, by Frances, by Andrew, by Colin, he did so,
holding the cane upright beside him, in the grip of a wonderfully-
kept right hand, that had a ring with a dark blue stone.

'I am taking the liberty of coming to talk to you about Julia,'
he said, looking at them one after the other, to impress them with
his seriousness. They waited. 'Your grandmother is not well,' he
said to the young men, and to Frances, 'I am well aware that it
is difficult to persuade Julia to do things she ought, for her own
good.'

The three pairs of eyes now gazing at him told him that he
had misjudged them. He sighed, almost got up, changed his mind,
and coughed. 'It is not that I think you have been neglectful of
Julia.'

Colin took it up. He was now a large young man, his round
face still boyish, and his heavy black-rimmed spectacles seemed

to be trying to keep those features that threatened, far too often, sardonic laughter, in order.

'I know she is not happy,' said Colin. 'We know that.'

'I think she may be ill.'

The trouble was that Julia had lost Sylvia. Yes, the girl was still in the house, this was her home, but events had forced Julia to conclude that this time it was for good. Surely Wilhelm could see this?

Andrew said, 'Julia is breaking her heart over Sylvia. It is as simple as that.'

'I am not such a stupid old man that I am unaware of Julia's feelings. But simple it is not.'

Now he was getting up, disappointed in them.

'What do you want us to do?' asked Frances.

'Julia should be less alone. She should be walking more. She goes out very little now and I must insist that it is not her age. I am ten years older than Julia and I have not given up. I am afraid that Julia has done that.'

Frances was thinking that in all those years Julia had never said Yes, when asked to go out to supper, or walking, or to a play, or to a picture gallery. 'Thank you, Frances, You are very kind,' she always said.

'I am going to ask your permission to give Julia a dog. No, no, not some great big growler, a little dog. She will have to take it for walks and care for it.'

Once again the three faces told him that he was not going to be informed what they were really thinking.

Did the old man really imagine that a little dog was going to fill the empty place in Julia? A swap: a little dog, for Sylvia!

'Of course you must give her a dog,' said Frances, 'if you think she would like that.'

And now Wilhelm, who had just confessed what they would not have guessed, that he was in his eighties, said, 'It is not a question of what I think would be good for her. I must tell you . . . I am at my wit's end.' And now the gravity, the high seriousness of his manner, his style, broke down, and before them they saw a humbled old man, with tears running into his beard. 'It will be no secret to you that I am very fond of Julia. It is hard to see her so . . . so . . .' And he went out. 'Excuse me, you must excuse me.'

Frances said, 'And who is going to say first, I'm not going to look after that dog?'

Wilhelm arrived with a tiny terrier that he had already named Stuckschel – a scrap, a little thing – and as a joke had put a blue ribbon around its neck. Julia's immediate reaction was to back away from it, as it yapped around her skirts, and then, seeing her old friend's anxiety that she like it, made herself pat the dog and try to calm it. She put on a good enough act to make Wilhelm think that she might learn to like the creature, but when he went, and she had to see to the dog's food, its toilet arrangements, she sat trembling on her chair and thought: He's my best friend and he knows so little about me he thinks I want a dog.

There followed unpleasant days: food for the dog, messes on her floors, smells and the restless little creature who yapped and drove Julia to tears. *How could he?* she muttered, and when Wilhelm arrived to see how things went, her efforts to be nice told him what a bad mistake he had made.

'But, my dear, it would be good for you to take him for a walk. What have you called him? Fuss! I see.' And he went off, wounded, so now she had to worry about him too.

Fuss, who knew this mistress hated him, found his way to Colin, who liked the creature because it made him laugh. Fuss became Vicious, because of the absurdity of this minute thing growling and defending itself, and snapping with its jaws the size of Julia's sugar tongs. Its paws were like puffs of cotton wool, its eyes like little black pawpaw seeds, its tail a twist of silvery silk. Vicious now went everywhere with Colin, and so the dog that had been meant to be good for Julia became good for Colin, who had no friends, went for solitary walks around the Heath, and was drinking too much. Nothing serious but enough for Frances to tell him she was worried. He flared up with, 'I don't like being spied on.' The real trouble was that he hated being dependent on Julia and his mother. He had written two novels, which he knew were no good, and was at work on a third, with Wilhelm Stein as a mentor. He was pleased that Andrew had returned to the condition of being dependent. Having done well in his exams, Andrew had left home to set himself up with a group of lawyers, but decided he wanted to do international law. He came home, and was going to Oxford, Brasenose, for a two-year course.

Sylvia had become a junior doctor, much younger than most, and was working as hard as they do. When she did come home she walked in a trance of exhaustion up the stairs, not seeing anyone, or anything; she was already in her mind in her bed, able to sleep at last. She might sleep the clock around, then take a bath and was off. Often she did not even say hello to Julia, let alone kiss her goodnight.

But there was something else. Sylvia's father, her real one, Comrade Alan Johnson, had died and left her money, quite a bit. The letter from the lawyer came accompanied by a letter from him, obviously written when drunk, saying he had understood that she, Tilly, was the only real thing in his life. 'You are my legacy to the world,' apparently considering the substantial legacy a mere derisory material contribution. She did not remember ever having seen him.

Sylvia dropped in to see Julia, to tell her the news and to say, 'You've been so good to me, but I won't need any more hand-outs.' Julia had sat silent, twisting her hands about in her lap, as if Sylvia had hit her. The gracelessness was because of exhaustion. Sylvia was simply not herself. She was not built for continuous over-strain and stress, was still a wisp of a girl, her big blue eyes always a little red. She had a bit of a cough, too.

Wilhelm met Sylvia as she came up the stairs after a week of work and almost no sleep, and asked her advice about Julia as a doctor, but Sylvia replied, 'Sorry, haven't done geriatrics' – and pushed past him to get to her bed, where she fell and was asleep.

Julia had overheard. She was listening from the upstairs landing. Geriatrics. She brooded, suffered; everything was an affront to her in her paranoid state – for it was that. She felt Sylvia had turned against her.

Sylvia had read the lawyer's letter when she was hungering for sleep like a prisoner under torture, or a young mother with a new baby. She went down to Phyllida with the letter in her hand, and found her looming about her flat in a kimono covered with astral signs. She cut into Phyllida's sarcastic, 'And to what do I owe the honour . . .' with, 'Mother, has he left you money?'

'Who? What are you talking about?'

'My father. He's left me money.'

At once Phyllida's face seemed to burst into anger, and Sylvia said, 'Just listen, that's all I ask, just listen.'

But Phyllida was off, her voice in the swell and fall of her lament, 'And so I count for nothing, of course I don't count, he's left you the money . . .' But Sylvia had flung herself into a chair and was asleep. There she lay, limp, quite gone away from the world.

Phyllida was suspicious that this was a trick or a trap. She peered down at her daughter, even lifted a flaccid hand and let it drop. She sat down, heavily, amazed, shocked – and silenced. She did know Sylvia worked hard, everyone knew about the young doctors . . . but that she could go off to sleep, just like that . . . Phyllida picked up the letter which had fallen on the floor, read it, and sat with it in her hand. She had not had the opportunity to sit and look at her daughter, really look, for years. Now she did look. Tilly was so thin and pale and washed out – it was a crime, what they expected of young doctors, someone should pay for it . . .

These thoughts ran out into silence. The heavy curtains were drawn, the whole house was quiet. Perhaps Tilly should be woken? She would be late for work. That face – it was not at all like hers. Tilly's mouth, it was her father's, pink and delicate. Pink and delicate would do to describe him, Comrade Alan, a hero, well let them think it. She had married two communist heroes, first one, and then the other. What was the matter with her, then? (This until now uncharacteristic self-criticism was soon to take her into the Via Dolorosa of psychotherapy and from there into a new life.)

When Tilly came down to tell her of the legacy, was that boasting? A taunt? But Phyllida's sense of justice told her it was not so. Sylvia was full of airs and graces and she hated her mother, but Phyllida had never known her spiteful.

Sylvia woke with a start and thought she was in a nightmare. Her mother's face, coarse, red, with wild accusing eyes, was just above her, and in a moment that voice would start, as it always did, talking at her, shouting at her. You have ruined my life. If I hadn't had you my life would have been . . . You are my curse, my millstone . . .

Sylvia cried out and pushed her mother away, and sat up. She saw her letter in Phyllida's hand, and snatched it. She stood up and said, 'Now listen, mother, but don't say anything, don't say anything, *please*, it's unfair he gave me all the money, I'll give you half. I'll tell the lawyer.' And she ran out of the room, with her hands over her ears.

Sylvia informed the lawyers, having consulted with Andrew, and the arrangements were made. Giving Phyllida half meant that a substantial legacy became a useful sum, enough to buy a good house, insurance – security. Andrew told her to get financial advice.

Suddenly there was only one set of fees to pay – Andrew's. Frances decided that the next time she was offered a good part she would take it.

Once again Wilhelm knocked on the kitchen door, but this time Doctor Stein was all smiles, and as bashful as a boy. Again it was Sunday evening, and Frances and the two young men were making a family scene at the supper table.

'I have news,' said Wilhelm to Frances. 'Colin and I have news.' He produced a letter and waved it about. 'Colin, you should read it aloud . . . no? Then I shall.'

And he read out a letter from a good publisher, saying that Colin's novel, *The Stepson*, would be published soon, and that great things were hoped for it.

Kisses, embraces, congratulations, and Colin was inarticulate with pleasure. In fact, the letter had been expected. Wilhelm had read and condemned Colin's two earlier attempts, but this one had been approved by him, and he had found the publisher – a friend. And Colin's long apprenticeship to his own patience and stubbornness was over. While the humans kissed and exclaimed and hugged, the scrap of a dog bounced and barked, its tiny yaps ecstatic with the need to join in, and then it leaped on to Colin's shoulder and stood there, its feather of a tail going like a windscreen-wiper all over Colin's face, and threatening his spectacles.

'Vicious, down,' chided Colin, and the absurdity choked him with tears and laughter and he jumped up, shouting, 'Vicious, Vicious . . .' and rushed up the stairs with the little dog in his arms.

'Wonderful,' said Wilhelm Stein, 'wonderful,' and having kissed the air above Frances's hand, departed, smiling, up to Julia, who, when she had been told the news by her friend, sat silent for some time, then said, 'And so I was wrong. I was very wrong.' And Wilhelm, knowing how Julia hated being in the wrong, turned away, so as not to see the tears of self-criticism in her eyes. He poured two glasses of madeira, taking his time over it, and said, 'He has a considerable talent, Julia. But more important, he knows how to stick at it.'

'Then I shall apologise to him, for I have not been kind.'

'And perhaps tomorrow you will come with me to the Cosmo? A little walk, Julia, that won't do you any harm.'

And so Julia apologised to Colin, who, because of her evident emotional disarray, took time and trouble to reassure her. Then, her arm in Wilhelm's, Julia descended the hill gently to the Cosmo, where he courted her with cakes and compliments, and all around them the flames of political debate leaped or smouldered.

Frances read *The Stepson*, and gave it to Andrew, who remarked, 'Interesting. Very interesting.'

Years before Frances had had to sit and hear Colin's criticism of her, and his father, angry and merciless, so that she felt she was being shrivelled up by rivers of lava. Here was all that anger distilled. It was the tale of a small boy whose mother had married a mountebank, a scoundrel with a magic tongue, who concealed his crimes behind screens of persuasive words that promised all kinds of paradises. He was unkind to the little boy, or ignored him. Whenever the child thought this tormentor had disappeared, he turned up again, and his mother succumbed to his charms. For charming he was, in a sinister way. The tale was told by the child to an imaginary friend, the lonely child's traditional companion, and it was sad and funny, because the distorted vision of a child could be interpreted by the adult reader as something exaggerated, distorted: the almost nightmare scenes like candle-shadows on a wall were in fact commonplace, and even tawdry. A publisher's reader had described the book as a little masterpiece, and perhaps it was. But the mother and older brother were seeing something else, how frightful unhappiness had been distanced by the magic of the tale: Colin showed himself in this book to be grown-up, and Andrew said, 'Do you know, I think my little brother has outreached me: I don't think I could achieve anything like this degree of detachment.'

'Was it so bad?' Frances asked, afraid of his answer which was, 'Yes, it was, I don't think you realise ... I don't see how he could have been a worse father, do you?'

'He didn't beat you,' said Frances feebly, trawling for something to make the history better.

Andrew said that there are worse things than beating.

But when it was decided to have a little dinner to celebrate *The Stepson*, Colin himself added his father's name to the list.

So the big table would again have 'everyone' around it. 'I've asked everyone,' said Colin. Sophie was the first to be asked and to accept. Geoffrey and Daniel and James, all habitués of Johnny's place, said they would come but would be late – a meeting. Johnny said the same. Jill, met by Colin in the street, said she would come. Julia said that no one wanted a boring old woman, and Wilhelm told her, 'My dear one, you are talking foolishly.' Sylvia said she would try to come, if her hours permitted.

The table was laid for eleven. Wilhelm had donated a wondrous and most un-English cake, in shape a plump blunt spiral, with a surface like crisp glistening tulle – cream and meringue, in fact. It was sprinkled with tiny gold flakes. Sophie said it should be worn, not eaten.

They sat down to eat with half the places unoccupied, and then Sophie rushed in, with Roland. The handsome young actor, extending potent charm to each one of them, said, 'No, no I'm not going to sit down, I've just come to congratulate you, Colin. As you know, I am an inveterate social climber, and if you are going to be an important writer, then I have to be in on the act.' He kissed Frances, then Andrew – who looked humorous, shook Colin's hand, bowed over Julia's, and directed a sweeping bow at Wilhelm. 'See you later, my darling,' he said to Sophie, and then, 'I have to be on stage in twenty minutes.' And they sat listening to the car go roaring away.

Sophie and Colin, seated next to each other, were kissing, embracing, rubbing their cheeks together. Everyone permitted themselves thoughts of how Sophie would at last leave Roland, who made her so unhappy and that Colin and she might . . .

Toasts were drunk. The food was served. The meal was halfway through when Sylvia came in. She was as always these days, only half herself: she was ready to drop and they knew she soon would. She had brought with her a young colleague whom she described as a fellow victim of the system. Both sat down, accepted glasses of wine, allowed food to be put on their plates, but they were drifting off to sleep as they sat. Frances said, 'You'd better be off to bed,' and they rose like ghosts and stumbled out and up.

'A very strange system,' came Julia's harsh voice, which these days sounded threatening, and sorrowful. 'How is it they can treat these young people so badly?'

Jill arrived late, and apologetic. She was now a large young woman with her hair in a wide frizz of yellow, and clothes designed to make her look public and competent – understood when she said she was going to stand as councillor in the next municipal election. She was effusive, kept saying how wonderful it was to be here again: she lived a quarter of a mile away. She volunteered, when no one asked, that Rose was a freelance journalist and 'politically very active'.

Julia enquired, 'And may I ask what cause is claiming her attention?'

Not understanding the question, since of course there was only one possible cause, Revolution, Jill said that Rose was involved 'with everything'.

Towards the end of a cheerful meal, Johnny came in. These days he was even more military, stern, unsmiling. He was wearing a war surplus camouflage jacket, and under it a tight black polo-neck and black jeans. His grey hair was half-inch stubble. He shot out his hand to Colin, nodded, said, 'Congratulations', and to his mother, 'Mutti, I hope you are well.' 'Well enough,' said Julia. To Wilhelm, 'Ah, so you are here too. Excellent.' He nodded at Frances. To Andrew he said, 'I am glad you are doing international law. That ought to come in useful.' He remembered Sophie, for he did give her a little bow, and Jill, whom he knew well, got a comradely salute.

He sat down and Frances filled his plate. Wilhelm poured wine for him, and Comrade Johnny lifted his glass to the workers of the world, and then continued with a speech he had just been making to the meeting he had left. First, though, apologies from Geoffrey, James and Daniel, who were sure that everyone would understand the Struggle must come first. American imperialism . . . the military–industrial machine . . . Britain's role as lackey . . . the Vietnam War . . .

But Julia was miserable about the Vietnam War, and stopped him by asking, 'Johnny, could you please give more details . . . I would really like to know about it. I simply do not understand why it is, this war.'

'Why? Surely you don't have to ask, Mutti. Because of profit of course.' And he went on with his speech, interrupting it to push in mouthfuls of food.

Colin stopped him with, 'Just a minute. Just stop for one minute. Did you read my book? You haven't said.'

Johnny laid down his knife and fork and looked severely at his son. 'Yes, I have read it.'

'Then, what do you think of it?'

This folly caused Frances, Andrew in particular, Julia too, incredulity, as if Colin had decided to poke an up-till-now unprovoked lion with a stick. And what they feared happened. Johnny said, 'Colin, if you are genuinely interested in my opinion, then I shall give it. But I must return to principles. I am not interested in the by-products of a rotten system. That is what your book is. It is subjective, it is personal, there is no attempt to set events in a political perspective. All this class of writing, so-called literature, is the detritus of capitalism, and writers like you are bourgeois lackeys.'

'Oh, do shut up,' said Frances. 'Just behave like a human being for once.'

'Really? How you do give yourself away, Frances. A human being. And what do you think I and all the other comrades are working for, if not humanity?'

'Father,' said Colin, who was already white, and suffering, 'I'd like to know, leaving all the propaganda aside, what did you think of the book?'

The father and son were leaning towards each other across the table. Colin was like someone threatened with a beating, his father was triumphant and in the right. Had he recognised himself in the book? Probably not.

'I told you. I read the book. I am telling you what I think. If there is one class of person I despise, it is a liberal. And that is what you are, all of you. You are the hacks spawned by the decaying capitalist system.'

Colin got up and walked out of the kitchen. They heard him go blundering up the stairs.

Julia said, 'And now Johnny, leave. Just go.'

Johnny sat, apparently in thought: it might be occurring to him that he could have behaved differently? He quickly shovelled in what remained on his plate, tipped what was in his wine glass down his throat, and said, 'Very well, Mutti. You are throwing me out of my house.' He got up, and in a moment they heard the front door slam.

Sophie was in tears. She went out to follow Colin, saying, 'Oh, that was so *awful*.'

Jill said into the silence, 'But he's such a great man, he's so wonderful . . .' She looked around, saw nothing but distress and anger, and said, 'I should go, I think.' No one stopped her. She went saying, 'Thank you so much for asking me.'

Frances showed signs of cutting the cake, but Julia was rising, aided by Wilhelm. 'I am so ashamed,' she said. 'I am so ashamed.' And, weeping, she went up the stairs, with Wilhelm.

There remained Andrew and his mother.

Frances suddenly began beating her fists on the table, her face raised, eyes streaming. 'I'll kill him,' she said. 'One of these days I'll kill him. How could he do that? I cannot understand how he could do it.'

Andrew said, 'Mother, just listen . . .'

But Frances was going on, and now she was actually tugging at her hair, as if wanting to pull it out. 'I will kill him. How could he hurt Colin like that? Colin would've been happy with just one little kind word.'

'Mother, do listen to me. Just stop. Listen.'

Frances let her hands drop, rested her fists on the table, sat waiting.

'Do you know what you've never understood? I don't know why you haven't. Johnny is stupid. He is a stupid man. How is it you've never seen it?'

Frances said, 'Stupid.' She felt as if weights and balances were shifting in her mind. Well, of course he was stupid. But she had never admitted it. And that was because of the great dream. After all she had taken from him, all the shit, she had never been able to say to herself, simply, that Johnny was stupid.

She persisted, 'It's the unkindness. That was such a brutal thing . . .'

'But, Mother, what are they if not brutal? Why do they admire all that, if they aren't brutal people?'

And then, a surprise to herself, Frances laid her head down on her arms, on the table, among all the dishes. She sobbed. Andrew waited, noting the freshets of tears that renewed themselves every time he thought she had recovered. He was white too now, shaken. He had never seen his mother cry, never heard her criticise his father in this way. He had understood that not attacking Johnny had been to shield him and Colin from the worst of it, but he had not really understood what an ocean of angry tears had remained unshed. At least, not shed where he or Colin could know about them. And she had done well, he was now thinking, not to weep and rage in front of them. He was feeling sick. After all, Johnny was his father . . . and Andrew knew that in some ways he resembled his father. Johnny was never to achieve even a grain of the self-understanding his son had. Andrew was doomed to live always with a critical eye focused on himself: a debonair, even humorous regard – but a judgement nevertheless.

Andrew sat on, turning his wine glass between his fingers, while his mother wept. Then he swallowed his wine, and stood up and put his hand on his mother's shoulder.

'Mother, leave all this stuff. We'll deal with it in the morning. And go to bed. It's no good, you know. He'll always be like this.'

And he went out. He knocked on his grandmother's door, and Wilhelm opened it and said in a loud voice, 'Julia's taken a valium. She's very upset.'

He hesitated outside Colin's door, heard Sophie singing: she was singing to Colin.

Then he glanced in at Sylvia. She had fallen asleep in her bed, dressed, and the young man was on the floor, his head on a cushion. It didn't look comfortable, but he was clearly beyond that.

Andrew went to his room, and lit a joint: he used pot for emotional emergencies, and listened to traditional jazz, mostly the blues. Classical music was for good moods. Or he recited to himself all the poems he knew – a good many – to make sure they remained there, intact. Or he read Montaigne, but about this he was secretive, for he felt this to be an old man's solace, not a young one's.

Julia had been left by Wilhelm tucked up in her big chair, with a rug, insisting she was not sleepy. But she did doze a little, then woke, the valium outwitted by anxiety. She shook off the rug irritably, listening to the dog, which she could hear making a nuisance of itself just below her. She also heard Sophie singing, but thought it was the radio. There was a light under Andrew's door. She crept down the stairs, hesitating whether to go in to him, but instead descended another flight, and was on the landing outside Sylvia's room. A crack of light showed that Frances was still awake. The old woman felt she ought to go in to Frances and say something, find the right words, sit with her, do something . . . *what* words?

Julia gently turned the handle of Sylvia's door and stepped in to a room where moonlight lay across Sylvia and just reached the young man on the floor. She had forgotten him, and now her heart reminded her of her terrible, inadmissible unhappiness. Wilhelm had told her, not so long ago, that Sylvia would marry, and that she, Julia, mustn't mind it. So that's all he thinks of me, Julia had complained – to herself, but knew he was right. Sylvia must marry, though probably not this man. Otherwise wouldn't he be beside her on the bed? It seemed to Julia terrible that any young man, 'a colleague', should come home with Sylvia and sleep in her room. They are like puppies in a basket, Julia thought, they lick each other and fall off to sleep just anyhow. It should matter that a man was in a young woman's room. It should mean something. Julia sat herself carefully in the chair where − but that seemed an age ago − she had coaxed little Sylvia to eat. Now she could see Sylvia's face clearly, and as the moonlight moved over the floor, the young man's. Well, if it wasn't going to be him, this quite pleasant-looking youth, it would be another one.

It seemed to her that she had never cared for anyone in her life but Sylvia, that the girl had been the great passion of her life − oh, yes, she knew she loved Sylvia because she had not been allowed to love Johnny. But that was nonsense, because she knew − with her mind − how much she had longed for Philip all through that old war, and then how much she had loved him. The beams of light on the bed and the floor resembled the arbitrariness of memory, emphasising this and then that. When she looked back along the path of her life, periods of years that had had a sharp and distinct flavour of their own reduced themselves to something like a formula: that was the five years of the First World War. That little slice there was the Second World War. But, immersed in those five years, loyal in her mind and emotions to an enemy soldier, they were endless. The Second World War, which was now like an uneasy shadow in her memory, when she had lost her husband to his fatigue and to the fact he could tell her nothing of what he did, was an awful time and she had often thought that she could not bear it. She had lain at nights beside a man who was preoccupied with how to destroy her country, and she had to be glad it was being destroyed − and she was, but sometimes it seemed the bombs were tearing at her own heart. And yet now she could say to Wilhelm, who had been a refugee from that monstrous regime which she refused to think of as German, 'That was during the war − no, the second one.' As if talking about an item on a list that had to be kept up to date and accurate, events one after another, or perhaps like moonlight and shadows falling across a path, each having a sharp validity as you moved through them, but then when you looked back there was a dark streak through a forest with splashes of thin light across it. *Ich habe gelebt und geliebt*, she murmured, the fragment of Schiller that still stayed in her mind after sixty-five years, but it was a question: Have I lived and loved?

The moonlight had reached Julia's feet. She had been sitting here for some time, then. Not once had Sylvia so much as stirred. They seemed not to breathe: she could easily believe them lying there dead. She found herself thinking, If you were dead, Sylvia, then you'd not be missing much, you'll only end up like me, an old woman with my life behind me, dwindling into a mess of memories, that hurt. Julia dozed off, the valium at last sinking her into a sleep so deep that she was limp in the hands of Sylvia, who was shaking her.

Sylvia had woken, her mouth dry, to reach out for water, and saw a little ghost sitting there in the moonlight, whom she expected to vanish as she came fully awake. But Julia did not vanish. Sylvia went to her, held her, rocked her as the old woman whimpered, a desolate heart-wrenching sound.

'Julia, Julia,' whispered Sylvia, thinking of the young man who needed his sleep. 'Wake up, it's me.'

'Oh, Sylvia, I don't know what to do, I'm not myself.'

'Get up, darling, please, you must go to bed.'

Julia got up, unsteadily, and Sylvia, also unsteady, since she was half-asleep, took her out of the room and up the stairs. Now there was no light under Frances's door, not under Andrew's, but yes, there was under Colin's.

Sylvia laid Julia down on her bed and pulled up a cover.

'I think I'm ill, Sylvia. I must be ill.'

This cry went straight to Sylvia's professional self, and she said, 'I'm going to look after you. Please don't be so sad.'

Julia was asleep. Sylvia, falling asleep, wrenched herself up and crept across the room supporting herself on backs of chairs, and got down at last to her own room where she found her colleague sitting up. 'Is it morning?' 'No, no, go to sleep.' 'Thank God for that.' He collapsed back and she fell on her bed.

And now they were all asleep except for Colin, who lay with his arms around Sophie, who was asleep, the little dog on her hip, dozing, though its wisp of a tail sometimes fluttered.

He was not thinking of beautiful Sophie, in his arms. Like his mother earlier he was insanely promising: 'I'll kill him, I swear I will.' Now here's a knot! If Johnny had recognised himself in the poisonous word-spinner, then he was being asked for the heights of dispassionate judgement: only the standards of literary excellence should fuel his thoughts, '*Is this a good novel or isn't it?*' – the memories perhaps of those novels he had read when he had been a well-read person, before he had succumbed to the simple charms of socialist realism. As when the victim of a savage cartoon is expected to say, 'Oh, well done! What a talent you have!' In short, from Comrade Johnny was being demanded conduct that his family had long ago agreed he was incapable of. On the other hand, if he had not recognised himself, then he was to blame for suspecting nothing of how at least one of his sons saw him.

Julia grieving, grieving, though she could not have said for what if it wasn't Sylvia, or her whole life, studied newspapers, flung them down, tried again, and when Wilhelm walked her to the Cosmo, she tried to take in what was being said around her. The Vietnam War, that was what they talked about. Sometimes Johnny came in, with his entourage, dramatic, forceful, and he might nod at her, or even give her the clenched fist salute. Often, Geoffrey was with him, whom she knew so well, a handsome young man, like Lochinvar from the West, as she said scornfully to Wilhelm. Or Daniel, with his red hair, like a beacon. Or James, who came to her saying, 'I am James, do you remember me?' But she remembered no one with a cockney accent.

'It's the correct thing, now,' Wilhelm explained. 'They speak cockney.'

'But what for, when it's so ugly?'

'To get jobs. They are opportunists. If you want to get a job in television or in films, you have to lose your educated voice.'

Around them, cigarette smoke, and often angry voices. 'Why is it when it's politics, then there's always quarrelling?'

'Ah, my dear, if we understood that . . .'

'It reminds me of the old days, when I visited home, the Nazis . . .'

'And the communists.'

She remembered the fighting, the shouting, the flung stones, the running feet – yes, waking at night to hear feet running, running. After some atrocious thing, they ran through the streets shouting.

Julia sat in her chair, surrounded by newspapers, until her thoughts pushed her up to prowl around her rooms, clicking her tongue with annoyance as she found an ornament out of place, or a dress anyhow on the back of a chair. (What was Mrs Philby thinking of?) All her sorrows were becoming focused on the Vietnam War. She could not bear it. Wasn't it enough, that old war, the first one, so terrible and then the second, what more did they want, killing, killing, and now this war. And the Americans, were they mad, sending their young men, no one cared about the young men, when there was a war the young men were herded up and driven off to be killed. As if they were good for nothing but that. Again and again. No one learned anything, it was a lie to say we learned from history, if any lessons had been learned, the bombs would not be falling into Vietnam, and the young men . . . Julia was dreaming about her brothers, for the first time in years. She had nightmares about this war. On the television she watched Americans fighting the police, Americans not wanting the war, and she didn't want it, she was on the side of the Americans who rioted in Chicago or at the universities, and yet when she had left Germany to marry Philip she had chosen America, she was on that side. Philip had wanted Andrew to go to school in the States, and if he had, then by now he would probably be part of that America that turned hoses and teargas on the Americans who protested. (Julia knew Andrew was conservative by nature, or perhaps better say, on the side of authority.) Johnny's new woman, who apparently had abandoned him, was fighting in the streets against the war. Julia hated and feared street fighting, even now she had nightmares about what she had seen in the Thirties, when she went home to visit, in Germany, which was being destroyed by the gangs that rioted and smashed and shouted and ran at nights through the streets. Julia's head and mind and heart were whirling with violently opposing pictures, thoughts, emotions.

And her son Johnny was constantly in the papers, speaking against this war, and she felt he was right. Yet Johnny had never been right, she was sure of that, but suppose he was right now?

Julia, without telling Wilhelm, put on her hat, the one that concealed her face best, with its close-meshed veil, and chose gloves that would not show every mark – she associated politics with dirt – and took herself off to hear Johnny speak at a meeting to oppose the Vietnam War.

It was in a hall she thought of as communist. The streets around it seethed with young people. The taxi put her down outside the main entrance, and as she went in young people dressed like gypsies or hoodlums stared at her. The ones who had seen her arrive by taxi told each other she must be a CIA spy, while others, seeing this old lady – there was not one person here over fifty – said she must be here by mistake. Some said that with that hat she must be the cleaning lady.

The hall was full. It seemed to heave and swell and sway. The smell was horrible. Immediately in front of Julia were two heads of greasy unwashed blonde hair – what girls could have so little self-respect? Then she saw that they were men. And they stank.

The noise was so loud that she did not at once see that the speeches had begun. Up there were Johnny, and Geoffrey, whose clean well-ordered face she knew so well, but he had Viking's hair, and stood with his feet apart, and his right hand pounding the air, as if stabbing something, and he was sneering agreement with what Johnny was saying, which was variations on what she had heard so often, American imperialism . . . roars of agreement; the indus-trial–military complex – groans and boos; lackeys, jackals, capitalist exploiters, sell-outs, fascists. It was hard to hear, the roars of agree-ment were so loud. And there was James, so much the public man, large and affable, who had become a cockney, and there was a black man beside Johnny she was sure she knew. A lot of people up there on the platform. Every face was alive and elated with conceit and self-righteousness and triumph. How well she did know all that, how it frightened her. They swaggered about up there, under strong lights, spilling out their phrases which she could anticipate, each one, before it arrived. And the audience was a unit, it was whole, it was a mob, it could kill or run riot, and it was aflame with – hatred, yes that is what it was. Yet strip off the stupid clichés, and she was agreeing with them, she was on their side; how could she be, when they were foul, they were frightful; yet the violence of war was everything she hated most. She was finding it hard to keep upright – she was standing against a wall, and surrounded by Yahoos who might as well be carrying clubs. She took a long last look up at the platform, saw her son had recognised her, and that his stare was both triumphant and hostile. If she did not leave he might be making her a target for his sarcasms. She pushed her way through the crowd back to the door. Luckily she was not far away from it. Her hat was knocked awry, Julia believed deliberately. She was right. The muttering that she was a CIA spy was following her. She tried to hold her hat on, and at the door saw a large young woman with a big face reddened by excitement and by alcohol. She had a steward's badge. Recognising Julia she said loudly for the benefit of her colleagues, 'Well, what do you know? It's Johnny Lennox's ma.' 'Let me get past,' said Julia, who by now was beginning to panic. 'Let me out.'

'What, can't you take it? Can't you take the truth?' sneered a young man whose smell was literally making her sick. She held her hand over her mouth.

'Julia,' said Rose, 'does Johnny know you're here? What are you doing? Keeping a check on him?' She glanced around, grinning, for approval.

Julia had got through the door, but the outer room was full of people who had not got in.

'Make way for Johnny Lennox's ma,' shouted Rose, and the crowd opened. Out here, where the speeches were being relayed, was less of the atmosphere of a mob, of imminent violence. Young people were staring at Julia, at her hat, which was crooked, and her distressed face. She got to the outer door. There, feeling faint, she clung to the door frame.

Rose said, 'Julia, do you want a taxi?'

'I don't remember asking you to call me Julia,' said the old woman.

'Oh, I'm so sorry, Mrs Lennox,' said Rose, glancing around for approval. And then, laughing, 'What *shit.*'

'The *ancien régime*, I guess,' said an American voice.

Julia had reached the edge of the pavement. She knew she was going to faint. Rose stood on the steps behind her and said loudly, 'Johnny Lennox's ma. She's drunk.'

A taxi came, and Julia waved, but it was not going to stop for this disreputable old woman. Rose ran after it, shouting, and it did stop.

'Thank you,' said Julia, climbing in. She still held the handkerchief to her face.

'Oh, don't mention it, please,' said Rose daintily, and looked around for laughs, which she got. As Julia was driven away she heard through the windows come bursts of applause, derision, shouts, chanting, 'Down with American imperialism. Down with . . .'

Rose took this lucky opportunity, when Johnny made his way out, to waylay Comrade Johnny the star and say to him, like an equal, 'Your mother was here.' 'I saw her,' he said, not looking at her: he always ignored her. 'She was drunk,' she dared, but he pushed past, not saying anything.

Sylvia had not forgotten her promise. She had made an appointment for Julia with a certain Doctor Lehman. Wilhelm knew him and that he was a specialist in the problems of the old. 'Our problems, dear Julia.'

'Geriatrics,' said Julia.

'What's in a word? You can make an appointment for me too.'

Julia sat in front of Doctor Lehman, a quite likeable man, she thought, if so young – in fact he was middle-aged. German, like her? With that name? Then, Jewish? A refugee from her kind? It was remarkable how often she found herself thinking these thoughts.

He had an impeccable English voice and accent: evidently doctors did not have to talk cockney.

She knew he had taken in a great many facts about her from watching her walk to the chair, and that he would have heard more from Sylvia, and that since he had analysed her urine, taken her blood pressure, and checked her heart, he knew more about her than she knew herself.

He said, smiling, 'Mrs Lennox, you have been sent to me because of problems to do with old age.'

'So it seems,' she said, and knew he had not missed the resentment. He smiled a little.

'You are seventy-five years old.'

'That is so.'

'That isn't very old, not these days.'

She succumbed with, 'Doctor, I sometimes feel I am a hundred.'

'You allow yourself to think you are.'

This was not what she had expected, and, reassured, she smiled at this man who was not going to oppress her with her age.

'There is nothing wrong with you, physically. Congratulations. I wish I were in as good a shape. But there you are, everyone knows doctors don't follow their own advice.'

Now she allowed herself to laugh, and nodded, as if to say, Very well, now get on with it.

'I see this quite often, Mrs Lennox. Somebody who has been talked into feeling old when it is too early for them.'

Wilhelm? wondered Julia. Did he . . .

'Or has talked themselves into feeling old.'

'Have I done that? Well . . . perhaps I have.'

'I am going to say something that may seem shocking.'

'No, doctor, I don't shock easily.'

'Good. You can decide to become old. You are at a crossroads, Mrs Lennox. You can decide to get old and then you'll die. But you can decide not to get old. Not yet.'

She sat thinking, and then she nodded.

'I believe you have had a shock of some kind. A death? but it doesn't matter what. You seem to me to be showing signs of grief.'

'You are a very clever young man.'

'Thank you, but I am not so young. I am fifty-five.'

'You could be my son.'

'Yes, I could. Mrs Lennox, I want you to get up from that chair, and walk away from – the situation you are now in. You can decide to do it. You are not an old woman. You don't need a doctor. I am going to prescribe you vitamins and minerals.'

'Vitamins!'

'Why not? I take them. And come back in five years time and we'll discuss whether it is time for you to be old.'

*　*　*

Hazy golden clouds were throwing down brilliants that scattered around and on the taxi, exploding into smaller crystals, or sliding down the windows, and their shadows made dots and splodges which imitated the theme of Julia's little spotted veil that was held on the crown of her head with a serious jet clasp. The April sky of sunshine and showers was a cheat, for in fact it was September. Julia was dressed as she always was. Wilhelm had said to her, 'My dear, liebling, my dearest Julia, I am going to buy you a new dress.' Protesting and grumbling, but pleased, she was taken around the best shops, where he enlisted the aid of superior, but then charmed, young women, and Julia ended up with a claret-coloured velvet suit indistinguishable from those she had been wearing for decades. Upright inside it she was supported by thoughts of the tiny silk stitches on collar and cuffs and the perfectly fitting pink silk lining which she felt as a defence against barbarians. On the seat beside her Frances was doubled low in the task of changing her stockings and sensible shoes for high-heeled ones and black sheers. Otherwise, her working clothes – Julia had picked Frances up from the newspaper – were clearly expected to be adequate. Andrew had said there would be a little celebration, but they mustn't dress up. What could he mean? Celebrate what?

They were making the inevitably slow progress towards Andrew, side by side, in companionable and wary silence. Frances was thinking that all the years of living in Julia's house had led to occasions when they sat together in a cab so few she could list them. And Julia was thinking that there was no intimacy between them, and yet the young woman – come on, Julia, she was certainly not that! – was able to strip off stockings, exposing solid white legs, without a moment's embarrassment. It was likely no one had seen Julia's naked legs except her husband and doctors since she became adult. Had Wilhelm? No one knew.

They had gone so far as to agree that the celebration was probably because Andrew had been offered a job in one of the great international organisations that inhale and exhale money and order the world's affairs. When he had gained his second degree in law – he had done very well – he had left his grandmother's house for the second time for a flat shared with other young people, but he did not expect to be there for long.

By the time they had reached Gordon Square the light had gone. Large raindrops fell from a dark sky and splashed invisibly about them. It was a good house, no one need be ashamed of it: Julia had wondered if the reason Andrew had not invited them before was because he was ashamed of his address and if so, why had he left home at all? It did not enter her mind that he found her and Frances a crushing weight of authority or at least of accomplishment. 'What *me*? – you're joking!' parents say, as this situation repeats itself through the generations. '*Me?* A threat? This small so easily crushed thing that I am, always just clinging on to the edges of life.' Andrew had had to leave home, for survival, but things had been better during his return to it, to obtain the second degree, because he discovered he no longer feared his strict disapproving grandmother or the thoughts aroused in him by his mother's unsatisfactory life.

There was no lift, but Julia went briskly up steep stairs whose carpet had once been a good one, and the flat, when it was opened to them by Andrew, continued the theme, for it was large and full of varied furniture, and some of it had been grand but was ending its days. This had been a students' flat, or for young people beginning their working life, for decades, and the next step for most things here would be the rubbish dump. Andrew did not take them into the big general room, but into a small one at one end, parted from it by a glass wall. There were a couple of young men and a girl reading, or watching television in the big room, but here was a prettily-laid table, for four – white linen, glass, flowers, silver and proper napkins. Andrew said, 'We are going to have to drink our aperitifs at the table, otherwise we won't be able to hear ourselves speak.'

And so they sat, the three of them, and a still empty place waited for its occupant.

Andrew, his mother thought, looked tired. With adolescents dark circles around the eyes, a pasty look, fatness, spots, or a certain trembling self-possession on the edge of a threatened collapse – all these are signs of expected emotional disarray, but when adults look like Andrew, one has to think, Life is so hard now, it's cruel . . . Andrew was smiling, he was all charm, as always, he was well-dressed enough for a big occasion, but he was radiating anxiety. His mother was determined not to ask, but Julia said, 'You're keeping us on the edge of our seats. What is your news?'

Andrew allowed himself a little chuckle – a delightful sound – and he said, 'Prepare yourself for a surprise.'

Here a young woman came in from a kitchen next door with a tray of drinks. She was smiling and at ease and said to Andrew, 'Andy, we're a bit low in the alcohol department. This is the last of the decent sherry.'

'This is Rosemary,' said Andrew. 'She's cooking for us tonight.'

'I cook to earn my keep,' said Rosemary.

'She's at London University, doing law,' said Andrew.

She dipped them a mock curtsy, and said, 'Tell me when you're ready for soup.'

'This isn't about my job,' said Andrew. 'I'm waiting to have that confirmed.' Now he hesitated, on the brink: something was about to become real that was still an airy or a sombre phantom: telling the family, now that's getting real, all right. 'It's Sophie,' he said at last. 'Sophie and me . . . We are . . .'

The women sat silent, stunned. Sophie and Andrew! For years Frances had wondered if Colin and Sophie . . . but they went for walks together, he was always at her first nights, and she came to weep on his shoulder when Roland was again being impossible. Mates. Siblings. So they said.

The same practical thoughts were making their way through the two women's minds. Andrew was going abroad to work, probably to New York, and Sophie was an increasingly well-considered actress in London. Was she planning to throw up her career for his? Women did: they did, too often, when they should not. And both were thinking that Sophie was unsuitable as the consort of a public man, being so emotional and dramatic.

'Well, thanks,' said Andrew at last.

'Sorry,' said his mother. 'It's the surprise, that's all.'

Julia was thinking of those years spent apart from her love, Philip, waiting for him. And had it all been worth it? This seditious little thought more and more often presented itself, fair and square, and was not refused admittance. The fact was, and Julia was prepared to think so now, Philip should have married that English girl, so right for him, and she – but her mind went into panic when she contemplated what she might have done instead, with Germany in such ruins, such disaster, and then the politics, and then the Second World War. No. Her conclusion was, had been for some time now, that she was right to have married Philip, but that he should not have married her.

At last she said, 'You must see it's a shock. She is so close to Colin.'

'I know,' said Andrew. 'But they are like brother and sister. They have never . . .' And here he called out, 'Rosie, let's have the champagne.' Not looking at his mother and grandmother he said, 'I think we should begin – she's late.'

'Perhaps something is keeping her – the theatre – something . . .' Frances said, trying to find words to smooth away the anguish – and it was that – gripping her son's face.

'No. It's Roland. He takes no notice of her when he's got her, but he's jealous. He doesn't want her to leave.'

'She hasn't left yet?'

'No, not yet.'

At this Frances felt better. She knew that Sophie would not easily leave that sorcerer Roland. 'He's my doom, Colin,' she had cried. 'He's my fate.' After all, she had tried to leave often enough. And if she came to Andrew . . . one had only to look at him to see him as an emotional lightweight, soothing perhaps, after the peacocking Roland, but no counter-balance. Scenes, shouts, thrown crockery – once a heavy vase, which broke her little finger – tears, pleas for forgiveness: what could civilised and ironical Andrew offer Sophie, who would certainly miss all that . . . but perhaps I am wrong, Frances admonished herself. I am much too ready to see the end of a story before it has even properly begun.

Now Julia spoke: 'Andrew, it will not be a good thing to ask her to give up her work.'

'I have no intention of doing that, Grandmother.'

'And you will be such a long way off.'

'We'll manage somehow,' he said, and went to open the door for Rosemary, who was bringing in the soup.

By mutual consent, the champagne was not opened. They ate their soup. The next course was delayed, but Rosemary said it would spoil, and so they ate it, while Andrew listened for the doorbell or for the telephone. Then at last the telephone did ring, and Andrew went into another part of the flat to talk to Sophie.

The two women sat on, united by foreboding.

Julia spoke, 'Perhaps Sophie is a young woman who needs unhappiness.'

'But I am hoping Andrew doesn't.'

'And then there is the question of children.'

'Grandchildren, Julia.' Frances spoke lightly, and did not know that Julia was smiling because she could smell freshly washed baby's hair, and that close to her seemed to be the ghost of – who? a young creature, a girl perhaps.

'Yes,' said Julia. 'Grandchildren. I see Andrew as someone who would like children.'

Andrew, returning, heard this. 'I would, very much. But Sophie sends apologies. She is . . . held up.' He was on the verge of tears.

'Well, has he locked her up?' enquired his mother.

'He applies – pressure,' he said.

This was all awful, as bad as it could be, and they knew it.

He said brokenly, and sounded like a valediction, 'I can't imagine going on without Sophie. She's been so . . .' And now he really was breaking down. He rushed out of the room.

'It won't happen,' said Frances.

'I hope not.'

'I think we should go home.'

'Wait until he comes back.'

It was a good half hour before he came back, and the young people in the room through the glass wall invited the guests who were sitting alone to come and join them. Julia and Frances were pleased to do this. They might, they felt, easily break down themselves.

By now there were half a dozen young men and a couple of girls, one being Rosemary. She knew that a disaster – major? minor? – had occurred, and was being tactful, making conversation. A charming young woman, thought Julia: pretty, clever – certainly a good cook. She was in law, like Andrew. Surely they would be just right for each other?

The young men and women were talking about what they had done during the long summer holidays: they were all still at university. It sounded as if between them they had visited most of the countries of the world. They talked about how things were in Nicaragua, Spain, Mexico, Germany, Finland, Kenya. They had all had a thoroughly good time, but they had also been in search of information, were serious travellers. Frances was thinking how well they contrasted with what had gone on in Julia's house ten or more years ago. These people seemed much happier – was that the word to use? She looked back on strain, difficulty, on damaged creatures. Not these. Well, of course these were older . . . but even so. Julia would say, of course, that these were none of them war children: the shadows of war were a long way behind them.

This half hour, which could have been agreeable, was spoiled by the worry over Andrew, who came in briefly to say that he had ordered a taxi for them. They must forgive him. From the way the others looked at him, surprised, the women could see that they were not used to debonair Andrew in disorder. In the street, he kissed them, a hug for Julia, a hug for Frances. He held the door of the taxi for them but he was not thinking about them. At once he went running back up the stairs.

'I wonder if these young ones know how fortunate they are?' said Julia.

'Certainly much luckier than either of us.'

'Poor Frances, you didn't have much chance of running about the world.'

'Then poor Julia, too.'

Feeling kindly towards each other, they finished their journey in silence.

'It won't happen, Frances,' was Julia's last word.

'No, I know it won't.'

'So we mustn't lie awake all night worrying about it.'

Sitting by herself in the kitchen at the table which was half the size, these days, Frances drank tea, and hoped that Colin might drop in. Sylvia hardly ever did. No longer a junior, but a proper doctor, she did not instantly fall asleep as she sat down, but she worked very hard, and the room on the landing across from Frances's room scarcely saw her. She might come for a bath and a change of clothes, or sometimes for the night, she might or might not run up to embrace Julia, but that was it. So it was Colin of all 'the kids' Frances saw these days.

She knew nothing about his life outside this house. One day a disreputable fellow with a big black mongrel dog rang the bell and enquired for Colin, who came running down to make an arrangement to meet on the Heath. At once Frances began worrying, was Colin a homosexual, then? Unlikely, surely? – but she was already at work on honing the appropriately correct attitudes, if he was, when a wan girl appeared, and then another, only to be told that he was out. But if he is not here, then why isn't he with me? – Frances knew they were thinking, because she would be, in their place. These incidents were hints at Colin's life. He roamed the Heath at all hours with Vicious, talked to people on benches, made friends with other dog-owners, sometimes went to a pub. Julia who had said to him, 'Colin, it is not healthy for a young man to have no sex life,' had been rebuked with, 'But, Grandmother, I have a dark and dangerous secret life, full of mad romantic encounters, so please don't worry about me.'

Tonight he came in, as always with the little dog, saw Frances, and said, 'I'll make myself a cup.' The dog jumped up on the table.

'Do get that little nuisance down.'

'Oh, Vicious, did you hear that?' He picked up the dog, and took it to a chair, told it to stay, and it did, wagging its tail and watching them with black inquisitive eyes.

'I know you want to talk about Andrew,' he said, sitting down with his tea.

'Of course. It would be a disaster.'

'Can't have disasters in this family.' His smile informed his mother that he was in combat mood. She braced herself, thinking that she could say anything at all to Andrew, but with Colin there was always an apprehensive moment while she waited to find out what mood he was in. She almost said, 'Forget it – another time' – but he was going on. 'Julia's been at me too. What do you expect me to do? Say, Do not be foolish, Andrew, do not be reckless, Sophie? The point is, she needs Andrew to get free of Roland.'

Here he waited, smiling. He was now a large bulky man, with curly black hair, and black-rimmed spectacles that gave him a studious air. He was always ready to go on the attack, because for one thing he was still partly dependent financially. Julia had said to Frances, 'Better for me to give him an allowance than you – psychologically better.' She was right, but it was his mother he took it out on. Frances waited too. Battle was about to commence.

'If you want a crystal ball, then you should consult dear Phyllida downstairs, but using my vast knowledge of human nature – the *TLS* says I have it – then I'd say she will stay with Andrew just long enough to let Roland cool off, and then she'll leave Andrew for someone else.'

'Poor Andrew.'

'Poor Sophie. Well, she's a masochist. You should understand that.'

'Is that what I am?'

'You do have a certain talent for long-suffering, wouldn't you agree?'

'Not now. Not for a long time now.'

He hesitated. This scene might have ended there, but he leaped up, put another teabag in his cup, poured on water that was not boiling, saw his error, fished out the teabag and threw it into the sink, swore, picked it out to drop it into the rubbish bin, caused the kettle to boil, chose another teabag, poured on boiling water – all this in clumsy haste that told Frances that he was not enjoying this encounter. He came back, he put down his cup. He got up and gave the little dog a hasty stroke, and sat down.

'It's not personal,' he said. 'But I've been thinking. It's your generation. It's all of you.'

'Ah,' said Frances, relieved that they had chosen the familiar ground of abstract principles.

'Saving the world. Paradise on every new agenda.'

'You are confusing me with your father.' Then she decided to go on the attack herself. 'I do get fed up with this. I am always implicated in Johnny's crimes.' She contemplated the word. 'Yes, crimes. You could call them that by now.'

'When could we not have called them that? And do you know what? I actually read in *The Times* that he said, Yes, mistakes have been made.'

'Yes. But I did not commit the crimes, nor condone them.'

'No, but you're a world saver, all the same. Just like him. The whole lot of you. What conceit you all have. Do you know that?

You must be the most conceited hubristic generation there has ever been.' He smiled still: he was enjoying this attack, but was feeling guilty too. 'Johnny for ever making speeches and you filling the house with waifs and strays.'

Ah, now they were at the nub of it. She said, 'I'm sorry, but I don't see what that has got to do with it. I don't remember him ever helping anybody.'

'Helping? Is that what you call it. Well, his place is full all the time of Americans dodging the draft – not that I've got anything against that – and *comrades* from everywhere.'

'It's not the same thing.'

'Has it ever occurred to you to ask yourself, what would have happened to them if you hadn't taken in Uncle Tom Cobbleigh and all?'

'One of them was your Sophie.'

'She never actually moved in.'

'She was practically living here. And how about Franklin? He was here for over a year. He was your friend.'

'And that bloody Geoffrey. I had him day and night at school and then all the holidays here, for years and years.'

'But I never knew you disliked him so much. Why didn't you say? Why don't children ever say when they're unhappy about something.'

'There you are – you didn't even have enough insight to see it.'

'Oh, Colin. And you're going to say we shouldn't have let Sylvia stay here.'

'I'd never say that.'

'You may not now but you certainly used to. You've made my life a misery with your complaints. Anyway, I'm fed up with this. It's a long time ago.'

'The results are not a long time ago. Did you know that little bitch Rose is going around saying that Julia is a lush and you are a nymphomaniac?'

Frances laughed. It was angry, but genuine. Colin hated that laugh: his stare at her was all miserable accusation. 'Colin, if you only knew what a chaste life I'd led . . .' But now, summoning the spirit of these times, she said, 'And anyway, if I had a new man every weekend, it was my right, why not? You'd have no right to say a bloody word.'

The absurdity of this showed itself at once. Colin went white, and sat silent. 'Colin, for God's sake, you know perfectly well . . .' The dog intervened. 'Yap, yap,' it went, 'yap, yap.'

Frances collapsed laughing. Colin smiled, bitterly.

The fact was, the weight of his main accusation lay there between them, a poisoned thing.

'Where did you get all that confidence? Father saving the world, a few million dead here, a few million dead there and you, Do come in and make yourself at home, I'll just kiss the sore places and make them better.' He sounded beaten into the earth by years of his miserable childhood, and he actually looked like a little boy, eyes full, lips trembling. And Vicious, leaving his chair, came to his master, leaped up on to his knee and began licking his face. Colin put his face – as much of it as would go – into the tiny dog's back, to hide it. Then he lifted it to say, 'Just where did you get it all from, you lot? Who the bloody hell *are* you – world-savers every one, and making deserts . . . Do you realise? We're all screwed up. Did you know Sophie dreams of gas chambers and none of her family was anywhere near them?' And he got up, cuddling the dog.

'Wait a minute, Colin . . .'

'We've dealt with the main item on the agenda – Sophie. She is unhappy. She will go on being unhappy. She will make Andrew unhappy. Then she will find someone else and go on being unhappy.'

He ran out of the room and up the stairs, the little dog barking in his arms, its high absurd yap, yap, yap.

★   ★   ★

Something was going on in Julia's house that none of the family knew about. Wilhelm and Julia wanted to get married, or at least, for Wilhelm to move in. He complained, humorously at first, that he was being forced to live like a teenager, with little assignations to meet his love at the Cosmo, or for visits to restaurants; he might spend all day and half the night with Julia, but then had to go home. Julia fended off the situation, with jokes to the effect that at least they were not yearning like teenagers for a bed. To which he replied that there was more to a bed than sex. He seemed to remember cuddles, and conversations in the dark, about the ways of the world. Julia did wonder about sharing a bed after so many years as a widow, but increasingly saw his point. She always felt bad, staying comfortably in her room, when he had to go home, through whatever weather there was. His home was a very large flat, where once his wife, who was dead long ago, and two children, now in America, had lived. He was hardly ever in this flat. He was not a poor man, but it was not sensible, keeping up his flat with its doorman and the little garden, while there was this big house of Julia's. They discussed, then argued, then bickered about how things could be arranged.

For Wilhelm to live with Julia in the four little rooms that were enough for her – out of the question. And what would he do with his books? He had thousands of them, some of them part of his stock as a book dealer. Colin had taken over the floor beneath Julia, had colonised Andrew's room. He could not be asked to move – why should he? Of all the people in this house, except Julia herself, he needed most his place, his little secure place in the world. Below Colin was Frances in two good rooms and a little one. And on that floor was the room that was Sylvia's, even if she only came back to it once a month. It was her home and must remain so.

But why should Frances not be asked to move? – Wilhelm wanted to know. She earned enough money these days, didn't she? But Julia refused. She saw Frances as a woman used by the Lennox family to do the job of bringing up two sons, and now

– out. Julia had never forgotten how Johnny had demanded that she should go away, into some little flat or other, when Philip died.

Beneath Frances was the big sitting-room that stretched from front to back of the house. It might take more shelves for Wilhelm's books? But Wilhelm knew Julia did not want this room to be sacrificed. There remained Phyllida. She could now well afford to find her own place. She had the money Sylvia had assured her and she earned steady money as a psychic and fortune teller, and – increasingly – a therapist. When the family heard that Phyllida was now a therapist, the jokes, all on the lines of 'but herself she cannot save', were unending. But she was attracting patients. To get rid of Phyllida and her persistent customers – no one in the house would object. Yes, one, Sylvia, whose attitude towards her mother was now maternal. She worried about her. And to what end would be Phyllida's moving out? Only useful if Frances would move down, or if Colin did. Why should they? And there was something else, very strong, which Wilhelm only guessed at. Julia's dream was that when Sylvia married or found 'a partner' – a silly phrase Julia thought – that she would move in to the house. Where? Well, Phyllida could leave the basement, and then . . .

Wilhelm began saying that he had at last understood: Julia did not really want him there. 'I have always loved you more than you have loved me.' Julia had never thought about this love to weigh and measure it. Simply, it was what she relied on. Wilhelm was her support and her stay, and now she was getting old (which she felt she was, despite Doctor Lehman), she knew she could not manage without him. Did she not love him then? Well, certainly not, compared with Philip. How uncomfortable this line of thought was, she did not want to go on with it, nor to hear Wilhelm's reproaches. She would have liked him to move in, if things hadn't been so difficult, if only to soothe her conscience over that big under-used place of his. She was even prepared to contemplate cuddles and bedtime conversations in her once connubial bed. But she had only shared her bed with one man in her long life: too much was being asked of her – wasn't it? Wilhelm's reproaches became accusations and Julia cried and Wilhelm was remorseful.

Frances was planning to leave Julia's. At last she would have her own place. Now that there were no school or university fees, she was actually saving money. Her own place, not Johnny's, or Julia's. And it would have to accommodate all her research materials and her books, now divided between *The Defender* and Julia's. A large flat. What a pleasant thing it is to have a regular salary: only someone who has not enjoyed one can say this with the heartfelt feeling it deserves. Frances remembered freelancing and precarious little jobs in the theatre. But when she had achieved enough money for the substantial down-payment, then she would resign from what she felt as an increasingly false position at *The Defender*, and that would be the end of regular sums arriving in her bank account.

She had always done most of her work at home, had never felt herself to be part of the newspaper. That she just came and went was her colleagues' complaint about her, as if her behaviour was a criticism of *The Defender*. It was. She was an outsider in an institution that saw itself as beleaguered, and by hostile hordes, reactionary forces, as if nothing had changed from the great days of the last century when *The Defender* stood almost alone as a bastion of wholesome open-hearted values: there had been no honest good cause *The Defender* had not defended. These days the newspaper championed the insulted and the injured, but behaved as if these were minority issues, instead of – on the whole – 'received opinions'.

Frances was no longer Aunt Vera (My little boy wets his bed, what shall I do?), but wrote solid, well-researched articles on issues like the discrepancy between women's pay and men's, unequal employment possibilities, nursery schools: nearly everything she wrote was to do with the difference between men's situation and women's.

The women journalists of *The Defender* were known in some quarters, mostly male (who saw themselves increasingly as beleaguered by hostile female hordes), as a kind of mafia, heavy, humourless, obsessed, but worthy. Frances was certainly worthy: all her articles had a second life as pamphlets and even as books, third lives as radio or television programmes. She secretly concurred with the view that her female colleagues were heavy-going, but suspected she could be accused of the same. She certainly felt heavy, weighed down with the wrongs of the world: Colin's accusation had been true enough: she did believe in progress, and that a stubborn application in attacking unfairness would put things right. Well, didn't it? At least sometimes? She had small triumphs to be proud of. But at least she had never flown off into the windy skies of the so fashionable feminism: she had never been capable, like Julie Hackett, of a fit of tearful rage when hearing on the radio that it was the female mosquito that is responsible for malaria. 'The shits. The bloody fascist *shits*.' When at last persuaded by Frances that this was a fact and not a slander invented by male scientists to put down the female sex – 'Sorry, gender' – she quietened into hysterical tears and said, 'It's all so bloody *unfair*.' Julie Hackett continued dedicated to *The Defender*. At home she wore *The Defender* aprons, drank from *The Defender* mugs, used *The Defender* drying-up cloths. She was capable of angry tears if someone criticised her newspaper. She knew Frances was not as *committed* – a word she was fond of – as she was, and often delivered little homilies designed to improve her thinking. Frances found her infinitely tedious. Aficionados of the prankish tricks life gets up to will have already recognised this figure, which so often accompanies us, turning up at all times and places, a shadow we could do without, but there she is, he is, a mocking caricature of oneself, but oh yes, a salutary reminder. After all, Frances had fallen for Johnny's windy rhetoric, been charmed out of her wits by the great dream, and her life had been set by it ever since. She simply had not been able to get free. And now she was working for two or three days a week with a woman for whom *The Defender* played the same role as the Party had done for her parents, who were still orthodox communists and proud of it.

Some people have come to think that our – the human being's – greatest need is to have something or somebody to hate. For decades the upper classes, the middle class, had fulfilled this useful function, earning (in communist countries) death, torture and imprisonment, and in more equable countries like Britain, merely obloquy, or irritating obligations, like having to acquire a cockney accent. But now this creed showed signs of wearing thin. The new enemy, men, was even more useful, since it encompassed half the human race. From one end of the world to the other, women were sitting in judgement on men, and when Frances was with *The Defender* women, she felt herself to be part of an all-female jury that has just passed a unanimous verdict of Guilty. They sat about, in leisure moments, solidly in the right, telling little anecdotes of this man's crassness or that man's delinquency, they exchanged glances of satirical comment, they compressed their lips and arched their brows, and when men were present, they watched for evidence of incorrect thought and then they pounced like cats on sparrows. Never have there been smugger, more self-righteous, unself-critical people. But they were after all only a stage in this wave of the women's movement. The beginning of the new feminism in the Sixties resembled nothing so much as a little girl at a party, mad with excitement, her cheeks scarlet, her eyes glazed, dancing about shrieking, 'I haven't got any knickers on, can you see my bum?' Three years old, and the adults pretend not to see: she will grow out of it. And she did. 'What *me*? I never did things like that . . . oh, well, I was just a baby.'

Soberness soon set in, and if the price to be paid for solid worth was an irritating self-righteousness, then surely it was a small price for such serious, scrupulous research, the infinitely tedious rooting about in facts, figures, government reports, history, the work that changes laws and opinions and establishes justice.

And this stage, in the nature of things, would be succeeded by another.

Meanwhile Frances had to conclude that working for *The Defender* was not unlike being Johnny's wife: she had to shut up and think her own thoughts. This was why she had always taken so much work home. Keeping one's counsel, after all, takes it out of you, wears you down, it had taken her much longer to see that many of the journalists working for *The Defender* were the offspring of the comrades, though one had to know them a while before the fact emerged. If one had a Red upbringing, then one shut up about it – too complicated to explain. But when others were in the same boat? But it was not only *The Defender*. Amazing how often one heard, 'My parents were in the Party, you know.' A generation of Believers, now discredited, had given birth to children who disowned their parents' beliefs, but admired their dedication, at first secretly, then openly. What faith! What passion! What idealism! But how could they have swallowed all those lies? As for them, the offspring, they owned free and roving minds, uncontaminated by propaganda.

But the fact was, the atmosphere of *The Defender* and other liberal organs had been 'set' by the Party. The most immediately visible likeness was the hostility to people not in agreement. The left-wing or liberal children of parents they might describe as fanatics maintained intact inherited habits of mind. 'If you are not with us, you are against us.' The habit of polarisation, 'If you don't think like us, then you are a fascist.'

And, like the Party in the old days, there was a plinth of admired figures, heroes and heroines, usually not communists these days, but Comrade Johnny was a prominent figure, a grand old man, one of the Old Guard, to be pictured as standing eternally on a platform shaking his clenched fist at a reactionary sky. The Soviet Union still held hearts, if not minds. Oh, yes, 'mistakes' had been made, and 'mistakes' had been admitted to, but that great power was defended, for the habit of it had gone too deep.

There were people in the newspaper that were whispered about: they must be CIA spies. That the CIA had spies everywhere could not be in doubt, so they must be here too: no one ever said that the KGB had its Soviet fingers in this pie, manipulating and influencing, though that was the truth, not to be admitted for twenty years. The USA was the main enemy: this was the unspoken and often loudly asserted assumption. It was a fascist militaristic state, and its lack of freedom and true democracy was attacked continually in articles and speeches by people who went there for holidays, sent their children to American universities, and took trips across 'the pond' to take part in demos, riots, marches and meetings.

A certain naive youth, joining *The Defender* because of his admiration for its great and honourable history of free and fair thought, rashly argued that it was a mistake to call Stephen Spender a fascist for campaigning against the Soviet Union and trying to make people accept 'the truth' – which phrase meant the opposite of what the communists meant by it. This young man argued that since everyone knew about the rigged elections, the show trials, the slave camps, the use of prison labour, and that Stalin was demonstrably worse than Hitler, then surely it was right to say so. There was shouting, screaming, tears, a scene that almost came to blows. The youth left and was described as a CIA plant.

Frances was not the only one who longed to leave this prickly dishonest place. Rupert Boland, her good friend, was another. Their secret dislike of the institution they worked for was what first united them, and then when both could have left to get work on other newspapers, they stayed – because of the other. Which neither knew, for it was not confessed for a long time. Frances had found she was in danger of loving this man, but then when it was too late, she did. And why not? Things progressed in an unhurried but satisfying way. Rupert wanted to live with Frances. 'Why not move in with me?' he said. He had a flat in Marylebone.

Frances said that once in her life she wanted her own home. She would have enough money in a year or so. He said, 'But I'll lend you the money to make the difference.' She baulked and made excuses. It would not be entirely her place, the spot on the earth where she could say, This is mine. He did not understand and was hurt. Despite these disagreements their love prospered. She went to his flat for nights, not too often, because she was afraid of upsetting Julia, afraid of Colin. Rupert said, 'But why? You're over twenty-one?'

When you are getting on there occur often enough those moments when whole tangles of bruised and bleeding history simply wrap themselves up and take themselves off. She did not feel she could explain it to him. And she didn't want to: let it all rest. Basta. Finis. Rupert was not going to understand. He had been married and there were two children, who were with their mother. He saw them regularly, and now so did Frances. But he had not been through the savage impositions of adolescence. He said, just like Wilhelm, 'But we aren't teenagers, hiding from the grown-ups.' 'I don't know about that. But in the meantime – it's fun.'

There was something that could have been a problem, but wasn't. He was ten years younger than she was. She was nearly sixty, he ten years younger! After a certain age ten years here or there don't make much difference. Quite apart from sex, which she was remembering as a pleasant thing, he was the best of company. He made her laugh, something she knew she needed. How easy it was to be happy, they were both finding, and with an incredulity they confessed. How could it be that things were so easy that had been difficult, wearisome, painful?

Meanwhile, there seemed to be no accommodation for this love, which was of the quotidian, daily-bread sort, not at all a teenagers' romp.

★   ★   ★

The crowds for the celebration of the Independence of Zimlia spilled from the hall on to the steps and the pavements and threatened to clog the streets, as had earlier jamborees for Kenya, Tanzania, Uganda, Northern Zimlia. Probably the larger part of these celebrants had been at all the earlier festivities. Every kind of victorious emotion was here, from the quiet satisfaction of people who had worked for years, to the grinning inflated elation of those who get as intoxicated on crowds as they do on love, or hate, or football. Frances was here because Franklin had telephoned. 'I must have you there. No, you must come. All my old friends.' It was very flattering. 'And where is Miss Sylvia? She must come too, please ask her.' That was why Sylvia was with Frances, pushing through crowds, though Sylvia had said, and kept on saying, 'Frances, I have to talk to you about something. It's important.'

Someone was tugging at Frances's sleeve. 'Mrs Lennox? You're Mrs Lennox?' An urgent young woman with red hair as rough as a rag doll's and an air of general disorientation: 'I need your help.'

Frances stopped, Sylvia just behind her. 'What is it?' Frances shouted.

'You were so wonderful with my sister. She owes you her life. Please I must come and see you.' She was shouting too.

Light did dawn, but slowly. 'I see. But I think you must be wanting the other Mrs Lennox, Phyllida.'

Wild suspicion, frustration, then dismay contorted those features. 'You won't? You can't? You aren't . . .'

'You have the wrong Mrs Lennox.' And Frances walked on, with Sylvia holding to her arm. That Phyllida was to be seen in this light — it needed time to take in. 'That was Phyllida she was talking about,' Frances said. 'I know,' said Sylvia.

At the door into the hall it could be seen it was crammed and there was no chance of getting in but Rose was a steward and so was Jill, both with rosettes the size of plates, in Zimlian colours. Rose cried out with enthusiasm on seeing Frances, and shouted

into her inclined ear, 'It's like old family night, everyone's here.'
But now she saw Sylvia and her face twisted into indignation. 'I
don't see why you think you're going to get a place. I've never
seen you at any of our demos.'

'You haven't seen me either,' said Frances. 'But I hope that
doesn't mean I'm a black sheep too.'

'*Black* sheep,' sneered Rose. 'Wouldn't you know it.'

But she stood aside for Frances, and then, of necessity, Sylvia,
but said, 'Frances, I must speak to Franklin.'

'Hadn't you better apply to Johnny? Franklin stays with him
when he's in London.'

'Johnny doesn't seem to remember me – but I was part of
the family, wasn't I – for *ages*?'

A roar went up. The speakers were pushing on to the platform,
about twenty of them, Johnny among them, with Franklin, and
other black men. Franklin saw Frances, who had pushed her
way up to the front, and leaped down off the platform, laughing,
almost crying, rubbing his hands: he was dissolving in joy. He
embraced Frances and then looked around and said, 'Where's
Sylvia?'

Franklin was staring at a thin young woman, with straight fair
hair tied back off a pale face, in a high-necked black sweater. His
gaze left her, wandered off, came back, in doubt.

'But here is Sylvia,' shouted Sylvia above the din of the clapping and shouting. On the platform just above them the speakers
stood waving their arms, clasping their hands above their heads,
and shaking them, giving the clenched fist salute to some entity
apparently just above the heads of the audience. They were smiling
and laughing, absorbing the crowd's love and sending it back in
hot rays that could positively be seen.

'Here I am. You've forgotten me, Franklin.'

Never has a man looked more disappointed than Franklin did
then. For years he had held in his mind that little fluffy girl, like
a new yellow chick, as sweet as the Virgin and the female saints
on the Holy Pictures at the mission. This severe unsmiling girl

hurt him, he didn't want to look at her. But she came from behind Frances, and hugged him, and smiled, and for a moment he was able to think, Yes this is Sylvia . . .

'Franklin,' they were shouting from the platform.

At this moment up came Rose, and insisted on embracing him. 'Franklin. It's me. It's Rose. Do you remember?'

'Yes, yes, yes,' said Franklin, whose memories of Rose were ambiguous.

'I have to see you,' said Rose.

'Yes, but I have to go up now.'

'I'll wait for you after the meeting. It's to your advantage, remember.'

He climbed up, and was now a shiny smiling black face among the others, and next to Johnny Lennox, who was like a mangy old lion, but dignified with it, greeting his followers down in the audience with a shake of his fist. But still Franklin's eyes roamed the hall, as if somewhere down there the old Sylvia was, and then when he stared, forlornly for that moment, at where the real Sylvia was, in a front seat, Sylvia waved at him and smiled. His own face burst out again into happiness, and he opened his arms, embracing the crowd, but really it was her.

Victory celebrations after a war do not have much to say about the dead soldiers, or rather, they say a good deal or even sing about the dead comrades 'who made this victory possible', but the acclamations and the noisy singing are designed to make the victors forget about the bones lying in a cleft of rock on a kopje, or in a grave so shallow the jackals have got there, scattering ribs, fingers, a skull. Behind the noise there is an accusing silence, soon to be filled with forgetfulness. In the hall that night were few people – they were mostly white – who had lost sons and daughters to a war, or who had fought in one, but the men on the platform, some of them, had been in an army, or had visited the fighters. There were also men who had been trained for political war, or for guerilla war, in the Soviet Union, or in camps set up by the Soviet Union, in Africa. And in that audience a good few had known various bits of Africa 'in the old days'. Between them and the activists were gulfs, but they were all cheering.

Twenty years of war, beginning with isolated outbreaks of 'civil unrest' or 'disobedience' or strikes, or sullen angers erupting into murder or arson, but all those rivulets had become the flood that was the war, twenty years of it and soon to be forgotten except in celebratory occasions. The noise in the hall was tumultuous, and did not abate. People shouted and wept and embraced each other and kissed strangers and on the platform speakers followed each other, black and white. Franklin spoke, then again. The crowd liked him, this round cheerful man who – so it was said – would soon be in a government formed by Comrade Matthew Mungozi who had unexpectedly won a majority in the recent elections: President Mungozi, until recently only one name among half a dozen potential leaders. And there was Comrade Mo, arriving late, grinning, waving, excited, jumping up on the platform to describe how he had just returned from the lines of freedom fighters giving up their weapons, and planning how to make real the sweet dreams that had kept them going for years. Comrade Mo, gesticulating, agitated, weeping, told the audience of those dreams: they had been so occupied with news of the war that they had not had time to think how soon they would hear, 'And now we shall build a future together.' Comrade Mo was not actually a Zimlian, but never mind, no one else there had actually so recently been with the freedom fighters, not even Comrade Matthew, who had been too busy with discussions with Whitehall and in international meetings. Most of the world's leaders had already assured him of their support. Overnight, he had become an international figure.

There was no way for Frances and Sylvia to leave, and the shouting and tears and speeches went on till the hall's caretaker came to say there were ten minutes left of paid-for time. Groans and boos and cries of *fascists*. Everyone pressed towards the doors. Frances stayed looking up at Johnny, thinking that surely he should at least acknowledge her presence, and he did give her a stern and unsmiling nod. There, climbing up on the platform was Rose, to greet Johnny, who did acknowledge her with a nod. Then Rose stood in front of Franklin, blocking the people who wanted to shake his hand, embrace him, or even carry him shoulder high out of the hall.

When Frances and Sylvia had reached the foyer Rose arrived, bursting with her triumph. Franklin had promised her an interview with Comrade Matthew. Yes, at once. Yes, yes, yes, he promised, he would speak to Comrade Matthew who would be in London next week and Rose would get her interview.

'See?' Rose said to Frances, ignoring Sylvia. 'And so I'm on my way.'

'Where to?' was the expected reply, and Frances made it.

'You'll see,' said Rose. 'All I wanted was a break, that's all.'

She went off to resume her duties as a steward.

Frances and Sylvia stood on the pavement, while happy people unwilling to part from each other, milled about them.

'I have to see you, Frances,' said Sylvia. 'It's important – not just you, everybody.'

'Everybody!'

'Yes, you'll see why.'

They would all meet in a week, and Sylvia would come home for the whole night, she promised.

Rose read every article she could find on comrade Matthew, President Mungozi. Not so much on Zimlia. A great deal was being said, and most of it complimentary, by people who had often written unpleasantly. For one thing, he was a communist. What was that going to mean, in the Zimlian context, was being asked. Rose did not intend to pose such questions, or at least not in a confrontational manner. She had written a draft of her interview before even meeting The Leader, all taken from other interviews. As a freelance journalist she had written little pieces about local issues, mostly on information supplied to her by Jill, now on several committees on the Council. She had always fitted together information, or other people's articles, to make her articles, so this job was the same, only larger in import and – she hoped – in consequences. She used none of the criticism of Comrade Matthew, and ended with a couple of paragraphs of optimistic euphemism of the kind she had heard so often from Comrade Johnny.

This article, she took, in draft, for her interview to The Leader, at his hotel. He was not a communicative interviewee, at least to start with, but when he had read her draft he lost his suspicions, and gave her some helpful quotes. 'As President Mungozi told me . . .'

It was a week later. Frances had extended the table to its former state, hoping people would say, Just like old times. She had cooked a stew and made a pudding. Who was coming? Told that Sylvia was, Julia said she would come down, and bring Wilhelm. Colin, hearing of the subject of what Sylvia was calling 'a meeting' said he would certainly be there. Andrew, who had been on a honeymoon with Sophie – his word, though they were not married – said they would both come.

Julia and Frances waited together. Andrew arrived first, but alone. One glance was enough: he had a depleted, even haggard look, and there was no sign of the debonair Andrew. He was sombre. His eyes were red.

'Sophie might be in later,' he said, and poured himself copious drafts of red wine, one after the other. 'All right, mother,' he said. 'I know. But I've taken a beating.'

'Has she gone back to Roland?'

'I don't know. Probably. The bonds of love are hard to break, quote unquote, but if that's love then give me the other thing.' His voice was already slurred. 'I'm really here because I never see Sylvia. Sylvia – who is she? Perhaps it is Sylvia I love. But you know what, Frances, I think she's a nun at heart.' And so he ran on, the stream of words slowing and thickening, until he got up, strode to the sink, and splashed water on his face. 'There is a superstition . . .' – he said thuperthtition – 'that cold water subdues the flames of alcohol. Untrue.' His head fell forward as he sat down, and he got up again and said, 'I think I'll have a bit of a lie down.'

'Colin's using your room.'

'I'll use the sitting-room.' He went noisily up the stairs.

Sylvia arrived and embraced Julia who could not prevent herself from saying, 'I never see you these days.'

Sylvia smiled, and took the other end of the table from Frances, and spread papers around her.

'Aren't you having supper with us?' asked Julia, and Sylvia said, 'Sorry,' and pushed the papers to one side.

Colin came down the stairs in big leaps. Sylvia's pale face warmed to him in a smile and she held out her arms. They embraced.

Wilhelm knocked, as he always did, enquired if he might join them, sat near Julia, having first kissed her hand and given her a close enquiring look. He was worried about her? She looked the same, they both did. He might be on his way to ninety but he was hale, he was hearty.

Having heard that Andrew was sleeping it off upstairs, Colin said, 'La belle dame sans merci. I told you so, Frances, didn't I?'

At which point Sophie herself arrived, full of apologies. She was in a loose white dress, her black hair cascading over it; her face seemed unmarked by love or by pain, but her eyes – now that was a different matter.

Frances was serving food, her hands occupied. She turned her head so that Sophie might kiss her cheek. Sophie slid into a chair opposite Colin, and found him gravely examining her.

'Darling Colin,' said Sophie.

'Your victim is upstairs, he's flaked out,' said Colin.

'That's not nice,' said Frances.

'It wasn't meant to be,' said Colin.

Sophie's eyes were full of tears.

Wilhelm said to Colin, 'Beautiful women should never be reproached for the damage they do. They have the permission of the Gods to torment us.' He gathered up Julia's hand, kissed it once, twice, sighed, laid down the old hand, and patted it.

Rupert arrived. Without a word of explanation offered or asked for, he was a fixture, and – Frances hoped – accepted. Colin was giving him a long, not unfriendly look, but it was a bleak one, as if loneliness had been confirmed. Rupert sat in the place next to Frances, and nodded to everyone.

'A meeting,' he said. 'But it's a meal.'

Frances was laying filled plates in front of everyone, family style, and setting bottles of wine down the middle of the table.

'This is marvellous, Frances, it's so wonderful – like old times, oh I often think of them, all of us sitting around here, wonderful evenings,' Sophie chattered. But she was on the point of tears and was destroying a piece of bread with the long thin fingers that were made for rings.

Here the little dog, having escaped from some confinement, rushed into the kitchen and up on to Colin's lap, where it stayed, its feathery tail like an energetic duster.

'Down, Vicious,' said Colin. 'Down at once.' But the creature had settled on Colin's lap, and was trying to lick his face.

'It is not healthy to let dogs lick your face,' said Sylvia.

'I know,' said Colin.

'That dog,' said Julia, 'couldn't you call it something sensible? Every time I hear Vicious I need to laugh.'

'A laugh a day keeps the doctor away,' said Colin. 'What do you say to that, Sylvia?'

'I wish we could just get on with the supper,' said Sylvia. She had hardly touched her food.

'This is so wonderful,' said Sophie, eating as if starved.

Now Andrew appeared, ill but upright. He and Sophie exchanged miserable glances. Frances put a plate of food before Andrew, who said, 'Couldn't we just begin? Sophie and I have to rush off.' His look at Sophie was a humble enquiry but she seemed embarrassed.

'Do we have to recapitulate?' asked Sylvia, pushing aside her plate with relief, and arranging her papers in front of her. 'I sent everyone a resumé.'

'And very good it was,' said Andrew. 'Thank you.'

This was the situation. A group of young doctors wanted to start a campaign to get the government to build shelters against fall-out; that first, and then possibly against a full-scale nuclear attack. The trouble was, the organisation in the field, the Campaign for Unilateral Nuclear Disarmament, a noisy, vigorous efficient force, opposed any attempt to provide shelter of any kind, or even inform the populace about elementary protection. The tone of their polemic was scornful of criticism, was violent, even hysterical.

Julia said, 'I need to have something explained to me. Why do these people complain so much that the government is making provision to shelter itself and the Royal Family?' A persistent jeer was that 'the government is making very sure that it will be protected, never mind about us'. 'I simply do not understand,' said Julia. 'If there is a war then it is essential to maintain a government, surely that is commonsense?'

'I do not think commonsense has much to do with this campaign,' said Wilhelm. 'These are people who have not experienced war, or they would not talk so foolishly.'

'They think like this,' said Colin. 'A bomb will fall and everyone in the world will be dead. Therefore there is no need for shelters.'

'But it is not logical,' said Julia. 'It is not consistent.'

Frances and Rupert were looking at the wodges of articles and cuttings, from *The Defender*, they looked at each other, they shared resignation. *The Defender* was committed to the campaign's 'line'. Members of its staff were on the campaign's committees. Its journalists wrote its articles.

'The argument is,' said Colin, 'that if the government thinks itself protected and safe, then it will be more ready to drop the bomb.'

'What bomb?' said Julia. 'Why one bomb? What is this bomb they keep talking about? In a war there is not one bomb.'

'That is the point, Julia. It is the point we have to get across,' said Sylvia.

'Perhaps Johnny could enlighten us,' said Wilhelm. 'He is on their committee.'

'What committee is Johnny not on?' enquired Colin.

'Why don't we telephone him and ask him to come and defend himself?' suggested Rupert.

People were impressed with this idea; it had not occurred to the family. Andrew went to the telephone. He dialled, Johnny answered. He was told there was a meeting, and he agreed to come.

While they waited they studied Sylvia's cuttings, and Julia said, 'This is the strangest thing I have ever known. These people are like children.'

'I agree,' said Sylvia, 'they are.'

Grateful for this little crumb, Julia took Sylvia's hand and held it. 'Ah, my poor girl, you do not eat, you do not look after yourself.'

'I'm fine,' said Sylvia. 'We all eat too much.'

Frances's stew, rebuked, was nevertheless being offered for second helpings.

Johnny arrived, but not alone. With him was James. Both men wore Mao-style black jackets, and boots from the army surplus shop. Johnny, who had recently been in Cuba with Fidel, wore a scarf in Cuban colours. James was a large man now, smiling, affable, everyone's good fellow. Not pleased to see James? Impossible! He embraced Frances, he clapped Andrew and Colin on the shoulders, he kissed Sophie, he hugged a bonily resistant Sylvia, he gave Julia the closed-fist salute, at shoulder level – modified for social purposes. 'Good to be here again,' he said. He sat in an empty chair, looking expectant, and Johnny came to sit by him, but, feeling lowered from the perpendicular and on the same level as the others, stood up and resumed his old stance, back to the window, arms out, hands resting on the sill. 'I've eaten,' he said. 'How are you, Mutti?'

'As you see.'

James was heartily at work on the food. 'You're missing a treat,' he said to his guide and mentor. He spoke in cockney, and Julia went Tsk, tsk, in annoyance.

Johnny hesitated, then succumbed and sat down as a plate arrived in front of him, Frances having known that this would be the outcome.

Sylvia said, 'This is serious. Johnny, James, we are having a serious discussion.'

'When are situations not serious?' said Johnny. He had nodded at his sons on arriving, and now said to Andrew, 'Pass the bread.'

'Life,' said Colin, 'as we all know, is intrinsically serious.'

'Seriouser and seriouser, as far as I am concerned,' said Andrew.

'Stop it,' said Sylvia. 'We've invited Johnny here for a reason.'

'Shoot!' said Johnny.

'There is a group of young doctors. We have formed a committee. We have all been worried for some time, but the clinching factor was a letter brought out of the Soviet Union . . .'

Johnny, with dramatic intent, laid down his knife and fork and held up a hand to stop her.

She went on. 'It was from a group of doctors in the Soviet Union. They say there have been accidents at nuclear plants, a lot of deaths and people dying. Large areas of country are contaminated with fall-out . . .'

'I am not interested in anti-Soviet propaganda,' said Johnny. He resumed his place, back to the window, leaving his plate. James, with reluctance, left his and stood by Johnny, captain and lieutenant.

Sylvia said, 'This letter was brought out by someone who was there on a delegation. Smuggled out. It reached us. It is genuine.'

'In the first place,' said Johnny, his speech becoming ever more clipped, 'the comrades in the Soviet Union are responsible and would never permit nuclear installations to be faulty. And in the second place, I am not prepared to listen to information which so obviously comes from fascist sources.'

'Oh, Lord,' said Sylvia. 'Aren't you ashamed of yourself, Johnny? Just going on and on saying the same old stuff everyone knows . . .'

'And who is this everybody?' sneered Johnny.

Julia broke in: 'I want to know why your – mob – insists that it is in some way criminal for a government and the Royal Family to be kept safe in the event of war? I do not understand you.'

'It is perfectly simple,' said Andrew. 'These are people who hate anybody in authority – as a matter of course.'

James said, laughing, 'And quite right too.' And repeated it, 'An' qui' righ' too.'

'Children,' said Julia. 'Idiot children. And they have such influence. If you had lived through a war you would not talk such nonsense.'

'You forget,' said James. 'Comrade Johnny fought in the Spanish Civil War.'

Now, a silence. The younger ones had scarcely heard of Johnny's feats, and the older ones had long ago tried to forget. Johnny only looked modestly downwards, and then nodded, taking control again, and said, 'If the bomb falls then that will be curtains, for everybody in the world.'

'What bomb?' said Julia. 'Why do you always talk about *the* bomb, *the* bomb?'

'It's not the Soviet Union we should be worried about,' said Johnny. 'It's American bombs.'

Sylvia said, 'Oh, Johnny, I do wish you'd be serious. You always talk so much nonsense.'

Johnny, goaded by this nonentity, this squit of a girl, slowly losing his temper. 'I do not think I am often told that I talk nonsense.'

'That is because you only mix with people who talk nonsense,' said Colin.

Frances, who was silent because from the moment Johnny had entered she knew nothing sensible could be said or achieved, was removing the plates and putting down glass bowls of lemon cream, apricot mousse and whipped cream. James, seeing this, actually groaned with greed, and resumed his place at the table.

'Who makes pudding these days?' said Johnny.

'Only lovely Frances,' said Sophie, tucking in.

'And not often,' said Frances.

Sylvia said, 'Very well, Johnny, let us assume that these terrible nuclear accidents in the Soviet Union never happened . . .'

'And of course they did not.'

'Then what is your objection to the people of this country being protected against fall-out? You won't even agree to information about how to prepare a house against fall-out. You won't agree to any kind of protection for people. I don't get it. None of us can. The mere idea of any kind of protection and you all start squealing.'

'Because once you agree to shelters then it assumes war is inevitable.'

'But that is simply not logical,' said Julia.

'Not to an ordinary mind,' said Rupert.

Sylvia said, 'It amounts to this, Johnny. No government in this country could even suggest protecting the people, even to the minor extent of fall-out shelters, because of you and your lot. The Campaign for Unilateral Nuclear Disarmament – it has such power that the government is afraid of it.'

'That's righ',' said James. 'That's how i' ough'a be.'

'Why do you talk in that ugly way?' said Julia. 'That isn't how you need to speak.'

'If you don't talk ugly then you're posh,' said Colin, talking posh. 'And you don't get work in this free country. Another tyranny.'

Johnny and James showed signs of leaving.

'I'm going back to the hospital,' said Sylvia. 'At least I can have an intelligent conversation there.'

'I want to see the letter you are talking about,' said Johnny.

'Why?' asked Sylvia. 'You aren't even prepared to discuss what it says.'

'Obviously,' said Andrew, 'he wants to inform the Soviet Embassy here of its contents. So that it can be traced, and the writers can be sent to labour camps or shot.'

'Labour camps do not exist,' said Johnny. 'And if they did once – to a certain extent – they have been exaggerated – then they don't exist now.'

'Oh, Lord,' said Andrew. 'You really are a bore, Johnny.'

'A bore isn't dangerous,' said Julia. 'Johnny and his kind are dangerous.'

'That is very true,' said Wilhelm, politely, as ever, to Johnny. 'You are very dangerous people. Do you realise, if there is a nuclear accident here, in this country, or if a bomb is dropped by some madman, let alone if there is a war, then millions of people could die because of you?'

'Well, thanks for the snack,' said Johnny.

'Thanks for nothing,' said Sylvia, almost in tears. 'I should have known there was no point even in trying.'

The two men left. Andrew and Sophie left, their arms around each other. Colin's sardonic smile at the sight did not go unnoticed by them or by anybody.

Sylvia said, 'Anyway, there's a committee. So far it's all doctors, but we are going to expand.'

'Enrol us all,' said Colin, 'but expect to find glass in your wine and frogs through the letterbox.'

Sylvia embraced Julia, and left.

'Don't you think it is strange that stupid people should have such power?' said Julia, almost weeping, because of Sylvia's careless farewell.

'No,' said Colin.

'No,' said Frances.

'No,' said Wilhelm Stein.

'No,' said Rupert.

'But this is England, this is England . . .' said Julia.

Wilhelm put his arm around her, and led her out and up the stairs.

There were left Frances and Rupert, Colin and the dog. A little situation: Rupert wanted to stay the night, and Frances wanted him to, but she was afraid – she could not help it – of Colin's reaction.

'Well, you two,' said Colin, and it was an effort for him, 'bedtime, I think.' Giving them permission. He began teasing the dog until it barked.

'There you are,' he said. 'He always has the last word.'

A couple of weeks later Frances with Rupert, Julia and Wilhelm, Colin, were at a meeting called by the young doctors. There were about two hundred there. Sylvia opened the meeting, speaking well. Other doctors, and then more people followed. Members of the opposition had got wind of the meeting, and there were a group of thirty, who kept up a steady shouting, whistling, and shouts of *Fascists! War mongers! CIA!* Some were from the staff of *The Defender.* As our group left, some youths waiting at the exit caught hold of Wilhelm Stein and threw him against railings. Colin at once laid into them and put them to flight. Wilhelm was shaken, it was thought no more than that, but he had cracked ribs and he was taken to Julia's house and put to bed there.

'And so, my dear,' he said, in a voice that was wheezy, and old. 'And so, Julia, I have achieved the impossible: I am living with you at last.' This was the first the others had heard Wilhelm wanted to move in.

He was put into the room that had been Andrew's and Julia proved a devoted if fussy nurse. Wilhelm hated it, having seen himself always as Julia's cavalier, her beau. And Colin too, that abrasive young man, surprised the others, and perhaps himself, by a charming attentiveness to the old man. He sat with him, and told him stories about 'my dangerous life on the Heath, and in the Hampstead pubs', in which Vicious figured as something not far off the Hound of the Baskervilles. Wilhelm laughed, and begged Colin to desist, because his ribs hurt. Doctor Lehman came, and told Frances and Julia and Colin that the old man was on his way out. 'These falls are not good at his age.' He prescribed sedatives for Wilhelm and a variety of pills for Julia whom he was at last permitting to think of herself as old.

Frances and Rupert at *The Defender* demanded their right to put an opposing view to that of the unilateral disarmament people, and wrote an article, which earned dozens of letters nearly all furiously opposing, or abusive. *The Defender* offices seethed and Frances and Rupert found curt or angry notes on their desks, some anonymous. They realised this rage was too deep in some part of the collective unconscious to be reasoned with. It was not about protecting or not protecting the population: they had no idea what it was really about. It was very unpleasant at *The Defender*. They decided to leave, well before it suited either of them financially. They were simply in the wrong place. Always had been, Frances decided. And all those long well-reasoned articles on social issues? Anyone could have written them, Frances said. Rupert almost at once got another job on a newspaper described as fascist by a typical *Defender* addict, but as Tory, by the populace. 'I suppose I must be a Tory,' said Rupert, 'if we are going to take these old labels seriously.'

The week they resigned a parcel of faeces was pushed through the door of Julia's house, but not the front door, the one into Phyllida's flat from the outside steps to the basement. A death-threat arrived, anonymous, to Frances. And Rupert too was sent a death-threat, together with some photographs of Hiroshima after the bomb. Phyllida came up – the first time for months – to say she objected to being drawn into this 'ridiculous debate'. She was not prepared to deal with shit, not on any level. She was leaving.

She was going to share a flat with another woman. And then she was gone.

As for the poisonous debates over protecting or not protecting the population, soon it would be generally agreed that war had been prevented for so long because the possibly belligerent nations had nuclear weapons and did not use them. There remained, however, questions that this admission did not answer. Accidents at nuclear installations might happen and often did, and were usually hushed up. In the Soviet Union there had been accidents that had poisoned whole districts. There were madmen in the world who would not hesitate to drop 'the bomb', or several, but it was at least strange that this threat was usually referred to in the singular. The population remained unprotected, but the violence, the poison, the rage of the debates, simply fizzled out – stopped. If there ever had been a threat, it existed now. But the hysteria evaporated. 'A strange thing,' said Julia, in her new, sorrowful, slow voice.

Wilhelm was still at Julia's, and his big luxurious flat was empty. He kept saying that he was going to bring all his books over, and put an end to this 'amazingly absurd situation', with him neither living with Julia, nor not. He kept making dates with the movers, and cancelling them. He was not himself. He had to be humoured. Julia was as distressed. The two of them together were now like sick people who wanted to be responsible for each other, but their own weakness forbade it. Julia had succumbed to pneumonia, and for a while the two invalids were on different floors, sending notes to each other. Then Wilhelm insisted on getting up to visit her. She saw this old man shuffling into her room, holding on to the edges of doors, and chair tops, and thought he looked like an old tortoise. He was in a dark jacket, wore a small dark cap, for his head was always cold, and he poked his head forward. And she – he was shocked by her, the bones of her face prominent, her arms like sticks of bone.

Both were so sad, so distressed. Like people in a severe depression, the grey landscape that lay about them now seemed

247

to be the only truth. 'It seems I am an old man, Julia,' he jested, trying to revive in him the courtly gent who kissed her hand and stood between her and all difficulties. That had been the convention. But he had been nothing of the sort, he now perceived, only a lonely old thing dependent on Julia for, well, everything. And she, the benevolent gracious lady, whose house had sheltered so many, though she had grumbled about it often enough, without him would have been an emotionally indigent old fool, besotted with a girl who was not even her granddaughter. So they seemed to each other and themselves, on their bad days, like shadows a bare branch lays on the earth, a thin and empty tracery, no warmth of flesh anywhere, and kisses and embraces are tentative, ghosts trying to meet.

Johnny heard that Wilhelm was living in Julia's house and came to say that he hoped there was no question of Wilhelm being left money. 'That has nothing to do with you,' Julia said. 'I shall not discuss it. And since you are here I shall tell you that I have had to support your abandoned wives and children and so I am not leaving you anything. Why don't you ask your precious communist party to give you a pension?'

The house had been left to Colin and to Andrew, and both Phyllida and Frances were provisioned with decent if not lavish pensions. Sylvia had said, 'Oh, Julia, please don't, I don't need money.' But Julia left Sylvia's name in her will; Sylvia might not need it, but Julia needed to do it.

Sylvia was about to leave Britain, probably for a long time. She was going to Africa, to a mission station in the bush, in Zimlia. When Julia heard this she said, 'Then I shall not see you again.'

Sylvia went to say goodbye to her mother, having telephoned first. 'Kind of you to let me know,' said Phyllida.

The flat was a large mansion block in Highgate, and the entry-phone said that here were to be found Doctor Phyllida Lennox and Mary Constable, Physiotherapist. A little lift ground up through the lower floors like a biddable birdcage. Sylvia rang, heard a shout, was admitted, not by her mother, but by a large and cheery lady on her way out. 'I'll leave you two to it,' said Mary Constable, revealing that there had been confidences. The little hall had an ecclesiastical aspect which, examined, turned out to be due to a large stained-glass panel, in boiled-sweet colours, showing Saint Frances with his birds – certainly modern. It was propped on a chair, like a signboard to spirituality. The door opened to show a large room whose main feature was a commodious chair draped with some kind of oriental rug, and a couch, inspired by Freud's in Maresfield Gardens, rigorous and uncomfortable. Phyllida was now a stout woman with greying hair in thick plaits on either side of a matronly face. She wore a kaftan of many colours, and multiple beads, earrings, bracelets. Sylvia, who had been carrying in her mind a limp, weepy, flabby female, had to adjust to this hearty woman, who clearly had acquired confidence.

'Sit down,' said Phyllida, indicating a chair not in the therapeutic part of the room. Sylvia sat carefully on its very edge. A spicy provocative smell . . . had Phyllida taken to wearing perfume? No, it was incense, emanating from the next room, whose door was open. Sylvia sneezed. Phyllida shut the door, and sat herself in her confessor's chair.

'And so, Tilly, I hear you are going to convert the heathen?'

'I am going to a hospital, as a doctor. It is a mission hospital. I shall be the only doctor in the area.'

The big strong woman, and the wisp of a girl – so she still seemed – were being made conscious of their differences. Phyllida said, 'What a pasty-face! You're like your father, a proper weed he was. I used to call him Comrade Lily. His middle name was Lillie, after some old Cromwell revolutionary. Well, I had to keep my end up somehow, when he came the commissar at me. He was worse even than Johnny, if you can believe that. Nag, nag, nag. That bloody Revolution of theirs, it was just an excuse to nag at people. Your father used to make me learn revolutionary texts by heart. I am sure I could recite the *Communist Manifesto* for you even now. But with you it's back to the Bible.'

'Why back to?'

'My father was a clergyman. In Bethnal Green.'

'So what were they like, my grandparents?'

'I don't know. Hardly saw them after they sent me away. I didn't want to see them. I went to live with my aunt. Obviously they didn't want to see me, sending me away like that for five years, so why should I want to see them?'

'Do you have any photographs of them?'

'I tore them up.'

'I would have liked to see them.'

'Why should you care? Now you are going away. Just as far away as you can get, I suppose. A little thing like you. They must be mad, sending you.'

'However that may be. But I've come to say something important. And what is this Doctor on your nameplate?'

'I am a Doctor of Philosophy, aren't I? I took Philosophy at university.'

'But we don't use Doctor like that in his country. Only the Germans do.'

'No one can say I am not a doctor.'

'You'll get into trouble.'

'No one has complained yet.'

'That is what I've come to see you about . . . mother, this therapy you're doing. I know you don't need any kind of training for it but . . .'

'I'm learning on the job. Believe me, it's an education.'

'I know. People have said you have helped them.'

Phyllida seemed to turn into someone else: she flushed, she sat forward clasping her hands, was smiling and confused with pleasure. 'They did? You've heard good things?'

'Yes, I have. But what I want to suggest is, why not actually take a course? There are some good ones.'

'I'm doing all right as I am.'

'Tea and sympathy are all very well . . .'

'I can tell you, there have been times I could have done with tea and sympathy . . .' and her voice was sliding into the knell of her complaint. Sylvia's muscles were already propelling her upwards, when Phyllida said, 'No, no, sit down, Tilly.'

Sylvia sat, and pulled from a briefcase a stack of paper, which she handed to her mother. 'I've made a list of the good ones. One of these days someone is going to say they have a headache or a stomach ache and you'll say it's psychosomatic, but it's cancer or a tumour. Then you'll blame yourself.'

Phyllida sat silent, holding the papers. In came Mary Constable, all confidential smiles.

'Come and meet Tilly,' said Phyllida.

'How are you, Tilly?' said Mary, actually embracing the reluctant Sylvia.

'Are you a psychotherapist too?'

'I'm physio,' said Phyllida's companion . . . lover? Who knew, these days? 'I train physio students. We say that between us we deal with the whole person,' said cheerful Mary, radiating a persuasive intimacy and faint aromas of incense.

'I must go,' said Sylvia.

'But you've just come,' said Phyllida, with satisfaction that Sylvia was behaving as she had expected she would.

'I've got a meeting,' said Sylvia.

'Said just like Comrade Johnny.'

'I hope not,' said Sylvia.

'Then, goodbye. Send me a postcard from your tropical paradise.'

'They have just finished a rather nasty war,' said Sylvia.

Sylvia rang Andrew in New York, was told he was in Paris, then from there, that he was in Kenya. From Nairobi she heard his voice, crackly and faint.

'Andrew, it's me.'

'It's who? Damn this line. Well, we won't get a better. Third World tech,' he shouted.

'It's Sylvia.'

Even through the crackles she heard his voice change. 'Oh, darling Sylvia, where are you?'

'I was thinking of you, Andrew.'

She had been, needing his calming, confident voice, but this distant ghost was discommoding her, like a message of how little he could do for her. But what had she expected?

'I thought you were in Zimlia,' he shouted.

'Next week. Oh, Andrew, I feel as if I am jumping over a cliff.'

She had had a letter, from Father Kevin McGuire, of St Luke's Mission, forcing her to look steadily at a future she had not envisaged at all, until that moment. Attached to the letter was a list of things she must bring. Medical supplies she had taken for granted, as basic as syringes, aspirin, antibiotics, antiseptics, needles for suturing, a stethoscope, on and on. 'And certain things ladies need, because you won't find them easily here.' Nail scissors, knitting needles, crochet hooks, knitting wool. 'And humour this old man, who loves his Oxford marmalade.' Batteries for a radio. A small radio. A good jersey, size 10, for Rebecca. 'She is the house girl. She has a cough.' A recent issue of the *Irish Times*. One of *The Observer*. Some tins of sardines, 'If you can slip them into a corner somewhere.' With greetings, Kevin McGuire. 'P.S. And do not forget the books. As many as you can. There is a need for them.'

'It was a bit rough out there,' she had been told.

'Andrew, I'm in a panic – I think.'

'It's not so bad. Nairobi's not so bad. A bit gimcrack.'

'I'll be a hundred miles from Senga.'

'Look, Sylvia, I'll drop in to London on my way back and see you.'

'What are you doing there?'

'Distributing largesse.'

'Oh, yes, they said. Global Money.'

'I'm financing a dam, a silo, irrigation . . . you name it.'

'*You* are?'

'I wave my magic wand, and the desert blooms.'

So, he was drunk. Nothing could have been worse for Sylvia then, than that braggart cry from the ether. Andrew, her support, her friend, her brother – well almost, being so silly, so shoddy. She shouted, 'Goodbye,' and put the phone down and wept. This was her worst moment: she was not to have another as bad. Believing that Andrew would have forgotten the conversation, she did not expect him, but he telephoned from Heathrow two days later. 'Now here I am, little Sylvia. Where can we go and talk?'

He rang Julia from the airport, and asked if he and Sylvia might come and have a good talk, in her house. His flat was let, and Sylvia shared a tiny flat near her hospital with another doctor.

Julia was silent, then said, 'I do not understand? You are asking if Sylvia and you may come to this house? What are you saying?'

'You wouldn't like it if we just took you for granted.'

A silence. 'You still have a key, I think?' And she put down the telephone.

When the two arrived, they went straight up to see her. Julia sat alone, and severe, at her table, with a patience spread on it. She inclined a cheek to Andrew, tried to do the same to Sylvia, could not keep it up, and stood to embrace the young woman.

'I thought you'd gone to Zimlia,' said Julia.

'But I wouldn't go without saying goodbye.'

'Is this goodbye?'

'No, next week.'

The old sharp eyes scrutinised the two, at length. Julia wanted to say that Sylvia was too thin, and that Andrew had a look about him she did not like. What was it?

'Go and have your talk,' she commanded, taking up her hand of cards.

They crept guiltily down into the big sitting-room, full of memories, and on to the old red sofa, into which they sank, arms around each other.

'Oh, Andrew, I'm more comfortable with you than anyone.'

'And I with you.'

'And what about Sophie?'

An angry laugh. '*Comfortable!* – but that's over.'

'Oh, poor Andrew. Did she go back to Roland?'

'He sent her a nice bouquet and she went back.'

'What, exactly?'

'Marigolds – for grief. Anemone – Forsaken. And of course about a thousand red roses. For love. Yes, he has only to say it with flowers. But it didn't last. He started behaving as comes naturally to him and she sent him a bunch that said War: thistles.'

'Is she with someone?'

'Yes, but we don't know who.'

'Poor Sophie.'

'But poor Sylvia first. Why don't we hear about you and some fantastically lucky chap?'

She could have shrunk away from him, but he held her.

'I'm just – unlucky.'

'Are you in love with Father Jack?'

And now she did sit up, pushing him away. 'No, how can you . . .' but seeing his face, which was sympathetic, she said, 'Yes, I was.'

'Nuns are always in love with their priests,' he murmured. She did not know if he meant to be cruel.

'I'm not a nun.'

'Come back here.' And he drew her close again.

And now she said in a tiny voice he remembered from little Sylvia, 'I think there is something wrong with me. I did go to bed with someone, a doctor at the hospital, and . . . that's the trouble, you see, Andrew. I don't like sex.' And she sobbed, while he held her.

'Well, I think I'm not as proficient in that department as I might be. Sophie made it very clear that compared to Roland I'm a dead loss'.

'Oh, poor Andrew.'

'And poor Sylvia.'

They cried themselves to sleep, like children.

They were visited, while they slept, first by Colin, because the little dog's uneasiness said there was someone in the house who shouldn't be. The room was in twilight. Colin stood for a while looking at the two, holding the dog's jaws closed, to prevent it from barking.

'You're a good little creature,' he told Vicious, no a shabby old dog, as he went down the stairs.

Later Frances came in. The room was dark. She switched on a tiny light, which had once been Sylvia's night-light, because of her fear of the dark, and stood, as Colin had done, looking down at what she could see, only their heads and faces. Sylvia and Andrew – oh, no, no, Frances was thinking, like a mother, as it were crossing her fingers to avert evil. It would be a disaster. Both needed – surely? – something more robust? But when were her sons going to get themselves settled, and safe – (*safe?* she was certainly thinking like a mother, apparently one can't avoid it) – they were both well into their thirties. All our fault . . . she was thinking: meaning all of them, the older generation. Then, to console herself, Perhaps it will take them as long as it has taken me, to be happy. So I mustn't give up hope.

Much later still, Julia came down the stairs. She thought there was no one in the room, though Frances had told her the two were still there, lost to the world. Then, by the glimmer of the tiny light, she saw the faces, Sylvia's below Andrew's, on his shoulder. So pale, so tired – she could see that even in this light. All around them a deep black, for the red sofa was intensifying the dark, as when a painter uses a crimson undercoat and the black intensifies and glows. At either end of the great room windows admitted enough light to grey the dark, no more. It was a cloudy night, without moon or stars. Julia was thinking, surely they are too young to look like that, so washed out. The two faces were like ashes spilled on the dark.

She stood there a long time, looking down at Sylvia, fixing

that face on her memory. And in fact Julia did not see her again. There was a muddle over the time of the flight departure and a call from Sylvia, 'Julia, oh, Julia, I'm so sorry. But I'm sure I'll be back in London soon.'

Wilhelm died. There was a funeral with a couple of hundred people. Everyone who had ever drunk a cup of coffee in the Cosmo must have come, people were saying. Colin and Andrew, with Frances, stood together supporting Julia, who was mute and tearless, and seemed as if cut out of paper. 'Good God, everyone in the book trade must be here,' they heard from all around them. They had had no idea of Wilhelm Stein's popularity, or of how he was seen by his compeers. There was a general feeling that in burying the courteous, kind, and erudite old book dealer they were saying goodbye to a past much better than was possible now. 'The end of an epoch,' people were whispering, and some were weeping because of it. The two sons, who had flown in that morning from the States, thanked the Lennoxes politely for any trouble they had incurred, over the funeral, and said that they would now take over: Wilhelm was leaving a good bit of money.

Julia took to her bed, and of course people said that Wilhelm's death had done for her, but there was something else, an appalling thing, a blow to her heart that none of the family understood.

When Colin's second novel came out, it was clear that *Sick Death* would not do as well as his first. And it was not as good, being virtually a tract about a criminally irresponsible government neglecting to protect its people from nuclear fall-out, bombs, and so on. An efficient propaganda campaign, inspired by agents of a foreign enemy power, created a hysterical atmosphere which made this government, concerned about its popularity, ignore its responsibilities. This novel evoked roars of indignation from the various movements concerning themselves with the Bomb. Some reviews were malignant, among them Rose Trimble's. Her profile of President Matthew Mungozi had put her on the map, she had all kinds of opportunities afforded to her, but she was now working on the *Daily Post*, famous for its virulence, and was at home there. She used Colin's novel as a starting point for an attack on those who wanted to build shelters, and in particular the young doctors, and most particularly Sylvia Lennox. As for Colin, 'It should be known that he has a Nazi background. His grandmother Julia Lennox was a member of the Hitler Youth.' Rose felt safe. For one thing the *Daily Post* was a newspaper that expected to pay out – often – compensation for libel, and for another she knew that Julia would not deign to notice such an attack. 'Nasty old bitch,' Rose muttered.

Wilhelm had been shown this article by a friend in the Cosmo. He debated whether to tell Julia, decided that he should: and it was just as well, because a well-wisher sent her the cutting anonymously. 'Take no notice,' she had said to Wilhelm. 'They are nothing but shit. I think I am justified in using their favourite word?' 'My *dear* Julia,' Wilhelm had said, amused, but shocked, too, at this word from her.

Julia sat up against the pillows, nurses coming and going, not expecting to sleep, with the cutting in her bedside table. So now, she, Julia von Arne, was a Nazi. What hurt was the carelessness of it. Of course that woman – Julia remembered an unlikeable girl – had not known what she was doing. They all used words like fascist all the time, anyone they might be having a tiff with was a fascist. They were so ignorant they did not know there had been real fascists, who had brought Italy low. And Nazi . . . there were newspaper articles, radio programmes, television, about *them*, which she watched because she felt so directly concerned, but obviously none of these young people had taken it in. They did not seem to know that fascist, Nazi, were words that meant people had been imprisoned, been tortured, had died in millions in that war. It was the ignorance, the carelessness, that filled Julia's eyes with angry tears. She felt cancelled out, obliterated: her history, and Philip's too, reduced to epithets used by an ambitious young journalist in a gutter newspaper. Julia sat sleepless (she quietly disposed of her sleeping pills when the nurses weren't looking), poisoned by her helplessness. Of course she would not sue, or even write a letter: why dignify that *canaille* by even noticing them? Wilhelm had brought her a drafted letter, saying the von Arnes were an old German family which had never had connections with the Nazis. She asked him to forget it, not to send it. She was wrong: it should have been sent, to ease her heart, if nothing else. And she was wrong, too, about Rose Trimble. Carelessness and indifference to history – yes, she was like her generation, but it was an immediate hatred of the Lennoxes that inspired her, the need to 'get back at them'. She had forgotten what had brought her to their house in the first place, or that she had ever claimed Andrew had made her pregnant. No, it was that house, the ease of it, the way they took everything for granted, and looked after each other. Sylvia, that prissy little bitch; Frances, the shitty old queen bee, wasp, rather; Julia bossing everyone. And the men, complacent bastards. Her article had been written from the wells of bile and malice that forever churned and seethed inside Rose, which could be mollified if only temporarily, when she was able to write words directed straight to the hearts of her victims. She imagined, as she wrote, how they gasped and writhed as they read. She imagined them crying out in pain. That was why Julia was dying before her time. She felt she had suddenly been attacked by malignity. She sat against her pillows in a room where light fell from the window, and moved from floor to bed to wall, and back around the walls to the window, such a feeble answer to the dark that was descending from invisible inimical forces, and which enclosed her. She had been running away from them all her life, she felt, but now she was being swallowed by a monster of stupidity and ugliness and vulgarity. Everything was distorted and spoiled. And so she stayed in bed, and went back in her mind to her girlhood when everything had been beautiful, so *schön, schön, schön*, but into that paradise had come that old war, and the world was full of uniforms. At night, when the tiny light that had been Sylvia's and had been brought up from the sitting-room to her room, was the only illumination in the dark, her brothers and Philip, handsome brave young men, stood about her bed, in smart uniforms that had not a spot nor spatter nor stain on them. She cried to them to stay with her, not to go off and leave her.

She talked softly in German, and in English, and in her *comme-il-faut* French, and Colin sat with her, sometimes for hours, holding the bundle of little bones that was her hand. He was unhappy, remorseful, thinking that he had never really heard about Ernst and Frederich and Max; he had scarcely heard of his grandfather. Behind him was a chasm or gulf into which normality had fallen, ordinary family life had taken a fall, and here he sat, a grandson, but he had not met his grandfather, nor Julia's German family. But it was his family too . . . He bent close to Julia and said, 'Julia, please, tell me about your brothers, about your father and mother, did you have grandparents? Tell me about them.' She came out of her dream and said, 'Who? Who did you say? They are dead. They were killed. There is no family now. There is no house now. There is nothing left now. It is terrible, terrible . . .'

She did not like being called back out of her memories, or dreams. She did not like the present, all medicines, pills and nurses, and she hated the ancient yellowish body that was revealed when they washed her. Above all, she had a persistent diarrhoea, which meant that no matter how often her bed was changed, and her nightdress, or how much they cleaned her, there was a smell in her room. She demanded that cologne be splashed about, and she rubbed it into her hands and face, but the odour of faeces was there, and she was ashamed and miserable. 'Terrible, terrible, terrible,' she muttered, a fierce old crone, who sometimes wept angry tears.

She died, and Frances found the cutting in her bedside table, saying that Julia had been a Nazi. She showed it to Colin and they laughed, because of the absurdity. Colin said that if he met Rose Trimble he might consider beating her up, but Frances, like Julia, said they were not worth bothering about, these people.

Julia's funeral was not as heartwarming as Wilhelm's.

It seemed that she was or had been some kind of a Catholic, but she had not asked for a priest in her last illness, nor was there anything about her funeral in her will. They decided on a non-committally interdenominational service, but it seemed so bleak, that they remembered she had liked poetry. Poems should be read. What poems? Andrew looked about on her shelves, and then found in her bedside drawer a copy of Gerard Manley Hopkins. It had been much read and some poems were underlined. They were the 'terrible' poems. Andrew said no, too painful to read those.

'*No worst there is none. Pitched past pitch of grief . . .*'

No.

He chose *The Caged Skylark*, which she had liked, for there was a pencil line beside it, and then the poem *Spring and Fall*, to a young child, beginning,

> *Margaret, are you grieving*
> *Over Goldengrove unleaving?*

This had a line beside it too, but it was the dark poems that had the double, triple heavy black lines beside them, and jagged exclamation marks too.

So the family felt they were betraying Julia, choosing the softer poems. And, too, they had to tell themselves that they had not known Julia, could never have guessed at those deep black lines beside

> *I wake and feel the fell of dark, not day.*
> *What hours, O what black hours we have spent . . .*

There ought to be some German poetry but Wilhelm was not there to advise.

Andrew read the poems. His voice was light, but strong enough for the occasion: there were few people there, apart from the family. Mrs Philby stood well away from them, in blackest black, from her hat, kept for funerals, to her boots, that shone, a reproach to them: she continued in her role which was to shame the sloppy ways of the family. None of them was in black, only her. Her face was vindictive with righteousness. She wept, though, at the end. 'Mrs Lennox was my oldest friend,' she told Frances, in severe reproach. 'I shall not be coming to you again. I only came because of her.'

Halfway through the proceedings a gaunt figure, his white locks and loose clothes fluttering in a wind that blew through the gravestones, appeared and wandered uncertainly towards the funeral group. It was Johnny, sombre, unhappy, and looking much older than he should. He stood well apart from any of them, half turned away, as if ready to run off. The words of the service were an affront to him, it was evident. At the end his sons and Frances went towards him, to ask him back to the house, but he only nodded, and stalked off. At the limits of the graveyard he turned and gave them a salute with his open right hand, palm towards them, at shoulder level.

Sylvia was not at the funeral. The telephone lines to St Luke's Mission were down, because of a bad storm.

Meanwhile Frances's life with Rupert was not going as they had expected. She was virtually living in his place, though her books and papers were at Julia's. It was not a big flat. The sitting-room, which was also where they ate, with a tiny kitchen through a hatch, was a third of the size of Julia's. The big bedroom was adequate. The two small rooms were for the two children, Margaret and William, who came at weekends. When Meriel had gone off to live with a new man, Jaspar, there had been plans to buy something bigger. Frances liked the children well enough and believed they did not dislike her: they were polite and obedient. From their mother's flat they went off to school, and with their mother and Jaspar went for holidays. Then one weekend they were strained, silent, and said that their mother wasn't well. And no, Jaspar wasn't there. The children did not look at each other, imparting this information but it was as if they exchanged looks full of dread.

It was at this moment that real life caught up with her again: that was how Frances felt it. In the months – no, years now – she had spent with Rupert she had become a different person, slowly learning to take happiness for granted. Good Lord, just imagine, if there had been no Rupert she would have gone on in the same dull willed routine of duty, and without love, sex, intimacy.

Rupert went off with the children to their mother's and found what he had dreaded. Years ago, after the birth of Margaret, she had suffered a depression, a real one. He had seen her through it, she had got better, but lived in terror that it might recur. It had. Meriel sat curled up in the corner of a sofa, staring at nothing, in a dirty dressing-gown, her hair unwashed and uncombed. The children stood on either side of their father, staring at their mother, then pressed close to him so he could put his arms around them.

'Where is Jaspar?' he asked the silent woman, who was evidently a long way off, inside the dreadful suffering of the depressive.

After a time he repeated the question, and she said, irritated at the interruption, 'Gone.'

'Is he coming back?'

'No.'

That seemed to be all he was going to get out of her, but then she said, in a thick indifferent mutter, not moving, not turning her head, 'Better take the kids. They'll get nothing here.'

Rupert collected up books, toys, clothes, school gear, under the direction of Margaret and William, and then back to Meriel. 'What are you going to do?' he asked. A long silence. She shook her head, meaning, Leave me alone, and then when the three were already at the door, she said in the same tone, 'Get me into hospital. Any hospital. I don't care.'

The children were installed again in their old rooms, and at once the whole flat was awash with their possessions. They were frightened, and silent.

Rupert rang their doctor, who would arrange for Meriel to go into a psychiatric ward. He tried to ring Jaspar, but his call was not returned.

Frances was having hard, cool thoughts. She knew that Jaspar was not likely to come back to Meriel, if he had gone off in fright at the experience of being with a depressive. He was ten years younger, was an ornament of the fashion world, designing sports clothes and making money. His name was often in the newspapers. Why had he taken on a woman with two half-grown children? Rupert had said he believed the young man had enjoyed seeing himself as mature and responsible, proving that he was a serious person. He had the reputation of being too trendy for his own good, drugs, wild parties – all that. To which scene he had presumably returned. That meant that Meriel was without a man, and would very likely want her husband back. And here were two children in emotional shock, and here she was, a mother substitute. And yes, she was suffering that awed and appalled feeling that comes when life recurs, in a familiar pattern. She thought, I am in danger of being landed with these kids – no, I *have* been landed with them. Do I want that?

Margaret was twelve, William was ten. They would soon be adolescent. She was not afraid that Rupert would let her down, relinquish responsibility to her, but that their intimacy would not only suffer – it would have to – and it might disappear, sucked into the insensate demands of teenagers. But she liked Rupert so much . . . she did so like him . . . she loved the man. She could say, seriously, she had not loved till now – yes, she would say yes to whatever turned up. And after all, even depressions take themselves off, and then the children would want to be with their mother.

From the hospital where Meriel was came scrawls, you could not call them letters, in wild handwriting. 'Rupert, don't let the children come here. It won't be good for them. Frances, Margaret has asthma, she needs a new prescription.'

The doctors, telephoned by Rupert, said she was very ill but would recover. Her previous illness had lasted two years.

Frances and Rupert lay side by side in the dark, her head on his right shoulder, his right hand on her right breast. Her hand lay on his inner thigh, her knuckles against his balls, a soft but self-respecting weight that was giving her confidence. This connubial and time-honoured scene was how they spent the half hour before sleep, whether love-making had taken place or not. The subject that both had been skirting around now had to be dealt with.

'Where was Meriel when she was ill, those two years?'

'Mostly in bed. She wasn't up to much.'

'She can't stay in hospital for two years.'

'No, she'll need looking after.'

'I suppose Jaspar isn't going to rally around?'

'Is it likely?'

He spoke quietly, even jauntily, but with a forlorn bravery that melted her heart. 'Look, Frances, this is just as bad as it can be for you. Don't imagine I don't know it.' She wasn't going to say it wasn't bad, so hesitated, and he came in quickly with, 'I won't blame you if you left . . .' His voice was thick.

'I'm not leaving. I'm just thinking.' He kissed her cheek, from which she learned that his face was wet.

'If you sold this flat and we put our money together, and bought a big flat, even then there would be the problem – it would be the first wife and the second incumbent in separate rooms, like an African polygamist.'

'Or like Thurber's cartoon. I don't really see Meriel on the top of a cupboard.'

264

They laughed. They did laugh.

'Do we have enough money for a house?' she asked.

'Not in any decent part of London. Not a big one.'

'I take it Meriel is not going to be earning?'

'She was never one for a career.' His voice was dry, indeed: she knew that here was a history. 'An old-fashioned woman, that's Meriel. Or the last word in feminism. And of course she wasn't working when she was with Jaspar, she was enjoying the high life. So, yes, we can take it that she will have to be kept.' A pause. 'They did say, the doctors, that we have to assume the depression will recur.'

'I've been thinking, Rupert. It would be two wives in one house, but at least not on the same floor.'

'I gather you've done that one already?'

'I'm an old hand at it.'

'Are you planning to marry me, Frances?'

'It would certainly be better for the children if I did. Fancy-woman into wife. Never underestimate the conservatism of children.'

Frances telephoned Colin, asked if they could talk, and he suggested she should come and he would cook. She found herself back in Julia's house, in the kitchen, at a table which was the smallest she had seen it. Two chairs. Colin arrived, all energetic welcome.

They embraced.

Frances said, 'Where's the little dog?'

He hesitated, turned his back to lift plates from the refrigerator – using it as she had done so often to avoid or postpone notice, set cold soup in front of her, and sat opposite her.

'Vicious is with Sophie. She's downstairs.'

She laid down her spoon, and absorbed the shock. 'Sophie and you are together?'

'She's ill. It's a kind of breakdown. The man after Andrew – no good. She appealed to me.'

She had taken all this in and now applied herself to the soup. He was a good cook. 'Well, that certainly puts a different face on it.'

'Enlighten me.'

She did, and he showed his grasp of the essentials with, 'Well, Ma, you're a glutton for punishment.'

'The thing is, I really do . . .' she had been going to say, like, but said, 'love this man. I do.'

'He's a good bloke,' said her son.

'Have you moved in to Julia's flat yet?'

'It's such a period piece, I can't bear to demolish it. But yes, of course we're going to use it.'

'Suppose we put Rupert's wife in the basement flat?'

'Just like poor Phyllida.'

'But I hope not for ever. Rupert says that Meriel couldn't wait to get rid of him. More fool her.'

'Right then. Meriel in the basement. Sophie and me at the top of the house. We will use Sylvia's old room, and I will go on working in the sitting-room. So you and Rupert and the two kids will have the six rooms, on Andrew's floor and mine, and your rooms. And of course, there is this ever faithful kitchen.'

'I wouldn't have thought of it if I didn't know the house was virtually empty. And it would give us a breathing space . . .'

'It's not a bad idea.' With the energy he brought to everything, he removed the soup plates and produced grilled fish. He poured wine, he drank his down, poured himself some more.

'And you and Sophie?'

'Andrew wasn't good for Sophie. It was more of the same. She says Roland was like a black hole when it came to the crunch, and Andrew – well . . . every good intention, but he is a bit of a lightweight, you'll have to agree to that? He doesn't *engage*,' explained her son, with a grin that expected complicity in understanding. 'Whereas I,' he said, stating his case, 'take people on. I have victims in my past to prove it, well-gnawed and mangled, but *taken on*. No, you don't know about them. I've taken Sophie *on*.'

'Two loonies in one house,' said Frances.

'Elegantly put.'

'And not for the first time. But never mind, with children at ten and twelve, they'll be grown-up soon, won't they?'

'In the first place, I haven't noticed Andrew and me – or Sylvia – not needing a family base, even when grown-up. And in the second place – well, I wouldn't have understood your peremptory ways with time until recently. What's four years? Six years? Ten? Nothing. A mere breath. There's nothing like a death to bring that home . . . and there's another thing. Has it occurred to you that the kids might prefer you to their delinquent mum?'

'Delinquent! She's ill.'

'She went off with her demon lover, didn't she? She ditched them?'

'No, she took them with her. But now they're – ditched.'

'I hope they're at least passable. Are they?'

'So far they've been on their best behaviour. I don't know.'

'Aren't you haunted by all this recurrence?'

'Yes. Oh, yes, I am. And it's worse than you know. Meriel is the daughter of Sebastian Heath – you probably don't remember that name? You do? He was a famous communist, just like Johnny. He was arrested by the comrades in the Soviet Union and disappeared for ever.'

'I suppose to have a father who was shot in the back of the neck by his own side is enough to explain a certain amount of emotional disarray.'

'And then her mother committed suicide. She was a communist too. Meriel was brought up by a communist family – but they aren't communists now, apparently.'

'So she had what might fairly be described as a broken childhood.'

'Hence my feeling of being pursued by more of the same.'

'Poor Ma,' he said cheerily. Never mind. And don't think your housing problems will be solved permanently if you come here. I intend to get married.'

'Sophie!'

'Good God, no. I'm not that mad. She's just my mate. We're mates. But I'm definitely on the look-out for a wife. And I shall get married and have four kids, none of your two and a half stuff. And then I'll need this house.'

'Right,' said his mother. 'Fair enough.'

Frances, supper over, remarked that it was getting late, and that it was time Margaret and William were in bed. The girl got up, and faced her, the fair maidenly lightly freckled forehead presented to Frances like a little bull about to charge. 'Why should we? You can't order us about. You aren't our mother.' And now William said the same. Clearly the two had discussed the situation and decided to make a stand. Two obstinate faces, two antagonistic bodies, and Rupert, watching, was pale, like them.

'No, I am not your mother, but while I'm looking after you I'm afraid you'll have to go along with what I say.'

'I'm not going to,' said Margaret.

'I'm not going to,' said William.

Margaret had a round little girl's face waiting to take on definition, features that at a few yards seemed to disappear into a pale outline where only a little pink mouth asserted itself. Now the mouth was primly virtuous with disapproval.

'We hate you,' said William carefully, having rehearsed the line with Margaret.

Frances was inordinately, irrationally angry.

'Sit down,' she snapped, and, surprised, the children slid back into their chairs.

'Now, you listen. I did not expect I would have to look after you. It wasn't something I wanted.' But here she glanced at Rupert, who was so hurt by the whole awful situation. She went on, 'I don't mind doing things for you. I don't mind cooking and your clothes and all that – but I'm not putting up with nonsense. You can forget about the sulks and making scenes, because I won't put up with them.' She was really getting into her stride, and the two pale dismayed faces were not enough to stop her. 'You don't know this – and why should you – but I've had all I'm going to take of slamming doors and adolescent rebellions and all that *infantile* rubbish.' She was shouting at them. Never, ever, had she shouted at a child before. 'Do you hear? And if you start all that I'm going to leave. So I'm giving you due warning. I shall simply go.' Lack of breath stopped her. Rupert's eyebrows, usually ready for irony, were signalling that she was overdoing it.

'Sorry,' she said – to him rather than to them. And then, 'No, I'm not at all sorry. I said that because I mean it. So think about it.'

Without a word the children got up and silently went off to their rooms. But they would join each other in either his or hers to discuss Frances.

'Well done,' said Rupert.

'Well, was it?' said Frances, sitting limp, trembling, dismayed at herself. She dropped her head on to her arms.

'Yes, of course it was. There was bound to be a confrontation at some point. And by the way, don't think I'm taking you for granted. I wouldn't blame you if you simply left.'

'I'm not going to leave,' – and she reached for his hand. It was trembling. 'Oh, God,' she said, 'this is all so . . .' He reached out for her and she pushed her chair up to his and they sat close, with their arms around each other, sharing dismay.

A week later there was a repetition of the 'You aren't our mother, so why should we . . .' and so on.

Frances had been trying all day to get on with the heavy sociological book which she was writing, interrupted by telephone calls from the children's schools, Meriel's hospital, and Rupert from his newspaper, asking what he should bring home for supper. Her nerves were grumbling, they jangled and they swore. She was feeling a reaction to the whole situation. What was she doing here? What a trap she was in . . . did she even like these children? That girl, with her virtuous prim little mouth, the boy (that poor boy), so frightened by what was happening he could hardly look at her, or his father, and who moved about like a sleepwalker, with a scared smile that he tried to make sarcastic.

'Right,' said she, 'that's it, and got up from her place at the table, pushing away her plate. She did not look at Rupert, for she was doing the unforgivable – hitting him when he was down.

'What do you mean?' asked the little girl – she was, after all, still that.

'What do you think? I'm going. I told you I would.'

And she went into the bedroom she shared with Rupert, slowly, because her legs were stiff, not with indecision but because she intended them to walk her away from Rupert. There she brought clothes down from cupboards, stacked them on the bed, found suitcases, and methodically began to pack. She was in a state of mind opposite to anything she had felt for weeks now. Like a bride or bridegroom who has been swept along on the tide of events with only an occasional moment of misgiving, to find themselves on the eve of the wedding wondering how they could have been so mad, so now, a situation that had seemed reasonable enough, if difficult, made her feel as if she were being carried, wrists and ankles tied, into a prison. What on earth had made her say she would take on his kids, even if only temporarily? And how did she know it would be temporary? She must run away now, before it was too late. The only part of her mind that remained anywhere near what it had been was the thought of Rupert. She could not give him up. Well, that was easy. She would finally buy herself her own place, *her* place, and . . . the door opened, just a little, then a little more, and the boy stood there. 'Margaret says, what are you doing?'

'I'm leaving,' said Frances. 'Shut the door.'

The door shut, in careful jerks, as if each little degree of closure had been stopped by a change of mind: should he go in again?

The cases were packed and standing in a row when Margaret came sidling in eyes lowered, the mouth half open, that prim pink little mouth, but now it was swollen with tears.

'Are you really leaving?'

'Yes, I am.' And Frances, who was convinced she was, said, 'Shut the door — quietly.'

Later she went out and found Rupert still sitting at the supper table. She said, 'That was badly done, I'm sorry.'

He shook his head, not looking at her. He was a solitary and brave figure, and his pain shut him away from her. She could not bear that. She knew she would not leave, at least, not like this. She was thinking, in a wild last moment of rebellion, I'll get my own place and he can deal with the mess of Meriel and the kids and he can come and visit me and . . . 'Of course I'm not going,' she said. 'How could I?'

He did not move, but then slowly held out the arm near to her. She pushed a chair close and sat inside the arm, and he inclined his head, so that their two heads rested together.

'Well, at least they won't give you a bad time again,' he said. 'That is, if you do decide to stay.'

The occasion demanded that they should cement their frailties with love-making. He went off to their bedroom, and she prepared to follow, switching off lights. She went to the girl's door, meaning to go in and say goodnight, 'Forget it, I didn't mean it.' What she heard was sobbing, a dreadful low helpless sobbing which had been going on for some time. Frances stood near the door, then rested her head against it, in a flare of *Oh, no, I can't I can't* . . . but the sound of the child's misery was undoing her. She took a breath and went into the room, and saw the girl start up from her pillow, and then found her in her arms, 'Oh, Frances, Frances, I'm sorry, I didn't mean it.'

'It's all right. I won't go. I did mean it then, but now I've changed my mind.'

Kisses, hugs, and a new start.

With the boy, it was going to be harder. A hurt child, holding himself inside an armature of pride, he refused tears, rejected consoling arms, including his father's; he did not trust them. He had watched his mother, so ill and silent, go so deep inside herself she did not hear when he spoke to her, and it was this sight that kept him company as he obediently did what he was told, went to school, did homework, helped clear the table, make his bed. If Frances and Rupert had known what went on inside William, understood his wild solitary misery – but what could they have done? They even were reassured by this conforming boy, who was turning out – surely – to be easier than Margaret?

Sylvia stood in Senga airport's Arrivals, which accommodated the luggage carousel, Immigration, Customs, and all the people off the plane, who at one glance could be defined as black, and in thick three-piece suits, and white, in jeans and T-shirts, with sweaters they had left London in tied around their hips. The blacks were exuberant, manoeuvring refrigerators, stoves, televisions and furniture into positions where they could be offered to Customs' approval, which was being given, for the officials were congratulatory, only too happy to be generous with their scrawls of red chalk as each vast crate arrived before them. Sylvia had a hold-all, for her personal possessions, and two large suitcases for the medical supplies and items Father McGuire had asked for: lists had been arriving in London, each accompanied by: Don't feel yourself obliged to bring these, if it is a trouble. On the plane Sylvia had heard whites discuss Customs, its unpredictability, its partiality to the blacks who were allowed to bring in whole households of furniture. Next to Sylvia had been sitting a silent man, dressed like others in jeans and T-shirt, but he had a silver cross on a chain around his neck. Not knowing if this was a fashion statement, she timidly enquired if he were a priest, heard he was Brother Jude from the something mission – the unfamiliar name slid past her ears – and asked if she might expect trouble with her big cases. Hearing her story, where she was headed – he knew Father McGuire – he said he would help her at Customs, where she found him just ahead of her in the queue. He was hanging back, letting others go past, because he was waiting for a young black man who greeted him by name, asked if the cases were for the mission, passed them, and then was introduced to Sylvia and her cases. 'This is a friend of Father McGuire's. She is a doctor. She is taking supplies to the hospital at Kwandere.' 'Oh, a friend of Father McGuire,' said this youth, all smiling friendship, 'please give him my best, my very best.' And he scrawled the mystic red sign on the cases. She did well at Immigration, with all the right papers, and then they were outside on the steps of the airport building, on a clear hot morning, and towards Sylvia came a young woman wearing baggy blue shorts, a flowery T-shirt, and a large silver cross. 'Ah,' said Sylvia's saviour, 'I see you are in good hands. Hello there, Sister Molly,' – and he was off, to a group waiting for him.

Sister Molly was going to drive her to St Luke's Mission. She said there was no point hanging about in Senga, and they should leave at once. And off they went, in a battered truck, straight into the landscape of an Africa which Sylvia was prepared to admire when she had got used to it. It was alien to her now. It was really very hot. The wind blowing through the cab of the truck was dusty. Sylvia gripped the door, and listened to Molly, who was talking all the time, mostly about the male side of her religious establishment, whom she complained were all male chauvinist pigs. This phrase which had lost the relish of novelty in London, came rolling new-minted from her smiling lips. As for the Pope, he was reactionary, bigoted, bourgeois, too old and anti-woman, and what a pity he seemed to be in good health. God forgive her for saying that.

This was not what Sylvia had expected to be listening to. She did not care much about the Pope, though as a Catholic she knew she should, and she had never found the language of extreme feminism matched up with her experience. Sister Molly drove very fast over at first good roads, then increasingly bad ones until an hour or so later the car stopped at a group of buildings which it seemed was a farm. There Molly unloaded Sylvia and her cases, saying, 'I'll leave you here. And don't you let Kevin McGuire push you around. He's a sweetie, I'm not saying he isn't, but all those old-fashioned priests are the same.' She jolted off, waving at Sylvia and anyone else who might be looking.

Sylvia found herself invited in to morning tea by Edna Pyne, whose voice, all unfamiliar vowels, had above all a tang of self-pity that Sylvia knew only too well. And the elderly face was dissatis-fied. Cedric Pyne had long, burned legs in the shortest shorts she had ever seen, and his eyes, like his wife's, were blue, and reddened. There was such a glare round the verandah where they sat that Sylvia kept her eyes on this couple, avoiding the harsh yellow light, and really saw nothing on this first visit but them. It was clear that dropping off people and things at the Pynes' place was part of a regular trafficking, for when they were again in a car, this time a jeep, there were bundles of newspapers, letters for Father McGuire, and two black youths, one of whom Sylvia saw at once was very sick. 'I'm going to the hospital,' said the sick one and Sylvia said, 'So am I.' The two were in the back and she was with Cedric who drove, like Sister Molly, as if for a bet. They jolted over a dirt road for ten miles or so, and were then in dusty trees, and ahead was a low building, roofed with corru-gated metal, and beyond that on a ridge were more buildings scattered about among more dusty trees.

'Tell Kevin I can't wait,' said Cedric Pyne. 'Come and visit any time.' And with that he was off, leaving dust clouds drifting. Sylvia's head ached. She was thinking that she had scarcely left London in her life, and this had seemed to her until now quite a normal thing, instead of the deprivation that she now suspected it was. The two black youths went off to the hospital, and said,

'See you by and by.' Which sounded relaxed enough but the sick one's face was a plea for immediacy.

Sylvia went on to a tiny verandah, of polished green cement, with her cases. Then into a smallish room that had in it a table made of stained planks, chairs seated with strips of hide, shelves of books filling all one wall, and some pictures, all but one of Jesus, that one being a misty sunset view of the Mountains of Mourne.

A thin little black woman appeared, all welcoming smiles, said she was Rebecca, and that she would show Sylvia her room.

Her room, off the main one, was large enough for a narrow iron bed, a small table, a couple of hard chairs, and some wall shelves for books. There were nails and hangers on the walls for her clothes. A little chest of drawers, of the kind that once hotels all had, had washed up here. Above her bed was a small crucifix. The walls were of brick, the floors of brick, and the ceiling of split cane. Rebecca said she would bring tea, and went off. Sylvia sank on to a chair, in the grip of a feeling she did not know how to identify. Yes, new impressions: yes, she had expected them, had known she would feel alien, out of place. But what was this? – waves of bitter emptiness attacked her, and when she looked at the crucifix, to get her bearings, felt only that Christ Himself must be surprised to find Himself there. But surely she – Sylvia – was not surprised to find Christ in a place of such poverty? What was it then? Outside doves cooed, and chickens kept up their talk. I'm just a spoiled brat, Sylvia told herself – the word surfacing from somewhere deep in her childhood. Westminster Cathedral – yes; a brick shack, apparently, no. Dust was blowing past the window. Judging from her outside view of it, this house could not have more than three or four rooms. Where was Father McGuire's room? Where did Rebecca sleep? She could make no sense of anything, and when Rebecca brought the tea, Sylvia said she had a headache, and would lie down.

'Yes, doctor, you lie down, and you'll be better soon,' said

Rebecca, her cheerfulness recognisable as Christian: the children of God smile and are ready for anything. (Like Flower Children.) Rebecca was drawing the curtains, of black and white mattress ticking, which Sylvia suspected would be found the last word in chic in certain circles in London. 'I'll call you for lunch.'

Lunch. Sylvia felt that it must be already evening, the day had been going on for so long. It was only just eleven.

She lay, her hand over her eyes, saw the light define her thin fingers, fell asleep, and was woken by Rebecca half an hour later with more tea and an apology from Father McGuire who said he was detained at the school, and would see her for lunch, and he suggested she should take it easy till tomorrow.

This counsel having been transmitted, Rebecca remarked that the patient from the Pyne farm was waiting to see the doctor, and there were other people waiting, and perhaps the doctor could . . . Sylvia was putting on a white overall, which action Rebeccca seemed merely to be observing, but in a way that made Sylvia ask, 'What should I wear, then?' Rebecca at once said that the overall wouldn't stay white long and perhaps the doctor had an old dress she could wear.

Sylvia did not wear dresses. She had on her oldest jeans, for travelling. She tied her hair back in a scarf, which made her like Rebecca, in her kerchief. She went down a path indicated by Rebecca, who retired to her kitchen. Along the dusty path grew hibiscus, oleander, plumbago, all dusty, but looking as if they were in their own right places, in dry heat and under a sun in a sky that had not a cloud in it. The path turned down a rocky slope and in front of her were some grass roofs on supporting poles stuck in reddish earth, and a shed, whose door was half open. A hen emerged from it. Other chickens lay on their sides under bushes, panting, their beaks open. The two youths that had been in the back seat of the car sat under a big tree. One got up, and said, 'My friend is sick. He is too sick.'

So Sylvia could see. 'Where is the hospital?'

'Here is the hospital.'

Now Sylvia took in that lying around under trees, or bushes, or under the grass shelters, were people. Some were cripples.

'A long time, no doctor,' said the youth. 'And now we have a doctor again.'

'What happened to the doctor?'

'He was drinking too-too much. And so Father McGuire said he must go. And so we are waiting for you, doctor.'

Sylvia now looked about for where her instruments, medicines – the tools of her trade – might be, and went to the shed. Sure enough, were three layers of shelves, and on them a very large bottle of aspirin – empty. Several bottles of tablets for malaria – empty. A big tub of ointment – unnamed and empty. A stethoscope hung on a nail on the back of the door. It wasn't working. The friend of the sick youth stood by her, smiling. 'All the medicines are finished,' he said.

'What's your name?'

'Aaron.'

'Aren't you from the Pynes' farm?'

'No, I live here. I went to be with my friend when we knew a car was coming.'

'How did you get there, then?'

'I walked.'

'But – it's quite a way, isn't it?'

'No, not too far.'

She went back with him to the sick youth, who had been limp and lifeless but was now shaking violently. She didn't need a stethoscope to diagnose that. 'Has he been taking any medicine? – it's malaria,' she said.

'Yes, he had some medicine, from Mr Pyne, but it is finished now.'

'For one thing, he should be drinking.'

In the shed she found three big plastic screw-top cans with water, but it smelled a bit stale. She told Aaron to take some water to the sick one. But there was not a cup, or mug, or glass – nothing.

'When the other doctor left I am afraid there was stealing.'

'I see.'

'Yes, I am afraid that was the position.'

Sylvia understood that she was hearing his 'I am afraid' as it must have sounded long ago, when it was new made. He was using the words as a statement of apology. Long ago, when they said, I am afraid, did they then expect a blow or a reprimand?

What a lucky thing she had brought a new stethoscope, and some basic medicines. 'Is there a lock for this door?'

'I am afraid I don't know.' Aaron made the motions of hunting around, as if the lock might be found in the dust. 'And yes, here it is,' he cried, finding it tucked into the thatch of the shed.

'And the key?'

He hunted again, but the key was too much to ask.

She was not going to trust her little store to a shed without a lock. While she stood, indecisive, thinking that she did not understand anything around her, that she needed a key, let alone the shed, Aaron said, 'And look, doctor, I am afraid things are not good here – look.' He pushed the bricks of the shed on the back wall, and they fell out. A patch had been carefully freed of their mortar, so that quite a large hole was possible: anyone could come in there.

She made a quick tour of her patients, lying about here and there, but it was sometimes hard to tell them from their friends or relatives who were with them. A dislocated shoulder. She put it back there and then, told the young man to stay and rest, not to use it for a bit, but he staggered off into the bush. Some cuts – festering. Another malaria, or she thought so. A leg swollen up like a bolster, the skin seemingly about to burst. She went back to her room, returned with a lancet, soap, a bandage, a basin got from Rebecca, and, squatting, lanced the leg, from which large amounts of pus soaked into the dust, making, no doubt, a fine new source of infection. This patient was groaning with gratitude; a young woman whose two children sat near her, one sucking at the breast, though he seemed to be at least four years old, the other clinging to her neck. Rebecca bandaged the leg, hoping to keep some of the dust out, told the woman not to do too much, although this was probably absurd, and examined a pregnant woman, near her time. The baby was in the wrong position.

She collected her instruments, and the basin and said she had to talk to Father McGuire. She asked Aaron what he and the malaria patient planned to eat. He said that perhaps Rebecca would be kind to them and give them some sadza.

Sylvia found Father McGuire at the table in the front room, eating his lunch. He was a large man, in a shabby robe, with a generous crop of white hair, dark sympathetic eyes, and an air of jovial welcome.

Sylvia was urged to join him in a little tinned herring – brought by her, and she did; and then, urged again, ate an orange.

Rebecca stood watching, and said that they were saying down in the hospital that Sylvia could not be a doctor, she was too small and thin.

'Shall I show them my certificates?' said Sylvia.

'I'd show them the weight of my hand,' said Father McGuire. 'What impertinence is this I am hearing?'

'I must have a shed that locks,' said Sylvia. 'I can't carry everything down and back several times a day.'

'I will tell the builder to mend the hole in the shed.'

'And a lock? A key?'

'And now that is not so easy. I'll have to see if we have one. I could ask Aaron to go across to the Pynes and ask for a lock and a key.'

He was lighting a cigarette, and offered one to Sylvia. She had smoked, hardly at all, ever, but now she was grateful for it.

'Ah, yes,' he said. 'You've had a long day. It is always the same the first day from home. Our day starts at half-past five and it ends – at least mine does – at nine. And you'll be ready for your bed then, no matter what you think now, with your London ways.'

'I'm ready now,' said Sylvia.

'And then you should have a little nap, as I will now.'

'But what about those people down there? May I have a mug, at least, to give them some water?'

'You may. That at least we can do. We have mugs.'

Sylvia slept half an hour, and was woken by Rebecca with tea. Had Rebecca slept? She smiled when Sylvia asked. Had Aaron and his friend had something to eat? Doctor Sylvia must not worry about them, she smiled.

Sylvia went back down to the assemblage of sheds, shelters and shady trees where the sick lay about waiting. A lot more had come, having heard there was a doctor. There were quite a few cripples now, without a leg or an arm, old wounds never properly stitched or cleaned. These were the wounded from the war, which had after all ended quite recently. She thought they had come creeping to the 'hospital' because here, at least, their condition was validated, was defined. They were war wounded, and entitled to pills – painkillers, aspirins, ointment, anything really, these very young men, no more than boys some of them, they were the heroes of the war, and they were owed something. But Sylvia had so few pills, and was being parsimonious. So they got mugs of water, and sympathetic enquiries. 'How did you lose that leg?' 'The bomb went off when I sat down.' 'I'm so sorry, that was bad luck.' 'Yes, that was too much bad luck.' 'And what happened to your foot?' 'A rock fell from the kopje, all the way down, and on to a landmine and I was there.' 'I am so sorry. It must have hurt a lot.' 'Yes, and I screamed and my comrades they made me be quiet, because the enemy was not far.'

Late that afternoon, when the sun was low and yellow, there appeared a very tall, very thin, angry-faced stooping man who said he was Joshua, and his job was to help her.

'Are you a nurse? Have you trained?'

'No, I have no training. But I work here all the time.'

'Then, where were you earlier?' asked Sylvia, wanting information, not intending a rebuke.

But he said, intending insolence, a formal insolence, like the words *Damn you*, 'Why should I be here when there was no doctor?'

He was under the influence of something. No, not alcohol – what then? Yes, she smelled marijuana.

'What have you been smoking?' 'Dagga.' 'Does it grow here?' 'Yes, it grows everywhere.' 'If you are going to work with me, then I can't have you smoking dagga.'

Swaying from foot to foot, arms dangling, he growled out, 'I did not expect to work today.'

'When did the other doctor leave?' 'A long time ago. A year now.' 'What do the sick people do when it rains?' 'If there is no room for them under the roofs, they get wet. They are black people, that's good enough for them.' 'But you have a black government now, so things will change.'

'Yes,' he said, or snarled. 'Yes, now everything will change and we will have the good things too.'

'Joshua,' she remarked, smiling, 'if we are going to work together then we shall have to try and get on.'

Now there did appear a kind of smile. 'Yes, it would be a good thing if we – got on.'

'I take it you didn't get on with the one who left. By the way, was he a white doctor or a black doctor?'

'A black doctor. Well, perhaps not a real doctor. But he drank too much. He was a skellum.' 'A what?' 'A bad man. Not like you.' 'I hope that at least I won't drink too much.' 'And I hope so too, doctor.' 'My name is Sylvia.' 'Doctor Sylvia.'

He was still stooping and swaying, and now his face was set in a scowl. This was as if he had decided: Now I must show antagonism.

'Doctor Sylvia is going up to Father McGuire,' she said. 'He told me to be there when it got dark, for supper.'

'And I hope Doctor Sylvia will enjoy her supper.' He went off on a path into the bush, laughing. Then she heard him singing. A rousing song, she thought: it was a revolutionary song from the war, insulting to all whites.

Father McGuire sat at the table, a hissing paraffin lamp beside him, drinking orange juice. A glass of it waited for her.

'We do have electricity, but there's a power cut,' he said.

Rebecca appeared with a tray and the information that Aaron sent a message that he would stay with his friend that night down at the hospital.

'Why, does he live here?'

The priest, not looking at her, said that Aaron had a family in the village but he was going to sleep in this house at nights now.

Rebecca's face and his told her that here was a situation they were embarrassed about, so she enquired. It was an absurd thing, said Father McGuire, a ridiculous thing, and he could only apologise, but the young man would be living in the house for the sake of appearances. Sylvia had not understood. The priest seemed impatient, even offended at her, making him spell it out. 'It is not considered suitable,' he said, 'for a priest to have a female living with him.'

'*What?*' said Sylvia. She was annoyed, as he was.

Rebecca commented that people always talked, and that was a thing to be expected.

Sylvia said bitterly, and primly, that people had dirty minds, and Father McGuire said placidly that yes, that was so.

He then went on to say, but after a pause, that it had been suggested Sylvia should live with the nuns up the hill.

'What nuns?'

'We have the good sisters, in a house up the hill. But since you are not a religious, I thought you would be better here.'

So much was not being said, and Sylvia sat looking from him to Rebecca.

'Our good sisters are supposed to be helping in the hospital, but not everyone is cut out for the dirty work of nursing.'

'They are nurses?'

'No, I would not say that. They have done courses in basic nursing. But I suggest you arrange for them to wash bandages and dressings and bedclothes. Well now, you will not be having stores of disposable dressings? No. You should arrange for Joshua to convey what needs to be washed to the sisters' house every day. And I will instruct them that they should do this work as a service to God.'

'Joshua will not like doing that, Father,' said Rebecca.

'And you would not like doing it either, Rebecca, so we are in difficulties.'

'It is Joshua's work, not mine.'

'And so here is a little difficulty for you to sort out, Sylvia, and I shall be waiting with interest to see how you do it.'

He got up, said goodnight and went to his bed, and Rebecca, without looking at Sylvia, said goodnight and left.

It was a month later. The hole in the shed wall was mended, and there was a lock and a key. Around two of the grass shelters were blinds made of the hessian used to bale tobacco, which could be adjusted to keep out wind and dust, if not heavy rain. A new hut had been built, with grass walls and grass roof, a big one, with holes cut in the walls to let in light. It was cool and fresh inside. The floor was of stamped earth. In it the really sick people could shelter. Sylvia had cured cases of long-standing deafness, caused by nothing worse than old impacted wax. She had cured cataracts. She had got medicines from Senga and was able to do something for the malaria cases, but most of them were old sufferers. She set limbs and cauterized wounds and sewed them up, and gave out medicines for sore throats and coughs, sometimes using, when they ran out, old wives' cures remembered by Father McGuire from Ireland. She had a maternity clinic, and delivered babies. All this was satisfactory enough, but she was in permanent frustration because she was not a surgeon. She needed to be. Bad and urgent cases could be driven to a hospital twenty miles away but sometimes delays were damaging, or fatal. She ought to be able to do caesareans and appendixes, amputate a hand, or open up a badly fractured knee. There was a shadowy area where it was hard to say if she was on the right side of the law or not: she might slice an arm to get at an ulcer, open up a suppurating wound to clean it, using surgeons' instruments. If only she had known how badly she would need a surgeon's skills then, when she was taking all kinds of courses that were not useful to her now . . .

She was also doing the kind of work that did not come the way of doctors in Europe. She had toured nearby villages to inspect water supplies, and found dirty rivers and polluted wells. Water was running low at this time of the year, and often stood in stagnant pools that bred bilharzia. She taught women from these villages how to recognise some diseases and when to bring sufferers in. More and more people came in to her, because she was being seen as a bit of a miracle worker, chiefly because of ears syringed free of wax. Her reputation was being spread by Joshua, for it helped his reputation, tarnished by association with the bad doctor. He and Sylvia were 'getting on', but she was overlooking his often violent accusations of the whites. Sometimes she cracked with, 'But, Joshua, I wasn't here, how could I be to blame?'

'That is your bad luck, Doctor Sylvia. You are to blame if I say so. Now we have a black government what I say goes. And one day this will be a fine hospital, and we'll have our own black doctors.'

'I hope so.'

'And then you can go back to England and cure your own sick people. Do you have sick people in England?'

'Of course we do.'

'And poor people?'

'Yes.'

'As poor as we are?'

'No, nothing like.'

'That is because you have stolen everything from us.'

'If you say so, Joshua, then so it is.'

'And why aren't you at home looking after your own sick people?'

'A very good question. I often wonder the same thing.'

'But don't leave just yet. We need you until we get our doctors.'

'But your own doctors won't come and work in poor places like this. They want to stay in Senga.'

'But this won't be a poor place. It will be a fine rich place, like England.'

Father McGuire said to her, 'No, listen to me, my child, I'm going to talk to you seriously, as your confessor and adviser.'

'Yes, Father.'

This had become a little comic turn: while it was not true to say she had shed her Catholicism, she was certainly having to redefine her beliefs. She had become a Catholic because of Father Jack, a lean austere man, consuming himself with an asceticism that didn't suit him. His eyes accused the world around him, and his movements were all vigilance against error and sin. She had been in love with him, and she believed he was not indifferent to her. So far, he had been the love of her life. Father Jack had stood for priesthood, for the Faith, for her religion, and now she was in this house in the bush with Father McGuire, an easy-going elderly man who loved his food. You would think that on a diet of porridge and beef and tomatoes and mostly tinned fruit, seldom fresh, that it was not possible to be a gourmet. Nonsense. Father Kevin shouted at Rebecca if the porridge wasn't right, and his beef had to be just so, medium rare, and the potatoes . . . Sylvia was fond of Kevin McGuire, he was a good man, as Sister Molly had said, but what she had responded to was the passionate abstinence of a very different man, and to the glories of Westminster Cathedral and – once – a brief trip to Notre Dame which burned in her memory like everything she loved most made visible. Once a week on Sunday evenings at a little church made of unadorned brick, furnished with local native stools and chairs, the people of the district came for Mass, and it was conducted in the local language, and danced . . . the women got up from their seats and powerfully danced their worship, and sang – oh, beautifully, yes, they did – and it was a noisy convivial occasion, like a party. Sylvia was wondering if she had ever really been a true Catholic, and if she was one now, though Father McGuire, in his role as her mentor, reassured her. She asked herself if in the little chapel where the dust drifted in, the service had been conducted in Latin, and the worshippers had stood and kneeled and responded, according to the old way, she would have liked that better. Yes, she would, she hated the Mass as conducted by Father Kevin McGuire, she hated the fleshy dancing, and the exuberance of the singing which she knew was a loosening of the bonds of their poor restricted lives. And she certainly did not like the nuns in their blue and white habits, like schoolgirls' uniforms.

He said to her, 'Sylvia, you must learn not to take things so hard.'

She burst out, 'I can't bear it, Father. I can't endure what I see. Nine-tenths of it is unnecessary.'

'Yes, yes, yes. But that is how things are. It is. How they are now. They will change, I am sure. Yes, surely they will change. But, Sylvia, I see in you the stuff of martyrs, and that is not good. Would you go to the stake with a smile, Sylvia? Yes, I believe you would. You are burning yourself up. And now I am going to prescribe for you, just as you do for these poor people. You must eat three proper meals a day. You must sleep longer – I see the light under your door at eleven or twelve, or later. And you must take yourself off for a walk every evening into the bush. Or go and visit. You can take my car and see the Pynes. They are good people.'

'But I don't have anything in common with them.'

'But, Sylvia, aren't they good enough for you? Did you know they sat the war out in that house – under siege they were. Their house was set on fire over their heads. They are brave people.'

'But in the wrong cause.'

'Yes, that is so, yes surely it was, but they aren't devils just because the new newspapers say all white farmers are.'

'I'll do my best to be better. I know I get too involved.'

'You and Rebecca – both of you are like little rock rabbits in a drought year. But in her case she has six children and none of them get enough to eat. You don't feed yourself out of some sort of . . .'

'I've never eaten that much. I don't seem to care about food.'

'A pity we couldn't share out some characteristics between us. I like my food, God forgive me, I do.'

Sylvia's life had become the circuit from her little room to the table in the main room, down to the hospital, then back, around and around. She had scarcely even been in the kitchen, Rebecca's domain, had never entered Father McGuire's room, and knew that Aaron slept somewhere at the back. When the priest was not at the supper table, and Rebecca said he was sick – yes, he often got sick – Sylvia went into his room for the first time. There was a strong smell of fresh and stale sweat, the sour odours of sickness. He was up on his pillows, but sliding sideways, his head loose on his shoulders. He was very still, though his chest heaved. Malaria. This was the quiescent part of the cycle.

Small windows, one cracked, stood open above wet earth, from where came freshness, to compete with the smells. Father McGuire was cold, he was damp, his sweaty nightshirt clung to him, his hair was matted. Hot season or not, he could catch cold. Sylvia called Rebecca and the two women heaved the protesting man to a chair, a grass one, which settled under his weight. Rebecca said, 'I want to change the bed when Father is sick but he always says No, no, leave me.'

'Well, I am going to change it.'

The change was accomplished, the patient lay back, and then, while he complained his head ached, Sylvia gave him a blanket bath. Rebecca averted her eyes from the evidence of the Father's manhood and kept muttering that she was sorry. 'I am so so sorry, Father, I am so so sorry.'

A fresh nightshirt. Lemonade. A new cycle began, with the savage shakings and sweats of malaria, while he clenched his teeth and clutched at the iron rails at the top of his bed. The ague, the quartan fever, the tertian fever, the shakes, the rigours, the seizures, the trembles, of the disease that not so long ago had bred in the London marshes, in the Italian marshes, and had been brought home from anywhere in the world where there were swampy places, had not been witnessed by Sylvia until she had come here, though she had read it up on the plane. And now it seemed there was never a day when some wan depleted person did not collapse on the reed mats under the grass roofs and lie shaking.

'Are you taking your pills?' Sylvia shouted – it makes you deaf, malaria does, or the pills do – and Father McGuire said he took them but, since he had the shakes three or four times a year, believed he had gone past the help of pills.

When he had finished with this bout, he was newly soaked, and the bed was changed again. Rebecca showed her weariness as she carried out the sheets. Sylvia asked if there was not a woman in the village who could help with the washing? Rebecca said they were busy. 'Then what about your sisters?' she said to the sick man. He said, 'I don't think Rebecca would like that.' Rebecca was jealous of her position, and did not want to share it. Sylvia had given up trying to understand these complicated rivalries, so now suggested Aaron. The priest attempted a jest, that Aaron was an intellectual now and could not be asked to do such work: he was at the beginning of a study with Father McGuire that would make him a priest.

Would Aaron be too good to go through and around the trees and shrubs to look for mosquito larvae? 'I think you will find he is too good for that.' 'Then, why not the nuns?' Sylvia refrained from saying that they did not seem to do much, but Father McGuire said they wouldn't know larvae when they saw some. 'Our good sisters are not all that keen on the bush.'

Mosquitoes lay their eggs in any water they can find. The black wrigglers, as energetic in this phase of their lives as they will be when seeking whom they may devour, can be in the furl of an old dried pawpaw leaf, or in a rusted biscuit tin lid hidden under a bush. Yesterday Sylvia had seen the wrigglers in a tiny hollow excavated by a rivulet escaping from a flood, under the arching roots of a maize plant. The sun was sucking up the water as she watched, the wrigglers were doomed, so she did not kill them, but two hours later there was a downpour, and if they had not been washed out on to the earth to die, they were triumphantly completing their cycle.

Father McGuire seemed semi-conscious. She thought that he was worse than he knew – long term; he would get over this attack soon. Because he was ruddy-faced, a certain underlying pallor, even yellowness, was not easily seen. He was anaemic. Malaria does that. He should take iron pills. He should take a holiday. He should . . .

Outside in the night white shapes swirled in the wind from approaching rain: the big wash Rebecca had done earlier. Sylvia sat by the dozing man, waiting for the next paroxysm, and looked round the room, her attention free.

Brick walls, like hers, the same split-reed ceiling, the brick floor. In a corner a statue of the Virgin. On the walls the Virgin again, conventional representations inspired, if distantly, by the Italian Renaissance, blue and white and with downcast eyes, and surely out of place here in the bush? But wait, on a stool of dark wood, and of the same dark wood, a native Mary, a vigorous young woman, was nursing a baby. That was better. Hanging from a nail on the wall near the bed, where the priest could reach it, was a rosary of ebony.

In the Sixties, the tumults of ideology that afflicted the world had taken a local shape in the Catholic Church, in a bubbling unrest that had attempted to dethrone the Virgin Mary. The Holy Mother was *out*, and with her went rosaries. Sylvia had not had a Catholic childhood, had never dipped her fingers into the Holy Water stoups, or wound pretty rosaries around them, or crossed herself or swapped Holy cards with other little girls. ('I'll give you three St Jeromes for one Holy Mother.') She had never prayed to the Virgin, only to Jesus. Therefore, when she joined the Church, she did not miss what she had never known, and only slowly, when meeting older priests or nuns or church members, had learned that a revolution had taken place which had left many in mourning, and particularly for the Virgin. (She would be reinstated, decades later.) Meanwhile, in places of the world where eyes vigilant for heresy or backsliding did not reach, priests and nuns kept their rosaries and their Holy Water, their statues and pictures of the Virgin, hoping that no one would notice.

For someone like Rebecca, who had a little card of the Holy Mother nailed on to the central pole of her hut, this ideological argument would have seemed too silly to think about: but she had never heard of it.

On the wall in Sylvia's room was tacked, straight on to the brick, a large reproduction of Leonardo's Virgin of the Rocks, and some other smaller Virgins. It could be easy to conclude from that wall that this was a religion that worshipped women. The crucifix was a paltry thing in comparison. Rebecca sometimes sat on the bottom of Sylvia's bed, her hands folded, looking at the Leonardo, sighing, tears running. 'Oh, they are so beautiful.' You could say that the Virgin had slipped through the interstices of dogma by the way of Art. Sylvia had not known that she cared particularly for the Holy Mother but did know she could not live without reproductions of the pictures she loved best. Fish moth were attacking the edges of the posters. She must ask someone to bring her new pictures.

She fell asleep on her chair, looking at Father McGuire's insipid statuette and wondering why anyone could choose that if they could have a *real* statue, a real picture. She would not dream of saying this to Father McGuire who had been brought up in Donegal, in a small house with many children in it, and had come here to Zimlia straight from theological college. Did he not like the Leonardo then? He had stood a long time in the doorway of Sylvia's room, because Rebecca had told him, 'Father, Father, come and see what Doctor Sylvia has brought us.' His hands folded together on his stomach, and enlaced by his rosary, rose and fell as he stood there, and looked. 'Those are the faces of angels,' he pronounced at last, 'and the painter must have seen them in a vision. No mortal woman ever looked like that.'

Next morning, while Rebecca's wash dried again after its dousing by the storm, Sylvia asked Aaron if he would ransack the bush for wrigglers, but he said he was afraid he had to read his books for Father McGuire.

She walked to the village, found some youths – who should have been at school – and said she would give them money to search the bush. 'How much?' – and she told them, 'I'll give you a lump sum and you can share it.' 'How much?' In the end they were demanding bicycles, textbooks for school, and new T-shirts. This was because they saw every white person as rich and with access to anything they wanted. She began to laugh, then they did, and it was settled they should have what she held in her hand, a clutch of Zimlia dollars, enough for some sweets at the store. Off they went, laughing in to the bush, and playing the fool: the search would be a desultory one. Then she went to the hospital where she found Joshua sewing up a long quite deep cut.

'You were not here, Doctor Sylvia.'

'I would have been here in five minutes.'

'How was I to know that?'

This was an issue between them. He now did sew up wounds, and did it well. But he was attempting wounds that needed more skill than he had, and she had told him to stop. They were both watching the face of the boy, who was staring down at his arm where the needle slid through wincing flesh. He was brave, biting his lips. Joshua finished the stitching clumsily – Sylvia took the needle from him and did it herself. Then she went to the lock-up shed to measure out medicines. He followed her, leaving the reek of dagga on the air. 'Comrade Sylvia, I want to be a doctor. All my life, that is what I wanted.'

'No one is going to accept a man who uses dagga, for training.'

'If I was training, I would stop smoking.'

'And who is going to pay for it?'

'You can pay for it. Yes, you must pay for me.'

He knew – and so everyone did – that Sylvia had paid for the new buildings, was paying for the medicines, and for his wages. It was believed that behind her was one of the international donors, an aid organisation. She had told Joshua that no, it was her money, but he did not want to believe her.

On an old kitchen tray, relinquished by Rebecca, Sylvia arranged mugs of medicine, little piles of pills, many of them vitamins. She went with the tray to the tree where most of the patients lay, or sat, and began handing out mugs, and the pills, with water.

'I want to be a doctor,' said Joshua, roughly.

'Do you know what it costs to train someone to be a doctor?' she said to him, over her shoulder. 'Look, show this boy how to swallow this, I know it doesn't taste nice.'

Joshua spoke, the boy protested, but he took the potion. He was about twelve, undernourished, but he had worms, several varieties of them.

'Then, tell me how much it costs?'

'Well, at a rough guess, with everything, probably a hundred thousand pounds.'

'Then you pay, for me.'

'I do not have that kind of money.'

'Then, who paid for you? Perhaps the government? Was it Caring International?'

'My grandmother paid for me.'

'You must tell our government to let me be a doctor and tell them I will be a good doctor.'

'Why should your black government listen to this terrible white woman, Joshua?'

'President Matthew said we could all have an education. That is the education I want. He promised us when the comrades were still fighting in the bush, our Comrade President promised us all a secondary education and training. So you go to the President and tell him to do what he promised us.'

'I see that you have faith in the promises of politicians,' she remarked, kneeling to lift up a woman who was weak from child-birth and who had lost the baby. She held her, feeling the black skin that should have been warm and smooth, rough and chilly under her hands.

'Politicians,' said Joshua. 'You call them politicians?'

She saw that the Comrade President, and the black govern-ment – his – were in a different place in his mind from *politicians*, who were white. 'If I made a list of promises your Comrade Mungozi made when the comrades were in the bush fighting, then we could all have a good laugh,' said Sylvia. She gently laid the woman's head down, on a folded bit of cloth that kept it from the earth, muddy from the rain, and said, 'This woman, does she have some relative to give her food?'

'No. She is living alone. Her husband died.'

'What did he die of?'

AIDS was just entering the general consciousness, and Sylvia suspected that some of the deaths she saw were not what they seemed.

'He got sores, and he was too thin, and then he died.'

'Someone should feed this woman,' said Sylvia.

'Perhaps Rebecca could bring her some soup that she is making for the Father.'

Sylvia was silent. This was the worst of her problems. In her experience hospitals fed their patients but here if there were no relatives, then no food. And if Rebecca brought down soup or anything else from the priest's table there would be bad feeling. If Rebecca would agree to bring it: a struggle went on between her and Joshua about who should do what. And, thought Sylvia, this woman was going to die. In a decent hospital, she would almost certainly live. If she were put in a car and taken to the hospital twenty miles away she would be dead before she got there. Sylvia had in her store some Complan, which she did not describe as food but as medicine. She asked Joshua to go and mix up some for the woman, thinking, I am wasting precious resources on a dying woman.

'Why?' said Joshua. 'She will be dead soon.'

Sylvia, without a word, went to the shed, which she had incautiously not locked, and found an old woman reaching up to a shelf to fetch down a bottle of medicine. 'What do you want?'

'I want *muti*, doctor. I need *muti*.'

Sylvia heard those words oftener than any others. I want medicine. I want *muti*. 'Then, come to where the others are waiting for me to examine them.'

'Oh, thank you, thank you, doctor,' giggled the old woman and she ran out of the shed and into the bush.

'She's a bad skellum,' said Joshua. 'She wants to sell the medicine in the village.'

'I didn't lock the dispensary.' She called it that, with an inward mock at herself.

'Why are you crying? Are you sorry for me because I can't be a doctor?'

'That too,' said Sylvia.

'I know what you know. I watch you and I learn what you do. Perhaps I would not need much training.'

She mixed the Complan and carried it to the woman who had gone past the need for it: she was nearly dead, her breath fluttering away in little gasps.

Joshua spoke to a little boy sitting with his sick mother, and said, 'Go back to the village and tell Clever to dig a grave for this woman. The doctor will pay him.' The child ran off. To Sylvia he said, 'I want you to teach my son Clever, teach him, he can learn here.'

'Clever? Is that his name?'

'When he was born his mother said his name must be Clever so that he will be clever. And he is, she was right.'

'How old is he?'

'Six years old.'

'He should be at school.'

'What is the good of going to school, when there is no head-master and no books to learn from?'

'The headmaster will be replaced.'

'But there are no books at the school.' This was true. Sylvia hesitated and Joshua attacked with, 'He can come here and learn what you know. I can teach him what I know. We can both be doctors.'

'Joshua, you don't understand. I don't use more than just a little part of what I know here. Don't you see? This isn't a proper hospital. A proper hospital has . . .' She despaired, turning away, shaking her head from the enormity of it, in exactly the same way as Joshua would, it was an African gesture; then squatted down and picked up a bit of twig, and began drawing a building in the soft wet earth. She was wondering, What would Julia say if she could see me now? She was squatting, knees apart, opposite squatting Joshua, but he sat lightly and easily on his thigh muscles, while she was balancing herself with one hand down beside her. With the other she drew a building of many storeys, and looked at Joshua and said, 'This is what a hospital is like. And it has X-rays – do you know what X-ray is? It has . . .' She was thinking of the hospital she had trained in, while she looked out at grass roofs over the reed mats, the dispensary shed, the hut where women gave birth, on mats. She was crying again.

'You are crying because this is a bad hospital, but it should be me, it should be Joshua crying.'

'Yes, you are right.'

'And you must tell Clever he can come here.'

'But he must go to school. He cannot be a doctor or even a nurse without getting his exams.'

'I cannot pay for him at school.'

Sylvia was paying fees for four of his children, and for three of Rebecca's. Father McGuire paid for two of Rebecca's, but he did not get much money, as a priest.

'Is he one of yours I am paying for now?'

'No. You are not paying for him yet.'

In theory, schools were free. And they had been, at the beginning. Parents all over the country, promised education for their children, helped to build schools, their labour free, their most heartfelt devotion building schools where no schools had been. But now there were fees, and every term they were higher.

'I hope you aren't going to have any more children, Joshua. It's just silly.'

'We know it is a plot by the whites, to stop us having children, so that we become weak and you can do as you like.'

'That's so ridiculous. Why do you believe that nonsense?'

'I believe what I see with my own eyes.'

'The same way you see a plot by the whites to kill you with AIDS' – he called it Slim. 'He's got Slim,' people might say; he, she, has the disease that makes you lose weight. Joshua had taken in all she knew about AIDS, and was probably better informed than members of the government who were still denying its existence. But he was sure that AIDS had been deliberately introduced by the whites, from some laboratory in the States, a disease created to weaken Africans.

The Selous Hotel in Senga had been inter-racial, earning much obloquy, long before Liberation, and now it was a comfortable old-fashioned place, often used for sentimental reunions of people who had been imprisoned under the whites – whites by whites – or been banned, or Prohibited or just harassed and made miserable. It was still one of the best hotels, but the new ones, of an international standard, were already racing up into the sky like arrows into the future – a remark by President Matthew often quoted in promotion brochures.

Tonight a table of twenty or so people stood prominently in the centre of the dining-room, where lesser guests told each other, 'Look, there's Global Money.' 'And there's the Caring International people.' At the head one end was Cyrus B. Johnson, who was boss of the section of Global Money that dealt with that Oliver Twist, Africa, a silver-haired much-groomed man with the habit of authority. Next to him sat Andrew Lennox, and on the other side Geoffrey Bone, Global Money and Caring International respectively. Geoffrey had been an expert on Africa for some years. His enterprise had caused hundreds of the latest most elaborate tractors donated to an ex-colony up north to lie rotting and rusting around the edges of as many fields: spare parts, know-how and fuel had been lacking, quite apart from the agreement of the local people, who would have liked something less grandiose. He had also caused coffee to be planted in parts of Zimlia where it instantly failed. In Kenya millions of pounds disbursed by him had vanished into greedy pockets. He was disbursing millions here, in Zimlia, which were suffering the same fate. These errors had in no way set back his career, as might have happened in less sophisticated times. He was deputy head of CI, in constant discussion with GM. Next to him was his ever-faithful admirer Daniel whose shock of red hair was as much of a beacon as it ever was: Daniel was rewarded for his decades of devotion by a starry job as Geoffrey's secretary. James Patton, now Labour MP for Shortlands in the Midlands, was here on a fact-finding trip, but really because Comrade Mo, visiting London, had run into him at Johnny's, and said, 'Why don't you come and visit us?' This did not mean that Comrade Mo was now a Zimlian, more than a citizen of any other part of Africa. But he knew Comrade Matthew – of course, as he seemed to know every new president – and when he was at Johnny's he would issue invitations as from some generic Africa, a benevolent burgeoning place with ever-open arms. It was because of Comrade Mo and his contacts that Geoffrey had reached his eminence; because of Comrade Mo's remark to some powerful person that Andrew Lennox was a clever up-and-coming lawyer, and he knew him well, 'had known him since he was a child', Global Money had headhunted him from some rival enterprise. Other people around that table, among them Comrade Mo, had been habitués of Johnny's: international aid was the legitimate spiritual heir of the Comrades. At the other end of the table from Cyrus B. – as he was affectionately known by half the world – sat Comrade Franklin Tichafa, Minister for Health, a large public man with a capacious stomach and a spare chin or two, always affable, always smiling, but his eyes these days had a tendency to wander away from questions. He and Cyrus B. were more splendidly attired than anyone else here, but not more pleased with themselves. These people, with an assortment of representatives of other charity organisations, scattered tonight around other hotels, had spent some days driving all over Zimlia, staying at towns that had acceptable hotels, and fitting in visits to beauty spots and some famous game parks. They had all agreed at lunches, dinners and on coach trips – which is where the decisions that affect nations are really made – that what Zimlia needed was a rapid development of secondary industry, already established if sometimes only in embryo, but there were problems with President Matthew who was still in his Marxist phase, which was thwarting all attempts to make a modern country of Zimlia, and a great many people were manoeuvring themselves into positions where they could be nourished by the lively flood.

Next day was the Celebration of the Heroes of the Liberation, and Comrade Franklin wanted them all to come. 'It would please our Comrade President,' he said. 'I will see that you all have good seats.'

'I'm booked to leave for Mozambique tomorrow morning,' said Cyrus B.

'Cancel it! I'll get you a good seat on the plane the day after.'

'I'm sorry. I have an appointment with the President.'

'*You* won't say no,' Franklin ordered Andrew, his voice rough because of some unpleasantness that he couldn't quite remember.

'I have to say no. I am driving out to visit Sylvia – do you remember Sylvia?'

Franklin was silent. His eyes moved aside. 'I think I remember. Yes, I seem to remember she was some kind of relative?'

'And she is working as a doctor in Kwadere. I hope I pronounce that right.'

Franklin sat smiling. 'Kwadere? I did not know there was a hospital there yet. It is not a developed part of Zimlia.'

'But I am going to see her and so I can't come to your wonderful ceremony.'

A sombreness had dashed Franklin's sparkle, he sat silent, his brows puckering. Then he threw it off and cried, 'But I am sure our good friend Geoffrey will be there.'

Geoffrey was now a solid handsome man, who drew eyes as he had done as a boy, and the millions he had at his command had given him an almost visible silvery sheen, the glisten of self-approval. 'I will certainly be there, Minister, I wouldn't miss it.'

'But such an old friend ought not to be calling me Minister,' said Franklin, offering Geoffrey dispensation in his smile.

'Thank you,' said Geoffrey, with a little bow. 'Minister Franklin, perhaps?'

Franklin laughed, a big satisfied laugh. 'And before you leave, Geoffrey, I want you to come to my office and I will show you around.'

'I was hoping you might invite me to meet your wife and children. I hear you have six children now?'

'Yes, six, and soon there will be seven. Children and money troubles,' said Franklin, looking hard at Geoffrey. But he did not invite him to his home.

Laughter, understanding laughter. More wine was called for. But Cyrus B. said he was an old man needing his sleep, and went off, remarking that he expected to see them at the conference in Bermuda next month.

'I believe that our old friend Rose Trimble has done very well,' said Franklin. 'Our President likes her work very much.'

'Rose is certainly doing well,' said Andrew, with a delightful smile, which Franklin misread.

'And you are all such good friends,' he cried. 'That is so good to hear. And when you see her, please give her my warmest regards.'

'When I do, I shall,' said Andrew, even more pleasantly.

'And so we may soon expect generous aid,' said Franklin, who was slightly drunk. 'Generous, generous aid for our poor exploited country.'

Here Comrade Mo, who had not yet contributed, said, 'In my view there should be no aid at all. Africa should be standing on her own two feet.'

He might just as well have thrown a bomb on to the table. He sat blinking a little, his teeth showing in an abashed grin, withstanding stares of surprise. He and all his coevals had overlooked or applauded every bit of news from the Soviet Union, and, with far fewer comrades, had celebrated every new massacre in China, he and still fewer had ruined the agriculture of his country by forcing unfortunate farmers into collective farms, the State's bully boys beating up and harrying any who resisted – few of the Causes he had encouraged or promoted had turned out anything but scandalous, but here, at this moment, at this table, in this company, what he was saying was inspired, was the truth, and for saying it, surely, he should have been forgiven all the rest.

'It will do us no good,' he said. 'Not in the long run. Did you know that Zimlia at Liberation was at the same level as France was, just before the Revolution?'

Laughter, relieved laughter. For one thing France had been invoked, the Revolution, they were on safe ground again.

'No, the Revolution was due to bad harvests, bad weather –

France was basically prosperous. And this country too – or it was until some perhaps slightly unfortunate policies were adopted.'

There was a silence that bordered on the panicky.

'What are you saying?' said Daniel, hot and offended, his face flaming under his red hair. 'Are you telling us this country was better off under the whites?'

'No,' said Mo. 'I did not say that. When did I say that?' His voice was slurring: with relief they all saw that he was a little drunk. 'I am saying that this is the most developed country in Africa, apart from South Africa.'

'So, what are you saying?' demanded Minister Franklin, polite, but concealing anger.

'I am saying that you should build on your very sound foundations and stand on your own feet. Otherwise Global Money and Caring International and this Fund and that Fund – present company excepted,' he said clumsily, raising his glass to them in a circling salute, 'they'll all be telling you what to do. It is not as if this country is a disaster area, like some we might mention. You have a sound economy and a good infrastructure.'

'If I did not know you so well,' said Comrade Minister Franklin, and he was actually nervously looking around to see if anyone had heard this dangerous talk, 'I'd say you were in the pay of South Africa. That you are an agent for our great neighbour.'

'Okay,' said Comrade Mo. 'Don't call the thought police yet.' Journalists had been arrested and jailed for wrong opinions, only a few days ago. 'I am among friends. I spoke my thoughts. I am saying what I think. That is all.'

A silence. Geoffrey was looking at his watch. Obediently Daniel looked at him. Various people were getting up, not looking at Comrade Mo, who sat on, partly out of stubbornness, partly because he was going to have trouble walking straight.

'Perhaps we could have a discussion on this subject?' he said to Franklin. He spoke easily, intimately: after all, had they not known each other for years, and discussed Africa noisily, but amicably whenever they met?

'No,' said Comrade Franklin. 'No, Comrade, I don't think I shall be saying any more on this subject.' He got up. A couple of until now silent black men at a near table got up too, revealing themselves as his aides or guards. He gave the clenched fist salute, shoulder level, to Geoffrey and to Daniel, and to various other representatives of international generosity, and went out, with a heavy on either side of him.

'I am going to bed,' said Andrew. 'I'm getting up early tomorrow.'

'I think Comrade Franklin may have forgotten that he has promised us seats for tomorrow's celebration,' said Geoffrey sulkily. He meant this as a rebuke to Comrade Mo.

'I'll see to it,' said Comrade Mo. 'Just give my name. I'll reserve you seats on the VIP stand.'

'But I want a seat too,' said MP James.

'Oh, don't worry,' said Comrade Mo, waving his hands about, as if they dispensed largesse, invitations, tickets. 'Don't lose any sleep. You'll get in, you'll see.' His moment of truth was past, defeated by the demon, *peer pressure*.

On that morning when Andrew was expected there was trouble at the hospital. When Sylvia walked down through the again dusty shrubs she saw chickens lying gasping, their beaks wide open, and this time it was not their defence against the heat. No water in their drinking tins. No food in their trough. She found Joshua standing swaying, a knife in his hand, over a young woman who was crouching terrified, both hands held up to ward him off. He stank of dagga. He looked as if he intended to murder the woman, who had a swollen arm. Sylvia took the knife from him and said, 'I told you that if you smoked dagga again then that would be the end. This is the end, Joshua. Do you understand?' His angry face and reddened eyes, his powerful threatening body, loomed over her. She said, 'And the chickens are dying. They have no water.'

'That is Rebecca's work.'

'You agreed between you that you would do it.'

'She must do it.'

'Now, leave. Go.'

He stalked off to a tree about twenty yards away, subsided under it, and sat, his face on his arms. Almost at once he fell over, asleep or unconscious. His little boy, Clever, was watching. He had taken to hanging around, anxious to do any little job given him. Now Sylvia said, 'Clever, will you feed the chickens and give them water?' 'Yes, Doctor Sylvia.' 'Now watch me while I show you how.' 'I know how to do it.' She watched while he fetched water, filled the tins, threw grain down. The chickens hustled to the water tins, and drank and drank but one hen was too far gone. She told him to take it up to Rebecca.

Andrew had trouble getting the kind of car he was used to from the car hire firm. They were all old and scary. 'Is that all you've got?' He knew that any new cars being imported went straight to the new elite, but on the other hand, tourists were being beckoned in. He said to the young black woman behind the desk, 'You've got to get better cars than these if you want to attract tourists.' Her face told him she agreed with him, but he wasn't going to criticise her superiors. He took a battered Volvo, asked if there was a spare tyre, was told there was, but it wasn't very good, and, since time was running by, he decided to risk it. He had detailed instructions from Sylvia on the lines of, Get on to the Koodoo Dam road, go through the Black Ox Pass, then when you see a big village, take the dirt road that bends to the right, go on about five miles, turn right at the big baobab, drive ten miles, you'll see the signpost for St Luke's Mission on the same signpost as Pyne's Farm.

He found the country impressive in a grand but hostile way, so dry, and the dust lying in the air, though he knew there had been rains recently. He had visited Zimlia many times, but had never had to find any place for himself. He lost his way, but at last was driving past the Pynes' signpost when he saw on the road in front a tall white man waving his arms. Andrew stopped, and this man said, 'I'm Cedric Pyne. Could you take this stuff to the Mission? We heard you were on your way.' A big sack was thrown into the back, and the farmer went sloping off, back to the house some hundreds of yards away. Andrew deduced that he, or someone, had been keeping an eye out for the dust of the car. He was still waiting to see the Mission, when he saw a low brick house, with gum trees around it, and beyond it the flat low buildings, like barracks, which he knew was a school. He parked. A smiling black woman came out on the verandah and said that Father McGuire was at the school and that Doctor Sylvia was coming just-now.

He followed her on to the verandah and into the front room where he was invited to sit.

Andrew's experience had been with the Africa of presidents and governments, officials, and attractive hotels, but he had not ever descended to the Africa he was seeing now. This wretched little room offended him, and precisely because it was a challenge. When he talked Global Money, dispensed Global Money, was a fount of ever-unfailing largesse, this was what it was all about – wasn't it? But this was a mission, for God's sake! This was the Roman Catholic Church, wasn't it? Weren't they supposed to be rich? There was a rent in the cretonne curtain which was attempting to exclude the glare from a sun that had only just climbed high enough not to strike it direct. Tiny black ants crawled over the floor. The black woman brought him a glass of orange juice. Warm. No ice?

The kitchen where the black woman was, opened to his right. Another door, standing ajar, was on his left. On the door a dressing-gown hung from a nail: he knew it was Sylvia's, he remembered it. He went into the room. The bare red brick floor, the brick walls, the gleaming pale reed ceiling which now was to Sylvia like a second skin, seemed to him offensively meagre. So small, this room was, so bare. On the little chest of drawers were photographs, in silver frames. There was Julia, and there, Frances.

And one of him, aged about twenty-five, debonair, whimsical, smiling straight back at him. It hurt, his younger self – he turned away, unconsciously passing his hands down over his face, as if to restore that confident unmarked face, that innocent face. He thought, mocking the surroundings, so inimical to him – that little crucifix – that he had not then eaten of the fruit of good and evil. He stared conscientiously at the crucifix, which defined a Sylvia he did not know at all, trying to accept it, accept her. Her clothes were hanging on nails on the walls. Her shoes, mostly sandals, stood along a wall. He turned and saw the Leonardo on the wall. The other pictures of Virgins and infants he ignored. Well, there was one decent thing in the room.

Now he heard that someone approached, and went to the window that opened on to the verandah, and watched Sylvia coming up the path. She wore jeans, a loose top similar to the one he had seen on the black servant, and her hair was bleached by the sun, and tied back with an elastic band. Between her eyes was a deep frowning furrow. She was burned by the sun a dry dark brown. She was as thin as he remembered ever seeing her. He went out, she saw him, rushed to him, and there was a long embrace full of love and memories.

He wanted to see the hospital: she was reluctant, knowing he would not understand what he saw: how could he, when it had taken her long enough? But they walked together down the path, and she showed him the shed she called the dispensary, the various shelters and the big hut which it seemed she was proud of. Some black people lay about on mats, under trees. A couple of men came from the bush, lifted a woman he had thought was sleeping on to a litter made of branches, the fronds of leaves tied down over it for softness, and went off with her into the trees. 'Dead,' said Sylvia. 'Childbirth. But she was ill. I know it was AIDS.' He did not know how she wanted him to respond – if she expected a response. She sounded – what? Angry? Stoical?

Back at the house, they found Father McGuire had come. Andrew disliked him and began talking, as was his way with difficult situations. He spent most of his life in committees or congresses or conferences, always presiding, and in control of people from a hundred countries representing conflicting interests and demands. Never has a man better deserved that technical adjective *facilitator*: that is what he was, and what he did, smoothing paths and opening avenues. Some facilitators use silence, sitting with unspeaking faces until at last they enter the fray with conclusive words, but others talk, and Andrew's urbane and affable rivers of words dissolved discords, and he was used to seeing angry or suspicious faces relax into hopeful smiles.

He was talking about the dinner last night which in his description became a mildly humorous social comedy, and would have made hearers laugh who knew something of the background. But these two – and that black woman standing there – did not smile, and Andrew was thinking, Of course, they are as good as peasants, they aren't used to . . . and still Sylvia and the priest stood by their chairs, while he was already sitting, ready to command, and waiting for them to smile. But he was not winning them, not at all, and a glance between them suddenly enlightened him: they wanted to say grace. Anger at himself made him go red. 'I'm so sorry,' he said, and stood up.

Father McGuire recited some Latin words which Andrew could not follow, and Sylvia said Amen in a clear little voice that Andrew remembered from that other distant life.

The three sat. Andrew was so discommoded by what he saw as his social gaffe, that he was silent.

The black woman, whom he knew was Rebecca, now served the lunch. There was chicken, the one that had died that morning from dehydration. It was tough. The priest said to Rebecca that there was no point in cooking a chicken just dead, but she said she wanted to cook something nice for the visitor. She had made a jelly, and Father McGuire, tucking in, said they should have visitors more often.

Sylvia knew that Andrew was watching, and tried to eat the chicken and spooned in the jelly as if it were medicine.

He wanted to know the history of the hospital. He had been shocked by it, and by Sylvia's being there. How could such a wretched thing be called a hospital? His dislike of the place, his suspicion, were being communicated, being felt, by Sylvia, by the priest and by Rebecca, who stood with her back to her kitchen, hands folded, listening. He did not like Rebecca. And he thoroughly distrusted Sylvia's looking like her – the native-style top, certain mannerisms, ways with the face and the eyes which Sylvia was unconscious of. Andrew spent most of his time with *people of colour* – and what could you call Sylvia, looking like that, almost as dark as Rebecca? He knew he did not suffer from race prejudice. No, but it was class prejudice, and the two are often confused. What was Sylvia doing, letting herself go like this?

These thoughts, all visible on his face, though he smiled and was his delightful social self, were putting the three against him. The trio, two of whom he thoroughly disliked, were united in criticism of him.

Father McGuire's emotions came out of him thus: 'That white suit of yours, what possessed you to put that on, to come and visit us in our dusty land?'

And indeed Andrew knew he had been foolish. He possessed a dozen or so white or cream linen suits, which took him to the Third World looking cool and smart. But there was dust on him today, and he had caught Sylvia's critical inspection of him, seeing the suit as a symptom.

'It's as well you didn't see the hospital as it was when I first came,' Sylvia said.

'That's true enough,' said the priest. 'If you are shocked by what you see now, what would you have said then?'

'I didn't say I was shocked.'

'I think we are used to seeing certain expressions on the faces of our visitors,' said Father McGuire. 'but if you want to understand that hospital, then ask the people in our village what they think.'

'We think Doctor Sylvia has been sent by God to us,' said Rebecca.

This silenced Andrew. They sat on at the table, drinking weak coffee, for which the priest apologised – decent coffee was hard to find, anything imported was so expensive, there were shortages of everything, and it was due to incompetence, that was all it was . . . He went on, a hard practised grumbling and then he heard himself, sighed and stopped. 'And God forgive me,' he said, 'to complain about a thing like bad coffee.'

The story of the hospital – it was not going to be told, Andrew saw, and knew it was his fault. He wanted to leave, but a visit to the school had been planned. They would have to go out into the dazzle of hot light that showed through the window. Father McGuire said he would get his forty winks, and off he went to his room. Sylvia and Andrew sat on, both wanting to sleep, but sticking it out. Then Rebecca came in to take the dirty plates.

'Did you bring the books?' she asked Andrew direct. The way Sylvia was keeping her eyes lowered meant that she had been wanting to ask this, but had been afraid to. She had sent him a list of books after he had telephoned to say he was coming. He had forgotten them, though she had written under the list, *Please, Andrew. Please*. He said to Rebecca, 'I forgot them, I'm sorry.' Her face stared: *No* – then she burst into tears and ran out of the room, leaving the tray on the table. Sylvia fitted plates and cups on to the tray and still did not look at him. 'It means a great deal to us,' she said. 'I know you won't be able to understand how much.'

'I'll send them to you.'

'They would probably be stolen on the way. Never mind, forget it.'

'Of course I won't forget it.'

Now he remembered that when he was in her room he had seen shelves on the wall, and above it a printed card: Library. 'Wait,' he said, and went into her room. She followed. There were two books on the shelves, one a dictionary and one, *Jane*

Eyre. Both were falling to pieces. A sheet of paper was nailed to the brick: Library Books. Taken out: Returned. *The Pilgrim's Progress. The Lord of the Rings. Christ Stopped at Eboli. The Grapes of Wrath. Cry, the Beloved Country. The Mayor of Casterbridge. The Holy Bible. The Idiot. Little Women. The Lord of the Flies. Animal Farm. Saint Teresa of Avila.* These were the books that Sylvia had brought with her, a store added to when people came, the books they had brought with them, begged for and donated to these shelves.

'A funny little collection,' said Andrew humbly. He was really moved to tears.

'You see,' said Sylvia, 'we need books. They love books and we can't get them. And these are all the worse for wear.'

'I'll send you what you asked, I will,' he said.

She did not say anything. She said nothing in a way that he knew she had learned and was practising. He suspected she was praying under her breath for patience. 'You see,' she attempted, 'you don't understand what books mean. You see someone sitting in a hut at night reading by candlelight . . . you see someone barely literate struggling.' Her voice trembled.

'Oh, Sylvia, I'm so sorry.'

'Never mind.'

The list she had sent was in his briefcase, which he had brought with him: why? but he always took it with him.

The Little Flowers of Mary. The Theory and Practice of Good Husbandry in Sub-Saharan Africa. How to Write Good English. The Tragedies of Shakespeare. The Naked and the Dead. Gawain and the Green Knight. The Secret Garden. The Centre Cannot Hold. Teach Yourself Engineering. Mowgli. The Diseases of Cattle in Southern Africa. Shaka the Zulu King. Jude the Obscure. Wuthering Heights. Tarzan. And so on.

He went back into the dining-room and found that Father McGuire had reappeared, refreshed. The two men exited into the hot glare and Sylvia tumbled on her bed. She wept. She had promised all the people who had come up to the house and come up again, and again, asking for books, that a new stock of books was coming. She felt abandoned. In her mind Andrew stood for perfect tenderness, kindness; he was the gentle big brother to whom she could say anything, whom she could ask for anything – but he was a stranger now. That brilliant white suit! I ask you, white linen, put on to visit St Luke's Mission! White linen that must be like rubbing thick cream between your fingers. She felt that in some subtle way that suit was an insult to her, to Father McGuire, to Rebecca. Once long ago she could have said this to him, they might have laughed about it.

She slept, woke and made tea – Rebecca would not return until supper time. She had made some biscuits for the visitor.

The two men returned. Andrew was smiling, but tight-lipped and looked washed out: well, he had not slept.

'And there is my tea,' said Father McGuire. 'I can tell you, my child, that I need it, yes I do.'

'Well?' said Sylvia to Andrew. She sounded aggressive, since she knew what he had seen.

Six buildings, each holding four classrooms, bursting with children, from small ones to young men and women. They were all exuberantly welcoming, and all complained to this representative from the higher places of power that they needed textbooks, they had no textbooks. There was sometimes one textbook for the whole class. 'How can we do our homework, sir? How can we study?'

There was not a globe, nor an atlas, in the whole school. When he had asked, the children did not know what they were. Harassed and frustrated young teachers took him aside to beg him to get them books to teach them how to teach. They were eighteen or twenty years old themselves, without hardly any qualifications and certainly none to enable them to teach.

Andrew had never seen a more depressing place: school it was not. Father McGuire had escorted him from building to building, striding through dust to get out of the sun and back into patches of shade, introducing him as a friend of Zimlia. His fame as Global

Money – though Father McGuire had not mentioned the magic name – had permeated the whole school. He was greeted with cries of welcome and with songs, and everywhere he looked were expectant faces.

The priest had said: 'I shall tell you the history of this place. We, the Mission, ran a school here for years – since the colony began. It was a good school. We had no more than fifty pupils. Some of them are in government now. Did you know that most of the African leaders came from mission schools? During the war Comrade President Matthew promised every child in the country a good secondary education. The schools were rushed up every-where, are multiplying now. There are not the teachers, there are not the books, there are no exercise books. When the government took over our school – that was the end. I do not think the children you saw today will end up in the cabinet, or indeed, not anywhere that requires an education.'

Then, when he had drunk some tea, he said, 'Things will get better. You are seeing the worst. This is a poor district.'

'Are there many schools like this one?'

'Yes, indeed,' said Father McGuire equably. 'Many. Very many.'

'And so what will happen to those children? Though some of them seem to be adults.'

'They will be unemployed,' said Father McGuire. 'They will be unemployed. Yes, surely they will.'

'I suppose I had better be driving back,' said Andrew. 'I have a plane to catch at nine.'

'And now, if I may be so bold as to ask, is there a possibility you may do something for us? The school? The hospital? Would you think of us when you return to the ease and the pleasantness of – where did you say you are located?'

'New York. And I think you have misunderstood. We shall be directing money – a big loan, to Zimlia, but not . . .'

'You mean, we are beneath your notice?'

'Not beneath mine,' said Andrew, smiling. 'But Global Money

aims at high levels of . . . but I'll speak to someone. I'll speak to Caring International.'

'We would be duly grateful,' said Father McGuire. Sylvia said nothing. The furrow between her eyes made her seem like a scowling little witch.

'Sylvia, why don't you come for a holiday to New York?'

'And indeed you should,' said the priest, 'so you should, my child.'

'Thank you. I'll think about it.' She did not look at him.

'And will you drop in something for us to the Pynes? Just drop it, no need to go in, if you are in a hurry.'

They went to the Volvo and the sack for the Pynes was put in the back.

'I'll send you the books, darling,' he said to Sylvia.

A couple of weeks later a sack arrived, by special messenger, from Senga, by motorbike. Books, from New York, delivered by plane to Senga, collected by InterGlobe, who attended to the Customs, and brought them all the way here. 'What did that cost?' asked Father McGuire, offering tea to the exile from the bright lights of Senga.

'You mean, all of it?' said the messenger, a smart young black man, in a uniform. 'Well, it's here.' He brought out the papers. 'That will have cost the sender just on a hundred pounds, to get them here,' he said, admiring the size of the sum.

'We could build a reading room with that, or an infant's nursery,' said Sylvia.

'We must not look a gift horse in the mouth,' said the priest.

'I'm looking at it in the mouth,' said Sylvia. She was scanning the list of books. Andrew had given her list to his secretary, who had mislaid it. So she went to the nearest big bookstore and ordered all the bestsellers, feeling complacent, and even sated, as if she had actually read them herself: she did fully intend to start reading soon. The novels were all unsuitable for Sylvia's library. In due course they were given to Edna Pyne, who complained continually that she had read all her books a hundred times. 'To her who has, it shall be given.'

The history of the hospital Andrew did not hear was this.

During the Liberation War this whole area, miles of it, had been full of the fighters, because it was hilly, with caves and ravines, good for guerilla war. One night Father McGuire had woken to see standing over him a youth pointing a gun at him, and saying, 'Get up, put your hands up.' The priest was stiff with sleep and slow at the best of times, and the youth swore at him and told him he would be shot if he didn't hurry. But this was a very young man, eighteen, or even younger, and he was more frightened than Father McGuire: the rifle was shaking. 'I'm coming,' said Father McGuire, clumsily getting out of bed, but he couldn't keep his hands up, he needed them. 'Just take it easy,' he said, 'I'm coming.' He put on his dressing-gown while the gun waved about near him, and then he said, 'What do you want?'

'We want medicine, we want *muti*. One of us very sick.'

'Then come to the bathroom.' In the medicine cabinet were not much more than malaria tablets and aspirin and some bandages. 'Take what you need,' he said.

'Is that all? I don't believe you,' said the youth. But he took everything there was, and said, 'We want a doctor to come.'

'Let us go to the kitchen,' said the priest. There he said, 'Sit down.' He made tea, put biscuits out, and watched while they vanished. He took a couple of loaves of Rebecca's new bread and handed them over, with some cold meat. These things vanished into a cloth bundle.

'How can I get a doctor here? What shall I say? You people keep ambushing this road.'

'Say you are sick and need a doctor. When you expect him tie a bit of cloth to that window. We shall be watching and we'll bring our comrade. He's wounded.'

'I'll try,' said the priest. As the youth disappeared into the night he turned to threaten: 'Don't tell Rebecca we were here.'

'So you know Rebecca?'

'We know everything.'

Father McGuire thought, then wrote to a colleague in Senga, saying a doctor was needed for an unusual case. He should drive out in daytime, not stop the car for anything, and be sure he had his gun with him. 'And be careful not to alarm our good sisters.' A telephone call: a discreet exchange, apparently about the weather and the state of the crops. Then, 'I shall visit you with Father Patrick. He has had medical training.'

The priest tied a cloth to the window and hoped Rebecca did not notice. She said nothing: he knew she understood much more than she let on. The car arrived with the priests in it. That night two guerillas appeared, saying their comrade was too ill to be moved. They needed antibiotics. The priests had brought anti-biotics, together with a good supply of medicines. They were all handed over, while Father Patrick prescribed. Again the larder was emptied of what was left while two half-starving young men had eaten as much as they could.

Father McGuire went on living in this house that anyone could enter at any time. The nuns lived inside a security fence, but he hated it: he said he felt like a prisoner even going inside it to visit them. In his own house, he was exposed, and he knew he was watched. He expected to be murdered: white people had been killed not far away. Then the war ended. Two youths came to the house and said they were there to say thank you. Rebecca fed them, when she was ordered to do it. She said to the priest, 'They are bad people.'

He asked what had happened to the wounded man: he had died. After that he saw them around: they were unemployed and angry because they had believed Liberation would see them in fine jobs and good houses. He employed one at the school as an odd-job man. The other was Joshua's eldest son, who started school in a class full of small children: he spoke pretty good English, but could not read or write. Now he was sick, very thin, and with sores.

Father McGuire did not mention these events to anyone, until he told Sylvia. Rebecca did not speak of them. The nuns did not know of them.

He had to keep an ever-enlarging supply of medicines in his house, because people came to ask for them. He built the shacks and shed down the hill, and asked Senga for a doctor to come: Comrade President Matthew had promised free medicine for everybody. He was sent a young man who had not finished his medical training, because of the war: he had intended to be a medical orderly. Father McGuire did not know this until one night the young man got drunk and said he wanted to finish his training, could Father McGuire help him? Father McGuire said, When you stop drinking, I'll write the letter for you. But the war had damaged this fighter, who had been twenty when it started: he could not stop drinking. This was 'the doctor' that Joshua had told Sylvia about. Father McGuire, in a chatty letter to Senga, complained that there was no hospital for twenty miles and no doctor. It happened that a priest visiting London had met Sylvia, with Father Jack. And so it had all happened.

But there was a good hospital planned for ten miles away, and when that opened, this disgraceful place – Sylvia said – could cease to be.

'Why disgraceful?' said the priest. 'It does good things. It was a good day for us all when you came. You are a blessing for us.'

And why had the good sisters up the hill not been a blessing?

The four who had seen out the dangers of the war had not always been behind their security fence. They taught at the school, when it had still been a good one. The war ended and they left. They were white women, but the nuns who replaced them were black, young women who had escaped from poverty, dreariness and sometimes danger into the blue and white uniforms that set them aside from other black women. They were not educated and could not teach. They found themselves in this place which was a horror to them, not an escape from poverty, but a reminder of it. There were four of them, Sister Perpetua, Sister Grace, Sister Ursula, Sister Boniface. The 'hospital' was not one, and when

Joshua ordered them to come every day they were back where they had escaped from: under the domination of a black man who expected to be waited on. They found excuses not to go, and Father McGuire did not insist: the fact was, they were pretty useless. Gentility was what they had chosen, not suppurating limbs. By the time Sylvia arrived the enmity between them and Joshua was such that every time they saw him they said they would pray for him, and he taunted, insulted and cursed them in return.

They did wash bandages and dressings while complaining they were dirty and disgusting, but their energies really went into the church which was as pretty and well-kept as the churches that had beckoned them to become nuns when they were girls. Those churches had been the cleanest and finest buildings for miles and now this one at St Luke's Mission, like those, never had a speck of dust, because it was swept several times a day, and the statues of Christ and the Virgin were polished and gleaming, and when dust swirled the nuns were up shutting doors and windows and sweeping it up before it even settled. The good sisters were serving the church and Father McGuire, and, said Joshua, mimicking them, they clucked like chickens whenever he came near.

They were often sick, because then they could return to Senga and their mother house.

Joshua sat all day under the big acacia tree while sunlight and shadow sifted over him, and watched what went on at the hospital, but often through eyes that distorted what he saw. He was smoking dagga almost continually. His little boy Clever was always with Sylvia, and then there were two children, Clever and Zebedee. They could not have been further from the adorable black piccanin with long curly lashes that sentiment loves. They were lean, with bony faces where burned enormous eyes hungry to learn and – it became evident – hungry for food too. They arrived at the hospital at seven, unfed, and Sylvia made them come up to the house where she cut them slabs of bread and jam, while Rebecca watched, and once remarked that her children did not get bread and jam, but only cold porridge, and not always that. Father McGuire watched and said that Sylvia was now the mother of two children and he hoped she knew what she was doing. 'But they have a mother,' she said, and he said no, their own mother had died on the violent roads of Zimlia, and their father had died of malaria, and so they had become Joshua's responsibility: they called him Father. Sylvia was relieved to hear this history. Joshua had already lost two children – another had just died – and she knew why, and what the real reason was – not the 'Pneumonia' that was on their death certificates. So these two were not Joshua's by blood: how useful, how painfully pertinent that old phrase had become. They were both clever, as Joshua had claimed for Clever: he said that his brother had been a teacher and his sister-in-law had been first in her class. The little boys watched every movement she made, and copied her, and examined her face and eyes as she spoke, so they knew what she wanted them to do before she asked; they looked after the chickens and the sitting hens, they collected eggs and never broke one, they ran about with mugs of water and medicines for the patients. They squatted on either side of her watching when she set limbs or lanced swellings, and she had to keep reminding herself they were six and four, not twice those ages. They were sponges for information. But they were not at school. Sylvia made them come up to the house at four o'clock, when she had finished at the hospital, and set them lessons. Other children wanted to join in: Rebecca's, for a start. Soon, she was running what amounted to a little nursery school. But when the others wanted to be like Clever and Zebedee and work at the hospital, she said no. Why did she favour them, it wasn't fair? She made the excuse that they were orphans. But there were other orphans at the village. 'Well, my child,' said the priest, 'and now you begin to understand why people's hearts break in Africa. Do you know the story of the man who was asked why he was walking along the beach after a storm throwing stranded starfish back into the sea, when there were thousands of them who must die? He replied that he did it because the few he could save would find themselves back in the sea and be happy.' 'Until the next storm – were you going to say that, Father?' 'No, but I might be thinking it. And I am interested that you might be thinking on those lines too.' 'You mean, I am thinking more realistically – as you put it, Father?' 'Yes, I do, I do put it like that. But I've told you often enough, you have too many stars in your eyes for your own good.'

The Studebaker lorry, an old rattler donated by the Pynes to the Mission, to replace the Mission lorry which had finally met its death, stood waiting on the track. Sylvia had told Rebecca to say in the village that she was going to the Growth Point and could take six people in the back. About twenty had already clambered in. With Sylvia stood Rebecca and two of her children – she had insisted they should have the treat, not Joshua's children, not this time.

Sylvia said to the people in the back that the tyres were very old and could easily burst. No one moved. The Mission had its name down for tyres, even second-hand tyres, but it was a forlorn hope. Then Rebecca spoke in first one local language and then another and in English. No one moved and a woman said to Sylvia, 'Drive slowly and it will be okay.'

Sylvia and Rebecca jumped into the front seat with the two children. The lorry set off, crawling. At the Pynes' turn-off they were waved down by the Pynes' cook who said he had to get into the Growth Point, there was no food in his house and his wife . . . Rebecca laughed, and there was much laughter at the back and he climbed up, and fitted himself in somehow. Rebecca sat beside Sylvia and turned to watch the back – where they were laughing and teasing the cook: there was some drama Sylvia would never know about.

The Growth Point was five miles from the Mission. The white government had created the idea that there should be a network of nuclei around which townships would grow: a shop, a government office, the police, a church, a garage. The idea was successful, and the black government claimed it as theirs. No one argued. This Growth Point was still in embryo but expanding: there were half a dozen little houses, a new supermarket. Sylvia parked outside the government office, a small building sitting in pale dust where some dogs lay asleep. Everyone piled out of the lorry, but Rebecca's boys had to stay in it, to guard it, otherwise everything would be stolen off it, including the tyres. They were given some Pepsi and a bun each, with instructions that if anyone at all looked as if theft was planned one must run and tell their mother.

The two women went together into the office, whose waiting-room already had a dozen people in it, and sat together at the end of a bench. Sylvia was the only white person there, but with her burned skin, and in her headscarf, for the dust, she and Rebecca were like each other, two small thin women, both with worried faces, in the timeless scene, petitioners waiting, lulled by boredom. From inside, beyond a door that had on it, *Mr M. Mandizi*, faded white paint on brown, came a loud hectoring voice. Sylvia grimaced at Rebecca who grimaced back. Time passed. The door suddenly opened and there appeared a young black girl, in tears.

'Shame,' said an old black man, who was well down in the queue. He clicked his tongue and shook his head, and said, 'Shame' loudly, as a large and imposing black man, in the obligatory three-piece suit, stood there and impressed them all. He said, 'Next', and stood back, shutting the door, so that the next petitioner had to knock, and hear, 'Come in'.

Time passed. This one came out successful: at least, he was not crying. And he clapped his hands together gently, not looking at anyone, so that the salutation or applause was for himself.

The loud voice from inside: 'Next.'

Sylvia sent Rebecca with some money to buy the children some lunch and a drink, and to make sure they were there. They were, asleep. Rebecca brought a Fanta back, which the two women shared.

A couple of hours passed.

Then, it was their turn, and the official, seeing that this was a white woman, was about to summon the man next on the bench when the old man said, 'Shame. The white woman is waiting like the rest of us.'

'It is for me to say who comes next,' said Mr Mandizi.

'Okay,' said the old man, 'but it is not right, what you are doing. We don't like what you are doing.'

Mr Mandizi hesitated, but then pointed at Sylvia and went back in.

Sylvia smiled thanks at the old man, and Rebecca spoke softly to him in their language. Laughter all around. What was the joke? Again, Sylvia was thinking she would never know. But Rebecca whispered to her as they went in to the office, 'I told him he was like an old bull who knows how to keep the young ones in order.'

They arrived in front of Mr Mandizi still smiling. He glanced up from papers, frowned, saw Rebecca was there, and was about to speak sharply to her when she began on the ritual greeting.

'Good morning – no, I see it is already afternoon. So, good afternoon.'

'Good afternoon,' he replied

'I hope you are well.'

'I am well if you are well . . .' and so on, and even truncated it was an impressive reminder of good manners.

Then, to Sylvia: 'What do you want?'

'Mr Mandizi, I am from St Luke's Mission, and I have come to ask why the supply of condoms has not been sent. It was due from you last month.'

Mr Mandizi seemed to swell, and he half rose from his desk, and his startled look became offended. He subsided and said, 'And why am I expected to talk to a woman about condoms? It is not what I expect to hear?'

'I am the doctor at the Mission hospital. The government last year said that condoms were being made available for all bush hospitals.'

Clearly Mr Mandizi had not heard of this ukase, but now he gave himself time by dabbing at his forehead, bright with sweat, with a very large white handkerchief. His was the kind of face that has to labour for authority. It was by nature amiable, and wanting to please: the frown he imposed on it didn't suit him. 'And what may I ask are you going to do with all these condoms?'

'Mr Mandizi, you must have heard that there is a bad disease . . . it is a new very bad disease and it is transmitted by sexual intercourse.'

His face was that of a man being forced to swallow unpleasantness.

'Yes, yes,' he said, 'but we know that this disease is an invention of the whites. It is to make us wear condoms, so that we do not have children and our people become weakened.'

'Forgive me, Mr Mandizi, but you are out of date. It is true that your government was saying that AIDS does not exist but now they say that perhaps it may exist, and so men should wear condoms.'

Ghosts of derision chased themselves across his large, black pleasant face, displacing the frown. And now Rebecca spoke, direct to him, in their language, and it seemed well, for Mr Mandizi was listening, his face turned towards her, towards this woman to whom in his culture, he would not have to listen on such subjects, at least not in public.

He addressed Sylvia: 'You think this sickness is here, in this district, with us? Slim is here?'

'Yes, I know it is. I know it is, Mr Mandizi. People are dying from it. You see, the problem is diagnosis. People may be dying of pneumonia or TB or diarrhoea or skin lesions – sores – but the real reason is AIDS. It is Slim. And there are a lot of sick people. Many more than when I first came to the hospital.'

Now Rebecca spoke again, and Mr Mandizi was listening, not looking at her, but nodding.

'And so you want me to telephone the head office and tell them to send me the condoms?'

'And we have not had the malaria tablets. We haven't had any medicines.'

'Doctor Sylvia has been buying medicines for us with her own money,' said Rebecca.

Mr Mandizi nodded, sat thinking. Then, a different man, a petitioner in his turn, he leaned forward and asked, 'Can you tell by looking if someone has Slim?'

'No. There are tests for it.'

'My wife is not well. She coughs all the time.'

'That needn't be AIDS. Has she lost weight?'

'She is thin. She is too too thin.'

'You should take her to the big hospital.'

'I did. They gave her *muti* but she is still sick.'

'Sometimes I send samples to Senga – if someone isn't too sick.'

'You are saying that if someone is very ill you don't send samples?'

'Some people come in to me when they are so ill I know they are going to die. And there is no point in wasting money on tests.'

'In our culture,' said Mr Mandizi, regaining his authority because of this so often used formula, 'in our culture, we have good medicine, but I know you whites despise it.'

'I don't despise it. I am friends with our local *n'ganga*. Sometimes I ask him for help. But he says himself he cannot do anything for AIDS.'

'Perhaps that is why his medicine didn't help her?'

But hearing what he had said, his whole body seemed to freeze up in panic and he sat rigid, staring, then jumped up and said, 'You must come with me now – yes, now-now – she is here, in my house, it is five minutes.'

He swept the two women before him out of the office and through the silent petitioners, saying, 'I will be back in my office in ten minutes. Wait.'

Sylvia and Rebecca were directed through the hot dusty glare to one of the new houses, ten of them in a row, like boxes sitting in the dust, but identical to the big new houses going up in Senga, scaled down to the importance of Kwadere Growth Point. Over them scarlet, purple and magenta bougainvillaeas marked them for distinction: here lived all the local officials.

'Come in, come in,' Mr Mandizi urged, and they were in a small room stuffed with a three-piece suite, a sideboard, refrigerator, pouffe, and then in a bedroom filled with a big bed where lay someone ill, and beside her a pretty plump black woman fanning the sleeper with a bunch of eucalyptus leaves, whose smell was trying to overcome the sickroom odours. But was the invalid asleep? Sylvia stood over her, saw with shock that this woman was ill, very ill – she was dying. She should have been a glossy healthy black, but she was grey, sores covered her face, and she was thin, the head on the pillow showed the skull. There was hardly any pulse. Her breath barely moved. Her eyes were half open. Touching her left Sylvia's fingers cold. Sylvia turned her face to the desperate husband, unable to speak, and Rebecca beside her began to wail softly. The plump young woman stared straight ahead, and went on with her fanning.

Sylvia stumbled out to the other room and leaned against the wall.

'Mr Mandizi,' she said, 'Mr Mandizi.' He came up to her, took her hand, leaned to stare into her face, and whispered, 'Is she very ill? My wife . . .' 'Mr Mandizi . . .' He let his body fall forward so that his face lay on his arm on the wall. He was so close to Sylvia she put her arm around his shoulders and held him as he sobbed.

'I'm afraid she will die,' he whispered.

'Yes. I am sorry, I think she is dying.'

'What shall I do? What shall I do?'

'Mr Mandizi, do you have children?'

'We had a little girl but she died.'

Tears were splashing on to the cement floor.

'Mr Mandizi,' she whispered – she was thinking of that plump healthy woman next door, 'you must listen to me, you must, please do not have sex without a condom.'

It was such a terrible thing to say at that moment, it was ridiculous, but the dreadful urgency of his situation compelled her. 'Please, I know how this must sound, and don't be angry with me.' She was still whispering.

'Yes, yes, yes, I heard what you said. I am not angry.'

'If you want me to come back later, when you are . . . I can come back and explain it to you.'

'No, I understand. But you don't understand something.' He pulled himself off the support of the wall and stood upright. He spoke normally now. 'My wife is dying. My child is dead. And I know who is responsible. I shall consult our good *n'ganga* again.'

'Mr Mandizi, you simply can't be saying . . .'

'Yes, I am saying it. That is what I am saying. Some enemy has put a curse on me. This is the work of a witch.'

'Oh, Mr Mandizi, and you are an educated man . . .'

'I know what you are thinking. I know how you people think.'

He stood there before her, his face contorted with anger and with suspicion. 'I will get to the bottom of this.' Then he commanded. 'Tell them at the office I will be returning in half an hour.'

Sylvia and Rebecca began to walk away towards the lorry.

They heard, 'And that so-called hospital at the Mission. We know about it. It is a good thing that our new hospital will soon be built and we shall have some real medicine in our district.'

Sylvia said, 'Rebecca, please don't tell me that you agree with what he is saying. It is ridiculous.'

Rebecca was first silent and then said, 'Sylvia, you see, in our culture it is not ridiculous.'

'But it is a disease. Every day we understand more about it. It is a terrible disease.'

'But why do some people get it but other people don't get

it? Can you explain that? And that is the point, do you understand what I am saying? Perhaps there is some person who wanted to harm Mr Mandizi, or who wanted to get rid of his wife? Did you see that young woman in the bedroom with Mrs Mandizi? Perhaps she would like to be Mrs Mandizi herself?'

'Well, Rebecca, we are not going to agree.'

'No, Sylvia, we are not going to agree.'

At the lorry people were already waiting to clamber in but Sylvia said, 'I am not driving home yet. And I will let six people come, only six. We are going to the new hospital and it is bad road.' She could see the beginnings of it, a rough track through the bush.

Rebecca issued urgent commands. Six women got in the back.

'I'll pick you up in half an hour,' Sylvia said, and the lorry lumbered and lurched over roots, stones, potholes, for another mile or so, and they arrived where the outlines of a building had been laid down in a clearing among trees. These were big old trees; this was old bush, a bit dusty, but full and green.

The two women and the children got out of the cabin of the lorry, and the six women followed them. The women stood staring at what was described as the new hospital.

Swedes? Danes? Americans? Germans? – some country's government, devoted to the sorrows of Africa, had caused a lot of money to be directed here, to this clearing, and in front of them were the results. As with an architect's plan, these observers had to use their minds to work out the shape of things to come from these foundations, and walls begun and not finished, for the trouble was, it had been a good while arriving, the next instalment of aid money, and the rooms, wards, corridors, operating theatres and dispensaries were filling with pale dust. Some walls stood waist high, some were at knee level, blocks of concrete had holes in them filled with water. The women from the village, seeing the hope of something useful, went forward and retrieved a couple of bottles, and half a dozen tin cans, which they shook, getting rid of dust, and then put them carefully into big hold-alls. Someone had had a picnic here or a wanderer had built a fire for the night to keep off animals. The faces of these visitors had on them the expressions seen so often in our time: we are not going to comment, but someone has blundered. And who had? And why? Rumour said that the money earmarked for this hospital had been stolen on the way; some said that the government in question had simply run out of funds.

On the other side of the clearing, under the trees, large wooden cases lay about. The six women went over to look and Sylvia and Rebecca followed. A case had split open. Inside was dental equipment: a dentist's chair.

'Pity I am not a dentist,' said Sylvia. 'We could certainly do with one.'

Another case, split at the sides, showed that inside was a wheelchair.

'Oh, doctor,' said one of the women, 'we must not take this chair. Perhaps one day the hospital will be built.' She was pulling the chair out.

'We need a wheelchair,' said Rebecca.

'But they'll want to know where it came from and our hospital doesn't run to a wheelchair.'

'We should take it,' said Rebecca.

'It's broken,' said the woman. Someone had tried to pull the chair out of its wooden shelter and a wheel had come loose.

Four more cases lay about. Two of the women went to one and began wrenching at the rotten wood. Inside were bedpans. Rebecca, without looking at Sylvia, took half a dozen bedpans to the lorry and came back. Another woman found blankets, but these were eaten by insects, and mice were nesting in them, and birds had pulled out threads to line their nests.

'It will be a good hospital,' said one woman, laughing.

'We shall have a fine new hospital in Kwadere,' said another.

The village women laughed, enjoying themselves, and then Sylvia and Rebecca joined in. In the middle of the bush, miles from the philanthropists in Senga (or, for that matter, London, Berlin, New York), the women stood and laughed.

They drove back to the Growth Point, picked up the waiting people, and proceeded slowly to the Mission, all listening for a burst tyre. Their luck held. Rebecca and Sylvia took the bedpans down to the hospital. The seriously ill people, in the big new hut built by Sylvia when she first came, had been using old bottles, cans, discarded kitchen utensils. 'What are those things?' asked Joshua's brother's little boys, and when they understood, they were delighted and ran about showing them to anyone well enough to care.

Colin opened the door to a timid ring, and saw what he thought was a mendicant child or a gipsy and then, with a roar of 'It's Sylvia, it's little Sylvia,' lifted her inside. There he hugged her, and she shed tears on his cheeks, bent down to rub hers, like a cat's greeting.

In the kitchen he sat her at the table, *the table*, again extended to its full length. He poured a river of wine into a big glass and sat opposite her, full of welcome and pleasure.

'Why didn't you say you were coming? But it doesn't matter. I can't tell you how pleased I am to see you.'

Sylvia was trying to lift her mood to his height, because she was dispirited, London sometimes having this effect on Londoners who have been away from it and who, while living in it, have had so little idea of its weight, its multitudinous gifts and capacities. London, after the Mission, was hitting her a blow somewhere in the stomach region. It is a mistake to come too fast from, let's say, Kwadere, to London: one needs something like the equivalent of a decompression chamber.

She sat smiling, taking little sips of wine, afraid to do more, for she was not used to wine these days, feeling the house like a creature all around her and above her and below her, *her* house, the one she had known best as home when she had been conscious of what was going on in it, the atmospheres and airs of every room and stretches of the staircase. Now the house was populous, she could feel that, it was full of people, but they were alien presences, not her familiars and she was grateful for Colin, sitting there smiling at her. It was ten in the evening. Upstairs someone was playing a tune she ought to know, probably something famous, like 'Blue Suede Shoes' – it had that claim on her – but she couldn't name it.

'Little Sylvia. And it looks to me that you need a bit of feeding up, as always. Can I give you something to eat?'

'I ate on the plane.'

But he was up, opening the refrigerator door, peering at its shelves, and again Sylvia felt a blow to her heart, yes it was her heart, it hurt, for she was thinking of Rebecca, in her kitchen, with her little fridge, and her little cupboard which to her family down in the village represented some extreme of good fortune, generous provisioning: she was looking at the eggs filling half the door of the fridge, at the gleaming clean milk, the crammed containers, the plenitudes . . .

'This is not really my territory, it's Frances's, but I'm sure . . .' he fetched out a loaf of bread, a plate of cold chicken. Sylvia was tempted: Frances had cooked it, Frances had fed her; with Frances on one side and Andrew on the other, she had survived her childhood.

'What is your territory, then?' she asked, tucking in to a chicken sandwich.

'I am upstairs, at the top of the house.'

'In Julia's place?'

'I, and Sophie.'

This surprised her into putting down her bit of sandwich, as if relinquishing safety for the time being.

'You and Sophie!'

'Of course, you didn't know. She came here to recuperate, and then . . . she was ill, you see.'

'And then?'

'Sophie is pregnant,' he said, 'and so we are about to get married.'

'Poor Colin,' she said, and then coloured up from shame – after all, she did not really know . . .

'Not entirely poor Colin. After all, I am very fond of Sophie.'

She resumed her sandwich, but put it down: Colin's news had clamped her stomach shut. 'Well, go on. I can see you are miserable.'

'Perspicacious Sylvia. Well, you always were, while apparently only little miss-I-am-not-here-at all.'

This hurt, and he had meant it to. 'No, no, I'm sorry. I really am. I'm not myself. You've caught me at a . . . Well, perhaps I am myself, at that.'

He poured more wine.

'Don't drink until I've heard.'

He set down his glass. 'Sophie is forty-three. It's late.'

'Yes, but quite often old mothers . . .' She saw him wince.

'Quite so. An old mother. But believe it or not Down's Syndrome babies – ever so jolly I hear they are? – and all the other horrors are not the worst. Sophie is convinced that I am convinced she coaxed the baby into her reluctant womb, to make use of me, because it is getting late for her. I know she didn't do it on purpose, it is not her nature. But she won't let it go. Day and night I hear her wails of guilt: "Oh, I know what you're thinking . . ."' – And Colin wailed the words, with great effect. 'Do you know something? yes, of course you do. There is no pleasure to compete with the pleasure of guilt. She is rolling in it, wallowing in it, my Sophie is, she's having the time of her life, knowing that I hate her because she has trapped me and nothing I can say will stop her because it's such fun, being guilty.' This was as savage as she had heard ever from savage Colin, and she saw him lift his glass and down the lot in a gulp.

'Oh, Colin, you're going to be drunk and I see you so seldom.'

'Sylvia – you're right.' He refilled his glass. 'But I will marry her, she is already seven months, and we will live upstairs in Julia's old flat – four rooms, and I shall work down at the bottom of the house – when it's empty.' Here his face, reddened and angry as it was, spread into that exhilaration of pleasure that goes with the contemplation of life's relentless sense of drama. 'You did know that Frances took on two kids with her new bloke?'

'Yes, she wrote.'

'Did she tell you there is a wife, a depressive? She is downstairs, in the flat where Phyllida was.'

'But . . .'

'No buts. It has worked out as well as might be. She has recovered from her depression. The two children are upstairs where Andrew and I used to be. Frances and Rupert are in the flat she always had.'

'So it has worked out?'

'But the two children reasonably enough think that now their mother has broken off with her fancy man, then why shouldn't their father and mother get together again, and Frances should just fade out.'

'So they are being horrible to Frances?'

'Not at all. Much worse. They are very polite and reasonable. The merits are argued out over every meal. The little girl, a real little bitch by the way, says things like, "But it would be so much better for us if you went away, wouldn't it, Frances?" It's the little girl really, not the boy. Rupert is hanging on to Frances for dear life. Understandably, if you know Meriel.'

Sylvia was thinking about Rebecca with her six children, two of them dead, probably from AIDS – but perhaps not – her usually absentee husband, working eighteen hours a day, and never complaining.

She sighed, saw Colin's look: 'How lucky you are, Sylvia, to be so far away from our unedifying emotional messes.'

'Yes, I am sometimes glad I am not married – sorry. Go on. Meriel . . .'

'Meriel – well, now she's a prize. She's cold, manipulative, selfish and has always treated Rupert badly. She's a feminist – you know? With all the law of the jungle behind her? She has always told Rupert that it is his duty to keep her, and she made him pay for her taking a degree in some rubbish or other, the higher criticism, I think. She has never earned a penny. And now she is trying to get a divorce where he keeps her in perpetuity. She belongs to a group of women, a secret sisterhood – you don't believe me? – whose aim it is to screw men for everything they can get.'

'You're making it up.'

'Sweet Sylvia, I seem to remember you never could believe in the nastier aspects of human nature. But now Fate has taken a turn, and you'll never believe . . . Meriel went to Phyllida for therapy. Frances paid for it. Then Frances went to see Phyllida who is quite a reasonable female after all – you are surprised?'

'Of course I am.'

'And she asked Phyllida to train Meriel as a counsellor, and she would pay.'

And now Sylvia began to laugh. 'Oh, Colin. Oh, Colin . . .'

'Yes, quite so. Because you see, Meriel is quite unqualified. She didn't finish her degree. But as a counsellor she will be self-supporting. Counselling has become the resource of the unqualified female – it has replaced the sewing machine, for earlier generations.'

'Not in Zimlia is hasn't. The sewing machine is alive and well and earning women's livings.' And she laughed again.

'At last,' said Colin. 'I had begun to think you would never smile.' And he poured her more wine. She had actually drunk all hers. And he poured more for himself. 'And so. Meriel is going to move out to live with Phyllida, because Phyllida's partner is setting herself up as an independent physio, and our flat downstairs will be free and I shall use it to write in. And of course to evade my responsibilities as a father.'

'Which doesn't solve the problem of Frances being set up as a cruel stepmother. Apart from the children, is she happy?'

'She's delirious. First, she really likes this Rupert, and who could blame her? But you haven't heard? She's back in the theatre.'

'What do you mean? I didn't know she was ever in it.'

'How little we know about our parents. It turns out that the theatre has always been my mother's first love. She is in a play with my Sophie. At this very moment the applause is ringing out for both of them.' And now his voice was slurred, and he frowned, concentrating on his speech. 'Damn,' he said. 'I am drunk.'

'Please, dear Colin, don't drink, please don't.'

'Spoken like Sonia. Well done.'

'Oh, Chekhov. Yes. I see. But I'm on her side, all right.' She laughed, but unhappily. 'There's a man at the Mission . . .' But how was she going to convey the reality of Joshua to Colin? 'A black man. If he's not high on pot he's drunk. Well, if you knew his life . . .'

'And mine doesn't justify alcohol?'

'No, it doesn't. So you'd rather it wasn't Sophie . . .'

'I'd rather it wasn't a woman of forty-three.' And now a howl broke out of him, it had been waiting there all this time. 'You see, Sylvia, I know this is ridiculous, I know I am a sad pathetic fool, but I wanted happy families, I wanted mummy and daddy and four children. I wanted all that and I'm not going to have anything like it with my Sophie.'

'No,' said Sylvia.

'No.' He was trying not to cry, rubbing his fists over his face like a child. 'And if you don't want to be here to greet my happy Sophie and my triumphant mother, both high on *Romeo and Juliet* . . .'

'You mean Sophie is playing Juliet?'

'She looks about eighteen. She looks wonderful. She is wonderful. Pregnancy suits her. You don't have to notice she's pregnant. The newspapers are making a thing of it, though. Sarah Bernhardt played Juliet aged a hundred and one with a wooden leg – that kind of thing. A pregnant Juliet adds an unexpected dimension to *Romeo and Juliet*. But the audiences love her. She's never had bigger applause. She is wearing white flowing robes and white flowers in her hair. Sylvia, do you remember her hair?' And now he began to cry, after all.

Sylvia went to him, persuaded him out of his chair, and then up the stairs, and where she had sat with Andrew, she held Colin and listened while he sobbed himself to sleep.

She didn't know where in this house she could find a bed. So she left a note for Colin. She told him she wanted him to 'write the truth about Zimlia'. Someone should.

She walked off into the streets and when she saw a hotel, went in.

She had said she would appear for lunch. In the morning she went to the bookshops and bought, and bought: two big containers of books arrived with her at Julia's house – it was still that, for Sylvia. She was admitted by Frances, who, as Colin had done, took her into the kitchen, embraced her like a long-lost daughter, and put her in the old place, next to her.

'Don't tell me I need feeding,' said Sylvia. 'Don't.'

Frances set on the table a basket full of cut-up bread, and Sylvia looked at it and thought how much Father McGuire would relish that sight: she would take a loaf of good bread back for him. A plate full of curls of sparkling butter: well, she couldn't take that. Sylvia looked at the food and thought of Kwadere, and Frances moved about, laying the table. She was a large handsome woman, her yellow hair – dyed – in a cut that had cost the earth. She was well-dressed: Julia would at last have approved.

Four places . . . who? In came a tall child who stopped to examine Sylvia, the stranger. 'This is William,' said Frances, 'and Sylvia used to live here. This is Sylvia, Meriel's friend Phyllida's daughter.'

'Well, hi,' he said, as formally as a how-do-you-do, and sat down, a beautiful boy, knitting his fair brows together and frowning as he tried to sort it all out. Then he gave it up with, 'Frances, I have to be at swimming at two. Please may I eat quickly?'

'And I have to be at rehearsal. I'll serve you first.'

What was being served was far from the abundant home food of the past. All kinds of bought dishes were appearing, and Frances put a pizza into the microwave and then in front of William. He at once began to eat.

'Salad,' commanded Frances.

With a look of heroic endeavour the boy forked two frills of lettuce and a radish on to his plate and ate them like medicine.

'Well done,' said Frances. 'I suppose Colin has told you all our news, Sylvia?'

'I think so.' The two women allowed their eyes to communicate. From which Sylvia gathered that Frances would say more if the child were not present. 'It seems I am going to miss a wedding,' she said.

'I would hardly call it that. A dozen people at the register office.'

'I'd like to be there, all the same.'

'But you can't. You don't like leaving your – hospital?'

That hesitation told Sylvia that Andrew had described the place unkindly, to Frances. 'You can't judge *there* by our standards.'

'I wasn't judging. We are wondering if your skills aren't being wasted. After all, you were in some pretty classy jobs.'

Now Sophie made an entrance. She wore something like an old-fashioned teagown, or peignoir, white with big black flowers, and was a vision, like Ophelia floating on the water, her long black hair streaked dramatically with white, her lovely eyes unchanged. Her pregnancy was the most elegant little lump imaginable.

'Seven months,' said Sylvia. 'How do you do it?'

She was lost in Sophie's embrace. Both wept, and while this was no more than could be expected of Sophie, and it became her, Sylvia said, 'Damn,' and wiped her eyes. Frances was crying too. The boy watched with detached seriousness over bites of pizza. Sophie reclined in the big chair at the foot of the table, her eloquent hands outlining her belly.

'Sylvia,' she said tragically, 'I am forty-three.'

'I know. Cheer up. Have you had the tests?'

'Yes.'

'Well, then.'

'But Colin . . .' and she began weeping again. 'Will he ever forgive me?'

'Oh, nonsense,' said Frances, impatient, having had too much of this particular tune.

'From what he was saying last night,' said Sylvia, 'I don't think forgiving or not forgiving is the point.'

'Oh, Sylvia, you are so kind. Everyone is so kind. And to come here to this house, *this* house, I've always felt it is my real home, and Frances . . . you were as much my mother as my mother and now she's gone, poor soul.'

'Not so much a mother as a nurse,' said Frances.

'Yes, did you know, she is playing the Nurse – oh, wonderfully,' said Sophie. 'But now we're going to have a real nurse in this house because I shall go on acting and of course Frances is acting too.'

'No, I don't think I am prepared to take on a small baby,' said Frances.

'Of course not,' said Sophie, but it was clear that she had in fact been hoping for just that.

'And besides,' said Frances, 'you forget, I and Rupert and the children will be moving out.'

'Oh, *no*,' mourned Sophie, 'please don't. Please. There's plenty of room for everyone.'

The boy was sitting straight up, eyes panicky, staring at them. 'Why, where are we going? Why, Frances?'

'Well, this is Colin's and Sophie's house now and they're going to have a baby.'

'But there's so much room,' said William loudly, as if shouting them all down. 'I don't see why.'

'Hush,' said Sophie ineffectually, and looked to Frances, who must soothe the boy's desperation.

'I like this house,' William insisted. 'I don't want to go away.

Why should we?' He began to cry, the difficult painful gulping tears of a child who cries a good deal, but alone, hoping no one will hear. He got up and rushed out. No one said anything.

Then, Sophie said, 'But, Frances, Colin hasn't said you must go, has he?'

'No, he hasn't.'

'I don't want you to go either.'

'We always forget Andrew. He is going to have ideas about what to do with this house.'

'Why should he? He's having a lovely time running the world. He wouldn't want us to be unhappy.'

Sylvia said, 'You shouldn't overdo things, Sophie. Surely you aren't going to go on acting till the end?' Now that Sophie was not aflame with the excitements of welcome, it could be seen that she was strained, drawn, and evidently overtired.

Sophie twisted her hands about over her lump. 'Well . . . I had thought . . . but perhaps . . .'

'Have some sense,' Frances said. 'Bad enough that . . .'

'That I'm so *old*, oh, yes, I know.'

'Well,' said Sylvia, 'I wanted a word with Colin.'

'He's working,' said Sophie. 'No one dares to interrupt when he's working.'

'That's too bad, because I must.'

As Sophie went past Frances on her way up she quickly hugged her and said, 'Don't go, Frances. Please don't. I am sure no one wants you to go.'

Frances followed her, and found William crouching on his bed, like an animal wary for danger, or like someone in pain. He was saying aloud, 'I don't want to go. I don't want to.'

She put her arms around him and said, 'Stop. It may never happen. It probably won't.'

'Promise, then.'

'How can I? You should never promise something if you aren't sure.'

'But you are nearly sure, you are, aren't you?'

'Yes, I suppose so. Yes.'

She waited, while he readied himself to go swimming, and then said, 'I don't think Margaret is all that keen on staying here, is she?'

'No. She wants to live with her mother. But I don't. Meriel hates me because I am a man. I want to stay with you and my father.'

Frances went to get ready for rehearsal, thinking that it was a long time since she had even remembered that she had intended to get her own place and live in it, self-sufficient and self-supporting. The money she had saved to pay for it had alarmingly dwindled. A slice had gone to pay for Meriel's therapy. She was also paying Meriel's monthly allowance. Rupert had sold the flat in Marylebone, and two-thirds of that had gone to Meriel. Rupert and Frances were jointly paying a fair rent for living here, in this house – the two of them and two children. He was paying the children's school fees. Frances earned money from various books, pamphlets, reprints, but when she did her little sums, a good part of it had gone to Meriel. She was in that familiar position for our times: she was supporting a first wife.

She went into the marital bedroom, with its two beds, the one where she had slept alone for so long, and the big bed which was now the emotional centre of her life. She sat on her spinster bed and looked over at Rupert's pyjamas, lying folded on his pillow. They were of a greeny-blue poplin, serious pyjamas indeed, but, when you touched them, silky and tender. Rupert, when you met him, must give the impression of solidity, strength, but then you saw the delicacy in his face, the sensitive hands . . . Frances sat on Rupert's side of the bed and caressed the pyjamas.

Did Frances regret having said yes to Rupert, his children, the situation – nor situation? Never, not for one moment. She felt as if she had stumbled so late in her life, as in a fairy tale, into a glade full of sunshine, and she even dreamed scenes like these, and knew it was Rupert she was dreaming of. Both of them had been married, had thought that these thoroughly unpleasant partners could be said to sum up marriage, but had found a happiness they had not expected or even believed in. Both had busy outward lives, he at his newspaper, she at the theatre, both knew what seemed to be hundreds of people, but all that was the outer life, and what was at the heart of it was this great bed, where everything was understood and nothing needed to be said. Frances would wake from a dream and tell herself, and then Rupert, that she had been dreaming of happiness. Let them mock who would, and they certainly did, but there was such a thing as happiness and here it was, here they were, both of them, contented, like cats in the sun. But these two middle-aged people – courtesy would call them that – cuddled to themselves a secret they knew would shrivel if exposed. And they were not the only ones: ideology has pronounced their condition impossible and so, people keep quiet.

To come back to a house that loved you, took you in, kept you safe, a house that put its arms around you, that you pulled over your head like a blanket, and burrowed into like a lost little animal – but now it is not your home, it is other people's . . . Sylvia went up those stairs, her feet knowing every step, every turn: here she had crouched, listening to the noise and laughter from the kitchen, thinking that she would never ever be accepted by it; and here Andrew had found her and carried her up to bed, tucked her in, given her chocolate from his pocket. Here had been her room but she must walk past it. Here had been Andrew's room, and Colin's. And now she was going up the last flight to Julia's and did not know on the landing which door to knock at, but guessed right, for Colin's voice said Come in, and she was in Julia's old sitting-room and Colin was at – no, that was not Julia's little desk, but a big one, that filled a wall. If all the things that had been Julia's had been removed, and now it was all new furniture, it would have been easy, but here was Julia's chair and her little footstool, and it was as if the room both welcomed and repelled her. Colin looked thoroughly dissipated. He was bloated, a big man who would soon be all puffy fat if he . . . He said, 'Sylvia, why did you just run away like that? When they told me this morning . . .'

'Never mind. It doesn't matter. I really want to talk to you about something.'

'And I am sorry. Forget what I said last night. You got me at a bad moment. If I was criticising Sophie – forget it. I love Sophie. I always did. Do you remember – we were always a – team?'

Sylvia sat in Julia's chair, knowing that her heart was going to ache if she didn't watch out, for Julia, and she didn't want that, didn't want to waste time on . . . Colin was opposite, his back to the big desk, in a swivel chair. He sprawled there, legs extended, and then he grinned, the savage self-criticism of his drunkenness.

'And there's another thing. What right have we to expect any sort of normality? With the history of our family? All war and disruption and the comrades? What nonsense!' He laughed, and the smell of alcohol filled the room.

'You'll have to stop drinking, if you're going to have a baby. You might drop it or . . .'

'What? I might what, little Sylvia?'

She sighed and said gently, humbly presenting this to him like showing him a picture in a book: 'Joshua, that's the man I told you about – a black man of course . . . he dropped his two-year-old into the fire. He was so badly burned that . . . of course, if it happened in this country there would have been proper treatment for him.'

'Well, Sylvia, I don't think I'm going to drop our child into a fire. I am perfectly aware that I am . . . that I could be more satisfactory.' This was so comical that she laughed and Colin did laugh but not at once. 'I'm a mess. But what do you expect of Comrade Johnny's progeny? But do you know something? As long as I was just a bear in a cave, sallying forth to a pub, or an affair here and a *relationship* – now that's a word that evades any real issue – well, I did not strike myself as a mess. But as soon as my Sophie moved in and it was happy families I knew I am just a bear that was never house-trained. I don't know why she puts up with me.'

'Colin, I would really like to talk to you about something.'

'I tell her that if she perseveres she may make a husband out of me yet.'

'Please, Colin.'

'What do you want me to do?'

'I want you to go out to Zimlia and see things for yourself and write the truth.'

A silence. His smile was gently satirical. 'How that does take me back! Sylvia, do you remember when the comrades were always going out to the Soviet Union or associated communist paradises to see for themselves and coming back to tell the truth? In fact, we are entitled to conclude, with all the hindsights we lucky inheritors have been endowed with, that if there is one way of not finding the truth it is going to somewhere to see for yourself.'

'So, you don't want to do it?'

'No, I don't. I don't know anything about Africa.'

'I could tell you. Don't you see? What's going on, it's got nothing to do with what the newspapers are saying.'

'Wait a minute.' He swivelled himself about, pulled out a drawer, found a newspaper cutting and said, 'Did you see this?' He held it out.

Byline: Johnny Lennox.

'Yes, I did. Frances sent it. It's such nonsense, the Comrade Leader is not as the newspapers describe him.'

'Surprise, surprise.'

'When I saw Johnny's name I couldn't believe it. He's turned into an expert on Africa, then?'

'Why not? All their idols have turned out to have feet of clay, but cheer up! There's an unlimited supply of great leaders in

Africa, thugs and bullies and thieves, so all the poor souls that have to love a leader can love the black ones.'

'And when there's a massacre or a tribal war or a few missing millions, all they have to do is to murmur, It's a different culture,' said Sylvia succumbing to the pleasures of spite.

'And poor Johnny has to eat after all. This way he is always the guest of some dictator or other.'

'Or at a conference discussing the nature of Freedom.'

'Or at a symposium on Poverty.'

'Or a seminar called by the World Bank.'

'Actually, that's part of the trouble – the old Reds can't spout about Freedom and Democracy, and that's what's on our agendas. Johnny is not as much in demand as he was. Oh, Sylvia, I do miss you. Why do you live so far away? Why can't we all live together for ever in this house and forget what goes on outside?' He was animated, had lost his hung-over pallor, he was laughing.

'If I give you all the facts, the material, you could write some articles.'

'Why don't you ask Rupert? He's a serious journalist.' He added, 'He's one of the best. He's good.'

'But when they are so well-known then they don't like taking risks. They're all saying Zimlia's wonderful. He'd be out on a limb by himself.'

'They are supposed to like being the first.'

'Then why isn't he one of them? I could ask Father McGuire to draft an article and you could use it as a basis.'

'Ah, yes, Father McGuire. Andrew said he had never understood the real meaning of a fatted capon before.' Sylvia was annoyed. 'I am sorry.'

'He's a good man.'

'And you are a good woman. We are not worthy of you – sorry, sorry, but little Sylvia, can't you see I'm envious of you? It's that clear-eyed single-hearted candour of yours – where did you get it? – oh, yes, of course, you are a Catholic.' He got up, lifted Sylvia on to his knee, and put his face into her neck. 'I swear you smell of sunlight. I was thinking last night when you were being so nice to me, She smells of sunlight.'

She was uncomfortable. So was he. It was incongruous, this position, for them both. She slid back to her chair.

'And you will try not to drink so much?'

'Yes.'

'You promise?'

'Yes, Sylvia, yes, Sonia, I promise.'

'I'll send you material.'

'I'll do my best.'

Sylvia knocked on the door to the basement flat, heard a sharp 'Who's that?', put her head around the door, and from the foot of the stairs a lean woman in smart tan trousers, tan shirt, with a copper-coloured Eton crop, stared up at her. A woman like a knife.

'I used to live in this house,' said Sylvia. 'And I hear you are going to live with my mother?'

Meriel did not abate her hostile inspection. Then she turned her back to Sylvia, lit a cigarette, and said into a cloud of smoke, 'That's the plan at the moment, yes.'

'I'm Sylvia.'

'I supposed you might be.'

The rooms Sylvia was looking into were as she remembered, more like a student's pad, but now very tidy. It seemed that Meriel was packing. She turned to say, 'They want this space. Your mother has kindly offered me a place to lay my head while I'm looking for something.'

'And you will be working with her?'

'When I have finished my training I shall work on my own account.'

'I see.'

'And when I get my own place I shall have the children with me.'

'Oh, well, I expect it will all work out. I'm sorry I disturbed you. I wanted just to – look, for old times' sake.'

'Don't slam the door. This is a very noisy house. The children do as they like.'

Sylvia took a cab to her mother's. Nothing much had changed there. Incense, mystical signs on cushions and curtains, and her mother, large and angry but all smiles of welcome.

'How nice of you to take the trouble to see me.'

'I'm off back to Zimlia tonight.'

Phyllida slowly and thoroughly examined her daughter. 'Well, Tilly, you look thoroughly dried out. Why don't you use skin creams?'

'I will. You're right. Mother, I met Meriel just now.'

'Did you?'

'And what happened to Mary Constable?'

'We had words.'

This phrase brought back to Sylvia a rush of memories, she and her mother, in this boarding-house or that furnished room, always on the move, usually because of unpaid rent; landladies who were best friends but became enemies, and the phrase, 'There were words.' So many words, so often. And then Phyllida married Johnny.

'I'm sorry.'

'Don't be. Plenty of fish. At least Meriel has had children. She knows what it is to have her children stolen from her.'

'Well, I'll be off, I just popped in.'

'I didn't expect you to sit down and have a cup of tea.'

'I'll have a cup of tea.'

'Those brats of Meriel's. Now, they're a handful.'

'Then perhaps she's well rid of them?'

343

'They're not coming here, so she needn't think it.'

'If we're going to have tea, let's have it. It's nearly time to leave for the airport.'

'Then you'd better go, hadn't you?'

Sylvia was again in the Arrivals of Senga airport, as crowded as it had been when she was last here, and with the same two kinds of people divided by colour, but much more by status. But there had been a change. Four – no, five, years before, this had been a vigorously confident crowd, yes, but so soon after that war faces and the set of bodies still showed a practised apprehension, as if the news of Peace had not really been taken in by the whole person. Nerves were still set for bad news. But now this crowd was exuberant, triumphant with successful shopping in London, which was overloading the small and creaking carousel to the point where great suitcases, refrigerators, luggage, furniture toppled off to be hustled away by their laughing owners. Never has there been a more openly self-congratulatory population of travellers than this one; on the plane among the whites the words *the new nomenklatura* had circulated with the relish of gossip.

And, again, here was the same division in dress, the new black elite in their three-piece suits, wiping copious sweat from their beaming faces, and the casual be-jeaned and T-shirted whites off to a hundred different humble stations in the bush, or in the town. Soon, both these so very different categories of being were staring at one focus: a young black woman of perhaps eighteen, very pretty, wearing the advanced clothes of some designer or other, high heels like skewers and the petulant frown of the spoiled young. She had commandeered two of the porters. Off the carousel were being lifted one, two, three, four – was that all? – no, seven, eight, Vuitton suitcases. 'Boy, bring that here,' she told them, in the high peremptory voice she had learned from the white madams of former times – none would dare to use it now.

'Boy – be quick.' She advanced to the front of the queue. 'Boy, show my cases to the officer.' A large black man in the queue said something to her, avuncular, proprietary, to establish his acquaintance with this dazzler to the crowd, while she tossed her head and gave him a smile half-pleased, and half Who are *you* to tell me what to do? All the blacks were proudly watching this accomplishment of their Independence, while the lesser mortals' white faces did not comment, though glances were certainly being exchanged. They would discuss the incident later when safely in their homes. At Customs she said, 'I am So and So's daughter' – a senior Minister – and to the porters, 'Boy . . . Boy – follow me.' And she went through Customs and then past Immigration as if it did not exist.

Sylvia had four large cases and a little hold-all for her clothes, and while watching whole households of goods being chalked okay by the Customs officials, she knew she could not expect the same. This time she had not been lucky in whom she had sitting beside her on the plane. She was looking along the faces of the Customs officials for the young, eager, friendly face of last time, but he was not on duty, or had evolved into one of these correct officials. When she got to the head of the line, a frowning man confronted her.

'And what is all this you have here?'

'These are two sewing machines.'

'And what do you want sewing machines for? Are they for your business?'

'No, they are presents for the women at the Mission at Kwadere.'

'Presents. And what will they be paying you for them?'

'Nothing,' said Sylvia, smiling at him: she knew that the sewing machines had touched this man, perhaps he had watched his mother or sister working on one. But duty won.

'They will have to go to the depot. And you will be informed what you must pay on them.' The two boxes were lifted off to one side: Sylvia knew she was unlikely to see them again. They would be 'mislaid'.

'And now what is all this?' He knocked on the sides of the two cases as if they were doors.

'Books. For the Mission.'

At once on to the man's face appeared a look she knew too well: hunger. He took a lever, prised up the top of one case – books. He picked one up, turning pages, taking his time, and sighed. He let the books fall back, used the lever to bang the top down, and stood undecided.

'Please – they are much needed, these books.'

It was touch and go. 'Okay,' he said. She had traded two sewing machines for the books, but she knew which the women at the Mission would choose.

She went through Immigration without difficulty, and there stood Sister Molly waiting, smiling, outlined by that brilliance of light that means rain has recently cleared the air. The rainy season had come. Late, but it was here. But now, the question had to be, was it going to stay: the last three or four years, rains had indeed broken the long dryness, but then had taken themselves off again. The region was officially in a state of drought, but today you'd not know it, with complacent white clouds sailing on the blue, and puddles everywhere. The sunlight dazzled off Sister Molly's cross, shone off her strong brown legs. Healthy, that was the word for her. And healthy was this scene, everything strong and vigorous, newly-washed trees and bushes and a good-natured crowd disappearing into official cars and lowly buses. Sylvia felt herself again. Her visit to London had not been a success, except for her boxes of books. But that experience snapped shut behind her. London seemed unreal to her: this was real.

The back seat of Sister Molly's old car sank under the weight of the big cases. She at once began to talk, with the news that there had been scandals. Ministers had been accused of taking bribes and of stealing. She spoke with the relish that confirms a satisfaction in everything going on as expected. 'And Father McGuire said there was trouble of some kind at the Mission. St Luke's has been accused of theft.'

'That's nonsense.'

'Nonsense can be very powerful.' And Sylvia thought that this nun's – she was that, after all – look at her was too admonitory – a warning? – for the occasion. There was something wrong. It did not do to dismiss anything she said. This was a very accomplished young woman. She ran a scheme that brought teachers from America and from Europe to teach for a couple of years in Zimlia, because of the shortage of black teachers, and this was – so far – welcomed by the black government because it saved on teachers' wages. Some teachers were in schools in remote areas, and Sister Molly was almost permanently on her rounds to see how her charges did. 'Some of them, they come from well-off families and they have no idea of what they are coming to, and then they find themselves at a school like the one at Kwadere and they can take it hard.' Breakdowns, fits of depression, collapses of all kinds were coped with by this competent young woman as a hazard of the work: and she was kind and consoling, and some sheltered young thing from Philadelphia or LA might find herself rocked on the bosom of the deep, 'There now, there now,' in the arms of this Molly who had started life in a poor home in Galway. 'And I hear there is trouble again at the school, the headmaster has absconded with the money, and Father McGuire is working double again. And now that is a curious thing, don't you think so? All these headmasters and naughty thieves they think they are invisible to the rest of us and to the police, and so what is it goes through their poor heads, do you think?' – but she did not want an answer, she wanted to talk, and for Sylvia to listen. Soon she was back on her real centre of gravity, which was the Holy Father and his deficiencies, for apart from being a man, he was 'putting ideas into the heads' of priests working in various parts of the world. To hear this sequence of words, in this context – for it had ever been a main grievance of the whites that missions 'put ideas' into black heads – was an odd exhilaration, the same used as fuel by Colin in his books – the infinite incongruity that life was capable of. (Not long before leaving for London, Sylvia had heard from Edna Pyne that the present delinquency of the blacks was due to having had ideas put into their heads too soon in their evolutionary development.)

'And what ideas may they be?' Sylvia did manage to interpolate, and heard only Molly's old refrain that the Pope was sexist and did not understand the trials of women. Birth control, said Sister Molly, that was the key, and the Pope might have the keys of Heaven, and she did not want to argue with that, but he did not understand this earth. Let him be brought up with a tribe of nine brats and not enough money to put food into their mouths, and he would sing to a different tune. And in a state of mild and agreeable indignation, Sister Molly drove all the way to St Luke's Mission where she left Sylvia with her boxes of books. 'No, I'm not coming in. Otherwise I'll have to visit the nun-house.' And Sylvia heard, as she had been meant to, hen-house.

The priest's house, standing in the dust, the raggedy gum trees, the sun marking the nuns' house and the half dozen roofs of the school on its ridge – so paltry did all this seem, such a shallow incursion on the old landscape – she was back home, yes she felt that – and it could all be blown away by a breath. She stood with the smell of wet earth in her nostrils and a warmth striking up from it on to her legs. Then Rebecca appeared, with the cry of, 'Sylvia. Oh, Sylvia', and the two women embraced. 'Oh, Sylvia I have missed you too much.' But Sylvia was feeling that what she was embracing matched her feelings of evanescence, impermanence. Rebecca's body was like the frailest bundle of light bones, and when Sylvia held her away to look into that face, she saw Rebecca's eyes deep in her head, under the old faded kerchief.

'What's wrong, Rebecca?'

'Okay,' said Rebecca, meaning, I shall tell you. But first she took Sylvia's hand and led her into the house, where she sat her down at the table with herself opposite. 'My Tenderai is sick.' No concealment, while the two pairs of eyes searched each other. Two of Rebecca's children had died, another had been sick for a long time, and now there was Tenderai. The source of the disease was Rebecca's husband, still apparently in good health, if thin and drinking. By all the rules of probability Rebecca should be HIV positive, but without a test, who could know? And if she were, what could be done? She was not likely to be sleeping around, spreading the fatal thing.

Sylvia had been away a week.

'Okay,' said Sylvia, in her turn, using this new, or newish idiom, which now seemed to begin every sentence. She meant that she had absorbed the information and shared Rebecca's fears. She said, 'I'll examine him and see. Perhaps it is just a temporary disease.'

'I hope it is,' said Rebecca, and then, putting behind her family worries, said, 'And Father McGuire is working too-too hard.'

'I heard. And what is this business about theft?'

'It is a foolishness. It is about the cases of equipment at the hospital we went to. They are saying you stole them.'

Now, Sylvia had been thinking, for in London her thoughts had been with the mission, that it was only commonsense to return to the ruinous hospital and take away anything that could be used. But there was something more here, and Rebecca was not coming out with it. She looked away into the air, and her face was tight with embarrassment and the apprehension of trouble.

'Please tell me, Rebecca. What is it?'

Rebecca still did not look at Sylvia, but said that it was all a big foolishness. There was a spell on the cases – she used the English word, and then added, 'The *n'ganga* said bad things would happen to anyone who stole anything from the hospital.' And now she got up, and said it was time to get Father McGuire's lunch, and she hoped Sylvia was hungry, because she had cooked some special rice pudding.

While Rebecca had sat opposite, and in their minds had been Tenderai and the other children, dead and living, between the two women had been an absolute openness and trust. But now

349

Sylvia knew that Rebecca would not tell her more, for on this subject Rebecca knew she would not understand.

Sylvia sat on her bed surrounded by brick walls, and looked at the Leonardo women, whom she felt were welcoming her home. Then she turned to the crucifix behind her bed, with a deliberate intention of affirming certain ideas that had been growing clamorous in her mind. Someone subscribing to the miracles of the Roman Catholic Church should not accuse others of superstition: this was her train of thought, and it was far from a criticism of the religion. On Sundays the congregations that came to take the Eucharist with Father McGuire were told that they drank the blood and ate the flesh of Christ. She had slowly come to understand how deeply the lives of the black people she lived among were embedded in superstition, and what she wanted was to understand it all, not to make what she thought of as 'clever intellectual remarks'. Of the kind Colin and Andrew would make, she told herself. But the fact remained: there was an area where she, Sylvia, could not go, and must not criticise, in Rebecca just as much as any black casual worker, although Rebecca was her good friend.

She would have to go over to the Pynes, if Father McGuire would not help. At lunch she brought the subject up, while Rebecca stood by the sideboard listening, and adding when the priest appealed to her for confirmation, 'Okay. It is true. And now the people who took the things are falling ill and people are saying it is because of what the *n'ganga* said.'

Father McGuire did not look well. He was yellow and the hectic patches on his broad Irish cheekbones flared. He was impatient and cross. This was the second time in five years he was having to teach twice his normal hours. And the school was falling apart and Mr Mandizi only repeated that he had informed Senga of the situation. The priest went back to the school without taking his usual nap, and Sylvia and Rebecca unpacked the books, and made shelves from planks and bricks and soon all of one wall, on either side of the little dressing-table, was covered with books.

Rebecca had wept to hear the sewing machines had been impounded – she had hoped to make a little extra money sewing on hers, but her tears when looking at and touching the books were from joy. She even kissed the books. 'Oh, Sylvia, it was so wonderful you thought of us and brought us the books.'

Sylvia went down to the hospital, where Joshua sat dozing under his tree, as if he had not left it in her absence, and where the little boys clamorously welcomed her, and she attended to her patients, many because of the coughs and colds that come with the sudden changes of temperature at the start of the rains. Then she took the car and went over to the Pynes, who filled a precise place in her life: when she needed information, that is where she went.

The Pynes had bought their farm, after the Second World War, in the Fifties, on that late wave of white immigration. They grew mostly tobacco and had been successful. The house was on a ridge, looking out over to tall tumbling hills that in the dry season were blue with smoke and haze, but now were sharply green – the foliage; and grey – granite boulders. The pillared verandah was wide enough to have parties on, and before Liberation parties had been many, but were few now, with so many of the whites gone. The floor was polished red, and on it were scattered low tables and dogs and some cats. Cedric Pyne sat gulping tea, while he stroked the head of his favourite dog, a ridgeback bitch called Lusaka. Edna Pyne, smart in her slacks and shirt, her skin glistening with sun-creams, sat by the tea tray, her dog, Lusaka's sister Sheba, as close as she could get by her chair. She listened to her husband holding forth about the deficiencies of the black government. Sylvia drank tea and listened too.

If she had had to hear Sister Molly out on the subject of the Pope and his inveterate maleness; had had to listen every day to Father McGuire saying he was an old man and he was no longer up to it, he was going back to Ireland; if she had had to listen to Colin lament his situation with Sophie, now she had to bide her time again before she could introduce her own concerns.

The bones of the situation – the white farmers – were easy

to understand. They were the main targets of the blacks' hate, were heaped with abuse every time the Leader opened his mouth, but they earned the foreign currency which kept the country going, mainly to pay the interest on loans insisted on by . . . in her mind's eye Sylvia saw Andrew, a smiling debonair fellow holding out a large cheque with lines of noughts on it, while accepting with the other hand another cheque with an equal number of noughts. This was the visual shorthand she had devised to explain the machinery of Global Money to Rebecca, who had giggled, sighed and said 'Okay.'

Because of the Leader's socialism, acquired late in life with all the force of a conversion, various policies he believed essential to Marxism had acquired the force of commandments. One was that no worker could be sacked, and that meant that every employer carried a dead weight of workers who, knowing they were safe, drank, did not work, lay about in the sun and stole everything – just like their betters. This was one item on the litany of complaints that Sylvia had heard so often. Another was that they could not buy spare parts for machines which broke down, and it was impossible to buy new machines. Those that were imported went straight to the Ministers and their families. These complaints, the most frequent, were of less importance than the main one, which like so many main, crucial, basic facts, was seldom mentioned simply because it was too obviously important to need saying. Because the white farmers were continually threatened with being thrown out and their farms taken, they had no security, did not know whether to invest or not, lived from one month to the next in doubt. Now Edna Pyne broke in and said she was fed up, she wanted to leave. 'Let them get on with it and they'll know then just what they've lost when we go.'

This farm, bought as virgin acres without so much as a cleared field on it, let alone this big house, was now equipped with every kind of farm building – barns, sheds, paddocks, wells, boreholes and, a recent development, a large dam. All their capital was in it. They had had none when they came.

Cedric said to his wife in a sharp rebuke that Sylvia had heard before, 'I'm not giving up. They're going to have to come and throw me off.'

Now Edna's plaint began. Since Liberation it had been hard to buy even basics, like decent coffee or a tin of fish. 'They' could not even keep a decent supply of mealiemeal coming for the workers, she had to keep a storeroom filled to the roof with meal for the next time when the labour force came up to beg for food. She was sick of being reviled. They – the Pynes – were paying school fees for twelve black children now, but none of those government black bastards ever gave the farmers credit for anything. They were all hot air and incompetence, they were inefficient and only cared about how much they could grab for themselves, she was fed up with . . .

Her husband knew she had to have her say out, just as she knew that he did, whenever a fresh face appeared on that verandah, and he sat in silence, looking out over the tobacco fields – in full green – to where the rainy season's clouds were building for what looked would be an afternoon storm.

'You're mad, Cedric,' said his wife direct to him, an evident continuation of many a private altercation. 'We should cut our losses and go to Australia like the Freemans and the Butlers.'

'We aren't as young as we were,' said Cedric. 'You always forget that.'

But she was going on. 'And the nonsense we have to put up with. The cook's wife is sick because she has had the evil eye put on her. She's got malaria because she doesn't like taking her pills. I tell them, I keep telling them, if you don't take the malaria pills then you'll get sick. But I'll tell you something. That *n'ganga* of theirs has got more to say about what goes on in this district than any government official has.'

Sylvia interposed herself into this gushing stream: 'That's what I want to ask you. I need your advice.'

At once two pairs of blue eyes attended to her: giving advice, that was what they knew they were equipped to do. Sylvia outlined the story. 'And so now I am a thief. And what is this spell that was put on the new hospital?'

Edna allowed herself a weak, angry laugh. 'And there it is again. You see? Just stupidity. When the money ran out for the new hospital . . .'

'Why did it? Sometimes I hear it was the Swedes, then it was the Germans, who was it?'

'Who cares? Swedes, Danes, the Yanks, Uncle Tom Cobbleigh – but the money vanished from the bank account in Senga and they pulled out. The World Bank or Global Money or Caring International or somebody, there are hundreds of these do-gooding idiots, they are trying to find new funding but so far no luck. We don't know what is happening. Meanwhile the cases of equipment are just rotting, so the blacks say.'

'Yes, I've seen them. But why send the equipment before the hospital was even built?'

'Typical,' said Edna Pyne, with the satisfaction of being proved right, yet again. 'Don't ask why, if it's bloody incompetence then don't even ask. The hospital was supposed to be up and running within six months, well I ask you, what rubbish, well what do you expect from the idiots in Senga? So the local Big Boss, Mr Mandizi as he calls himself, went to the *n'ganga* and asked him to put it about that he had put a curse on anyone who stole from the cases or even laid a finger on them.'

Cedric Pyne let out a short barking laugh. 'Pretty good,' he said. 'Come on, Edna, that's pretty clever.'

'If you say so, dear. Well, it worked. But then it seemed you went over and helped yourself. That broke the spell.'

'Half a dozen bedpans. We didn't have even one at our hospital.'

'Half a dozen too many,' said Cedric.

'Why didn't anyone tell me? Six women from our village came with me and Rebecca. They just – helped themselves. They didn't tell me anything.'

'Well, they wouldn't, would they? You're the Mission, you're

God the Father and the Church and Father McGuire is on at them for being superstitious. But with you there, they probably thought God's *muti* was stronger than the medicine man's.'

'Well, it hasn't turned out to be. Because now people are dying and it is because they stole from the cases. So Rebecca says. But it's AIDS.'

'Oh, AIDS.'

'Why do you say it like that? It's a fact.'

'It's the last bloody straw,' said Edna Pyne, 'that's why. They come up from the compound and want *muti*. I tell them there isn't *muti* for AIDS, and they seem to think I've got *muti* but won't give it to them.'

'I know the *n'ganga*,' said Sylvia. 'Sometimes I ask him to help me.'

'Well,' said Cedric, 'that's an innocent walking into the lion's den, if you like.'

'Don't touch it –' said Edna, sounding peevish, at the end of her tether, and intending to sound it.

'When I have cases our medicine doesn't reach – such as I've got – I ask him to come when Rebecca tells me they think they've got the evil eye put on them. I ask him to tell them they haven't been – cursed, or whatever . . . I say to him, I don't want to meddle in his medicine. I just wanted his help. Last time he went to each of the people who were lying there – I thought they were going to die. I don't know what he said, but some of them just got up and walked off – they were cured.'

'And the others?'

'The *n'gangas* know about AIDS – about Slim. They know more about it than the government people do. He said he couldn't cure AIDS. He said he could treat some of the symptoms, like coughs. Don't you see – I'm glad to use his medicine, I have so little. Half the time I don't even have antibiotics. When I went into the medicine hut this afternoon – I've been in London – there was hardly anything there, most of what I had was stolen.' She was sounding shrill, then tearful.

The Pynes glanced at each other, and Edna said, 'It's getting on top of you. It's no good taking things to heart.'

'And who's talking?' said Cedric.

'Fair enough,' said Edna. And to Sylvia. 'I know how it is. You get back from England, and you're on a rush of adrenalin and you just go on, and then – whoomph, you're whacked, and can't move for a couple of days. Now you go and lie down for an hour. I'll ring the Mission and tell them.'

'Wait a minute,' said Sylvia, remembering the most important thing she wanted to ask them. At lunch Sylvia had heard that she – Sylvia – was a South African spy.

Weeping, because it seemed she was unable to stop, she told them this, and Edna laughed and said, 'Think nothing of it. Don't waste tears on that. We are supposed to be spies too. Give a dog a bad name and hang it. You can steal farms off South African spies with a good conscience.'

'Don't be silly, Edna,' said Cedric. 'They don't need that. They can just take them.'

Inside the circle of Edna's strong arm Sylvia was led to a large room at the back of the house, and put on a bed. Edna drew the curtains and left. Over the thin cotton of the curtains cloud movements laid swift shadows, the yellow sunlight of late afternoon came back, then there was sudden darkness, and thunder crashed, and the rain came down on the iron roof in a pandemonium. Sylvia slept. She was woken by a smiling black man with a cup of tea. During the Liberation War the Pynes' trusted cook had shown the guerillas the way into the house, and then had left, to join them. 'He didn't have any alternative but to join them,' Father McGuire had said. 'He's not a bad sort of man. He's working now for the Finlays over at Koodoo Creek. No, of course they don't know his history, what good would that do?' The priest's comments on passing events were as detached as a historian's, even if his personal grumbles were not. Interesting that: judging by the tones of a voice, Father McGuire's indigestion was of the same scale of importance as Sister Molly's disapproval of the Pope, the Pynes' complaints about the black government – or Sylvia's tears because her medicine hut was empty.

Sundowners on the verandah: the storm had gone, the bushes and flowers sparkled, the birds were singing their hearts out. Paradise. And if she, Sylvia, had made this farm, built this house, worked so hard, would she not have felt as the Pynes did, for a violent sense of injustice was poisoning them. As the drinks were poured, and titbits thrown to Lusaka and Sheba, while their claws scraped and clacked on the cement, as they jumped up, jaws snapping, and while Sylvia listened, the Pynes talked and talked, obsessed and bitter. Once she had said on this verandah – but she had been a neophyte then – 'But if you, I mean the whites, had educated the blacks, then there wouldn't be all this trouble now, would there? They'd be trained and efficient.'

'What do you mean? Of course we educated them.'

'There was a ceiling in the Civil Service,' said Sylvia. 'They couldn't go higher than a pretty low level.'

'Nonsense.'

'Not nonsense,' Cedric had conceded. 'No, we made mistakes.'

'Who is we?' said Edna. 'We weren't here then.'

But if *mistakes* are writ into a landscape, a country, a history, then . . . A hundred years ago the whites had arrived in a country the size of Spain, with a quarter of a million black people in all that enormous territory. You'd think – the *you* here is the Eye of History, from the future – that there had been no need to take anyone's land, with so much. But what that Eye, using a commonsensical view, would be discounting were the pomps and greed of Empire. Besides, if the whites wanted land to have and to hold, with tidy fences and clear-cut boundaries, while the blacks' attitude to land was that it was their mother and could not be individually owned, then there was also the question of cheap labour. When the Pynes had come in the Fifties there were still only a million and a half blacks in all this fair land, and not even 200,000 whites. An empty landscape, according to the eyes

357

of overcrowded Europe. When the Pynes had taken on this farm, the national movements of Zimlia had not been born. Innocent, not to say ignorant, souls, they had come from a small country town in Devon, prepared to work hard and prosper.

Now they sat watching the birds swoop from poinsettias sparkling with raindrops to the birdbath, saw the hills standing close because of the clean-washed air, and one of them said that nothing would induce him to leave, and the other that she was fed up with being called a villain, she had had enough.

Sylvia thanked them for their kindness, from the heart, knowing that they thought her an odd little thing with over-sentimental ideas, and she drove herself back through the darkening bush to the Mission. There she again brought up the subject, at supper, of being a South African spy, and Father McGuire said he had been accused of that himself. It had been when he was protesting to Mr Mandizi that the school was a disgrace to a civilised country, where were the textbooks?

'There is a pretty advanced form of paranoia around, my child,' he said. 'It would be a good thing if you were not to fret your brains about it.'

At five next morning, the sun still a small yellow glow behind the gums, Sylvia came out on to the little verandah and saw in the dawn light a tragic figure, hands squeezed together in front of him, his head bent in pain, or in grief . . . she recognised Aaron.

'What is the matter?'

'Oh, Doctor Sylvia. Oh, Doctor Sylvia . . .' he came up to her in a sideways dawdle, slowed by conflict: tears ran down his usually cheerful face. 'I didn't mean it. Oh I am so-so-so-sorry. Forgive me, Miss Sylvia. The devil got into me. I am sure that is the reason I did it.'

'Aaron, I have no idea what you are talking about.'

'I stole your picture, and that is why Father beat me.'

'Aaron, *please* . . .'

He collapsed on to the brick floor of the verandah, put his head against the thin pillar there and sobbed. It was too early for Rebecca to be in the kitchen. Sylvia sat beside the lad, and did not say anything, merely was there. And there a few minutes later Father McGuire found them, coming out to taste the early morning freshness.

'And now what is this? I told you not to tell Doctor Sylvia.'

'But I am ashamed. And please tell her to forgive me.'

'Where have you been these last three days?'

'I am afraid. I have been hiding in the bush.'

That accounted for his shivering – he was cold because he was hungry: heat was already emanating from the East.

'Go into the kitchen, make yourself some good strong tea with plenty of milk and sugar and cut yourself some bread and jam.'

'Yes, Father. I am very sorry, Father.'

Aaron went off, in no hurry for his restoring meal, though he must have been desperate for it: he was looking over his shoulder as he went at Sylvia.

'Well, Father?'

'He stole your little photograph in its pretty silver frame.'

'But . . .'

'And no, Sylvia, you must not now give it to him. It is back on your table. He said he liked the face of the old woman. He wanted to look at it. I think he has no notion of the value of the silver.'

'Then it's over and done with.'

'But I beat him, and I beat him too hard. There was blood. This old man is not at his wisest and best.' The sun was up, hot and yellow. A cicada started, then another, and a dove began its plaint. 'I shall have extra time to do in purgatory.'

'Have you been taking your vitamin pills?'

'In my defence I must say that these people understand far too well that to spoil the child you must spare the rod. But –

that's no excuse. And I am supposed to be teaching Aaron to be a man of God. And he cannot be allowed to steal.'

'It's vitamin B you need, Father. For your nerves. I brought you some from London.'

Voices in altercation from the kitchen, Rebecca's, Aaron's. The priest called out, 'Rebecca, Aaron must be fed.' The voices stilled. 'It's getting hot, let's go in.' He went in, she followed, and on the table Rebecca was setting down the tray with the early morning tea.

'He has eaten all the bread I baked yesterday.'

'Then, Rebecca, you must bake some more.'

'Yes, Father.' She hesitated. 'I think he meant to put back the picture. He wanted to look at it while Sylvia was away.'

'I know. I beat him too hard.'

'Okay.'

'Yes.'

'Sylvia, who is that old lady?' asked Rebecca. 'She has a nice face.'

'Julia, her name was Julia. She is dead. She was my – I think she probably saved my life when I was very young.'

'Okay.'

A man may be austere by temperament rather than as a result of a decision to punish the flesh. The Leader was hardly one to examine his life with a view to improving his character, feeling that having been accepted by the Jesuits was enough of a guarantee for Heaven; and when it did come to his attention that frugality was supposed to be a good thing, he remembered an early childhood where he had often been short of food and everything else. In some parts of the world the virtues of abstinence come easily. His father worked on a Jesuit mission as a handyman, and was often drunk. His mother was a silent woman, usually sick, and he was the only child. When drunk his father might beat him, and his mother was beaten because of her inability to have more children. He was still not ten years old when he confronted his father, shielding his mother, and the blows meant for her reached his arms and legs, leaving scars.

He was a clever little boy, was noticed by the Fathers, and chosen for higher education. Thin as a stray dog – Father Paul's description of him – short, physically clumsy, he could not play games and was often a butt, and particularly of Father Paul, who disliked him. There were other Fathers, teachers and curers of souls, but it was Father Paul who was the child's experience of the white world, a meagre little man from Liverpool, formed by a bitter childhood, with a tongue that ran contempt for the blacks. The kaffirs were savages, animals, not much better than baboons. Even more than the other teachers, he did not spare the rod. He beat Matthew for obstinacy, for insolence, for the sin of pride, for speaking his own language, and for translating a Shona proverb into English and using it in an essay. 'Don't quarrel with your neighbour if he is stronger than you.'

It was a major responsibility, so Father Paul saw it, to rid his pupils of such backwardness. Matthew loathed everything about Father Paul: his smell revolted him, he sweated freely, did not wash enough, and his black robes had a sour animal odour. Matthew hated the reddish hairs that sprouted from his ears and nostrils and on the backs of his thin bony white hands. The boy's physical dislike was sometimes so strong, waves of pure murder rose up in him, and he contained them, trembling, his eyes burning.

He was a silent boy. At first he read devotional books, and then a pupil from a fellow mission came on a Retreat and Matthew fell under the spell of an ebullient joky personality, but even more, of his opinions. This boy, older than him, was political in the unformed way of that time – long before the national movements – and gave him black authors to read, from America, Richard Wright, Ralph Ellison, James Baldwin, and the pamphlets of a black religious sect that advocated killing all the whites as the devil's progeny. Matthew, still brilliant, still silent, went to college, leaving Father Paul behind, and there he was described long after, when he had become the Leader, as 'a silent observing youth, an ascetic, always reading political books, clever, not able to make friends – a loner'.

When the national movements exploded, Matthew found his place, and quickly, as a leader of his local group. Because he did not find it easy to join in argument and discussion, because he often sat rather out of things, really longing to be like the others, so easy and companionable, he acquired a reputation for cool judgement and political nous, and, of course, for information, since he had read so much. Then he was leader of the Party, after a nasty little jostle for power. The end justifies the means: his favourite saying. The Liberation War began and he was head of one of the rebellious armies. He made promises of every kind, as politicians do, the most productive of later harm being that every black person in the country would be given enough land to farm. Minor absurdities, like saying that to dip cattle was a white man's devilry, and to maintain contour ridges merely kow-towing to white prejudice, were trifles compared to this primal deception – that there would be land for everybody. But then, he did not know he would end up as the Leader of the whole country. When at Liberation his party came first, he secretly found it hard to believe that he could be chosen over more charismatic candidates for power: he did not believe he could be liked. Respected . . . feared . . . oh, yes, he needed that, the stray dog needed it and would for the rest of his life. When he had become converted – by, again, a strong and persuasive personality – to Marxism, he made rhetorical speeches copied from other commu-nist leaders. He admired to the depths of his nature strong and brutal leaders. When he was head of a nation he travelled all the time, as Leaders do, always in America or Ethiopia or Ghana or Burma, seldom choosing the company of whites, for he disliked them. Because he had to put on the front of a statesman he had to conceal what he felt, but he loathed the whites, disliked even being in the same room. Abroad he gravitated by instinct to dictators, some of whom would soon be dislodged from power, like the statues of Lenin that would litter the former Soviet Union. He loved China, admired the Great Leap Forward, the Cultural Revolution, had visited there more than once, taking with him in his entourage Comrade Mo who had instructed him in the necessities of power long before he had attained it.

No sooner had he got power than he became a prisoner of his fear of people. He was meeting no one but a few cronies, and a young woman from his village, with whom he slept; he never went out of his residence without an armed escort; his car was bullet-proofed – the gift of one dictator – and he had a personal guard offered to him by the most hated despot in Asia. Every evening, as the sun went down, the street outside his residence was closed to general traffic, so that the citizens had to drive streets out of their way. Meanwhile, while he was immured as much as any victim in a story who is compelled to build the wall around himself with his own hands, there was no Leader in all of Africa more loved by his people, and from whom more was expected. He could have done anything with the populace, for good or ill: like peasants in former times they looked up to him as a king who would put right everything that was wrong; where he led, they would follow. But he didn't lead. This frightened little man cowered in his self-made prison.

Meanwhile, too, the 'progressive opinion' in the world adored him, and all the Johnny Lennoxes, all the former Stalinists, the liberals who have ever loved a strong man, would say, 'He's pretty sound, you know. A clever man, that's Comrade President Matthew Mungozi.' And people who had been deprived of the soothing rhetoric of the communist world found it again in Zimlia.

Into this fortress buttressed by fear, it might have happened that no one could find a way, but someone did, a woman, for at a reception for the Organisation of African Unity he saw her, this handsome black Gloria, who had all the men clamouring around her while she flirted and bestowed smiles, but really she had her eyes on the man who stood well to one side, following her every movement as a hungry dog watches food being conveyed to mouths not his. She knew who he was, had known, had laid her plans, and expected it would be a walkover – as it was. Close to, she fascinated, every little thing about her enthralled him. She had a certain way of moving her lips, as if she was crushing fruit with them, and her eyes were soft and they laughed – not at him, he was making sure of that, so convinced was he that people did. And she was so at ease where he was not, in the flesh, in that magnificent body of hers, in movement and in pleasure in movement, and in food, and in her own beauty. He felt that he was being liberated simply by standing next to her. She told him he needed a woman like her, and he knew it was true. He was in awe of her too because of her sophistication. She had been in university in America and in England, she had friends everywhere among the famous because of her nature, not because of politics. She talked of politics with a laughing cynicism that shocked him, though he tried to match her. In short, it was inevitable that soon there would be a brilliant wedding, and he lived dissolved in pleasure. Everything was easy where it had been difficult – no, often impossible. She said he was sexually repressed, and cured him of that in so far as his nature permitted. She said he needed more fun, had never known how to live. When he told her of his meagre much-punished childhood she kissed him with great smacking kisses and pulled his head down into her massive breasts and cuddled it.

She laughed at him for everything.

Now, Matthew had at the start of his rule discouraged the comrades, his associates, the leadership, from indulging their greed. He forbade them to enrich themselves. This was the last of the influences from his childhood, and then the Jesuits, who had taught him that poverty was next to Godliness: whatever else the Fathers might have been, they were poor and did not indulge themselves. Now Gloria told him he was mad, and that she should buy this big house, that farm, then wanted another farm, and some hotels that were coming on to the market as the whites left. She told him he must have a Swiss bank account and make sure there was money in it. What money? he wanted to know, and she scorned him for his naivety. But when she talked of money he still saw in his mother's thin hands the pitiful notes and coins put there by his father at the month's end, and at first, when he voted himself a salary, he had been careful it should be no higher than a top civil servant's. All this Gloria changed, brushing it away with her scorn, her laughter, her caresses and her practicality, for she had taken over his life and as the Mother of the Country could easily see to it that money flowed her way. It was she who quietly diverted big sums that flowed in from charities and benefactors into her own accounts. 'Oh, be a fool then,' she cried when he protested. 'It's in my name. It's not your responsibility.'

Battles for someone's soul are seldom as clear and easy to see – and as short – as the one where the devil battled for Comrade Matthew's. And Zimlia, ill-governed before on ill-digested Marxism and tigs and tags of dogma, or remembered sentences from textbooks on economics, now rapidly plunged into corruption. Immediately the currency began its steady, but rapid devaluation. In Senga the fat cats got fatter every day, and out in places like Kwadere money that had descended in a trickle now dried up altogether.

Gloria grew more fascinating, more beautiful, and richer, acquiring another farm, a forest, hotels, restaurants – and wore them like necklaces. And now when Comrade President Matthew went abroad to meet his favourite people, the immensely rich, dissolute and corrupt rulers of the new Africa and new Asia, he did not sit silent when they displayed their wealth and boasted of their avarice. Now he could boast of his and did, and when these men showed how they admired him, giving him gifts and flattery, that empty place in him where there would always be a thin stray dog with its tail between its legs was filled, at least for a time, and Gloria caressed and stroked and petted and nuzzled and licked and sucked and held him against those great breasts and kissed the old scars on his legs. 'Poor Matthew, poor poor little boy.'

The evening before Sylvia had left for London she had stood on the path just where the oleanders and hibiscus and plumbago bushes ended, and looked down at the hospital with more than the forgivable amount of pride. Anyone could use the word 'hospital' now of that cluster of buildings. No money had come through Comrade Mandizi for a long time, but the plunging Zimlia currency meant that small sums in London became large ones here. Ten pounds, the cost of a small carrier bag of groceries in London, here built a grass hut or replenished the stock of painkillers or malaria tablets.

There were two 'wards' down there now, long grass-roofed sheds, the grass close to the ground on one side where rain most often came, and high on the other. In each were a dozen pallets with good blankets and pillows. She was planning another shed, for the existing beds were filling up with the victims of this AIDS, or Slim, that the government had just decided to fully and frankly acknowledge, with appeals to foreign donors for help. Sylvia knew that in the village these were called 'the dying huts', and she planned to build another, for patients who were merely malarial, or in labour – more ordinary pains of the flesh. She had had built a proper little house of brick, which she called the consulting-room, and in it was a high bed, made by lads from the village, of leather thongs stretched on a frame and on that a good mattress. Here she examined people, prescribed, set arms and legs, bound up wounds. In all this she was assisted by Clever and Zebedee. She had paid for the new buildings, and for medicines – paid for everything. She knew that in the village some said, And why should she not pay? She stole it all from us in the first place. It was Joshua who inspired this grumbling. Rebecca defended her, telling everyone that without Sylvia there would be no hospital.

On the evening after Sylvia returned from London, standing exactly in the same spot, she looked down at her hospital and was attacked by that failing of the heart and purpose that so often afflicts people just back from Europe. What she saw down there, the assemblage of poor huts or sheds, was tolerable only if she did not think of London, or Julia's house, with its solidity, its safety, its permanence, each room so full of things that had an exact purpose, serving a need among a multiplicity of needs, so that every day any person in it was supported as if by so many silent servitors with utensils, tools, appliances, gadgets, surfaces to sit on or to put things on – an intricacy of always multiplying things.

In the early mornings Joshua rolled from his place near the log that burned in the middle of the hut, reached for the pot where last night's porridge congealed, dug out from it with the stirring stick some lumps which he ate swiftly, supplying his stomach with its necessity, drank water from a tin jug that stood on the ledge that ran around the hut, then walked a few steps into the bush, urinated, perhaps squatted to shit, took up his stick that was made from bush wood, and walked the mile to the hospital, where he slid his back down the tree, to sit there, all day.

Surely she, a 'religious' as Rebecca called her – 'I told them in the village that you are a religious' – should be admiring this evidence of the poor in wealth, and probably of spirit, though she did not see herself as equipped to judge that. That great heap of a city, covering so many square miles, so rich, so *rich* – and then this group of paltry sheds and huts: Africa, beautiful Africa, which oppressed her spirits with its need, wanting everything, lacking everything, and everywhere people white and black working so hard to – well, what? To put a little plaster on an old weeping wound. And that was what she was doing.

Sylvia felt as if her own real self, her substance, the stuff of belief, was leaking away as she stood there. A sunset, a rainy season's going down of the sun ... from a black cloud low on the red horizon shot heavy thick rays like spikes of gold that radiate around a saint's head. She felt mocked, as if a clever thief were stealing from her and laughing as he did it. What was she doing here? And what good did she really do? And above all where was that innocence of faith that had sustained her when she first came? What did she believe in, really? God, yes, she could say that, if no one pressed for definitions. She had suffered a conversion, as classic in its symptoms as an attack of malaria, to The Faith – which is what Father McGuire called it, and she knew that it had begun because of ascetic Father Jack, with whom she had been in love, though at the time she would have said it was God she loved. Nothing was left of all that brave certainty, and she knew only that she must do her duty here, in this hospital, because Fate had set her down here.

The state of her mind could also be described clinically: it was, in a hundred religious textbooks. The doctors of her Faith would say to her, Disregard it, it is nothing, seasons of dryness come to us all.

But she didn't need these experts on the soul, she did not need Father McGuire, she could diagnose herself. So why then did she need a spiritual mentor at all, if she was not going to tell him, simply because she knew what he would say?

But the real question was, why would it be so easy for Father McGuire to say 'a season of dryness', but for her it was like a sentence of self-excommunication? What she had brought to her conversion was a hungry needful heart, and anger too, though she had not recognised that until recently. She could see herself, as she had been then, in Joshua, where anger burned always, forced out of him in bitter accusations and demands. Who was she ever to criticise Joshua? She had known what it was to be angry to the point she was poisoned by it, though at the time she had thought she was wanting comforting arms, Julia's. And now was she criticising Julia, because her love had not been enough to still that wanting, so that she had gone on to Father Jack? What had stilled the wanting? Work, always, and only, work. And so there she was, on a dry hillside in Africa, feeling that everything she did or might ever do was as effective as pouring water from a (tin) cup into the dust on a hot day.

She thought: There is no person in Europe (if they have not been here and seen) who could comprehend this level of absolute need, a lack of everything, in people who had been promised everything by their rulers, and that was the point where a quiet horror seemed to seep into her. It was like the horror of AIDS, the silent secretive disease that had come from nowhere – monkeys, it was said, perhaps even the monkeys that sometimes played about in the trees here. The thief that comes in the night – that was how she thought of AIDS.

Her heart hurt her . . . she must tell Zebedee and Clever to tell the builders that there must be another good brick building here and she would say yes to the demands from the village for more classes.

Father McGuire heard that there would be more classes and said that she looked tired, she must look after herself.

Here was where she could have mentioned her season of dryness and even joked about it, but instead she said he must remember to take his vitamins and why was he not taking his nap? He listened to her strictures patiently, smiling, just as she listened to him.

Colin had been appealed to by Sylvia to 'do something for Africa' – he saw how he had described this to himself and mocked – himself. 'Africa!' As if he didn't know better. There was that continent down there, imaged in most people's minds by a child holding out a begging bowl. But what Sylvia had said was not Africa, but Zimlia. It was his duty to help with Zimlia. And how often had he joked that Dickens's Mrs Jellaby summed it all up, people fussing over Africa when they might be attending to local needs. Why Africa? Why not Liverpool? The Left in Europe as usual concerning itself with events elsewhere: it had identified itself with the Soviet Union and as a result had done itself in. Now there was Africa, India, China, you name it, but particularly Africa. It was his duty to do something about it. Lies – Sylvia had said. Lies were being told. Well, what's new? What did anyone expect? So Colin muttered and grumbled, a caged bear in rooms that were too small now that the baby was born, a bit drunk, but not much, because he had taken Sylvia's strictures to heart. And what made her think he was equipped to write about Africa? Or that he knew people who would care? He knew no one in that world, newspapers, journals, television; he stuck pretty close to his last, writing his books . . . but wait, he knew just the person, yes, he did.

During that long time when he had frequented pubs and talked to people on park benches, with the little dog, he had acquired a crony, a boon companion. The Seventies: Fred Cope was spending his young life as was *de rigueur* then, demonstrating, assaulting policemen, shouting slogans and generally making himself noticed but when with Colin, who despised all that, could be persuaded at least sometimes to criticise it too. Both young men knew that the other was an aspect of himself kept on a leash. After all, if his judgement had not forbidden, Colin's temperament was one to enjoy noisy confrontation. As for Fred Cope, he discovered responsibility and sobriety in the Eighties. He married. He had a house. Ten years before he had mocked Colin for living in Hampstead: the word was being used as a pejorative by anyone aspiring to be in tune with the times. The Hampstead socialists, the Hampstead novel, Hampstead as a place, these were always good for a sneer, but as soon as they could afford it, these critics bought houses in Hampstead. And so had Fred Cope. He was now the editor of a newspaper, *The Monitor*, and sometimes the two met for a drink.

Has there ever been a generation that has not watched, amazed – though surely by now it has to be expected? – the roustabouts and delinquents and rebels of their youth becoming mouthpieces of considered judgement? Colin telephoned Fred Cope reminding himself that the possessors of considered judgement often found it hard to remember past follies. The two met in a pub, on a Sunday, and Colin plunged in. 'I have a sister – well, a kind of sister, who is working in Zimlia, and she came to see me to say we are all talking nonsense about dear Comrade President Matthew: he's really a bit of a crook.'

'Aren't they all?' murmured Fred Cope, back in his former role of practised sceptic about any kind of authority, but added, 'Surely he is one of the good ones?'

'I'm in a false position,' said Colin. 'This is the voice of Colin, but they are the words of Sylvia. She came to see me. She was in a state. I think it might be worth your while to . . . get a second opinion.'

The editor smiled. 'The trouble is, it doesn't do to judge them by our standards. Their difficulties are immense. And it's a completely different culture.'

'Why doesn't it do? That's surely patronising. And haven't we had our bellies full of not judging others by our standards?'

'Yeeeees,' said the editor. 'I see your point. Well, I'll look into it.'

Having got over what both felt as an awkwardness, they tried to regain the glorious irresponsibility of their earlier times, when Colin's views had been such that he had scarcely dared voice them outside the safety of his home, and Fred's young life now seemed to him like a prolonged festival of licence and anarchy. But it was no good. Fred was expecting a second baby. Colin as usual was thinking only of the novel he was writing. He knew he probably ought to be doing more about Sylvia, but when has being in the middle of a novel not been the best of excuses? Besides, he always felt guilty about her and did not understand why he did. He had forgotten how much he had resented her coming to Julia's house, and how he had railed at his mother. He looked back on that time with pride now: he and Sophie, both, and anyone else who had come and gone then, might talk affectionately about what fun it had all been. But he did know he had always envied his brother's ease with Sylvia. Now he found her religion and what he saw as her neurotic need for self-sacrifice irritating. And this last visit of hers which had ended in his scooping her up to sit on his knee – what embarrassment for both of them! And yet he was fond of her, yes he was, and he had been bound to do something about Africa and he had done it.

But wait, there was Rupert, who heard him out, and said like Fred Cope that they (meaning Africa, all of it?) shouldn't be judged by our standards. 'But what about the truth?' said Colin, knowing, from such long and painful experience that truth was always going to be a poor relation. Now, Rupert was not one of Comrade Johnny's spiritual heirs: if he had been, then he might have found aiding and abetting the truth a bit of a clarion call. Although 'the truth' had not yet emerged more than in drips and drops from the Soviet Union, compared to the great dollops of it that would be available in ten years' time; although that great empire still existed (though no one even vaguely on the left would dream of even thinking of describing it as an empire), enough had come out, was coming out, to be a perpetual goad and reminder that truth ought to be on everyone's agenda. But Rupert had never been anything but a good liberal and now he said, 'Wouldn't you say that telling the truth sometimes does more harm than good?'

'No, I most certainly would not,' said Colin.

Then Colin forgot Sylvia's appeal in the business of moving his work down to the basement flat, Meriel having taken herself off. He had to get this new book done: after all, the money Julia had left was not so much that any of them could slack, take things easy.

Fred Cope summoned up from his newspaper's and other archives, articles about Zimlia and concluded that it was true, Zimlia was always being given the benefit of any doubt. One of the experts whose name was often on articles about Zimlia was Rose Trimble. Well, she had never been critical, so who else? *The Monitor* had a stringer in Senga, and he was invited to write an article, 'Zimlia's first decade'. The article that arrived was more critical than most, while reminding readers that Africa was not to be judged by European standards. Fred Cope sent a copy of this article to Colin. 'I hope this is more on the lines of what you suggest?' And then, a postscript. 'How would you fancy writing a piece about whether Proudhon's "All property is theft" has been responsible for the corruption and collapse of modern society? I would be the first to admit that my thoughts on the subject have been prompted by the fact our house has been burgled three times in two years.'

The article in *The Monitor* was noticed by the editor of a newspaper for whom Rose Trimble had regularly written about Zimlia and Comrade President Matthew, and now she was invited to return to Zimlia and see if what she found there supported the critical article in *The Monitor*.

Rose was by now a name in the newspaper world. She had owed this to her timely praise for Zimlia but that had been only her start. Everything had gone right for her. She could easily have said, 'God be thanked who has matched me with His hour,' – if she had ever read a line of poetry or could use the word God without a smirk. Living in Julia's house she had felt inferior, but once out of it, it was they who seemed inferior. She was matched with the Eighties. Her qualities were what were needed now, in the time when getting on, getting rich, doing down your fellows, were officially applauded. She was ruthless, she was acquisitive, she was by instinct contemptuous of others. While she kept a connection with the comparatively serious newspaper for which she wrote her pieces on Zimlia, she had found her niche in *World Scandals*, where her task was to hunt out weaknesses, or rumours, and then hound some victim day and night until she could triumphantly come up with an exposé. The higher this unfortunate was in public life the better. She camped on people's doorsteps, rummaged in rubbish bins, bribed relatives and friends to reveal or invent damaging facts: she was good at this scavenger's work, and she was feared. She was particularly famous for her 'portraits', bringing journalism to new heights of vindictiveness, and found the work easy because she was genuinely incapable of seeing good in anyone: she knew that the truth about them had to be discreditable, and that it was in the unpleasant that the real essence of a person lies. This kind of jeering, derision, this ridicule, came from her deepest self, and matched a generation of similar people. It was as if something ugly and cruel had been exposed in England, something that had been hidden before, but was now like a beggar pulling aside rags to show ulcers. What had been respected was now scorned; decency, a respect for others, was now ridiculous. The world was being presented to readers through a coarse screen that got rid of anything pleasant or likeable: the tone was set by Rose Trimble and her kind who could never believe that anyone did anything except for self-interest. Rose hated most of all people who read books, or who pretended to – it was only a pretence; loathed the arts, denigrated particularly the theatre – she boasted she had invented the word 'luvvies' for theatre people; and liked violent and cruel films. She met only people like herself, frequenting certain pubs and clubs, and they had no idea that they were a new phenomenon, something that earlier generations would have despised, and dismissed as the gutter press, fit only for the lowest depths of society. But the phrase now seemed to her something vaguely complimentary, a guarantee of bravery in the pursuit of truth. But how could she, or they, know? They scorned history because they had learned none. Only once in her life she had written with approval, admiration, it was about Comrade President Matthew Mungozi, and then, more recently, Comrade Gloria, whom she adored because of her ruthlessness. Only once had her pen not dripped poison. And she read the article by *The Monitor*'s stringer with fury, and, too, with something like the beginnings of fear.

Meeting a journalist who worked on *The Monitor* she heard that it was Colin Lennox who had prompted it. And who the hell was Colin to have an opinion about Africa?

She hated Colin. She had always seen novelists and poets as something like counterfeiters, making something out of nothing and getting away with it. She had been too early on the scene for his first novel, but she had rubbished his second and the Lennoxes, and his third had caused her paroxysms of rage. It was about two people, apparently unlike each other, who had for each other a tender and almost freakish love – that it continued at all seemed to both of them a jest of Fate. While involved with other partners, other adventures, they met like conspirators, to share this feeling they had, that they understood each other as no one else ever could. Reviewers on the whole liked it and said it was poetic and evocative. One said it was 'elliptical', a word that goaded Rose to extra frenzy: she had to look it up in the dictionary. She read the novel, or tried to: but really she could not read anything more difficult than a newspaper article. Of course it was about Sophie, that stuck-up bitch. Well, let them both watch out, that's all. Rose had a file on the Lennoxes, all kinds of bits and pieces, some stolen from them long ago, when she went sniffing about the house for what she could find. She planned to 'get them' one day. She would sit leafing through the file, a rather fat woman now, her face permanently set in a malicious smile which, when she knew she had found the word or phrase that could really hurt, became a jeering laugh.

On the plane to Senga she was next to a bulky man who took up too much room. She asked for a change of seat, but the plane was full. He shifted about in his seat in a way that she decided was aggressive and against her, and he gave her sideways looks full of male dishonesty. His arm was on the rest between them, no room for hers. She put her forearm beside his, to claim her rights, but he did not budge, and to keep her arm there meant she had to concentrate, or it would slide off. He did remove it when he demanded from the attendant who was offering drinks a whisky, threw it to the back of his throat at once, asked for another. Rose admired his authoritative handling of the attendant, whose smiles were false, Rose knew. She asked for a whisky and took it in a swallow, not to be outdone, and sat with the glass in her hand, waiting for a refill.

'Bloody skivers,' said this man, whom Rose knew was her enemy as a woman. 'They think they can get away with murder.'

Rose did not know what he was complaining of, and only said, in an all-purpose formula, 'They're all the same.'

'Right on. Nothing to choose between any of them.'

Now Rose saw two black men, who had been at the back of the plane, being waved forward by an attendant through to Club Class – or perhaps even First.

'Look at that! Throwing their weight around, as usual.'

Ideology demanded that Rose should protest, but she refrained: yes, this was one of the unregenerate whites, but there were nine hours ahead of close proximity.

'If they spent less time showing off and more on running the country then that would be something.'

His arm and shoulder now threatened to oppress Rose.

'Excuse me, but these are small seats.' And she vigorously shoved him back in his seat with her shoulder. He opened half-shut eyes to stare. 'You are taking up too much room.'

'You're not exactly a lightweight yourself,' – but he withdrew his arm.

Here supper was served, but he waved it away – 'I'm spoiled for good grub on my farm.'

She accepted the little tray, and began eating. She was sitting next to a white farmer. No wonder she loathed him. Again she wondered if she should insist on changing her seat. No, she would make use of this opportunity and see if she could get an article out of it. He was openly watching her eat. She knew she ate too much and decided to reject the fancy pudding.

'Here, I'll have that if you don't want it,' he said reaching out for the little glass of cream goo. And he had it swallowed in a gulp. 'Not up to much,' he said. A boor, as well. 'I'm used to good grub. My wife's a zinger. And my cook boy's another.'

Cook*boy*.

'So you're well served,' she said, using the political jargon of the moment.

'Pardon?' He knew she was criticising him but not what for. She decided not to bother. 'And what do you do with yourself when you're at home? And by the way, where is home, are you going back to it or leaving it?'

'I'm a journalist.'

'Oh, Christ, that's all I needed. So I suppose you are planning another little article about the joys of black government?'

Her professionalism switched in and she said, 'All right then, you talk.'

And he did. He talked. All around them went on the bustle of the meal service and drinks and duty free, and then the lights were switched off and still he talked. His name was Barry Angleton. He had farmed in Zimlia all his life and his father before him. They had just as much right as . . . and so on. Rose was not listening to his words, because by now she had understood she fancied him, though she most certainly disliked him, and that hot grumbling voice made her feel as if she were being dissolved in warm treacle.

Rose's relations with men had been geared to misfortune, because of the times. She was, of course, a strict feminist. She had married in the late Seventies, a comrade met while demonstrating outside the American Embassy. He agreed to everything she said about feminism, men, the lot of women: he matched her, smiling, with formulations as progressive as hers, but she knew this was merely surface compliance, and that he did not really understand women or his fatal inheritance. She criticised him for everything and he went along with her, agreeing that thousands of years of delinquency could not be put right in a day. 'I daresay you've got a point there, Rosie,' he'd say, equably, with a little air of judicious assessment, as she ended a harangue that took in everything from bride-price to female circumcision. And he smiled. He always smiled. His fair, plump eager-to-please face infuriated her. She loathed him while she told herself that he was essentially good material. She was confused because, since she disliked almost everything, disliking her husband was not ground enough for self-examination, though she did sometimes wonder if her habit of keeping up irritated admonitions when they were in bed might possibly account for his becoming impotent. But the more he agreed with her, the more he smiled and nodded and took the words out of her mouth, the more she despised him. And when she demanded a divorce, he said, 'Fair enough. You're too good for me, Rosie. I've always said so.'

This man Barry – now that would be a different matter.

On the steps outside the airport building she saw him give money to a porter in a way that made her seethe, so commanding and lordly was it. Now, observing her with her big suitcase, looking about her for the car she had ordered, he strode over and said, 'I'll drop you in town.' He heaved his case to stand with hers, and went off to the car park. In a moment a big Buick stood before her, the front door open. She got in. A black man had materialised and put her cases and his into the car. Barry dispensed more money.

'I ordered a car.'

'Too bad. He'll find someone else.'

On the plane he had ended a perforation with, 'Why don't you come to the farm and see for yourself?' and she had refused and now she was sorry she had. At this moment he said, 'Come out to the farm and have breakfast.'

Rose was familiar with the approaches to the city of Senga, and thought it a tedious little place and full of self-importance. In fact what she really thought about Zimlia was the opposite of what she wrote about it. Only Comrade President Matthew had justified it, and now . . .

She hesitated, and said, 'Why not?'

'Why not she says, and expects an answer.'

They did not drive through the town but past it and were in the bush in a moment. Not everybody loves Africa, and, having left it, longs only to go back to an eternally smiling and beckoning promise. Rose knew that such people existed: how could she not, when the lovers of the continent are so vociferous, always talking as if their love were proof of an inner virtue? It was too big, for a start. There was a disproportion between the town – which called itself a city – and cultivation, and the wildness. Too much bloody bush and disorderly hills, and always the threat of an untoward dislocation of order. Rose had scarcely been out of the towns except for brief walks in a park. She liked pavements and pubs and town halls with people making speeches in them, and restaurants. Now she told herself it was a good thing that she was actually experiencing a white farm and a white farmer, though she could not of course write down his complaints, which were nearly all about the blacks, and that was simply not on. She could say, truthfully, that she was broadening her mind.

When they stopped outside a big raw brick-house in a clump of gum trees that she thought ugly, he remarked that she must go around to the front and up the steps and in, while he went to the kitchen to order breakfast. It was still only half past seven, a time when normally she would expect to sleep another hour. The sun stood high, it was hot, the colours were too bright, all scarlets and purples and strong greens and a pinkish dust lay about every-where. Her shoes almost disappeared into it.

As he went off she had heard, 'My wife's away this week. I've got to organise the bloody kitchen myself.' This had not sounded like an invitation to get into bed and skip the preliminaries. As she reached the top of the steps, and was on a verandah open on three sides that at first she thought was a still unfinished room, he appeared briefly to say, 'There's a bloody crisis with the barns. Go in and the boy'll give you your breakfast. I'll be with you shortly.'

She did not eat breakfast. She did not want any now. But she went into a big room which made her think it could do with some softening up, nice cushions perhaps? – and through it to a room where a large table stood, with an old black man, smiling.

'Sit down, please,' said this servitor and she sat down and saw all around her plates of eggs, bacon, tomatoes, sausages.

'Do you have any coffee?' she said to this servant, it being the first time in her life she had addressed one – a black one, that is.

'Oh yes, please, coffee. I have coffee for the missus,' said the old man eagerly and poured coffee which she was agreeably surprised to see coming strong from the silver spout.

She served herself an egg, and a curl of bacon, and then in strode the master. He flung down some bit of metal on to a chair, pulled out a chair with a scrape and sat.

'Is that all?' said Barry, despising her plateful and piling his. 'Go on, force yourself.'

She took another egg and asked, knowing she did not sound as casual as she had intended, 'And where is your wife, did you say?'

'Gadding. Woman gad, didn't you know?'

She smiled politely: she had understood some hours ago that feminist revolution had not reached everywhere in the world.

He piled on eggs and bacon, he drank cup after cup of coffee, then said he had to go around the farm to see what the kaffs had got up to while he was away. She should come too, and see for herself. At first she said no, but then yes, at his frowning stare. 'Always hard to get,' was his comment, but apparently without anything behind it. She would have liked it if he had said, Go into that room, you'll find a bed, get into it and I'll be along. Instead she spent some hours bumping in an old lorry from one point on the farm to another, where a group of blacks, or some mechanic or overalled person waited for him, and where he gave orders, argued, disagreed, gave in with, 'Yeah, okay, you may be right, we'll try it your way,' or 'For Christ's sake look what you've done, I told you, I told you, didn't I? Now do it again and get it right this time.' She had no idea what she was seeing, what everyone was doing, and while smelly cows did appear, which she knew was to be expected on a farm, she did not understand anything at all and her head ached. Back at the house tea appeared when he clapped his hands. He was sweaty, his face was red and wet, he had grease on his sleeve: she was finding him irresistible, but he said he would bloody well have to go and do some paper-work, this government was killing them with paper, and could she look after herself until lunchtime. She sat on the verandah that was closed in around her by glare, on some reassuringly recognisable cretonne, and looked at magazines, from South Africa. Presumably his wife's world: and hers, too.

An hour passed. Lunch. Meat, a lot of it. Rose did know that meat was politically incorrect, but she adored it and ate a lot.

Then she was sleepy. He was giving her looks that she thought might be interpreted as a come on but it seemed not, for he said, 'I'm for a kip. Your room's through there.'

With this he strode off in one direction, and she found her case standing on a stone floor beside a bed on which she fell and slept until she heard a loud clap of hands and the shout of 'Tea'. She tumbled off the bed, and found Barry on the verandah, his long brown legs stretched out in front of him for what seemed like yards, in front of a tea tray.

'I could sleep for a week,' she said.

'Oh, go on, you didn't do too badly last night, snoring away on my shoulder.'

'Oh, I didn't . . .'

'Yes, you did. Go on, pour. You be mother.'

Outside spread the African afternoon, all yellow glare and the songs of birds. There was dust on her hands, and on the floor of the verandah.

'Bloody drought. It hasn't rained properly on this farm for three years. The cattle aren't going to last out if it doesn't rain soon.'

'Why this farm?'

'Rain shadow. Didn't know that when I bought it.'

'Oh.'

'Well, I hope you're beginning to get the hang of it. Well, at least if you're going to go back and write that we are a lot of Simon Legrees you'll have taken the trouble to see for yourself.'

She did not know who Simon Legree was, but supposed that, logically, he must be a bit of a white racist. 'I'm doing my best.'

'And no one can do better than that.'

He was fidgeting again, and up he jumped. 'I'm going to have a look at the calves. Want to come?'

She knew she should say yes, but said she would stay and sit.

'Pity my better half isn't here. You'd have someone to gossip with.'

Off he went, and returned as the dark came down. Supper. Then there was the radio news where he swore at the black announcer for mispronouncing a word, and then said, 'Sorry, I've got to get my head down. I'm all in.' And off he went to bed.

And that was how a stay of what turned out to be five days went on. Rose lay awake in her bed and hoped that the sounds she heard were his feet moving stealthily towards her, but no such luck. And she did go around the farm with him, and did try to take in what she could. During the course of conversations which always seemed to be too brief and curtailed by some urgency or other, all of them dramatic in a way that seemed – surely? – excessive – a broken-down tractor, a bush fire, a gored cow – she had learned that her old pal Franklin was 'one of the worst of that gang of thieves', and that her idol Comrade Matthew was as corrupt as they come, and had as much idea of running a country as he, Barry Angleton, had of running the Bank of England. She dropped the name Sylvia Lennox, but while he had heard of her, all he knew was that she was with the missionaries in Kwadere. He added that once, when he was a kid, no one had a good word for the missionaries, who were educating the kaffs above their station, but now people were beginning to think, and he agreed with them, mind you, that it was a pity they hadn't been educated all the way, because a few properly educated kaffs were what the country needed. Well, you live and learn.

His wife did not return while Rose was there, though she telephoned with a message for her husband.

'Good thing you're there,' said this complacent wife, 'give him something to think about beside himself and the farm. Well, men are all the same.'

This remark, in the time-honoured words of the feminist complaint, but so far from the sophistications of Rose's women's group, allowed her to reply that men were the same the whole world over.

'Anyway, tell my old man that I'm going over to Betty's this afternoon and I'm bringing back one of her puppies.' She added: 'And now you just be fair to us for once and write something nice.'

Barry received this news with, 'Well, she'd better not think that dog is going to sleep on our bed the way the last one did.'

The next stop on Rose's itinerary, which had been planned to be the first, had not Fate and Barry Angleton intervened, was an old friend of Comrade Johnny's, Bill Case, who had been a South African communist, had been in jail, had fled to take refuge in Zimlia, and to continue his career in law, speaking for the underdog, the poor, the maltreated who were turning out to be more or less the same under a black government as under a white one. Bill Case was famous, and a hero. Rose was looking forward to hearing from him at last, 'the truth' about Zimlia.

As for Barry, for whom she would have parted her legs any time, the most she got out of him in that way was his remark when he dropped her in town that if he wasn't a married man he would ask her out to lunch. But she recognised it as a gallantry as routine as his, 'So long. Be seeing you.'

Bill Case . . . about the South African communists under apartheid it has to be said first that few people have ever been as brave, few have fought oppression more wholeheartedly – wait, though: at the very same time the dissidents in the Soviet Union were confronting the communist tyranny with equal dedication. Rose had dealt with the problem of how the Soviet Union was turning out by not thinking about it: it wasn't her responsibility, was it? And she had not been in Bill Case's house an hour before she learned this was his attitude too. For years he had claimed that the Soviet Union was a new civilisation which had for ever abolished the old inequalities, race prejudice for the present purpose being the most relevant. And now even in the provinces, which is where Senga was situated, capital city or not, it was being admitted that the Soviet Union was not what it had been cracked up to be. Not admitted of course by the black government, committed to the glories of communism. But Bill was not talking about that great failed dream, but a local one: Rose was hearing from him what she had been listening to for days from Barry Angleton. At first she thought Bill was amusing himself and her by parodying what he must know she had been hearing, but no, his complaints were as real and as detailed and angry as the farmer's. The white farmers were badly treated, they were the scapegoat for every government failure, and yet they had to provide the foreign currency, they were being taxed unfairly, what a pity this country had allowed itself to become the little arselicker and lackey of the World Bank and the IMF and Global Money!

During those days Rose finally understood something painful: she had backed the wrong horse with Comrade Matthew. She was going to have to climb down, retrack, do something to recover her reputation. It was too soon for her to write an article describing the Comrade Leader as he deserved: after all her last eulogy had been only three months ago. No, she would sidetrack, find a little diversion, use another target.

From Bill Case's house she moved to Frank Diddy's, the amiable editor of *The Zimlia Post*, a friend of Bill's. The easy hospitality of Africa appealed to her: it was winter in London, and she was living free. *The Post*, she knew, was despised by anyone of intelligence – well, most of the country citizens. Its editorials all went something like this: 'Our great country has successfully overcome another minor difficulty. The power station failed last week, due to the demands of our rapidly growing economy, and, it is being said, to the efforts of South African secret agents. We must never relax our vigilance against our enemies.

We must never forget that our Zimlia is the focus for attempts at de-stabilisation of our successful socialist country. Viva Zimlia.'

Frank Diddy, she discovered, regarded this kind of thing as a sop thrown out to appease the government watchdogs who suspected him and his colleagues of 'writing lies' about the country's progress. The journalists of *The Post* had not had an easy time of it since Liberation. They had been arrested, kept without charges, released, rearrested, threatened, and the heavies of the secret police, known in the offices of *The Post* simply as 'The Boys', dropped in to the newspaper's offices and the journalists' homes threatening arrest and imprisonment at the slightest signs of recalcitrance. As for the rest, the truth about Zimlia, she heard the same as at Barry Angleton's and at Bill Case's.

She was trying to get an interview with Franklin, not daunted, though she intended to ask him something like, They are saying you own four hotels, five farms, and a forest of hardwoods, which you are illegally cutting down. Is this true? She felt the worm of truth must come wriggling out of the knotholes of concealment. She was equal to him. He was a friend, wasn't he?

Though she always boasted of this friendship, in fact she had not seen him for some years. In the matey days of early Liberation she had arrived in Zimlia, telephoned and was invited to meet him, though never alone, because he was with friends, colleagues, secretaries, and on one occasion his wife, a shy woman who merely smiled and never once opened her mouth. Franklin introduced Rose as 'My best friend when I was in London'. Then, telephoning him from London, or on arrival in Senga, she heard that he was in a meeting. That she, Rose, could be fobbed off with this kind of lie was an insult. And who the hell did he think he was? He should be grateful to the Lennoxes, they had been so good to him. *We* had been so good to him.

This time when she telephoned Comrade Minister Franklin's office, she was amazed to hear him come on the line at once, and a hearty, 'So, Rose Trimble, long time no see, you are just the person I want to talk to.'

And so she and Franklin sat together again, this time in a corner of the new Butler's Hotel lounge, a fancy place designed so that visiting dignitaries should not make unfavourable comparisons between this capital city and any other. Franklin was enormous now, he filled his armchair, and his big face overflowed in chins and shiny black cheeks. His eyes were small, though she remembered them as large, winsome and appealing.

'Now, Rose, we need your help. Only yesterday our Comrade President was saying that we need your help.'

Professional *nous* told Rose that this last was like her own 'Comrade Franklin is a good friend'. Everyone spoke of Comrade Matthew in every other sentence, to invoke or curse him. The words *Comrade Matthew* must be tinkling and purring through the ether like the signature tune of a popular radio programme.

'Yes, Rose, it is a good thing you are here,' he said smiling and shooting at her quick suspicious looks.

They are all paranoid, she had heard from Barry, from Frank, from Bill and from the guests who flowed in and out of the Senga houses in easy colonial – whoa there! – *post*-colonial manner.

'So, Franklin, you are having problems, I hear?'

'Problems! Our dollar fell again this week. It is a thirtieth of what it was at Liberation. And do you know who is responsible?' He leaned forward, shaking his plump finger at her. 'It is the International Community.'

She had expected to hear, South African agents. 'But the country is doing so well. I read it only today in *The Post*.'

He actually sat energetically up in his chair, to confront her better, supporting his big body on his elbows. 'Yes, we are a success story. But that is not what our enemies are saying. And that is where you come in.'

'It was only three months ago that I wrote a piece about the Leader.'

'And a fine piece it was, a fine piece.' He had not read it, she could see. 'But there are articles appearing that damage the good name of this country and accuse our Comrade President of many things.'

'Franklin, they are saying that you are all very rich, buying up farms, you all own farms and hotels – everything.'

'And who says that? It is a lie.' He waved his hand about, dispelling the lies, and fell back again. She did not say anything. He peeped at her, raising his head to do it, let it fall back. 'I'm a poor man,' he whined. 'A very poor man. And I have many children. And all my relatives . . . you do understand, I know you do, that in our culture if a man does well then all his relations come and we must keep them and educate all the children.'

'And a very fine culture it is,' said Rose, who in fact did find this concept heartwarming. Just look at herself! When she had found herself helpless all those years ago, where had her family been? And then the rich son of an exploiting capitalist family had taken advantage of her . . .

'Yes, we are proud of it. Our old people do not die alone in cold nursing homes, and we have no orphans.'

This Rose knew was not the truth. She had been hearing of the results of AIDS – orphans left destitute, ancient grandmothers bringing up children without parents.

'We want you to write about us. Tell the truth about us. I am asking you to describe what you see here in Zimlia, so that these lies do not spread any further.' He looked around the elegant hotel lounge, at the smiling waiters in their liveries. 'You can see for yourself, Rose. Look around you.'

'I saw a list in one of our newspapers. A list of the Ministers and the top civil servants and what you all own. Some own as many as twelve farms.'

'And why should we not own a farm? Am I to be barred from owning land because I am a Minister? And when I retire how shall I live? I must tell you, I would much rather be a simple farmer, living with my family on my own land.' He frowned. 'And now there is this drought. Down in the Buvu Valley all my animals have died. The farm is dust. My new borehole dried up.'

Tears ran down his cheeks. 'It is a terrible thing to see your mombies die. The white farmers are not suffering, they all have dams and boreholes.'

It was occurring to Rose that here might be a subject. She could write about the drought, which it seemed was afflicting everyone, rain shadows or not, and that meant she would not have to take sides. She didn't know anything about droughts, but she could always get Frank and Bill to fill her in, and she could cook up something that would not offend the rulers of Zimlia: she did not want to end this profitable connection. No, she could become an ecological warrior ... these thoughts wandered through her mind as Franklin made a speech about Zimlia's stand in the forefront of progress and socialist accomplishment, ending with the South African agents and the need for vigilance.

'These South African spies?'

'Yes, spies. That is the right word. They are everywhere. It is they who are responsible for the lies. Our Security people have proof. It is their aim to destabilise Zimlia so that South Africa may take over our country and add it to their evil empire. Did you know how they are attacking Mozambique? Now they are spreading everywhere.' He peered at her to see what effect he was having. 'And so you will write some articles for us, in the English newspapers, explaining the truth?'

He began struggling out of his chair, panting a little. 'My wife tells me that I should go on a diet, but it is hard when you are seated in front of a good meal – and unfortunately we Ministers have to attend so many functions . . .'

The moment of parting. Rose was hesitating. A flush of reminiscent warmth for the boy Franklin, for whom she had after all stolen clothes – no, more, taught him how to steal for himself – insisted she should put her arms around him. And if he did embrace her that would count for a lot. But he held out his hand and she took it. 'No, that's not the way, Rose. You must use our African handclasp, like this, like this . . .' and indeed it was inspiring, the handshake that said it was hard to let go of a good friend. 'And

I am waiting to hear good news from you. You will send me copies of your articles. I am waiting for them.' And he went off to the door of the Lounge where a couple of bulky men were waiting for him – his bodyguards.

She had told Frank Diddy that she achieved an interview with the Minister Franklin, had seen that he was impressed. Now she described the interview as if it had been an achievement and, more, one up on him, but all he said was, 'Join the club. Perhaps you'd like to try your hand at one of our little editorials?'

She decided she did not want to write about the drought, anyone could do that. She needed something . . . in *The Post* which she was reading with professional contempt at the breakfast table she saw: 'Police report the theft of equipment from the new hospital in Kwadere. Thousands of dollars' worth has disappeared. It is suspected that local people are the thieves.'

Rose's pulses definitely quickened. She showed the item to Frank Diddy, but he shrugged and said, 'That sort of thing goes on all the time.'

'Where could I find out?'

'Don't bother, it's not worth it.'

Kwadere. Barry had said Sylvia was there. Yes, there was something else. When Andrew came to London this was often announced in the papers: Andrew was News, or at least Global Money was. Last time, months ago, she had rung him, 'Hi, Andrew, this is Rose Trimble.'

'Hi, Rose.'

'I am working on *World Scandals* these days.'

'I don't think my doings would interest *World Scandals*.'

But there had been a previous time, some years ago, when he had agreed to meet her for a cup of coffee. Why had he? Her first thought was, guilt, that was it! While she had forgotten she had ever said he had made her pregnant – liars having bad memories – she did know that he owed her. And that meeting reminded her she had once found him so attractive she had not been able to let him go. He was still attractive: that casual elegance, that charm.

She told herself it had broken her heart. She had been ready to elevate Andrew into the position of 'The man I loved best in my life', but slowly realised that he was warning her. All this smiling waffle was meant to tell her that she must lay off the Lennoxes. Who did he think he was! As a journalist it was her job to tell the truth! Just like that upper-class arrogance! He was trying to subvert the freedom of the Press! The cup of coffee lasted for quite a time, while he ponced about hinting this and that, but she had got out of him news of the family, for one that Sylvia was in Kwadere, she was a doctor. Yes, that was what had been at the back of her mind. Now she had the fact that Sylvia, whom she still hated, was a doctor in Kwadere, where hospital equipment was being stolen. She had found her subject.

Some days after Sylvia and Rebecca had arranged the new books along the walls in Sylvia's rooms, a group of villagers stood waiting as she emerged to go down to the hospital. A youth came forward, smiling. 'Doctor Sylvia, please give me a book. Rebecca has told us you have brought us books.'

'I have to go to the hospital now. Come back this evening.'

How reluctantly they went off, with glances back at Father McGuire's house, where the new books were calling to them.

All day she worked with Clever and Zebedee, who had been holding the fort while she was in London. They were so quick, so nimble, and they made her heart ache, because of their potential and what was likely to happen to them. She was thinking – had to think – where in London, no, where in England, or in Europe, are children as hungry for knowledge as these? They had taught themselves to read English off the print on food packets. Both, when they finished work with her, sat at home reading, by candle-light, progressively more difficult books.

Their father still sat all day drowsing under this tree, one big skeleton hand drooping over a raised knee, which was a bony lump between two lanky bones covered with dry greyish skin. He had had pneumonia several times. He was dying of AIDS.

At sundown there was a crowd of a hundred waiting outside Father McGuire's house. He was standing there as she came up from the hospital. 'And now, my child, it is time, you must do something.'

She turned to the crowd and said she was going to disappoint them tonight, but she would arrange for the books to be stationed in the village.

A voice asked: 'And who will keep them safe for you? They will be stolen.'

'No, no one will steal them. Tomorrow I'll do it all.'

She and the priest watched as the again disappointed people wandered off into the darkening bush, through boulders, through grasses, along ways not visible to them, and he said, 'I sometimes think they see with their feet. And now you will come inside and you will sit down and you will eat and then share your evening with me, and we will listen to the radio. We have the new batteries you brought us.'

Rebecca was not there in the evenings. She prepared some sort of meal, and left it on plates in the refrigerator, and was in her own home by two in the afternoon. But today she came in while they were eating and said, 'I have come because I must tell you.'

'Sit down,' said the priest.

There was a protocol, apparently never formally agreed to, that Rebecca would not sit at the table with them when she was in her capacity as a servant, and suggestions from Father McGuire that she should had been vetoed, by her: it would not be right. But when she was paying a visit, as now, she sat, and when invited took a biscuit from a plate and laid it down before her: they knew she would take it to her children. Sylvia pushed the plate towards her and Rebecca counted five more biscuits. At their enquiring looks – she had three surviving children – she said she was feeding Zebedee and Clever.

'We must arrange for the books. I have been talking about it with everyone. There is an empty hut – Daniel's, you know who he was.'

'We buried him last Sunday,' said the priest.

'Okay. And his children died too before. But no one wants to take that hut now. They say it is unlucky' – she was using their word.

'Daniel died of AIDS, and not because of any nonsense about bad *muti*.' Using her word for the *n'ganga*'s potions.

Rebecca and the priest had had in their long association many bouts of argument, which he had to win because he was the priest and she was a Christian, but now she smiled, and said 'Okay'.

'You mean, it isn't unlucky for books?'

'No, Sylvia, that is true, it is okay for books. And so we will take the shelves and bricks from your room and we will make the shelves in Daniel's hut, and my Tenderai will look after them.'

This youth was very sick, with probably only a few months to live: everyone knew he had had a curse put on him.

Rebecca read their faces, and said quietly, 'He is well enough to guard the books. And he can enjoy the books and so he will not be so unhappy.'

'There are not enough books for everyone.'

'Yes, there are enough. Tenderai will make them take a book out for one week, and bring it back. He will cover the books in newspaper. He will make everyone pay . . .' And, as Sylvia was about to protest, 'no, just a little bit, perhaps ten cents. Yes, it is nothing, but it is enough to tell everyone the books are expensive and we must all look after them.'

She got up. She did not look well. Sylvia scolded her that she worked too hard, with her sick children who woke her at night, and she said again now, 'Rebecca, you work too hard.'

'I am strong, I am like you, Sylvia. I can work well because I am not fat. A fat dog lies in the sun with the flies crawling over it and sleeps but a thin dog is awake and snaps at the flies.'

The priest laughed. 'I shall use that for my sermon on Sunday.'

'You're welcome, Father.' She made her curtsy to him as taught her at school, due to anyone older. She pressed her thin hands together and smiled at him. Then to Sylvia she said, 'I'll get some boys to come and carry your books down to the hut, and the planks and bricks. Put your books on your bed, so they don't take them too.'

She went out.

'What a pity Rebecca couldn't run this poor country instead of the incompetents we're saddled with.'

'Do we really have to believe that a country gets the government it deserves? I don't think these poor people deserve their government.'

Father McGuire nodded, then spoke. 'Have you thought that perhaps the reason these gross clowns have not had their throats cut is because the *povos* would like to be in their place, and know they would do the same if they had the chance?'

Sylvia said, 'Is that really what you believe?'

'It is not for nothing that we have the prayer, "Lead us not into temptation". And there is the other, its companion, "Thank you, Lord, for delivering me from evil".'

'Are you really saying that virtue is merely a question of not being tempted?'

'Ah, virtue, now there's a word I find it hard to use.'

Sylvia, it was clear, was not far off tears, and the priest saw it. He went to a cupboard, returned with two glasses and a bottle of good whisky – she brought it back with her. He poured generously for himself and for her, nodded at her and drank his down.

Sylvia looked at the golden liquid making patterns in the lamplight, a rich oily swirl that settled into a pond of amber. She took a sip. 'I have often thought I could become an alcoholic.'

'No, Sylvia, you could not.'

'I understand why in the old days they had sundowners.'

'Why the old days? The Pynes have their sundowners on the dot.'

393

'When the sun goes down I often think I'd give anything to drink a bottle empty. It's so sad, when the sun sets.'

'It is the colour in the sky, reminding us of the splendours of the Lord that we are exiled from.' She was surprised: he did not usually go in for this kind of thing. 'I have many times wished myself away from Africa but I have only to see the sun go down over those hills and I'd not leave for anything in the world.'

'Another day gone and nothing achieved,' said Sylvia. 'Nothing changed.'

'Ah, so you're a world-changer, after all.'

This struck into a sensitive area. She thought: Perhaps Johnny's nonsense got into me and spoiled me. 'How could one not want to change it?'

'How could one not want it changed? But wanting to change it oneself – no, there's the devil in that.'

'And who could disagree, after what we have learned?'

'And if you have learned that, then you have done better than most. But it is too potent a dream to let its victims go.'

'Father, when you were a young man, are you telling me that you never had a fit of shouting in the streets and throwing stones at the Brits?'

'You forget, I was a poor boy. I was as poor as some of those people down there in the village. There was only one way out for me. I only ever had one road. I didn't have a choice.'

'Yes, I cannot see you as anything other than a priest, by nature.'

'It is true – no choice, but the only one for me.'

'But when I hear Sister Molly go on and on, if she didn't have a cross on her chest, you'd never know she was a nun.'

'Have you ever thought that for poor girls anywhere in Europe there was only one choice? They became nuns to spare their families the cost of feeding them. And so the convents have been stuffed with young women who'd have been better off raising families or – or any kind of work in the world. Sister Molly fifty years ago would be going mad in a convent, because she should never have been in it. But now – did you know? – she said to her Superiors, I am leaving this convent and I shall be a nun in the world. And one day I expect that she will say to herself, I'm not a nun. I never was a nun. And she will simply leave her Order, just like that. She was a poor girl and she took the way out. That is all. Yes, and I know what you are thinking – it will not be so easy for those poor black sisters up the hill to leave as it is for Sister Molly.'

When Sylvia walked down to the village after lunch every day she found that outside every hut, or under the trees, or on logs or on stools, the people were reading, or, with an exercise book propped in front of them or on their knees, they laboured to learn to write. She had told them she would come from one to half past two and supervise classes. She would have said from twelve, but she knew Father McGuire would not let her skip lunch. But she did not need to sleep, after all. Within a couple of weeks something like sixty books were transforming the village in the bush where children went to school but did not get an education, and where most adults might have done four or five years at school. Sylvia had driven herself to the Pynes who were going into Senga, had gone with them, and bought a quantity of exercise books, biros, pencils, an atlas, a little globe, and some textbooks on how to teach. After all, she had no idea how a professional would go about it, and the teachers in the school on the rise where the dust these days was lying in heaps or blowing about in clouds had had no training in how to teach either. She had also gone to the depot to find her sewing machines, but they had not been heard of.

She sat outside Rebecca's hut, where a tall tree threw deep shade in the middle of the day, and taught up to sixty people, as well as she could, hearing them read, setting writing models, and propped the atlas on a shelf on a tree trunk to illustrate geography lessons. Among her pupils might be the teachers from the school who helped her, but were learning as they did.

The doves cooed in the trees. It was the sleepy time of the day for all of them, and Sylvia's need for sleep dragged down her lids, but she would not sleep, she would not. Rebecca handed around water in stainless steel and aluminium basins stolen from the abandoned hospital. Not much water: the drought was biting, women were getting up at three and four in the morning to walk to a further river, the near one having run low and foetid, carrying jugs and cans on their heads. Not much washing was going on: clothes were certainly not being washed. It was as much as the women could do, to keep enough water for drinking and cooking. The smell from the crowd was strong. Sylvia now associated that smell with patience, with long-suffering, and with contained anger. When she took a sip from Rebecca's stolen basins she felt as she should do, but did not, when she drank the blood of Christ at Communion. The faces of the crowd, of all ages from children to old men and women, were rapt, hushed, attentive to every word. Education, this was education, for which most had hungered all their lives, and had expected to get when it had been promised by their government. At two thirty Sylvia called up from the crowd some boy or girl more advanced than the others, set them to read some paragraphs from Enid Blyton – a great favourite: from *Tarzan* – another; from the *Jungle Book*, which was more difficult, but liked: or from the prize of them all, *Animal Farm* which was their own story, as they said. Or the atlas was passed around at a page they had just done, to hammer in what they knew.

She visited the village anyway, every morning after making sure her hospital was going well. She brought with her either Clever or Zebedee, for one of them had to be left in charge of the patients. She had patients in the huts, the ones with the slow lingering diseases, over whom she and the *n'ganga* would exchange looks that acknowledged what they were careful not to say. For if there was one thing this bush doctor understood as well and better than any ordinary doctor, it was the value of a cheerful mind; and it was evident that most of his *muti*, spells, and practices were elaborated for this one purpose: to keep going an optimistic immune system. But when she and this clever man exchanged a certain kind of look, then it meant that before long their patient would soon be up among the trees in the new grave-yard, which was in fact the AIDS or Slim cemetery, and well away from the village. The graves were dug deep, because it was feared the evil that had killed these people could escape and attack others.

Sylvia knew, because Clever had told her — Rebecca herself had not — that this sensible and practical woman, on whom both she and the priest relied, believed that her three children had died and a fourth was ill because her younger brother's wife, who had always hated her, had employed a stronger *n'ganga* than the local one to attack the children. She was barren, that was the trouble, and believed that Rebecca was responsible, having paid for charms and potions and spells to keep her childless.

Some believed she was childless because in her hut were to be found more stolen things from the abandoned hospital than any other. The object known to be most dangerous among the stolen goods was the dentist's chair that had once been in the middle of the village, where children played over it, but it had been taken away and thrown into a gulley, to get rid of its malign influences. Vervet monkeys played over it, without harm, and once Sylvia had seen an old baboon sitting in it, a piece of grass between his lips, looking around him in a contemplative way, like a grandfather sitting out his days on a porch.

Edna Pyne got into the old lorry to drive to the Mission because she was being pursued by what she called her black dog, which even had a name. 'Pluto is snapping at my heels again,' she might say, claiming that the two house dogs Sheba and Lusaka knew when this shadowy haunter was present and growled at it. Cedric would not laugh at this little fantasy when she made a joke of it all, but said she was getting as bad as the blacks with their superstitious nonsense. Even five years ago Edna had had women friends, on nearby farms, whom she could drive over to visit when she was down, but now none was left. They were farming in Perth (Australia), in Devon; they had 'taken the gap' to South Africa – they had gone. She hungered for women's talk, feeling she was in a desert of maleness, her husband, the men working in the house and garden, the people coming to the house, government inspectors, surveyors, contour ridge experts, and the new black busybodies always imposing more and more regulations. All were men. She hoped to find Sylvia free for a bit of a chat, though she did not like Sylvia as much as Edna knew she deserved: she was to be admired, yes, but she was a bit of a nut. When she got to Father McGuire's house, it seemed empty. She went into the cool dark inside, and Rebecca emerged from the kitchen with a cloth in her hands that should have been cleaner. But the drought was limiting the cleanliness in her own house too: the borehole was lower than it had ever been.

'Is Doctor Sylvia here?'

'She is at the hospital. There's a girl in labour. And Father McGuire has taken the car and gone to visit the other Father at the Old Mission.'

Edna sat as if her knees had been hit. She let her head fall back against the chair, and shut her eyes. When she opened them Rebecca stood in front of her still, waiting.

'God,' said Edna, 'I've had enough, I really have.'

'I shall make you some tea,' said Rebecca, turning to go.

'How long do you think the doctor will be?'

'I don't know. It's a difficult birth. The baby's in the breech position.'

This clinical phrase made Edna open her eyes wide. Like most of the old whites she had a mind in compartments – that is, more than most of us. She knew that some blacks were as intelligent as most whites, but by intelligent she meant educated, and Rebecca was working in a kitchen.

When the tea tray was put in front of her and Rebecca turned to leave, Edna heard herself say: 'Sit down, Rebecca.' And added, 'Do you have time?'

Rebecca did not have time, she had been chasing after herself all morning. Since her son, the one who went to fetch the water for her from the river, was with his father, who had drunk last night to the point of raging insanity, she, Rebecca, had had to carry water down from this kitchen, having asked permission from the Father, not once but five times. The water in the house well was low: water seemed to be creeping back down into the earth everywhere, always harder to reach. But Rebecca could see that this white woman was in a state, and needed her. She sat and waited. She was thinking it was lucky Mrs Pyne was here with her car because the Father had taken the car and Sylvia had said it might be necessary to run the patient into hospital for a caesarean.

Words that had been bubbling and simmering inside Edna for hours, for days, now came out in a hot, resentful accusing self-pitying rush, though Rebecca was not the right auditor for them. Nor was Sylvia, if it came to that. 'I don't know what to do,' Edna said, her eyes wide and staring, not at Rebecca but at the edge of blue beads on the fly net over the tea tray. 'I'm at my wits' end. I think my husband has gone mad. Well, they are mad, aren't they, men, aren't they, wouldn't you agree?' Rebecca who last night had been dodging blows and embraces from her raving husband smiled and said that yes, men were sometimes difficult.

'You can say that again. Do you know what he's done? He's actually bought another farm. He says that if he didn't one of the Ministers'd grab it, so why not him. I mean, if you people got it, that would be all right, but he says he can pay for it, it was offered to the government and they didn't want it so he's buying it. He is building a dam there, near the hills.'

'A dam,' said Rebecca, coming to life: she had been drowsing as she sat. 'Okay . . . a dam . . . okay.'

'Well, the moment he's built it one of those black swine'll grab it, that's what they do, they wait until we do something nice, like a dam, and then they grab. So what are you doing this for, I ask him, but he says . . .' Edna was sitting with a biscuit in one hand and a cup in the other. Her words were tumbling out too fast to let her drink. 'I want to leave, Rebecca, do you blame me? Well, do you? This is not my country, well you people say so and I agree with you but my husband says it is his as much as yours, and so he's bought . . .' A wail escaped her. She set down the cup, then the biscuit, shook a handkerchief from her handbag and wiped her face with it. Then she sat silent a moment, leaned forward and frowningly rubbed the blue bead edging between her fingers. 'Pretty beads. Did you make that?'

'Yes, I made it.'

'Pretty. Well done. And there's another thing. The government criticises us all the time, they call us all these names. But in our compound there's three times the number of people that should be there, they come in every day from the communal land, and we feed them, we are feeding all these people because they are starving on the communal land in the drought, well you know that, don't you, Rebecca?'

'Okay. Yes. That is true. They are starving. And Father McGuire has set up a feeding point at the school, because the children come up to school so hungry they just sit and cry.'

'There you are. But your government never has a good word for any of us.'

She was crying, a dismal weeping, like an over-tired child. Rebecca knew this woman was not weeping for the hungry people but because of what Rebecca called all-too-much. 'It's all-too-much,' she would say to Sylvia, 'too-much for me to bear.' And she would sit herself down, and put her hands up to her face and rock and set up a regular wailing, while Sylvia fetched pills – sedatives – which Rebecca obediently swallowed down.

'I sometimes think that everything is too much, it gets on top of me,' wept Edna, but actually sounded better. 'Bad enough before the drought, but now the drought and the government and everything . . .'

Here Clever appeared in the doorway to say to Rebecca that Doctor Sylvia said he must run over to the Pynes and ask someone to bring a car to take the woman in labour to the hospital.

And there was Edna Pyne! His face lit up and he actually did a little dance right there on the verandah. 'Okay. Now she won't die. The baby's stuck,' he informed them, 'but if she can get to hospital in time . . .' He darted off down the hill and soon Sylvia appeared, supporting a woman draped in a blanket.

'I see I'm some use after all,' said Edna, and went to help Sylvia hold up the woman, who was sobbing and moaning.

'If only they'd get on with that new hospital,' said Sylvia.

'Dream time.'

'She's scared of the caesarean. I keep telling her it's nothing.'

'Why can't you do the operation?'

'We make these mistakes. The one awful stupid ridiculous unforgivable mistake I made was not to do surgery.' She spoke in a flat dry voice, but Edna recognised it as the same as her emotional outburst: Sylvia was letting off steam and no notice should be taken. 'I'm sending Clever with you. I've got a really sick man down there.'

'I hope I'm not going to have to deliver a baby.'

'Well, you'd do as well as anyone. But Clever's very good. And I've given her something to delay the baby a little. And her sister's going too.'

At the car a woman was waiting. She extended her arms, the woman in labour went into them and began wailing.

Sylvia ran back down to her hospital. The car set off. It was bad road, and the drive took nearly an hour, because the patient cried out when the car went over a bump. Edna saw the two black women into the hospital, an old one built under the whites, meant to serve a few thousand people but now expected to care for half a million.

Edna got into the driver's seat and Clever got in beside her.

He should be in the back seat, she thought, but without much heat. She listened while he chattered about Doctor Sylvia and the classes under the trees, the books, the exercise books, the biros, much better than the school. She became curious and instead of dropping the boy at the turn-off to make his way back to the Mission, drove him there and parked.

It was still only half past twelve. Sylvia was sitting at the dining table with the priest, having lunch, where she, Edna, had been not so long before. Invited to sit down for lunch, Edna was going to, but Sylvia said she had to get down to the village, Edna mustn't take it personally. So Edna, a woman who liked her food, let the priest make her a sandwich of some tomato slices between unbuttered bread – yes, butter was hard to get at the moment, with the drought – and she followed Sylvia. She did not know what to expect, and was impressed. Everyone knew who Mrs Pyne was, of course, and smiles of welcome came her way. They brought her a stool, and forgot she was there. She sat with the sandwich pushed into her bag, because she suspected some of those present would be hungry, and she could not eat in front of them. Good Lord, she thought. Who could ever believe that I'd see a couple of bits of dry bread and a slice of tomato as a wicked luxury?

She listened to Sylvia reading, in English, slowly pronouncing every word, from an African writer she had never heard of, though she did know that blacks wrote novels, while the people listened as if . . . God, they might be in church. Then Sylvia invited a young man, and then a girl, to tell the others what the story was about. They got it right, and Edna realised she was relieved that they did: she wanted this enterprise to be a success and was pleased with herself that she did.

Sylvia was asking an old woman to tell them all about a drought she remembered when she was a little girl. The old woman spoke a jolting fumbling English, and Sylvia told a young woman to repeat it in better English. That drought didn't sound much different from this one. The white government had distributed maize in the drought areas, said the old woman, and there was some appreciative clapping which could only be a criticism of their own government. When the tale was finished Sylvia told the ones who could to write down what they remembered, and the ones who couldn't to make a story which they could tell tomorrow.

It was two thirty. Sylvia set the old woman who had told the drought story over the others, about a hundred of them, and went with Edna back up to the house. Now there would be a cup of tea and she and Sylvia could sit and talk, she could have her talk at last . . . but oddly, it seemed the need to talk and to be heard had left her.

Sylvia said, 'They are such good people. I can't bear it, the way they are being wasted.'

They were standing outside the house, near the car.

'Well,' said Edna, 'I suppose we are all of us better than we are given a chance to be.'

She could see from the way Sylvia turned to look hard at her, that this was not the kind of thing people expected to hear from her. And why not? 'Would you like me to come and help you with your school – or the patients?'

'Oh, yes, would you, would you really?'

'Let me know when you need me,' said Edna, and got into the car and drove off, feeling she had made a big step into a new dimension. She did not know that if she had said to Sylvia then and there, 'Can I start now?' Sylvia would have gratefully said, 'Oh, yes, come and help me with this sick man, he's got malaria so badly he's shaking himself to death.' But Sylvia decided that politeness had spoken out of Edna and did not think about her offer again.

As for Edna she felt all her life that she had missed an opportunity, a door had opened but she had chosen not to see it. The trouble was, she had been joking about do-gooders for years, and for her to become one, just like that . . . yet she had made the offer and had meant it. For a moment she had not been the Edna

Pyne she knew but someone very different. She did not tell Cedric about driving the black woman into hospital: suppose he grumbled about the petrol, and how hard it was to get any. She did mention that she had seen the village where stuff stolen from the unfinished hospital was evidence. 'Good for them,' was his comment. 'Better that than it lies rotting in the bush.'

Mr Edward Phiri, Inspector of Schools, had written to the head-master of Kwadere Secondary School to say he would arrive at 9 a.m. and would expect to have his midday meal with him and the staff. His Mercedes, third-hand when bought – he wasn't a Minister and worthy of a new one – had broken down not far from the Pynes' signpost. He left his car and in a foul temper walked the few hundred yards to the Pynes' house. There he found Cedric and Edna at breakfast. He announced himself, said that he must speak to Mr Mandizi at the Growth Point to come and fetch him and drive him to the school, but heard that the telephone line was down and had been for a month.

'Then why has it not been mended?'

'I am afraid you must ask the Minister for Communications that question. The telephone system is always breaking down and it can take weeks to be mended.' Edna spoke, but Mr Phiri looked at the husband – the man, whose role it was to lead. Cedric seemed unaware of his responsibility, and said nothing.

Mr Phiri stood looking at the breakfast table. 'You have break-fast late. I had mine it seems many hours ago.'

Edna said in the same accusing voice, 'Cedric was out in the fields just after five. It wasn't properly light. Perhaps you would like to sit down and have some tea – or perhaps some more breakfast?'

Mr Phiri sat, good humour restored. 'And perhaps I will. But I am surprised to hear that you are at work so early,' he said to Cedric. 'I was under the impression that you white farmers take it easy.'

'I think you are under a good many false impressions,' said

Cedric. 'But now I must ask you to excuse me. I have to get back to the dam.'

'Dam? Dam? There is no dam marked on the map.'

Edna and Cedric exchanged glances. They now suspected this official of having faked a breakdown for the purpose of having a look at their farm. He had as good as admitted it, when mentioning the map.

'Shall I have fresh tea made?'

'No, this tea in the pot will do me well. And perhaps those eggs you have left over? A pity to waste them, I think.'

'They wouldn't be wasted. The cook will have them for his breakfast.'

'And now that surprises me. I don't believe in spoiling staff. My boys get *sadza*, certainly not farm eggs.'

Mr Phiri was apparently unaware of his incorrectness and sat smiling as Edna filled his plate with fried eggs, bacon, sausages. As he began eating he said, 'Perhaps I could accompany you to see the dam? Since clearly I am not destined to get to the school this morning?'

'Why not?' said Edna. 'I'll run you there in my car. And when you are finished someone at the Mission will take you to the Growth Point.'

'And what about my car sitting helplessly on the road? It will be stolen.'

'That seems to me more than likely,' said Cedric, in the same dry disliking tone he had used from the start, such a contrast to the rawly emotional voice of his wife.

'Then, perhaps you could order one of your workers to guard my car?'

Again husband and wife exchanged looks. Edna, returned to her responsible self by her husband's rage, which Mr Phiri was unaware of, was silently urging compliance. Cedric got up, went out to the kitchen, returned, said, 'I have asked the cook to ask the garden boy to guard your car. But perhaps we should be taking steps to get it restarted?'

'What a fine idea,' said Mr Phiri, who had finished his eggs and was eating lumps of sugary sweets, which he clearly approved of. 'And how shall we do that?'

Edna knew that Cedric was suppressing something like, 'And why should I care?' – and said quickly, 'Cedric, you could try the radio.'

'Ah, so you have a radio?'

'The batteries are low. There are none available in the shops just now, as I expect you have found yourself.'

'That is true, but you could try?'

Cedric had not wanted to confess to the radio because he didn't want to waste what power there was on Mr Phiri. 'I'll try, but I won't promise anything.' He disappeared again.

'What is this delightful stuff I am eating?' said Mr Phiri, tucking in.

'Crystallised paw paw.'

'You must give me the recipe. I'll tell my wife to make me some.'

'She must have it already. I got it from the radio programme, *Making the Best of Our Produce*.'

'I am surprised you listen to a programme for poor black women.'

'This poor white woman listens to women's programmes. And if your wife is too good for it then she is missing a lot.'

'Poor . . .' Mr Phiri laughed, heartily, genuinely, and then realising there had been a remark which he was sure had been meant as a rudeness, said sourly, 'Now that is a good joke.'

'I am glad you like it.'

'Okay.' Meaning, enough of that.

But Edna went on. 'It is a very good programme. I have learned a lot from it. Everything you see on this table is made on the farm.'

Mr Phiri took his time surveying the spread, but did not want to confess some of it was unfamiliar to him – fish pâté, liver pâté, curried fish . . . 'The jams, of course, and may I taste this one?'

He reached for a pot, 'Rosella . . . rosella – but this grows wild everywhere?'

'So what, if it makes good jam.' Mr Phiri pushed the pot away without tasting it. 'I was told the nuns at the Mission won't eat the marvellous peaches growing in the garden, they'll only eat tinned peaches, because they don't want to be thought primitive people.' She laughed, spitefully.

'I hear your husband has bought the farm next to this one?'

'It was for sale. You people didn't want it. It was offered to you. It was much against my will, I assure you.'

Here they looked at each other, but really, as had not happened till now; their eyes had been doing anything but expressing a willingness to try and like each other.

Mr Phiri did not like this woman. First, on principle: she was a white farmer's wife, whom he thought of first of all as one of the females who had taken up guns in the Liberation War and defended homesteads, roads, ammunition points: this district was an area where the war had been fierce. Yes, he could just see her in battledress with a gun, aimed perhaps at him. Yet he had been a boy in the war, safe in Senga: the war had not touched him at all.

She disliked this class of black official, called them little Hitlers, and delighted in repeating every bad thing she heard about them. They treated their black servants like dirt, worse than any white person had ever done, the blacks didn't want to work for other blacks, tried to work for whites. They abused their power, they took bribes, they were – and this was the real sin – incompetent. And this particular man she had disliked from the first glance.

The two people, the over-tense dried-out white woman, the large and confident black man, sat looking at each other, letting their faces speak for them.

'Okay,' said Mr Phiri at last.

Luckily, in came Cedric. 'I got a message through just before the bloody thing faded. Mandizi will be along. But he says he's not well today.'

'Mr Mandizi I am sure will be as quick as he can, but we shall have time to see your new dam.'

The two men went out to the lorry, parked under a tree, and neither even looked at the woman. She smiled to herself, the practised bitter twist of the lips of one who feeds on bitterness.

Cedric drove fast, over the rough farm roads, through fields, kopjes, patches of bush. Mr Phiri had scarcely in his life been out of Senga, and like Rose did not know how to interpret what he saw.

'And what is this growing here?'

'Tobacco. It is what is keeping your economy going.'

'Ah, so that is the famous tobacco?'

'You mean you've never seen tobacco growing?'

'When I go out of Senga inspecting schools I am always in such a hurry, I am a busy man. That is why I am so pleased to have this chance of seeing a real farm, with a white farmer.'

'Some of your black farmers are growing good tobacco, didn't you know that?'

Mr Phiri was silent, because they were driving along the base of a tumbling hill and there, in front of them, was a waste land of raw yellow soil in heaps and piles and ridges, and an excavator was labouring away, balancing on improbable slopes and declivities. 'Here we are,' said Cedric, leaping out, and he went forward without looking to see if the Inspector was following. A black man, the excavator driver's mate, came forward to the farmer and the two stood close together, conferring over a map of some kind, on the edge of a hole in the dense yellow soil. Mr Phiri went cautiously forward among the yellow heaps, trying to keep his shoes clean. Dust blew off the tops of the heaps. His good suit was already dusty.

'Well, that's it.' Cedric returned.

'But where is the dam?'

'There.' Cedric pointed.

'But – when it is finished how big will it be?'

Cedric pointed again. 'There . . . there . . . from that line of trees to the kopje, and from there to where we are standing.'

'A big dam, then?'

'It won't be the Kariba.'

'Okay,' said Mr Phiri. He was disappointed. He had expected to see a lake of sweet brown water, with cows standing in it up to their middles, and over it thorn trees where weaver birds' nests dangled. He could not consciously remember ever seeing this scene, but that is what a dam meant to him. 'When will it be full?'

'Perhaps you could arrange for some good rain? This is our third season with practically no rain.'

Mr Phiri laughed, but he was feeling like a schoolboy and didn't like it. He could not imagine the sweep of water that would be here under the hills.

'If you want to catch Mandizi, we should go back.'

'Okay.' This was okay in its primal sense: Yes, I agree.

'I'll take you back another way,' said Cedric, though it was against his interests to impress this man who intended to steal his farm. He wanted to share his loving pride in what he had made from the bush. A mile from the house a herd of cattle stood eating dry maize cobs. They had the frantic look of drought-stressed animals. What Mr Phiri saw was cattle, saw *mombies*, and he longed to own them. His eyes filled with the wonder of these beasts: he did not realise they were in trouble.

Cedric said, 'I am having to shoot the calves as they are born.' His voice was harsh. Mr Phiri was shocked, and he stammered out, 'But, but . . . yes, I read in the paper . . . but that is terrible.' He saw that tears were running down the white man's cheeks. 'It must be terrible,' he said, sighing, and tactfully tried not to look at Cedric. He was feeling a real warmth for him, but he did not know what he would do if the white man broke down and wept. 'Shooting calves . . . but is there nothing . . . nothing . . .'

'No milk in the udders,' said Cedric. 'And when cows are as thin as that, the calves are poor quality when they are born.'

They were at the house.

Mr Mandizi was just arriving, but Cedric at first thought it was a deputy: the man was half the size he had been.

'You've lost a lot of weight,' said Cedric.

'Yes, that is so.'

He had dropped the mechanic at the Mercedes and now he opened the back door of the car and said to Mr Phiri, 'Get in, please.' And to Cedric in an official voice, 'You should get your radio fixed. I could hardly hear you.'

'That would be the day,' said Cedric.

'And now to the school,' said Mr Phiri, who was in low spirits because of the calves. He did not talk as he was driven to the Mission.

'This is the priest's house.'

'But I want the headmaster's house.'

'There is no headmaster. I am afraid he is in prison.'

'But why is there no replacement?'

'We have asked for a replacement, but you see this is not an attractive posting. They would rather go to a town. Or as near as they can to a town.'

Anger restored Mr Phiri's vitality, and he strode into the little house, followed by his subordinate. No one was about. He clapped his hands and Rebecca appeared. 'Tell the priest I am here.'

'Father McGuire is up at the school. If you walk up that path you will find him.'

'And why will you not go?'

'I have something in the oven. And Father McGuire is waiting for you.'

'And why is he there?'

'He teaches the big children. I think he is teaching many classes, because the headmaster is not here.' Rebecca turned to go into the kitchen.

'And where are you going? I have not said you can go.'

Rebecca made a deep, slow curtsy and stood with her hands folded, eyes down.

Mr Phiri glared, did not look at Mr Mandizi, who knew he was being mocked.

'Very well, you can go now.'

'Okay,' said Rebecca.

The two men set off up the dusty path with the sun hitting down hard on their heads and shoulders.

Since eight that morning the many classrooms of this school had been a pandemonium of excited children, waiting for the big man. Their teachers who were after all not so much older than some of them, were as elated. But no car came, there was only the sound of doves, and some cicadas in the clump of trees near the water tank, which was empty. All the children had been thirsty for weeks, and some were hungry and indeed had had nothing to eat but what Father McGuire had given them for breakfast, lumps of the heavy white sweet bread, and reconstituted milk. Nine o'clock, then ten. Teaching resumed, the din of several hundred voices chanting the repetitions necessary because of no schoolbooks, no exercise books, was audible for half a mile from the school, and only ceased when Mr Phiri and Mr Mandizi appeared, hot and sweating.

'What is this? Where is the teacher?'

'Here,' said a meek youth, smiling in an agony of apprehension.

'And what class is this? What is all this noise? I do not remember that oral lessons are part of our curriculum? Where are the exercise books?'

At this fifty exuberant children chorused, 'Comrade Inspector, Comrade Inspector, we have no exercise books, we have no books, please give us some exercise books. And some pencils, yes, some pencils, do not forget us, Comrade Inspector.'

'And why do they not have exercise books?' said Mr Phiri impressively to Mr Mandizi.

'We send in the requisition forms, but we have not been sent exercise books or textbooks.' It had been three years, but he was nervous of saying so in front of the children, and their teacher.

'And if they are delayed, then hurry them up, in Senga.'

There was no help for it. 'It has been three years since this school received any books or exercise books.'

Mr Phiri stared at him, at the young teacher, at the children.

The young teacher said, 'Comrade Inspector, sir, we do our best, but it is hard without any books.'

The Comrade Inspector felt trapped. He knew that in some schools – well, just a few – there was a shortage of books. The fact was, he rarely went out of the towns, made sure the schools he inspected were urban. There were shortages there, but it was not a terrible thing, was it, for four or five children to share a primer, or to use waste wrapping paper for writing lessons? But no books, nothing at all. Flashpoint: he exploded into rage. 'And look at your floors. How long since they were swept?'

'There is so much dust,' said the teacher in a low shamed voice. 'Dust . . .'

'Speak up.'

Now the children came in with, 'The dust comes in, and as soon as we sweep it up it comes in again.'

'Stand up when you speak to me.'

Since the officials had arrived without ceremony at the door, the young teacher had not ordered the children to stand, but now there was a great scraping of feet and desks. 'And how is it these children do not know how to greet the representative of the government?'

'Good morning, Comrade Inspector,' came the much-rehearsed greeting from the children, all still smiling and excited because of this visit which would result in their at last getting exercise books, pencils, and even perhaps a headmaster.

'See to the floor,' said Mr Phiri to the teacher, who was smiling like a beggar refused. 'Mr Phiri, Comrade Inspector Sir . . .' he was running after the officials as they made their way to the next classroom. 'What is it?' 'If you could ask the department to send us our supplies of books . . .' Now he was running beside them like a messenger trying to deliver an urgent despatch, and, all pretence of dignity gone, he was pressing his hands together and weeping, 'Comrade Inspector, it is so hard to teach when you have no . . .'

But the officials had gone into the next classroom, from whence almost at once came the shouts and imprecations of Mr Phiri's rage. He was there only a minute, went on to the next classroom, again the storm of shouts. The teacher from the first classroom who had been standing listening, giving himself time to recover, now pulled himself together and returned to where his pupils sat waiting, still full of hope. Fifty pairs of eyes shone at him: *Oh, give us some good news*.

'Okay,' he said, and their faces lost their shine.

He was trying his hardest not to cry. Tongues clicked in sympathy and there were murmurs of 'Shame'.

'We shall have a writing lesson.' He turned to the blackboard and with a fragment of chalk wrote in a clear round child's hand, 'The Comrade Inspector came to our school today.'

'And now, Mary.' A large young woman, perhaps sixteen, looking older, came out of the mass of crammed-together desks, took the bit of chalk, and wrote the sentence again. She bobbed a curtsy to him – the teacher had been a member of this class two years before – and returned to her place. They were silent, listening to the shouts coming from a classroom in the next block. The children were all hoping they would be called up to show what they could do on the board. The trouble was the shortage of chalk. The teacher had the fragment, and two whole sticks, which he kept hidden in his pocket, because school cupboards got broken into, even if they were as good as empty. It was out of the question to have all the children up, one after the other to copy the sentence.

The storm of noise that was Mr Phiri and Mr Mandizi approaching was just outside the classroom – oh, were they coming back in? at least there was the nice sentence on the blackboard – no, they were striding past. The children rushed to the windows to see their last of the Comrade Inspector. Two backs were disappearing down to the priest's house. Behind them came a third, the dusty black robe of Father McGuire, who was waving and shouting at them to stop.

Silently the children went back to their desks. It was nearly twelve, and time for the lunch break. Not all brought food, but would sit watching their fellows eat a lump of cold porridge or a piece of pumpkin.

The teacher said, 'There will be physical culture after the break.'

A chorus of pleasure. They all loved these exercises that took place in the dusty spaces between buildings. No equipment, no bars, no vaulting horse, or climbing ropes, or mats they could lie on. The teachers took it in turns.

The two men burst into the priest's house, with the priest just behind them.

'I did not see you at the school,' said Mr Phiri.

'I think you did not inspect the third row of classrooms, which is where I was.'

'I hear you teach at our school. And how is that?'

'I give remedial lessons.'

'I did not know that we have remedial lessons.'

'I teach children who are three or four years behind their proper level, because of the poor state of their school. I call that remedial. And it is voluntary. There is no salary attached. I do not cost the government anything.'

'And those nuns I saw. Why aren't they teaching?'

'They do not have the qualifications, not even for this school.'

Mr Phiri would have liked to rage and shout – perhaps hit something, or someone – but he felt his head swell and pound: he had been told by his doctor not to get over-excited. He stood, looking at the lunch set out on the table, some slivers of cold meat and some tomatoes. A new loaf emitted delightful odours. He was thinking of *sadza*. That is what he needed. If he could only get the comforting weight and warmth of a good plate of *sadza* into his poor stomach, which was churning with a hundred emotions . . . 'Perhaps you would like to share our meal?' said the priest.

Rebecca entered with a plate of boiled potatoes.

'Have you cooked *sadza*?'

'No, sir, I did not know you were expected for lunch.'

Father McGuire moved swiftly in, with, 'Unfortunately, as we all know, a good *sadza* takes half an hour to do well, and we would not insult you by giving you inferior *sadza*. But perhaps some beef? I am sorry to say there is plenty of beef around, with the poor beasts dying from the drought.'

Mr Phiri's stomach which had been relaxing, in the expectation of *sadza*, now knotted again and he shouted at Mr Mandizi, 'Go and find out if my car is mended.' Mr Mandizi was eyeing the bread, and looked in protest at his chief. He was entitled to his meal. He did not move. 'And come back and tell me if it is not ready, and I can return with you to your office.'

'I am sure he will have finished by now. He has had a good three hours,' said Mr Mandizi.

'And how is it you are defying me, Mr Mandizi? Am I or am I not your chief? And this in addition to the incompetence I have seen today. You are supposed to be keeping an eye on the local schools and reporting deficiencies.' He was shouting, but his voice was strained and weak. He was about to burst into tears from impotence, from anger, and from shame at what he had seen that day. Just in time, Father McGuire saved him, from the same impulse that earlier had made Mr Phiri avert his eyes from Cedric Pyne's tears over his calves. 'And now, please sit down, Mr Phiri. And I am so happy to have you here because I am an old friend of your father – did you know that? He was my pupil – yes, that chair there and Mr Mandizi . . .'

'He will do as he is told, and go and find out about my car.'

Rebecca, never looking at Mr Phiri, came forward to the table, cut two hefty slices of bread, put meat between them, and offered them to Mr Mandizi, with a little curtsy, which was far from mocking. 'You are not well,' she said to him. 'Yes, I can see you are not well.'

He did not reply, but stood with the sandwich in his hand.

'And what is wrong with you, Mr Mandizi?' said Mr Phiri.

Without replying, Mr Mandizi went out to the verandah where Sylvia met him, coming up from the hospital.

She put her hand on his arm, and was talking to him in a low persuasive voice.

From inside the room they heard, 'Yes, I am sick and my wife is sick too.'

Sylvia, with her arm around Mr Mandizi – he had lost so much weight it was easy – went with him to the car.

Father McGuire was talking, talking, pushing the meat plate towards his guest, the potatoes, the tomatoes. 'Yes, you must fill your plate, you must be so hungry, it has been a long time since breakfast and I too am hungry, and your father – is he well? He was my favourite pupil when I was teaching down at Guti. What a clever boy he was.'

Mr Phiri was sitting with his eyes closed, recovering. When he opened them, opposite him sat a small brown woman. Was she coloured? – no, that was the colour they went when they had too much sun, oh yes, she was the woman just now with Mr Mandizi. She was smiling at Rebecca. Was this smile a comment on him? Rage, which had been leaving him under the influence of the good beef and potatoes, returned, and he said, 'And are you the woman they tell me has been taking our school equipment for your lessons, so-called lessons?'

Sylvia looked at the priest, who was signalling to her, with a tightening of his lips to say nothing. 'Doctor Lennox has bought exercise books and an atlas with her own money, you need have no concern on that score, and now if you could give me news about your mother – she was my cook for a while, and I can say truly that I envy you with such a cook for a mother.'

'And what are those lessons you are giving our pupils? Are

you a teacher? Do you have a certificate? You are a doctor, not a teacher.'

Again, Father McGuire made it impossible for Sylvia to reply. 'Yes, this is our good doctor, she is a doctor and not a teacher, but there is no need for a teacher's certificate if you are reading to children, if you are teaching them to read.'

'Okay,' said Mr Phiri. He was eating with the nervous haste of one who uses food as a pacifier. He pulled the bread to him and cut a great slab: no *sadza*, but enough bread would do almost as well.

Rebecca suddenly chimed in: 'Perhaps the Comrade Inspector wants to come down and see how our people like what the doctor is doing, how she is helping us?'

Father McGuire managed to control severe irritation. 'Yes, yes,' he said. 'Yes, yes, yes. But on a hot day like this I am sure Mr Phiri would prefer to stay here with us in the cool and have a nice good strong cup of tea. Rebecca, please make the Inspector some tea.' Rebecca went out. Sylvia was about to tackle Mr Phiri about the missing exercise books and textbooks and the priest knew it, and he said, 'Sylvia, I am sure the Inspector would like to hear about the library you have made in the village?'

'Yes,' said Sylvia. 'We have about a hundred books now.'

'And who paid for them, may I ask?'

'The doctor has very kindly paid for them herself.'

'Indeed. And then I suppose we must be grateful to the doctor.' He sighed, and said, 'Okay,' and that was like a sigh.

'Sylvia, you haven't eaten anything.'

'I think I'll just have a cup of tea.'

In came Rebecca with the tea tray, set out the cups, the saucers, all very slow and deliberate, arranged the little net fly-shield with its beaded blue edge over the milk jug, and pushed the big teapot towards Sylvia. Normally, Rebecca poured the tea. She returned to the kitchen. The Inspector frowned after her, knowing there had been insolence, but he could not put his finger on it.

Sylvia poured, never lifting her gaze from what her hands

were doing. She put a cup near the Inspector, pushed the sugar bowl towards him, and sat making heaps of crumbs with her bread. A silence. Rebecca was humming out in the kitchen, one of the songs from the Liberation War, designed to annoy Mr Phiri, but he didn't seem to recognise it.

And now, luckily, there was the sound of a car, and then it had stopped, sending showers of dust everywhere. Out stepped the mechanic in his smart blue overalls. Mr Phiri got up. 'I see that my car is here,' he said vaguely, like someone who has lost something, but does not know what or where. He suspected that he had behaved in an improper manner, but surely not, when he had been in the right about everything.

'I do so hope you will tell your father and your mother that we met, and that I pray for them.'

'I will, when I do see them. They live out in the bush beyond the Pambili Growth Point. They are old now.'

He went out to the verandah. There were butterflies all over the hibiscus bushes. A lourie was making itself heard, half a mile away. He walked to his car, got in at the back, and the car drove off in rivers of dust.

Rebecca came in, and unusually for her, sat at the table with them. Sylvia poured her some tea. No one spoke for a while. Then, Sylvia said, 'I could hear that idiot shouting from the hospital. If I ever saw a candidate for a stroke, it is the Comrade Inspector.'

'Yes, yes,' said the priest.

'That was disgraceful,' said Sylvia. 'Those children, they have been dreaming of the Inspector for weeks. The Inspector will do this, he will do that, he will get us the books.'

Father McGuire said, 'Sylvia, nothing has happened.'

'What? How can you say . . .'

Rebecca said, 'Shame. It is a shame.'

'How can you be so reasonable about it, Kevin?' Sylvia did not often called the priest by his Christian name. 'It's a crime. That man is a criminal.'

'Yes, yes, yes,' said the priest. A pretty long silence. Then, 'Have you not ever thought that that is the story of our history? The powerful take the bread out of the mouths of the povos – the povos just get along somehow.'

'And the poor are always with us?' said Sylvia, sarcastic.

'Have you ever observed anything different?'

'And there is nothing to be done and it will all go on?'

'Probably,' said Father McGuire. 'What interests me is how you see it. You are always surprised when there is injustice. But that is how things always are.'

'But they were promised so much. At Liberation they were promised – well, everything.'

'So politicians make promises and break them.'

'I believed it all,' said Rebecca. 'I was a real fool, shouting and cheering at Liberation. I thought they meant it.'

'Of course they meant it,' said the priest.

'I think all our leaders went bad because we were cursed.'

'Oh, may the Lord save us,' said the priest, snapping at last. 'I will not sit to listen to such nonsense.' But he did not get up from the table.

'Yes,' said Rebecca. 'It was the war. It is because we did not bury the dead of the war. Did you know there are skeletons over there in the caves on the hills? Did you know that? Aaron told me. And you know that if we do not bury our dead according to our customs then they will come back and curse us.'

'Rebecca, you are one of the most intelligent women I know and . . .'

'And now there is AIDS. And that is a curse on us. What else can it be?'

Sylvia said, 'It's a virus, Rebecca, not a curse.'

'I had six children and now I have three and soon there will be two. And every day there is a new grave in the cemetery.'

'Did you ever hear of the Black Death?'

'How should I hear? I did not get beyond Standard One.'

This meant, that she had heard, knew more than she would let on, and wanted them to tell her.

'There was an epidemic, in Asia and in Europe and in North Africa. A third of the people died,' said Sylvia.

'Rats and fleas,' said the priest. 'They brought the disease.'

'And who told the rats where to go?'

'Rebecca, it was an epidemic. Like AIDS. Like Slim.'

'God is angry with us,' said Rebecca.

'May the Lord save us all,' said the priest. 'I'm getting too old, I'm going back to Ireland. I am going home.'

He was querulous, like an old man, in fact. And he did not look well either – in his case, at least, it could not be AIDS. He had had malaria again recently. He was tired out.

Sylvia began to cry.

'I'm going to get my head down for a few minutes,' said Father McGuire. 'And I know it is no use telling you to do the same.'

Rebecca went to Sylvia, lifted her, and the two went together to Sylvia's room. Rebecca let Sylvia slide down on her bed where she lay with a hand over her eyes. Rebecca knelt by the bed and slid her arm under Sylvia's head.

'Poor Sylvia,' said Rebecca, and crooned a child's song, a lullaby. The sleeve of Rebecca's tunic was loose. Just in front of her eyes, through her fingers, Sylvia could see the thin black arm, and on the arm a sore, of the kind she knew only too well. She had been dressing them on a woman down in the hospital that morning. The weeping child that Sylvia had been until that moment departed: the doctor returned. Rebecca had AIDS. Now that Sylvia knew, it was obvious, and she had known, without admitting it, for a long time now. Rebecca had AIDS and there was nothing that Sylvia could do about it. She shut her eyes, pretended to slide into sleep. She felt Rebecca gently withdraw herself and go out of the room.

Sylvia lay flat, listening to the iron roof crack in the heat. She looked at the crucifix, where the Redeemer hung. She looked at various Virgins in their blue robes. She took a glass rosary off its hook by her bed, and let it rest in her fingers: the glass of the beads was warm, like flesh. She hung it back.

Opposite her the Leonardo women filled half a wall. Fish moth had attacked the beautiful faces, the edges of the poster were lace, the children's chubby limbs were blotched.

Sylvia got herself out of that bed and went down to the village, where a great many disappointed people would be waiting for her.

Granddaughter of a notorious Nazi, daughter of a career communist, Sylvia Lennox has found a rural hideyhole in Zimlia, where she owns a private hospital, supplied by equipment stolen from the local government hospital.

The problem was, this ignorant country had not yet caught up with the fact that communism was politically incorrect, and then, the word Nazi did not get the reactions it did in London. A lot of people here liked the Nazis. There were only two epithets that could be guaranteed to get a reaction. One was 'racist', the other 'South African agent'.

Rose knew Sylvia was not a racist, but, since she was white, most blacks would be ready to say she was. But it needed only one letter in the *Post* from a black saying Sylvia was a friend of the blacks – no, but how about *spy*? That was tricky too. In that time just before apartheid collapsed, the spy fever in South Africa's neighbours was boiling over. Anyone who had been born in South Africa, or had lived there; who had gone there for a holiday recently; who had relations there; anyone criticising Zimlia for anything, or who suggested things might be better done; people who 'sabotaged' an enterprise or a business by losing or damaging equipment, such as a box of envelopes, or half a dozen screws – anyone at all who had become the focus of even mild disapproval, could be, and usually was, described as the agent of South Africa

– which of course was doing everything it could to destabilise its neighbours. So, in such an atmosphere, it was easy for Rose to believe that Sylvia was a South African spy, but when so many were, it was not enough.

Then Rose had a stroke of luck. A telephone call from Franklin's office invited her to a reception for the Chinese Ambassador, where the Leader would be present. At Butler's Hotel. At the best. Rose put on a dress and took herself there early. Already, after only a few weeks, if she was at a party for what she described to herself as the 'alternative crowd', she knew them all, at least to greet. Journalists, editors, the writers, the university people, the ex-pats, the NGOs – a mixed crowd, and a clever one, a quality she distrusted, since she always imagined people laughing at her – and it was still more white than black. They were informal, irreverent, hardworking, and most of them still full of faith in the future of Zimlia, though some were bitter and had lost faith. The other crowd, the one she would be with this evening, was where she felt at home – rulers and bosses, leaders and ministers, the ones with power, and more black than white.

Rose stood in a corner of the great room whose general style and elegance soothed her, telling her she was in the right place, and waited for Franklin to come in. She was being careful not to drink too much – yet. She would get drunk later. The room was filling, then it was full, and still no Franklin. She was standing next to a man whose face she knew from *The Post*. She was not going to say she was a London journalist, a breed so hated by this government, but said, 'Comrade Minister, it is an honour to be in your wonderful country. I am visiting here.'

'Okay,' said he, pleased, but certainly not ready to spend time on this unattractive white woman who was probably somebody's wife.

'Am I right in thinking of you as the Minister for Education?' said Rose, knowing he was not, and he replied, amiable but indifferent, 'No, as it happens the Under Minister for Health. Yes, I have the honour to be that.'

He was craning his head over and around the heads in front of him; he wanted to catch the eye of the Leader when he came in, who, while he was renowned throughout the world as a man of the people, gave his Ministers little chance to see him. At the rare cabinet meetings he appeared, made his views known and departed: not a comradely man, the Comrade Leader. The Under Minister had been for some time wanting an opportunity to discuss certain things with the Boss, hoped for even a few words tonight. Besides, he was secretly in love with the fascinating Gloria. Who was not? This big exuberant irrepressible sexy woman with her face like an invitation . . . where was she? Where were they, the Comrade President and the Mother of the Nation?

'I wonder if you know anything about a hospital in Kwadere?' Rose was saying – was repeating, for he had not heard her the first time. Now this was a solecism indeed. In the first place, at his level he could not be expected to know about individual hospitals, and then this was an official reception, it was not the place or the time. But as it happened he did know about Kwadere. The files had been on his desk that day, three hospitals, begun but not finished, because the funds had been – not to mince words – stolen. (No one could regret more than he did that these things happened, but then, one had to expect mistakes.) For two of the hospitals, angry and by now cynical donors had put forward a plan that if they, the original benefactors, raised half the necessary sums, then the government would have to match them. Otherwise, too bad, no go, goodbye hospitals. In Kwadere the original donor had sent a delegation out to the derelict hospital and then said, no, they did not propose to fund it. The trouble was, that hospital was badly needed. The government simply did not have the money. There was a sort of hospital, at St Luke's Mission, with a doctor, but a report had not been encouraging. The fact was it was embarrassing, that hospital, so poor and so backward: Zimlia expected better. And then there had been a report from the Security Services, saying the doctor's name was on a list of possible South African agents. Her father was a well-known communist, hand in glove with the Russians. Zimlia did not like the Russians, who had cold-shouldered Comrade Matthew when he was fighting – or rather, his troops were – in the bush. It was the Chinese that had supported Comrade Matthew. And here was the Chinese Ambassador now, with his wife, a tiny slice of a woman, both smiling away and shaking hands. He must move forward fast now, because where the Chinese Ambassador was, then that is where the Leader would be.

'You must excuse me,' he said to Rose.

'Please may I come and see you – perhaps in your office?'

'And what for, may I ask?' – said rudely enough.

Rose improvised: 'The doctor at the Kwadere hospital is – well, she is a cousin of mine and I heard that . . .'

'You heard right. Your cousin should be more careful with the company she keeps. I have it on reliable authority that she is working for – well, it doesn't matter who.'

'And – please, wait a minute, what is this about her stealing equipment from . . .'

He had heard nothing about this, and was annoyed with his advisers that he had not. The whole business was irritating, and he did not want to think about it. He had no idea how to solve the problem of the Kwadere hospital.

'What is this?' he said, turning to speak as he edged away into the crowd. 'If this is true then she will be punished, I can assure you, and I am sorry to hear she is related to you.'

And he went to where the lovely Gloria had appeared, in scarlet chiffon and a diamond necklace. Where was the Leader? But it appeared he was not coming, his wife was doing the honours.

Rose quietly left and went to a café that was always full of gossip and news. There she reported on the formal reception, on the Leader's absence, on the Mother of the Nation's red chiffon and diamonds, and the Under Minister's remarks about the Kwadere hospital. There was a Nigerian official, a woman, in Senga for the conference on the Wealth of Nations. Told about the spy at Kwadere, this woman said she had heard nothing but spies, spies, since she had arrived in Zimlia, and speaking from her experience in her own country, spies and wars were useful when things weren't going well with an economy. This provoked animated discussion, and soon everyone in the café was involved. One man, a journalist, had been arrested as a spy, but let go. Others knew people who were suspected of being agents and . . . Rose realised that now they would talk about South African agents all evening, and she slipped out and went to a little restaurant around the corner. Two men who had followed her from the café, though she had not noticed them, asked if she minded sharing her table: the place was full. Rose was hungry, a bit tight, and she rather liked these two men whom she found impressive in a hard-to-define way. Probably anyone in Zimlia would have seen at a glance that they were secret police, but to use that so useful formula, it has been so long since Britain was invaded that its citizens have a certain innocence. Rose was actually thinking that she must be looking attractive tonight. In most countries in the world, that is to say, those with an energetic secret service, it would have been instantly evident that with such men one should keep one's mouth shut. As for them, they wanted to find out about her; why had she left the café so precipitously when they started talking about spies?

'I wonder if you know anything about the mission hospital at Kwadere?' she chattered. 'I have a cousin working there, a doctor. I've just been speaking to the Under Minister for Health and he told me she is suspected of being a spy.'

The two men exchanged looks. They knew about the doctor at Kwadere, because they had her name on their list. They had not taken it particularly seriously. For one thing, what harm could she possibly do, stuck out there in the sticks? But if the Under Minister himself . . .

These two had not long been in the Service. They had got jobs because they were relatives of the Minister. They were not from pre-Liberation days. Most new States, even though enjoying a complete change of government, keep the Secret Service of the previous government, partly because they are impressed by the range and extent of the knowledge of these people who have so recently spied on them, and partly because a good few have secrets they do not want revealed. These men still had to make names for themselves, and needed to impress superiors.

'Has Zimlia ever had to expel someone for being an agent?' enquired Rose.

'Oh, yes, many times.'

This was not true, but it made them feel important, belonging to such stern and efficient service.

'Oh, really?' said Rose excitedly, scenting a story.

'One was called Matabele Smith.' The other amended, 'Matabele Bosman Smith.'

One evening, in the café Rose had just left, some journalists had joked about the spy rumours, and had invented a spy with a name that embodied as many unpleasant characteristics − to the present government's mind − as they could. (They had vetoed Whitesmith, on the analogy of Blacksmith.) This character was a South African frequently in Zimlia on business, and he had tried to blow up the coal mines at Hwange, Government House, the new sports stadium, and the airport. He had entertained the café for a few evenings, but they lost interest. Meanwhile he had reached the police files. In the café the name Matabele Bosman Smith became shorthand for the spy mania and the agents who frequented the place were hearing the name but could never actually find out more.

'And you deported him?' said Rose.

The two men were silent, exchanged glances again, then one said, 'Yes, we deported him.' And the other, 'We deported him back to South Africa.'

Next day Rose completed her paragraph about Sylvia with, 'Sylvia Lennox is known to have been a close friend of Matabele Bosman Smith who was deported as a South African spy.'

The general style and attack of this piece was right for the papers she liked to use as a receptacle for her inspirations in Britain, but she decided to show it to Bill Case, and then Frank Diddy. Both men knew the origin of the famous deportee, but did not tell her. They did not like her. She had long ago outstayed her welcome. Besides, they did like the idea of this famous Smith being injected with new life, to provide an evening or two's amusement in the café.

The piece was in *The Post*, which was not likely to notice one inflammatory paragraph among so many. She sent it to *World Scandals*, and it reached Colin, under the rule that if anything unpleasant is printed about one then it will be sent you by some well-wisher. Colin at once sued the paper for a hefty sum and an apology, but as is the way with such newspapers, the correction was put in tiny print where few people were likely to notice it. Julia was again branded as a Nazi; the suggestion that Sylvia was a spy seemed to Colin too ludicrous to bother with.

Father McGuire saw the paragraph in *The Post*, but did not show it to Sylvia. It found its way to Mr Mandizi, who put it in the file for St Luke's Mission.

Something happened that Sylvia had been dreading all the years she had been at the Mission. A girl who had acute appendicitis was carried up to her from the village by Clever and Zebedee. Father McGuire had taken the car to visit the Old Mission. Sylvia could not telephone the Pynes; either their telephone or the Mission's was not working. The girl needed an immediate operation. Sylvia had often imagined this emergency or something like it, and had decided that she would not operate. She could not. Simple – and successful – operations, yes, she could get away with that, but a fatality, no, they would be down on her at once.

The two boys in their crisp white shirts (ironed for them by Rebecca), with their perfectly combed hair, their scrubbed and scrubbed again hands, knelt on either side of the girl, inside the thatched shed that was called a hospital ward, and looked at her, their eyes filled with tears and brimming over.

'She's on fire, Sylvia,' said Zebedee. 'Feel her.'

Sylvia said, 'Why didn't she come up to me before? If we had caught this yesterday. Why didn't she? This happens again and again.' Her voice was tight, and rough, and it was from fear. 'Do you realise how serious this is?'

'We told her to come, we did tell her.'

It would not be her fault, if the girl died, but if she, Doctor Sylvia, operated and the girl died then it would be judged her fault. The two young faces, washed with tears, begged her, please, please. The girl was a cousin, and a relative too of Joshua.

'You know I am not a surgeon. I have told you, Clever, Zebedee, you know what that means.'

'But you must do it,' said Clever. 'Yes, Sylvia, please, please.'

The girl was pulling her knees up to her stomach and groaning.

'Very well, get me the sharpest of our knives. And some hot water.' She bent so her mouth was at the girl's ear. 'Pray,' she said. 'Pray to the Virgin.' She knew the girl was a Catholic: she had seen her at the little church. This immune system was going to need all the help it could get.

The boys brought the instruments. The girl was not on 'the operating table', because she should not be moved, but under the thatch, near the dust of the floor. Conditions for an operation could not have been worse.

Sylvia told Clever to hold the cloth she had soaked in chloroform (saved for an emergency) as far as possible from his own face, which he must turn aside. She told Zebedee to lift the basin with the instruments as high as he could from the floor, and began as soon as the girl's groans stopped. She was not attempting keyhole surgery, which she had described to the boys, but said, 'I am doing an old-fashioned cut. But when you do your training I think you'll find this kind of big cut will be obsolete – no one will be doing it. As soon as she cut, she knew she was too late. The appendix had burst and pus and foul matter were everywhere. She had no penicillin. Nevertheless she swabbed and mopped and then sewed the long cut shut. Then she said in a whisper to the boys, 'I think she will die.' They wept loudly, Clever with his head on his knees, Zebedee with his head on Clever's back.

She said, 'I am going to have to report what I have done.'

Clever whispered, 'We won't tell on you. We won't tell anyone.'

Zebedee grabbed her hands, which were bloody, and said, 'Oh, Sylvia, oh, Doctor Sylvia, will you get into trouble?'

'If I don't report it and they find out that you knew you will get into trouble too. I have to report it.'

She pulled up the little girl's skirt, and pulled down her blouse. She was dead. She was twelve years old. She said, 'Tell the carpenter we must have a coffin soon-soon.'

She went up to the house, found Father McGuire there, just back, and told him what had happened. 'I must tell Mr Mandizi.'

'Yes, I think you must. Don't I remember telling you that this might happen?'

'Yes, you did.'

'I will ring Mr Mandizi and ask him to come himself.'

'The telephone's not working.'

'I'll send Aaron on his bicycle.'

Sylvia went back to the hospital, helped to get the girl into her coffin, found Joshua where he was asleep under his tree, told him the girl was dead. The old man took time these days to absorb information: she did not want to wait to hear him curse her, which he was going to do – he always did, no necromancy was needed to foretell this – told the boys to say in the village she would not come that afternoon, but that they, Clever and Zebedee, would hear the people read, and correct their writing exercises.

At the house the priest was drinking tea. 'Sylvia, my dear, I think you should take a little holiday.'

'And what would that do?'

'Give it time to blow over.'

'Do you think it will blow over?'

He was silent.

'Where shall I go, Father? I feel now that this is my home. Until the other hospital is built these people need me here.'

'Let us see what Mr Mandizi says when he comes.'

These days Mr Mandizi was a friend, and it was a long time since he had been rude and suspicious, but what was coming was an official doing his duty.

When he came, there was nothing to know him by but his name. This was Mr Mandizi, he said he was, but really he was dreadfully ill.

'Mr Mandizi, should you not be in bed?'

'No, doctor. I can do my job. In my bed, there is my wife. She is very sick. Two of us, side by side – no, I do not think I would like that.'

'Did you have the tests done?'

He was silent, then sighed, then said, 'Yes, Doctor Sylvia, we had the tests.'

Rebecca brought in the meat, the tomatoes, the bread for lunch, saw the official and said, shocked, 'Shame, oh shame, Mr Mandizi.'

Since Rebecca was always thin and small and her face bony under her kerchief, he could not see she was ill, and so he sat there like the doomed man at the feast, surrounded by the healthy.

'I am so sorry, Mr Mandizi,' said Rebecca and went out to her kitchen, crying.

'And so now you must tell me everything, Doctor Sylvia.'

She told him.

'Would she have died if you didn't operate?'

'Yes.'

'Was there a chance of saving her?'

'A bit of a chance. Not much. You see, I don't have penicillin, it ran out and . . .'

He made the movement of his hand she knew so well: don't criticise me for things I can't help. 'I shall have to tell the big hospital.'

'Of course.'

'They will probably want a post mortem.'

'They will have to be quick. She is in her coffin. Why don't you just say it was my fault. Because I am not a surgeon.'

'Is it a difficult operation?'

'No, one of the easy ones.'

'Would a real surgeon have done anything different?'

'Not much, no, not really.'

'I don't know what to say, Doctor Sylvia.'

It was clear he wanted to say more. He sat with his eyes lowered, glanced up at her, doubtfully, then looked at the priest. Sylvia could see they knew something she didn't.

'What is it?' she said.

'Who is this friend of yours, Matabele Bosman Smith?'

'Who?'

Mr Mandizi sighed. He sat with his untouched food in front of him. So did Sylvia. The priest ate steadily, frowning. Mr Mandizi rested his head on his hand, and said, 'Doctor Sylvia, I know there is no *muti* for what I have, but I am getting these headaches, headaches, I didn't know there could be headaches like these.'

'I have something for your headaches. I'll give you the pills before you go.'

'Thank you, Doctor Sylvia. But I have to say something . . . there is something . . .' Again, he glanced at the priest, who nodded reassurance. 'They are going to close down your hospital.'

'But these people need this hospital.'

'There will be our new hospital soon . . .' Sylvia brightened, saw that the official was only cheering himself up, and she nodded.

'Yes, there will be one I am sure of it,' said Mr Mandizi. 'Yes, that is the situation.'

'Okay,' said Sylvia.

'Okay,' said Mr Mandizi.

A week later arrived a short typewritten letter addressed to Father McGuire, instructing him to close down the hospital 'as from this date'. On the same morning a policeman arrived on a motorbike. He was a young black man, perhaps twenty, or twenty-one, and he was ill at ease in his authority. Father McGuire asked him to sit down, and Rebecca made them tea.

'And now, my son, what can I do for you?'

'I am looking for stolen property.'

'Now I understand. Well, you won't find any in this house.' Rebecca stood by the sideboard. She said nothing. The policeman said to her, 'Perhaps I will come with you to your house and look around for myself.'

Rebecca said, 'We have seen the new hospital. There are bush pig living in it.'

'I too have visited the new hospital. Yes, bush pig, and I think baboons too.' He laughed, stopped himself, and sighed. 'But there is a hospital here, I think, and my orders are that I must see it.'

'The hospital is closed.' The priest pushed over the official letter, the policeman read it, and said, 'If it is closed, then I do not see any problem.'

'That is my opinion too.'

'I think I must discuss this situation with Mr Mandizi.'

'That is a good idea.'

'But he is not well. Mr Mandizi is not well and I think we shall soon have a replacement.' He got up, not looking at Rebecca, whose house he knew he ought to be investigating. Off he went, his bike roaring and coughing through the peaceful bush.

Meanwhile Sylvia was supposed to be closing down her hospital.

There were patients in the beds, and Clever and Zebedee were doling out medicines.

She said to the priest, 'I am going in to Senga to see Comrade Minister Franklin. He was a friend. He came to us for holidays. He was Colin's friend.'

'Ah. Nothing more annoying than the people who knew you before you were Comrade Minister.'

'But I'm going to try.'

'Wouldn't you perhaps think to put on a nice clean dress?'

'Yes, yes.' She went into her room and emerged in her going-to-town outfit, in green linen.

'And perhaps you should take a nightdress or whatever you need for the night?'

Again she went into her room and emerged with a hold-all.

'And now shall I ring the Pynes and ask if they plan a trip to Senga?'

Edna Pyne said she would be glad of an excuse to get away from the bloody farm, and was over in half an hour. Sylvia jumped into the seat beside her, waved at Father McGuire, 'See you tomorrow.' And so did Sylvia leave for what would be an absence of weeks.

Edna kept up her complaints all the way into town, and then said she had something shocking to tell, she shouldn't be mentioning it but she had to. Cedric had been approached by one of those crooks to say that in return for giving up his farms 'now-now' a sum amounting to a third of their value would arrive in his bank account in London.

Sylvia took this in, and laughed.

'Exactly, laugh. That's all we can do. I tell Cedric, just take it, and let's get out. He says he's not accepting a third of the value. He wants to stick out for the full value. He says the new dam alone will put up the value of the new farm by a half. I just want to get out. What I can't stand, is the bloody hypocrisy. They make me sick.' And so Edna Pyne chattered all the way in to Senga where she dropped Sylvia outside the government offices.

When Franklin was told that Sylvia Lennox wanted to see him he panicked. While he had thought she 'might try something on', he did not expect it so soon. He had signed the order to close the hospital a week ago. He temporised: 'Tell her I am in a meeting.' He sat behind his desk, his hands palms down in front of him, staring dolefully at the wall which had on it the portrait of the Leader which adorned all the offices in Zimlia.

When he thought of that house he had gone to for his holidays, in north London, it was as if he had touched some blessed place, like a shady tree, that had no connection with anything before or since. It had been home when he felt homeless, kindness when he had longed for it. As for the old woman, he had seen her, like an old secretary bird going in and out, but he had scarcely noticed her, this terrible Nazi. But he had never heard any Nazi talk in that house, surely? And there had been little Sylvia, with her shining wisps of gold hair, and her angel's face. As for Rose Trimble, when he thought of her he found himself grinning; a proper little crook, well he had benefited, so he shouldn't complain. And now she had written that nasty piece . . . surely she had been a guest in that house, like him? Yet she had been there much longer than he had, and so what she wrote had to be taken seriously. But what he remembered was welcome, laughter, good food, and Frances, in particular, like a mother. Later, when it was Johnny's place he stayed at, now that was a different thing. It wasn't a large flat, nothing like that great house where Colin had been so kind, yet it was always crammed with people from everywhere, Americans, Cubans, other countries in South America, Africa . . . It was an education in revolution, Johnny's flat. He remembered at least two black men (with false names) from this country who were training in Moscow for guerilla war. And the guerilla war had been won, and he owed his sitting here, behind this desk, a senior Minister, to men like those. While he kept an eye out for them, at rallies and big meetings, he had never seen them since.

434

Presumably they were dead. Now something confusing was happening. He knew what was being said about the Soviet Union, he was not one of the innocents who never left Zimlia. The word communist was becoming something like a curse: elsewhere, not here, where you had only to say *Marxism* to feel you were getting a good mark from the ancestors. (And where were they in all this?) A funny thing: he felt that that house in London had more in common with the ease and warmth of his grandparents' huts in the village (as it happened not all that far from St Luke's Mission) than anything since. And yet in the file on his desk was that nasty piece. He was feeling with every minute deeper resentment – against Sylvia. Why had she done those bad things? She had stolen goods from the new hospital, she had done operations when she shouldn't, and she had killed a patient. What did she expect him to do now? Well what *did* she expect? That hospital of hers, it had never had any real legal existence. The Mission decides to start a hospital, brings in a doctor, nothing in the files recorded permissions being asked or given . . . these white people, they come here, they do as they like, they haven't changed, they still . . .

He sent out for sandwiches for lunch, in case Sylvia was hanging about somewhere waiting to catch him, and when Sylvia's second request arrived, 'Please, Franklin, I must see you', scribbled on an envelope – who did she think she was, treating him like this – he ordered that she must be told he had been called away on urgent business.

He went to the window, and lifted the slats of the blind and there was Sylvia walking down there. Passionate accusations which he might reasonably have directed against Life Itself were focused on Sylvia's back with an intensity that surely she should have felt: little Sylvia, that little angel, as fresh and bright in his memory as a saint on a Holy Card, but she was a middle-aged woman with dry dull hair tied by black ribbon, no different from any of these white wrinkled madams whom he tried not to look at, he disliked them so much. He felt Sylvia had betrayed him. He actually wept

435

a little, standing there holding up the slat and watching the green blob that was Sylvia merge into the pavement crowd.

Sylvia walked straight into a tall distinguished gentleman who took her in his arms and said, 'Darling Sylvia'. It was Andrew, and he was with a girl in dark glasses with a very red mouth, smiling at her. Italian? Spanish?

'This is Mona,' said Andrew. 'We've got married. And I am afraid the ramshackle streets of Senga are a shock to her.'

'Nonsense, darling, I think it's cute.'

'American,' said Andrew. 'And she's a famous model. And as beautiful as the day, as you can see.'

'Only when I have all my paint on,' said Mona and excused herself saying she must lie down, she was sure they had a lot to talk about.

'The altitude is getting to her,' said Andrew, solicitously kissing her and waving her off into Butler's Hotel, a few steps away.

Sylvia was surprised to hear that 6,000 feet was considered altitude, but did not care: this was her Andrew and now she was going to sit and talk to him, so he said, in that café there. And there they went, and held hands, while fizzy drinks arrived and Andrew demanded to know everything about her.

She had opened her mouth to begin, thinking that here was one of the important men in the world, and that surely the little matter of the closing of the hospital at St Luke's could be reversed by a word from him, when a group of very well-dressed people filled the café, and he greeted them and they him and a lot of badinage began about this conference they were all attending here, in Senga. 'It's quite the coolest new place for conferences, but it's not exactly Bermuda,' someone said.

Sylvia did know that Senga was being touted as just the place for any sort of international get together, and, seeing these bright clever smart people, understood how much she had slid away, in the stark exigencies of Kwadere, from being able to take part in this talk.

Andrew continued to hold her hand, smiled at her often, then said perhaps this was not the place to have a chat. More delegates crowded in, joking at the café's smallness, which was somehow being equated with Zimlia's lack of sophistication, and these experts on absolutely everything you can think of, in this particular case, 'The Ethics of International Aid', sounded rather like children comparing the merits of parties their respective parents had recently given. There was so much noise, laughter and enjoyment that Sylvia begged Andrew to be allowed to leave. But he said she must come to the dinner tonight: 'There's the big end of conference dinner, and you must come.'

'I don't have a dress.'

He gave her a frank once-over, making allowances, and said, 'But it's not evening dress, you'll do.'

And now she had to find somewhere to spend the night. She had come away without enough money: had come away, she saw now, inefficiently, in an unplanned and foolish way. It was all a bit of a haze: she remembered Father McGuire taking command. Had she been a bit sick, perhaps? Was she now? She didn't feel herself, whatever that meant, for if she was not the Doctor Sylvia everyone knew at her hospital, who was she?

She rang Sister Molly, who was in, and asked to stay the night. Sylvia took a taxi there, was welcomed, and heard a good deal of on the whole good-natured mockery of the conference on the Ethics of International Aid, and all similar conferences.

'They talk,' said Sister Molly. 'They get paid to travel to some beauty spot and talk nonsense you'd not believe.'

'I'd hardly call Senga a beauty spot.'

'That is true, but they are off every day to see the lions and the giraffes and the dear little monkeys and I don't think they notice that the land is perishing from the drought.'

Sylvia told Molly about the dinner, said she had only what she had on, heard that it was a pity Molly was at least four sizes larger than Sylvia, who could otherwise borrow her one and only dress but as it was she personally would see to it that the suit was cleaned and ready by six o'clock. Having forgotten these amenities of real civilisation, Sylvia was perhaps disproportionately moved, and took off her suit, lay down on her little iron bed, just like the one she had at the Mission, and was asleep. Sister Molly stood over her for a while, the green suit folded over her arm, her face shedding beams of benevolent enquiry, judicious and experienced: after all, she did spend her life assessing people and situations from one end of Zimlia to the other. She did not like what she saw. Bending closer she checked up on this and that feature, sweaty brow, dry lips, flushed face, and lifted Sylvia's hand to look at the wrist where visibly pounded an intemperate pulse.

When Sylvia woke, her suit, nicely pinned and presented, hung on the door. On the chair was a selection of knickers, and a silk slip. 'I got too fat for these ages ago.' Also some smart shoes. Sylvia washed dust out of her hair, got dressed, put on the shoes, hoping she could still manage heels, and took a taxi to Butler's. She suspected she was feverish, but because it would be so inconvenient to be ill, decided she wasn't.

Outside Butler's the international crowd stood chatting, waving to each other, resuming conversations that might have been interrupted in Bogota or Benares. Andrew was waiting for Sylvia, on the steps. Mona was beside him in a pink floaty dress that made her look like one of the species tulips, jagged petals, that seemed cut out of crystallised light. Sylvia knew Andrew was anxious about how she might look, for if evening dress was not obligatory then none of the women was less smart than Mona. But his smile said, You're all right, and he took her arm. The three went to the staircase which was grand enough for a film set, though in the best possible taste. It delivered them to a terrace where little flowering trees and a fountain filled the dusk with freshness. Lights from inside picked out a face, the dazzle of a white suit, the flash of a necklace. People greeted Andrew: how popular he was, this handsome and distinguished grey-haired gentleman, who must deserve the glamorous girl with him, since the *fait accompli* of the marriage proved he did.

When they went into dinner it was a private room, but large

enough for the hundred or so guests, and what a delightful room it was, achieving what its designers had intended, that the privileged people who used it would not be able to say whether they were in Benares or Bogota or Senga.

Sylvia knew some faces from this morning in the café, but at others she had to look and look again . . . yes, Good Lord, there was Geoffrey Bone, as handsome as ever, and beside him the incendiary head, now subdued to a well-brushed russet, of Daniel, his shadow. And there was James Patton. For some people you have to wait decades before understanding what Nature has intended for them all along: in this case he had reached his culmination as man of the people, affable and amiable, comfily rotund, his right hand ever at the ready to reach out and clasp whatever flesh presented itself. There he was, a Member of Parliament in a safe Labour seat, and on this occasion a guest of Caring International, at Geoffrey's invitation. And Jill . . . yes, Jill, a large woman with a greyish coiffure, senior councillor in a London borough notorious for its mismanagement of funds, though the word corrupt could never, surely, be associated with this solid citizen whose police-bashing, rioting, American-Embassy-storming days were so long behind one could be pretty sure she had forgotten them or was murmuring, Oh, yes, I was a bit of a Red once.

Sylvia had not been put next to Andrew who was at the head of the table, flanked by two important South Americans, but beside Mona, some places away. Sylvia knew she was as invisible as an anonymous little brown bird next to a displaying peacock, for people looked so often at Mona whose name everyone knew if they followed fashion at all. And why was Mona here? She said to Sylvia that she was attending the conference as Andrew's personal assistant, and congratulated Sylvia, giggling, on her new status as Andrew's assistant secretary, which is how she was being described when introduced. Sylvia was able to sit quietly and observe, and imagine how Clever and Zebedee would look in these attractive uniforms, scarlet and white and so striking on the black skins of the smiling waiters. She knew, very well, how these youths had had to work, intrigue, beg for these jobs, and how their parents had sacrificed for them, so they could serve these international stars with food most of them had never heard of until coming to this hotel.

Sylvia was offered the choice of crocodile tails, in pink mayonnaise, and palm hearts imported from South East Asia, and all the time her heart was weeping, yes it was, a quiet wailing went on inside her, as she sat there beside Andrew's beautiful bride. It would not last, this marriage, you had only to look how they presented themselves, with the sleek complacency of well-fed cats, to know that she had said yes to Andrew probably for no better reason than she enjoyed saying, 'I have always liked older men,' to annoy younger ones, and he, who had not been married and had had to suffer the usual rumours, although he had been the 'friend' of a dozen well-known women, had finally needed to show his colours and make his statement, and he had, for here she was, his child bride.

Sylvia looked around, and despaired, and thought of her hospital, closed while people in the village were ill or had broken limbs or . . . there were never less than thirty or forty people a day needing help; she thought of the lack of water, the dust, the AIDS, she could not prevent all these stale old thoughts, which have been thought too often, and to no purpose. She imagined Clever and Zebedee's faces, disconsolate because they had dreamed of being doctors . . . how badly she had managed everything, she must have, for it all to end like this.

Mona was chatting to the man on her left about her poverty-stricken origins in a slum in Quito: she had been noticed by a visiting delate to a conference on the Costumes of the World. She was confiding to him that Zimlia was the pits, she saw too much on the streets to remind her of what she had escaped from. 'Basically, what I like is Manhattan. It has everything, hasn't it? I don't see why anyone should ever leave it.'

Now everyone was talking about the annual conference due

soon, with two hundred delegates from all over the world, which would last a week, with a keynote speech on 'The Perspectives and Implications of Poverty'. Where should it be held? The delegate from India, a handsome woman in a scarlet sari, suggested Sri Lanka, though they would have to be careful because of the terrorists, but there was no more beautiful place in the world. Geoffrey Bone said he had spent three nights in Rio for a conference on the World's Threatened Ecostructure, and there was a hotel there ... but, said a Japanese gentleman, the last annual conference had been in South America, and there was a fine hotel in Bali, that part of the world should have the honour. Talk about hotels and their attractions went on for most of the meal, and the consensus was it was time they favoured Europe, how about Italy, though probably strict policing would be essential, because they were all of them luscious targets for kidnappers.

In the event, they were all to go to Cape Town, because South Africa's apartheid was just about to disappear, and they wished to show their approval of Mandela.

Coffee was served in an adjacent room, where Andrew made a speech as it were dismissing them all, but saying how much he looked forward to seeing them again next month in New York – a conference; and then Geoffrey, Daniel, Jill and James came to Sylvia to say they had not recognised her, and how lovely it was to see her. The smiling faces told Sylvia how shocked they were at what they saw. 'You were such a beautiful little thing,' Jill confided. 'Oh, no, I'm not saying . . . but I used to think you were like a little fairy.'

'And look at me now.'

'And look at me. Well, conferences don't do much for one's figure.'

'You could try dieting,' said Geoffrey, who was as thin as ever.

'Or a health farm,' said James. 'I go to a health farm every year. I have to. Too many temptations in the House of Commons.'

'Our bourgeois forebears went to Baden Baden or Marienbad

to lose the fat accumulated in a year of over-eating,' said Geoffrey.

'Your forebears,' said James. 'I am the grandson of a grocer.'

'Oh, well done,' said Geoffrey.

'And my grandfather was a surveyor's clerk,' said Jill.

'And mine was a farm labourer in Dorset,' said James.

'Congratulations,' said Geoffrey. 'You win. None of us can compete with that.' And off he went, with a wave of his hand to Sylvia, Daniel just behind him.

'He was always such a poseur,' said Jill.

'I would have said a pouf,' said James.

'Now, now, the least we can expect here is political correctness.'

'You can expect what you like. As far as I am concerned, political correctness is just another little sample of American imperialism,' said the man of the people.

'Discuss,' said Jill.

And, discussing, they went off.

On the steps of Butler's, Rose Trimble agitatedly hovered, in a smart outfit bought in the hope Andrew would invite her to the dinner: but he had not answered her messages.

Jill appeared and ignored Rose, who had described her Council as a disgrace to the principles and ideals of democracy.

'I was only doing my job,' said Rose to Jill's back.

Then, cousin James, whose face hardened: 'What the hell are you doing here? Short of muck in London?' And he pushed her aside.

When Andrew came down the steps with Mona and Sylvia, he at once said, 'Oh, Rose, how utterly delightful to see you.'

'Didn't you get my messages?'

'Did you send me messages?'

'Give me a quote, Andrew. How did the conference go?'

'I am sure it will all be in the papers tomorrow.'

'And this is Mona Moon – oh, do give me a quote, Mona. How is married life?'

Mona did not reply, and went on with Andrew. Rose did not

recognise Sylvia, or rather only much later thought that boring little thing must have been Sylvia.

Abandoned, she said bitterly to the delegates who were streaming past, 'The bloody Lennoxes. They were my *family*.'

Sylvia was embraced by Andrew, kissed prettily by Mona and put into a taxi: they were off to a party.

Sister Molly's house was dark and locked. Sylvia had to ring and ring again. The snap of locks, the grind of chains, the click of keys, and Molly stood there in a blue baby-doll nightdress, the silver cross sliding over her breasts. 'Sorry, we all have to live in a fortress these days.'

Sylvia went to her room, carefully, as if she might spill about like a jelly. She felt she had eaten too much and knew wine didn't suit her. She was light-headed, and trembled. Sister Molly stood watching as she lowered herself to her bed and flopped.

'Better take that off,' and Molly pulled off an outer layer of linen and shoes and stockings. 'There. I thought so. When did you last have malaria?'

'Oh – a year ago – I think.'

Then you have it now. Lie still. You have the devil of a temperature.'

'It'll go.'

'Not by itself, it won't.'

And so Sylvia went through her bout of malaria, which was not the bad kind, cerebral, which is so dangerous, but it was bad enough and she shivered and she shook, and swallowed her pills – back to the old-fashioned quinine, since the new ones were not working with her – and when she was finally herself, Sister Molly said, 'That was a go, if you like. But I see you are with us again.'

'Please telephone Father McGuire and tell him.'

'Who do you take us for? Of course I rang him weeks ago.'

'*Weeks?*'

'You've had it bad. Mind you, I'd say it was malaria plus, a bit of a collapse generally. And you're anaemic, for a start. And you have to eat.'

'What did Father McGuire say?'

'Oh, don't you worry. Everything's going on as usual.'

In fact, Rebecca had died, and so had her sick boy Tenderai. The two children who stayed alive had been taken away by the sister-in-law whom Rebecca suspected of poisoning her. It was too early to tell Sylvia the bad news.

Sylvia ate, she drank what seemed to be gallons of water, and she went to the bath, where the sweats of the fever were finally swilled away. She was weak but clear-headed. She lay flat on her little iron bed and told herself that the fever had shaken foolishness out of her that she could well do without. One thing was Father McGuire: through difficult times she had been telling herself that Father McGuire was a saint, as if that justified everything, but now she was thinking, Who the hell am I, Sylvia Lennox, to go on and on about who is a saint and who isn't?

She said to Sister Molly, 'I have understood that I am not a Catholic, not a real one, and I probably never was.'

'Is that so? So you either are or you aren't. So it is a Protestant you are, after all? Well, I have to confess to you that in my view the good God has better things to do than worry about our little squabbles, but never tell them I said that, in Belfast – I don't want to find myself knee-capped when I go on leave next.'

'I have been suffering from the sin of pride, I know that.'

'I daresay. Aren't we all? But I'm surprised Kevin never mentioned it if you are. He's a great one for the sin of pride.'

'I expect he did.'

'Well, then, and now take it easy. When you are strong enough, give some thought to what you are going to do next. We have suggestions for you.'

And so Sylvia lay and took it in that she was not expected back at the Mission. And what was happening to Clever and Zebedee?

She telephoned. Their voices, so young, desperate: Help me, help us.

'When are you coming? Please come.'

'Soon, as soon as I can.'

'Now Rebecca's not here, things are so hard . . .'

'What?'

And so she heard the news. And lay on her bed and did not weep, it was too bad for that.

Sylvia lay propped up on her bed, absorbing nourishing potions while Sister Molly, hands on her hips, stood smiling, watching forcibly while Sylvia ate, and all day and as far into the night as was possible for Zimlia's early-rising citizens, came people of the kind Andrew Lennox, or the tourists or visiting relatives or people who under the white government had not been welcome, never met. And Sylvia had not met them either until now.

She was being made to reflect that while places like Kwadere existed in Zimlia, far too many of them, perhaps her experiences had been as narrow in their way as those of people who would not have believed that villages like St Luke's Mission could exist. After all, there were schools that actually taught their pupils, which had at least some exercise books and textbooks, hospitals that had equipment and surgeons and even research laboratories. It was her nature that had seen to it that she was in as poor a place as possible: she understood that as clearly as she did that fretting over her degrees of faith or lack of it was absurd.

On a level far from the embassies or the lounges of Butler's Hotel, or the trade fairs, or the corrupt bosses at the top (referred to by Sister Molly as 'chocolate cake') were people who ran organisations with small budgets, sometimes funded by single individuals, who accomplished more with their money than Caring International or Global Money could dream of, and who laboured in difficult places to achieve a library, a shelter for abused women, provision for a small business, or provided small loans of a size that ordinary banks must despise. They were black and they were white, Zimlian citizens or ex-pats, forming a layer of energetic optimism which spread up to embrace minor officials and lower civil servants, for there has never been a country that relied so much on its minor officials, who are competent, not corrupt, and hard-working. Unsung they are, and mostly unnoticed. But anyone who understood, would go for help to some comparatively lowly office run by a man or a woman who, if there were any justice, would be openly running the country, and who in fact were what everything depends on. Sister Molly's house and a dozen like it formed a layer or web of sane people. Politics were not discussed, not because of principle but because of the nature of the people involved: in some countries politics are the enemy of commonsense. If the Comrade Leader was mentioned at all, or his corrupt cronies, it was as one talks about the weather – something that had to be put up with. A great disappointment, the Comrade President, but what's new?

Sylvia was being presented with a dozen possibilities for her future. She was a doctor, people knew she had created a hospital in the bush where none had existed. She had fallen foul of the government, too bad, but Zimlia was not the only country in Africa.

A sentence in our textbooks goes something like this: 'In the latter part of the nineteenth century, and until the First World War, the Great Powers fought over Africa like dogs over a bone.' What we read less often is that Africa, considered as a bone, was not less fought over for the rest of the twentieth century, though the dog packs were not the same.

A youngish doctor, a native of Zimlia (white), had returned recently from the wars in Somalia. He sat on the hard upright chair in Sylvia's room and listened while she talked compulsively (Sister Molly said this was a self-cure) of the fate of the people at St Luke's Mission, dying of AIDS, and apparently invisible to the government. She talked for hours and he listened. And then he talked, as compulsively, and she listened.

Somalia had been part of the sphere of influence of the Soviet Union, which set up its usual apparatus of prisons, torture chambers and death squads. Then by a smart little piece of international legerdemain, Somalia became American, swapped for another bit of Africa. Naive citizens hoped and expected that the Americans would dismantle the apparatus for Security and set them free, but they had not learned that lesson, so essential for our times, that there is nothing more stable than this apparatus. Marxists and communists of various persuasions who had flourished under the Russians, torturing and imprisoning and killing their enemies, now found themselves being tortured and imprisoned and killed. The once reasonable enough State of Somalia, was as if boiling water had been poured into an ants' nest. The structure of decent living was destroyed. Warlords and bandits, tribal chiefs and family bosses, criminals and thieves, now ruled. The international aid organisations, stretched to their limits, could not cope, particularly because large parts of the country were barred to them by war.

The doctor sat for hours on his hard chair and talked, because he had been watching people kill each other for months. Just before he left he had stood on the side of a track through a landscape dried to dust, watching refugees from famine file past. It is one thing to see it on television, as he said (trying to excuse his garrulousness), while he stared at her, but not seeing her, seeing only what he was describing, and it was another thing to be there. Perhaps Sylvia was as equipped as most to visualise what he was telling her, because she had only to set in her mind along that dusty track two thousand miles to the north people from the dying village in Kwadere. But he had watched, too, refugees fleeing from the killing troops of Mengistu, some of them hacked and bleeding, some dying, some carrying murdered children: he had watched that for days, and Sylvia's experience did not match with it and so it was hard to see it. And besides there was no television in Father McGuire's house.

He was a doctor, and he had watched, helpless, people in

need of medicines, a refuge, surgery, and all he had had to aid them had been a few cartons of antibiotics which had disappeared in a few minutes.

The world is now full of people who have survived wars, genocide, drought, floods, and none of them will forget what they have experienced, but there are, too, the people who have watched: to stand for days seeing a people stream past in thousands, hundreds of thousands, a million, with nothing in your hands, well, this doctor had been there and done that, and his eyes were haunted and his face was stricken, and he could not stop talking.

A woman doctor from the States wanted Sylvia for Zaire, but asked was Sylvia up to it – it was pretty tough up there, and Sylvia said she was fine, she was very strong. She also said that she had performed an operation without being a surgeon but both doctors were amused: in the field, doctors not surgeons did what they could. 'Short of transplant operations, and I wouldn't actually go in for a by-pass.'

In the end she agreed to go to Somalia, as part of a team financed by France. Meanwhile she had to go back to the Mission to see Zebedee and Clever, whose voices when she spoke to them over the telephone sounded like the cries of birds caught in a storm. She did not know what to do. She described these two boys, now no longer children, but adolescents, to Sister Molly and to the doctors, and knew that one, who saw children like these every day of her working life, thought that both were destined for future unemployment (but she would keep a look out, perhaps they could be found work as servants?), and the others, with their minds full of starving thousands, endless lines of poor victims, could only with difficulty bend their imaginations to think of two unfortunates who had dreamed of being doctors but now . . . So what's new?

*   *   *

Sister Molly had to drive out fifty miles beyond Kwadere to resume work interrupted by Sylvia's illness. She had arranged that Aaron would collect Sylvia from the turn-off. Her complaints about the Pope and the churchly male hierarchy were interrupted by the sight of six great grain silos along the road whose contents – last season's maize – had been sold off by a senior Minister to another drought-ridden African country, the proceeds pocketed by himself. They were driving through hungry country; for miles in every direction stretched bush dry and starved because of the overdue rainy season.

'I wouldn't like to have his conscience,' said Sylvia, and Sister Molly said that it seemed some people had not yet understood that there were people born without consciences. This set Sylvia off on her monologue about the village at the Mission, and Sister Molly listened, saying, 'Yes, that is so,' and, 'You are in the right of it there.' At the turn-off Aaron was waiting in the Mission car. Sister Molly said to Sylvia, 'Well, that's it, then. I expect I'll see you around.' And Sylvia said, 'Fine. And I'll never forget what you've done for me.' 'Forget it.' And off she drove with a wave of the hand that was like a door shutting.

Aaron was vivacious, eager, on the verge of a new life: he was going to the Old Mission to continue his studies to become a priest. Father McGuire was leaving. Everyone was leaving. And the library? 'I am afraid the books are not many now, because you see, with Tenderai dead, and Rebecca dead and you not here, who was to look after them?'

'And Clever and Zebedee?'

Aaron had never liked them, nor they him, and all he said was, 'Okay.'

He parked the car under the gum trees and went off. It was late afternoon, the light going fast from gold and pink clouds. On the other side of the sky a half moon, a mere whitish smear, was waiting to acquire dignity when the dark came.

As she arrived on the verandah the two lads came running. They stopped. They stared. Sylvia did not know what was wrong.

While ill she had lost her sunburn, had become white as milk, and her hair, cut off because of the sweats, was in wisps and fronds of yellow. They had only known her as a friendly and comfortable brown. 'It is so wonderful to see you' – and they came rushing at her, and she put her arms around them. There was much less substance to them than she was used to.

'Isn't anyone feeding you?'

'Yes, yes. Doctor Sylvia,' they hugged her and wept. But she knew they had fed badly. And the bright white shirts were dingy with dirt because Rebecca was not there to do them. Their eyes through the tears said, Please, please.

Father McGuire arrived, asked if they had eaten and they said yes. But he took a loaf from the sideboard, and they tore it in half and ate hungrily as they went down to the village: they would return at sunrise.

Sylvia and the priest sat in their places at the table, the single electric lightbulb telling him how sick she had been, and she that he was an old man.

'You'll see the new graves on the hill, and there are new orphans. I and Father Thomas – he's the black priest at the Old Mission – we're going to set up a refuge for the AIDS orphans. We've got funding from Canada, God reward them, but Sylvia, have you thought that there will be perhaps a million children without parents, the way we are going?'

'The Black Death destroyed whole villages. When they take pictures of England from the air they can see where the villages were.'

'This village will not be here soon. They are leaving because they say the place is cursed.'

'And do you tell them what they should be thinking, Father?'

'I do.'

The electric light suddenly failed. The priest lit a couple of emergency candles, and they ate their supper by their light, served by Rebecca's niece, a strong and healthy young woman – well, she was now – who had come to help her dying aunt, and she would leave when the priest left.

'And I hear there's a new headmaster at last?'

'Yes, but you see, Sylvia, they don't like coming out to these far-out places, and this one's already had his problems with the drink.'

'I see.'

'But he has a big family and he will have this house.'

They both knew there was more to be said, and at last he asked, 'And now, what are you going to do with those boys?'

'I should not have set up their expectations and I did. Though I never actually promised them anything.'

'Ah, but it is the great wonderful rich world there that is the promise.'

'And so, what should I do?'

'You must take them with you to London. Send them to a real school. Let them learn doctoring. God knows this poor country will be needing its doctors.'

She was silent.

'Sylvia, they are healthy. Their father died before there was AIDS. Joshua's real children will die, but not these two. He's waiting to see you, by the way.'

'I am surprised he is still alive.'

'He is alive only to see you. And he is quite mad now. You must be prepared for that.'

Before giving her a candle to take to her room, he held his high to look into her face, and said, 'Sylvia, I know you very well, my child. I know you are blaming yourself for everything.'

'Yes.'

'It is a long time since you have asked me to confess you, but I do not need to hear what you have to say. In the state of mind you are in, when you are low from the illness, you must not trust what you are thinking about yourself.'

'The devil lurks in the absence of red corpuscles.'

'The devil lurks where there is bad health – I hope you are taking your iron pills.'

'And I am trusting you to take yours.'

They embraced, both needing to weep, and turned away to go to their rooms. He was leaving early, and said he probably wouldn't see her, meaning he didn't want to go through another parting. He was not going to say, like Sister Molly: See you around.

Next morning he was gone: Aaron had taken him to the turn-off where he would be picked up by the Old Mission's car.

Zebedee and Clever were waiting for Sylvia on the path to the village. Half the huts were empty. A starving dog was nosing about in the dust. The hut where Tenderai had looked after the books stood open, and the books had gone.

'We tried to look after them, we tried.'

'Never mind.'

The village before she had left had been afflicted, it had been threatened, but it had been alive: now its spirit had gone. It was Rebecca who had gone. In institutions and villages, in hospitals and in schools, often it is one person who is the soul of the place, though he or she may be the janitor, a chairman, or a priest's servant. When Rebecca died, the village died.

The three went up through the bush to where the graves were, getting on for fifty of them now, Rebecca's and her son Tenderai's among the newest, two oblongs of red dust under a big tree. Sylvia stood, looking, and the lads, seeing her face, came to her and she held them close and now she did weep, their faces on her head: they were taller than she was.

'And now you must see our father.'

'Yes, I know.'

'Please do not be cross with us. The police came and took away the medicines and the bandages. We told them you paid for them, with your money.'

'It doesn't matter.'

'We told them it was stealing, they were your medicines.'

'Really, it doesn't matter.'

'And the grandmothers are using the hospital for the sick children.'

Everywhere in Zimlia old women and sometimes old men whose grown-up children had died were left trying to feed and keep young children.

'How are they feeding them?'

'The new headmaster said he will give them food.'

'But they are too many, how can he feed them all?'

They stood on a small rise, opposite the one where the priest's house stood, looking down into Sylvia's hospital. Three old women sat in the shade under the grass roofs, with about twenty small children. Old, that is, by third world standards: in luckier countries these fifty-year-old women would be dieting and finding lovers.

Under Joshua's big tree lay a heap of rags, or something like a big python, mottled with shadow. Sylvia knelt beside him and said, 'Joshua.' He did not move. There are people who, before they die, look as they will after they are dead: the skeleton is so close under the skin. Joshua's face was all bone, with dry skin sunk into the hollows. He opened his eyes and licked scummy lips with a cracked tongue. 'Is there water?' asked Sylvia, and Zebedee ran to the old women, who seemed to be protesting, why waste water on the nearly dead? But Zebedee scooped a plastic cup through water that stood in a plastic pail open to dust and any blown leaves, and brought it to his father, knelt, and held the cup to the cracked lips. Suddenly the ancient man (in late middle age by other standards) came alive and drank desperately, the cords of his throat working. Then he shot out a hand like a skeleton's and grasped Sylvia's wrist. It was like being held in a circlet of bone. He could not sit up, but he raised his head and began mumbling what she knew must be curses, imprecations, his deep-sunk eyes burning with hatred.

'He doesn't mean it,' said Clever. 'No, he doesn't,' pleaded Zebedee.

Then Joshua mumbled, 'You take my children. You must take them to England.'

Her wrist was aching because of the tight bone bracelet. 'Joshua, let me go, you're hurting me.'

His grip tightened, 'You must promise me, now-now, you must promise.' His head was lifted up off his nearly-dead body as a snake lifts its head when its back is broken.

'Joshua, let my wrist go.'

'You will promise me. You will . . .' And he mumbled his curses, his eyes hard on hers, and his head fell back. But his eyes did not close, nor did he stop his mumbled hatred.

'Very well, I promise, Joshua. Now let me go.' His grip did not relax: she was wildly thinking that he would die and she would be handcuffed to a skeleton.

'Don't believe what he says, Doctor Sylvia,' whispered Zebedee. 'He doesn't mean what he says,' said Clever.

'Perhaps it is just as well I don't know what he's saying.'

The bone handcuff fell off her wrist. Her hand was numb. She squatted beside the near-corpse, shaking her hand.

'Who is going to look after him?'

'The old women are looking after him.'

Sylvia went to the women and gave them money, nearly all she had, leaving enough to get back to Senga. It would keep these children fed for a month, perhaps.

'And now get your things, we're leaving.'

'Now?' They fell back from her, with the shock of it; what they had longed for was here, was close – and it was a separation from everything they knew.

'I'll get you clothes, in Senga.'

They went running down to the village, and she walked up the hill between the oleanders and the plumbago to the house, where everything she was going to take was already in her little hold-all. To Rebecca's niece she said that if she wanted her books,

454

she could take them. She could take anything she wanted. But what the girl asked for was the picture of the women on the wall. She liked those faces, she said.

The lads appeared, each with a carrier bag – their possessions. 'Have you had anything to eat?' No, clearly they had not. She sat them at the table, and cut bread and set the jam-jar between them. She and Rebecca's niece stood watching them fumble with the knives, spreading the jam. All that had to be learned. Sylvia's heart was as heavy with dismay as it was going to be: these two – orphans, for it was what they were – were going to have to take on London, learn everything, from how to use knives and forks, to how to be doctors.

Sylvia rang Edna Pyne, who said that Cedric was sick, she couldn't leave him – she thought bilharzia.

'Never mind, we'll take the bus into Senga.'

'You can't go on those native buses, they're lethal.'

'People do.'

'Rather you than me.'

'I'm saying goodbye, Edna.'

'Okay. Don't fret. In this continent our deeds are writ in water. Oh dear, what am I saying, in sand then. That's what Cedric is saying, he's got the blues, he's got my black dog. "Our deeds are writ in water," he says. He's getting religion. Well, that's all it needed. Goodbye, then. See you around.'

The three were where the road to the Pynes and the Mission joined one of the main roads north. It was a single belt of tarmac, much potholed, and as eaten away at the edges as the poster Rebecca's niece had taken off the wall that morning. The bus was due, but would be late: it always was. They stood waiting and then sat waiting, on stones placed there for that purpose under a tree.

Not much of a thing, you'd think, this road, curving away into the bush, its grey shine dimmed where sand had blown over it, but along it, a host of the smartest cars in the country had sped not long ago to the Comrade Leader's wedding to his new wife – the Mother of the Country having died. All the leaders of the world had been invited, comrades or not, and they had been conveyed on this bush road or by helicopter to a Growth Point not far from the birthplace of the Comrade Leader. Near it, among trees, two great marquees had been erected. Inside one trestle tables offered buns and Fanta to the local citizens, while the other had a feast laid out on white cloths, for the elite. But the church service where the marriage was being solemnized went on too long. The povos, or plebs, having consumed their buns, surged into the tent for their betters, and consumed all the food, while waiters futilely protested. Then they vanished back into the bush to their homes. More food had to be flown by helicopter from Senga. This event, so aptly illustrating . . . but one that is so like a fairy tale does not have to be annotated.

Along this road, in not much more than ten years, the bully-boys and thugs of the Leader's Party would run with machetes and knives and clubs to beat up farm workers who wanted to vote for the Leader's opponents. Among them were the young men – former young men – to whom Father McGuire had given medicine in the war. Part of this army had turned off from this road on to the minor road to the Pynes' farm, which they did not appear to know had already been forcibly acquired by Mr Phiri, though the Pynes had not yet left. About two hundred drunks arrived on the lawn in front of the house and demanded that Cedric Pyne should kill a beast for them. He killed a fat ox – the drought having relaxed its grip – and on the front lawn a great fire was built and the ox was roasted. The Pynes were dragged down from the verandah and told to chant slogans praising the Leader. Edna refused. 'I'm damned if I'm going to tell lies just to please you,' she said, and so they hit her until she repeated after them, 'Viva Comrade Matthew.' When Mr Phiri arrived to take possession of the two farms, the garden of the house was black and fouled and the house well was full of rubbish.

Along this road eight years ago Sylvia had been driven, dazed and dazzled by the strangeness of the bush, the alien magnificence, listening to Sister Molly warn her against the intransigence of the male world: 'That Kevin now, he hasn't caught on that the world has changed around him.'

By this road, not far from here, in a hilly area full of caves and rocky clefts and baobabs, is a place where the Comrade Leader was summoned at intervals by spirit healers (*n'gangas*, witch-doctors, shamans) to night sessions where men (and a woman or two), who may be working in a kitchen or a factory, painted, wearing animal skins and monkey hair, danced themselves into a trance and informed him that he must kill or throw out the whites or he will displease the ancestors. He grovelled, wept, promised to do better – then was driven back to town to take up his residence again in his fortress house, to plan for his next trip to meet the world's leaders, or a conference with the World Bank.

The bus came. It was old, and it rattled and shook and emitted clouds of black greasy smoke that trailed for miles behind it, marking the road. It was full, yet a space appeared and admitted Sylvia and her two – what were they, servants? – but the people on the bus, prepared to be critical of this white woman travelling with them – she was the only white among them – saw her put her arms around the lads, who pressed up close to her, like children. They were doleful, trying not to cry, afraid of what they were facing. As for Sylvia, she was in a panic. What was she doing? What else could she have done? Under the rattling of the bus she asked them, low, 'What would you have done if I hadn't come back?' And Clever said, 'I don't know. We have nowhere to go.' Zebedee said, 'Thank you for coming to fetch us. We were too-too afraid you wouldn't come for us.'

From the bus station they walked to the old hotel that had been so thoroughly diminished by Butler's, and she took a room for the three of them, expecting comments, but there were none: in the hotels of Zimlia a room may have half a dozen beds in it to accommodate a whole family.

She went with them to the lift, knowing that they had never seen one, nor, probably, heard of them, explained how they worked, walked along a corridor where a dusty sun was laying patterns, and in the room showed them the bathroom, the lavatory: how to turn taps and cistern handles, open and shut windows. Then she took them to the restaurant and ordered *sadza* for them, saying they must not use their fingers to eat it, and then a pudding, and with the aid of a kindly waiter, they managed that too.

Then it was two o'clock and she took them back upstairs, and telephoned the airport, booking seats for the following evening. She said she was going to get them passports, explained passports, and said they could sleep if they wanted. But they were too excited, and were bouncing on the beds when she left, letting out cries that could have been joy, or a lament.

She walked to the government offices and as she stood on the steps wondering what next, Franklin stepped out of his Mercedes. She grabbed his arm and said, 'I'm coming in with you and don't you dare say you have a meeting.' He tried to shake her off, and was about to shout for help when he saw it was Sylvia. He was so astonished he stood still, not resisting, so she let him go. When he had seen her weeks ago she had been an imposter who called herself Sylvia, but here was what he remembered, a slight creature, whose whiteness seemed to gleam, with soft golden hair and enormous blue eyes. She was wearing a white blouse, not that horrible white madam's green suit. She seemed positively transparent, like a spirit, or a gold-haired Madonna from his long-ago schooldays.

Disarmed and helpless, he said, 'Come in.' And up they went along the corridors of power, up stairs, and into his office where he sat, sighing, but smiling, and waved her to a chair.

'What is it you want?'

'I have with me two boys from Kwadere. They are eleven and thirteen. They have no family. Everyone has died of AIDS. I am taking them back to London and I want you to arrange passports for them.'

He laughed. 'But I am the wrong Minister. It is not my department.'

'Please arrange it. You can.'

'And why should you steal away our children?'

'Steal! They have no family. They have no future. They learned nothing in your so-called school where there aren't any books. I've been teaching them. They are very bright children. With me they'll be educated. And they want to be doctors.'

'And why should you do this?'

'I promised their father. He is dying of AIDS. I think he must be dead by now. I promised I would educate his sons.'

'It is ridiculous. It is out of the question. In our culture some-one will look after them.'

'You never go out of Senga, so you don't know how things are. The village is dying. There are more people up in the cemetery than in the village now.'

'And is it my fault their father has AIDS? And is this terrible thing our fault?'

'Well, it's not ours, as you keep saying. And I think you should know that in the country districts people are saying that AIDS is the fault of the government because you've turned out to be such a bunch of crooks.'

His eyes wandered. He took a gulp of water. He wiped his face. 'I'm surprised you listen to such gossip. They are rumours spread by South African agents.'

'This is wasting time. Franklin, I've booked seats for tomorrow night's flight to London.' She pushed across a piece of paper with the boys' names on it, their father's name, their birthplace. 'Here you are. All I need is a document to get them out of the country. And I'll arrange for them to have British passports when we get to London.'

He sat looking at the paper. Then he cautiously lifted his eyes and they were full of tears. 'Sylvia, you said a very terrible thing.'

'You ought to know what the people are saying.'

'To say such a thing, to an old friend.'

'Yesterday I was listening to . . . the old man cursed me, to make me take his sons to London. He cursed me . . . I am so full of curses that they must be spilling out of me.'

And now he was really uneasy. 'Sylvia, what are you saying? Are you cursing me too?'

'Did I say that?' But between her eyes was the deep tension furrow that made her look like a little witch. 'Franklin, have you ever sat beside an old man dying of AIDS while he curses you up hill and down dale? – it was so terrible his sons won't tell me what he was saying.' She held out her wrist, that had around it a black bruise, like a bracelet.

'What's that?'

She leaned across the desk and gripped his wrist, in as tight a hold as she had felt yesterday. She held it, while he tried to shake her away, then released it.

He sat, head bowed, from time to time giving her panicky glances.

'If your son wanted to go tomorrow night to London and needed a passport, don't tell me you couldn't fix it.'

'Okay,' he said at last.

'I shall wait for the boys' documents at the Selous Hotel.'

'Have you been ill?'

'Yes. Malaria. Not AIDS.'

'Is that meant to be a joke?'

'Sorry. Thank you, Franklin.'

'Okay,' he said.

When Sylvia rang home from the airport before boarding she said she was arriving tomorrow morning with two boys, yes black ones, and she had promised to educate them, they were very clever – one was called Clever, she hoped it wasn't going to be too cold because of course the boys wouldn't be used to that, and she went on until Frances said that the call must be costing a fortune and Sylvia said, 'Yes, sorry, oh, I'm so sorry,' and at last rang off saying she would tell them everything tomorrow.

Colin heard this news and said that evidently Sylvia intended the boys to live here. 'Don't be silly, how can they? Besides, she is going to Somalia, she said.'

'Well, there you are.'

Rupert after some thought, as was his way, remarked that he hoped William would not be upset. Which meant that he too thought the boys would be left with them.

Neither Frances nor Rupert could be there to welcome Sylvia, they would be at work, but Frances suggested a family supper. This family conference was handicapped by lack of information. 'She sounded demented,' said Frances.

It was Colin who opened the door to Sylvia and the boys. In his arms was his daughter and Sophie's, Celia, an enchanting infant, with black curls, black flirty eyes, dimples, all set off by a little red dress. She took one look at the black faces, and howled.

'Nonsense,' said her father, and firmly shook the boys' hands, which he noted were cold and trembling. It was a bitter November day. 'She's never seen black faces so close,' explained Sylvia to them. 'Don't mind her.'

They were in the kitchen, then at the faithful table. The boys were evidently in a state of shock, or something like it. If black faces can be pale, then theirs were. They had a greyish look, and they were shivering, though each had a new thick jersey. They felt themselves to be in the wrong place, Sylvia knew, because she did: too fast a transition from the grass huts, the drifts of dust, the new graves, at the Mission.

A pretty young woman in jeans and a jolly striped T-shirt came in and said, 'Hi, I'm Marusha,' and stood by the kettle while it boiled. The au pair. Soon big mugs of tea stood before Sylvia and the boys, and Marusha set biscuits on a plate which she pushed toward them, smiling politely. She was a Pole, and absorbed in mind and imagination in the disintegration of the Soviet Union, which was in energetic process. Having gathered Celia on to her hip, she said, 'I want to see the News on the telly,' and went up the stairs singing. The boys watched Sylvia putting biscuits on to her plate, and how she added milk to her tea, and then sugar. They copied her exactly, their eyes on her face, her movements, just as they had watched her for the years at the hospital.

'Clever and Zebedee,' said Sylvia. 'They have been helping me at the hospital. I shall get them into school the moment I can. They are going to be doctors. They are sad because their father has just died. They have no family left.'

'Ah,' said Colin, and nodded welcome to the boys, whose sad scared grins seemed permanently fixed. 'I'm sorry. I do see that all this must be terribly difficult for you. You'll get used to it.'

'Is Sophie at the theatre?'

'Sophie is intermittently with Roland – no, she hasn't actually left me. I would say she is living with both of us.'

'I see.'

'Yes, that's how things are.'

'Poor Colin.'

'He sends her four dozen red roses at the slightest excuse or meaningful messages of pansies or forget-me-nots. I never think of things like that. It serves me right.'

'Oh, poor Colin.'

'And from the look of you, poor Sylvia.'

'She is sick. Sylvia is very sick,' the boys came in. Last night on the plane they had been frightened, not only of the unfamiliar plane, but Sylvia kept vomiting, going off to sleep, and coming awake with a cry and tears. As for them, she had shown them how the toilets worked, and they thought they had understood, but Clever had pushed what must have been the wrong button, because next time he made his way there the door had Out of Order on it. They both felt the stewardesses were looking at them critically, and that if they did something stupid the plane might crash because of them.

Now, when Sylvia put her arms around them, as she sat

between them, they could feel that she was cold, through her clothes, and was shivering. They were not surprised. The view out of the window coming from the airport, all oozing grey skies and endless buildings and so many people bundled up like parcels made them both want to put their heads under a blanket.

'I take it none of you slept a wink on the plane?' asked Colin.

'Not much,' said Sylvia. 'And the boys were too overcome with everything. They are from a village, you see. All this is new to them.'

'I understand,' said Colin, and did, as far as anyone can who has not seen for himself.

'Is there anyone in Andrew's old room?'

'I work in it.'

'And in your old room,'

'William is in it.'

'And in the little room on that floor? We can get two beds in there.'

'Bit crammed, surely, with two beds?'

Zebedee said, 'There were five people living in our hut until my sister died.'

'She wasn't really our sister,' said Clever. 'She was our cousin, if you reckon by your ideas. We have a different kinship system.' He added, 'She died. She got very sick and died.'

'I know they are not the same. I look forward to your explaining it to me.' Colin was just beginning to distinguish the boys from each other. Clever was the thin, eager one with enormous appealing eyes; Zebedee was bulkier, with big shoulders and a smile that reminded him of Franklin's.

'Can we look at that fridge? We have never seen a fridge as big as that before.'

Colin showed them the fridge, with its many shelves, its interior lighting, its freezing compartments. They exclaimed, and admired and shook their heads, and then stood yawning.

'Come on,' said Colin, and he went up the stairs, with his arms on their shoulders, Sylvia behind them. Stairs, stairs – the boys had not seen stairs until the Selous Hotel. Up they went, past the living-room floor, past Frances's and Rupert's, and the little room where once Sylvia had had her being, to the floor that had housed Colin's and Andrew's growing up. In the little room was already a big bed, and just as Colin was saying, 'We'll fix you up with something better,' the two flung themselves down on it and were asleep, just like that.

'Poor kids,' said Colin.

'When they wake they'll be in a panic.'

'I'll tell Marusha to keep her eyes open . . . and where are you sleeping, have you thought of that?'

'I can doss down in the sitting-room until . . .'

'Sylvia, you aren't thinking of dumping the boys on us and taking off to – where did you say?'

'Somalia.'

Sylvia had not been thinking. She had been carried along on a tide of accomplishment since her promise to Joshua, and had not allowed herself to think, or to fit together the two facts, that she was responsible for the boys, and that she had promised to be in Somalia in three weeks' time.

They went back down the stairs, sat at the table and smiled at each other.

'Sylvia, you had remembered that Frances is getting on a bit, she is past seventy? We gave her a big party. Not that she looks it or acts it.'

'And she has Margaret and William already.'

'Only William.' And now, at his leisure – they had all the time in the world – he told her the story. Margaret had decided, without discussing it with them, that she would live with her mother. She had not asked her either, but had turned up at Phyllida's and said to Meriel, 'I'm coming to live with you.'

'There's no room,' said Meriel promptly. 'Not until I get a

you must get a place,' ordered her daughter. 'We've money, haven't we?'

The trouble was this: Meriel had decided to go to university and take a degree in psychology. Frances was furious: she had expected Meriel to start earning some money, but Rupert was unsurprised. 'I always said she had no intention of ever earning a living for herself, didn't I?' 'Yes, you did.' 'No one would believe it, looking at her, but she's a very dependent woman.' 'Are we going to have to keep her in perpetuity?' 'I wouldn't be surprised.'

This was why Meriel did not really want to leave Phyllida: she did not want to be by herself. Phyllida meanwhile wanted Meriel to go. There had been some dark satisfaction, never really analysed, in having Rupert's former wife, here, with her, like an extension of the Lennox household, but enough was enough. She did not actively dislike Meriel, but her sharp cutting ways could depress. When Margaret moved in, Phyllida felt she was reliving an old nightmare, seeing herself in Meriel, with the girl, mother and daughter, snapping and snarling and kissing and making up and noisy, so noisy, tears and rows and shouts and the long silences of reconciliation.

Then Meriel had a relapse and was in hospital. Phyllida and Margaret were together. Phyllida suggested that now her mother was not there Margaret might go back to the Lennox house, but Margaret said she liked it better with Phyllida. 'Frances is an old cow,' she said. 'She doesn't really care about anything but Rupert. I think it's disgusting, old people like that, holding hands. And I really do like being with you.' She said this last shyly, tentative, afraid of a rebuff, offering herself as it were to this mother surrogate: 'I want to be with you.'

Phyllida was in fact moved by this, hearing that the girl liked her. How unlike sly and deceiving Sylvia, who couldn't wait to get away from her.

'All right, but when your mother is better, I think you should have your own place.'

Meriel showed no signs of being better. Margaret would not go and see her, she said it upset her too much, but William went nearly every evening, and sat by the woman curled on her bed, in the grey absence that is depression, and he told her, in the careful, guarded thoughtful way that was his, about his day, about what he had been doing. But she did not reply nor move nor look at him.

And when Colin had finished telling about Meriel, there was Sophie, and Frances, who was writing books, part history and part sociology, that did very well. And about Rupert, whom Colin said was the best thing that had happened in this house. 'Just imagine, somebody really sane, at last.'

The two talked the afternoon away, while the little girl made charming appearances in the arms of Marusha, who grew more exultant every moment with new instalments of the News, of the thorough humiliation of Poland's old enemy, and then Frances arrived, with arms full of food, just like the old days. The three pulled the table out to its former length, as if setting the stage for past festivals.

While Frances cooked, in came William, just as the two black boys came down the stairs. They were introduced. 'Clever and Zebedee are going to stay here for a bit,' said Colin. Frances said nothing, but began laying the table for nine people. Sophie would join them later.

Frances took her place at the head of the table, with Colin at the foot, and a place beside him for Sophie, then Marusha's place and next to her the baby's high chair. Ten, if you counted Celia. Rupert was next to Frances on one side, William on the other. Sylvia and the two boys were in the middle. Sylvia told about the big dinner at Butler's Hotel, and all the expensive people, some of them who had once been around this table, and then about Andrew's bride, saying flatly that it couldn't last. She was speaking in an empty voice, giving information, none of the relish ~ossip, of life's improbable workings. The boys kept looking ~o see what she was feeling since her voice seemed deter- ~ to say: it was their uneasiness that alerted the others ~ld be worried about Sylvia. In fact she felt that she was floating off somewhere, and this was not just lack of sleep. She was tired, yes, so tired, and it was hard to keep her attention here, and yet she knew she had to, because the boys were depending on her, and she was the only person who could understand how hard it was for them. Rupert put questions, like a good journalist, but it was because he knew she was needing to be held down, like a too buoyant kite: he was sensitive to her distress, because of his long attention to William, who suffered so much and who depended on him, Rupert, to understand him. And through it all the little child prattled and babbled and made flirtatious eyes at them all, the black boys too, now that she was used to them.

Sophie came rushing in, in a wave of scent. She was fatter than she had been and 'more Madame Bovary than the Lady of the Camellias', as she said herself. She wore elegant voluminous white, and her hair was in a chignon. She gave Colin passionately guilty looks until he kissed her and said, 'Now, just shut up, Sophie. You can't be the centre of attention tonight.'

'What's wrong with you, Sylvia, for God's sake?' cried Sophie. 'You look like death.'

The words struck a chill, but Sophie could not know the boys' father was just dead, and that their Saturday afternoons for months now had been spent at the funerals of people they had known all their lives.

'I think I'll have a little sleep,' said Sylvia, and pushed herself up out of her chair. 'I feel . . .' She kissed Frances. 'Darling Frances, to be back here with you, if you only knew . . . dear Sophie . . .' She smiled vaguely at everyone, then put her hand shakily on Clever's shoulder and then on Zebedee's. 'I'll see you later,' she said. She went out, holding on to the door's edge and then the door frame.

'Don't worry,' said Frances to the boys. 'We'll look after you. Just tell us what you need, because we don't understand the way Sylvia does.' But they were staring after Sylvia, and it was easy to see it was all too much for them. They wanted to go back up to bed, and went, Marusha accompanying them, with Celia. Then, Sophie followed: it seemed she intended to stay the night.

Frances, Colin and Rupert faced William, knowing what was coming.

He was now a tall slender fair youth, handsome, but the pale skin was tight over his face, and often there was strain around his eyes. He loved his father, was always as near to him as he could get, though Rupert told Frances he did not dare put his arms around him, hug him: William did not seem to like it. And he was secretive, Rupert said, did not share his thoughts. 'Perhaps it is just as well we don't know them,' said Frances. She experienced William, who would consult her about small difficulties, as a controlled anguish which she did not believe a hug or a kiss could reach. And he worked so hard, had to do well at school, seemed always to be wrestling with invisible angels.

'Are they coming to live here?'

'It seems that they are,' said Colin.

'Why should they?'

'Come on, old chap, don't be like that,' said his father.

William's smile at Colin, whom they had to deduce he loved, was like a wail.

'They have no parents,' said Colin. 'Their father has just died.' He was afraid to say, of AIDS, because of the terror of the word, even though in this house AIDS was as distant as the Black Death. 'They are orphans. And they are very poor . . . I don't think it's possible for people like us to understand. And they've had no school except for Sylvia's lessons.' In all their minds briefly appeared an image of a room with desks, a blackboard, a teacher holding forth.

'But why here? Why does it have to be us?' This routine reaction – *But why me?* – cannot be answered except with appeals to the majestic injustices of the universe.

'Someone has to take them in,' said Frances.

'Besides, Sylvia will be here. She'll understand what to do. I agree that we're not up to it,' said Colin.

'But how can she be here? Where's she going to stay? Where's she going to sleep?'

If Sylvia's mind was a blur of panic because of the impossibility of being in Somalia and London at the same time, then these three adults were in a similar state: William was right.

'Oh, we'll manage somehow,' said Frances.

'And we'll all have to help them,' said Colin.

This meant, as William knew very well, We expect you to help them. They were younger than him, but that made it even more likely they would depend on him. 'If they don't get on here, will they go away?'

Colin said, 'We could send them back. But I understand everyone in their village has died of AIDS or is going to.'

William went white. 'AIDS! Have they got AIDS?'

'No. Nor can they have it, Sylvia says.'

'How does she know? Well, all right, she's a doctor but why does she look so sick, then? She looks ghastly.'

'She'll be all right. And the boys'll have to be tutored first, to catch up, but I am sure they will.'

'They can't be called Clever and Zebedee, not here. They'll be killed, with names like that. I hope they aren't going to my school.'

'We can't just take their real names away from them.'

'Well, I'm not going to fight their battles for them.'

He said he had to go up: he had homework. He left: before homework, they knew, he would play a little with the baby, if she was awake. He adored her.

Sylvia did not reappear. She had flung herself down into the bosom of the old red sofa, her arms outstretched: she was at once asleep. She sank deep into her past, into arms that were waiting for her.

Rupert and Frances were in their rooms undressing when Colin came in to say he had checked on Sylvia, who was sleeping like the dead. Later, about four in the morning, uneasiness woke Frances, and she crept down and returned to tell Rupert, who had been awakened by her going, that Sylvia was dead asleep. She was about to slide into bed, but now heard what she had said and, retrospectively, what Colin had said. 'I don't like it,' she said. 'There's something wrong.' Rupert and Frances went down and into the sitting-room where on the sofa Sylvia was indeed dead asleep: she was dead.

The boys lay weeping on their beds. Frances's instinct, which was to put her arms around them, was stopped by that oldest of inhibitions: hers were not the arms they wanted. As the day wore on and the weeping did not cease, she and Colin went to the little room, and she with Clever and he with Zebedee, made them sit up and were close, arms around them, rocking them, saying that they should stop crying, they would be ill, they must come down and have a hot drink, and no one would mind if they were sad.

The first bad days were got through, and then the funeral, with Zebedee and Clever in prominent positions as mourners. Attempts were made to telephone the Mission, but a voice the boys did not know said that Father McGuire had taken all his things away and the new headmaster was not here yet. Messages were left. Sister Molly, left a message, at once rang back, loud and clear though she was miles from anywhere. She said at once, 'Are you thinking what to do about the boys?' She believed that probably work could be found for them at the Old Mission, looking after the AIDS orphans. When the priest rang back the line was so bad that only intermittently could be made out his concern over Sylvia, 'Poor soul, she did have to work herself into the grave.' And, 'If you could see your way to keep the boys it would be best.' And, 'It is a sad business here.'

The boys' grief was terrible, it was inordinate, it was frightening their new friends, who agreed that everything had been too much: after all, these children – and that was all they were – had been torn from what they had known, then thrust into . . . but 'culture shock' was hardly appropriate when that useful phrase may describe an agreeable dislocation felt travelling from London to Paris. No, it was not possible to imagine what depths of shock Clever and Zebedee had suffered, and therefore no notice should be taken of faces like tragic masks and tragic eyes. *Haunted* eyes?

There was something that the new friends had no conception of, and could not have understood: the boys knew that Sylvia had died because of Joshua's curse. Had she been there to laugh at them, and to say, 'Oh, how can you think such nonsense?' they might not have believed her, but the guilt would have been less. As it was, they were being crushed by guilt, and they could not bear it. And so, as we all do with the worst and deepest pain, they began to forget.

Clear in their minds was every minute of the long days while they waited for Sylvia to return from Senga to rescue them, while Rebecca died and Joshua lay waiting to die until Sylvia came. The long agony of anxiety – they did not forget that, nor that moment when Sylvia reappeared like a little white ghost, to embrace them and whisk them away with her. After that the blur began, Joshua's bony grip on Sylvia's wrist and his murderous words, the frightening aeroplane, the arrival in this strange house, Sylvia's death . . . no, all that dimmed and soon Sylvia had become a friendly protective presence whom they remembered kneeling in the dust to splint up a leg, or sitting on the edge of the verandah between them, teaching them to read.

Meanwhile Frances kept waking, her stomach clenched with anxiety, and Colin said he was sleeping badly too. Rupert told them that not enough thought had gone into this decision, that was the trouble.

Frances, waking with a start and a cry, found herself held by Rupert, 'Come on downstairs. I'll make you some tea.' And when they reached the kitchen, Colin was already at the table, a bottle of wine in front of him.

Outside the window was the dark of 4 o'clock on a winter's

night. Rupert drew the curtains, sat by Frances, put his arm around her. 'Now, you two, you've got to decide. And whatever it is you do decide, then you've got to put the other choice clean out of your minds. Otherwise you'll both be ill.'

'Right,' said Colin, and shakily reached for the wine bottle.

Rupert said, 'Now look, old son, don't drink any more, there's a good chap.'

Frances felt that apprehension a woman may feel when her man, not her son's father, takes the father's role: Rupert had spoken as if it were William sitting there.

Colin pushed away the bottle. 'This is a bloody impossible situation.'

'Yes, it is,' said Frances. 'What are we taking on? Do you realise, I'll be dead by the time they qualify?'

Rupert's arm tightened around her shoulder.

'But we have to keep them,' said Colin, aggressive, tearful, pleading with them. 'If a couple of kittens try to crawl out of the bucket they're being drowned in, you don't push them back in.' The Colin who was speaking then Frances had not seen or heard of for years: Rupert had not met that passionate youth. 'You just don't do it,' said Colin, leaning forward, his eyes holding his mother's, then Rupert's. 'You don't just push them back in.' A howl broke out of him: a long time since Frances had heard that howl. He dropped his head down on to his arms on the table. Rupert and Frances communed, silently.

'I think,' said Rupert, 'that there is only one way you can decide.'

'Yes,' said Colin, lifting his head.

'Yes,' said Frances.

'Then, that's it. And now put the other out of your heads. Now.'

'I suppose once a Sixties' household, then always a Sixties' household,' said Colin. 'No, that's not my little *aperçu*, it is Sophie's. She thinks it's all lovely. I did point out that it was not she who would be doing the work. She said she would muck in – with everything, she said.' He laughed.

Back in bed Rupert said, 'I don't think I could bear it if you died. But luckily women live longer than men.'

'And I can't imagine not being with you.'

These two people of the word had hardly ever said more than this kind of thing. 'We don't do too badly, do we?' was about the limit. To be so thoroughly out of phase with one's time does take a certain bravado: a man and a woman daring to love each other so thoroughly – well, it was hardly to be confessed, even to each other.

Now he said, 'What was all that about the kittens?'

'I have no idea. Not in this house, and I am sure not at his school. Progressive schools don't drown kittens. Well, not so their pupils can see.'

'Wherever it happened, it went deep.'

'And he's never mentioned it before.'

'When I was a boy I saw a gang of kids torturing a sick dog. That taught me more about the nature of the world than anything else ever has.'

Lessons began. Rupert tutored Clever and Zebedee in maths: beyond knowing their multiplication tables they were as blank sheets, he said, but they were so quick, they could catch up. Frances found that their reading had been extraordinary: their memories retained whole tracts of *Mowgli* and Enid Blyton, and *Animal Farm* and Hardy, but they had not heard of Shakespeare. This deficiency she proposed to remedy; they were already reading everything on the shelves in the sitting-room. Colin came in with geography and history. Sylvia's little atlas had done good service, the boys' knowledge of the world was wide, if not deep; as for history, they did not know much beyond *The Renaissance Popes* – this being a book on Father McGuire's shelves. Sophie would take them to the theatre. And then, without being asked, William began teaching them from old textbooks, and it was this that really did them good.

William said he was unnerved by their application: he himself had to do well, but compared to them . . . 'You'd think their lives depended on it,' and added, making the discovery for himself, 'I suppose their lives do depend on it. After all, I can always go and be . . .' 'What?' enquired the adults, grasping at this opportunity to glimpse what really went on in his mind. 'A gardener. I could be a gardener at Kew,' said William gravely. 'Yes, that's what I'd really like. Or I could be like Thoreau and live by myself, near a lake and write about Nature.'

Sylvia had died intestate, and so, the lawyers said, her money would go to her mother, as the next of kin. A good sum it was, well able to see the boys through their education. Andrew was appealed to, as Phyllida's old mate, and, dropping into or through London, he went to see Phyllida, where this conversation ensued.

'Sylvia would have wanted her money to educate the two African boys she seems to have adopted.'

'Oh yes, the black boys, I have heard about them.'

'I'm here formally to ask you to relinquish that money, because we are sure that is what she would have wished.'

'I don't remember her saying anything to me about it.'

'But, Phyllida, how could she?'

Phyllida gave a little toss of her head, with a small triumphant smile, that was amused, too, like someone applauding the vagaries of Fate, having won a fortune in the sweepstake, perhaps. 'Finders keepers,' she said. 'And anyhow, something nice is owed to me, that's how I see it.'

There was a family discussion.

Rupert, though a senior editor in his newspaper, and adequately paid, knew that even when he had finished paying for Margaret's school fees (Frances now paid for William) he would have to keep Meriel.

Colin's intelligent novels, described by Rose Trimble as 'elite novels for the chattering classes', were not going to provide for more than the child, and Sophie, who as an actress was often resting. He spent so little on himself he hardly counted.

Frances found herself in a familiar situation. She had been offered a job helping to run a small experimental theatre: her heart's desire, a lot of fun but not much money. Her reliable and serious books, bought by every library in the land, brought in good money. She would have to say no to the theatre and write books. She said she would be responsible for Clever, and Andrew would pay for Zebedee.

Andrew proposed to start a family, but he earned so well he was sure he could manage Zebedee. Things did not turn out as he expected. The marriage was already in trouble, would soon dissolve, after not much more than a year, though Mona was pregnant. Years of legal wrangling would follow, but when Andrew did wrest time with his child from the jealous mother, the little girl was mostly with her cousin Celia, sharing whatever au pair was around, and Celia's daddy's attention. Colin, as Sophie often wailed, was such a wonderful father, and she was such a rotten mother. ('Never mind,' prattled Celia, when Sophie said this, 'you are such a pretty yummy mummy we don't care.')

Where was everyone going to fit in?

Clever would have Andrew's old room, Zebedee Colin's. Colin would use the sitting-room to work in. William was in a room on Frances's and his father's floor. The au pair used Sylvia's old room.

And the basement flat? Someone was in it. Johnny was in it.

Frances had been on her way to a bus stop when she heard hurrying steps behind her and, 'Frances, Frances Lennox.' She turned to see a woman whose white hair was being blown about while she tried to keep a scarf in place. Frances did not know her . . . yes, she did, just: it was Comrade Jinny, from the old days, and she was chattering, 'Oh, I wasn't sure, but yes it's you, well we're all getting on aren't we, oh dear, I simply had to . . . it's your husband you see, I'm so worried about him.'

'I left my husband fit and well not five minutes ago.'

'Oh dear, oh dear, silly me, I meant Johnny, Comrade Johnny, if only you two knew what you meant to me when I was young, such an inspiration, Comrades Johnny and Frances Lennox . . .'

'Look, I'm sorry, but . . .'

'I hope I'm not speaking out of turn.'

'Just tell me, what is it?'

'He's so old now, poor old thing . . .'

'He's my age.'

'Yes, but some people wear better than others. I just felt you ought to know,' said she, running off and sending back scared but aggressive waves of the hand.

Frances told Colin who said that as far as he was concerned his father could sink or swim. And Frances said that she was damned if she was going to pick up Johnny's pieces for him. That left Andrew, who dropped over from Rome for the afternoon. He found Johnny in a quite pleasant room, in Highgate, in the house of a woman he described as the salt of the earth. He was a frail old man with fans of silvery hair around a shiny white pate, all pathos and vulnerability. He was pleased to see Andrew but he wasn't going to show it. 'Sit down,' he said. 'I'm sure Sister Meg will make us all some tea.' But Andrew remained upright, and said, 'I've come because we hear you've fallen on hard times.'

'Which is more than you have done, so I'm told.'

'I'm glad to say what you hear is all true.'

Not many people in the world would see Johnny's lot as a hard one, but after all, he had spent probably two-thirds of his life in comradely luxury hotels in the Soviet Union, Poland, China, Czechoslovakia, Yugoslavia; in Chile and Angola and Cuba – wherever there had been a comradely conference, Johnny had been there, the world his barrel of oysters, his honeypot, his ever-open jar of Beluga caviar, and here he was, in one room – a nice room, but one room. On his old-age pension. 'And of course the senior bus pass helps.'

'A good member of the proletariat at last,' said Andrew, smiling benevolently from the windows of his gravy train at his dispossessed father.

'And you got married, I hear. I was beginning to think you must be a queer.'

'Who knows these days? But never mind all that, we thought you might like to come and live in the bottom flat?'

'It's my house anyway, so don't make a favour out of it.'

But there were two good rooms, and everything paid for, and he was pleased.

Colin went down to help settle him in and said that he mustn't expect Frances to wait on him.

'It's news to me that she ever did. She was always a lousy housekeeper.'

But Johnny was far from dependent on his family for company. His visitors brought him gifts and flowers as if to a shrine. Johnny was in the process of becoming a holy man, the follower of a senior Indian holy man, and was now often heard to remark, 'Yes, I was a bit of a Red once.' He would sit cross-legged on his pillows on his bed, and his old gesture, palms extended outwards as if offering himself to an audience, fitted in nicely with this new persona. He had disciples, and taught meditation and the Fourfold Sacred Way. In return they kept his rooms clean for him and cooked dishes in which lentils played a leading role.

But this was his new self, perhaps one could describe it as a role, in a play where Sisters and Brothers and Holy Mothers replaced the comrades. His older self did sometimes resurface, when other visitors, old comrades, came around to reminisce as if the great failure of the Soviet Union had never happened, as if that Empire was still marching on. Old men, old women, whose lives had been illumined by the great dream, sat about drinking wine in an atmosphere not unlike that of those far-off combative evenings, except for one thing: they did not smoke now, whereas once it would have been hard to see across a room for the smoke that had been through their lungs.

Late, before the guests left, Johnny would lower his voice and lift his glass, and propose a toast, 'To Him.'

And with tender admiration they drank to possibly the cruellest murderer who has ever lived.

They say that for decades after Napoleon's death old soldiers met in taverns and bars and, secretly, in each other's hovels, raised their glasses to The Other: they were the few survivors of the Grand Armée (whose heroic feats had achieved precisely nothing, except the destruction of a generation), crippled men, whose health had gone and who had survived unspeakable sufferings. But so what, it is always The Dream that counts.

Johnny had another visitor, Celia, who would descend on the hand of Marusha or Bertha or Chantal and run to Johnny. 'Poor little Johnny.'

'But that's your grandfather! You can't call him that.'

The faery child took no notice, stroked the old chastened head, kissed it, and sang her little song, 'That's my little grand-father, that's my poor little Johnny.'

The conjunction of Colin and Sophie had produced a rare being: everyone felt it. The big lads, William and Clever and Zebedee, played with her delicately, almost humbly, as if this was a privilege, a favour she was doing them.

Or they all sat around the table, Rupert and Frances, Colin and William, Clever and Zebedee, and quite often Sophie too, at the evening meal that might go on and on, and the child came running in, evading bedtime. She wanted to be near them, but not to be picked up, held, or sat on a knee. She was deep inside her game, or play, talking softly to herself confidentially, in voices they learned to recognise. 'Celia's here, yes she is, this is Celia, and there is my Frances and there is my Clever . . .' The tiny child, in her scrap of a coloured dress, chattering there, but to herself, perhaps using a bit of cloth, or a flower, or a toy to stand in for some person or character or imagined playmate – she was so perfectly beautiful that she silenced them, they sat watching, charmed, awed . . . 'And there's my William . . .' she reached out to touch him, to be sure of him, but she was not looking at him, perhaps at the flower or toy, 'and my Zebedee . . .' Colin got up, the big clumsy man, so coarse and heavy beside her, and stood looking down. 'And there – my Colin, yes, it's my daddy . . .' Colin, tears running, bent down to her in something like an obeisance of his whole being, holding out his hands with a groan, 'Oh Frances, oh Sophie, did you ever see anything so . . .'

But the little girl did not want to be gathered in and held, she spun around on herself, singing for herself and to herself, 'Yes, my Colin, yes, my Sophie, yes, and there's my poor little Johnny . . .'

Doris Lessing

Under My Skin

Volume One of My Autobiography,
to 1949

'Passionate and compelling, a book so packed with extraordinary images that it has obliterated almost everything else I
read in 1994.'   ROSE TREMAIN

This, the first volume of Doris Lessing's autobiography, begins
with her childhood in Africa and ends on her arrival in London in
1949 with the typescript of her first novel, *The Grass is Singing*, in
her suitcase. It charts the evolution first of her consciousness, then
of her sexuality and finally of her political awareness with an
almost overwhelming immediacy, and is as distinctive and challenging as anything she has ever written. It is already recognized
as one of the great autobiographies of the twentieth century.

'By putting her life on the page, Doris Lessing has created her
greatest work of art. An immediate, vivid, beautifully paced
memoir.'   HILARY MANTEL, *London Review of Books*

'The book pulsates with life. The intensity of the sensory world is
brilliantly evoked. Not just the story of the first thirty years of
one life, this is the biography also of an age.'

JANE DUNN, *Observer*

'No mere review can do justice to an autobiography which is not
just about a particular childhood, but about all childhoods, not
just about white marginality, but about all forms of interior exile,
rebellion, subversion and secret self-making. A voice of wise and
fearless honesty cuts through this book, the best Doris Lessing
has ever written.'   LYNDALL GORDON, *THES*

Doris Lessing

Love, Again

'This is a grand novel, boldly hewn, more literary than it declares, and yielding the occasional swooning glimpse of beauty. An encounter with a magnificent mind and temperament in artistic maturity, capable of turning her equal gaze on George Eliot.' CANDIA McWILLIAM, *Independent on Sunday*

Love, Again is the story of Sarah Durham, a sixty-year-old producer and founder of a leading fringe theatre, who commissions a play based on the journals of Julie Vairon, a beautiful and wayward nineteenth-century mulatto woman. The play captivates all who come into contact with it, and dramatically changes the lives of all who take part in it. For Sarah, the change is profound – she falls in love with two younger men, one after the other, causing her to relive her own stages of growing up, from immature and infantile love (the beautiful and androgynous Bill) to the mature love, Henry.

Love, Again is a fierce and compelling examination of the nature and origins of love, of its remorseless ability to overwhelm and surprise us.

'Lessing's mixture of passionate involvement and the capacity to stand back and take a long look at what was going on, or will go on, is unlike that of any novelist writing now, except perhaps Saul Bellow, and the late Anthony Burgess. It grips, maddens, depresses and excites the reader from the first page to the last.' A.S. BYATT, *The Times*

'A wholly compelling book, as vigorous and thought-provoking as anything she has ever written.' RUTH BRANDON, *New Statesman & Society*

Doris Lessing

The Fifth Child

Four children, a beautiful old house, the love of relatives and friends, Harriet and David Lovatt's life is a glorious hymn to domestic bliss and old-fashioned family values. But when their fifth child is born, a sickly and implacable shadow is cast over this tender idyll. Large and ugly, violent and uncontrollable, the infant Ben, 'full of cold dislike,' tears at Harriet's breast. Struggling to care for her new-born child, faced with a darkness and a strange defiance she has never known before, Harriet is deeply afraid of what, exactly, she has brought into the world . . .

'*The Fifth Child* has the intensity of a nightmare, a horror story poised somewhere between a naturalistic account of family life and an allegory that draws on science fiction. Read it and tremble.'   CLARE TOMALIN, *Independent*

'*The Fifth Child* is a book to send shivers down your spine, but one which it is impossible to put down until it is finished.'
Sunday Times

'A powerful fable. Like the story of Frankenstein or the Minotaur, it generates all sorts of uneasiness. Its strength is expressive not didactic. A disturbing vision, *The Fifth Child* offers a faithful if chilling reflection of the world we live in.'
Sunday Telegraph

Doris Lessing

Ben, in the World

'A wonderful novel, flawless as a black pearl'   *Daily Mail*

'Outstanding . . . A *tour de force* that poses stark questions about modern-day Britain and what it is to be human.'
Sunday Times

'*Ben, in the World* picks up the story of Ben Lovatt, the neanderthal anti-child who in *The Fifth Child* experiences the family as an engine of hatred, rejection and perfectionism mobilised against him. Now an adult, Ben inhabits the world of the modern freak: the world of the homeless, the unregistered, the unwanted. With the mind of a child in a giant, simian body, he is at once vulnerable and threatening, capable of violence and terribly dependent upon approval and trust . . . Lessing has a striking ability to illustrate human moral worth through such a simple lens. In this short, gripping and tragic novel, she conveys a powerful message about the limits of love and the destructive power of selfishness; and most of all about our brutal desire to live our lives unfettered by the helpless, by those who slow us down with their need for kindness.'   *Sunday Express*

'*Ben, In the World* is huge in scope, humanity and pathos. Lessing created a monster; her triumph is that he not only personifies the human yearning to belong, but that we also come to love him.'   *Daily Telegraph*